# MAN'S BOOK

# TOUCHFEATHER, TOO
Jimmy Sangster

★

# NORTH CAPE
Joe Poyer

★

# THE HAWSER PIRATES
Oswald Wynd

ODHAMS BOOKS
LONDON

MADE AND PRINTED IN GREAT BRITAIN
BY ODHAMS (WATFORD) LTD.

SBN.600778886

7.71

# CONTENTS

---

# TOUCHFEATHER, TOO

## Jimmy Sangster

*'Touchfeather, Too' is published by
Triton Books*

## The Author

Jimmy Sangster is in his early forties and has been writing for twelve of them. He lives in Jersey and travels extensively; his favourite places being St. Tropez, Los Angeles and London. This is his fourth novel; he has also sweated out over forty-five screenplays. He has himself produced nine of them as films. He likes good food, pretty girls, expensive motor cars, pretty girls, comfortable living and pretty girls. Any offers will be gratefully received.

### AUTHOR'S NOTE

To the best of my knowledge and belief there is not—and never has been—a Katherine Touchfeather on the roster of air stewardesses employed by BOAC, TWA, PanAm, Air India, or any other member of IATA. Katy, as my story makes clear, is employed by Mr. Blaser. How he contrives to have her appear in the right aeroplane at the right moment, wearing the right uniform and exhibiting the ready smile and warm friendliness of the perfect air stewardess, is his secret. I would like to assure SAS, United, Qantas, American, Lufthansa and all other member companies of IATA that I make no suggestion that any of their employees could, or should, do the things Katy does—despite some recent airline advertisements which may have given their readers ideas to the contrary, e.g. 'Save Friday night for Ingeborg Bechtel. She puts the fun in flying'. Or 'Sometimes our stewardesses take young men home with them'. Katy Touchfeather is to be regarded entirely as fiction. Whereas my admiration and affection for that unique race of young women, the air stewardesses, is demonstrably fact!

J. S.

# CHAPTER ONE

'GOLD, MISS TOUCHFEATHER,' Mr. Blaser had said. 'Gold. That's what we are looking for.' I refrained from commenting 'Aren't we all?' and he continued in that self-righteous, pompous way that I used to find quite impressive, but which now annoys me intensely. I even made up my mind to tell him about it once, but he frightens me too much.

'This gold,' he said, 'is being smuggled into South America, and the man you are being sent to follow is the one who will be carrying it.'

'Follow' had been Mr. Blaser's word for what I was doing, although it hardly seemed to fit the situation I was currently involved in. Here I was, wrapped in a large bath towel, in a luxurious suite on board one of the most glamorous yachts in the world, busily going through the luggage of one of Spain's great heroes of the bullring, while said hero snored lustily in the background, dreaming no doubt about the Great Bull that all matadors are supposed to dream about; or perhaps just dreaming about me and the rather energetic couple of hours we had just spent together.

I'm a pretty dab hand when it comes to searching someone's personal effects, but I was handicapped slightly in this case in that I didn't know what I was looking for. I knew what it was, but not what it would look like.

Mr. Blaser had been his usual enigmatic, pompous self when he briefed me. 'If we knew what it looked like, Miss Touchfeather, we would simply bribe a member of the crew or a harbour official to take it from his cabin. But that is not the object of the exercise. If it was, we would not be spending good money to send you on this high-life jaunt where no doubt you will have a most enjoyable time at Her Majesty's expense.'

He was right there. I'd had a ball. I've always had a soft spot for Spaniards, and when that Spaniard turns out to be a bull-fighter to boot . . . Well, all I can say is 'Ole!'

'We know this bullfighter has an invitation to join one of Galipolodopolo's yachting orgies in Cannes. You will endeavour to effect an introduction before that time and use your . . . ingenuity to be invited on the same trip. Do I make myself clear?'

'Perfectly,' I said.

'I have arranged for you to fly on his flight from Mexico City to Madrid. It is a ten-hour journey. You shouldn't have any problems.'

I pulled my skirt a little lower down my thighs and tried to look prim but when you're built like I am and have been dragged from a swinging party somewhere off the King's Road at quarter past midnight on a Saturday evening, neither one's state of mind nor one's wardrobe is conducive to primness. It had been a friendly party, too, and I'd had a couple too many to drink; while not actually falling all over the place, I was nevertheless reasonably high. I hadn't mentioned this to Mr. Blaser, of course, It's doubtful that he would have appreciated or made allowances for such a lapse on the part of one of his people; we weren't supposed to have any spare time in which to indulge ourselves. If he had had his way we would all have been locked up in a sterile padded cell each time we finished a task, there to languish until he decided he needed us for a fresh piece of nastiness. And there's no point in asking me what Mr. Blaser himself was doing in his office at 0015 hours on a Sunday morning. Even if I'd asked him, which I wasn't about to, he wouldn't have told me.

'You will fly to New York tomorrow,' he had said. 'And from there, straight to Mexico City. Your man is booked out on the midday flight on Thursday. The three days beforehand you will spend in Mexico City brushing up on your Spanish. To that effect I have arranged that you will fly a local airline between Mexico City and Tampico.'

I knew those local flights. The passengers all had ten pairs of hands and brought their goats along with them. I could as well have brushed up on my Spanish lying by a pool in Acapulco; but there didn't seem to be any point in mentioning it. Then Mr. Blaser removed his pipe from his mouth, and proceeded to gouge out the bowl, spilling ash all over his blotter. Here comes the crunch, I thought. He always started to disembowel his pipe when he had something unpleasant to say.

'Should you meet with any unforeseen complications when dealing with this man, you will do everything you consider necessary to cover up your tracks. The man himself is of no importance, but it is essential that his companions do not learn they are under any sort of suspicion from any source. Understood?'

Here he raised his eyes from the business of the pipe and fixed them on me. They are greyish eyes, perhaps more blue than grey, but grey nevertheless. Buried beneath a pair of formidable eyebrows, they peer out at you like a predator watching from beneath a shaggy bush.

'Yes, sir,' I said.

Virtually he was telling me that if anything went wrong, I was expected to push my man overboard or poison his aperitif or fuck him to death; in any event, to call an abrupt halt to his short, happy life.

Fortunately, up to now, nothing had gone wrong. Antonio, who was rather a sweety, was snoring away contentedly whilst I was busy disembowelling his personal effects. It had all been ridiculously simple and remarkably enjoyable. Two hours after taking off from Mexico City wearing the neat uniform of an Iberian Airlines stewardess, I had emptied a tray of dry martinis into his lap. By the time I had sponged him dry and dried him out he had plotted my seduction to the last gasp. So as not to appear obvious, once we got to Madrid, I had made him lay seige for a few days. Finally after a particularly good afternoon in the Plaza de Toros, where the President of the *corrida* had awarded him two ears, I awarded him the tail . . . mine. Two days after that we had flown to Nice, driven from there to Cannes and boarded the *Maria*, the Galipolodopolo yacht.

If Mum could only see her Katy now, I had thought as soon as I had discovered who our fellow guests were. Apart from Galipolodopolo himself, reputed to be among the five richest men in the world, if one excluded the Arabs, there was his current (number three) wife who was conveniently named Maria. This stroke of fortune had saved Galipolodopolo from changing the name of the yacht when he married her; it had been named after his second wife who was also called Maria. She was a quiet little Greek girl, twenty-five years his junior, and quite plainly terrified of her husband, his friends, the crew, the sea and everything else. Her one comfort and joy was a nasty little Pekinese which followed her everywhere and bit the crew constantly. I gave the dog three days before it disappeared mysteriously overboard. Then there was Gary Brian, forty years old, American, top box-office draw in the cinemas of the world for the past five years, and as camp as a row of tents. The only problem I had with this one was keeping him away from Antonio. There was Sir Roger Bleak, accompanied by a predatory little dolly bird who obviously proposed to change it to Lady Bleak or die in the attempt. There was an Italian Count with a roving eye and hands to match and his lesbian wife, and there was a French textile magnate who distinguished himself by bringing three girls along and insisting that all four of them share the same stateroom. The girls were lean, cool, brown, and as near as made no difference, identical. Then there was Antonio, number one Matodor de Toros, and of course there was Katy; in with the jet set at last and at this moment rifling the personal belongings of her lover.

I glanced at him as I finished the top drawer and started on the next. Apart from being a sweety, he was also a dish. Twenty-six or thereabouts, and unlike most of his contemporaries in the bullring, from a very good Spanish family. He hadn't started to fight bulls from hunger, but because he wanted to. The critics had started by saying he would never make a truly good matador because he had never starved. And it was probably true he would never be a Manolete or a Belmonte, but he was bloody good from where I was sitting. I'm neither pro nor anti bullfighting, and I suppose if I were asked to analyse it I would have to admit that it is basically cruel; but then so are *paté de foie gras* and battery chickens. Having convinced myself of that, I become an *afficionado*. With someone like Antonio, it had been easy. There's something about sleeping with a bullfighter that's like nothing else. I suppose a racing driver might be similar, but not to such a large extent. It's the proximity to death that does it. It heightens sexual awareness; each time you get into bed may be the last, so everything becomes that much more important.

There was nothing in the first two drawers and I started on the third.

'Why not have the customs go through his bags and take it off him?' I had asked Mr. Blaser, not unreasonably I thought.

'We are not interested in the gold, that's why,' he said.

'Oh,' I said, not sure where on earth we were going.

'Allow me to enlarge on that,' he continued. Thank you very much, I thought. 'We are not interested in preventing the smuggling of the gold, only in ascertaining what kind of gold it is.' To me, gold was gold; obviously I'd been wrong all my life. 'What do you know about the refining of gold, Miss Touchfeather?'

'Absolutely nothing, sir.'

'I thought as much.' He tossed a folder across his desk towards me. 'I suggest you read this as soon as possible.'

'What is it?'

'It is a short report on the methods and processes involved in the refining of gold.'

It was about an inch thick and looked as short as a telephone directory. I pulled it towards me and flipped back the cover; single space typing on foolscap sheets; it would take me a week to wade through. But I started anyway.

'Later, Miss Touchfeather,' snapped Mr. Blaser.

I sat back quickly. 'Yes sir.'

'When you locate what we are looking for you will take a sample and then replace the gold so that no one will know it has been disturbed. Clear?'

'Not very, sir.'

'When you have read that, it will be,' he said.

I doubted it, but the after effects of my party were beginning to creep up on me, and I wanted to go home. I got to my feet and headed for the door.

'Miss Touchfeather,' he said just before I went out. I turned back to him. 'The next time you come into this office, try to do so sober,' he said bleakly. Which only goes to show that he is not as dim as I would sometimes like to believe.

The third drawer yielded nothing either, and I was beginning to get heartily sick of the whole affair. Antonio was still rumbling away in the background and I dearly wanted to join him. But duty called, and I started on the built-in wardrobes. Gold can be disguised into practically any shape, but even I know that it ends up still being metal; it may be sprayed silver, bronze or grey but, however ingenious the smuggler is, he can't make it look like a Christian Dior necktie or a pair of silk Y fronts. And all this speculation seemed pretty stupid when I reached the second wardrobe, because that's where I found it. It wasn't disguised as a model of the Eiffel Tower or a 'present from the Cote d'Azur'; it wasn't disguised at all. In the bottom of one of Antonio's small hand cases, the sort that one usually carries on to the aeroplane, were three gold bars. And that's exactly what they were, bars of gold, ingots, or whatever they're called. I lifted one gingerly from the bottom of the bag. God, it was heavy! Multiply it by three and one had to admire Antonio; I knew he was pretty strong in more ways than one, but to heft that bag around making it look as though it carried nothing more than a toothbrush and a pair of pyjamas was going to take some doing. He would have to carry it as hand luggage, that way he could avoid having it weighed at the airport. And for Antonio, the celebrated Matador de Toros, customs would prove no problem either out of Spain or into South America.

I replaced the ingot next to its companions and scampered back to bed. Shaving samples off gold bars wasn't something that one could do at dead of night with someone sleeping not ten feet away. But at least I had located the stuff, and tomorrow or the next day I would find time to do the necessary. Antonio grunted something as I grabbed my share of the sheet, but he didn't even wake up. Normally, after making love long and well, all I want to do is sleep, but this time I was so wide awake I doubted I would ever sleep again. I lay on my back for a while, contemplating the ceiling and wondering how much trouble Antonio was going to get into as a result of all this. And wondering why. Because money he just didn't need. Apart from the fact that his family seemed to own two-thirds of Spain, he earned enough each Sunday afternoon to keep an average family in luxury for a year. But then, everyone aboard the *Maria* was filthy stinking rich; one of them must have passed the stuff to Antonio, because he certainly didn't have it before we came aboard. I suppose it was just a case of the more you've got, the more you want.

Mr. Blaser had been as tight as a clam; just get the samples and turn them over to the first contact I could make. Then I was to extricate myself from the high-life and return to London. Whys and wherefores weren't my concern, apparently.

I tucked myself into the crook of Antonio's body and tried to persuade myself into sleep. But it still wouldn't come and after ten minutes the sweat created where our bodies touched became uncomfortable. I rolled clear again and continued my earlier contemplation of the ceiling. And, as is my wont on occasions like this, my reflective turn of mind carried me back beyond the present assignment, beyond even the previous one; right back, in fact, to the time when Mr. Blaser entered my life.

Six months before meeting Mr. Blaser, my existence had been neat and well ordered. I was an air stewardess. We used to call ourselves hostesses, but the connotation smacked of night clubs and call girls; and while most of us enjoy night clubs, and some of us even moonlight in the latter profession, it wasn't the image we wished to put over to the travelling public. So there I was, free, white and twenty-one, a fully fledged, paid up, member-in-good-standing, air stewardesss. Then I met this sweet, lovely man. He was captain on one of my early flights to Beirut. I fell like a ton of bricks, and our two day stopover in Beirut turned into a sort of pre-nuptial honeymoon. We were married very soon after, and three months later I was a widow. An accident, they had said; and I had believed them because I was like that in those days.

Then Mr. Blaser crept into my life. He convinced me that it had been no accident, and he presented me with a formidable pile of evidence to back up his claim. My husband had been murdered. The Touchfeather blood started to boil and I greedily accepted Mr. Blaser's offer to square the books. One thing led to another and, before I fully realized it, I was no longer a common or garden air stewardess, but a cross between a female James Bond and Mata Hari.

I still flew, but one day it would be for BOAC, the next Air India and the third Pan Am. This was what they call in the trade my 'cover'. Mind you, I'm a good air stewardess, too. I'm built right, everything evenly distributed; my bust is a little prominent perhaps, but I've never found that a particular disadvantage. My reddish hair and greenish eyes seem to go well with most of the airline uniforms I'm required to wear, and I can pour a martini, serve a meal, empty a sick bag, calm a frightened passenger and fend off a wandering hand, all at the same time if necessary.

Mr. Blaser started me off on nice simple jobs when I first entered his department; I suppose he hadn't wanted to scare me off before I found my sea legs. There were a couple of simple tailing jobs from London to Tokyo and back, via Sydney and Calcutta. I delivered some mysterious packages to equally mysterious individuals in Tangier, Beirut, Bombay and Rangoon.

Then, apparently satisfied, he sent me back to school where I was handed over to the care of a WRAC sergeant of vast proportions and strong lesbian inclinations. Bessie was her name and she was rather a sweety, actually. She taught me the six most horrendous things a girl can do to a man. I've only used two of them since and I still go quite cold when I recall the effect they had. I've cause to be grateful to Bessie, wherever she is. She did try to teach me the joys of lesbianism as well but, while I have dabbled—I'll try anything once—it isn't really my speed at all. I'm a normal type girl and I enjoy normal sex— whatever that may be.

What I really mean is that I like a man involved somewhere and, provided I am equally involved, as frequently as possible. I don't go along with that theory about men needing it more than women. Most women need it just as much, but they're better equipped mentally to control themselves if they're not getting it. Being a freelance air stewardess has its advantages: one gets to meet a vast number of attractive men, with the added bonus that, if one is careful geographically, there's very little chance that they'll trip over each other.

Not being a greedy girl, I make do with three on a semi-permanent basis. One of them is the airport manager in one of the South American countries; another is a flight captain on the New York-Los Angeles run; and my home number is just a nice man who sells motor cars and considers a trip to the Isle of Wight as foreign travel. They're all nice men, and I suppose I'm a little in love with all three of them. No doubt all three would marry me if I gave them the faintest encouragement, but marriage I can do without at the moment. Strange as it may sound, I actually enjoy working for Mr. Blaser. It has drawbacks, of course; like the time I was locked in an Italian cellar with two crazy American hoods who were making patterns all over me with lighted cigarettes,* but they're both dead now and there's not much point in bearing grudges.

In any event, such situations I have learned to relegate to the area of occupational hazards, and the drawbacks are amply compensated for by the enormous satisfaction I get from a job well done. And I am good at my job. Fortunately I don't need Mr. Blaser to tell me so, because he never says a word except to criticize. But I usually accomplish what I set out to do, and up to now

* Touchfeather.

I've managed to stay in one piece. I have scars, of course, but you can get scarred from knocking over a frying pan, or banging your foot on the vacuum cleaner. All in all, I am a pretty well adjusted girl who enjoys her work and does it well. I'm not overly modest either, but you will have probably gathered that.

I drifted off to sleep about four a.m. so I was a bit miffed when Antonio woke me up at ten-thirty. Then I realized why he had awakened me, and it was alright again. We made soft, gentle love most of the morning and probably would have gone through the best part of the afternoon as well, except that the engines stopped suddenly. Antonio tottered over to the window and looked out.

'Where are we?' I asked from the bed.

He came back towards me shrugging. 'Everywhere looks the same at sea.' he said. He climbed back into bed.

'Let's go ashore for lunch,' I said.

'You're all I want to eat right now,' he said, reaching for me again. He really was the most marvellous lover. His body was hard and lean and, if one discounted the scars of his profession, each one looking dramatic enough to have killed six ordinary men, he was also very beautiful. I felt a rush of tenderness towards him and he started nuzzling me gently, driving me right up the wall. If that was how he wanted to take his lunch, who was I to argue? I rolled myself around and joined the feast.

Afterwards we dozed off again, and I woke up half an hour later still in his arms. He smelled warm and very sexy. I'm a great one for smells as long as they're clean and, lying there with him sleeping all over me, I'm damned if I didn't start to turn on again. Enough Katy, I thought, this is ridiculous. I slid away from him gently and padded over to the bathroom where I had a quick shower and slipped into a bikini. Then I tip-toed back into the stateroom. He was still asleep. I planted a little kiss on his bare backside and went up on deck, feeling as warm towards him as I had towards anyone for a long long time. This, of course, exposes an essential flaw in my makeup; one that I have tried to suppress, but which every now and then rears its ugly head inconveniently. The flaw is simply that I am still able to become personally involved with people I have no business to. Mr. Blaser had made it very clear that, should things go wrong on this job, I was expected to do something about removing Antonio from the scene permanently. I suppose, if it came to the crunch, I *could* do it, but it would keep me awake nights for at least a week.

The deck was as hot under foot as the sun was overhead, the dry, flat heat of the Mediterranean. I love the South of France; I suppose you could call me a France-ophile (as opposed to a Francophile). Gary Brian was the only one of my fellow guests present. He had a large drink in his hand and a jaundiced look in his eyes. I sat in the chair next to him and ordered a champagne orange from the steward who had appeared beside me instantly.

'Godawful trip darling,' said Gary for openers.

'I'm having a ball.'

'I'm not at all surprised,' he said. Then he leaned forward. 'I suppose there's no chance you might get tired of your beautiful bullfighter?'

'By him, not of him,' I said, a little smugly.

He relaxed in his chair. 'It figured that way,' he said without rancour. 'Godawful trip.'

'Why don't you go ashore?' As soon as I had come up on deck, I had recognized that we were lying off La Siesta at Antibes. I knew the place well. 'You're bound to get lucky there.'

'Too risky, sweety. Before I get involved I've got to inspect the pedigree. Vulnerable, that's my problem.'

'Once bitten?' I asked, rather liking him.

He gave me a wicked grin, the one that had formed queues outside more cinemas than I have had hot dinners. 'More than once sweety. Delicious.'

'Antonio's not right for you, anyway,' I said.

'I can see that by the bags under your eyes. I'll be alright once we get to St. Tropez. I have my contacts there. But that's a couple of days away.'

'Why don't you go ashore and drive there? It only takes an hour. You can pick up the boat again when we arrive.'

He gave the suggestion a moment of quiet thought, then got to his feet abruptly. 'Brilliant, darling. I'll see you on Thursday. Make my apologies.' He loped off to find a boat to take him ashore. I felt I'd done him a big favour he looked so happy.

The steward brought me my drink a moment later. Not just a glass, of course, but a bottle of Dom Perignon in a silver ice bucket, and a beautiful cut glass jug of fresh orange juice. He opened the champagne immaculately, tipped ice out of the glass, and poured my breakfast, half champagne, half orange juice. Then he stood respectfully while I tasted it.

'*Formidable*,' I said. He bowed and disappeared as quietly and as efficiently as everything else on this floating palace. A word about the *Maria*: everyone has heard of the *Christina*; well add an extra quarter of a million pounds and you've got the *Maria*. It is impossible to describe the indescribable, so there is no point in wasting my time trying. I took another sip of my drink. My God, Katy, this is the life, I thought. I'd had my share of luxury since working for Mr. Blaser, but there was usually something pretty nasty lurking in the vicinity; something I had just done, or was about to do. But in this case I was required to harm no one; a simple two minutes alone in our stateroom; a contact in St. Tropez two days from now, and that was that. In the meantime, eat, drink and make love. Life was very good and I raised my glass in a silent toast to Mr. Blaser. Perhaps it was that which did it; one shouldn't provoke the deities and Mr. Blaser is the only deity I know personally. If I'd kept my mouth shut and just drunk my champagne, perhaps things wouldn't have gone as wrong as they sure in hell did.

The other guests drifted back to the boat about five-thirty. They'd had too much food, sun and booze and looked a pretty bedraggled lot; all except the textile man's three companions who looked as cool as three glasses of iced lager, complete to the frosting on the outside. And Galipolodopolo looked as smooth as he ever did. He must have been at least sixty years old, but he looked a well preserved fifty, and very dishy if one liked one's men short, dark and Greek. Personally I don't, but if the world's press were even half way accurate, there were plenty who did. His name had been linked with every international beauty on the scene for the past fifteen years, and this notwithstanding the fact that he had been married all that time. Much to my surprise he came over and sat down next to me while everyone else staggered below to sleep off the day.

'I'm sorry you weren't able to join us for lunch,' he said.

I pointed to the remains of the caviar the steward had brought me. 'I was well taken care of.'

He smiled showing his immaculate teeth. 'I'm glad. And Antonio?'

'Still sleeping.'

'I envy the ability of the young to sleep,' he said. 'If I manage more than four hours out of each twenty-four, I consider myself lucky—you are a very beautiful girl, Katherine.'

This caught me way off guard on two counts; first he tucked the phrase on to the end of his sentence without pause or change of tone; and second, I wasn't even aware that he knew my name. We had been introduced, of course, when we first came aboard, but that had been the sum total of our acquaintance to date.

'Thank you,' I said and, believe it or not, I started to blush. I mean, I know I'm quite attractive and all that, but when one of the richest men in the world tells you you're beautiful . . . well, it just gets to a girl where it matters.

'I would like to make love to you,' he said, still without changing his tone. The blush, which had started to recede, now re-blossomed like the rising sun, and for a moment I really couldn't think of anything to say. Then I did the unpardonable: I giggled; not chuckled or laughed, but giggled like an embarrassed school-girl. His eyes didn't go cold because they were always that way; in fact, his expression didn't change one iota. He looked at me steadily for a few seconds, then he got to his feet. 'Let me know when Katherine,' he said, and walked away without a backward glance.

Not let me know 'if', but let me know 'when'. Antonio would probably run him through with his *espada* if I told him. But then again, he probably wouldn't. The group of people I was now moving with passed their girlfriends round like cigarettes, and all of a sudden I decided I didn't care as much for the high-life as I had at first thought. Galipolodopolo's remark had even cast a shadow over my relationship with Antonio. But it was just as well I suppose; I had started to forget my position in the whole affair. I was here to work, so the best thing I could do would be to get the work done and get out of here while my sense of values was still intact. And, as though to help me on my way, Antonio came on deck at that moment, looking quite beautiful in his swimming trunks and with a towel slung over his shoulders. He came over to join me.

'I woke up and you weren't there,' he said.

'I'm resting up.'

He reached out and gently squeezed one of my nipples through my bikini bra. I felt it creep to attention. 'I'll have a swim and then we'll find out how much good your rest has done you. Alright?'

I nodded. 'I'll go down and make myself sexy.'

'Twenty minutes,' he said. 'Then I'll make you sexy.'

'You already have,' I said, removing his hand gently.

I watched him move over to the deck rail. He threw his towel on to the deck, jumped lightly on to the rail, posed for a brief moment, and then dived overboard into the incredible blue of the sea. There was a pool on board, of course, but Antonio was a long distance swimmer: he didn't believe in paddling about splashing water on each other. He liked plenty of space and I knew he would swim at least half a mile from the boat before turning bask. That gave me the twenty minutes he had promised with a probable fifteen more on top. I got to my feet and went below.

Gold: a dense, bright yellow metal; symbol Au; atomic number 79; atomic weight 197·2. The dossier handed to me by Mr. Blaser had started out like that. Then it had gone on for sixty-two closely typed pages which, if I had read and understood them, would probably have told me more about the stuff than anyone needs to know. As it was, I had skimmed through it, missing out the parts that seemed too complicated, comprising about two-thirds of the report, but at the end I still knew more about gold than anyone not intimately connected with the stuff. And I think it was just bloody mindedness on Mr. Blaser's part making me read it anyway, because all I had to do was to take the samples. I wasn't going to be the one who had to analyse them.

The stateroom struck very cold as I came down from the deck. I turned down the air conditioner and wrapped myself in a towelling robe. From my manicure case I produced a small, scalpel type knife which had been provided by the department. Had anyone been interested in my manicure case, the knife *could* have been something to do with nail paring or cuticle cutting; but in fact it was as sharp as a razor and God knows how many times tougher. It would cut gold like an ordinary knife cuts butter, I had been told. I hadn't believed it particularly, but now was the time to find out.

I removed one of the gold bars from Antonio's case and carried it over to the light. I examined it carefully for any markings, but it was as clean as a whistle. I had been told to expect none but to make sure just in case. Then I took the knife and placing the blade flat along the base of the gold bar, I drew it towards me. Whoever had designed the knife, knew his job. There was a fractional curve along the flatness of the blade, invisible to the naked eye. But this curve sliced a sliver of gold from the base of the bar thinner than a cigarette paper. I drew the knife towards me half an inch, then relaxed the pressure slightly. As I did this, the wafer of gold was detached. Holding my breath in case I blew it away, I picked it up with a pair of eyebrow tweezers and slipped it into a small plastic envelope. It was so thin that when I held it up to the light I could see through the gold as well. I examined the gold bar minutely before I replaced it. A microscope might have shown where I had removed my sample, but you certainly couldn't see anything with the naked eye; at least, I couldn't.

I repeated the whole business with the other two bars, replacing each one exactly where I had found it. The knife and the plastic envelope I replaced in my manicure set, the envelope slipping neatly between the lining and the case. And that was it. That was what I had travelled half way round the world for. All that remained was to pass it to a contact in St. Tropez. If for any reason we didn't go to St. Tropez, then the contact would be made at the first port of call we *did* make. And then Katy could go home. But that was two days away which meant I had forty-eight more hours of the high-life, if I could stand the pace.

I went to the bathroom, stripped off and showered. Then I

settled back on the bed to wait for Antonio to finish his swim and get down to work again. I must have dozed off, because when I next became aware of the time, more than an hour had passed, and I was very cold. I got up, turned the air conditioner off altogether and, pulling on a pair of slacks and a sweater, I went up on deck to find out what had happened to my bullfighter.

There was no one around, which wasn't surprising when one remembered the condition they had all been in when they returned from lunch. I didn't expect any of that lot to put in an appearance before nine p.m. at the earliest, if then. The sun was going down in a molten sky behind the old fort and the sea was as calm and flat as a sheet of polished glass. Two miles away a speedboat swept out from behind the Cap, heading across towards Nice, but apart from that nothing moved except for the cars just visible on the road backing the long stretch of stony beach. Antonio's towel was still where he had dropped it before going in for his swim. Quite suddenly, cold as I had been, I became even colder. I rang the bell for the steward who appeared as though he had been waiting on tenterhooks all day for this summons.

'Have you seen Senor Fuentes?'

He shook his head. 'No Madame.'

I thought about it for a moment. 'Would you tell the Captain I'd like to see him,' I said.

He bowed and disappeared, leaving me looking out to sea, searching for I know not what. The Captain, a Greek of indeterminate age and antecedents, joined me in less than a minute.

'I know this may sound silly.' I said. 'But I think we've lost Senor Fuentes.'

'Lost?'

'He went for a swim. He doesn't seem to have returned.'

'How long ago?' Not much concern yet.

'Over an hour.' A little concern now.

'What makes you think he hasn't come back on board?'

I pointed to Antonio's towel. 'It's exactly where he left it when he dived in.'

The Captain digested this for a moment, then he saluted politely and walked quietly away.

I remained where I was while the boat was searched, and I remained there when the others came up on deck to watch the crew launch the two speedboats. I was still there two hours later when Antonio's lifeless body was carried back on board.

## CHAPTER TWO

'YOU SEEM to have mismanaged the whole affair abominably, Miss Touchfeather,' said Mr. Blaser.

'Yes, sir.'

'A perfectly simple task which could have been carried out by a disinterested girl guide. And what do you do?'

'I ball it up, sir.'

He frowned, the lines in his already weatherbeaten face becoming positively canyon like. 'If I thought for one moment that you were treating this affair with anything but deadly seriousness, I would take you off duties and bury you so deep you'd never emerge again.' He wasn't given to idle threats, was Mr. Blaser; but then neither was I trying to be facetious.

I *had* balled it up, and that's all there was to it. He settled back in his chair. 'Perhaps I have missed something out, Miss Touchfeather,' he said. 'Shall we go over the whole thing once more?'

He had missed nothing, but we went over it again anyway.

Antonio had been fetched aboard and laid out on the deck. Resuscitation had been attempted in the speedboat as soon as he had been dragged from the water. But he was long dead and, once he was lifted aboard the *Maria*, all they did was to spread a blanket over him and wait for the arrival of the police who had been summoned by ship to shore telephone. My fellow passengers grew very bored very quickly, and after a short time I was the only one of us who remained with Antonio. Galipolodopolo had tried to talk me into going below, but I had shaken my head through a mist of tears and he had diplomatically left me to wallow in my misery.

The police arrived half an hour later. They asked me some preliminary questions and we were about to get down to serious business when the very junior man in charge took a look at the passenger list. He wilted visibly and disappeared into the radio shack for a few minutes. When he re-emerged he walked as though on broken glass, taking care not to step on any of the very influential toes the *Maria* abounded with. Very politely he asked the Captain if he would ask Mr. Galipolodopolo if he would mind terribly putting into Nice for a short time. He didn't mind, and that's where we went.

Someone on board had got a big mouth for, when we arrived an hour later, there were enough people on the quay to seriously disrupt the traffic. We were all requested to remain aboard, and Antonio's body was carried ashore and driven off in an ambulance. A strong police guard was put on the gangway to stop unwelcome visitors from overrunning us and, a few minutes after we docked, a full blown Chief Inspector lumbered aboard, looking like a cross between Maigret and Robespierre. We were all questioned as the Inspector endeavoured to put together the facts. Not that there was much problem. Antonio had gone for a swim, something had happened, and he had drowned; all very unfortunate, but straightforward.

Half an hour after the Inspector came aboard, the Captain informed him that Mr. Galipolodopolo wished to take the *Maria* out of Nice as soon as possible and would the Inspector kindly remove his finger, as Mr. Galipolodopolo didn't like to be kept waiting. The Inspector didn't like to be talked to in this fashion and, naturally enough, he became a little stroppy. But the poor dear man didn't stand a chance; within fifteen minutes there arrived on board a Frenchman with diplomatic corps written all over him. He was accompanied by a Superintendent of police and a man from the Mayor's office. There was a fourth man, too, who claimed to be a junior police officer, but who I knew was no such thing. I'd met him before a couple of times and, while he may have appeared to work for the Nice police department, he also worked for the Deuxième Bureau, the CIA, MI5, 6 and 7 and, for all I knew, the NKVD and KGB as well. He also worked on and off for Mr. Blaser, which is why I recognized him.

While the heavy guns were attacking the Chief Inspector, beating him over the head with his pension, my man managed to get it across to me that I was expected to leave the boat there and then. And that's exactly what I did do. I started to cry all over again. The first time had been when Antonio had been lifted aboard, and that had been for real. This time I squeezed a few tears and managed a minor attack of hysterics. Shouting that I couldn't bear to remain aboard for another second, I staggered ashore. Unfortunately, I forgot to take my luggage with me. And in my luggage, of course, reposed the object of the whole exercise, my gold samples.

'Perhaps you had too much sun,' said Mr. Blaser.

'Yes, sir.' I felt the less said the better at this stage.

'Have you *no* excuses?'

I did have a slender one and I thought that here was as good a time as any to try it out. 'It would have been all right if you hadn't recalled me.'

'I recalled you for the simple reason I assumed the whole venture had aborted.'

'Why?'

'Your instructions were that if you got into trouble you were to . . . dispose of the man. I assumed that was what you had done. I merely wanted to get you out of the predicament I thought you had got yourself into.'

That was nice of him, I thought.

'With you dead or incapacitated,' he continued, 'I would have to have assigned someone else to the affair, and at this moment there is no one else available.'

So up you, too, I thought. But I threw him a crumb. 'Well I didn't kill Antonio,' I said. 'Someone else did.'

He didn't bat an eyelid.

'The Coroner in Nice describes it as death by drowning.'

'And no doubt that's what it was,' I said. 'But there is more than one way to skin a cat.'

'Stop being obtuse, Miss Touchfeather.'

'Sorry, sir. There was a frogman lurking around.'

I had been on deck when the speedboats had left to search for Antonio and, because I'm trained for such trivialities, I had noticed something that none of my fellow passengers had. The boats had left with four crew members apiece; one of them had returned with five. Later, on our way to Nice, I had taken a quick look into this boat, which had been hoisted back on deck. Under the rear seat squab had been a frogman's suit, and it was still wet.

'You are suggesting that someone from the *Maria* swam out after this man and deliberately drowned him?'

'I'm not suggesting anything, sir. I'm just telling you what I saw.'

'Assumptions?'

'As long as you're asking, sir, yes, I do think someone from the *Maria* drowned Antonio. He was a magnificent swimmer and in perfect physical health. There can be no other explanation.'

'Reason?'

'You've never told me what this is about, so how can I be expected to come up with a reason?' This was a little bold of me but, after all, he had asked. He digested this for a moment, making up his mind whether to tell me anything or not.

'Mmm,' he said, after a few seconds. I waited, and after another lengthy pause, he said 'Mmm' again. Finally he dragged himself back to awareness of me. 'Could you get back on board?'

'The *Maria*?'

He nodded.

'If it's the gold samples you're worried about, surely the easy thing to do would be to have my luggage picked up at their next port of call?'

'Answer my question, please, Miss Touchfeather!'

I thought about Galipolodopolo. 'Tell me when, Katherine,' he had said. He wasn't bad looking; and he *was* one of the richest men in the world; and I badly wanted to have a go at someone for Antonio; and Mr. Blaser was the boss.

'Yes, sir,' I said.

'When?'

'I'll have to send a cable.'

'Send it.'

'From Nice. That's where I'm supposed to be.'

'Miss Moody will take care of it.'

'Then I've got to be invited,' I added.

'See that you are,' said Mr. Blaser, and that seemed to be that.

Miss Moody took down my cable for me. She is Mr. Blaser's secretary-cum-right-hand; a little grey haired body of indeterminate age who never smiles. This isn't because she is unfriendly, but she possesses a very badly fitting set of false teeth which on occasions have been known to drop out in her lap. So she tries to keep her mouth shut at all times, talking as much as possible through her nose.

'You look lovely and brown,' she said, after despatching my cable through the Nice office. I liked Miss Moody. Apart from the fact that she usually says something nice to me, she is the person responsible for checking my expenses and she has been known to pass items that Mr. Blaser didn't even know existed. She had looked a little puzzled when I dictated the cable, but she hadn't said a word as she took it down. I asked her to take a copy in to Mr. Blaser. Let him work that one out, I thought.

GALIPOLODOPOLO SS MARIA C/O GALIPOLODOPOLO ATHENS WHEN STOP WHERE QUERY KATHERINE

Galipolodopolo would get it even if Mr. Blaser didn't. And I hied me to the South of France once more.

The Hotel Byblos at St. Tropez is truly a wondrous place. It's about the best hotel for a hundred miles in any direction but, even if it wasn't, it would still be my idea of heaven. It is a low, rambling place, cool and faintly Eastern in design, with all the luxuries of the West thrown in. There are beautifully tiled courtyards, small arches leading to enchanting little hideaways, and a split level bar that perches out over the swimming pool. The service is impeccable, with just the right mixture of the personal and impersonal. Film stars stay there, so do film producers; millionaires stay there either *en famille* or most definitely *sans famille*; the only qualification the Byblos makes of its guests is that they be rich; it provides the best that money can buy and you need plenty of money to buy it. But I was a guest of Galipolodopolo, and I received the bridal suite and the royal treatment. A reply to my telegram had been phoned through from Nice within two hours of sending mine.

TOUCHFEATHER NEGRESCO NICE
SAINT TROPEZ THURSDAY WAIT AT BYBLOS CONSTANTIN

As I wasn't supposed to have any luggage, I caught the first plane back to Nice. There I checked into the Negresco, arranged to have a bill falsified and back dated two days, and promptly checked out again. I hired a car and drove to St. Tropez. At the Byblos I was greeted like the Queen of Sheba. I was informed deferentially that instructions had been given that I was to buy anything I wanted in the town and charge it to my hotel bill. Never having been one to miss an opportunity, and mindful of my role as that of a jet set courtesan who would have no scruples in that direction, I trotted down to the town and spent a fortune on clothes I would probably never wear, but which were fun to have lying around. This was Wednesday and the *Maria* wasn't expected until the next day. I wasn't supposed to know anyone in St. Tropez, so I was agreeably surprised when my phone rang at six o'clock, just about cocktail time. It was Gary Brian.

'Katy, darling. I heard you were in town. Are you in mourning?'

'Not particularly.'

'Oh, the fickleness of youth. Meet you in the bar in ten minutes. I've something to show you.'

The something turned out to be the most beautiful boy I have ever seen. His name was Gaston and he was tall, willowy, with coal black hair and light blue eyes and a mouth to send anyone wild. He smiled gently at me as Gary introduced us and took my hand in his. He had a grip like a steel trap and then, as he bent low over my hand, he tickled my palm with the tip of his forefinger. Poor Gary, I thought; here was one pedigree he hadn't checked too carefully. But it turned out that Gaston did what he did for a living and, be it with male or female, he believed in giving value for money. Gary was ecstatic.

'It's all your doing, beloved,' he told me. 'It was your idea that I came here in the first place.' Then he remembered suddenly that I'd had a personal tragedy, and he went all Hollywood on me. 'What can I say, Katy? You poor, poor child! What you must be going through,' and all that jazz. I stood it for a couple of minutes then I drew the line.

'I'm rejoining the *Maria* tomorrow,' I said.

'Oh! Under whose auspices?'

'Constantin Galipolodopolo's.'

He patted me on the head. 'There's a brave girl,' he said. 'Clever, too.'

And in truth I wasn't mourning any longer. Anger, yes; misery, no. Because, in my line of business, reflecting on the past is strictly for the birds. I had been fond of Antonio, yes; but I hadn't been in love with him. We had swung together and it had been simply marvellous. But now he was dead, and tomorrow was another day. We Touchfeathers are realists, if nothing else.

I had dinner with Gary and Gaston on the poolside patio of the hotel, where it seemed half St. Tropez had come to dine. All the women fancied Gary, all the men fancied me, and all the in-betweens fancied Gaston. We were the centre of attraction as everyone tried to work out what sort of arrangement we had going between the three of us—who had who while who did what. We were the best looking *ménage a trois* you ever did see, and I felt like the belle of fifteen different balls all at the same time.

Afterwards we went to *Les Caves du Roy,* the club built beneath the hotel where the noise was stupendous and the atmosphere stifling. Then we moved on to the *Voom Voom* and, later, the *Papagayo,* our party growing larger by the minute. It was half past five when we started back to the hotel. We were tottering along the quay playing hopscotch over the mooring ropes of the floating gin palaces that seem to spend their entire sea-going lives tied up in exotic ports, when Gary suddenly hove to.

'Ship ahoy!' he said.

I looked out to where he was pointing. Just outside the harbour bar, riding gently in a lazy swell, lay the *Maria.* Fun over, Katy, I thought. Back to business.

Gary opted out of rejoining the boat. Gaston couldn't or wouldn't get away and Gary decided that where Gaston stayed, he would stay, too. He sent a message out to the *Maria* and had his luggage brought ashore.

I travelled out to the *Maria* on the same speedboat that had carried Antonio's body and was delighted to find I didn't feel a thing.

Constantin Galipolodopolo was waiting for me at the top of the gangway. He kissed my hand elegantly and said how delighted he was to see me again, then turned me over to a steward who escorted me down to a stateroom. Not the same one used by Antonio and me, but one which had a connecting door to another stateroom; and it didn't take much working out to know where the owner's cabin was located. My luggage from the previous voyage had been transferred and I watched while the steward hung up and put away all the new stuff I had picked up yesterday. Then, as soon as he left, I made a beeline for my manicure case. My samples were still there.

\* \* \*

'We still need those samples Miss Touchfeather,' Mr. Blaser had said. 'And the same arrangements will apply. There will be a contact waiting for you in each port you call at. As for this new business, if you have any information to pass, you will do so at the same time that you pass the samples.'

This new business was simply for me to find out as much as I could about Antonio's death. Not who killed him, because apparently that wasn't important; all that mattered were the reasons for his being murdered. And finally Mr. Blaser just had to tell me the details of the whole affair. He explained it to me once and, in case I hadn't got it, he explained it a second time.

He told me Galipolodopolo was engaged in smuggling gold. 'So what?' I had replied. 'Everybody smuggles gold these days.' But it seemed that the gold that Constantin was shifting all round the globe had no business being in existence in the first place. The world supply of gold is kept under pretty tight control; the people whose job it is to know about such things keep accurate reports on how much gold is dug out of the ground; how and where it is refined; and what happens to it later. So much is used for jewellery, *objets d'art* and other trivialities; so much is returned to the ground from whence it came in innumerable vaults, banks, safe deposits, tin trunks and old boxes; so much is shipped back and forth between Governments trying to balance their budgets; and so much just disappears, God knows where. But, at all times, a check is kept on it to the nearest five or six million dollars' worth. In other words, it is known at any one time that there is umpty-four million dollars worth of gold floating around somewhere, and everyone is reasonably happy knowing more or less where it is.

But during the past couple of years the boys with their adding machines had started to get worried. It seemed there was no longer umpty-four million dollars' worth, but umpty-five or even six. And no one knew where it was coming from. The Russians, notoriously tight-lipped normally, had been approached through tortuous channels to find out whether they were digging out more than usual, but it turned out that they were just as concerned as were our lot. They'd noticed it, too, and had wondered themselves. They were asked if they could make discreet inquiries from the Red Chinese, but Russia and Red China weren't talking any more and they had declined.

About here I had made one of my stupid remarks which I occasionally do, and which never fails to get up Mr. Blaser's nose.

'Surely,' I had said. 'The more gold there is, the better?'

He doesn't often actually snarl at me, but he did this time. He must have been getting it pretty strong from up top, I decided.

'Controls, Miss Touchfeather! We must have controls. Think

for one moment what would happen if there was a sudden glut of gold.'

I thought, and I must admit the idea sounded attractive.

'Chaos,' said Mr. Blaser. 'Absolute chaos. The monetary systems of the world would collapse.' I hung my head, not quite knowing why. 'International finance is a delicately balanced operation,' he went on. 'Our entire economy is built on gold. Flood the market with gold and gold becomes worthless. Now do you understand?' I didn't, but I let him go on. 'Gold is appearing all over the world,' he continued. 'Gold which, to the best of our knowledge, doesn't exist. It has been mined and refined by people we know nothing about in a place we can't identify. It may be Red China, it may be one of the emergent African nations, it may be South American in origin, we just don't know. But we must find out. Right?'

'Yes, sir.'

'That is why we want the samples that you idiotically forgot about. It may be that the analysts will be able to ascertain point of origin from the chemical properties. Gold dug up in Africa differs from gold dug up in Alaska. Most of the differences are refined out of the finished product, but we may be lucky.' He offered me one of his wintry smiles which, if anything, are worse than his snarls. 'If you'd had even half your wits about you, we would already have completed that phase of the operation, Miss Touchfeather.'

'Yes, sir,' I said.

There had been a little more. It seemed that Constantin Galipolodopolo had been tied into the whole thing somewhere along the line. On three occasions the pirate gold had been traced back as far as him. A distributor he most certainly was; my job was to try to find out if he was anything more and, if he wasn't, to find out who the hell was. Antonio must have been some sort of courier, carrying gold into South America or Mexico or Spain. Being no end of a celebrity in bullfighting countries, he was never likely to have trouble with customs, so he was ideal for the job. The only point that still puzzled me as far as Antonio was concerned, why someone as rich and successful as he would even have bothered. I mentioned this to Mr. Blaser.

'Mr. Galipolodopolo is also rich and successful, Miss Touchfeather. Much more so than your late friend who fought cows for a living.' And that had been that.

Now here I was, a member of the jet set once more, and about to be seduced by one of the richest men in the world. My seduction was obviously going to take place on the high seas because, before I had been in my stateroom for ten minutes, I felt the

engines start up and we were under way again. I mooned around
the stateroom for another half hour, then I decided that I had
better put in some sort of appearance for the benefit of my fellow
passengers. It would be as well to set the record straight as far as
they were concerned as soon as possible. I climbed into a bikini
and, wearing one of the towelling robes supplied by the *Maria*,
I wandered up on deck. With the rather obvious exception of
Mrs. Galipolodopolo, they were all there, all except Constantin.
Sir Roger, the Count, the Countess and the textile magnate were
playing bridge on the aft deck; the other ladies were engaged in
oiling themselves, swimming in the pool and generally doing
what everyone does on a million pound yacht in the middle of
the Mediterranean. Sir Roger's little bird flashed me a glacial
smile; the three companions of the Frenchman didn't even bother
to do that. They formed a complete entity in themselves; their
lack of communication with the rest of us was complete. They
would murmur quietly among themselves and only address an
outsider with a request to pass the salt or pepper. Trying to work
out what went on between the three of them and their lord and
master once they were all tucked away in their communal stateroom, was something that had occupied everyone else on board
at one time or another.

I borrowed some sun oil from Sir Roger's lady friend, desperately trying to remember her name. She was exceedingly frosty
at first, until I casually mentioned that I had rejoined the party
at the request of our host. After that she started to blossom. Poor
dear, she had been worried that I might be after the title that
she was angling for. Looking across at Sir Roger, it could only
have been the title. He was rich, admittedly, but it all ended
there. He was a shade under six foot tall, with sandy coloured
hair, a minimal chin and red-rimmed pale grey eyes; he possessed
very prominent teeth which weren't particularly clean, and when
he talked he managed to drench you before he had squeezed out
two sentences. He was perhaps the only man on board who didn't
fit the pattern. The French textile man was a hard, cruel, barrel-
shaped man who had hacked his own way to the top; the Count
was smooth and bland and as tough as granite; Constantin, we all
knew about. But Sir Roger . . . I just couldn't see it at all. I
decided that he was along for window dressing, like Gary Brian
had been.

We lolled away the afternoon, becoming stupefied by the sun.
About four p.m. I thought I heard a speedboat starting up somewhere nearby, but I wasn't paying much attention and nobody
else seemed to bother, so it made no real impression. Then at five
o'clock I decided that I'd had enough sun for one day and
staggered down to my stateroom for a bath and a nap before the

evening's festivities. As I opened the door, the first thing I saw
was an envelope lying on my bed, propped up against the pillow.
It was addressed simply to Katherine. I opened and read it.

Katherine my dear,
A thousand apologies, but business has dragged me away. I
will be returning to the *Maria* at Capri in two days' time.
Until then, anything you want just ask.

Constantin.

So my honour was to remain intact for at least another forty-
eight hours. I have to admit, I wasn't sorry. I hadn't been looking
forward to going to bed with Constantin Galipolodopolo; not
that I doubted for a moment he was very adept in that area, but
I really do prefer to choose my own lovers rather than have Mr.
Blaser do it for me.

So Capri was going to be our next port of call. No doubt Mr.
Blaser already knew about it and was arranging my contact there.

I spent half a day poking around and asking questions of any
member of the crew who would stand still long enough to talk to
me. One never knew, perhaps I would turn up new information
on the death of Antonio. But they were either very well trained
or extremely stupid, because nobody knew anything. So now I
had nothing to do except enjoy myself. But somehow without
Antonio, the gilt seemed to have worn off the jet set bit and, as I
bathed and tried to decide what I was going to wear for dinner,
all I could see before me was two days of stupefying boredom.

And that's how it turned out. In fact I spent most of the time
in my stateroom, sleeping. I had my meals sent in, despatching
apologies to my fellow guests. They probably imagined that I
was heartbroken that Constantin had deserted me as soon as
I came back on board and, apart from fighting off the Count
once, when he took it upon himself to come into the stateroom
to inquire about my health, nothing else happened to break the
monotony until we reached Capri.

We dropped anchor at six o'clock on the evening of the second
day and everyone immediately piled ashore. I accompanied them,
and we climbed up to the main square where two tables had
been commandeered for us, to take care of the cocktail hour. As
always, the arrangements had been impeccable, our arrival having
been announced and prepared for. Within seconds of sitting down
the booze was flowing like water and nothing to pay, of course.

The evening promenade in Capri is a sight to behold. It seems
that the entire island moves into the main square, there to see
and be seen. There are the boys and girls, the boys and boys and
the girls and girls. There are the middle-aged, trying to recapture
something; and the downright old who gave up trying to recap-

ture it years ago and now while away their lives in sorrowful reminiscing. There are the starlets and the film men, the has-beens and the never-weres; there are the Italians and the Germans and Scandinavians, a few French and practically no English. And there are the Americans, the individual tourists and their package counterparts, the women with blue hair and the men in Bermuda shorts, festooned with Japanese cameras. And, of course, there is my contact whoever and wherever he is.

But it turned out that I didn't have to worry. I spotted him almost at the same time as he spotted me. It was an old friend, Signor Bertelli, who ran Mr. Blaser's Rome operation. He was sitting at a table a few yards from ours, sharing it with a group of young people who were chattering among themselves in Swedish. Here then was my contact. It would be interesting to see how he would go about it. Perhaps he would signal for me to go to the ladies, or some-such; perhaps he would follow us later and try to waylay me in a dark alley. But whatever he decided to do, I knew it would be efficient. Because beneath the appearance of a lightweight de Sica, Bertelli was solid steel. He had been a founder member of the Italian Resistance during the war and, if the records were accurate, had done things to make even my hair curl. So I sat back and waited for him to make his play.

I didn't have to wait long. He finished his drink, left some money and, getting to his feet, he started to thread his way through the tables, no easy feat considering how closely packed they were. Then came the acting bit. He pretended to see me for the first time, then he did a double take as he looked again. A smile came over his face and he changed direction and started to plough his way towards our table. He started speaking while he was still a good ten feet away, oozing Italian over everyone.

'Miss Touchfeather! Dear, dear Katherine! Is it really you? Can it be you? Dear, dear Katherine . . .'

Everyone was looking at him by now, and by everyone I don't just mean my party, but practically the entire square.

'Dear sweet Miss Touchfeather . . . Katherine! After all this time. Say it's you . . . Say you remember me . . .'

Tripping over a pair of legs he finished up practically in my lap, grabbing my hand and then kissing it as though his very life depended on it.

'Signor Bertelli!' I said, trying to appear surprised, which wasn't all that difficult after watching his performance. 'How nice to see you again.'

He looked crestfallen. 'Umberto, please! Not Signor Bertelli! After all we have been to each other, it must be Umberto.'

The others were agog, and even I was beginning to think he was piling it on a bit thick.

'It's been a long time, Umberto,' I said, trying to drag his feet back on to the ground.

'Too long, dear Katherine ... Katy ... Dear, dear Katy!'

'I'd like you to meet my friends, ' I said, wanting to step out of the blinding limelight that his entrance had switched on. Immediately he released my hand and stood to attention.

'Signor Umberto Bertelli,' he said, damn near clicking his heels. I floated through the names I could remember, stumbling a little over the textile man's three companions. But no one seemed to notice unduly. Then Bertelli took over once more, which was just as well, because I hadn't the faintest idea how to play it.

His face crumpled suddenly. 'You deserted me, Katherine. You left me without a word.' He looked at the others. 'She left me without a word ... at dead of night. I wake up one morning and she is gone ... all her luggage is gone ... I am devastated.' He looked back at me. 'Why Katherine? Why did you do it?' I thought about here that I had better take a hand.

'Please, Umberto!' I said. 'Not here.'

'Not here? Why not here? Are you ashamed? Tell me truly, are you ashamed?'

'Please, Umberto, that's enough.'

'You are ashamed! I know it! You are ashamed of what you did to Umberto Bertelli.'

I got to my feet and turned to the others. 'Please excuse us,' I said. 'I'll see you back on board.' I took Bertelli's arm but he was enjoying himself far too much to leave without a final flourish.

'On board? On board what? What are you on board?'

'Please, Umberto ...' I pleaded, practically dragging him away. And finally he decided that he'd had his fun.

'We will talk Katherine, you and I.' He turned to the others. 'You will excuse us, please.' He bowed once more; then allowed me to drag him away.

We found a quiet little cafe away from the square where we chose a table at the back, away from any chance of being overheard.

'What the bloody hell was all that about?' I said.

He smiled. 'Good?'

'It'll take me a week to explain it all,' I said. 'Especially as I've got to make everything up.'

'But it could have been, Miss Touchfeather. It could have been,' he said, reaching for my hand again. He never failed to make a pass at me. I think he did so because he felt that as an Italian it was expected of him, a matter of national honour. I retrieved my hand quickly.

'We're alone Signor Bertelli. There's no more need for acting.'

'I am not acting,' he said, breathing heavily.

'Yes, you are,' I said. 'And if you don't stop, I shall tell Mr. Blaser.' This didn't seem to deter him unduly, so I added my topper. 'And Signora Bertelli as well.' That stopped him dead as it always did, and he immediately became very businesslike.

'You have the samples?' I took them from my purse and passed them to him beneath the table. He slipped them into his pocket without even looking. 'And information?' he asked.

'No information.'

'Mr. Blaser will not be pleased.'

'Tell Mr. Blaser that Galipolodopolo hasn't been around since we left St. Tropez. He's supposed to be rejoining us here.'

'Then you will go to bed with him.'

I put on my icy expression. 'That's none of your business, Signor Bertelli,' I said.

He looked at me steadily for a brief moment, his eyes calculating and shrewd. Then he nodded.

'You are right, Katherine. It is none of my business. But one day, one fine day . . .'

'Don't hold your breath,' I said.

He smiled at me. 'Have fun, Miss Touchfeather,' he said, and a moment later he was gone.

We all had dinner ashore that evening. Constantin still hadn't turned up when we went back to the boat to change, but dinner had been arranged at one of the best restaurants and we were all ferried there in taxis. Nobody mentioned the encounter in the square, which was just as well because I hadn't quite got my story worked out. Sir Roger's bird looked at me a little slant-eyed a couple of times during the evening, wondering I suppose whether there would be any profit in mentioning it to Constantin, but that was all. I'd found out her name by now, it was Deirdre as if it could have been anything else. I decided that I hoped Sir Roger would pop the question soon; they deserved each other.

After dinner the others decided to go dancing. I begged off and walked back to the boat alone, hoping that Constantin still hadn't put in an appearance. He hadn't, and by midnight I was tucked up safe, sound and alone. Mr. Blaser had told me to hang around a bit after passing the samples, so nobody would get suspicious by my taking off in a hurry. I was still wondering just how long I was going to have to hang around when I drifted off to sleep.

The steward brought me my breakfast the following morning at nine o'clock, which was a bit inconsiderate of him, because I hadn't ordered any breakfast. There was a small note on the tray saying would I please see the Captain at my earliest convenience, and in any event before ten o'clock.

The Captain was in his cabin when I went to see him. He was very polite and most apologetic. Mr. Galipolodopolo had telephoned the previous night; unfortunately he was unable to rejoin the *Maria* at this time and, that being the case, was sure that Miss Touchfeather would understand that there was little point in her remaining on board. The steward was already packing my things, a speedboat was waiting to take me across the bay to Naples, and here was a first class one-way ticket from Naples to London. It's been very pleasant, see you again sometime.

Two hours later I was at Naples airport. I managed to bung off a cable to Mr. Blaser telling him I was homeward bound, and two hours after that I was in London.

When I fly into London Airport I usually check at the office Mr. Blaser keeps there to see if there are any messages or instructions; also to bum a lift into town. That was my intention this time. I came through immigration and out into the customs hall. I was waiting for my bags to come up when a porter sidled up to me.

'Porter, Miss?'

I agreed that I needed a porter and I identified my bags for him as the conveyor regurgitated them on to the turntable. He collected them all and I headed over towards the green customs exit.

'This way, Miss,' said my porter, heading towards one of the red exits. 'It'll be quicker.'

It wouldn't be quicker, but I knew he must have his reasons, so I followed him to the end bench. There I waited behind a young couple who were frantically declaring all their cigarettes and duty-free liquor in the vain hope that the inspector would overlook the camera they had bought as well. He didn't, and I waited patiently while the invoice was made out and the duty paid. Then it was my turn.

'Have you read this?' said the Inspector, shoving the board at me. I said I had read it.

'Have you anything to declare?'

'No,' I said, looking him straight in the eye.

'Would you open that one,' he said, pointing to the case holding all the gear I had bought in St. Tropez. I opened it and waited while he rummaged through it, carefully checking all the St. Tropez labels in the dresses. Then he closed the case, snapping it shut.

'Thank you,' he said. He looked past me at the porter who was still hovering. 'You may take the lady's cases to the bus.'

The porter nodded, gathered up the cases, and I followed him out. A nod is as good as a wink they say and, if someone wanted me to take the bus, that was it. I climbed aboard, paid my seven shillings, and forty minutes later I was deposited at the West London Air Terminal. There I hailed a taxi and twenty minutes after that I was home in my own little pad.

The place smelt musty with disuse and the first thing I did was to go round and open all the windows in the sitting-room. Then I moved through into the bedroom and noticed immediately that the cleaners had delivered back to me my Iberian uniform. This was a little odd because, apart from the one trip I had made with Antonio, I hadn't flown that airline for months and the uniform I'd been wearing on that particular occasion I'd mislaid somewhere in Madrid.

I opened the suitcase that had interested the Customs Inspector, and the note was just under the top dress. 'You're being followed,' it said, and that was all.

I burned the note and set about opening a few tins for my dinner. It wasn't much after the gastronomic high-life I had been living over the past few days, but even baked beans can taste good after all that caviar, pheasant and stuff. So I had a fry up, just like my Mum used to do, and washed it down with Brooke Bond '69.

So I was being followed; that meant I would have to play the game according to the pattern I had set myself. I had met Antonio as an Iberian stewardess, and that was supposed to be what I returned to now that my jaunt into the high-life was over. I called in to the airline office and reported myself for duty. They were expecting my call. A flight to Mexico City tomorrow, departure from London, ten-thirty a.m. 'Thank you very much,' I said, and that was that. I brushed my teeth, switched on the television and settled down for a domestic evening. But the television wasn't particularly absorbing and I found myself wondering.

If I was being followed, it had to be from the *Maria*, to see where I went and with whom I made contact. And if I was being followed today, it was a pretty fair bet that I was being followed yesterday. And if I had been followed yesterday, then they, whoever they were, would also have followed Signor Bertelli after his diabolical acting bit in the main square. I hoped he was all right, because in spite of the occasional disagreements we have, I quite like him, and he really is very good at his job. But I was good at my job, too, so why was I being followed? Where had I slipped up?

But I didn't spend too much time wondering about this, because I knew that if I had made a mistake, Mr. Blaser would tell me in his own good time, hammering it home with considerable relish. About half-past nine, I debated whether to call my motor car salesman, but decided not to; I had to get up reasonably early next morning and fly the Atlantic. So instead I took a sleeping pill and went to bed.

In fact I flew the Atlantic three times the following week. I was on the regular duty roster and I worked just like all the other girls. There wasn't a word from Mr. Blaser, so I assumed that I was still being followed. Whoever was responsible for watching me was doing a very good job and must have been using a dozen different people, because never once did I get the slightest clue that I was being tailed; and never once did I spot anyone I even vaguely recognized. They must have been spending a fortune on aeroplane tickets alone. I think Mr. Blaser assumed that if I continued to play the part I had been cast in, they would eventually give up. But he was wrong there. They were prepared to play a waiting game, but they weren't going to wait forever. They allowed me eight days to make my move and when I didn't they moved themselves.

I was picked up in London. I was tired and little grotty after a particularly nasty flight and I accepted a lift into town with a captain I knew rather than take the crew bus. He tried to talk me into coming out to dinner with him, but I begged off. Sulking, he dropped me off outside my apartment and drove off, no doubt going home to his wife. I picked up my suitcase and headed towards the front door, feeling pretty bloody about everything.

The man was waiting just inside the front door of the building. The landlord didn't consider it necessary to light the hall and passages and a small army could have lurked in our building unseen.

'Miss Touchfeather?' inquired the man politely. He was short. That much I could tell from the level that his voice was coming from, but that was all.

'Yes,' I said, too tired to even suspect anything.

'I wonder if you'd mind coming with me?' he said. And still I didn't get it.

'Where?' I asked, wondering what the hell he was talking about.

'We'll talk about it in the car,' he said. He got through to me then all right. Play it cool, Katy, I thought. I didn't doubt that I could take care of the man in front of me. After all, that's what I'm trained for, but I didn't know how many there were behind me and, even more important, I had been playing the role of an air stewardess all week, and air stewardesses just don't go around breaking men's arms and suchlike. So I did my indignant bit.

'I don't know who you are,' I said. 'And I'll thank you to get out of my way.'

'Don't give us any trouble, Miss Touchfeather.' He was still being polite.

'Look here,' I said in my best Roedean accent. 'If you don't leave me alone, I shall call the police.' My eyes had become used to the darkness now and I could see him better. He was smiling, actually enjoying himself.

'I shouldn't do that,' he said. I was inclined to agree with him, but I was still acting a part, so I had to follow it through.

'I'll scream,' I said.

'No you won't,' he said equably.

Let's see who's right, I thought, knowing full well that he was. I opened my mouth to yell, and that was that. He poked four stiff fingers into my midriff, just below and between my breasts; then he caught me as I fell. I was still trying to get a breath of air into my tortured lungs when he swung me up into his arms. Then he carried me out of the door, across the pavement and deposited me in the back of a waiting car. It had all been so simple and straightforward. There were even people walking about in the street, but no one took a blind bit of notice. This goes towards proving a theory of mine; you can commit a major crime in full view of umpteen people and, providing you don't make too much noise about it, the chances are that no one will notice and, if they do notice, they won't do anything about it in case they make fools of themselves.

My abductor got into the back of the car with me and I saw that there was a driver sitting in the front. Without a word, the driver started the engine and the car pulled away. I lay where I was for a good ten minutes trying to get my breath back, while the cause of my trouble just ignored me. I took a closer look at him, seeing him clearly for the first time. I was right; he was short, but barrel shaped and obviously very strong. He had fair hair and a nothing sort of face, except for the mouth which was thin and hard. You wait, my lad, I thought. One day I'll get you when I'm not pretending to be someone else, and that will be a day you'll remember. We can be very vindictive, we Touchfeathers.

By the time I pulled myself together, we were out of London on the Western Avenue and, as I noticed this, I started to worry about something else. If my captors weren't concerned that I knew where they were taking me, then it was a pretty fair assumption that they didn't think I was going to be in any position to do anything about it at a later date. Very ominous, I thought. I gave the indignant bit one more try. 'I have never . . .'

'Shut up,' said my companion. Soft soap then, I thought.

'Please, won't you . . .'

He told me to shut up again, and this time there was a look in his eyes which warned me to take notice. I didn't think there would be much point in chatting up the driver: apart from leaning over to open the door when I'd been shoved into the car, he had done nothing but drive, and hadn't said a word. I tried to see what he looked like through the driving mirror, but it was angled wrongly. So I gave it up, sat back, and tried to prepare myself for what was bound to follow.

I may be all sorts of a tough chick when it cames to handling myself; turn me loose with most people and providing the odds aren't too heavily stacked against me, I can generally make out. But this doesn't mean that I enjoy violence and particularly not when it's directed at me. After all, I *am* a girl, a member of the weaker sex and, like ninety-nine per cent of my sex, my basic desire is to be cossetted and nurtured, looked after and loved. I don't like hurting people and, even more, I don't like being hurt. If I read the signs correctly, I was due to be hurt extensively when we arrived at wherever it was we were heading for. These people had been following me for a week, hoping that I would give something away. I hadn't, and now they were tired of waiting; they wanted me to start talking and I had no illusions about how they would go about it. I felt very vulnerable all of a sudden, wishing I had taken up cooking or drama instead of my chosen profession.

We drove for two hours, turning off the main Oxford road on the other side of High Wycombe, there losing ourselves in the maze of small country roads that interlace the Chilterns. Although I didn't reckon it would do anyone any good, I kept a check on where we were going. In the unlikely event that I would be given a chance in the future, at least I'd be able to find my way back. Then abruptly we turned off the road through a pair of high, ornate wrought-iron gates, and headed up a long drive flanked by parkland. It was very dark and all I could see was the area picked out by the headlamps, which wasn't much.

The house lay at the end of the drive; a vast, hideous Victorian folly that looked as though demolition would be doing it a kindness. The car stopped and the driver got out. He was almost as indistinguishable as his companion, an anonymous sort of man whose face looked as though it had been put together by an Identi-kit. I was urged out of the car and across the ten feet of drive to the front door. One of my escorts opened the front door, not even having to use a key, and we went through into the hall. Somewhere somebody clicked the lights on.

The house was as ugly inside as it was out. Perhaps some of the furniture may have been good, but it was all covered with dust-sheets so I couldn't see. And it was very cold, the dank cold of disuse. I almost expected to see water running down the flock wallpaper. I was nudged across the hall and through a pair of doors into what I assumed was the sitting-room. Sixty feet long and as inhospitable as the rest of the place.

'Sit,' said one of my companions. I sat in the high back wing chair he indicated and a small cloud of dust blew up from the sheet that covered the chair. The two men didn't even bother to sit; they took up station, one leaning against the fireplace, the other with his arms resting along the back of what I took to be a settee. And they just looked at me, neither of them making any sort of move at all. So it seemed that if nastiness were to follow, they weren't going to be the ones to inflict it. The house had had the emptiness of a tomb about it when we arrived, so I assumed that the principal in this little drama wasn't even here yet.

This was confirmed twenty minutes later when we all heard a car crunch across the gravel outside. One of my escorts detached himself from the fireplace and walked out into the hall. I heard the low murmur of voices and a moment later he came back, followed by the new arrival.

It was a woman. She was about thirty years old, very dark, and with a strong Eurasian look about her. I'm not particularly charitable when it comes to describing members of my own sex, but even I had to admit that this one was very beautiful indeed. Her skin was a pale creamy colour, her eyes black and enormous; she had a classic line to her cheekbones, and her mouth was very full, the sort of mouth to drive men crazy. She was wearing a full length sable coat over a white evening gown.

She hardly glanced at the man who had been standing watching me. She came straight over to my chair and stopped about three feet away. A swift kick with my sensible stewardess type shoes and I could have crippled her for life. But there didn't seem much point unless I could incapacitate her two heavies with the same kick. Instead I thought once more that I had better try to recapture my supposed identity.

'I don't know who you are,' I said in my best outraged manner. 'But I demand to be released.'

'My name is Lucia,' she said. She pronounced it Luchia. 'And yours is Katherine.' She spoke quite softly, even gently, her accent carrying strong French overtones.

'All right, Lucia,' I said, continuing to flog a dead horse. 'What is the meaning of this outrage?'

'Please, Katherine, don't waste our time by continuing this act. Just answer my questions and we can have an end to the affair.'

I knew what the end would be, too, as far as Katy was concerned.

'What questions?'

'Very simply, who do you work for?'

'Iberian Airlines.'

'We know that, dear. Who else?'

'No one else,' I said.

She looked at me for a bit, then she opened her handbag. From it she took a small, leather case. She opened it and drew out a hypodermic syringe and a small phial containing a colour-less fluid. Whoops, I thought, here we go with the truth drug. But I must admit I felt a slight feeling of relief. At least they were going about this in a civilized way, thumb screws obviously weren't their speed at all.

'Do you know what this is, Katherine?' she asked, as she expertly charged the hypodermic, drawing into the shaft what looked like a half pint of drug.

'No,' I said.

'It's a truth drug,' she said. 'With this in your veins you will be incapable of lying to me. Incidentally, it will also kill you fifteen minutes after administration.'

That didn't sound like any truth drug that I had ever heard of, but I believed her implicitly. And if I was going to die in fifteen minutes, I thought that about here I had better do some-thing about it. After all, it wasn't as though I had anything to lose. And anyway I *hate* injections. The one leaning against the fireplace looked the most dangerous, if you discounted Lucia who was more dangerous than the two of them lumped together and multiplied by four. But he was ten feet away from me, and that was an awful lot of ground to cover. God only knew what weapons he was carrying on him, but at least they didn't want me dead before I had talked so he probably wouldn't do anything too drastic. I glanced quickly at the other one. He was still leaning up against the settee watching the whole business with a casual disinterest as though he had no part in it. Then Lucia did me a big favour. 'Come and hold her,' she said.

Both men approached my chair as Lucia held the needle up and squirted out the air. The men took up station either side of me.

'Roll up her sleeve,' said Lucia. One of them started to do just that, and Katy did what she had to do. I broke his arm quickly and painfully. The crack of breaking bone sounded like a pistol shot, rivetting everyone in the room for the brief moment I needed to deal with the other one. To him, I did Bessie's number three trick for disabling a man. It worked like a charm. Unfor-tunately I had underestimated the calibre of the first man. Broken arm he might have had, but he still had one good arm left and a job to do. As I turned back to him he had just finished pulling a wicked looking cosh from his pocket. I tried to grab his wrist, but I was off balance. The first blow caught me on the shoulder, knocking me to my knees. I heard Lucia scream something at the man before he hit me again. Then came a roar like thunder, and I slid off to hell and gone.

\*      \*      \*

'Fortunately we arrived on the scene at that precise moment,' said Mr. Blaser. By 'we' he didn't mean himself personally, but the two men who had been following me to find out who was following me, if you get my point. They had seen my abduction from outside my apartment and had tailed the car, only breaking into the house just before Katy was beaten to death by an irate man with a broken arm.

'What happened to them?'

'Your two kidnappers are under lock and key,' said Mr. Blaser. 'Both in hospital I might add.'

'What about Lucia?'

'I assume by Lucia you mean the woman?' I agreed that I meant the woman. Mr. Blaser cleared his throat. 'Unfortunately she escaped. Those responsible have been severely reprimanded.' I started to say something, but he continued, 'In any event, it is doubtful that she would have led us anywhere, so there is no real harm done.'

'She was going to kill me,' I said.

'I know,' said Mr. Blaser. 'We analysed the chemical she was going to inject you with. Most interesting.'

'Can the men tell you anything?'

'They're just a couple of small time criminals engaged for one job only.'

'Engaged by whom?'

'By the woman, Lucia.'

'Cosy,' I said. Then I had an idea. 'What about the house? Is there a lead there?'

'That at least proved interesting,' said Mr. Blaser as though all else was a crashing bore. 'It belongs to Sir Roger Bleak.'

'The plot thickens,' I said.

'Not for you it doesn't, Miss Touchfeather. You are no longer of any use to me on this venture. You have been identified.'

'But I didn't say anything,' I said. 'They could still think I'm what I claimed to be.'

'Airline stewardesses don't have special agents coming to their rescue when they get into trouble.' He said it as though he regretted having rescued me in the first place. But he was right. My cover was blown, as they say in the trade.

'What about Galipolodopolo?'

'What about him?'

'Aren't you going to do anything about him? I mean, he was responsible for all this.'

'Come, Miss Touchfeather. That blow must have affected your thought processes.' Again he was right. Nobody could tie Galipolodopolo in with my abduction, except perhaps Lucia, and she was long since gone. All that we had left were two unfortunate heavies who had been paid for a job that had gone sour, and who knew nothing about their employer except that she was female.

'So what happens next, sir?'

'As far as you are concerned, nothing,' said Mr. Blaser. 'You will be re-assigned as soon as I have something else for you to do.'

I grew bold here; after all, I was interested and I knew the people involved. 'No, sir. I mean, what happens about the whole gold business?'

Mr. Blaser looked at me as though I had just committed sacrilege. 'You know better than to ask a question like that.'

'Yes, sir.'

And the miserable old idiot was right again. It was bad organisation to allow too many people to know what was going on; the less anyone knew, the more secure the whole operation. Just before I left the office, I asked him something I had been wanting to for quite a long time, and hadn't up to now in case the answer upset me: 'What happened to Signor Bertelli?'

'Nothing,' said Mr. Blaser. 'Why?'

'As they were on to me I assumed they would be on to him as well.'

He smiled at me thinly. 'Fortunately all my people are not as inept as you, Miss Touchfeather,' he said. 'Good day.'

The next three days I spent on the London-New York run, behaving like any normal air stewardess, which of course I am when I'm not doing things for Mr. Blaser. It makes quite a pleasant change knowing that the passengers are just passengers and not assorted villains liable to beat you over the head, shoot you, or stick needles into you. Not that the normal passenger can't be a menace: some are positively diabolical in their cunning. They devise elaborate schemes to harass the stewardess, and one such individual can make a girl's life a living hell for the six or seven hours it takes to cross the Atlantic. I had one on my second trip, a sandy haired lecher of twenty-two, who behaved like every dirty old man who had ever existed. He pestered me rotten, and every time I came anywhere near him, he tried to look down my blouse or up my skirt. Two hours out of New York, he nearly succeeded in trapping me in the toilet and it was only the timely arrival of the Captain, doing his rounds, that saved me from a fate worse than death. What some people expect for the price of an aeroplane ticket is quite extraordinary. The other trips were uneventful and, whereas normal scheduled flying can make a pleasant change, it can also turn out to be a drag if it goes on too long.

*       *       *

I was soaking in a hot bath after my fourth round trip, wondering how many more times I was going to have to walk across the Atlantic, when the phone rang. It was Miss Moody.

'Mr. Blaser would like to see you,' she said.

'Tomorrow?'

'Tonight.'

'It's ten-thirty already.'

'Is it as late as that?' she said. 'I hadn't noticed. How long will you be?'

'I'm in the bath.'

'Shall we say an hour then?' And she hung up before I could think of an excuse. A pox on the both of them, I thought, as I clambered out of the bath. Then the thought of not having to fly the Atlantic again tomorrow cheered me up a little. I dressed, put on my war-paint, called a minicab, and went to see what little goodies Mr. Blaser had in store for me next.

# CHAPTER THREE

BORAMI is a country, believe it or not. It has its own President and elected representatives; the only trouble is that it is the President who elects them. It also has a huge hydro-electric project in the pipeline, and the Russians and Chinese fighting with each other over who is going to pay for it. Once it is completed it will provide electricity for the whole of Borami; and it is a matter of record that only two per cent of the population of the entire country are equipped technically or psychologically to handle electricity. Borami also has its own bank, a seat on the United Nations, its own import and export councils and, of course, like all emergent African nations, it has its own airline.

I looked up the airline in the trade books; two 707s and three Dakotas. One of the 707s was reserved exclusively for the President himself and, as the Borami people were notoriously frightened of flying, the other was used almost entirely by foreigners who flocked to the country, vying with each other to see who could offer the largest bribes thereby landing some of the huge contracts which were being financed by roubles or yen or dollars. Borami was like a very small boy with three frantically rich uncles each of whom, for reasons best known to himself, wanted to become the only uncle, and was willing to empty his pockets for the privilege.

Miss Moody gave me her customary nod of encouragement as I

waited for the light on Mr. Blaser's door lintel to change to green.

'You look very nice, dear,' she said.

Before I could reply, the light went to green and I tapped on the door and went in. Mr. Blaser unbent sufficiently to ask how I was, but he didn't wait for me to tell him before ploughing straight on.

'Borami, Miss Touchfeather. You're due there the day after tomorrow.'

'Yes, sir.'

'You fly BOAC to Nairobi and check in with Borami National Airlines there.'

'Yes, sir.'

'You will report direct to Captain Chalmers and no one else. He knows about you.'

'What does he know?'

'He knows that you are going to report to him,' said Mr. Blaser crossly. 'Naturally he doesn't know what your assignment is.'

That makes two of us, I thought.

Then Mr. Blaser went on to explain what it was all about.

And that's why I was standing in the Main terminal building at Nairobi Airport, while the public address system searched for Captain Chalmers on my behalf. The air conditioning had broken down about ten minutes after I arrived, and the temperature had rapidly climbed up into mid-nineties. The journey from London had been grotty in the extreme; the job I was supposed to be doing was pretty foul viewed by any standards; I hadn't slept a wink in nineteen straight hours; I hadn't even bathed for seventeen. All in all I felt like half a dozen different versions of hell rolled into one.

I had reported to the Borami Airlines desk as soon as I arrived, asking for Captain Chalmers. The desk was manned by a snotty-nosed adolescent with pimples, who told me to wait. I waited for half an hour while he did absolutely nothing, so I asked him again. He exposed some very grubby teeth at me and told me to wait some more. I told him to go and take a jump at himself and asked the main information desk if they could assist me in locating my Captain Chalmers. They started by telling me to check with the Borami Airlines desk. I told them I had already done that and if I had to go back there I would probably commit homicide. They must have had dealings with my pimply adolescent, because I detected a note of sympathy as they promised to try to locate Captain Chalmers for me. And locate him they did.

As he introduced himself I thought that here was the only good thing to happen to me for over a week. He was a large, slow-moving man, fair, with blue eyes and little wrinkles in the corners that came from long hours spent staring out of flight

deck windows. He was just like a commercial for an airline
captain and he was exactly my type. Because, although I might
swing with the Antonios of this world, it is usually in the line of
duty and, if the truth be known, I have a very soft spot for these
large capable men with gentle voices and even gentler touch. I
cursed the fact that I looked such a mess, but he didn't seem to
notice; or, if he did, he didn't show it. In fact he looked as agreeably surprised when he saw me as I felt on seeing him.

'Miss Touchfeather?'

'Captain Chalmers.'

We shook hands, in spite of the heat his hand was cool and
dry and I wished I'd wiped my palm before offering it.

'Sorry you've been kept waiting.'

'Snot nose at your counter was no help at all,' I said.

'He never is. Let's get out of here.'

We went to the crew room, where miraculously the air conditioning was still working. Fortunately the place was empty so
we were able to talk.

'I know almost nothing of why you are here, Miss Touchfeather,' he said, when he had assured himself that I was comfortable and wanting for nothing. 'I was asked by certain parties in
London to get you the job of junior stewardess on the presidential
707.'

'How did you manage?' I asked.

'When the junior stewardess went sick I put your name forward.
I'm in charge of recruiting personnel for our illustrious airline.'

'She went sick very conveniently, didn't she?' I asked.

He looked puzzled for a moment. 'Funny about that,' he said.
'The doctors say it was food poisoning, but as far as I know I'd
eaten the same food as she had for the previous twenty-four
hours.' I detected the long arm of Mr. Blaser here, but I certainly
wasn't going to say anything.

'Well,' I said. 'All's well that ends well.'

He looked at me steadily for a moment. 'I'm sure it will end
very well indeed,' he said.

Why not, Katy? I thought. After all, I didn't have a regular
boyfriend in Africa. If I was going to be in Borami for any length
of time, I was going to be seeing a great deal of Captain Chalmers
and, from where I was sitting at this moment, I had to admit to
liking the idea.

'I suppose you can't tell me what it's all about?' he asked.

'What?' I asked innocently.

'The reason you're here.'

'You needed a stewardess. You've got one.'

'I could have picked up a stewardess here in Nairobi,' he said.
'Not that I'm complaining.' he added quickly.

'Then how did you manage to get me engaged all the way from London?' And here he actually started to blush under his warm brown tan. 'I had to tell a couple of lies.'

'Affecting me?'

'Actually yes,' he said. 'I'm in the President's good books at the moment. He likes the way I fly.' That'll make two of us, I thought. 'Anyway, I told him I had a girl friend . . . a sort of fiancée . . . in London, and please could I give her the job?' Better and better I thought, all the ground work had already been done for me. Then he returned to his original question about what I was doing here.

'I don't think the certain parties in London would be too keen on my telling you,' I said, trying to make it sound as pleasant as posible. 'In fact I would get into terrible trouble if they thought . . .'

He leaped in like the gentleman I knew he was. 'Enough said. Not one more word. And now I'll take you to your hotel.'

He picked up my bags from where I had left them and ten minutes later we were in a car heading into town.

'What's our flying programme?' I asked. Then I remembered that I was junior stewardess and he was Captain. 'Sir,' I added.

'That's all right for the flightdeck,' he said. 'Otherwise it's Peter.'

'And I'm Katy,' I said coyly.

'As to our flight programme, we act on the whim of the President. He's in Nairobi conferring with other despots at the moment. When the fancy takes him, he'll expect to be whipped out of here at one hour's notice.'

'Back to Borami?'

'I think Borami's the only other country that'll put up with him.'

'What's wrong with him then?'

'Delusions of grandeur. A third rate, coffee-coloured Caligula. I don't know why old man Kenyatta even allows him into Kenya.'

'Politics,' I said, as though it covered the entire spectrum of human behaviour.

Peter nodded his big, beautiful head. 'You're right, Katy. It's a great comfort to have an honest trade at one's fingertips.' I didn't want to disillusion him too soon in our relationship, so I kept my mouth shut on that one. Five minutes later he handed me the key to my hotel room and told me he would expect me downstairs for dinner at seven p.m.

The room was airy and cool. I stripped off everything and threw it in the dirty linen basket. Then I took a long cool bath. While I was soaking I went over my last conversation with Mr. Blaser.

'Politically Borami is a powder keg, Miss Touchfeather. The

president is playing all ends against the middle. America, China and Russia are all pouring money into the place in an attempt to buy the old pirate's allegiance. But as long as the money continues to arrive, he's going to remain firmly on the fence. Her Majesty's Government, needless to say, are extremely interested in the outcome of this sordid affair. After all, we ruled in Borami for over a hundred years, and we *know* President Calmooni. Despot and tyrant he may be, but he still has a hearty respect for the British. It is not beyond the bounds of possibility that he will take all the money that is handed out, and eventually throw out the Americans, the Russians and the Chinese, and return to the fold. After all, Borami *is* a member of the Commonwealth. Should any of the three Big Powers get wind of this, it is quite likely that they will work towards having the President removed permanently and replaced by a man who is more sympathetic to their own particular cause. Chaos would of course result, forcing Her Majesty's Government to send troops to restore order. Needless to say, we have neither the desire nor the facilities to mount an operation of this sort. Apart from that the publicity would be extremely bad. "Colonialist" has become a dirty word, Miss Touchfeather.' He paused.

'Now, as to your specific instructions, they are simply keep your eyes and ears open. You will be working aboard the President's own aircraft. When he is not using it, it is employed extensively to fly foreign diplomats in and out of Borami. You will merely listen, take everything in, and send your reports back to me from time to time. You will make no attempt to evaluate what you hear. You're not equipped for that kind of work. In the event, however, that you hear something that you feel requires immediate action, you will be given a contact you can approach in Borami. That's all, Miss Touchfeather.'

'How long will I be there, sir?' I had ventured to ask.

'As long as I choose to keep you there,' he said.

I should have known better than to ask.

Bath over, I managed to get a couple of hours' sleep before going down to meet Peter. We had a slow, leisurely dinner and he behaved like the perfect gentleman afterwards, leaving me outside my room with just a brotherly peck on the cheek by way of good night. But the chemistry between us was right; we both knew it and we both knew that it was only a matter of time. A couple of days lolling around the pool, I thought; perhaps a drive up country to the National Parks; a few more cosy meals *a deux* and we'd be away. With this pleasant thought at the back of my mind, I drifted off into the best night's sleep I'd had for a long time. I awoke about eight o'clock and wondered why

I was feeling so good; then I remembered and started to plan the day. Peter had promised to call for me at about ten o'clock, so there was no hurry. I phoned down for my breakfast and prepared to spend a quiet couple of hours getting ready for the day. At eight-fifteen the phone rang. It was Peter.

'We take off at ten-fifteen,' he said.

'Take off what?' I wasn't quite awake.

'The president, God damn his soul, has decided he wants to go home. I've got to go straight out to the airport to file a flight plan. Be there no later than nine-thirty.'

'It's a quarter past eight already,' I wailed.

'Be there, Katy.' Then, in case he had sounded too authoritative and grotty, he added, 'Please . . .'

'Yes, sir,' I said and, for the same reason, I blew him a kiss over the phone. I heard him chuckle just before he hung up. I leaped out of bed and into the bathroom. My breakfast arrived and I ate it while I was getting ready. It was only when I went to the wardrobe that I realized that I had no uniform. There was no point in calling Peter because he would have already left for the airport, and I certainly wasn't going to call the airport office in case snot nose answered the phone. Finally I decided that the President would have to take me as he found me. I chose my most conservative suit in pale blue linen and, with a white blouse underneath, I had to admit I looked pretty svelte.

Then came the problem of my luggage. Were we coming back here or weren't we? I decided better to be safe than sorry and repacked everything, bidding a fond farewell to the stuff that I had sent to the cleaners the night before. I would put in an expense chit when I returned to London. Miss Moody would see me all right. I rang for a porter to carry my bags down, and when he arrived travelled down in the elevator with him. My bill had already been taken care of by the airline, and I asked for a taxi. But the porter who had brought my bags down indicated that he had put them in a waiting car. I walked over to the car, climbed into the back, and met Gloria.

Gloria Glover was the senior stewardess, and my superior. A startlingly beautiful girl of twenty-seven or thereabouts, with the blondest hair I had seen for a long time. She smiled a big smile as I parked myself next to her and the driver started the car.

'You're Katy. I'm Gloria. Call me Glo,' she said.

'Hello, Glo.'

'Peter asked me to pick you up.' I felt my hackles rise slightly. This was competition with a capital C.

'That was nice of him.'

'He's like that,' said Glo. 'He's going to be our best man.' I warmed towards her immediately. Lovely girl, I thought. She chattered on as we drove to the airport. It seemed she was about to marry a Great White Hunter she had met in Nairobi. The only trouble was he kept running off on safari and she couldn't pin him down long enough to name the day. Glo was an American; a former TWA stewardess, who had met her GWH on an African trip, fallen like a ton of bricks, and taken a job which at least allowed her to see him occasionally. He hadn't wanted her to work but she had tried the idle life for a few weeks and then given it up. 'He was always dashing off into the bush to kill something,' she said. 'I never knew whether he'd be home to dinner this side of Christmas.'

She was a nice girl, I decided; a little scatterbrained for twenty-seven, but looking like she did I couldn't see it worrying anyone. Just before we reached the airport, I asked what my inflight duties would be.

'Keep the booze flowing and your back to the bulkheads at all times,' she said.

'It's like that is it?'

'It's worse than that,' she said. 'But there's plenty of room for manoeuvring.'

I saw what she meant about there being plenty of room, the moment we went aboard. The original interior of the aircraft had been stripped out and re-designed as a rather plush, overblown boardroom-cum-living room, with decoration strongly reminiscent of a Victorian bordello. There were numerous large overstuffed armchairs bolted to the floor around the outside edge of the cabin, and a large oval dining table complete with ten chairs in the centre. This occupied forty-five feet of the aircraft. The rear end, sheltered behind a bulkhead, was reserved as a private suite for the President himself. It consisted of sitting room, bedroom, dressing room and bathroom. All very luxurious and vastly extravagant.

The President came aboard about twenty minutes after we did. Peter came through from the flight deck and told Glo and me that the tower had just called to say he was on his way. The two of us lined up inside the open hatch while Peter went down the gangway to meet him. Three Mercedes 600's drew up and out piled about a dozen coloured men and, by coloured, I don't mean their skin. They were black certainly, but it was the clothes they were wearing that blinded. Bright red robes, blue head-dresses, yellow sashes, orange pantaloons sticking out beneath green three-quarter length jackets; feathers dipped in all colours and shades; and the whole group flocking around the President himself, who was dressed in a blue kaftan shot with gold thread. He was a mountain of a man, over six feet tall and weighing somewhere in the region of twenty stone. He had a great moon-shaped face, with heavy Negroid features. He moved slowly, rather like a hippopotamus, while his minions fluttered around him like a flock of exotic tropical birds. He grinned widely at Peter and shook his hand. As he stepped aboard the aircraft I could have sworn I felt the springs sag. He smiled at Glo, then looked at me. Before Peter could present me, he grinned hugely, exposing what looked like enough teeth for three ordinary people.

'You must be Peter's young lady,' he said in impeccable English. He held out a huge hand and engulfed mine.

'Miss Katherine Touchfeather,' said Peter from behind him.

'Welcome, Katherine,' he said. Then he turned to Peter. 'Now you are happy, Peter?'

'Very happy, sir. Thank you.'

Then he turned further, addressing the entourage who were queueing up behind him, waiting to get into the aircraft.

'This is the fiancée of Captain Chalmers,' he said very loudly. 'If anyone dares to lay a finger on her, I will have his hand cut off at the wrist.' He meant it, too; I could see that by the expression on everyone's face. It was only later that I discovered he was addressing his Prime Minister, Foreign Secretary, Minister of Finance, two Generals and countless Under Secretaries. He certainly had *his* government where he wanted them.

Glo and I settled everyone in their seats, and checked that they were strapped in. President Calmooni patted my bottom as I adjusted his outsized seat belt, but it was avuncular rather than anticipatory, and I didn't mind a bit. Glo and I strapped down on a couple of spare seats, and five minutes after everyone coming aboard, we were up, up and away.

The President's warning seemed to have had its effect and I had no trouble whatsoever with the passengers. I served their booze and, when the time came, their lunch. Glo and I were the only cabin staff. On the flight deck, apart from Peter, there was a co-pilot, a middle-aged Sikh, and the third crewman was an African, a young, gentle-faced lad who never failed to smile politely at me and who called me 'ma'am' at all times.

The flight itself was completely uneventful and, once lunch had been cleared away, the President retired to his own quarters and everyone else got their heads down where they were sitting. I had just finished clearing up when the co-pilot came back to ask if I would like to sit up front with Peter for a while. Peter flashed me a smile as I slid into the co-pilot's seat. He was on automatic pilot, with his feet resting on the instrument panel in front of him. I like it on the flight deck, all around is blue nothing; there may be clouds, but they're fifteen thousand feet straight down, and the main impression one gets is of enormous, clear, fresh space; you feel you can breathe better up here.

'I hate to appear ignorant,' I said after a couple of minutes' companionable silence. 'But how far is Borami from Nairobi?'

'Four and a half hours,' said Peter. 'We'll be there just before fifteen hundred.' As though to confirm this, the polite African handed him a paper at which he glanced. 'Fourteen fifty-five.'

I looked at my watch. There's a clock somewhere on the flight deck, but who could ever find it with all the other junk that festoons the place? It was already a quarter past two.

'What's Borami like?' I asked.

'Borami is the country. We're going to Calmooniville, the capital.'

'So what's Calmooniville like?'

'Hot,' he said.

'Where will I be staying?'

'The hotel. There's only one.'

'Do you live there?'

'I have a house,' he said, giving me a sideways glance. 'It's a large house.'

I'm not usually so forward, but what with the height and the rarefied atmosphere, I made my pitch. 'Wouldn't it be better if . . .' I paused. Perhaps I *was* coming on a bit strong. He helped me off my own hook.

'I was thinking, Katy,' he said. 'I mean, after all, you're supposed to be my fiancée. It's a big house, four bedrooms actually. Wouldn't it be better if you moved in with me? Strictly kosher, of course.' That's what you think, I thought.

'It sounds like a very good idea,' I said, as though I hadn't thought about it.

He beamed broadly at nothing in particular. 'I've got a couple of house servants, use of the presidential swimming pool, and a cook I can borrow from the French Embassy from time to time. How does it sound?'

It sounded marvellous, and I said so.

Ten minutes later I went back to the cabin to wake everyone up for the landing. Glo did the necessary with the President, and five minutes before touchdown he lumbered out from his own quarters and subsided into one of the armchairs. I decided that he was a bad daytime sleeper, because he was foul tempered. The Prime Minister said something to him in language I didn't understand, and promptly got his head bitten off at the neck. After that it was dead silence until we had landed and taxied to our dispersal point.

The original designer of Calmooniville airport had visualized nothing larger than an occasional Dakota, and when in a fit of lunacy the airline bought two 707s an extra mile of runway was slapped on to the end of the one already in existence. The wind was always blowing in the same direction in Calmooniville, so there was only need for the one. Then, in another fit of national pride, work had commenced on the airport buildings. Something like a cross between Kennedy and Heathrow had been proposed; foundations had been dug; and work had started. Six months later everyone seemed to get fed up with the idea, and it had just stopped. There remained a couple of acres of half-built terminal buildings, and a small corrugated iron hut which had originally been the site foreman's office. This hut now housed customs, immigration, passenger waiting area, the lot. There was a maintenance hangar on the far side of the main runway, and at least this was run efficiently. Peter saw to that. Major maintenance had to be done elsewhere, but at least he could replace a gasket or mend a puncture on his home field.

Two Rolls-Royces and a Cadillac followed the aircraft for the last half mile of taxiing and, by the time we had stopped and opened the hatch, the gangway was in place and the cars waiting at the bottom. The President and his party piled off the aircraft and into their respective cars which drove off to God knows where. I waited for Peter while he turned the aircraft over to the co-pilot with his instructions as to its disposition. Then he joined me and I set foot on Borami soil for the first time.

Peter had been right about the heat. As I stepped on to the gangway and allowed the sun to give me its first belt, I damn near passed out straight away. It must have been well over a hundred degrees and in two seconds I was soaking wet and feeling like hell. Peter took my arm as we walked down the gangway.

'Good job we didn't arrive at noon,' he said. 'It's as hot as hell then.'

He must have been here longer than I thought. He had a small saloon car parked at the back of the unfinished terminal building. It was standing in the sun and I drew back as we approached it.

'I'm not getting into that,' I said. 'I'll cook.'

'No, you won't,' he said.

Two Africans were already stowing our luggage in the boot and I noticed the engine was running. When Peter opened the front door and pushed me in, it was like getting into an ice box.

'It's refrigerated,' said Peter, climbing in beside me. 'They come across from the control tower and switch it on when I make my last approach call.' My God, was he organized!

The drive from the airport to his house was unrelieved in its depression. Calmooniville had started off as a few mud huts a hundred and fifty years ago. The British had done their bit and put up a few hideous Victorian style buildings, which since Independence seemed to have been left strictly alone, apart from the groups of squatters that had taken up residence. So there were still mud huts, and shanty-like buildings, and a couple of grubby houses, and more shanties, another relic of the Raj, and a few more mud huts. And suddenly there was the Palace. Originally Government House, it had been extensively enlarged and renovated; what had been good enough for a succession of Governor Generals and High Commissioners certainly wasn't good enough for a home-grown President.

I saw it all later, and from that time on I never wondered where all those millions of dollars of aid had gone. But that was later; right now, Peter drove round the perimeter of the palace walls to an area which had been neatly laid out like a very upper class American suburb. There were cool, elegant houses, with well-kept lawns and gardens, and a proper road meandering through the whole area. I could see gardeners working industriously and, in a lot of cases, built-in lawn sprinklers were throwing water around every whichway. It looked like any normal Sunday in Beverly Hills.

Peter's house wasn't quite as grand as some of the others, but it was pretty nice from where I was sitting. It was on the far side of the development, a couple of miles from the Palace. A lawn sloped up from the road to the house itself which was surrounded by a screened verandah. It was a one storey building and it looked cool and inviting. As we drew up two jolly looking Africans came bowling out of the place and running down to meet us. They greeted Peter in atrocious English, exposing masses of teeth and rolling their eyes.

'Diogenes and Archimedes,' said Peter.

'You've got to be kidding.'

'So help me God.'

'Which is which?'

Peter shrugged. 'I don't know.'

He managed to get it across to them that I was to be a house guest and their delight knew no bounds. They fought over my luggage fiercely, and then compromised by dividing it between them; Peter's they left by the side of the road. They preceded us up to the house, looking back over their shoulders to make sure I didn't disappear in a cloud of smoke. One couldn't really blame them I suppose, but they dumped all my luggage in Peter's bedroom. When Peter made them take it out they looked almost as disappointed as I did. Still, if he wanted to play it all proper and above board, I wasn't about to give him any arguments. I allowed myself to be led to the room he had chosen for me and was considerably encouraged to find there was a connecting door to his. I had a spot of trouble stopping Diogenes and Archimedes from doing my unpacking. I finally got them out of my room, but they continued to stick their heads round the door every two minutes giggling something or other to me which I didn't understand. Finally I heard Peter bellow something at them and they didn't appear again until dinner time.

Obviously this was one of the nights when Peter hadn't been able to borrow the Embassy chef, because the food was pretty grotty. But I didn't mind, because everything else was pure romance; the soft night outside, the candlelight, good wine, and dinner *a deux*.

And after dinner? Well, it was inevitable. We had both made up our minds on that ten minutes after we met. He allowed me thirty minutes before he had tapped on the connecting door. I had made the best of that time, too. I looked smashing and I smelled divine. He was very gentle as I had known he would be. I've had my share of kinks and the caveman bit, and they're all very nice if the company and the situation is slanted that way; but basically I'm an old fashioned girl and I like it warm and tender the first time round. He kissed my breasts; he nuzzled around my navel with his tongue, and he put his finger where he had no business to, but which I approved of most highly. I tried to get him inside me after five minutes, but he was having none of that for some time yet. He had the willpower of a superman and he did everything to me that I had ever heard of and a few things that I hadn't before he finally came to the crunch. He woke me up twice during the night for repeats. I don't know what the staple diet is in Borami, but it certainly worked wonders for Peter. I mean, it wasn't as though he were twenty any longer. But he managed to have me begging for mercy before the dawn sun edged through the venetian blinds. He left me at seven a.m. and I zonked out until after mid-day.

Archimedes woke me up, or was it Diogenes? I managed to make enough of his garbled English to learn that I had a visitor. I must have nodded my head or something because he suddenly disappeared and a moment later Glo was pushed into the room. She slapped his hand away vigorously, and after getting him out of the room she slammed the door in his face.

'My God, you look terrible,' she said.

'So would you,' I replied smugly.

'Funny really,' she said. 'I never fancied Peter.'

'Start now and I'll cut your heart out,' I said. I meant it, too. She smiled. 'Don't worry I've got all I can handle.'

'That's in Nairobi.'

'I didn't say that,' she said, and we left it at that. 'Peter asked me to look after you today. He had to go to the airport,' she went on.

'I'm a big girl now.'

'You are indeed,' said Glo, eyeing my breasts which were sticking out over the sheet. Hello, I thought, had I missed something in the beautiful Gloria's hormone make-up? I stored the idea at the back of my mind where I kept other such trivia.

'He told me to show you the sights,' she said.

'Are there any?'

'You'll be surprised. Don't wear slacks or a mini,' she added, and left me to get dressed. That rather put the knockers on my entire wardrobe, and I was wondering what the hell I was going to do, when I made a discovery. Diogenes and Archimedes had been very eager to unpack for me yesterday and I had assumed it was because they wanted to fondle my undies or somesuch. When they had reluctantly surrendered the privilege at my insistence, they had nevertheless shown me the closet I was to use. Now, in my sleep dazed way, I climbed out of bed and opened the wrong closet. It was crammed with clothes, women's clothes. Some were new, some were used. My opinion of how well organized Peter was shot up fifty per cent. Also I felt a little disappointed. Unreasonable of me I know, but show me the girl who wouldn't be. I rifled the closet and came up with a sari that looked as though it could have been made for the Begum.

Hoping that wherever Glo was going to take me, I wouldn't bump into the owner of the sari, I bathed quickly and wrapped myself in its soft coolness. It's a delicious thing to wear is a sari; sexy, subtle, comfortable and elegant. On the odd occasions I had flown Air India I had worn one and, once I had got into the habit, I'd bought myself a couple for my personal wardrobe.

Half an hour after waking up, I was ready and I went to see what little treats Glo had in mind. She made an 'Oooh' of approval as I swept in, and Diogenes and Archimedes went into paroxysms of ecstasy when they saw me. So we set forth.

Peter had left his car and, with the refrigeration turned well up, we took the full tour of Calmooniville. My first impression hadn't been all that wrong, but what I hadn't seen was the new town that was going up. It was a sort of poor man's Brasilia, being constructed ten miles from the main town. A huge area had been chopped out of the jungle, and here were the high buildings, the massive sculptures, the landscaped architecture and the immaculate planning of a bankrupt nation. Mind-boggling schemes had been started, but over all hung the hideous certainty that none of it would ever be finished. Like the grand new airport, interest had seemed to fade about halfway through the operation. There were odd groups of dispirited looking Africans moving around wheeling barrows and mixing cement, but they looked as though they would still be at it a hundred years from now. And as though to confirm everything I was thinking, the jungle was starting to creep back in to reclaim its territory.

'The money is running out,' said Glo. 'Everyone leaped in with open purse strings at first; then when the Russians found they were working next to the Americans with the Chinese in between they all decided they were being taken for a ride. Which they were, of course. So the bottomless purse was snapped shut. It only opens nowadays for things like power stations, dams, irrigation projects and factories; something that the financier can point to proudly at the end and say, "Look! We built that. Aren't we kind, generous and far sighted?" '

It was all very depressing, and I said so.

'You'll get used to it,' said Glo.

We spent a couple of hours viewing the remains; then we headed back towards town. 'Where now?' I asked.

'The Club,' said Glo. It seemed that the entire social life of Borami revolved around the Club. Everyone who was anyone, and a good few people who were nobody at all, used the Club as their meeting place, and as the clearing house for information and gossip. Nothing happened in Borami without news of it going the rounds at the Club almost simultaneously. Glo told me all this on the way back to town, so I was half expecting everyone to know who I was and with whom I was staying; I also had a sneaky feeling that everyone would recognize the sari I was wearing; which turned out to be exactly right.

The Club was housed in a new building on the outer perimeter of the palace grounds. The President was fully aware of its value in keeping him informed on who was doing what to whom in his little domain, so he had presented the land and donated a considerable sum towards its construction. Then he made sure that at least seventy per cent of the staff were on his own payroll. He never used the place himself, but he knew more about what went on under its roof than the resident manager. The place was crowded when we arrived, the car park full of opulent looking automobiles of British, Russian and American origin.

'It's always crowded,' said Glo, as we headed across the cool green lawn to the clubhouse. On the left I could see the swimming pool, and beyond that half a dozen hard tennis courts, none of them being used. 'Eighty per cent of government and ninety per cent of commerce is done from here,' she added. It sounded the right sort of place for me, bearing in mind my current assignment.

I was introduced to the manager as soon as we set foot on the terrace that surrounded the whole building. He was a sandy-coloured Englishman wiht piggy eyes and a mean-looking mouth. His name was Beamish and he had once served in the navy.

'Welcome aboard, Miss Touchfeather,' he said, stripping my sari from me with his first glance. 'We're delighted to welcome any friend of Captain Chalmers.'

He made 'friend' sound like a dirty word and I decided that I didn't like Mr. Beamish one little bit. I found out later that very few people did, but that he was good at his job. He ran the place well without putting his hand too deep into the till, so he stayed where he was. He escorted us straight through to the bar, which covered one entire half of the building, opening on all sides to the terrace. The place was crowded and until the moment I arrived, it was noisy, too. Then, as I appeared, there was an abrupt and absolute silence for one brief moment. Every eye in the place swivelled towards me; everything was noted, clear down to my false eyelashes. Then, as though by command, all eyes swung away and the noise was resumed at exactly the same level. Welcome to Borami, I thought. But one pair of eyes had not swung away and now their owner bore down on us like an eager little retriever fumbling his way towards the kill.

'God,' said Glo. 'Here comes the faggot.'

The faggot turned out to be called Henry Henry. That's not a misprint, his family name was Henry and his parents in a fit of lunacy had christened him with the same given name. He was a little roundish man about thirty-five years old. He babbled effusively, but always with a faint underlying impression of panic. It was as though one only had to say 'Boo!' to him and he would collapse into floods of tears. Glo introduced us.

'Katy Touchfeather. Henry Henry.' I must have looked a little surprised, but obviously he was used to it. He smiled rather sweetly.

'Terrible, isn't it? I thought about changing it, but I never quite got round to it.' He seemed the sort of man who would never quite get around to anything in this life.

'I'll call you Hank,' I said.

The poor darling nearly kissed my hand. 'Would you?' he said. 'Would you really?'

'Hank it is,' I said, feeling impossibly noble.

'Please come and have a drink with me to celebrate my new name.'

I glanced at Glo, who shrugged. 'Love to,' I said.

I started towards a corner of the room, but imperceptibly Hank touched my elbow, steering me in the opposite direction. It was only much later that I learned he had spotted the owner of my sari sitting with a party at the far side of the room, and wanted to keep me as far away from her as possible. I was rather sorry when I found out because I would have liked to have taken a look at her. But when I did find out, it only confirmed the nice feelings I already held about Hank. I don't know what it is, but queers like me. I mean it's not as though I'm butch or anything like that, but for some reason they take to me on sight and remain dear and devoted friends; at least until such times as I have my eye on a fellow they also have designs on. Then they can be bitchier than any woman born. But in general, they like me, and I like them. They're invariably good company, polite, amusing, and there's never any complications at the end of the evening.

We spread ourselves around a spare table and Hank ordered the drinks. Then he beamed at us both.

'The two most beautiful girls in the room, and I've got them both,' he said.

'No, you haven't,' said Glo.

Hank was about to say something; then he shut up. Glo got to her feet, excused herself and headed across the bar towards a group of people who were standing on the far side. Hank smiled at me, apologizing for her.

'Gloria has so many friends,' he said. I could see one of them from where I was sitting: six feet two, fair haired, brown as a berry, and looking as though he had just stepped off a movie set.

'She'd only need one like that,' I said.

'Karl Brenner,' said Hank. 'He fools around with a small import export business.'

'That's not all he fools around with,' I said. He was leaning over Glo and whispering something to her, his arm wrapped around her in a proprietary fashion.

'They're very discreet,' said Hank. It didn't look that way to me, but I let it go. 'How do you like Borami?' he went on.

'Not much,' I said. 'Although it does have its compensations.'

'Everyone loves Peter,' he said.

I fluffed the edge of my sari at him. 'I'm beginning to find that out,' I said.

He smiled apologetically. 'It can get very lonely out here. After all, it's not as though he really means anything to you.'

'He's my fiancé,' I said. 'Where I come from, that means something.'

'Ah, yes,' said Hank. 'Your fiancé. And who's going to give you away at the wedding? Mr. Blaser?' Big deal, I thought. So now I know who my contact is.

We talked inconsequentials for the next half an hour. A couple of people drifted over, were introduced, and left again. Hank gave me a brief rundown on the social and sexual lives of most of the people in the room and it all sounded highly entertaining, rather like Peyton Place in a hot climate. Then Peter joined us, thanked Hank for looking after me and dragged me off.

'We're going to a palace reception,' he said.

'Who's being received?'

'The usual. Diplomats, business men, promoters and gangsters. You name it and it'll be represented there this evening.'

'Do we have to go?'

'I do,' said Peter. 'I suppose I could make excuses for you.'

'I was just wondering if one of your ex girl-friends has as good a taste in reception type gowns as she has in saris?'

He didn't bat an eyelid, for which I was grateful. 'You'll find something,' he said.

'Just so long as no one is going to come up to me in the palace and rip it off my back.'

'The only ripping will be done by me, and it won't be at the palace,' said Peter. And with that thought to warm me for the evening, I went to get ready for my first palace reception.

President Calmooni headed the receiving line, which was composed of the Prime Minister, the Minister of Finance, and assorted males and females whose names and functions I never quite did get hold of. But it wasn't really my fault, because the moment I walked into the reception room, before I had even started along the line, I recognized someone across the room. He saw and recognized me at the same moment. I would like to have said he blanched or rocked back on his heels or somesuch. But he didn't. But then men like Constantin Galipolodopolo very rarely do.


## CHAPTER FOUR

I MANAGED to locate Hank without too much trouble. He, too, was at the reception. It was only later that I learned he was at all the Palace binges; he was a sort of unofficial master of protocol. Calmooni relied on him to make sure that the functions he gave were reasonably well run and the social gaffes not too monumental. Peter had me chatting with a party of Americans when I caught Hank's eye across the room. I made some vague sort of signal in his direction which he must have understood because a moment later he moved over to our group. He stood chatting for a few minutes, then asked Peter if he could borrow me for a short time. Peter agreed, and Hank led me back across the reception room towards what he hoped would be a quiet corner. At one moment I saw the cold eyes of Constantin resting on me from across the room, but he made no attempt to make any sort of contact. Finally Hank throught we had sufficient privacy for whatever it was that I wanted. But he thought he would do me a favour before we got down to the nitty gritty.

'Do you want to meet one of the richest men in the world?' he asked.

'I most certainly do not,' I said. 'I already know him. And I

want you to let Mr. Blaser know he's here and what am I supposed to do about it?'

'Like for instance?'

'Like run like bloody hell before Galipolodopolo sets his dogs
on me again.'

'Oh dear!' said Hank. 'Oh dear me.' Which didn't strike me
as being any help at all.

'How long before you can get word back?' I asked.

He glanced at his watch. 'A couple of hours,' he said.

'Then be a love and get moving. In the meantime I'll plead
sick and go home.' He offered to escort me back to Peter, but I
didn't want to risk that walk across the room again. The longer
I remained here, the more chance there would be that I would
be confronted with Galipolodopolo; and I had absolutely no
idea how I would handle the situation. Added to all this, there
was a fair old chance that Constantin would tell everyone that
I was not all that I was supposed to be. Altogether it seemed
that I was batting on an extremely sticky wicket and the quicker
I extricated myself, the better.

Hank left to do the necessary with his radio, and I sent a
message to Peter saying I'd come over queer and had to go home.
I located the car in the forecourt, manoeuvred it out, and drove
back to the house. Archimedes and Diogenes fussed around me
like two mother hens when they heard I wasn't well. I managed
to prevent them calling a doctor and, after considerable effort, I
also managed to dissuade them from undressing me and putting
me to bed. I allowed them to bring me a medicinal brandy, then
sent them both to bed. After that, I just waited. It was an even
money bet as to who would get to me first: Hank, with some sort
of instructions; Peter with tender solicitude; or Galipolodopolo
with a meat axe.

Fortunately Hank arrived first. I heard him arguing in the hall
with Archimedes-or-was-it-Diogenes and, after making out
phrases such as 'Missy sleeping' and 'Missy not well' and 'No
disturb Captain's lady,' I pulled on a dressing gown, courtesy of
another Captain's lady, and went to learn my fate.

'Did you speak to him?' I asked. Hank looked horrified, as
though I'd asked if he'd spoken to God.

'Of course not. Not personally anyway.'

'But you found out what I'm supposed to do?'

'Well yes, in a way.'

'In what way?' I asked, not liking the sound of it at all.

'Your instructions are to play it by ear.'

More specifically, the report had come through that Miss
Touchfeather was to use her discretion in the matter. I thought

of the hundred times that Mr. Blaser had told me that I was
totally lacking in discretion.

'Are you sure you contacted the right Mr. Blaser?' I asked.
Hank looked horrified again.

But those were the instructions and Katy prepared to play it
by ear. And the first thing my ear told me to do was to get
the hell out of there; to put as much distance between myself
and Galipolodopolo as I could. Because it was a pretty fair bet
that where Galipolodopolo lurked, then not far behind lurked
Lucia of the happy hypodermic. Truth drugs are all very fine
in their place, but truth drugs that kill you stone dead I can do
without.

Then reason prevailed. If Galipolodopolo was going to go after
me, it was a pretty safe bet that somewhere, sometime he would
eventually get me. And apart from all that, I couldn't see myself
sitting across from Mr. Blaser and telling him that I had run
because I was scared. His people weren't supposed to get scared
about silly little things like their own skins. So I decided to stay
where I was. Perhaps if Galipolodopolo was handed enough rope
he'd hang himself; my main concern was that he would do it
before he hanged me.

I thanked Hank and asked him to keep an avuncular eye on
me for the next couple of days in case I suddenly dropped from
view.

'I could get you a gun,' he said doubtfully.

But guns are for shooting people and there didn't seem to be
anyone around I could shoot, except myself, so I declined the
offer. Apart from that, a girl like me, with a trim little form-
fitting uniform to wear, has absolutely no place where she can
conceal a gun, except in her handbag; and my bag is always
so full of junk, I'm hard pressed to find room for a spare lipstick.
So I patted Hank's cheek, thanked him very much, and sent him
on his way. Then I went to bed.

Peter crept home an hour or so later. I heard him open the
connecting door between our rooms and stand there looking
towards my bed. But I just wasn't in the mood, so I breathed
steadily and pretended to be asleep. He tiptoed out a moment
later and two minutes after that I really was asleep. It's a funny
thing with me; when all around is grotty in the extreme and
disaster lurks around every bend, all I want to do is sleep. I
know I shall miss the Day of Judgment because I'll be asleep at the
time; and this night I died for ten straight hours.

When I emerged it was after ten and the day's heat had started
to build up alarmingly. I rang for Archimedes-or-was-it-Diogenes
and asked him what had happened to the air conditioning which,

along with every other electrical appliance, wasn't working because the electricity supply had packed up again. Apparently it did this with monotonous regularity. Archimedes-or-was-it-Diogenes explained that the power station usually remained out of action for five or six hours so there was nothing to worry about. I disagreed with him; it meant a day without air conditioning in a temperature that reached 110° in the shade at noon. I thought for a moment about going to sit in the car all day, but that didn't seem very practical. Nor did it seem practical to go swimming, either at the Club or at the Palace pool which Peter had use of; either of these places could be swarming with Galipolodopolo.

So I took a cold shower, wrapped myself in a damp sheet and prepared to sulk the day away. Peter had gone out to the airport at nine o'clock and wasn't expected back until the evening. He had left a note for me in which he hoped I was feeling better and would look after myself and have a nice day. I wandered round the house for a couple of hours being nosy and pretending I was looking for something to do. Peter's library was woefully inadequate, all James Bond and technical journals. I found a couple of minor pornographic works on one of the top shelves, but I don't go much for solitary reading of pornography and, anyway, I'd read them both before.

I was still sulking around the house two hours later when Peter called from the airport.

'How are you feeling?' he asked. I told him I was feeling fine. 'Good. There'll be a car there in fifteen minutes. We're flying upcountry.'

'Where's upcountry?'

'Manboola,' said Peter, leaving me none the wiser. 'There's a uniform in the closet that should fit you. It may be a little tight around the bust though,' he said, no doubt recalling the chest measurements of its former owner.

'They don't build them like me these days.'

'They certainly don't,' he agreed, and hung up.

Delighted to have something to do, I showered again, made up, and climbed into the uniform of Borami Airlines. It wasn't bad as uniforms go, lightweight and not as tight around the bust as Peter had supposed. Obviously his memory of things past was going. Then I made the mistake of telling Archimedes-or-was-it-Diogenes that I was going to Manboola. I only told him because he asked me if I would be back for dinner and I said I didn't know because I didn't know how far away Manboola was. His eyes opened wide, as did his mouth, and yelled excitedly for Diogenes-or-was-it-Archimedes. He gabbled something to him and there was the same reaction. Immediately they started running round in circles, and ten minutes later, just as I was about to leave, they handed me an old carrier bag, containing God knows what. It seemed they had three or four aunts and untold cousins in Manboola, and would Missy be so kind as to locate one of the clan and hand over the carrier bag. It contained, they assured me, scraps from Peter's table, food that would otherwise be thrown out, but which would be very gratefully received by the poor, half starved upcountry cousins.

On the way to the airport I peered into the carrier bag; among other things were two jars of caviar, a bottle of scotch, one of gin, and three tins of turtle soup; hardly perishable foodstuffs, but then obviously Peter could afford it, and it wasn't really any of my business anyway.

Peter met my car at the airfield. 'We've got a very very V.I.P. today,' he said, when he had given me a kiss.

'Don't tell me,' I said. 'Let me guess.'

And of course, I was right.

It seemed we weren't taking the 707 because the airfield at Manboola wasn't big enough to accommodate it. Today it was to be one of the renovated Dakotas. As we walked across the baking apron towards the aircraft, I started to plot and scheme. Perhaps I should just throw a faint here and now; perhaps I should tell Peter I couldn't fly when I had the curse, which I didn't have; perhaps I should say Dakotas made me air sick; or perhaps I should just cut my throat and call it a day.

Then Peter handed me the topper. 'I was going to use Gloria on this trip,' he said. 'But our V.I.P. asked for you especially.'

With the scales weighed that heavily against me, there didn't seem much point in fighting it any more. I grinned weakly and allowed Peter to take my hand and lead me up the short gangway into the aircraft.

'Incidentally, you must have made quite an impression on him,' said Peter, just before he went forward. 'I didn't know you were at the reception long enough to meet anyone.'

This meant that up to now, my antecedents weren't being shouted around. I didn't know whether to be relieved or otherwise; and on reflection it didn't seem to make much difference either way. I moved around the aircraft numbly, getting things ready for the flight. It was only two hours, so no food was to be served, but we had enough ice and booze on board to stupefy a regiment.

'How long are we going to be gone?' I asked Peter, just before the passengers came aboard.

'We'll be back this evening,' he said. 'Galipolodopolo just wants to visit the mines at Manboola.'

'What does he want to do that for?' I asked, thinking that I might as well continue on the job up to the bitter end.

'Who knows why a man like him does anything?' replied Peter, and with that I had to be contented.

The two engines were run up and we taxied as close to the airport entrance as we reasonably could. The passengers arrived in two of the palace cars. The group consisted of three Borami representatives and three Europeans whom I took to be Galipolo-dopolo's men. And, of course, Constantin himself. He came up the gangway first while I buried my head in the galley and hoped he would forget I existed. Then, as Peter moved back on to the flight deck, I was simply forced to put in an appearance. I moved down the aisle checking the seat-belts, and eventually I came face to face with Constantin.

'Is your seat-belt fastened correctly, sir?' I asked feeling like a complete twit.

He looked at me steadily with those cold brown eyes of his and, if you think it's difficult for brown eyes to be cold, you should take a look at Constantin's.

'I would still like to make love to you, Katherine,' he said. And that was all. Not 'Sorry I had you kidnapped and tried to have you killed at the same time'; not 'Now you're for it, Katy Touchfeather'; not even 'You're looking well,' or 'Long-time no see'. Just 'I would still like to make love to you.' Sex mad, that was his problem.

He gave me absolutely no trouble on the trip. When I asked him if he would like a drink, he thanked me very much and said he'd have a vodka on the rocks. When I asked him if he would like another, he said, 'No, thank you'. And that was the extent of our inflight communication.

Two hours later on the dot Peter announced that we were about to land. Seat belts were fastened and I sneaked a look out of the window. For a moment I thought Peter had suffered heat stroke or something, because it seemed we were going to put down slap in the middle of the jungle. And it was real jungle. Even from up here one could tell that. This wasn't a Hollywood jungle with Tarzan swinging through the trees; absolutely nobody or nothing could swing through that tangled mass of vegetation that stretched as far as the eye could see. It looked like a very shaggy green carpet that went on forever. Then, as we dropped lower and lower and I could still see no break in the surface, I thought that perhaps we were going to land on top of the trees, they certainly looked solid enough. We seemed about to do just that when a gash opened up in front of us, cement stretched out ahead, the wheels banged down on to something solid, the brakes screamed, held, and we had arrived. We turned at the end of the runway and taxied back along half its length. Then we turned off on to a tiny apron, and a moment after that the engines started to wind down. Peter appeared up front.

'I don't know how much business you have to conduct here, gentlemen,' he said to no one in particular. 'But I would be grateful if you would allow me to take off before dark. There are no runway lights here and things get a bit tricky come night-fall.'

It was Constantin who answered him. 'We will be exactly two hours, Captain. Will that be alright?'

Peter glanced at his watch. 'That will be fine, sir. Thank you.'

The gangway was trundled up outside and the passengers disembarked to get on with their undoubtedly nefarious business.

This left Peter and Katy alone together.

'Drink?' suggested Peter.

'Drink,' concurred Katy.

We walked over to the corrugated iron hut that was the only building in sight, and while Katy belted a large scotch on the rocks, Peter had a coke. Being a well brought up flight captain he never touched a drop of booze when he was working. And I needed that scotch. Apart from the flight which had been nerve racking in the extreme, Manboola was enough to drive anyone to drink on its own account. It had been chopped out of the jungle and consisted of a collection of huts crouched among the trees which loomed over the settlement as though they were about to devour it. Three land-rovers had met the aircraft and the passengers, Constantin included, had driven off into the jungle. Peter explained that the mine was about two miles from the airstrip and he had never seen it, because he had never been asked. Indeed, on one occasion when he had expressed an interest in visiting the place, he had been convincingly dissuaded. He hadn't actually been ordered not to visit the place, but it had been made clear to him that a lot of people in high places would have disapproved strongly. So he hadn't bothered.

'What do they mine up there?' I asked.

'Manganese,' he said. 'Or is it nickel? Anyway, there's a railway line that goes through to Calmooniville. They ship the ore there, then it's switched to the main line and goes on to the coast.'

'What's so secret about a nickel mine?' I asked.

He shrugged. 'Perhaps they're digging up uranium at the same time.' He didn't really care, and there was no reason why he should.

'May I have another scotch?' I asked. He looked at his watch. There was still an hour and a half before the passengers could reasonably expect to be back, so he agreed.

'A small one this time,' he said. Then he trotted out to supervise the refuelling and check on the weather for the return flight. The waiter serving us spoke English so I asked him if he knew any of the cousins of Archimedes/Diogenes. He did better than that, he *was* one of the cousins. So I gave him the carrier bag I had toted from Calmooniville, and won a friend for life in the process. No, he had never been up the mine, but three of his cousins worked there, and would I like to meet them? I said I would like to very much, but there wasn't much chance as we were due out in the next ninety minutes. Never mind, he said, next time. I agreed that next time would be fine and I ordered another scotch. Landing here had been pretty traumatic and I wanted to be well insulated by the time we came to take off again. He brought me my scotch and, because we were now bosom buddies, it was a big one. I'd like to think it was this that set my head reeling five minutes later; after all I had started with a double, then a single, now another double; five scotches may not sound too much, but in that stupefying heat, and with my nerves being as uptight as they were, it seemed a reasonable enough explanation. I stood it as long as I could, then I told my new-found friend to tell Captain Chalmers that when he needed me I'd be in the ladies loo, throwing up. I never even made the ladies; I hit the sun outside, the sun belted me back, and I keeled over. I was vaguely aware of catching my elbow an awful bang as I tried to break my fall, and that was all I remembered.

When I emerged, it was to see a rather pleasant face bending over me, the face of a blond young man with blue eyes and a nice smile. 'Hi!' he said.

I tried to reciprocate, but nothing came out. I tried again. 'Hi yourself,' I managed.

'Feeling OK?' he asked. I shook my head, then grabbed it before it fell off and rolled under the bed.

'Take it easy,' he said. 'Drink this.' He held me partially upright while I swallowed some vile tasting concoction which surprised me by muffling the bells that were ringing in my head.

'What happened?' I asked, when he had lowered me back on to the pillow.

'You passed out and you were brought here.'

'Where's here?'

'The hospital.'

'What hospital?'

'Manboola Mining.'

'Oh, I said. 'Where's Captain Chalmers?'

'He and his party left hours ago. You've been out for quite a time.'

'Galipolodopolo, too?'

'I believe so.' At least that was relief. 'I'm Doctor Petrie,' he went on. 'You're Katy Touchfeather.'

'I wouldn't bet on it,' I said, still feeling like absolute death.

He grinned pleasantly. 'You're a real treat for me,' he said. 'All I usually get here are VD cases and broken arms.'

'Shouldn't there be a nurse in the room or something,' I said, recognizing a far off gleam in his blue eyes.

'Don't worry,' he said. 'You're far too sick for me to take advantage of you. Not that I wouldn't like to.'

'What's wrong with me?' I asked, trying to change the line of the conversation.

He shrugged. 'I don't know,' he said. 'I thought you might be pregnant, but you're not.'

'I know it,' I said. 'How do you?'

'I looked.' Fair enough, I thought. After all, he was a doctor. 'Food poisoning probably,' he went on. But he didn't sound too happy about that either.

'So what happens now?' I asked.

'As soon as you're well enough, I call Captain Chalmers and he'll come and fetch you.'

'How about calling him now?' I didn't fancy staying in Manboola any longer than was absolutely necessary.

'Let's leave it until tomorrow,' he said. 'Is there anything you want?' I shook my head again, and this time it stayed in place. 'I'll send a nurse in to give you something to help you sleep. See you in the morning.'

'Are we actually at the mine?' I asked, game to the end.

'We're in the compound,' he said. 'There's no hospital at Manboola proper.'

'I thought this place was off limits to outsiders.'

He looked puzzled. 'Who told you that?'

'Well, isn't it?'

He shrugged, 'We don't get many outsiders here I admit, but that doesn't mean they're not welcome. You're very welcome.'

'I must have misunderstood,' I said.

He smiled, rather sweetly. 'If I played my cards right I could keep you here for a couple of weeks,' he said. 'Doctor's orders.'

I managed a smile in return. 'I'm a pretty generous type girl,' I said. 'But never when pushed.'

He looked at me from the door for a moment, a speculative gleam in his eye. Then he smiled again.

'See you tomorrow,' he said, and left.

I looked around my room. It was sterile, functional and completely without any warmth or charm whatsoever. There was a small wardrobe in one corner, one chair, a wash basin and a bedside table. That was it; exactly the sort of hospital room one would expect to find anywhere in the world. But I wasn't anywhere in the world. I was in Manboola, in the middle of the jungle and a thousand miles away from absolutely everything. I didn't like it and I started to feel miserable; really miserable. At times like this Mr. Blaser invariably comes to mind, because he is the one who is responsible for me being where I am. 'Play it by ear', indeed.

Had he any idea at all what he was talking about, the silly old fool. I'd like to play it by his ear, all around Calmooniville, Manboola and points between. Still, Constantin Galipolodopolo was gone, so I didn't have to worry about him any longer, which was a consolation. And having indulged myself in a small ration of self pity, I started to cheer up again.

The nurse arrived ten minutes later, a cheerful coloured girl. I thought I was going to get a sleeping pill, but she had other ideas. She prepared an injection, swabbed down my arm, and shot me full of something that perched me for a moment on the edge of a delightful cottonwool abyss, and then slid me gently over the edge, way over my head.

This was some drug I had been given. It was better than an LSD trip. There were hallucinations, colour, movement, noise, people, more movement and more noise. All this was interspersed with periods of nothing. It was exactly as though I were lightly sleeping and occasionally surfacing to wakefulness when I would grasp an impression of something, and slip back to sleep once more. All very cosy, I thought, in one of my semi-lucid moments. I must remember to get the name of the stuff. Whoops, now I was flying. Not by myself as in a proper LSD trip, but in an aeroplane, a warm comfortable aeroplane. I've always said that the best way to fly is by aeroplane. Then off to sleep again. Perhaps the next time I surfaced I'd be floating. But I wasn't, I was still flying. Cheap old drug I thought. It doesn't even vary the pattern. I dozed off once more and, damn me, if I wasn't still flying the next time I emerged. Ridiculous, I thought. This needs investigation. So I fought against drifting back to sleep this time and managed to stay awake initially for thirty straight seconds. After that, it was no problem because my fright pumped enough adrenalin into my system to keep me awake for the next ten years. Because Goddamn it, I *was* flying.

Without advertising the fact, I took a peek around. I was in a small cabin holding six very luxurious seats with plenty of leg and elbow room. I was at the back, and there may have been someone else in the cabin with me, but they would be obscured by the rear of their seats. The engine noise was that of a jet, and glancing out of the window I could see by the vague light of the night sky that there were no wing engines. That meant aft engines. So what did we have? One; a small aircraft. Two; rear mounted jet engines. It had to be the sort of aircraft owned by film stars and captains of industry—the executive jet, they call it. And it didn't need three guesses to work out which executive *this* aircraft belonged to.

After five minutes I managed to convince myself that I wouldn't drop off to sleep again. I thought about now would be a good time to try to garner some information. I unfastened my seatbelt and lurched to my feet. I wasn't as well as I had supposed, because if I hadn't been able to grasp the backs of the two seats in front of me, I would have fallen flat on my face. But, standing up, I was able to see across the backs of the other seats. I was alone in the cabin. This was a certain comfort, but not much, because I obviously wasn't going anywhere except where the aircraft took me. I tottered towards the front of the cabin where the door led through to the flight deck. Should I try it or not? It would probably be locked, and in trying it I would only advertise the fact that I was up and about. The best thing I could do would be to make preparations for the nastiness that was to follow.

By now I had worked out exactly what had happened; a mickey finn in one of my scotches, sufficient to make me pass out and be taken to hospital; something heftier and more subtle in my late night injection. While all this was going on, Galipolo-dopolo would have arranged for one of his private aircraft to slip into Manboola and have me lifted out of there at dead of night. Altogether a very smooth operation especially if one bore in mind Peter's earlier statement that there were no runway lights at Manboola. Whoever was up front driving this thing was a hell of a pilot.

I spent a few minutes working out the permutations that would follow my disappearance. No doubt Peter would call to see how I was. If Doctor Petrie was in on the deal, then I would be reported as OK but not yet well enough to travel. If Petrie wasn't in on it, then he would tell Peter that I had disappeared in the middle of the night. And what would Peter do then? And would Hank hear about it? And if he did, what the hell would Mr. Blaser be able to do about it? Because one thing was for sure, wherever we were heading, it was a pretty fair bet that very few people would get to hear about it and Mr. Blaser was way at the bottom of the list. No, Katy was strictly on her ownsome, and pretty sick about it to boot.

A look out of the window told me absolutely nothing, except that dawn wasn't far away. Below there was just cloud. The first light of the day did tell me we were travelling roughly north west, but that was all. If there had been a parachute available I would probably have used it, preferring the unknown to what I reckoned was waiting for me. But there wasn't a parachute so I was saved from making the choice. But while there wasn't a parachute there was something else. In the rear bulkhead there was a hatch marked 'Emergency Equipment'.

This seemed as dire an emergency as would come my way for quite a time, so I opened the hatch. Behind it was a deep locker holding a couple of inflatable rubber dinghies, half a dozen inflatable life jackets, and a small box marked 'survival kit'. I opened the box and sorted through the glucose tablets, sea-sick pills, water purifiers, chocolate bars and first aid gear until I found what I was looking for. It was a roll of fine nylon thread on a spool, half a dozen extremely large fish hooks and a knife. Every survival kit worth its salt carries the equipment necessary for fishing, and for gutting the fish if you're fortunate enough to catch anything. The knife was very sharp, with one plain and one saw edge. This I tucked down the back of my blouse. flat under the back strap of my bra, giving silent thanks to whoever it was had dressed me at the hospital. God knows where I would have hidden the knife if I hadn't been wearing a bra. I wasn't quite sure what use the fish hooks would be, but they were very large and looked exceedingly vicious; these I hooked into the underside hem of my skirt. The nylon cord I started to wrap around my waist under my blouse and skirt. When I had wound what seemed like ten miles of the stuff around my middle, I pulled the knife out again and cut the cord; then I tied the end so that it wouldn't unravel and fall around my ankles. I put everything else back in the emergency locker, closed it, and resumed my seat at the rear. When we landed it would be advisable to look as though I had just regained consciousness. That way they wouldn't bother to poke around my person wondering if I had been up to anything.

It was almost daylight now, but there was still one hundred per cent cloud cover below, so it was no help. What I did manage to see was the aircraft registration letters. They showed that the aircraft was registered in Greece. Surprise, surprise! And then, just as I was about to drift off to sleep again, having nothing better to do, the door to the flight deck started to open. I closed my eyes quickly and tried to look unconscious. I sensed someone come into the cabin and then there was silence. I stood it for as long as I could and then I risked a peek. A rather dishy face was a foot away from mine, brown eyes regarding me steadily. I squeezed out a little groan, closed my eyes again, opened them once more and rolled them about a bit. All told, not a bad performance; at least it managed to convince him.

'How do you feel?' he asked.

I focused once more. He really was dishy; dark, with soft brown eyes like Omar Sharif. He wore a plain blue uniform with no sleeve rings, and he smelled faintly of an expensive after shave lotion.

'Oh dear,' I groaned. 'Oh dear.'

There was a flash of concern in his eyes; a hell of a kidnapper this one.

'What is it? Can I get you anything?'

'I'm going to be sick,' I said.

He moved quickly and returned a moment later with a sick bag. He handed it to me, and then, because he was obviously a gentleman, he turned his back to me so that I wouldn't be embarrassed at throwing up in front of a complete stranger. He was the one to be embarrassed. I made convincing throwing up noises just for the time necessary to unstrap my seat belt and reach into the back of my blouse for the knife. The first intimation he had that all was not as it should be was when I struck the point of the knife up under his ear. He wasn't used to this sort of caper because he made the mistake of trying to turn round to see what was going on, and I had to jab the knife in a little way.

'Perfectly still,' I said. 'Or it goes all the way in.'

He looked so shocked I almost felt sorry for him, especially as there was a trickle of blood running down his neck into his clean white shirt collar.

'Madre mia!' he exclaimed. 'Be careful with that knife.'

'Sit down!' I said. He sat, while I kept the knife stuck where it was. 'Anyone else up front?'

He was about to nod, then, working out he would probably impale himself, he settled for saying, 'Yes'.

'Just one?'

'Yes.'

'Where are we going?'

I think about here he decided to see if I was bluffing, because he shut his mouth firmly and a small jab with the knife, while making him wince, didn't open it again.

'Is the money Galipolodopolo pays you worth getting your throat cut for?' I inquired politely. Still he didn't answer.

This would be quite a problem I thought. I could hardly stand there digging him with the knife if he was determined not to say anything. And at any moment his companion might come trotting through the door. I didn't want to cut his throat because, believe you me, the mess is indescribable. I hardly had time to tie and gag him, and I hadn't got a club to beat him over the head with. So, hoping I remembered the anatomy that Bessie had taught me, I reached for the vital pressure point that could cut off the flow of blood to the brain. I gave it a good whack with the edge of my free hand and he keeled over as though he had been poleaxed. For a moment I wondered whether I had killed him. But I wasn't about to waste time finding out. Leaving him where he was, I moved up to the front part of the cabin. He had left the door half open, and peering through it I could see his companion flying the aircraft like he didn't have a care in the world. Maybe at that moment he didn't, but he sure as hell did ten seconds later when I came up behind him and clouted him with the fire extinguisher I took from the wall just inside the flight deck. He keeled over and the aircraft immediately put its nose down in sympathy, starting earthwards at a vast rate of knots. I dragged him clear, slipped into the seat, and levelled off five thousand feet lower down. I located the automatic pilot, switched it on and checked for a moment to see that it was operational. Then I slipped out of the seat again and went to tidy up. Ten minutes later I was back, looking at the controls and trying to work out how to fly the bloody thing.

By now, my two companions were back in the cabin, wrapped up in fishing cord. Even when they regained consciousness, they weren't going to be able to do anything except strangle themselves if they struggled too hard. Katy was on her own with five hundred and fifty miles per hour of aeroplane at her fingertips, and without the faintest idea what to do with it. I'd flown aeroplanes, of course—all part of the training—but there is a vast difference between a conventional prop aircraft and a jet. Books have been written about this difference, but unfortunately I'd never read any of them.

I looked at the dials and levers and gadgets for a full five minutes before I said the hell with it. But one thing I could do was to go down and take a look at what was below. The fuel gauges read half full, so there was no screaming rush to land, or anything like that, but it would be comforting to know roughly where we were. Then perhaps if things worked out I could take a chance on the radio; one never knew who might be listening in.

I dipped the stick forward and started a long, gentle downward track. The clouds came up three minutes later and, gritting my teeth, I continued to head downwards. There may have been a mountain lurking someplace but I had to take a chance. The altimeter was reading six thousand feet when we went into the cloud and two thousand when we came out. As soon as I saw the ground, I eased back on the stick and levelled off. I wish I hadn't bothered. I should have left the flying to the two boys back in the cabin. At least they knew where we were going, and how to get there. We were flying over desert; not your Californian type desert, or even your Arizona type desert. This was full blown, king-sized number one, top grade, umpty thousand mile type desert. Seeing as we were still travelling roughly north west, and bearing in mind where we started from, it had to be the Sahara; the daddy of all deserts. Sand went on forever, without any sort of a break, not even a camel to relieve the monotony. All right Katy, I thought, what are you going to do now? Either you can fly this thing until you see something below you, or until you run out of fuel; or you can go back into the cabin, untie the pilot, apologize, and let them get on with what they are equipped for, namely to take this flying coffin to someplace where they can put it down on the ground. Because even if I found a place I considered good for landing, I didn't think I would be able to do it. It was all to do with stalling speed, flap angles, drag and inertia, and a few things I'd never even heard of, let alone understood. Perhaps I could force one of the pilots into flying me to where I wanted to go. Let's give it a try, I thought.

I reset the automatic pilot and went into the cabin. Both men had regained consciousness and both started talking as I came in.

'Please lady you'll get us all killed.'

'Let me fly the aeroplane.'

'Do you know what you are doing?' And similar remarks in that vein.

I chose the pretty one, the one I had stuck the knife into. At least he hadn't received a bang on the head to upset his judgment.

'I'm going to cut you loose,' I said. He didn't say anything, but his eyes spoke volumes. 'But please don't get any ideas. I may be sugar on the outside, but I'm just plain mean underneath it all. And if I have to stick this knife into you, I'll do it, even if it's only to convince your friend that I'm that type of person. Now, are you going to behave yourself?'

'Yes ma'am.'

He sounded reasonably impressed with what I had told him, so I cut him loose. Which only goes to show how you can't trust a soul these days. Because as I cut the last strand of nylon he proved just how untrustworthy he was by grabbing for my wrist where I held the knife. I stepped back quickly but the gangway wasn't all that wide and I didn't have as much room to manoeuvre as I would have liked.

'Get her, Andrei,' shouted the one who was still tied. And Andrei did his best. In fact he did so well, I had to do something I'd hoped to avoid; namely stick the knife into him.

The mess was unbelievable, and by the fuss he made you would have thought I'd castrated him. He rolled around the cabin, shedding blood copiously and swearing that he was as good as dead. All I had done was to slash his wrist; painful, yes; bloody,

certainly; but fatal, no; not so long as a tourniquet was applied.
I told him this and let him get on with it while I untied the
second man, who was as quiet as a two day old kitten by now.
As I urged him towards the flight deck, Andrei appealed to me.

'Please help me,' he said. 'I can't put a tourniquet on by myself.'

'Use your other hand,' I suggested. 'Just clamp it above your
wrist. Don't forget to ease the pressure every few minutes or
your arm will drop off.'

With that I escorted the other man through to the flight deck,
where I closed and locked the door. He knew more or less what
was wanted of him, because he sat straight down, switched off
the automatic pilot, and quickly checked all the instruments to
make sure I hadn't fouled up anything. Then, satisfied, he turned
to me.

'All right lady,' he said. 'What happens now?'

Where the other man was Greek, this one was English, obviously ex R.A.F. He was about thirty years old with a rather tired
face as though he had seen it all and didn't much like any of it.

'First things first,' I said. 'Where are we going?'

'Babout.'

'Where's Babout?'

He pulled a flight chart towards him, turned a couple of
sheets, and pointed to Babout. It was, as near as made no difference, slap in the middle of the Sahara.

'What's at Babout?'

He shrugged. 'It's an oasis.'

'With a private airfield of course,' I prompted. He nodded.
'Whose?'

There was a moment of silence so I encouraged him with the
knife under his ear.

'Constantin Galipolodopolo,' he said reluctantly, no doubt
seeing his pension going out of the window. I looked at the map
again.

'We'll go on to Casablanca,' I said.

He shook his head. 'Not enough fuel.'

'Where have we got enough fuel for?'

'Babout,' he said. And so help me if he didn't grin.

'What's your name?' I asked.

'Thomas Wise,' he said, not catching the drift.

'All right, Tom,' I said. 'Let's see how funny you'll find it with
your ear in your lap.'

He stopped grinning and went quite white.

'And having exhausted our comical repertoire, perhaps you'll
tell me where else we can put down.'

'Lady, there isn't anywhere,' he said, with shades of panic

beginning to edge his voice. 'There's nothing this side of Babout and nothing for six hundred miles the other.'

'We haven't got six hundred miles?'

'We haven't got sixty if you make me keep to this altitude. We're burning fuel down here like there's no tomorrow.'

'Take her back up where you want her,' I said.

He breathed a silent sigh of relief, eased back on the stick and we started to climb back into the clouds. I let him fly the aeroplane for the next five minutes, until he had levelled off at his former altitude. 'So tell me all about Babout,' I said finally.

It seemed there were a few oil wells, owned by Galipolodopolo, and the great man also kept an establishment there which, while not exactly being a palace, came pretty close. All the world knew of his houses in London, New York, Paris, Athens and Rio, but I was willing to bet that very few people also knew he had a pad in Babout.

'What's going to happen when we land?' I asked.

Tom didn't look pale any more as he realized I wasn't going to try to put us down in the middle of the Sahara.

He shrugged. 'I suppose a car will call for you to take you up to the house.'

'And then?'

'That's your problem, lady. We were just told to pick you up at Manboola. We've done it before.'

'Done what before?'

'Picked up birds . . . ladies, and flown them in.'

'Unconscious ladies?'

'We thought you'd had too much to drink,' he said. 'That's what we were told anyway.'

It sounded reasonable. They must have had quite a shock when I turned as grotty as I did. Ladies visiting *chez* Galipolodopolo weren't supposed to play around with knives.

'How far is the airfield from the house?' I asked.

'A couple of miles.'

'What else is at Babout?'

'A small Arab village, the water hole, the airstrip, the oil encampment, and that's it.'

'How does the oil go out?'

'Pipe line.'

'Where to?'

'Bir el Mers.' That was in Spanish Morocco, on the coast.

'And there's nothing else?'

'Like what, lady?'

I didn't know, but somewhere there had to be something I could use. I'd done pretty well up to now; it would be a crying shame if it all went to waste.

'How long before we arrive?' I asked.

'I don't know till I get a fix.'

'So get it,' I said.

He switched on the radio and I prodded him gently with the knife just to remind him that he still had company. He called Babout and received a strength two reply. He received his fix and, after doing a couple of calculations, informed me that we would be in Babout in a shade under ninety minutes.

Having extracted a promise from him that he would behave himself, I went back into the cabin to see whether Andrei had bled to death yet. I was grasping at straws by now, and there was only one way out that I could see. It wasn't a good one, and I didn't honestly expect it to work, but beggars can't be choosers.

Andrei hadn't bled to death, but he looked pretty sick nevertheless. He was sitting on the edge of a seat, clutching his wrist like it would drop off if he let it go for a second. I fixed a tourniquet for him, and he seemed pathetically grateful. 'Thank you, Miss,' he said.

'A couple of dozen stitches and you'll be as right as rain,' I said. He looked at me doubtfully and I tried to give him a smile of encouragement. A silence followed which grew positively companionable.

'You'll be judged as accessories,' I said finally.

He looked at me blankly. 'To what?'

'Murder.'

'Who's been murdered?'

'Me, shortly.'

'I don't know what you're talking about,' he said, meaning it.

'That won't help you in court,' I said. 'And rest assured there will be a trial. A lot of people will be looking for me. They're very efficient, and eventually they'll find me. What's left of me,' I added.

He shook his head slowly from side to side. 'You really are a case. I've flown all sorts of girls all over the world for Mr. Galipolodopolo, but there's never been one like you.'

'That's because all the others wanted to go.'

'Don't you?'

'Does it look like it?'

He had to admit that it didn't. 'So why are you going?'

'Because I was drugged and then handed over to you and your friend Tom.'

'They said you were drunk.'

'Well I wasn't. And in about five hours from now I'm going to die.'

About here he started to take me seriously. He still wasn't convinced by a long chalk, but at least he was listening and taking things in. He asked me a couple of questions and I gave him a couple of answers. They weren't strickly true, but by the time I'd mentioned white slavery a couple of times and repeated the fact that I was going to wind up dead, he had started to look worried.

'Does Tom know all this?' he asked.

'Why not tell him.'

He decided to do just that and asked my permission to go forward, which I graciously granted. After all, at this stage there wasn't much that the two of them could get up to and at least I'd got one of them thinking. Perhaps if he could convince the other that they were batting on a sticky wicket, something could be salvaged yet. Andrei was up front about ten minutes; then they both came back looking very worried.

'Is all this true?' Tom asked me.

'I have certain information Galipolodopolo wants from me. After he has got it, he will have me killed,' I said, laying it as flat on the line as I could.

'Can you prove it?' asked Tom. Obviously he was to be spokesman.

'If I was a normal type dolly bird off for a dirty weekend with one of the richest men in the world, is it likely I would have acted the way I did?'

He agreed that it wasn't likely. 'Anything else?' he asked.

'How great a radio range have you got up front?'

'On the aircraft radio about five hundred miles. But we've got the guvnor's radio on board as well.'

'What's the range?'

'Unlimited, more or less. He uses it to call all over the bloody world when he's flying.' That was a bit of luck.

'London?' I asked.

'On the key,' he said. 'Not on R/T.'

'Good enough,' I said. I gave him a call sign, and told him to make the call and verify my identity. I also gave him my code name, always a source of embarrassment to me.

'I beg your pardon,' said Tom.

'Virgin,' I said. 'You heard right the first time.'

He would like to have smiled, but the circumstances didn't seem to call for it and, anyway, he already knew the call sign, very hush hush, top secret and all that jazz. Like all pilots he was aware of its existence, but he had never used it. It clears the airways quicker than a Mayday signal. He and Andrei had a couple of quiet words, then he disappeared up front to do the necessary. He came back five minutes later and almost bowed to me, he was so impressed. Then he turned to Andrei. 'She's a big wheel,' he said.

They both looked at me as though it was quite beyond all belief, and I only just refrained from gloating as I asked them what they intended to do in the light of their newfound information. And whereas thirty minutes ago, it was me who had no idea, now it was them. They still had to land at Babout, it was the only place, and once they landed things were out of their hands. But then Katy came up with an idea she should have had hours ago.

'Send out a Mayday call,' I said. They looked at me blankly for a moment. 'Say you *hope* to land at Babout, but you don't know if you'll make it.' They thought about it for a couple of minutes.

'It's a good idea,' said Tom finally.

And that's what we did. The Mayday call went out on the wavelength reserved for such emergencies, and within five minutes we were being tracked and reported on by a dozen different radio beacons. Fast aircraft took off from Casablanca and Spanish Morocco, converging on Babout. We may have been in the middle of the Sahara, but everyone jumps at a Mayday call because they never knew when they were going to have to make one themselves. We now had so much publicity that Mike Todd would have envied us.

I suggested to Tom that he drop our altitude a little to burn up fuel; it was important to both he and Andrei that they arrive at Babout with empty tanks, hence the reason for the distress call. Also they would be able to tell Galipolodopolo that the wild woman they had picked up had created havoc in the aircraft, slashing wrists and beating people about the head. After all, they weren't supposed to know that I was anything other than just another girl for their master, and they couldn't be blamed when I turned grotty and forced them to fly low and burn up fuel; neither could they be blamed for sending out a Mayday call. Galipolodopolo would be livid, of course, but he wouldn't be able to touch them without giving away the plot.

Then, to make sure we had a good sized reception committee, we continued to call on the radio that we had an injured man on board in urgent need of medical attention.

'Loosen your tourniquet just after we land,' I told Andrei. 'Spread a bit more blood about the place.'

'I don't think I have any more to spare,' he said, almost enjoying himself by now.

Ten minutes out of Babout, Tom seriously started to wonder whether we would in fact make it after all. He and Andrei did a quick re-calculation of the remaining fuel and arrived at different conclusions. So we all crossed our fingers and sweated it out together. We did make it, just. We ran out of fuel as we were taxiing back to the dispersal point. Then, before everyone piled into the aircraft, I gave them both a big kiss, apologized for treating them badly, and said I hoped we never met again. They both wished me luck and prepared for their acting bits.

It didn't really need much acting on their parts. All they had to do was to tell the truth. A nutty female had run beserk with a knife, tried to take over the aircraft and forced them to fly low so they burned up too much fuel. Finally they managed to overpower her and here she is. For God's sake take her off our hands. All this to a perfectly charming young Arab police officer stationed at Babout. He met us as we landed, actually driving along the runway beside us as we began to taxi in. Big noises were made over the telephone and, while Galipolodopolo's people stood by impotently, I was locked in a tiny cell to await my fate. The cell was a little larger than an oven, and twice as hot. But I didn't have to put up with it for long. The Arab lieutenant brought me a coke and told me I was in serious trouble, so serious that one of the aircraft alerted by the Mayday call had been instructed to put down at Babout and transport me direct to Casablanca.

'Why Casablanca?' I asked, not caring.

'The offence you committed was done over Moroccan airspace,' said the Arab in impeccable French. 'Therefore you will come under the jurisdiction of the Moroccan courts.'

'Courts? What courts? What have I done?' I, too, could act when necessary.

'You are going to Casablanca to stand charges of piracy,' he said. Strong stuff and music to my tired old ears. 'The penalty for piracy in Morocco is death,' he added as an afterthought.

All I had to worry about now was whether Mr. Blaser's contacts in Casablanca carried sufficient weight to do the necessary once I got there. It would be an interesting problem for him to work out. Running a worldwide department as he did, he was forever moving on tiptoe along international boundaries taking enormous care not to overstep the laws of any particular country. In a case like this, it would never have surprised me if he were to wash his hands of me entirely and let me take the consequences. However, he was probably thinking that I had suddenly become a mine of information on the Galipolodopolo case, so he would move hell and high water to get me out. Or so I hoped.

My air taxi arrived half an hour later. Papers were signed and exchanged, and Katy, escorted by a young Arab constable who was ecstatic about a free trip to Casablanca, was driven out to the boarding point. As we took off, I could see Tom talking heatedly to the men who had been sent to meet me. A moment before we turned away, heading north, I saw Andrei, his arm in a neat sling, move over to join the group. A lot of people were going to get fleas in their ears over this, and I didn't care one little bit.

## CHAPTER FIVE

CASABLANCA; a sea port on the coast of Morocco at 33 degrees 27 north, 7 degrees 46 west. The capital city of Morocco and one of the largest on the African continent. So say the gazetteers. They're undoubtedly right, but all that had nothing to do with the Casablanca that I know. I know the beaches just outside the city, the incredibly white villas along the coast, the languor and indolence of weeks spent there before and after assignments. There are a number of places scattered around the globe that I keep a soft spot for, and Casablanca is quite high on the list. A place is attractive solely through the memories of times spent there, and I had spent some incredible times in Casablanca.

All this was resting comfortably at the back of my mind on our flight from Babout. I knew there would be inconveniences; after all, I was under arrest charged with a major crime. But the Touchfeather optimism is renowned and I was warmed by the thought that as soon as the legalities were disposed of, I would probably be able to con Mr. Blaser into allowing me to spend a week or two recuperating. Which only goes to show how time and distance can dull even the most perceptive of minds. Because in the cold light of day I have long been aware that Mr. Blaser wouldn't offer a dying man a glass of water if he were sitting with his feet dangling in a swimming pool.

The flight wasn't too uncomfortable if one discounted the fact that I was handcuffed to my Arab policeman. I had tried to get him to unlock them after we took off. After all, I told him, I could hardly run away. But he was having none of it. He had been lurking in the background when they searched me at Babout, and had seen them extract the fishhooks one by one from my skirt. As far as he was concerned, any girl who would hide that sort of thing away couldn't be trusted to blow her own nose. Added to that, he made an interesting discovery once we were airborne. Being handcuffed to someone brings you in very close physical touch. He was only a lad, but an Arab lad, and they mature early I've been told. I worked it out that, if my escort was anything to go by, they must mature in the womb. He became hornier than a pond full of toads, pressing up to me, rearranging his legs in seventeen different positions, all of them embarrassing. I may be fluent in half a dozen languages, but

Arabic doesn't happen to be one of them. I tried glowering at him, snarling, frowning, scowling; and still he came on strong. I could hardly break his arm or otherwise maim him. I was in enough trouble with the law already. So I put up with it, struggling as far away from him as our united wrists would allow.

We landed at a military airport at Casablanca, the authorities obviously convinced I was far too dangerous to be allowed anywhere near the general public. From there we transferred into a police car and, escorted by three motor cycle outriders, we drove into town to police headquarters. There I was finally cut asunder from my Arab admirer, who disappeared to enjoy the fleshpots of the city before he returned to Babout. I was turned over to an Akim Tamiroff type character, who introduced himself as Inspector Ahmed Ben Mullah.

'Miss Toochfeather,' he said, pronouncing it exactly like that. 'You will explain your actions, please.'

Without guidance from Mr. Blaser, I had no idea how far I was supposed to go in my explanations, so I compromised by asking to see the British Consul. It appeared he was playing golf, so the Embassy sent me a minor Under-Secretary instead. His name was Bernard Philpot and he was remarkable only to the extent of his B.O. He must have been to police headquarters before, because the Arabs, who aren't usually too particular in that area, recoiled visibly the moment he walked into the room. I got the message two seconds later as he came close to me to shake my hand. It had to be glandular I decided, because he looked perfectly clean, in fact well scrubbed. It was a crime sending a man like him to a hot country; in a place like Iceland he could probably have carved quite a career for himself. Here, he didn't stand a chance. Inspector Ahmed Ben Mullah was delighted to leave us, rushing out of the room at the first opportunity.

'Sorry about this,' said Philpot, as soon as we were alone.

'About what?'

'The pong,' said Philpot. 'It's glandular. Can't do a thing about it.'

I warmed to him immediately. 'It doesn't bother me a bit,' I said, lying like a cheap carpet.

'Stay upwind of me and, believe it or not, you'll get used to it. And now down to business. What have you been up to?'

'Haven't you heard anything from London?' I asked.

'Not about you. Should I have done?' I'd obviously drawn the wrong Under-Secretary.

'Would you be an angel and call them for me?' I asked.

I gave him the diplomatic callsign and he turned me back to Ahmed Ben Mullah and toddled back to the Embassy to alert the radio room.

Ben Mullah opened all the windows in his office before coming over to sit down opposite me.

'Filthy pig,' he said.

'It's glandular,' I offered. Either he didn't know the meaning of the word or he was just plain stubborn.

'Filthy pig,' he said, and left it at that.

However, the 'filthy pig' had spoken up on my behalf, waving his Union Jack all over the place, and nothing was to be done with me until he contacted the police again. I was shown to a cosy little cell deep in the bowels of the building, which smelled even worse than poor Philpot. When I asked for some nourishment, not having eaten for more than twenty-four hours, I was reluctantly handed a bowl of inedible slop, which I ate anyway.

Two hours after leaving me, Philpot was back. I was escorted back to the Inspector's office to enjoy another blast of *eau de Philpot*.

'Would you believe that I've taken two showers since I last saw you?' he said companionably as I came in. At least he had learned to live with his affliction.

'Did you make the call?' I asked.

'The call was made. Strings are now in the process of being pulled.'

'When do I get out?'

He shrugged. 'It's out of my hands. Whatever happens now is up to the big wheels. I'm only a little one.'

'Can you use your influence to get me some decent food sent in?'

He nodded. 'If anyone will let me get close enough to talk to them, I'll organize it,' he said. He bowed to me, and saying that it was unlikely we would meet again, he wafted out, clearing a wide path in front of him. Ahmed Ben Mullah returned and we went through the window opening bit once more, and then I was escorted back to my cell. An hour later a reasonable meal was brought to me, along with a bottle of dubious wine. I ate the meal, drank the whole bottle and, feeling like I hadn't slept for ninety-six hours straight, I hit the sack.

They had to choose that particular night to raid one of the brothels. I was rudely awakened at three a.m. by my cell door being slammed open. Suddenly I seemed to be fighting for my life. In fact, nobody was attacking me; it was just that six people were now occupying a cell designed to hold one. They were all highly painted, three-quarters nude, very loud and, as it turned out, a load of laughs. After we had introduced ourselves and they had ascertained that I wasn't one of them, they insisted that I retain the bunk, while they all squatted around the floor, cursing the police in general and Ahmed in particular. It seemed that he was a man of vast and extraordinary sexual appetites; he had slept with all of them at one time or another and not necessarily one at a time. Needless to say, they had let him have it on the house, charging him nothing, him being a police inspector and all, and now he had the barefaced effrontery to throw them all in the pokey. The conversation drifted from there to tales of an autobiographical nature, all wildly erotic, and most of them highly entertaining. Nobody asked me who I was, or what I was in for, and altogether it was quite a pleasant hen party.

At seven a.m. the door crashed open once more and standing there, in a brightly shining newly pressed uniform, was Inspector Ahmed Ben Mullah. He scowled at the whores who all scowled back at him. Then he located me. He beamed and bowed low.

'Miss Toochfeather, can you ever forgive me?'

Obviously the strings had been well and truly pulled, and now Ahmed was dancing at the end of them. He escorted me out of the cell, bowing and scraping and apologizing, surreptitiously trying to kick some of my new found companions en route.

'Bye girls,' I called out just before the cell door was closed, and they chorused their reply.

'Trash,' said Ahmed. 'Gutter scrapings.'

'I thought they were rather pleasant,' I said. 'And they're very cross with you, Inspector.'

'Cross with me? Why should they be cross with me? I only do my duty. And who cares if they are cross with me anyway. They are trash.'

'The one named Maris said the next time you ask her to . . .' I went on to describe one of the wild things I had heard in the cell. It is difficult for an Arab to blush, but Ahmed Ben Mullah managed it admirably. I've never seen anyone so delighted to get rid of me. He turned me over to my new escort and practically bolted. My new companion was a young Frenchman, very handsome and very sure of himself. He greeted me as though we had been on intimate terms for years. This wasn't particularly remarkable because we had, on and off. Pierre Boulard was Mr. Blaser's man in Casablanca, and he was one of the reasons why Casablanca held fond memories for me.

'Katy my darling,' he said as soon as he saw me. 'You look . . .' He groped for the right word and finished up by shaking his head. '*Merde*,' he said.

I must admit that up to that moment I hadn't given much thought to my appearance. Now I did, recalling that I hadn't washed for as long as I could remember and hadn't been out of the clothes I stood in since I had been bundled into them at the hospital at Manboola two, or was it three, days ago. And I had complained about Philpot. Bless him, he probably smelled like a rose garden up against me. Doing his best to conceal his obvious distaste, Pierre, who had always been a shade too fastidious for my liking, escorted me into a waiting car.

'I'll be all right as soon as I've had a bath,' I said, settling back.

'There's no time, *chérie*. The aircraft is waiting.'

'What aircraft? Where am I going?'

He gave a Gallic shrug. 'My instructions were to get you out of jail and take you to the aircraft. I don't know any more than that.'

'Was it difficult getting me out?'

He shook his head. 'The difficult thing was getting you in. It was the only way we could guarantee your safety at Babout. Under official arrest even Galipolodopolo wouldn't try to spirit you away.'

I thought for a moment about my arrest, my amorously inclined police escort and my night in a dirty cell with half a dozen whores. I opened my mouth to complain, and then I recalled what the alternative could have been and shut it again. Just before we reached the airfield, Pierre overcame his distaste sufficiently to take my hand and turn on the soulful Frenchman bit.

'Dear Katy, is it possible that you will be returning soon to Casablanca? The city is a desert without you.' Considering I hadn't been here for close on eight months, he must have been going through a pretty dry time. I tried to get close to him metaphorically; I didn't want to get too close physically in case he recoiled in horror.

'I'll be back as soon as I can, Pierre. I promise you that.' After all, a girl never knows when she'll be in need of a friend; and he was a sensational lay.

At the military airfield I had landed at the previous day, I was delivered into the care of an RAF Squadron Leader who looked seventeen years old and behaved like a courteous old man of seventy. I don't know what he had been told about me, but he treated me like he would have the Queen Mother. He actually bowed slightly as Pierre introduced us.

'Have I got time for a bath?' I asked as soon as Pierre left us.

He was desolate. 'My orders ma'am. They are specific. We are to leave the moment that you arrive at the airfield.' He nearly burst into tears he was so upset at not being able to grant such a simple little request. I didn't want to upset him more than necessary.

'OK,' I said. 'Lead on.'

We drove out to where an RAF Transport Command Comet was waiting, a whole Comet, just for Mrs. Touchfeather's little girl. At least there would be wash and brush up facilities aboard, I thought. Wrong again. The aircraft had been stripped out as a troop carrier, and troops weren't supposed to wash it seemed. So I sat in lonely, dirty, isolation for the hour that it took us to fly to Gibraltar. I had nursed a secret hope that London was to be our destination. Visions of my cosy little pad were floating before my eyes. About the last place I would have chosen to go to right then was Gibraltar. Aldershot by the sea, I called it. However, that's where we were.

My Squadron Leader bowed me off the aeroplane and into an official car driven by a Corporal in the WRACS, who took one look at my condition and came over all smug and superior.

'I suppose I couldn't stop off somewhere for a bath?' I asked, as we swept out of the airfield gates. She looked even more smug in her trim little uniform and deodorized underwear.

'Orders are to drive you straight to headquarters,' she said Then, in case she had misjudged my rank or importance, she took out a little insurance. 'I'm sorry Miss,' she added reluctantly, not sorry at all.

Headquarters was a nondescript looking building flying the Union Jack. In these troubled times with all the Spanish arguments going on, everybody flew the Union Jack in Gibraltar; it was as though they were beating everyone over the head with how British they really were. Why anyone could actually *want* to be ruled by the current British Government is beyond me entirely, but then I don't live in Gibraltar, so it's none of my business. My WRAC Corporal handed me over to a sergeant in the Royal Marines who escorted me down miles of grey corridor, finally stopping outside an unmarked door. Just before he knocked I tried it for the last time.

'Is there anywhere I can get a wash and brush up?' I asked, almost desperate now. His stubby little moustache bristled as he looked down at me.

'Orders Miss,' he said. 'You are to . . .'

I didn't even let him finish; the whole thing was obviously a conspiracy to keep me dirty. 'Never mind,' I said.

He knocked on the door and was bidden enter. He opened the door and stood back for me to go in. I went in.

'How dare you come into my office looking like that! For heaven's sake go away and get yourself cleaned up,' said Mr. Blaser.

I'd never before seen Mr. Blaser outside his office in Pandam Street, London W.C.2. At one time I had even worked out a theory that he never left the place, living out his entire existence in a small bedroom in the back somewhere. I suppose he must have had a smart little two up and two down somewhere in the suburbs, but I could never picture it; he was part of the furniture and fittings of Pandam Street as far as I was concerned. I couldn't have been more surprised at seeing him here in Gibraltar. It would have been easier for me to accept the presence of the Archangel Gabriel or, to be more precise in my similes, Mephistopheles. But there he was, as large as life and as objectionable as ever.

After being thrown out of his office, I looked around for someone who could tell me where I could clean up and get a change of clothes. The only person I could find was the Marine Sergeant. And I was in luck. It seemed that he had a daughter of my age and build, and he took pity on me. He phoned his wife and five minutes later she arrived at headquarters in a beat-up old car. She collected me and drove me to their home in the naval married quarters. Grace was her name, a homely body of fifty-five or thereabouts, worn down by the uncertainty of being a service wife all her married life.

'Look after her, Grace,' her husband told her. 'And get her back here as soon as possible.'

The bath was heaven and I lay soaking in it until Grace banged on the door for the third time. Then I hauled myself out reluctantly and Grace showed me to her daughter's room. The girl's make-up wasn't exactly what I would have chosen for myself, but it was adequate; about as adequate as the slacks and sweater I chose from the wardrobe. Mr. Blaser hated women in slacks; so up yours, Mr. Blaser, I thought. And an hour later I was shown back into the office that he had requisitioned.

Apart from being his normal grotty self, he was livid at having to come to Gibraltar. This was the week of the Royal Regatta at Henley, a positive must for Mr. Blaser, and he had issued instructions that I was to be flown through to London. But the RAF had dug their heels in, and said they would only transport Katy as far as Gib. Added to that, Mr. Blaser had needed to get into heavy discussions with the Moroccan authorities to arrange my entry and exit. Reasonably enough, they hadn't even heard of Henley and they weren't prepared to travel all the way to London to do Mr. Blaser a favour.

'Sit down, Miss Touchfeather,' he said.

I sat, trying to look respectful and mutinous at the same time; I felt in my water that he was about to come up with something pretty drastic for Katy, and Katy was rapidly getting tired of the whole bit. Whatever he was going to ask me to do, I was going to go down fighting.

'You made a bit of a mess of your assignment, didn't you,' he said.

'Which one, sir?'

'Both of them. Or, if we go back to the beginning, all three. First you let Galipolodopolo get on to you on his yacht. Second, you blow your cover in Borami . . .' I started to say something, but he lifted his hand imperiously. 'I haven't finished. Then when I send through instructions that you are to play the new situation with the utmost discretion, you get yourself kidnapped . . . for the second time. You alert half of North Africa with a Mayday signal; you force me to go cap in hand to the Moroccan authorities to arrange for your arrest in Babout and your release in Casablanca; you tie up a Comet that I had to borrow from the Royal Air Force; and, to cap it all, Miss Touchfeather, you come into my office looking as if you had slept in your clothes for two nights running.'

'I had, sir.'

'That's beside the point,' he snapped. 'I'm seriously displeased with you, Miss Touchfeather. Seriously displeased.'

So do me a favour and sack me you silly old twit, I thought.

'I'm sorry, sir,' I said.

'Still,' he went on. 'Perhaps all is not lost.' He took his unlit pipe from his mouth and started to gouge away at the bowl with a letter opener. Here we go, I thought, he's about to tell me to go and cut someone's throat or, worse still, my own. I braced myself in the chair waiting for the bomb to drop. When he finally spoke it was without looking up at me.

'As from this moment you can consider that you are off the Borami assignment,' he said. I tried to remember what the hell it had been, it seemed so long ago. 'I am re-assigning you to the Galipolodopolo case.'

It seemed to me that if anyone had done the re-assigning, it had been Constantin himself, but I didn't say so.

'Only we will now approach it from an entirely different angle.' He paused a moment, giving his pipe an extra savage stab and breaking the letter opener in the process. He looked at the ruined letter opener and then at his pipe. Satisfied that the latter was undamaged, he stuck it in his mouth and sucked it experimentally a couple of times; revolting in the extreme, I found it.

'Let us examine your involvement from the point of view of Galipolodopolo's side. They know you are on to them; they know you are working for someone. It is imperative for them to find out who it is and how much we know. To that end, you have been abducted twice. Given the opportunity, they will try it a third time.' Fat chance I thought; from here on you wouldn't even find me entering a Greek restaurant. 'On our side, it is necessary for us to put a stop to Galipolodopolo's activities as soon as possible.'

'What are they?' I blurted out before I could stop myself.

He looked at me a little strangely for a moment, as though he believed I must have suffered a severe blow on the head. Then he decided to pretend that he hadn't heard me.

'To this end I have decided on a course of action which could loosely be described as a last resort.'

I decided that I just couldn't let it go. 'Please sir, what exactly are Mr. Galipolodopolo's activities that you are going to put a stop to?'

'I thought you knew, Miss Touchfeather. I certainly told you at considerable length, if memory serves me.'

'No sir, you didn't. You told me he was digging up gold and not telling anyone about it.'

'That's part of it, certainly. But only the visible portion of the iceberg.' When Mr. Blaser became metaphorical he sometimes became difficult to follow, so I started to concentrate.

'It is what he is doing with the gold that we wish to put a stop to. As you know, in the vast majority of countries, the barter of gold is illegal. In fact, it is forbidden for any of the citizens to own gold. There are exceptions, of course, but we are not concerned with those. Are you following me so far Miss Touchfeather?' Now he was getting sarcastic as well as metaphorical. It wasn't going to be easy, so I concentrated even harder.

'This state of affairs is designed to maintain an evenly balanced economy. It prevents the outflow of money from the country in question. Let us take a hypothetical case.' Let's do that, I silently agreed.

'A Mr. X in India is very wealthy, but he is unable to take his rupees out of India. And he wants very much to take them out because there isn't all that much he can spend them on in his home country. He wants to travel; he wants a house in the South of France and a castle in Spain; he has the money to buy these things ten times over, but he is prevented by law from doing so. Even if he can smuggle his rupees out of India, he can't sell them, because nobody wants rupees. So he buys gold, paying in rupees four times what the gold is worth on the official market. Now he owns gold, which is freely saleable in most countries of the world.'

I put in my two cents' worth. 'But if Galipolodopolo sells the gold, it means that he now owns a lot of Indian rupees. What does *he* do with them?'

'He uses the rupees to buy things in India. Things like ships, guns, aeroplanes. He buys them in India and he uses Indian money to pay for them.'

'It all sounds very reasonable to me.'

'That's because you haven't even begun to grasp what I am getting at, Miss Touchfeather,' he said testily. 'Let us assume he buys a ship for fifty million rupees. After six months he transfers the registration of the ship to one of his merchant navy flags, and that's the last the Indians ever see of it.'

'But he's paid fifty million rupees to the shipbuilder; the money has stayed in India.'

'No. The shipbuilder is Mr. X, and the money has left India in illegally purchased gold. Added to that, of course, Galipolodopolo has paid for the ship with money that he purchased at twenty-five per cent of its face value.'

It all sounded like admirable business to me. No wonder Constantin was so bloody rich. I ventured to say so.

'Pressure is being brought to bear, Miss Touchfeather. If we continue to use our hypothetical case, the Indian Government become very annoyed indeed and questions heavily loaded with political overtones start to be asked. We need all the friends we can get these days, and we are losing them rapidly because of the activities of Mr. Galipolodopolo.'

'Why us? He's not English.'

'He operates through two main companies. One English, the other American. Unlike some of his fellow shipowners, he does not operate under a flag of convenience. His fleet, some one hundred and fifty vessels, is divided equally; half of them fly the Red Ensign, the other half the Stars and Stripes. He pays all his taxes, he's on very good terms with the merchant seamen's unions in both countries and, all in all, he provides the United States and our Treasury with considerable amounts of foreign currency.'

It sounded to me as though we should be giving him a medal or the Queen's Award for Industry. But I didn't bring it up, and Mr. Blaser continued.

'The Americans, too, are feeling the pressure from affected countries, notably those on the South American continent. But while they are embarrassed and even annoyed, they are not prepared to do anything about it at the moment.'

'There's not much they can do,' I said boldly. 'Any more than we can. I can see that what Galipolodopolo is doing is illegal, but it's hardly earth shattering enough to have him locked up.'

'Well put, Miss Touchfeather,' said Mr. Blaser, leaving me wondering what the hell I had said. 'You're quite right, of course; our case it hardly one we can bring into International Court. Even if we did have all the evidence, it would still be too tenuous to hold up. Therefore he must be stopped in a different way.'

'What way?'

'One, we must find his gold mines.'

'I've found one of them . . . I think.'

'Manboola?' I nodded. 'I assumed as much. Then, having found them, we must close them down.'

'How do we do that?'

'We simply get the countries where they are located to nationalize them.' That seemed straightforward enough. 'Two, we must prove to him that he is going to lose considerable amounts of money on the operation. To do that, we must make sure that the gold he is already holding is confiscated.'

'Confiscated?'

'All right,' he said testily. 'Stolen. And if all else fails, three, we must remove Mr. Galipolodopolo himself.'

That was like saying we must remove Mount Everest, but there didn't seem much point in my mentioning it, as Mr. Blaser knew as well as anyone what he was talking about. I thought about here that it was time for me to get down to the crunch.

'How am I to figure in all this, sir?' I asked. 'I have no cover as far as Galipolodopolo is concerned.'

'Exactly,' said Mr. Blaser, sitting back as though he had produced a rabbit out of a hat. I waited for an explanation, not at all sure that I was going to get one. But he gave me one, and listening to it curled my hair.

From Gibraltar to Tangier is a couple of hours by boat. One leaves Gibraltar, which is painfully English, and two hours later one lands in Tangier, which is overwhelmingly Arab. Following orders to the letter, I caught the eight a.m. boat and landed in Tangier at ten a.m.

All this was two days after my meeting with Mr. Blaser, who had climbed on an aeroplane the moment he had briefed me and returned post haste to the wet warm comfort of his Whitehall office and the last two days at Henley.

I disembarked from the ferry-boat and fought my way to a taxi waiting at the dockside. I gave the driver the address of the hotel that had been booked for me. It wasn't one I would have chosen for myself, but I wasn't in any condition to worry about it. To say that I was numb would have been an understatement; I was a walking paralysis case. And having checked in, still following instructions, I prepared to wait. Not that I would have to wait long; that much I was sure of. Because, although Tangier is quite a large harbour, there's not much room to hide a boat like the *Maria*; and it was the *Maria* that had hypnotized me for the last twenty minutes of our trip across the Straits of Gibraltar. There she lay, unbelievably elegant and outrageously opulent. But to me she no longer resembled a rich man's plaything; to me she looked like a stinking prison hulk.

\* \* \*

Assisted no doubt by the connivance of Mr. Blaser, the Galipolo-dopolo organization knew of my arrival in Tangier before I had even landed. I suppose long distance telephone calls resulted and instructions were issued. The two hours they gave me after checking into my hotel was longer than I could have reasonably expected, and by the time they arrived I was nearly ready for them.

Behaving as I had been instructed, I had unpacked my newly purchased wardrobe as soon as I checked in and spread myself around the suite as though I had every expectation of remaining there for a couple of weeks at least. And, like I said, they gave me two hours. I had just got out of the bath when there was a polite tap on the sitting room door. I wrapped myself in a large bath towel, and went to answer it.

'Who is it?' I called.

'Room service,' came the reply. I hadn't asked for any room service. But I opened the door nevertheless and then indulged in the full, indignant, angry, frightened bit, as two men sidled into the room behind two large guns. They were gentlemen of few words and all of these to the point.

'Get dressed,' said one; and while I got dressed and he watched me like a hawk, the other one threw all my stuff back into the suitcase. The one who was watching me didn't bat an eyelid while I was getting dressed, having already declined my request that I be allowed to do so in privacy. He just stood there while I fumbled with my pants and bra beneath the bath towel, making like Grandma trying to dress on the beach at Blackpool. In the end I said to hell with it and I dropped the bath towel and got dressed the normal way. After all, my modesty was the least of my worries from this point on. And he still didn't bat an eyelid; although his companion looked up from his packing long enough to go slightly glassy-eyed. They were a couple of real heavies these two; dark skinned, immaculately dressed, cold blue eyes and as alike as two maggots in an apple. They were tidy and professional in their operation. They knew exactly what they were doing and the most efficient way to go about it. They wasted no time or effort, and five minutes after they came into the suite we were all ready to leave.

One of them carried my suitcase, the other held my arm just above the elbow in a grip that looked like cotton wool but felt like a steel trap. We travelled down in the elevator and stepped out into the lobby. While I was escorted straight out to a waiting car, the one carrying my suitcase went over to the reception desk and checked me out. Ten minutes later we were pulling up at the dockside where the *Maria* was berthed. They may have been kidnapping me, but they weren't about to be sneaky about it. I was escorted up the gangway like a very important guest and they even had the Captain waiting at the top for me. He saluted me gravely.

'Welcome aboard, Miss Touchfeather,' he said. 'It's nice to see you again.'

Before I could reply he was already shouting out orders like 'single up aft' and 'belay the mainbrace' or somesuch. In fact we put to sea so quickly that my two man escort barely had time to scamper ashore before the gangplank was hauled up from under them.

A steward had taken my bag and now he escorted me below. I had given up the protesting bit by now, there didn't really seem much point any longer. After all, not a soul believed me, so I decided not to waste my time or my breath. Believe it or not, they put me in the same stateroom that I had occupied before, the one with the connecting door to the owner's suite. Perhaps I'd got the whole thing wrong; perhaps Constantin was only after my lily-white body. Then I remembered Lucia and her happy hypodermic and I decided that Katy was just pipe dreaming. And as though to confirm this, I tried the stateroom doors only to find they were both locked on the outside. So here we were, Katy. Everything going according to Mr. Blaser's plan.

'You will allow yourself to be abducted by Galipolodopolo,' he had said. 'Then when he or his employees demand information from you you will give it to them.'

'You bet your life I will,' I said. Then I added 'Sir' in case I sounded too flippant. I mean, honestly, I had escaped the clutches of the arch villain twice, at considerable peril to life and limb, and now I was being told to forget it and start again at page one. It was too much, and I felt like bursting into tears.

'We will of course tell you exactly what you can and cannot say,' Mr. Blaser had said.

'That won't be much good if they give me a truth drug.'

'It is unlikely,' said Mr. Blaser. 'The last time they were acting in haste. This time they will have all the time in the world. Added to that there is the fact that information divulged under the influence of a drug is not as succinct and accurate as that given under threat or torture. The subject is not in control of his or her faculties and the information is liable to be bogged down among the rubbish that lies around in the subconscious. It takes someone used to such things to sift out the accurate from the supposed. No, I think they will threaten you with something painful and unpleasant.' He was a great comfort was Mr. Blaser. 'However,' he said. 'If they do threaten to use a drug on you, you must feign terror, fear, revulsion, call it what you will, and then divulge your information before they can administer the drug. On no account are you to allow them to weaken your mental defences by allowing them to inject you with any drugs. Understood?'

I was too flabbergasted to do anything but nod my head.

'Good,' he said. 'Now the *Maria* is due in Tangier tomorrow evening, so we have all night and all day tomorrow to go over what you are to tell them. You will leave for Tangier yourself by the first boat on Thursday morning.

The briefing session had been long and involved. I was tired when it started. I was practicaly unconscious by the time Mr. Blaser was satisfied that I was reliable enough to be turned loose. And all this accounted for the fact that now, with the engines of the *Maria* throbbing gently under my feet, I decided that the best thing I could do would be to catch up on some sleep. I had no idea when the fun was due to start, but I wanted to be in full possession of my faculties while I still had faculties to be in possession of. We Touchfeathers have always had the ability of being able to drop off to sleep at the damnedest of times; one Jeremiah Touchfeather was reported to have snatched forty winks on the tumbril taking him from Newgate jail to the gallows at Tyburn. And feeling that my situation was not unlike that of Jeremiah, I took off my shoes, lay down on the bed and zonked out.

I must have slept for a couple of hours at least. When I awoke the first thing I did was to look out of the window. There was no sign of land and the sea had changed colour from Mediterranean blue to Atlantic green. That meant we had turned left after leaving the harbour, heading out to God knows where. I unpacked my suitcase, hanging up the stuff I had bought in Gibraltar, the inevitable loss of which wasn't going to bother me one little bit. I intended putting in an expense chit for twice what they had cost me as soon as I got back to London; *if* I got back to London. After that I took a bath. By the time I emerged I was feeling hungry. I was still debating whether or not to ring for the steward when he arrived, bringing me one of the finest meals I have had for a long time. Hoping that it wasn't the traditional 'condemned man's breakfast', I tucked in vigorously. Another Touchfeather family accomplishment is that when all around is doom and despair, we can still eat like there was no tomorrow; and, in this case, there quite possibly wouldn't be.

After my meal there was nothing left to do but wait. I assumed that Constantin wasn't aboard, or surely he would have been to see me before now. But on the other hand, perhaps he wished to remain aloof from personal involvement. He had all sorts of minions drifting about, and it was unlikely that he would actually tighten the thumbscrews himself. He wasn't built that way. He was the sort of man who could give the orders quite cold bloodedly as long as there was no chance that any of the blood would splash over his five hundred dollar suit. For carrying out the orders, he had people like Lucia, and it was she who turned up in my cabin twenty minutes later. She wasn't dressed as an inquisitor at all; she was wearing a Pucci style number and looked gorgeous. She had obviously worked out that there was very little I could get up to on the high seas, because she arrived alone and unarmed. She let herself in quietly and stood looking at me for a long moment. 'Hello, Katherine,' she said finally.

'Hello, Lucia.' There didn't seem much point in doing the ignorant bit with these people any longer; they had me well documented and it wasn't going to fool anyone.

'May I sit down?' she asked politely.

It was interesting to speculate what she would have done if I had said 'No,' but, like the perfect hostess, I nodded towards a chair and she sat, arranging herself immaculately before she got down to business.

'You are a girl of infinite resource,' she said.

'Thank you.' There was no point in being ungracious.

'And, knowing this, we wonder why you have allowed yourself to fall into our hands for the third time.'

'I didn't arrange anything,' I said. 'Your thugs picked me up in Tangier.'

'But what were you doing in Tangier?'

'Working. At least I was going to.'

'Which brings us back to the original question. For whom do you work?'

It would have been so easy right there to trot out my carefully rehearsed story. That way, all the subsequent unpleasantness would be avoided; but, equally, they wouldn't have believed a word of it. Girls of infinite resource only open their mouths under duress.

I smiled sweetly at her. 'I can't tell you that.'

'What were you doing in Borami?'

'I can't tell you that either.'

'Why were you in Gibraltar?' I shook my head, still smiling. She looked at me speculatively for a moment. 'This wouldn't be a suicide mission would it, Katherine?' she asked, getting far too close for comfort. 'You haven't got a neatly prepared story to tell us?'

'I haven't got anything to tell you,' I said. 'Except that I shall be missed and people will start looking for me. In fact, they're probably already doing so.'

She dismissed this as of no importance whatsoever. 'Rest assured they won't find you unless we want them to. Now, you have one more chance. The next time I ask you, you will be made to answer. Who do you work for?'

I just shook my head, wishing like hell I could tell her; because I don't like pain. Especially I don't like it when it is inflicted on me. And Lucia had developed a glint in her eyes which rather pointed to the fact that I was about to suffer considerable unpleasantness in the very near future. She stood up and left the stateroom without a word. More from habit than anything else, I tried the door after she had closed it behind her; it was locked, of course. So I took a couple of deep breaths in an effort to slow the beating of my heart, and then I finished the bottle of very good wine that they had sent me with my meal. Then I lay myself on the bed and prepared myself. One problem that had reared its ugly little head was just how much I should put up with before I trotted out my story. If I threw a fit of hysterics too soon after they started on me and babbled all, there was a chance they wouldn't believe me. In this case it wasn't beyond the bounds of credibility that they would keep on trying, to see whether I came up with anything else. And if they tried hard enough, I sure as hell would. I would tell them the lot, even the colour of Mr. Blaser's waistcoat. On the other hand, I didn't want to last out too long because, as I have mentioned before, I don't like being hurt. So the whole thing evolved into a matter of rather fine judgment—not too soon, not too late; rather like working out how many fingernails one was prepared to let them extract before one called a halt. Two would be insufficient; four would be insupportable.

But, as it turned out, my fingernails were to remain inviolate. It seemed that whatever was to happen, they didn't want to leave any external marks. No doubt the plan was to deposit my remains somewhere, so that death could reasonably be attributed to natural causes. I worked all this out as Lucia got to work on me. And, as it turned out, I didn't have to worry about how much pain I could stand, because I didn't stand any at all; discomfort, yes; pain, no.

She returned twenty minutes after she had left me with three crew members. They must have been lately recruited, because I didn't recall any of them from my previous trips on board the *Maria*. Obviously Constantin kept one crew for pleasure, another for business; and this was definitely the business crew. They were all three vaguely Middle Eastern, large, silent and very capable.

Two minutes after coming into the cabin, they had me as helpless as a babe and stark naked to boot. I was spreadeagled on the bed, face down, my wrists and ankles secured with leather belts to the four corners of the bed. I must have looked like a stranded starfish. I twisted my head to try to see what Lucia was doing. I couldn't see her at first, but then she walked into my line of vision. She was still wearing her Pucci number, but she had pulled on a white laboratory overall over the top and she was carrying an enamel tray; the sort that one finds in hospitals, complete to the white towel draped over what it was holding, lest the contents disturb the patient. She put this down on the bedside table and then pulled a chair up so that she was sitting close to me.

'I don't want to do this to you, Katherine,' she said. 'But you leave me no alternative.' I tried to see what was in the tray but the towel covered everything completely.

'Do what?' I asked, not keen to know.

'You'll see,' she said. 'But first, one more chance.'

She ran the flat of her hand down across my back and over my backside. It was gentle, almost a caress. Hello, I thought, perhaps I've read her hormones wrong; but that was the least of my problems at the moment. She allowed her hand to linger where it had no business to for a moment, and then, almost as though she had read my mind, she withdrew it abruptly.

'Just one more chance, Katherine,' she said, as though she were reluctant to do what came next.

Enough of this procrastination, Katy, I thought. If it's got to happen, let's get it over with. 'Go fuck yourself,' I said.

She looked at me steadily for a moment, then she sighed. 'Very well,' she said. Then she stood up. 'I'm going to give you an enema,' she said.

I nearly burst out laughing, it was so preposterous. 'You're going to do what?'

'You heard me.'

She pulled the towel off the tray and, by God, there it was, an ordinary common or garden enema, something I hadn't even seen since I was fourteen years old and had my appendix out. Beside it was an enamel bowl, and beside that a small medical bottle unlabelled.

'This is water,' she said, pointing to the bowl.

But I wasn't interested in the water, I wanted to know what was in the bottle.

'This is sulphuric acid,' she said.

And naturally, as soon as she told me that, I started singing like the proverbial canary. While I could possibly have withstood the bamboo splinters or hot pliers for a short time, what Lucia was proposing was quite out of the question. In spite of the fact that she intended to use a diluted solution to start off with, I didn't want to know.

She had been very specific, 'I will dilute the sulphuric acid in the ratio of ten to one to start with,' she said, impassively. 'Subsequently, if you survive and don't go out of your mind, I shall decrease the dilution. But I don't think that will be necessary.'

I maintained my cool long enough to watch her mix the potion, and even long enough for her to charge the enema. But once she started to reach for the vaseline, I turned the whole thing in. Visions of that stuff sloshing around inside me, burning holes through the walls of my intestines, swam before me. Enough is enough, and sod Mr. Blaser and everyone connected with him.

'World Bank,' I said.

She paused in the business of charging the enema. 'What did you say?'

'I work for the World Bank.'

Almost reluctantly she put down her equipment of persuasion. She went to the door of the stateroom and opened it. There must have been someone waiting outside because she returned to my line of vision almost immediately carrying a small portable tape recorder. We both waited while she set it down and switched it on. Then she turned to me once more. 'All right, Katherine, start at the beginning. Who do you work for?'

'Can't you untie me?'

She shook her head. 'Not yet. First you talk. Who do you work for?'

'The World Bank.'

'Doing what specifically?'

'Investigation.'

'What have you discovered about Constantin Galipolodopolo, and why is the World Bank interested?'

'He's mining gold unofficially. He's selling gold illegally.'

'How did the World Bank find out?'

'I haven't the faintest idea,' I said.

She paused for a moment wondering whether it was worth the effort to get me to try to enlarge on this statement. She decided that it wasn't.

'And what is the intention of your employers now that they have this information?'

'I just investigate,' I said. 'Then I turn in a report. What happens after that is none of my business.'

'You must have some ideas.'

'Some,' I said. 'But they're only ideas.'

'Let me hear them.'

'They'll close down the mines. Or at least wrest them from Galipolodopolo's control.'

'They don't know where they are.'

'Yes, they do. At least that's what they told me.'

'Is that why you were sent to Borami?' I nodded, no easy feat if you're strapped down face first.

'And is that all they intend to do? Close down the mines?'

'No,' I said. 'They also intend to confiscate all the gold that Galipolodopolo holds at present.'

There was a long pause as she digested all of this. Then she started again.

'That deals with the generalities,' she said. 'Now let's get down to specifics.'

This is where the hard work started; now I had to start remembering details of the briefing I had been given; names, places, more names, dates, memos, code words, and all the paraphernalia that had been so carefully prepared for me under the auspices of Mr. Blaser. Everything would check out, Mr. Blaser had assured me. He knew that nothing I said would be taken on trust and he had prepared everything accordingly. There wasn't one word that I delivered to Lucia that couldn't be proved as fact once Constantin's organization swung into operation. She untied me after the first half hour and from then on I was allowed to sit in a chair, wrapped in a dressing-gown, while a large seaman with a gun watched me like a hawk and the tape recorder continued to record.

About nine o'clock, Lucia seemed satisfied with all she had learned and decided to call it a day. Before she left me she had one final word.

'I hope that all you have told me so far is accurate,' she said. I assured her that it was.

'We will continue at a later date.' And with that she left me to my own devices. The seaman cum guard also left and Katy was alone once more. Dinner was brought down half an hour later, but with visions of a burned out digestive system, my appetite seemed to have evaporated, and I was only able to do justice to the wine that accompanied the meal. An hour later I was tucked up in bed and asleep.

The following day I was left strictly alone. I was allowed on deck for a couple of hours, but it was cold and there was a heavy swell running, so it wasn't much fun. It was amazing the difference between the *Maria* I had known before, and this particular vessel. Apart from the fact that the deck furniture and the sun awnings had been stowed away, it was exactly the same ship, but now, instead of indolence she carried an air of efficient menace; efficient because here in the Atlantic she was able to show herself off as a proper ship and not just a floating gin palace; and, as for the menace, well you know all about that. Nobody spoke to me all day, and I didn't see Lucia. While I was on deck, the same large seaman remained within grabbing distance at all times. It was difficult to imagine what they thought I would be capable of, a couple of hundred miles out in mid-Atlantic, but obviously they thought that a girl of infinite resource needed close watching.

While trotting around the deck, I relearned the geography of the ship as best I could; quickest way up to the bridge; quickest way down to the engine room; quickest way over the side; stuff like that. I tried pumping the steward who brought me my food, just to find out where we were heading, but if he knew, which was doubtful, he certainly wasn't going to talk about it.

Around nine p.m., just as I was about to go to bed, the engines stopped suddenly. I wandered over to the window and peered out. Three hundred yards away was an oil tanker, her bridge and deck lights blazing. She, too, had stopped engines, and was wallowing gently in the swell. There was some clattering on the deck above me, and a couple of minutes later I heard a speedboat start up. A moment later it emerged into my line of vision, heading towards the tanker. It remained there just long enough for someone to climb down the side of the tanker, then headed back towards the *Maria* carrying one passenger. It passed out of my line of vision beneath the deck rail of the *Maria,* as the Captain appeared from somewhere above me to welcome aboard the owner.

The engines started up soon after, and at the same time the tanker swung away to continue her normal business. I debated for a time whether I should continue what I had been doing, namely going to bed; then decided that it probably wasn't a very good idea. The chances were that Constantin would want to talk to me, and one is at a disadvantage when woken out of a deep sleep. So I got dressed again and, when Constantin arrived twenty minutes later, I was sitting in an armchair reading a particularly dull book. He entered without knocking and, not being a lady, I just glanced up from my book, looked him straight in the eye for a second, and then continued reading. He closed the door quietly behind him and, after a couple of minutes of total silence, I just had to look up at him again. He had remained standing just inside the door, staring at me. He had changed since coming aboard, and was now wearing the standard seduction gear of a smoking jacket.

'I hope you are comfortable, Katherine,' he said, when I looked up.

'Not particularly.'

'That's a pity, because you will be staying with us for some little time.' At least that was a relief; it meant that they had decided not to kill me right away. Now he moved across the stateroom and sat himself down oposite me. 'I am still in the process of having your credentials checked,' he went on.

'And?'

'So far they seem genuine enough,' he said. 'Are you sure you left nothing out?'

'Nothing.'

He smiled a thin smile. 'Lucia is very efficient in affairs of this kind.'

'Lucia is going to get her neck broken if she's not very careful.'

'Possibly,' he agreed. 'But not by you.'

'Don't take any money on it,' I said. 'And now, unless you've got anything to talk about, I'd like to go to bed.' Then, in case he got the wrong idea, I added a rider. 'Alone.'

'Aren't you interested in what we are going to do as a result of the information you have given us?'

'Not very,' I lied. 'But tell me anyway.'

'The people you work for are going to close down my mines. This is inconvenient, but not disastrous. Let them go ahead, if they can find them. But, thanks to your timely warning, I am having all the gold already in existence shipped to one place. It's worth a great deal of money, Katherine. Some three hundred million pounds on the black market. So you can see, it's enough to last me through my old age.'

'They're also planning to confiscate the gold you already have,' I reminded him. 'Or didn't Lucia tell you that?'

'She told me,' he replied. 'But before they can confiscate it, they've got to find it. And they won't.'

'Where can you hide that much gold?' I asked. 'Fort Knox?'

He smiled again. 'That I shan't tell you. But rest assured, no-one will get their hands on it. Now, is there anything you need?'

I shook my head. 'Just peace and quiet.'

He looked at me speculatively for a moment. 'I would still like to make love to you, Katherine.'

I smiled sweetly. 'I'll tell you what you do then. Get half a dozen of your crew in here to hold me down, and then you go ahead. But make sure they're holding me securely, or I shall very likely break your back.'

He got to his feet. 'You are an extremely exciting woman, Katherine, because I am sure you could do just that if you put your mind to it. And you would do it without second thoughts, without any qualms whatsoever.'

'You'd better believe it,' I said, and returned to my book.

He left a moment later and I was alone once more. All right, Katy, I thought, mission accomplished. Mr. Blaser had grudgingly admitted that once I had given them my story, and they had checked it out, then I was on my own with full permission to extricate myself in any way that I could. Meanwhile his people would start to close in on the Galipolodopolo enterprises. Vast amounts of gold need vast amounts of transport and organization to shift it around. If enough people kept their eyes open in enough places, then somewhere along the line there would be a slip up, and Mr. Blaser's men could swoop. My only other brief had been to try and learn the whereabouts of the gold that Mr. Galipolodopolo already had in stock, and even Mr. Blaser had admitted that this would be difficult; so he had generously left it to me whether or not I should fulfil this last instruction. Also in the back of his mind he obviously thought that I would have very little chance of passing on anything I learned, so there hadn't been much point in his getting grotty and laying down the law about it.

So now all that was left was for Katy to disable a crew of twenty-five, take over the ship, and sail her to a friendly port. So come on, Katy. It shouldn't be too difficult for a girl of your infinite resource. I thought about it for a minute or two. A plan here, a scheme there. I made a couple of mental calculations, permuting a sequence of events. I tore them up and made a few more. And then I decided upon the one thing I was fit and capable of doing at that precise moment. I went to bed.


CHAPTER SIX

THE BAHAMA ISLANDS stretch as a loose group for about a thousand miles. Starting with Grand Bahama, less than a hundred miles from the coast of Florida, they finally trail out into the Turks and Caicos Islands about one hundred miles north of the Dominican Republic. There are big islands and little islands, well populated islands and deserted islands; some are well charted and some aren't charted at all because the last time the charts were revised, either someone forgot to put them in because they were so small, or because at that time they didn't even exist, some undersea upheaval having thrust them up into view without anyone being aware of the fact.

I don't really know for sure how I was aware that we had reached West Indian waters; the weather was better certainly, and the sea was bluer; but that only meant that we had reached a more temperate climate. No, there's something about the West Indies, something in the air that you can't put your finger on, but which, if you've been there, you never forget. Even so, I had no idea what part of the West Indies we had reached, because any land that was visible was never nearer than five miles away.

It had taken us two more days to reach here, and during those two days I had kept myself to myself. Constantin had asked me whether I would like to take my meals with Lucia and himself,

but I had told him that it would give me flatulence and heart-
burn, so he had not asked me again. Apart from that, by taking
my meals alone in my stateroom, I had been able to start putting
together a small armoury. A steak knife and a lobster pick may
not sound like much in the way of aggressive or defensive
weapons, but they did wonders for my morale. Also I had rigged
up an interesting little electric gizmo, using the stateroom's
domestic appliances, whereby I could electrocute anybody who
tried to switch on the bathroom light; all I needed was ten
seconds' notice to join up a couple of wires and pow!

It was during these experiments that I made an interesting
discovery. Tucked away in the panelling in the far corner of the
room, well obscured with carved curlycues and cupids, was the
lens of a television camera. It wasn't much of a problem to keep
out of its way once I had located it, but it did provide the answer
to a question I had almost forgotten existed. Assuming every
stateroom was similarly equipped, it would explain away the
death of Antonio, my bullfighting lover of what seemed like
another age. Having viewed our amatory gymnastics over the
course of the few days we were aboard, whoever was watching
would have seen me going through Antonio's luggage and, later,
slice off my gold samples. They must have assumed that Antonio
was in cahoots with me outside the sack as well as in. So exit
Antonio. One thing was for sure. If the TV camera was connected to any sort of videotape or film recorder, somebody had
some extremely blue movies lying around that would be worth
a fortune.

Anyway, here we were, two days after Constantin's arrival
aboard, cruising the waters of the West Indies. I was still allowed
up on deck for a few hours each day, guarded by one of the
crewmen, and I spent a considerable time leaning on the deckrail
trying to identify some of the humps and bumps of the distant
land line. But it was hopeless; the only way I would find out
what island lay off our port bow would be to swim ashore and
ask someone. And, bearing in mind it could turn out to be Cuba
or Haiti, I didn't give the idea too much consideration. Anyway,
most of the time we never came any nearer to land than five or
six miles, and I'm strictly a feet on the ground type of swimmer.
By that, I mean that I can swim very well, as long as I know the
water isn't too deep, but tell me that it goes on down forever
beneath me and I start to panic. Silly, I know, and I believe
they've even got a medical term for it but, whatever it's called,
that's what I've got. So I just continued to lean up against the
rail and watch the long line of land drift by in the distance.

My dinner was later than usual. The steward, obviously not

realizing my true status aboard, had the good grace to apologize.

'I am sorry about this, Miss,' he said. 'But the Captain has had all hands working below.'

'What on earth for?'

'Clearing some forward cargo space.'

'Cargo? On this boat?'

'Oh, we carry it from time to time. Leastways we've got room for it. There's a big hold up front where we keep junk most of the time. But every now and then the guvnor wants something moved in a hurry, and he uses the *Maria*.'

Interesting, I thought. Cargo to be taken on. It didn't take much working out what that cargo would be. Also it didn't take much working out that Katy's days were definitely numbered. If Constantin was going to take on gold, it could only be because he intended to deliver it someplace—the ultimate hiding place. And he wasn't going to do that with me lurking around. The fact that I was still around at all was only due to the consideration that I might be able to answer questions as they came up regarding my fictitious employers. Indeed, Lucia had come to see me on the third day, seeking clarification on a point I had made during our long chat in the shadow of the hot enema. But now had come the crunch, and Katy was going to have to pull her finger out while she still had some fingers left.

After the steward left, I checked over my armoury. Like I said, a steak knife and a lobster pick—hardly the equipment of which revolutions are made. What I really needed was a gun, and as long as I was dreaming there was no point in not throwing in a bazooka and an armoured car as well.

We hove to three hours after I had eaten my dinner. For the benefit of anyone who was looking in on me, I had climbed into bed, but had stayed wide awake. As soon as the engines stopped, I was out of bed and over to the window like a shot. There was a land mass looming up a couple of miles away, only just distinguishable in the clear moonless night. On land there was no sign of any lights at all; either it was a deserted island or everyone had gone to bed early. We lay at rest for half an hour before anything happened, the engines restarting occasionally as we drifted off our point a couple of times. I assumed the Captain didn't want to drop anchor in case a quick getaway was called for. From my window I could see a dozen crewmen and one of the officers gathered at the rail a little forward of midships—it's amazing what three or four days on board a boat can do for your vocabulary. Before I had come aboard I would have said they were hanging around halfway up towards the sharp end. They didn't seem impatient, as though whatever it was they were waiting for would get here in its own good time. And get here it did. There was the sound of engines first, drifting across the water, growing closer and closer; a few minutes later the vague outline of a small coastal cutter could be picked out. The men at the rail doused their fags and prepared to start work. Katy did likewise.

The lock on the cabin door was absolutely no problem; I could have opened it at any time since coming aboard, but there hadn't seemed much point in doing so before now. But now there was and I went into my little pantomime for the benefit of anyone who may have been watching telly. I went back to bed as though I had grown bored with what was going on outside. I turned off the lights and settled down. I lay where I was for five minutes, then got up again and padded across to the bathroom like any girl who needs to take a pee in the middle of the night. I closed the bathroom door behind me and dressed in no time flat, using the clothes I had left hanging behind the door. Then I wired up my electrical booby trap and, one minute after entering the bathroom, I was out again.

Only this time I didn't cross the room into the range of the TV camera. I hugged the wall of the stateroom making my way round to the door. Like I said, it proved no problem at all; a couple of judicious jabs with my lobster pick and I heard the tumblers click back. The trouble was that if there was anyone outside, he would have heard them, too. But I had to take a chance on that.

There was no one. I closed the door quietly behind me and started up the corridor which led eventually up on to the main deck. It was as though this section of the *Maria* had been abandoned; there wasn't a soul around. A great deal of noise was coming from the deck part and obviously everyone was up there, either helping or just watching. Remembering my geography, I turned left when I reached the open air and made my way aft to where we had all sipped our cocktails in happier times. But now the deck furniture had gone and so had the sun awning.

But one thing had stayed the same, and that was the location of the Captain's cabin. If everything I knew about ships and suchlike were correct, this was where they kept the guns. I'd seen dozens of movies where the Captain breaks open the armoury and hands out weapons to his loyal officers with which to defend themselves against the mutinous dogs clamouring outside.

I was taking a hell of a lot for granted, because apart from the fact that I may have been seeing the wrong movies, and there wouldn't be any guns, I was also assuming that the Captain himself wouldn't be in his cabin. And that turned out to be mistake number one. I opened the cabin door and there he was. He was sitting at his desk working on some papers. Why he wasn't going about his rightful business conning the ship or somesuch, I don't know. But he wasn't and ten seconds later he was heartily wishing that he had been. He looked up at me as I came in, and for a moment he didn't get it. He had become used to seeing me walk around the deck during my exercise periods, and he assumed no doubt that I had taken to exercising at night. He even started to smile.

'Good evening, Miss Touchfeather,' he said.

'Good evening, Captain,' I replied, sticking the point of my steak knife up under his chin. Hardened old sea dog he may have been, but twenty years before the mast hadn't equipped him for this sort of situation. He started to get to his feet until I pricked him with the knife.

'I'll cut your throat Captain,' I said, trying not to sound like Long John Silver. It was very important that he believe me because, if he didn't, I was going to be in trouble; not as much trouble as he would be in, but trouble enough. Fortunately he decided that he did believe me, and he subsided into the chair again, his weathered old hands gripping the arms as though they were my neck.

'I need a gun, Captain,' I said. 'Two if you can manage.'

'There are no guns here,' he said, lying vigorously.

'Either you tell me where they are or I'll have to look myself, and I can't do that with you hanging around,' I said, and gave him another jab, sending his head snapping back, just so he would understand what I was getting at. Then came the soul searching bit as he weighed up the pros and cons of doing what I asked. On the one hand he would get into terrible trouble with Galipolodopolo, probably lose his job, his pension, and find himself scrubbing decks again; on the other hand he would get his throat cut. It was an unfair contest. The breath went out of his body like a deflating tyre, and suddenly he wasn't the salty old skipper any longer, but a rather tired little man. He nodded down towards the desk.

'Top right hand drawer,' he said.

I leaned across him, careful to keep the knife in place and tried to open the drawer. It was locked. I glanced round at him and he almost burst into tears he was so apologetic.

'I'm sorry,' he said. 'I forgot.'

He fumbled in his pocket for a bunch of keys, selected one and unlocked the drawer. He was about to assist me further by pulling it open for me when I stopped him.

'I'll do it Captain.'

I pulled open the drawer and there was the gun lying there in isolated splendour. It was a Colt .45 automatic, a veritable cannon. Anybody firing that who didn't know about guns was liable to get their arm broken. Fortunately I knew about guns. Together with the gun was a spare clip which looked full. Assuming the gun was also full, that gave me sixteen shots—hardly enough to mount a full scale battle, but a hell of a sight better than a steak knife and a lobster pick. I reached across him again and took the gun out. It weighed a ton, but to me it felt as light as a feather.

I think the Captain had worked out what I was going to do next a second before I did it. Now that I had got what I had come for, he reasoned, I was going to have to do something about him. I could hardly thank him for the gun and just walk out. No, he decided, I was going to have to incapacitate him. He started to say something, but we'll never know what it was because, before he could get a word out, I clouted him gently with the barrel of the gun just behind his ear. All his doubts and uncertainties vanished at once; he slid from his chair as though I had suddenly extracted every bone from his body. And there I was, on my own, with a lovely, lovely gun and sixteen beautiful bullets.

Go down I might but I was going to take a hell of a lot of people with me. Why, if I could line them up in groups of two, I could probably shoot thirty-two of them. I pulled back the breach and fed a cartridge into the barrel. The gun was well oiled and moved like a dream, and suddenly I felt ten feet tall. I hate guns in the normal course of events; they're nasty, vicious, dangerous things; and, apart from anything else, they can give a person delusions of grandeur. But I had been sat upon, pushed around and threatened with all kinds of nastiness for long enough, and delusions of grandeur was exactly what I wanted right now.

I glanced down at the Captain who was sprawled untidily at my feet. He'd give no trouble for an hour at least. I don't think I had fractured his skull, but he was going to feel like hell when he came round. I turned out the light and closed the door when I left. I didn't know how long I was going to remain undiscovered, but the longer the better.

The deck area outside the captain's cabin was deserted when I came out, which was fortunate for any person who might have been there, because I would have shot them without batting an eyelid.

I suppose I could have swiped a boat about here and just escaped, but I was feeling grotty in the extreme, and I wanted to spread a bit of my grottiness around where it would cause the most trouble.

So now I put phase two of my plan into operation. I called it a plan, but the loose conglomeration of my intentions couldn't really be distinguished with such a high sounding word. A plan is something that has been worked out in detail; all that I had was an intense desire to stay alive and to do as much peripheral damage as possible in the process. As far as the former was concerned, optimist I might have been, but I didn't rate my chances very high; but, as for the damage I could cause, there I was convinced I could pick up top marks.

All the kerfuffle of the loading was still going on on the port side, so I kept to the starboard, making my way forward to midships. I reached the corner of the main deck superstructure and risked a peek round the edge. A portable winch had been rigged and this was being used to transfer stuff from the smaller coastal vessel on board the *Maria*. The deck area in use was floodlit and I could see Constantin and Lucia standing arm in arm watching the proceedings. Whatever it was being loaded—and it just had to be gold—was coming aboard in small wooden crates about two feet by one foot by one foot. They were winched aboard two at a time and lowered on to the deck. Then two men would take one of the crates at either end. And they were heavy. You could see that by the effort the men put into carrying them. Using rope handles fixed to the crates, the men lugged them across the foredeck and down an open companionway halfway up towards the bow. It was a scene of efficient industry, fascinating when one knew what the crates contained. A ship's officer was checking the loading against a manifest, and Constantin was checking the officer. Two shots, I thought, and I would dispose of both Constantin and Lucia. It was a pleasant thought, but hardly practical in the circumstances. All right Katy, just what in hell are you going to do? I was saved further speculation, however, when there came a sudden scream from somewhere in the ship and simultaneously all the lights went out.

Clever Katy, I thought, someone has tried to switch on your bathroom light. In fact, as I learned later, it was the steward who had been passing my cabin and had decided to collect my dinner dishes. He had put his key in the door, found it already open, and gone in. No Katy, and no light on in the bathroom; better just take a look before reporting to the Old Man. Into the bathroom, switch on the light and, bingo, instant shock. And instant darkness too, by way of a bonus. As the lights went out, the group around the winch froze into temporary immobility. They were still lit by the lights from the other boat behind them, but that was below the *Maria*'s deck level, and it was pretty dark by most standards. Added to that, up until a moment before they had all been standing in the bright glare of two powerful floodlights; the sudden contrast must have left them in what seemed like total darkness, while their eyes slowly adjusted.

Constantin pulled himself together first. He ordered the officer to go and check the electrics, then detailed two men to accompany Lucia and himself aft to investigate the scream. As soon as the owner was out of sight, the others all sat down and lit their fags. Now or never Katy, I thought. I slipped around the corner and padded across the deck to the open companion way. Just before I climbed in, I heard a couple of voices cursing from below at having been left halfway down the stairs in the pitch dark. I slipped round to the back of the hatch and waited until the owners of the voices reached the deck once more. Then, as they crossed towards their companions, I ducked round the edge and promptly fell down a flight of metal stairs.

I picked myself up painfully. There didn't seem to be anything broken, but I wasn't prepared to take any money on it. And, having got here, I started to wonder what I was going to do next. Because, apart from the glimmer of light from the open hatchway above me, I couldn't see a bloody thing. The darkness was like black velvet, complete and unrelieved; there was absolutely no point in my trying to move around, because I could break both legs three times over before taking more than half a dozen steps. I was still pondering my predicament and ready to shoot anyone who poked their head over the hatchway, when someone did me a big favour. All the lights went on again. Two seconds to orientate myself, and I was off once more.

I was in a narrow passage, with closed doors either side and one at the end, which was open; it was obviously there that the crates had been carried. Acting on the premise that a place safe enough for all that loot must be safe enough for Katy, I made straight for the open door. I stepped over a rising bulkhead and found myself in what could only be the forward hold. It was as wide as the ship herself, but narrowing rapidly at the bow. The ceiling was low and the whole place was strictly functional in that this was the inside of the hull, and looked exactly that. Elsewhere in the *Maria* the walls may have been decorated with oak panelling or flock paper, but here we were down to basics, and nothing separated the hold from the sea outside other than half an inch of steel plate. I started to look around, and then I decided first things first, and closed the door behind me. It was a heavy door and it fitted in a watertight fashion into the bulkhead. There were four levers for securing it, one at the top, one at the bottom, and two down the edge. They were one sided levers only; and could only be operated from my side. The outside had its own set. I slammed all the levers home, leaning on them to make sure they were secure; and that seemed to be that for the time being. Now I took a closer look around me. The crates had been stacked down either side of the hull and, at first, it looked as though there were hundreds of them. In fact there were two hundred, because I counted them later. Also later, I prised one of them open. It contained twenty gold bars and, remembering some of my homework, I was able to estimate each bar as being worth approximately five thousand pounds. That made it one hundred thousand pounds per crate; and two hundred crates made it twenty million pounds actual value, and probably two or three times that much on Constantin's black market. I'd certainly chosen the right place to make my last stand; around that sort of money everyone would have to tread very carefully. I say 'my last stand' because that was what I knew it was going to have to be. I never really expected to hide aboard the *Maria*. By a simple process of searching the ship from stem to stern, they were bound to find me. All I could hope for was to make things as uncomfortable as possible for everyone on board.

It took them half an hour to work out where I was. During that half an hour they had obviously found the electrocuted steward, the unconscious Captain and checked that there wasn't a missing lifeboat. There wasn't and, like I said, after thirty minutes there was a great clang on the door outside. Just to be sociable I pulled out a bar of gold and clanged back at them. That little exchange was followed by two minutes silence, which in turn was followed by another clang, this time more positive. I clanged back a couple of times until between clangs I heard someone shouting from the other side of the door. I pressed my ear up against the cold metal and listened. It was Constantin, obviously yelling at the top of his voice to make himself heard through half an inch of steel watertight door.

'Katherine! Can you hear me?'

'I hear you,' I yelled back.

'I will give you two minutes to come out.'

'What are you going to do if I don't?' I yelled back at him.

There was a long silence while everyone outside realized that there was absolutely nothing they could do. After a couple of minutes I grew bored with the silence. 'Constantin,' I shouted.

'Yes, Katherine?'

'I have a proposition for you.'

'What is it?'

'Are you listening carefully?'

'I'm listening.' I judged his height roughly, visualizing more or less where his ear would be, seeing it pressed up hard against the metal of the door. 'Are you sure you're listening?' I screamed at him, just to be doubly sure.

His voice came back to me faintly as he yelled at me. 'I'm listening, Katherine.'

I drew back the gold bar I was holding and clouted the door so hard I nearly broke my arm. The reverberations were still going through my body ten minutes later when the engine started.

A tomb is still a tomb; even a twenty million pound coffin, despite the elbow room. And taking a good look around me, it seemed that was what I was confined in. Having got myself into it, safely sealed off from the vicissitudes of the outside world, there didn't seem to be a thing I could do except wait for their next move. It was noisy down here with the engines running, a little bit murky, and the place smelled of oil and bilge water. Apart from the gold, there was very little else. There were some links of anchor chain coiled up at the far end, a few miles of rope, some tools, some oxy-acetylene equipment and, rather incongruously, a pair of oars. There were some drums of what I assumed to be oil, but which could equally well have been petrol and, wrapped in protective polythene, neatly stowed away, there was the summertime deck awning. And, of course, there was Katy, all alone and, now that the euphoria was evaporating, very miserable. One small consolation was that Constantin couldn't be all that happy either. Bar cutting his way through the bulkhead, there was no possible way that he could get to me or his loot. And that gave me an idea. But before I could investigate its possibilities, a noise from outside the door attracted my attention. I moved back to the door and stuck my ear up against it, then jerked my head back quickly, clapping a hand to my ear. The door was hot and I immediately identified the noise I had heard. It was the roar of an oxy-acetylene torch.

Great minds must think alike. No sooner had I promulgated the theory that cutting his way in was all that Constantin had left than here he was, doing just that. Well, someone was in for a nasty shock in the very near future. I moved away and sat patiently on a million pounds' worth of gold and watched the door turn a dull red on my side. A few minutes later the metal fractured and a lance of flame came through the half inch gap it had cut in the steel. I remained watching the flame as it started to move sideways and ten minutes later there was a four inch slash in the door, half an inch deep. Now is the time, Katy, I thought. I moved over to the door and, keeping to the opposite side to which they were cutting, I risked a quick peek through the slit. I received a vague impression of a man's head masked with heavy goggles and, past him, farther down the narrow passage, a couple more men sitting on the steps that led up to the deck; the relief crew, obviously.

Satisfied that my efforts would not be in vain, I pulled out my gun. I lined up the barrel with the half inch slit in the door and, without bothering to aim at anything, I pulled the trigger. The noise was catastrophic, nearly blowing my head off and setting all the bells in the world clanging in my ears. But that was nothing compared to what happened out in the passage. The bullet neatly clipped the ear of the man doing the cutting, and then went off on a merry little jaunt of its own, ricocheting off the steel walls and taking one of the men on the stairs with it en route. It was bloody marvellous. A bullet fired at an angle into that passageway could do the work of a machine gun.

Feeling safe, I took a good look through the slit this time. The man on the stairs was bleeding profusely. His companion had disappeared entirely. The one whose ear I had shot off was busy crawling on all fours towards the end of the passage, presenting me with the almost irresistible target of his backside scurrying away from me. If it had been Constantin or Lucia, I would certainly have used another bullet, but on some poor fellow I didn't even know, the operation would have been spiteful. So I let him scuttle to safety up the steps dragging his more seriously shot companion with him. Constantin may have been all sorts of an international big wheel, but it wasn't going to count for much in getting any more of his crew down into the passageway, now that Katy had shown her hand.

In fact, they did try it once more, using a large piece of sheet steel carried in front of them. I had been peering through the slit on and off while I was making my own plans, and the first thing I saw was this two feet by three feet piece of flat steel moving towards me. I could see a pair of legs sticking out from beneath it, and had a vague glimpse of a shock of red hair over the top. I let him get halfway down the passage and then, judging the angle of deflection carefully, I fired at the wall halfway between him and me. The bullet screamed off the wall like a banshee. A fraction of a second later the steel shield was dropped and the man was beating it back up stairs dragging a badly bleeding leg. What about that? I thought. I've got a gun that shoots around corners.

And that was the extent of outside interference for the next few hours. I think Constantin must have decided that he would starve me to death because, although I took frequent looks through the slit, nobody appeared again. Between looks I went about my business.

Briefly this was that if they could cut their way in, I could cut my way out. The oxy-acetylene equipment was to hand, and I'd once done a short course on its use when Mr. Blaser had wanted me to take the back off a safe in Rio during carnival week. (Remind me to tell you about that sometime.) I paced around the hold for a few minutes weighing the pros and cons of exactly

where I was going to cut a hole in the *Maria*. Eventually I settled
for a point about ten feet back from the prow on the port side.
The only reason I selected this particular place was because that
was where the oxy-acetylene equipment happened to be. The
cylinders are very heavy and I didn't fancy having to drag them
around the confined space in which I was trapped. I checked the
cylinder gauges and the hose connections. Everything looked
fine. I calculated the mixture I would need for the most effective
cutting flame. I even found a pair of goggles and gloves where
they had been left by the last person to use the equipment. I
took one more peek down the corridor to make sure I was still on
my own, and I was ready for work. But I didn't have a bloody
match.

I found one eventually in a box of lifeboat supplies stacked
away at the back. Also among the supplies were three bottles
of brandy; obviously there for medical purposes, I decided that
if anyone needed medicine right now, it was Katy. I broke open
one of the bottles and took a couple of healthy slugs. Then, feeling primed like a well tuned pump, I went to work. The first,
and most important, calculation I had to make was the height
of the waterline outside. I could hear the stuff slopping away
against the hull, but it was difficult to judge exactly how high the
true level was. We were moving and, by the vibration, we were
making good speed. That would mean a bow wave was being
sent up, and the true water line would become lower for the first
few feet of hull. On the other hand, if I took this level as accurate,
when we slowed down or stopped I could find myself trying to cut
a hole into the sea. I took another slug of brandy and gave the
matter considerable thought; I took one more slug, and nearly
decided to forget the whole thing. Then I started cutting. The
height I cut at was finally resolved by my taking up the most
comfortable position I could find, crossing my fingers, taking
another swig from the bottle and praying.

It's a very simple piece of equipment is an oxy-acetylene cutter.
It's the same as they use for welding, but it carries an extra jet
which blows pure oxygen on to the oxidised metal, shoving it
out of the way, thus forming the cut. All things being equal, it
can be operated by anyone with a strong wrist and an ounce of
common sense. But here, all things were most definitely not equal.
The boat was rolling and I was three parts pissed. And that was
just for openers. The actual burning flame reaches a temperature
of 6000 degrees fahrenheit and, although that is only a minute
portion of the flame, the result can still be a great deal of spread
around heat.

After ten minutes I was sweating like a pig and, worse, I wasn't making much of an impression on the hull. What with the heat, the rolling of the boat and the rolling of Katy, I seemed completely incapable of holding the flame still for long enough for it to bite into the metal. All I was getting was a large area of scorched hull and a terrible headache. I decided to start all over again. I switched off the flame, then stripped off to bra and pants. Resisting another pull at the brandy bottle, I took one more peep through into the still empty corridor; then gritted my teeth and really concentrated. Using one of the crates of gold as a support I managed to hold the flame reasonably still, and was rewarded a few minutes later by seeing the metal start to give way under the onslaught. A moment later the sea came in and my torch went out.

It was only a small hole, but it must have been well below the waterline because a sudden jet of water doused the torch and hit me straight on the goggles. Feeling heartily fed up with the whole thing, I tore myself off a strip of polythene from the deck awning wrapping and plugged the hole. It wasn't difficult, but the event did act as a pointer as to what could happen if I cut in the wrong place again. I dried off the torch, relit it, and started cutting two feet higher. This time everything went swimmingly and I even started to hum a little tune while I worked. It must have been the effect of that bloody brandy again because, all things considered, I was in a hell of a mess whichever way you sliced it. Still there's not much point in dwelling on your problems; they don't get any smaller that way. If anything, they seem to get larger. Neither is there much point in projecting your plans too far ahead because as sure as hell something will crop up which you haven't foreseen and which will trip you up leaving you flat on your arse with egg all over your face.

Half an hour later I had a neat cut, eighteen inches long. I paused for a while for a short bout of stocktaking. Outside, the sea seemed very close. When the metal had cooled sufficiently, I took my goggles off and had a proper look. My God, it *was* close. I was eighteen inches above the operative waterline. Outside the water seemed to be flowing by at approximately seventy-five miles an hour, and it whispered and gurgled at me in a terrifying manner. I had intended to make the next cut vertically downwards from the first one. To hell with that, I thought, and started the next cut at an angle of forty-five degrees from the original, cutting upwards. I reckoned that if I could remove a triangle eighteen inches by eighteen by eighteen, I would be able to wriggle through; my 36, 24, 36 notwithstanding. It would be a tight squeeze and I would probably scrape myself raw, but that was my plan. And that's what I did.

With periodic checks to make sure I was still being left alone, I managed to cut through the hull within the hour. The last couple of minutes were a bit traumatic as I didn't know whether the section I had cut away was going to fall inwards or outwards. If it fell inwards, it could do Katy a nasty injury. But nothing ventured nothing gained, and I continued to cut away. Fortunately it fell outwards and there I was staring out at sea eighteen inches away from my nose. From this low eyeline it seemed to stretch away forever.

While I was still staring at it, a hundred odd gallons suddenly sloshed through the opening, drenching me and frightening me out of my life to boot. I was still spluttering and coughing when another hundred gallons spilled through. The engine noise was still the same so obviously we hadn't decreased our speed. This could only mean that the weather was getting worse. Just what I needed with sea water coming in by the ton, and an overloaded forehull, the boat would soon become unmanageable. She'd start to carry so much weight forward that she'd lose steerage-way. At least, that's what I thought. With any luck she might sink too, which raised the rather interesting theory as to what the hell I was going to do if she did. It was all right for that lot up there—they'd got life jackets, boats, rafts, rubber rings and all sorts of stuff for keeping afloat. Me, I had my bra and pants, and twenty million pounds worth of gold; a nice nest egg, but pretty useless when it comes to keeping your head above real wet-type water.

Another couple of hundred gallons of sea sloshed into the hold and the water line outside seemed a fraction closer. The more water that came in, the lower the *Maria* would settle forward, which in turn would let in more water. A vicious little circle, with Katy at the dead centre. More water spilled in, and suddenly the engine noise changed and I heard the far off clang of the engine telegraph. They had obviously noticed the change in the *Maria*'s trim and were about to investigate its cause.

So it was now or never. I waded across to the door that led to the passageway and looked through the slit. Two heads were peering down from the top of the stairs, one of them belonging to an officer. I banged a couple of shots and the heads disappeared miraculously as the bullets sang and whistled their way from bulkhead to bulkhead and back again. Then I tore off another piece of polythene from the deck awning cover and used it to wrap the gun in what I hoped was a watertight fashion. I tied this little package around my neck with a short piece of nylon rope, because where I was going I would need both hands free. Then, hoping that I had discouraged outside interference for the next few minutes, I opened the watertight door as quietly as possible. The oxy-acetylene equipment used in the attempt to

winkle Katy out was still where it had been abandoned in such
a hurry when I had started to make like Annie Oakley. I lit
the flame, adjusted it quickly, and in two minutes I had wrecked
the hinges of the door, melting them into blodges of shapeless
metal. The devil himself wouldn't be able to close that door now.

Fortunately nobody felt inclined to see what I was up to,
because, in spite of frequent looks over my shoulder, nothing
happened at the top of the stairs—which was just as well, because
my gun was now nicely wrapped in a waterproof parcel around
my neck and it would have taken me five minutes to get it into
action once more.

Having sealed open the door, I went back into the hold. The
water was knee deep now and, instead of sloshing in through
the hole I had cut, it had started to flow in steadily. The *Maria*
had definitely settled a fraction and, if I knew anything about
marine architecture, which I didn't, she was very likely for the
knackers yard if someone didn't do something soon. I waded
across to my do-it-yourself exit and, gritting my teeth and sucking in my chest, I started to squeeze through. It was no easy feat
because, apart from anything else, the water was really coming in
now at a steady rate of knots. It had already spilled over into
the passageway outside and, in a couple of minutes those on deck
looking down into the passageway would be able to see it. When
they did, it was doubtful that even the threat of Katy's gun was
going to keep them from coming down to investigate.

I managed to get my upper half through the hole and, in
imminent danger of drowning, I tried to get the rest of me
through. Obviously however, I wasn't the 36-24-36 that I had
thought I was. If I was still 36 up top then I must have suddenly
developed a frightening 38 down below—the outcome no doubt
of too much luxury cruising because I wedged solid. Now I was
in real trouble. If anyone decided to risk coming down to investigate, they were going to be presented with Katy's nether regions,
apparently growing out of the hull like so many barnacles. Apart
from the indignity of the situation, I would be completely helpless. Added to that, I was proving to be an effective cork, because
no more water was spilling into the hold, which wasn't the object
of the exercise at all. I pulled and I heaved; I wriggled and I
squirmed; I braced my arms against the outside of the hull and
pushed hard. Nothing! I took a deep breath and tried again;
still nothing. One last try, Katy, I thought, then you'd better turn
the whole thing in. I sucked in my breath, then I blew it all out;
I braced my arms agains the hull, counted to five, and then
shoved hard. I shot out of that hole like a cork from a well
shaken bottle of champagne, and in seconds I was coughing
and spluttering with a mouth and nose full of sea water. I

righted myself after a moment and took stock. The hull of the now stationary *Maria* rose in front of me as high and as solid looking as the United Nations building. And the water was really making it into the hold now; in fact I had to pull myself along the hull a little way to avoid being dragged back in by the suction. Bullets or no bullets, somebody was just going to have to come down and have a look. Then the fun would start. And by that time I wanted to be somewhere else.

I felt my way along the hull, trying not to think of the mile or so of water beneath me. Fortunately being nose heavy the *Maria* wasn't drifting as much as she might have been and by half swimming and half pushing myself along I made my way aft. The foredeck was going to be as busy as Piccadilly Circus on Cup Final Night, and I couldn't see myself climbing over the deckrail into all that excitement. If anyone managed to lay hands on me, they would probably be so livid with what I had done that they would use me to plug the hole. The further back I moved, the higher the stern seemed to rise. There was a line on the hull down by the water line which had been a foot beneath the sea up front but here, more or less midships, it was a foot out of the water.

I could hear a lot of noise from the deck above me. There was shouting and yelling and running feet and more shouting. Obviously they knew something was seriously wrong up front and now it only remained for someone to pluck up enough courage to go down and have a look. What they would do when they discovered there was a bloody great hole in the ship was anybody's guess. If they got to it very soon they might be able to weld a patch over it, but even that was doubtful because by now the sea must be gurgling in good and fast and, with the watertight door sealed open, it wasn't going to be just the fore-hold that was flooded. A boat like the *Maria* could cope with that and still stay afloat. But what I had done was to lay open the means for the sea to flood back into the passageway, into the cabins either side, on under the staircase, back God only knew how far; probably between a third and a half of the length of the entire boat. Smashing ship she may have been, but she wasn't smashing enough to hold that much water and still stay on the top of the sea where she belonged.

I was thinking so hard on all this as I worked my way back along the hull that I nearly missed my chance. I had reached about three-quarters of the way towards the stern when from a point just above my head and slightly to one side, I heard a thump of sound and something banged gently against the hull. I looked up, and in the vague light that leaked down from the deck above I could just make out the shape of a bucket tied to a length of rope which disappeared up on to the deck. Somebody had been pulling in sea water to scrub the decks or some such and had left his bucket dangling when he had been called away to more important things. The only question now was how tightly he had secured the rope up on the deck. Hoping he had paid attention to his knot-tying instructions when he was in sailors' school, I reached up and grabbed the rim of the bucket with both hands. I gave it an experimental tug and it remained secure. Still, it didn't really tell me much. The only way I was going to find out if it would take my weight was to start climbing the bloody thing. Metaphorically crossing my fingers, I braced my feet against the hull and, shifting my grip from the rim of the bucket to the rope, I started upwards.

Two minutes later my head was just below deck level, and offering up a silent blessing to the sailor who had tied the knot. I shifted my grip to the lower rail. There was a hell of a racket going on above me, but most of it seemed to be coming from the forward area and, apart from a scurrying pair of feet inches from my head just before I reached the top, my part of the boat seemed deserted. I held my breath for a moment, plucking up some heretofore undiscovered courage or foolhardiness, and then hauled myself upwards.

Two seconds later I was crouched in the shelter of one of the lifeboats unwrapping my gun. I was shivering like a maniac. It was cold, certainly, and I was soaking wet in just a bra and pants. But it wasn't that cold and I realized that the brandy-induced euphoria of the last couple of hours had been washed away by all that salt water, leaving just a frightened little girl.

Praying that the gun was in working order, and praying too that I wouldn't have to use it, I poked my head out from my place of concealment. Looking forward I could see what looked like a veritable army of men gathered on the foredeck around the hatch that led down to my passageway and hold. From where they were standing they must have been able to see the water pouring into the passageway and points beyond, but it looked as though, as yet, nobody had decided to risk his neck and go down to take a closer look. As far as they were concerned, down there lurked Katy and her itchy trigger finger. Soon they would work out that it would be six of one against half a dozen of the other; drown or get shot. Then someone would go down. But by then I hoped to be well on my way. Because I had finished playing this affair by ear. Now I *did* have a plan. When we Touchfeathers are frightened, we really come to the fore. I suppose it's all that adrenalin shooting around inside that does it but, the more frightened we become, the more coldbloodedly efficient we seem to act. And I was just about as frightened as any girl has any business to be.

# CHAPTER SEVEN

'ALL RIGHT, MISS TOUCHFEATHER. You have described the build up with your customary flair for rhetoric,' said Mr. Blaser. 'Shall we now get down to what actually happened?'

He's a bastard that Mr. Blaser. He won't give me the satisfaction of basking in my own reflected glory for longer than it takes him to fix me with that basilisk stare of his, bringing me down to earth with a dirty great thump.

It was three days later and I considered that I had dried out sufficiently to make a full report. Had Mr. Blaser had his way, I would have been back two days earlier, but I was in Jamaica and as long as I didn't answer the phone, he couldn't get to me. Of course, he had done so in the end. He always does, practically dragging me back to London by the scruff of my neck. Now, with his tape recorder devouring everything that I said, and without even so much as a 'Good to see you're still alive, Miss Touchfeather,' he was getting at me again.

'You had regained the deck of the *Maria*,' he prompted. 'And you had formulated a plan. What went wrong?'

'Nothing went wrong, sir,' I said, trying to keep righteous indignation out of my voice.

His eyebrows went up a millimetre. 'Do you mean to sit there and tell me that everything that happened subsequently was by deliberate action on your part?'

'Yes, sir,' I said proudly.

He still didn't get it. 'This fiasco was intended?'

The Touchfeather blood started to simmer gently; it wasn't boiling yet, but it would do so very shortly. 'Yes, sir,' I said. 'This fiasco was intended.'

He regarded me steadily for a moment, then something that could have been a sigh vaguely disturbed his frame.

'Very well, Miss Touchfeather. Explain it to me.'

The explanation wasn't nearly as difficult as the actual operation. There I was, cold, wet and frightened, standing on the deck of the *Maria*, which had put her nose down so alarmingly that I could almost hear the Lutine bell ringing at Lloyds. I had three objectives; the bridge, Constantin and a boat—in that order. Assuming, with all the excitement up front, that the bridge would be sparsely occupied, I made for it straight away. I had been on the *Maria* enough times by now to know the geography accurately, and I went to the bridge by the back way, circling the main deck aft, and keeping as much boat as possible between

myself and the foredeck at all times. I was right about the
occupants of the bridge; there were only two men, both officers.
One was looking down towards the foredeck; the other was in
the radio room, just aft of the bridge proper, sending out subtle,
ambiguous signals, trying to ascertain whether there were any
rescue boats in the area, without actually committing himself
until everyone knew what was what. He had earphones clamped
to his head, so I ignored him for the moment, concentrating on
the other one. So fascinated was he with what was going on below
that he allowed me to get right up to him without his being
aware that I was there. I peered past him down on to the foredeck where the entire ship's company were standing around the
open hatchway.

'What's happening?' I asked.

'Christ knows,' he said without turning. 'But someone had
better go down there pretty bloody soon before . . .'

Then he twigged. He turned to me and his mouth fell so far
open that I could see his back teeth. I had to admit that he had
good cause. There was Katy, dripping wet, as naked as made
no difference, and with a cannon in her hand. I now stuck the
cannon hard into his stomach. That had the effect of snapping
his mouth shut again, bringing him back to earth with a nasty
jolt. His eyes remained blank for one second, then I read a change
of expression in them. It was an expression I had seen many
times before. It meant that he was about to do something foolish
and, if I didn't nip it in the bud, I was going to have to shoot
him. So I nipped. I stepped back a couple of paces to give myself
swinging room and, without reversing the gun, I hit him across
the side of the head. His mouth fell open once more and this
time it stayed that way. He toppled backwards losing all further
interest in me, the *Maria* and everything else.

So now all I had to cope with was the Sparks, who was still
sitting in the radio room with his back towards the bridge. He
was still fiddling with his morse key, wondering whether he dare
send out an SOS. Constantin wouldn't want anyone creeping
around the *Maria*, with the cargo she was carrying, and he had
probably given strict instructions about it. But the radio officer
was no fool; he had a slip of paper in front of him giving the
exact position of the *Maria* and, orders or no orders, he was
going to bang that message out as soon as he felt the need to.
But I relieved him of having to make the decision. I crept up
behind him and pushed the cold barrel of the gun up against
the back of his neck. This one was no hero and, like I said before,
he was no fool either. He froze immobile, his hands flat on the
table in front of him. In fact he remained like that for so long I
wondered whether I had killed him from shock and instant rigor

mortis had set in. But he wasn't going to move a muscle until he received permission, so I had to use my other hand to pull his earphones from around his ears. 'You can turn round,' I said.

He did so very carefully, using the revolving seat of his chair. He was sweating profusely and his eyes were glazed with panic.

'Up!' I said.

He stood up. I indicated with the gun that he should move out on to the bridge. After one brief moment, I followed him. He went three shades whiter when he saw his companion stretched out and I thought that any moment now he was going to faint dead away. But he managed to keep his feet by supporting himself on the compass housing.

'Get on the public address and ask for Galipolodopolo to come to the radio room,' I said.

He looked at me blankly so I repeated the message, punctuating the words with periodic jabs of the gun into his stomach. At last I managed to get through to him. He switched on the public address and a moment later I saw all heads on the foredeck turn towards the speaker as it crackled into life.

'Mr. Galipolodopolo to the radio room please,' the voice boomed out.

I jabbed him with the gun again. 'Urgent,' I hissed.

'Urgent,' he said, with remarkable lack of invention.

I saw Constantin detach himself from the group on the foredeck and head towards the bridge and, joy of joys, Lucia decided to come with him.

'Sorry about this,' I said to the radio officer, and despatched him to join his companion. Then I threw a couple of charts on to the floor, put a match to them, and went out to greet Constantin and Lucia.

'You deliberately destroyed the charts?' said an incredulous Mr. Blaser.

'Yes, sir. I used them to start the fire.'

'Why did you need a fire?'

'It seemed like a good idea at the time.'

'Couldn't you have used something else? *Anything* else.'

'There wasn't anything handy,' I said.

He sighed again. 'Why did you want Galipolodopolo and the woman?'

'I wanted them with me.'

'I realize that,' he said tetchily. 'But why?'

'After what they'd done to me, I didn't feel inclined to leave them to disappear to some South American haven to live happily ever after.'

'Personal revenge?' said Mr. Blaser ominously.

I back tracked quickly before I re-blotted my copy-book. 'I needed them to insure my getaway,' I said.

There was a moment's pause. 'Carry on, Miss Touchfeather,' he said finally.

I met Constantin and Lucia halfway up to the bridge. I would like to say he looked surprised or shocked when he saw me, but he didn't. Obeying the obvious threat he saw in my hand, he just stopped and waited for me to handle the ball which was so well and truly in my court. Lucia went a couple of shades paler beneath her immaculate make-up, but she too behaved impeccably. 'We're going aft,' I said.

He gave me no argument; just turned and started aft, Lucia by his side. He did, however, express a certain amount of interest. 'What's aft, Katherine?' He asked without turning.

'The number two speedboat,' I said, seeing no reason why I should keep it secret.

'Where are we going then?'

'Anywhere, so long as it's off this ship,' I said. 'She's about to sink.' I detected a slight stiffening of his neck muscles as the impact of this hit him fully.

'The *Maria* is a very seaworthy vessel,' he said, fishing.

There didn't seem any reason now why I shouldn't tell him. 'Not with a bloody great hole in the hull and a fire on the bridge,' I said. And of course they just had to do something. You can push people just so far, then they reach a point where there ain't nothing going to move them any further. Funny, but it was Lucia who reached this point first. She stopped suddenly.

'We seriously under-estimated you, Katherine,' she said coolly.

'Yes, you did, didn't you?' I said with equal aplomb. Constantin had stopped, too, and was watching both of us. 'But I haven't got time to stand around and talk about it,' I said, waving the gun at her. But she didn't move.

'You're going to have to shoot me, Katherine,' she said.

'Don't continue to under-estimate me,' I said, but she didn't move a muscle. And gradually into her eyes came a gleam of satisfaction like a poker player gets when he calls a bluff and comes out on top. It was that expression that did it, that and the mental images I conjured up quickly of poisonous truth drugs and sulphuric acid enemas. I had to conjure up these to help me do what I did, because I'm not a vindictive girl by nature. It's just that I can get a bit stroppy when self preservation is in the balance.

'You're going to have to shoot me, Katherine,' she had said. 'Very well,' I said. And I shot her.

*       *       *

The rest was easy. Using the automatic winch, Constantin lowered the speedboat over the side and we both climbed in. As we drew away from the *Maria* we could see just how dire were the straits she was in. She was really settling forward now, her bows six feet deeper in the water than they had any right to be. That meant that the hole I had cut was way, way below the water line and the sea would be coming in under pressure now. There was absolutely nothing that could keep her afloat much longer. Added to that, the fire on the bridge was now going great guns and, from five hundred yards away, Constantin and I watched the tiny figures of the crew running this way and that, like so many disorganized lemmings. Finally someone must have given the order to abandon ship, because boats started to come down the side. And once the *Maria* decided to go, she didn't hang around. There was a huge, metallic crash that carried clearly across the water, as her machinery gave up the effort of trying to withstand the steep angle of incline, and broke loose. The whole lot must have slid forward, increasing the weight at the bows to an impossible degree. Fine ship that she undoubtedly was, she gave a desperate clang of despair, stuck her nose down, and two minutes later there was nothing left but isolated pieces of debris and a couple of life rafts which were gradually filling with crew.

'That's all?' said Mr. Blaser.

'You know the rest, sir,' I said. 'I made land three hours later, reported the wreck and caught the first plane to Jamaica.'

'And Galipolodopolo?'

Here was my big disappointment. I had cosseted and nurtured him across three hours of water, beached the boat single-handed because I didn't trust him to do it, and then proudly marched him off at gunpoint to the nearest authorities I could find. I had left him there while I had toddled off to make a couple of calls. An hour later, when I returned, he had gone.

'Did you know that he had a charter plane fly in within the hour to pick him up and take him out?' asked Mr. Blaser.

'No, sir,' I said. 'But I guessed as much.

'Don't you care?'

I *did* care and, if I had known it was going to happen, I would probably have pushed him over the side before we landed. But there was no point in crying over spilt milk. 'Not much,' I said.

He looked at me shrewdly for a moment before continuing. 'There's nothing we can do with him, of course. We've clipped his wings considerably. His mines have gone, and from here on he'll have to make his living honestly.'

'Not too much of a hardship with a hundred and fifty ships of his own,' I said.

'One hundred and forty-nine,' said Mr. Blaser. 'Which brings me to another point.' I knew he would get to it in the end, but it had been interesting seeing just how long he had been able to hang out. 'We are very interested in pinpointing the exact position where the *Maria* went down.'

'Yes, sir,' I said.

He waited. 'Well?' he said.

I looked at him innocently. 'Sir?'

'Come, Miss Touchfeather. You can read charts. Before you burned them didn't it occur to you to check the exact position of the *Maria*?'

'No, sir,' I said.

He looked at me steadily for a long time, then growled a dismissal. Before I walked out of the door to present Miss Moody with an expense chit that was going to curl her hair, Mr. Blaser acknowledged in his own way that I had been through a great deal and was entitled to something.

'You can have two days off, Miss Touchfeather,' he said.

'Thank you, sir,' I replied sweetly, and I left.

It's a great comfort to a girl to know that she's got a twenty million pound nest egg. It's a thought that will keep her warm on those long winter nights when, because of the passing years, the phone has stopped ringing. Because naturally I know where that gold is. The position was written on that slip of paper in the radio room and I memorized it very carefully before I threw it on the fire that I had started.

Of course, all this is pipe dreaming. Eventually I shall have to tell Mr. Blaser. It's absolute hell being a basically honest person —it causes one to do the most stupid things. But if I can't keep the money for myself, at least I can use it as a lever. Even Mr. Blaser will budge under the pressure of a twenty million pound solid gold lever. I think I shall ask him for three months leave on full pay and a round trip ticket to Calmooniville. On the other hand, he pulls a lot of weight; perhaps I shall get him to exert some of it to have Peter Chalmers transferred to London for a couple of months. I'd like to see Peter again; we never really got much of a scene going together, what with Archimedes and Diogenes lurking about all over the place and my early abduction. Yes, that sounds like fun. The only trouble comes in knowing just how much pressure to exert on Mr. Blaser. Not enough, and the result is a big fat zero; too much, and the lever is liable to spring back and inflict serious injury on Katy. Push that man too far and he'll have me flying some grubby milk run in the Outer Hebrides for the rest of my working days—probably without the aid of an aeroplane.

# NORTH CAPE

## Joe Poyer

'North Cape' is published by
Victor Gollancz Ltd.

## *The Author*

Joe Poyer was born in 1939 in Battle Creek, Michigan. Escaping from the confines of the Midwest he has tackled about every type of job requiring writing skills, and he considers that the easiest people to write for are magazine and book editors, because they are real professionals, whereas outside publishing everyone considers he could be an expert at writing—if only he had the time, of course. He is married with two children, he lives in California and claims to be a confirmed Anglophile.

For my father and mother,
in some small return for their
forbearance and love.

# CHAPTER ONE

FIFTY-EIGHT DEGREES *of frost. Twenty-six below zero F . . .*
From two hundred thousand feet, the surface of the earth below
was void of all but the largest geological features. The land was a
mixture of browns and grays, overlain with the misty white of a
thin ice cover at sixty thousand feet. A barely discernible range of
mountains stretched to the northeast beyond the narrow scope of
vision allowed by the slit window. From this altitude, the lofty
sixteen-thousand-foot peaks of the Urals appeared as softly
rounded mounds almost lost in the sere browns of the surrounding plains. A thread of a river snaked down through these plains
from the narrow valleys and snowfields of the mountains and
disappeared into the mist and cloud on the horizon. The land
below spoke of peace and serenity; but the height obscured the
hidden missile sites that could fling their deadly cargoes of
thermonuclear death across continents and oceans; hid the military camps and bases scattered across the Asian mainland to meet
the threat of enemies on two fronts.

The weather screen shifted focus to the northwest. Here the
contrast was startling. Stretching far into the north of the continent and out across the Arctic Ocean, the northwestern swell of
the Scandinavian Peninsula was covered with a huge storm that
built even as Teleman watched. A hundred-mile-long streamer of
cloud twisted around the tiny eye of the cyclonic storm sweeping
down across the Great Barrier. All but the foremost edges of the
storm were lost below the horizon, but in his imagination Teleman could picture the whole storm, covering five hundred
thousand square miles on its leading edge, and God only knew
how much in total. On the surface, one-hundred-mile-an-hour
winds would be lashing the ocean into sixty- and seventy-foot
waves to send them crashing onto the northern edges of the continental shelf. Salt spray blown off the crests of the waves would be
turned instantly to ice and would batter to death all but the
strongest ships that had the misfortune to be caught in the storm.
This was an Arctic storm at its worst, a gale that could laugh at
the puny efforts of the largest of its Mid-Atlantic and Caribbean
cousins, a storm even more powerful and deadly than the coastal
typhoons of the China Sea. For the next hour he would watch it
grow through the forward observation slits and on his screen as
he approached the Barents Sea.

Lazily the pilot read the course plot and made a minor correction. He felt the plane bank over, the gulping ramjets running

up with a steady murmur. He checked the instrument panels, all 573 dials, verniers and digital readouts. Airspeed, course fix, engine temperature, fuel, contact point countdown, ambient temperature, internal temperatures in a hundred different locations throughout the aircraft, star fix coordinates, metal flex, accumulators, liquid oxygen generators, batteries, hydraulics, altitude, trim, generators, cameras, blood pressure, acid-base balance, $p^{co2}$, $p^{o}s$, renal function, EKG . . . all checked themselves green on the boards.

Teleman—Major Joseph Teleman, USAF Ret.—lay back in the acceleration couch and relaxed, suffused with the languid feeling of tranquilizers as the Physiological Control and Monitoring System (PCMS) accomplished its programed tasks and he was fully in control of his body again.

The airspeed indicated was slightly over Mach 1.5, with contact less than one hour away. The on-board computers had decided that he was fully capable of handling the aircraft at this relative crawl and had withdrawn all booster drugs. He settled back, one hand casually resting on the finger controls, and enjoyed the comfortable murmur of the engines and the passing scene below.

For the next twenty minutes the reconnaissance plane would drone on across the roof of Soviet Russia, skirting the Moscow anti-aircraft missile defense ring by 250 miles, as it headed for the Barents Sea and rendezvous with the US Navy battle cruiser that would accept the cargo of precious military information.

Above, traveling in overlapping polar orbits at six hundred nautical miles in carefully calculated paths that would circumscribe the earth every thirty minutes, a complex of Advanced SAMOS 3 satellites relayed information between one another and their ground point in Virginia. Shortly, the encoder on board clicked softly to itself and began displaying, in digital shorthand, information on a particularly suspicious ground location. One of the SAMOS 3 satellites had observed a small area of low-level infrared radiation where none had existed before. The location was in the vicinity of Magnitogorsk, the center of the Soviet electronics research.

Teleman smiled grimly. *At last.* He had been searching this entire mission for this patch of infrared as had his sister aircraft the week before. Word had been passed from the Defense Intelligence Agency of the sudden move of a very vital part of the new Soviet missile warhead countermeasures research operation. The testing location had been shifted for some unknown reason; perhaps it had something to do with the latest KGB announcement of a blown Western spy ring. Whether genuine or not, there was no way of knowing, but the fact remained that a large research installation had been moved, almost overnight it seemed. Thoughtfully, he programed the coordinates for his next sweep. Maybe the pieces of this little puzzle would finally begin to fall into place.

But, for the remainder of this flight, it would be a milk run until he orbited the ship still a thousand miles north. Beneath his aircraft he could see the cloud- and snow-covered landscape of northern Russia turning black with its covering of pine. The forest, the taiga of Asian fame, stretched north for four hundred miles without a break—a last holdout of commercial enterprise in the Soviet Union, the home of hundreds of fur trappers and family lumbering concerns, and the deathtrap into which whole divisions of the Moscow Army of the Nazi Wermacht had been lured to their destruction in the winters of 1942 and '43.

Ahead, the terrain of Soviet Russia, slipping by the needle nose of the AR-17, was being covered by a heavy cloud layer. The cover thickened rapidly during the next ten minutes until a solid overcast was spread from horizon to horizon. Teleman reached forward and warmed up the infrared detectors and switched on the radar. The wide-scan radar beam knifed through the clouds to lay the pattern of the land below. Infrared came on-line moments later, laying a composite picture of heat patterns as it hunted through the lower frequencies to build a black and white image on the screen. The white, washed-out picture was quickly highlighted here and there with sharp black dots and patches as the warmer formations jumped out of the blizzard- and storm-covered ground below.

After a further ten minutes, an insistent code pattern containing airspeed and direction corrections appeared on the digital readout screen. Teleman altered course once more to suit the final rendezvous location. As the aircraft settled on to the new course, the code pattern for rendezvous changed to that for the battle cruiser, his contact point for this portion of the mission. Still fifteen minutes short, he nevertheless began the check-out procedure on the transmission batteries.

## CHAPTER TWO

FORTY DEGREES *of frost. Eight degrees below zero F at sea level.* The nuclear-powered *Robert F. Kennedy* came around sharply, bows swinging into the crushing fury of a Force 11 wind, twin screws churning furiously as she clawed her way up a towering wave rising nearly twenty feet above her superstructure, then rocketed down into the pounding waters of the trough. The bows smashed deep into green Arctic waters. Tons of water sprayed over her decks, mast-high, turning instantly to ice that rattled against the bridge like cannon shot. What liquid, not frozen instantly in the frigid air, clung to the bridge, the shrouds, any exposed part of the ship, added yet another microlayer of ice to the tons already weighting her down. Again and again the ship smashed into the waves, each time rising half submerged from an encounter that would have sent lesser vessels to the bottom with all the careless thought of a glacier crushing a hillock beneath its advance.

Fifty- to seventy-foot waves, whipped to a froth by the Arctic gale, marched down from the Great Barrier across two hundred miles of open sea. What was possibly the worst Arctic storm in more than thirty years hunted through the desert wastes of the Arctic in a cyclonic storm of unbelievable proportions.

Formed from a katabatic storm somewhere on the Greenland Icecap and fed by a smaller low pressure area of relatively warmer, moister air, the two centers had met; the colder, moist, and therefore heavier air had settled down on to the glacier. The Greenland Icecap rises from the coast to nearly two thousand feet in the interior. The settling cold air had merely flowed down the eastern side of the icecap, encountered a low-pressure area off the foggy coast into which it rushed, picked up more moisture and speed, and spewed itself out into the Greenland Sea as a full-scale cyclone. Now, the storm, fully built and overpowering everything in its path, was sweeping in a huge curving arc up into the Norwegian and Barents seas.

Lieutenant Commander Peter Folsom swiveled on his high seat as Captain Henly Larkin, commanding officer of the *RFK*, came on to the bridge, peered out through the driving wipers, and shuddered. Folsom indicated the coffee pot and grinned as Larkin poured his famous oversized cup and carefully took a sip of the steaming black liquid as he came over to stand by Folsom.

'How's she look, Pete?'

'A real ball coming up, Captain. The wind is about seventy-five knots and rising. The barometer is 28.52 and still falling—fast. We've had a four-tenths drop in the last half hour.'

'Anything coming in over the weather channel?'

'Thule's forecasting what they call "heavy weather" again. They claim that little breeze two days ago was only a prelude. At least 125-knot winds, possibly higher for this area in the next twenty-four hours.'

Folsom passed over the sheaf of flimsies that had come in since Larkin went off watch four hours before. Larkin took them over to his console and settled into the high stool with a muffled sigh of weariness and began to read. The picture was not good.

Arctic cyclones are not to be fooled with. Any shipping without dire need steered well clear of such storms and even submarines moved down to the two-hundred-foot level to avoid the angry currents and crosscurrents churned up by the furious winds above. Larkin read on. The volume of meteorological information that had been gathered, collated, and disseminated in the past four hours was far more complete than that available to commercial shipping. In addition to the reports from the civilian agency weather satellites, the Department of Defense maintained a series of its own, devoted exclusively to gathering weather information strictly for the military. Larkin therefore had available to him more data about the storm and more accurate projections as to its future course than did commercial shipping. But Larkin had one other thing that commercial captains did not have—strict orders to maintain station in the Barents Sea at all costs, short of losing his ship. However, if it should become clear to Larkin that he was about to lose his ship, it would probably be too late to save her.

Larkin rubbed his eyes and swiveled around to face Folsom at the adjacent panel. 'Ah . . . my aching back. How long till contact?' He peered at his watch and checked it against the chronometer readout above his command console.

'Five minutes to go. Communications tells me everything is set. There shouldn't be any trouble on this end.' Folsom slid out of the seat and walked over to the forward ports and stared out through the revolving screen into the wind- and wave-filled night. The ship crested another wave, tipped, slid and smashed again into the Arctic seas. Folsom hung on to the coaming, riding easily with the ship's motion, and winced involuntarily as solid spray rattled like grapeshot against the tempered glass.

'Thule also said that we can expect snow toward the end. It seems to be one of those blasted Greenland storms, and when this one finally spilled over the edge it found a low-pressure area along the coast and kept coming . . . bringing everything in its path with it.'

Larkin merely grunted as he continued to stare thoughtfully into the storm. His mind was churning with dozens of lines of thought, all ending at one consideration . . . the safety of the ship. Fourteen years of sea duty in every ocean of the world had taught him one certain lesson: the sea can never be trusted. Even the weather satellite system, with its computerized data reduction processes, was not to be trusted completely. There were too many unknowns, too many variables in the billions of cubic miles that comprised the ocean of air and the ocean of water that always obscured the pattern. Larkin had weathered both Mid-Atlantic hurricanes and South Pacific typhoons. He had seen a destroyer almost turned turtle in a South China Sea typhoon off the coast of Taiwan and rode out the Pacific typhoon of '57 in a light cruiser. If nothing else, Larkin had immense respect for the sea. He was worried about this storm. If the predictions were right, it was going to get an awful lot worse before it got better. And, he remembered, it was here in the Barents Sea in 1942 that two lend-lease British destroyers had been sunk by just this same kind of Arctic cyclone. The *RFK* was a much more powerful and stouter ship than those two World War I tin cans—'tin cans' built in a day when they were really not much more than that—but still, every ship, every crew had its limit. One small mistake could be extremely fatal.

He turned to survey the bridge quickly, noting each station manned with all of the ship's electronic and visual eyes and ears turned outward to register the slightest alteration in the storm or the condition of the sea. Radar units quested ceaselessly to pinpoint the most insignificant object revealed by an instant's break in wave or cloud that might turn out to be the conning tower of a submarine or rocket-loaded fighter bomber. For all intents and purposes, the Barents Sea, edging the northern coasts of the Union of Soviet Socialist Republics as well as Norway and Finland, was enemy water. The panel above the ECM—electronic counter-measures—console was lit a bright red, indicating that the highly secret sonar, radar, and infrared jamming devices were in full operation. Any contact with a Soviet vessel—or that of any nationality—would be a matter of pure, blind luck in these seas, but Larkin was not one to trust to luck any more than he trusted the sea.

'Helmsman, course and speed,' he called out. Folsom glanced at him for a moment, then went back to staring out the ports.

'026° at sixteen knots sir.'

Larkin considered a moment. 'Sixteen knots against these headwinds, not bad. Let's cut her back to ten. I don't want to carry any more pressure on that bow patch-up than we absolutely have to have.'

Folsom nodded agreement and called out the changed speed, then ordered communications to make the proper correction in the rendezvous location and time and get it off. As he finished talking, the screen door swung open with a bang and a fur-shrouded figure stumbled in, followed by the banshee shriek of the wind. A howled chorus of 'shut the door' rose from the bridge crew as they swung around as one man from their consoles to glare at the snow-covered apparition. The hatch was jerked from the man's grip by the wind and thudded back against the stops, then just as perversely swung the other way and slammed shut, abruptly ending the noise. Lieutenant Commander Joel

Bridges leaned wearily against the hatch and stripped the Arctic mask from his face with a great deal of care. The mask and his nylon all-weather gear were coated with an inch of solid ice. Bridges worked the zipper on the parka loose and pulled it down. The parka then fell away of its own volition and the ice coating clumped on to the deck plates in thick chunks.

Bridges stood swaying among the ruins of his parka, his face flushed in the sudden ninety-degree temperature change. His expression, as circulation began returning to his legs and arms, was almost comical.

'It's colder than a bitch kitty out there!'

'Now, now, that's no way to talk in the presence of your ranking officers, is it, Lieutenant?' Folsom asked innocently.

Bridges delivered a muffled comment, glaring from the corner of his eyes as he stumbled around in a wobbly circle looking for the coffee. Larkin chuckled and poured coffee for him. 'I take it that it is *cold*. Anyone else out there?'

'No, sir, I sent them in about twenty minutes ago.'

'Good, there is no need to stand watch outside tonight. You can't see anything anyway.'

'Amen. Your eyeballs freeze.' Bridges took the coffee and stumbled over to the second officer's console and pulled himself up into the high seat and began massaging his legs.

Twenty minutes passed slowly, twenty minutes in which the ship fought the angry seas while Larkin calmly continued to study the weather reports and maps displayed by his console. Only the intenseness of his concentration betrayed his worry.

Larkin turned sharply at the buzz of the intercom. Folsom picked up the handset.

'Communications is ready. Shall I have them pipe it up here, sir?'

Larkin nodded. He lit a cigarette and made himself comfortable at his console, then picked up the handset and pressed the button that cut in the secrecy circuits and slipped the ear-plug wire around his ear. Immediately he heard the operator two decks below begin his 'ident' call on the ultratight FM scrambled frequency.

'Got him, sir.'

'Beatle to Target One . . . I read your signal . . . five by five . . . stand by . . . for transmission.'

The characteristically drowsy voice of the reconnaissance pilot came through on the FM channel clearly in spite of the storm and havoc raging in the intervening twenty thousand feet between ship and aircraft. Larkin pressed a third tab and glanced around quickly to make sure the banks of tapes were all running, and then took a long drag at his cigarette.

'Clear, go ahead.'

High-frequency chatter sounded briefly over the handset. The tape reels spun madly and the bridge echoed to the tortured squeal of the telemetry. The guard stood looking straight ahead impassively. Folsom sat on his stool at the executive officer's console and tried to appear disinterested in the little drama being played out at the next console. He did not succeed any more than did the eight other officers and enlisted men on the bridge. Only Larkin knew who was aloft or why. Only the captain of the rendezvous vessel was entrusted with the knowledge of the trite but very true phrase—supersecret mission—so secret that the entire project did not possess a code name. The identification label was changed with every mission flown. Tonight the mysterious pilot and aircraft were known as *Target*. Two weeks ago in the Indian Ocean the name had been *Phoebus*.

Larkin became aware of a faint hissing noise filling the background as the pilot began to speak. For God's sake, he thought, not again. The last rendezvous had taken three hours while the communications section had struggled to maintain contact. For three hours Larkin had steamed a zigzag pattern around a fixed point while the aircraft had flown long, looping orbits around a rotating imaginary point and the ionosphere had wreaked havoc with the radio transmission. For three hours Larkin had sweated blood, knowing that even the vastness of the southern Indian Ocean was not big enough to hide both an aircraft and a large battle cruiser from hostile submarines or roving ASW patrols. Now he was praying that they would not experience similar trouble only 170 miles off the coast of the Soviet Union.

But after a few moments the hissing began to fade and the pilot's voice came through once again, slow and measured but clear:

'Transmission complete . . . fuel load . . . low . . . proceeding to refueling . . . point . . . at minus . . . thirty-five minutes . . . everything in clear . . . working like a charm . . . no . . . trouble from . . . Reds . . . ECM gear . . . working . . . perfectly.'

Larkin hunched forward and spoke directly into the handset. 'It looks as though you won't be completing this sweep . . . or returning to base for a while,' he said.

'We have new orders for you in supplementary transmission coming up. I have been instructed to tell you by voice that you are to review them *after*'—he stressed the word—'refueling. We will remain on station here, waiting for you to report in. The mission should be completed by 1800 hours tomorrow. You will rendezvous with us tomorrow night, same location.'

Larkin paused and unconsciously lowered his voice. 'I have also been instructed to add that this mission is of the highest importance to East-West relations and must be completed at all costs, short of detection.'

'I . . . understand . . .'

Larkin did too, only too well in fact. What he would pass along, locked into the tapes, was an almost impossible task. 'Stand by for transmission.' Larkin keyed the tape decks to transmit to the circling aircraft.

Teleman sat thinking while the encoder clicked out the receipt of the transmission from the ship. He too understood only too well what Larkin's verbal instructions meant. And he was rather puzzled. This certainly did not sound like a routine patrol, the last of this watch before returning to base. Never before had he flown a mission pattern that in any way brought him in range of enemy rockets or aircraft. Heretofore all missions over hostile territory—which was anywhere in the world, including the United States—had been flown at altitudes above eighty thousand feet. He glanced out the slit beside his head and banked the aircraft a few degrees to see the storm below.

Darkness was only an hour away, but the setting sun shed enough light on the cloud cover to highlight the intensity of the storm, even from twenty thousand feet. The storm, seen from above, resembled a devilish badlands: long, twisting canyons and arroyos of saw-edged cloud. The depths of the canyons were filled with hell's own blackness, contrasting sharply with the evil red of the peaks and ridges. The late afternoon sunlight filtered suddenly as he passed beneath a thick blanket of high-flying ice crystals. The sun dipped below the rim of the storm and immediately its light turned a somber gray, deathly solid in its low intensity. In spite of himself, Teleman shivered involuntarily.

'Looks . . . awfully rough . . . down there . . . you be able to hold . . . through that stuff?'

'I don't anticipate any real trouble,' Larkin replied. 'So far it's nothing we can't handle.'

Inwardly though, Larkin was worried. Although the *RFK* was new and built to more exacting specifications than any other ship in history, she had been damaged a week previously. Steaming slowly out of Newport, Rhode Island, Naval Base she had collided with a destroyer in a freak accident. In the heavy fog the destroyer had come off second best, but her sharply raked bow had gashed a hole in the *RFK's* port bow, slashing through several structural members. An emergency patch had been rigged at the almost deserted Portsmouth, New Hampshire, Naval Yards by a skeleton crew and the bow section shored up with temporary braces. This mission was too important to delay and there had been no other ship with the required equipment anywhere within steaming range.

Now, the weather satellite information and photographs that had come in just prior to contact had shown the entire Arctic region as far east as Novaya Zemlya and west to Iceland in for the worst Arctic gale in years—worse in all appearance than the Great Storm of 1942. And now, the *RFK*, less than 170 miles from the Soviet coast and forty miles off Norway's North Cape, was also directly in the storm's track.

'We'll be here,' he said with considerably more confidence than he felt at the moment. The seas were increasing and the stabilizers were just about useless in the heavy waters. He noted that Folsom, bent over the console, had just ordered the RPM's on the engines stepped up to furnish stabilizing air around the hull.

'We are going to start quartering a fifty-mile circuit in fifteen minutes.' Out of the corner of his eye he saw the white flicker of another wave break mast-high and come crashing down against the forward ports 'So we'll be here.'

'Good . . .' The transmission garbled and quickly cleared.

'Say again,' Larkin requested.

'Good . . . take it . . . easy . . . down there . . . see you tomorrow.'

'Right, clear.' Larkin stubbed his cigarette out and got up from the console. He waved to the marine and ordered Folsom to stand down from security. He thought for a moment, leaning against the console, feeling again the crushing weight of responsibility come down over him just as it had the night the destroyer sheared through the bow, or that afternoon off the North Vietnamese coast. He took a deep breath and shook his head reluctantly, then beckoned Folsom to join him at the plotting table, and quickly explained that they would stay on station for another twenty-four hours.

For the next ten minutes they discussed the advantages and disadvantages of various courses that would allow them to take the brunt of the storm in the easiest manner possible. Finally, they settled on a straight run to the northeast that would bring them abreast of the North Cape, some one hundred miles north by 1100 hours. Both were convinced that it would be better to ride directly into the teeth of the gale now, before it unleashed its better than one-hundred-mile-an-hour winds, as it was expected to do late tomorrow. They would then be able to run before the storm, arriving back on station at 1700 hours. This allowed a one-hour lead time for any unexpected delays or heavier seas than predicted.

Folsom picked up the maps and spread them out on the chart table. He drew a fine line in red between their present position and the expected turn-around point north of the Cape.

He pointed with the pencil at the exposed position. 'Actually it might be better to come farther west to bring us under the lee of the Cape.' He waited expectantly for Larkin's answer.

Larkin shoved his cap back and rubbed his forehead. 'Ordinarily, yes. But in this weather, I just don't trust these waters. They shoal too damned easily and the average depth runs less than ten fathoms. If we pick up any more ice, and it looks like we're going to, we'd be in big trouble. No, I think I'd prefer to make the turn in the open sea and take my chances with the wind and waves.'

'You're the boss.' Folsom nodded and bent over the table again to begin the intricate task of plotting a course that would take them into the teeth of eighty- to ninety-knot headwinds that had a tendency to quarter unexpectedly. Even with the latest in inertial gyroscopes aboard, he still had a tricky problem in navigation on his hands—to take them a total of 223 nautical miles in twenty-four hours and bring them back to a starting point less than half a mile wide, all with terrible winds and towering waves that would combine to push the battle cruiser in a myriad of directions during the voyage.

Larkin nodded to himself and turned away, satisfied that the ship was in capable hands with Folsom at the helm. He went below for breakfast.

## CHAPTER THREE

TELEMAN fell off to the north and west at a leisurely pace for the refueling point. Beneath him, the storm-filled Arctic Ocean gave way to the frozen wastes of the Great Ice Barrier, now at its farthest point of advance south in late March, well past the Norwegian outpost of Bear Island. Only the Great North Atlantic Drift, still retaining some of the slightly warmer waters of the Gulf Stream, kept the vast plateau of ice from moving farther south toward the European mainland. Crumpled and torn, the jagged edges of ice near the rim, twisted and warped by the pressure of billions of tons of slowly, insidiously moving ice from its vast interior, threw up blinding sheets of minute ice crystals that filled the frozen air to a height of twenty feet with fiery, needle-sharp spicules that screamed through the pressure ridges and hummocks, which carved them into tortured shapes. A frozen hell from insanity's worst imaginings.

Teleman climbed slowly to one hundred thousand feet and held. Here the air, what little there was of it, was quiet, knifing past the razor-sharp leading edges of his half-extended wings as he flew westward, overtaking the sun. After another hour of flight, the trailing edge of the storm appeared low on the horizon, and within minutes he could see the gray shape of the ice surface below. The low Arctic sun broke suddenly through the edge of the cloud cover that reached westward to Greenland and flooded a two-dimensional pyramid of burnished ice with blood. The sunlight shining through the small observation slit to his right carried no warmth, only the cold glare of death.

He flew on for another twenty minutes, lulled by the muffled sound of the engines working in a throttled-down ramjet mode and by the slow infusion of relaxant drugs seeping into his bloodstream. He was eight hundred miles north of Greenland when the radar contact panel lit suddenly. Instantly the computers responded and the PMC injected a neutralizer followed by a timed release of an Adrenalin derivative that jumped his heart rate to double the normal rate of 72 beats per minute, with a correspondingly increased respiration ratio. Teleman hunched forward, taking in the full signicance of the radar signal and the digital readout that was feeding closing range and speed into the display. At the same time, his body, acting in a blur of motion —a controlled berserk reaction—took over the aircraft and prepared for a series of evasive actions. Teleman knew that the blip on the radar screen could only be the refueling aircraft climbing up to meet him. But this made no difference to his reflex patterns. Friend or foe, he repeated the drill precisely as laid down in his subconscious by intensive training. The digital panel displayed a 'friendly contact' signal and one second later flashed the recognition pattern for the refueling tanker.

The computers stepped down the flow of reaction drugs and Teleman relaxed slightly. He was now in full control of the aircraft and approaching the tanker, still two hundred miles distant, at a closing rate of better than three thousand miles an hour. The radar screen indicated that the craft was a KB-58 tanker. His speed was close to Mach 2, near his limit, and Teleman's was Mach 2.1. The tanker did not slack his speed and Teleman barely caught a glimpse of him as he pulled past and below his nose in a tight turn to take up his station ahead and above.

Only then did Teleman cut back his speed to match that of the KB-58. The boom was out of the tanker and he maneuvered carefully, bringing the aircraft up and just off the boom. Teleman watched it waver in the nebulous slipstream and, judging the right moment, increased power slowly to slip the nozzle into the housing aft of the cockpit. The maneuver was all performed by Teleman. The KB-58 pilot merely brought his straining aircraft up to the one-hundred-thousand-foot altitude for which it had been specially modified with TF-30 fanjets and outboard ramjet wing-tip engines and held her steady. The juggling for position, too precise even for the most advanced computer-controlled instrumentation, was performed by Teleman, who depended upon the extended reach that the controlling drugs provided his body.

When he felt the sharp bang of the nozzle slamming home and saw the safety light go on, he signaled the KB-58 and high-pressure pumps forced the two-hundred-thousand pound cargo of liquid hydrogen into the cryogenic tanks. Eight minutes later the refueling process was complete, and he broke away. Speed was of the essence during these midair refuelings, as both aircraft were totally helpless. Due to the advanced electronic detection and countermeasure equipment carried by Teleman, it was not likely that hostile aircraft would have the capability to track and ambush the two planes, but then in this operation nothing had been left to chance. Once, nearly twelve years before, it had been, and the one in a million gamble had occurred—with disastrous results. The United States Government was determined that it would not happen again.

The KB-58, gleaming and sharply defined in the reddish light, dropped down and pulled ahead. Teleman answered the cocky, rocking wings and watched as the KB-58 pulled into a wide turn to the south that would take it back to its base at Thule. Then he settled into an orbiting pattern and keyed in the contents of the taped orders that Larkin had transmitted from the ship.

For long minutes, Teleman sat silently, waiting for his next command and absorbing the message encoded on the tape while the aircraft described a vast orbit nearly fifty miles in diameter. When he finished, he sat for a few moments thinking that his orders amounted to international blackmail on a grand scale.

From all outward appearances, the Soviet Union and the United States had been moving toward a rapprochement ever since the days of the Cuban Missile Crisis, when both nations, and indeed the world, had teetered on the brink of the nuclear abyss. Teleman knew that, although the outward hostilities had been submerged fairly well from public view, they had not disappeared. Now it was a much more subtle thrust and counterthrust. The Cold War had become economic war; carefully conducted war in which both great nations vied for the largest slice of world trade and world influence. Espionage had increased to such an extent that close to one percent of the national budget of both countries went to support their numerous 'spy' establishments. Overt hostilities were engineered and carried out through third and fourth parties as insurgency-counterinsurgency wars in Southeast Asia, the

Middle East, and Africa testified. But lately the world had tired of playing patsy for these two giants.

Both NATO and the Warsaw Pact had all but died in the past two years. The Southeast Asian nations had subtly declared that neither Western nor Eastern influences were welcome any longer, only trade. To reinforce their new demands, they had formed the Southeast Asian Common Market, in effect a revival of the old Southeast Asian Sphere of Greater Co-Prosperity dominated and led by, naturally enough, Japan. What could not be achieved by war was finally won by the ancient oriental traits of patience and discipline. Since the Great Chinese Cultural Revolution had elevated Mao Tse-tung to the status of a semidivinity—a new Confucius—the flagging Chinese resolve had been stiffened by the infusion of a new spirituality into a people that had always existed in its soul. This newly revived and expansionist character, foiled by the SACM, had turned on the Soviet Union for the fuel of hatred to replenish the Communist Revolution. The Soviets had been challenged in fact as well as word for the leadership of the Communist world and for the 'Uncommitted nations.' Fortunately enough for the world, the smaller developing nations had tired of the empty promises of Communism, found the exhortations and money of the United States to be quite unapplicable to their own problems, and discovered that on a planet where the farthest neighbor was no more than eight hours away by supersonic transport and milliseconds by communication satellites, that even nationalism no longer held the key. Suddenly the wave of nationalist sentiment of the 1960s was dead.

By the mid-1970s a new trend—the first tentative edgings toward international cooperation that far surpassed that of the 1930s and completely disregarded the regional blocism of the late 1940s and early 1950s—was gaining momentum.

And so, rebuffed like the other two giants, Red China turned again, as historically she had done for thousands of years, to fomenting trouble on her frontiers—her Asian frontiers. And not without some small justification.

Between the Soviet Union and Red China stretches nearly two thousand miles of common border. That this borderland includes some of the most worthless land on the face of the earth made absolutely no difference to either party—just as it never had in four hundred years of struggle. In the mid-1800s the troops and diplomats of the Romanov tsars, after their rebuff at the Dardanelles by Britain and France during the Crimean War, turned their attentions toward the still mythical lands of Cathay. By the turn of the century they had managed to annex some fifty million square miles of former Chinese territory in a fashion that not even the wily Ch'ing emperors completely understood. That fifty million square miles of desolate and useless land remained a bone of contention ever since. Most of it consisted of a northeastern extension of the Himalayas called the Tien Shan Range; the Takla Makan, a cold, wind-swept, and totally barren desert ranging from three to six thousand feet in altitude; and the equally desolate and useless western reaches of the Gobi Desert. Since the late 1950s, China and the Soviet Union had continually fought a series of small-scale battles up and down the border and throughout the land on either side; the Chinese side was known as Sinkiang and the Russian, the Kazakh S.S.R. So isolated was this area, so far removed from human civilization was this region, that very little word of conflict ever leaked out to the Western world. Teleman recalled that it was in this same area, along these same borders, that in 1938-39 the Soviets and the Japanese fought a small-scale war—so small in fact that in 1940 over three thousand Soviet officers were decorated for war action—and promptly shipped off as badly needed reinforcements for Soviet troops in Finland.

As Soviet and Chinese relations worsened following the de-Stalinization campaign of the Khrushchev regime, the intensity and frequency of Sino-Soviet border clashes increased until finally, less than a year ago, both sides, in a carefully secreted meeting, worked out a compromise that was to have settled the entire affair. It seemed that the Chinese had already broken their side of the bargain.

Teleman's orders directed him to fly to the Sinkiang-Kadakh border where the Red Chinese were reported to have attacked in strength. It appeared to Western observers, from the sketchy reports available, that the Chinese had pulled a surprise attack and caught the Russians flat-footed. They were steadily being pushed back all along the border and Chinese troops were reported to be firmly established on Soviet territory. Both sides were extremely quiet about the fighting, as indeed they always had been. The war was being conducted on a non-nuclear basis at the moment, rather a gentlemen's agreement, although Teleman could not think of two less likely candidates.

Teleman thoughtfully considered the implications of such an attack as he continued to enjoy a rare moment of relaxation. If the war was being fought without the use of nuclear weapons, the Chinese would be at a distinct advantage. They could mobilize one field army at a strength equal to the entire Soviet forces. The Soviets now must be feeling the same way about the Chinese that the United States had felt about the North Vietnamese and the Viet Cong, and, before them, the magnificent French Army about the Viet Minh. The Chinese troops were equipped and trained for this type of 'conventional' guerrilla war, a conventional war that involved the proper use and maneuvering of small battle units in guerrilla tradition, small but in vast numbers of independently acting units. Units able to hit and run, always edging and prodding the Soviet forces into territory where the Chinese troops could overwhelm the less mobile Soviet troops by sheer weight of numbers.

The Soviet generals and political leaders would be in Moscow fingering their arsenal of nuclear missiles and bombs, just as the United States generals had done in Southeast Asia, knowing that they could never use them unless the Chinese did so first, or unless a disastrous defeat endangering the entire nation appeared imminent. They would learn, thought Teleman, just the way the United States had, how best to fight such a war—by practical experience. All the reading and observing could never furnish what one year's defeats and questionable victories would provide.

The Soviets could ill afford to risk the loss of prestige that would follow if the world knew that the stepson was challenging the stepfather, a very untutored and ill-equipped stepson at that. The State Department and the Pentagon apparently felt that, if the Soviet Union should wind up on the losing side, it would not take long for them to run screaming to the United States for help.

And why not? he thought sarcastically. Everyone else did as soon as their backs were to the wall. Why should they be different? For the moment the Soviets did not want it known that the much poorer Red Chinese had had the effrontery to attack one of the strongest nations on earth and the leader of World Communism to boot, at least spiritually. Seven to five, he thought, the State Department wants to know how deeply both are involved so that they can start cooking up one of their own brews to ease the pressure somewhere else in the world. Perhaps an announcement in the United Nations General Assembly, or better yet a call to two (tongue in cheek) distinguished nations to settle their differences before nuclear bombardments began would steal a march on both as well as promote general world condemnation. The other nations, particularly the non-nuclear nations, had become very leery of the big three of late whenever they had differences to settle in a nondiplomatic manner. After Cuba and the Tel Aviv incident, Teleman did not blame them the least bit.

Another thought occurred to him. The Red Chinese, who had taken some pretty embarrassing reverses in Africa and Southeast Asia in the past five years and who were presently torn apart internally, would not want their preoccupation with the Soviets widely known. Although they could put a much larger army into the field than could the Soviets, a correspondingly greater portion of their total national effort would have to be devoted to supporting that army. And the Chinese Central Government would not logically want to risk their very shaky position in China at the moment. The neo-warlords would certainly be ready and able to take advantage of the situation. If the war got too far out of hand, the Chinese could be damn sure that the United States and the Soviet Union would in due course make plenty of trouble for them elsewhere. The more Teleman thought about it, the more he was ready to lay odds that the Soviets had initiated this particular fight by baiting the Chinese somehow. They must be realizing full well that they could not much longer tolerate the supercilious attitude of the present Peking leadership. That the Russians might have bitten off more than they could chew was also quite possible. Teleman shook his head at the childishness and complexity of international politics and began to set up his flight plan.

The orders directed him to proceed to the war area—the desolate and rugged hills of the northern Sinkiang plateau and border region—some of the worst territory for fighting a war in the world, territory that made the Dakota badlands look like a children's playground, he thought.

Teleman made the necessary final corrections and keyed the program into the computer. Seconds later the aircraft broke out of its orbiting mode and headed westward on a course that would intercept the 90° meridian. He would pick up the meridian over Uedineniya Island in the Arctic Sea, less than seventy-five miles from the Soviet Mainland of the Taimyr Peninsula. He would then cross the Soviet Union from north to south at 150,000 feet with negative 4 radar disruption to avoid Soviet observation.

For the next hour Teleman sat staring out the observation slit at the frozen wastes of the Arctic slipping past below. He sat and stared and thought about the coming mission. He had no qualms about performing it, had no questions about its importance. But he was puzzled about the motives involved on either side. It was not spelled out in the orders, but years of intensive training, covering a good bit more than flying this aircraft, had taught him that he must seek the reason behind anything the opposition did. He knew that he could not rely on the busy clerks and service officers in the State Department to read the correct interpretations into the intelligence that he gathered. It was, by its very nature, often nothing more than a broad overview. And then again, sometimes, the most minute details were found that brought the entire picture into focus. The trouble with the State Department was its size. Its thousands of employees were all too often engaged simply in running a bureau where forty thousand people worked. His own agency had fallen into the same pattern of late.

There were just too many people involved, too many in decision-making positions, too many incapable of making the correct decisions or, for that matter, any decisions at all. Too many that spent all of their time pushing their own ideas, interpretations, and motives no matter how they conflicted with the evidence at hand. Nor were the problems of bureaucracy the problems of the United States alone. The interrupted mission to locate the new Soviet electronics research center after its recent move was a prime example. The present theory popular in his agency was that A. Sovulov Semechastky had been responsible. Semechastky was Second Party Secretary and he had come up the hard way in the new generation of Soviet leaders. He also had a son who was general manager of the Electronics Assembly Plant No. 2 in Magnitogorsk. The cocktail talk around Moscow was that Semechastky had been pressured by his son to shift the location of the research center closer to the assembly plant, ostensibly for reasons of efficiency. Covertly, for reasons of increasing family power. Several million roubles would be spent in making such a change, but it was reportedly common knowledge that Semechastky, Jr., was about to be named the new director of the research center.

Teleman could confirm the rumor by photographs from 120,000 feet that would identify the make, model, and, if lucky, the license plate number of the automobile in the factory manager's parking space.

Teleman sighed. Such was the stuff of modern spying. License plates from 120,000 feet. He knew that he must look for similar signs along the Kazakh-Sinkiang border. In the meantime, he had nearly six thousand miles to go and it looked like a long day. He keyed the computer and PCMS into action and slept.

## CHAPTER FOUR

IN 1964, as the A-11 project—later to become the SR-71 Fighter Interceptor in an attempt to cover up its reconnaissance and intelligence-gathering role—came to conclusion, it had become extremely clear that the United States was badly in need of a stop-gap method of acquiring intelligence information beyond the limited capabilities of the original SAMOS project. SAMOS was a classified Air Force satellite system, launched from 1958 to 1972 from both Cape Kennedy and Vandenberg AFB near Santa Barbara, California. Always shrouded under heavy secrecy, SAMOS—and later the expanded ADVANCED SAMOS—had one and only one objective: to keep an eye on Soviet and Red Chinese territory.

The state of the art in photographic techniques, lenses, and films in the early part of the project's life was such that only fairly gross data could be obtained. The SAMOS satellites were at first limited to one-hundred-nautical-mile orbits in an equatorial path that covered, at best, only limited portions of USSR terriory. But as more powerful launch vehicles became available and as the Vandenberg launch site was completed, the SAMOS satellites were launched with increasing frequency into polar orbits of altitudes from six to ten thousand miles, which provided coverage of Communist territory every two hours. By increasing the number of satellites in orbit and launching them into carefully prepared, overlapping orbits, complete coverage every three minutes was obtained.

Sensor technology increased quickly as industry was funded for billions of dollars. From the first crude infrared and black and white lenses, which were limited to coverage of open, daylight, cloudless territory, faster films, computerized programing, sensitive day-night television cameras, tape storage, and widely dispersed, secretly located mobile and fixed ground stations continually received microsecond-duration transmissions that were impossible to locate and fix, and relayed them to a central monitoring station deep in the Virginia hills. From there, especially prepared abstracts were transmitted to Washington.

But, even with sensors able to photograph a Russian guard sneaking a smoke on duty at the Number 3 gates at Kasputin Yar, or record the identification numbers on the locomotive and each of the freight cars moving along the Trans-Siberian Railroad with supplies for the naval base at Vladivostock, there were often, all too often, sites and areas spotted that needed further investigation.

In the 1950s, before the SAMOS satellites were available, this portion of the job had been performed in large part by a series of aircraft, the three most important of which were the U-2 and the reconnaissance versions of the B-47 and B-66. But in 1960, just prior to the ill-fated Paris Summit Conference, a U-2 had been shot down over the Soviet Union with a new type of missile. Nikita Khrushchev had used the incident to stop reconnaissance flights over Soviet territory. For some years after, the U-2 had continued to be operated over Red Chinese territory by the Nationalist Chinese, in spite of the ever-increasing number of the outmoded aircraft shot down and destroyed.

By the late 1960s, both the United States and the USSR realized that the continual surveillance of each other's territory by their respective 'spy-in-the-sky' satellites was doing a great deal of harm to their defense efforts. Such a great deal of harm that both nations on differing occasions were able to report such incidents as the explosion of a nuclear test rocket and the resulting destruction of a complete test complex—and several key officials—in the Soviet Union, and the similar explosion of the highly secret nuclear rocket-engine project at Jackass Flats, Nevada, before the capitols were aware that the disaster had occurred.

As sensor technology improved, steps were taken to move highly classified work into underground or camouflaged locations not visible to the spying satellites. It was this problem that brought several key officials, the director of the Central Intelligence Agency, the Chief of Staff, the secretaries of State and Defense, and the president of a large aircraft corporation together in the President's office in late 1967. From this meeting had come the decision to build an aircraft that would carry many of the same sensors that were incorporated in the Advanced SAMOS. The aircraft to be designed would have long loiter time—on the matter of days rather than hours—coupled with high speed and an extremely high altitude ceiling, well beyond the range of high-altitude anti-aircraft rockets.

For two years the lights had burned twenty-four hours a day on the back lot of the aircraft plant, the same lights that had burned for the U-2 and the A-11. Only the two hundred men virtually hand-building the aircraft ever knew what was being built, and of these, only five knew the reason why. A specially constructed and programed computer was used to design and refine the basic structure of the aircraft taking shape in the 'skunk works', as the back lot of the aircraft plant, the same lights that had burned evidence at all times, hard-bitten men from the AP's. They brooked no attempts to cross the gate and were as likely to level a shotgun at a general as a wandering employee. It was contrary to normal American industrial security procedures, usually unobtrusively present, but it was thought better to be safe than sorry.

On the day the aircraft was rolled out, shrouded in nylon and airlifted to Edwards Air Force Base, there was no celebration, no rejoicing over a job well done, only relief that it was at last out of the plant and gone. A Lockheed C-141 flew the parts of the aircraft to the desert flight-testing base at the foot of the Sierra Nevadas, and it was quickly rolled into a hangar and disassembled, then trucked deeper into the Mohave to Gillon Advanced Test Site on the northern rim of the desert. Here, in a specially constructed and closely guarded base annex, the aircraft was reassembled and the testing began.

Teleman's first look at the aircraft came on a day three years after he had signed his contract with the CIA and entered training. Previously, he had served as a reconnaissance pilot with the U.S. Air Force during the Vietnamese war, with some eighty-three missions to his credit before the armistice. He was a bachelor, with no more than the usual family ties and a fierce devotion to his country that had been tested and found fully complete in a North Vietnamese prison camp. His three years of training, covering a range of subjects from aeronautical engineering to geopolitics, and including education equivalent to a masters degree in the psychology of political power and government structures, had taught him more than he had ever suspected there was to learn.

Teleman stood in the hangar that August day, feeling the fierce heat of the Mohave sun burning down on his back. It was nothing compared to the white heat of excitement generated by the sleek black needle of an airplane that reached back into the gloom of the hangar.

He shook his head wonderingly as he walked back along its DC-9 length. The body was 120 feet long, yet nowhere was it more than eight feet in diameter. The fuselage carried the distinctive contours of a supersonic aircraft: a pinched waist, Coke bottle shape halfway along its length. The wing began less than ten feet from the tip of the nose. Starting at a width of half an inch, it grew to two feet at mid-length, where it then flared out into a severely flattened and cambered parallelogram. Twin vertical stabilizers rode the wing, reaching four stories toward the ceiling of the cantilevered hangar. Each was demurely painted with the symbol of the United States, a six-by-nine-foot representation of the American flag. Other than that red, white, and blue flag, the aircraft was a gleaming black, a deadly killer whale of an aircraft for all that she was completely unarmed.

Teleman climbed the ladder affixed to the fragile side, half expecting the fuselage to collapse under his weight. He wriggled down into the cockpit and stretched out in the same acceleration couch he had sat in so many times in the mock-up at Elgin AFB. Every instrument, every control was exactly where it should be. With eyes closed he ran through the complete check-out of the instrument and computer panels. The only difference that he could detect was the complete satisfaction of sitting in the actual aircraft rather than the fiberglass and plywood mock-up.

Teleman was the first to fly the A-17. She was rolled out the next day and he climbed into the cockpit again and wriggled down into the couch, feeling the soft push of the oil-filled cushions against his back as the couch adjusted itself to his body. He made the first flight without the PCMS—the Physiological Control Monitoring System—in operation and the aircraft was all his to control. Teleman taxied to the far end of the runway and set the brakes. Then he ran the engines up slowly to full-military-rated thrust. The two great Pratt & Witney TRR-5e turbo-ram-rocket engines took two minutes to build thrust to the maximum allowable for takeoff, nearly 53,000 pounds apiece. Teleman lay in the acceleration couch wondering at the tremendous vibration that shook every rivet, every seam in the entire aircraft until his teeth ached. Then he released the brakes. And in spite of its two-hundred-thousand-pound dead weight, the A-17 bounded forward. He was off the runway before he realized it. Automatically his body went through all the motions: gear up and locked, engines throttled back to low cruising speed of 470 knots, ground control tuned to 126.6 Mc, eyes sweeping the instrument panels. All instruments were reading into the green, and for a moment he ignored the check list and concentrated on getting the feel of the aircraft.

While the chase planes took up their stations around him, he tentatively tried the control system and whistled excitedly as the A-17 responded with all the firmness of an F-4 Phantom. Then test control was on the radio demanding to know if he had started through the check list yet. Regretfully he dropped back into the proper pattern while his two chase pilots, one on either side, grinned at each other from their stations well back and below his tail assembly.

For the next year, Teleman got to know the A-17 better than he had ever known any other aircraft. Under the supervision of the design engineers, he took apart and reassembled the aircraft. Then he took the A-17 up for hours on end, always flying the same tight pattern at one hundred thousand feet, well above the allow-able levels for commercial planes. Gradually, as he came to know exactly what the airplane would do, flight altitudes and speeds were increased until he was flying routinely at Mach 5 and two hundred thousand feet.

Now he was nearly on his own. He spent so many hours in the aircraft that without the log he would have lost all count. Of the hours spent cramped in the cockpit, sitting in the closely guarded hangar flying computer-devised emergency conditions, he did lose track. At the end of the year he came to feel that the A-17 was an extension of himself. And then the medical people moved in to make it so.

It had been recognized when the A-11 cum SR-71 was completed that man had just about reached his limits in controlling his own aircraft. The A-11 was capable of Mach 3 and nearly Mach 4 by the time the Pratt & Witney J-58 engines had been up-rated to their fullest extent. The A-11 was only marginally effective as an interceptor aircraft. At Mach 3, fifty miles was needed to complete a 180° turn. Almost 90 percent of the aircraft was composed of fuel tanks and her cruising range was severely limited at speeds above Mach 1.5, allowing little or no loiter time to contact a target. Because of the immense fuel load needed to keep her in the air, her reconnaissance payload, and therefore her cameras and other sensors, were severely limited also. In effect, and compared to the A-17, she was little help to the satellite surveillance system. Some stopgap measure was needed so that aircraft could spend time over enemy territory without being detected and could gather the smallest details necessary until large, manned satellites could be placed in orbit—still four years in the future.

For nearly ten years the X-15 series of rocket craft had been providing behavior and engineering data on hypersonic aircraft. The X-15 was used as the basic design for the A-17. The X-15 was rocket-powered, and this provided the tremendous speeds necessary—but powered flight time was limited to a few minutes' duration. The A-17 needed days of flight time.

The turbojet engine is the most efficient of all propulsion systems for speeds between Mach .9 and Mach 2.5, where fuel load, speed, range, and weight are the critical factors. Beyond Mach 2.5 and one hundred thousand feet, the ramjet becomes the most efficient. Beyond 12,000 feet, where the air is too thin to support even the ramjet, the rocket engine, with its self-contained oxidizer, becomes the most efficient.

To avoid Soviet anti-aircraft missiles, the A-17 needed an altitude greater than 125,000 feet. Since the late 1950s, a combination of the three types of propulsive systems had been the research goal of aeronautical research laboratories all across the world. The approach finally adapted to the A-17 was the U.S. Air Force concept called the TURBO-RAM-ROCKET. Below eighty thousand feet and Mach 2.5, the twin power plants in the A-17 functioned as turbojets—air sucked in through the inlet and forced into a combusion chamber, where it mixed with fuel, burned fiercely and the hot gas was forced past a turbine and expelled from the nozzle. The turbine was in turn coupled to the compressor behind the air inlet to compress air and force it into the combustion chamber. An improvement was made on the basic system by adding another stage in front of the compressor assembly called a fan. The fan was just that. Huge blades, coupled to and spun by the turbine, pulled in far more air than the combustion process needed. The excess air was ducted out the side of the engine casing to add as much as 30 percent more thrust.

The turbofan, as it was properly called, was capable of pushing the A-17 to speeds above Mach 2.5. Depending upon the altitude and various atmospheric conditions that necessitated the change —somewhere above Mach 2.5 to 3—the engine switched from the turbojet mode to ramjet. It was in this versatility that the twin engines differed radically from earlier jet aircraft engines. These assemblies are composed of a thick disk of high-strength steel alloy upon which are mounted cambered blades. The blades are twisted to assume an airfoil shape. In the usual turbojet engine, these blades are mounted rigidly. The turbine assembly is constructed the same way and the blades are made of various materials, selected to withstand temperatures in excess of 1600°F as the hot gases exit from the burner chamber. As a rule of thumb, Teleman had been taught, the hotter the temperature of the gases leaving the burner—the Turbine Inlet Temperature (TIT)—the greater the thrust developed by the engine. The A-17's TIT was in excess of 3200 degrees.

To allow the power plant to enter the ramjet mode, the blades were mounted upon variable stator disks and could be turned edge-on to the airstream. In addition, the air inlet plug, a large rounded cone of metal mounted in front of the air inlet, could be moved forward to increase the air compression.

A ramjet engine works by ramming air into its combustion chamber at high speeds, where it is mixed with fuel and ignited by a glow plug. Because the ramjet must have a certain flow velocity of air before it will begin to operate, it usually must be carried aloft by another engine to the proper speed and altitude. But once in the thin reaches above eighty thousand feet, the two engines, now operating as ramjets, far surpass the potential and efficiency of the turbojet or turbofan.

A ramjet of this efficiency has a rather narrow operating 'envelope.' When the air inlet plug is rammed forward to compress the air while the compressor blades are turned edge-on to the airstream, a carefully designed tolerance between plug and inlet must be maintained to provide the maximum flow of air to the combustion chamber for the altitude and speed. This tolerance mechanically limits the altitudes and speed beyond which the ramjet may be operated in direct proportion to the growing lack of atmosphere. Beyond 170,000 feet, Teleman could elect, if the extra speed and altitude were needed, to go to the rocket mode.

Now, clamshell doors closed down the area ahead of the combustion chamber—or burner ring in the case of the A-17 engines—and liquid oxygen was fed directly into the burner ring to mix with the fuel—liquid hydrogen—thereby providing a rocket engine that was capable of taking the A-17 to Mach 5.9, only two thousand miles per hour less than would be needed to achieve sub-orbit. Teleman had never had occasion to use the rocket mode except on practice missions. It was a last-ditch stand when all else failed. The rocket mode could use six hours worth of carefully metered fuel in two minutes of burning time.

Most experienced military pilots who had received their training during the Vietnamese War were now edging toward the age where their efficiency was slowly being whittled away by the heavy demands placed upon them by their aircraft. Many had gone into the Vietnam War well past the age that a World War II flight surgeon would have considered them capable of controlling even the relatively slower and much less technically complicated fighter aircraft of that period. The younger pilots who had received their baptism of combat flying in the mid-1960s had left the service in droves at the end of the war to answer the lure of high salaries and lifetime sinecure in commercial airlines, which were expanding tremendously in the wake of the giant airliners, supersonic transports, and rapidly growing travel markets.

The human organism is still the most reliable of all mechanisms in spite of the strides that had been made in automation. Rather than load the aircraft down with servo-mechanisms and complicated gear to perform many of the tasks that the pilot could do, the designers had opted for the human factor.

The A-17 had been on the threshold of man's ability to control under the difficult and microsecond decision points that had to be reached and gated properly when the aircraft was closing on its target at nearly four thousand miles an hour. The elapsed time from the moment a ground target—often less than a hundred feet across—came into sight until the A-17 had left it behind was often no more than four seconds. During this time, the information displayed on the screens had to be accepted, interpreted, a decision for action made, and the decision implemented; all with enough time remaining to allow the cameras and other recording devices to do their job.

Even in those instances where circumstances dictated that Teleman could loiter the aircraft over the target and select his objectives, someone had to decide what should be recorded, what must be searched for to make the picture complete, and handle the volumes of data that poured in, constantly interpreting, redeciding and shifting objectives—and often targets. No computer could handle this job.

Teleman was trained in the use of certain psychic energizer drugs of the amphetamine and lysergic acid families that could boost his body system output to fantastic heights in relation to normal physiological response. The LSD derivatives extended his powers of concentration and, through their hallucinogenic effect, made him feel that he was actually part of the aircraft. They also increased his comprehension and ability to deal with a multitude of facts in a very short time.

The amphetamines provided the same effect for his bodily responses, increasing his reaction time and slowing his time sense to compensate for the demands of the aircraft's speed.

Teleman's physiological and biochemical status was monitored constantly during the mission through a specially tailored system of instruments blended together to form the Physiological Control and Monitoring System. At the start of the mission, an intravenous catheter was inserted into the superior vena cava vein through a plug implanted surgically in his shoulder. A glass electrode was brought into intimate contact with his bloodstream at this nearest acceptable point to the heart. Through the electrode a series of minute pulses, set up by an electrochemical reaction with his blood, informed the computer continually of his body status. The computer was programed to receive inputs directly from various parts of the aircraft's controlling instrumentation that, coupled with the *in vivo* status reports, determined the time and dosage of the drugs he received. If the instrumentation, directed by the flight plan or by instructions from Teleman, called for a state of physiologically alert and expanded consciousness, proper drugs were fed into his bloodstream through the catheter and his body responded accordingly. Because of the duration of the flights, often lasting six to seven days, when Teleman was not needed to respond to specific tasks, the computer instructed the PCMS to feed in barbiturate derivatives and he slept. Teleman had once calculated that at least 65 percent of all of his missions were spent sleeping.

Although great pains had been taken to develop a high tolerance in Teleman to the drugs he was constantly being infused with, he was thoroughly poisoned by the end of a mission.

In short, Teleman was carefully tailored to the aircraft and its missions. The reach the drugs allowed was marginal, yet enough to provide the control needed to handle his craft as no other airplane had ever been flown. Drugs kept him awake, or put him to sleep, instantly. Others kept him at the peak of alertness for as long as required and his mind focused on his mission, his instruments, and his aircraft.

## CHAPTER FIVE

THE GREAT BEND in the Ob River, one hundred miles east of the Siberian city of Tomsk, lay 180,000 feet below when the PCMS nudged Teleman out of sleep. Within three seconds he was awake and scanning the information displayed on the screen. The Electronics Countermeasures (ECM) bank had detected a series of searching radar beams within the past few minutes. Teleman got busy with the source detectors, concentrating closely on the sweep of the searching finger on the ECM screen. So far the radar beams were searching below eighty thousand feet, well below his present altitude.

After a few minutes of concentrated work, he tracked the radar signals to their location—about where he had suspected. Four hundred miles farther down the Ob was the ancient city of Novosibirsk, one of the oldest of the tsarist Siberian exile camps. Now it was a booming industrial and mining center, containing one of the largest Soviet air bases. Novosibirsk was located 1800 miles north of the Soviet-Chinese border, and he suspected that the local commander of this tempting target was feeling just a bit jumpy this close to a hot war.

At the moment it appeared to be nothing more than routine searching by omni-radar. But the closer he approached to Novosibirsk, the more intense the weaving net of radar became and the greater the search altitude. For a minute his feeling of apprehension tightened, and Teleman wondered if they were on to him.

Fifteen minutes later he was approaching the northern rim of the Altai Mountain chain that ringed the western rim of the Mongolian Plateau. Beneath, the ground was still shrouded in darkness, sparsely broken by patches of light signifying inhabited communities. As he flew farther across the mountain range the lights became more and more scattered, until finally they ceased altogether. Now, far on the eastern horizon, he could make out the darker band of horizon that in less than an hour would be touched by the first tinges of dawn.

The night-light television cameras displayed a scene of hellish grandeur in the uninhabited recesses of this most desolate of mountain ranges. The Altai range sprawled to three hundred miles wide on its north-south axis, with peaks of thirteen thousand feet and higher thrusting jaggedly into the black sky. On either side of the range, deep, forbidding stretches of badland had been strewn about as if by a giant's hand. The southern reach of badland and foothill was Teleman's immediate destination, the stretch of land between the Altai and the smaller, but no less lofty, Tarbagatai range. More out of curiosity than anything else, he cranked the image up, increasing the magnification and resolution on the electronic telescopes until he was watching a strip of land less than three hundred yards wide slipping past. He was still on the northern face of the range, the gentler side, if that term could be applied to this waste of rock and ice. A few stunted trees, in miniature, appeared here and there. But nowhere could he find a trace of human habitation. This range of mountains was so barren that it was shunned even by the nomadic tribes of Mongolian sheepherders who drew a living from the wastes of the Gobi.

For the next half-hour the A-17 passed over the mountains thirty-six miles below, until, on the eastern horizon, Teleman could make out the first indications of the approaching dawn. It would still be another hour and a half before the sun would reach into the valleys and canyons of the Tien Shan ahead, but the aircraft, reacting to the carefully prepared flight plan, began to throttle back and lose altitude.

For long minutes Teleman watched the far-off ground sliding past; he was too slept out to sleep any longer and loath to request a barbiturate from the PCMS. As he sat debating with himself, the radar panel blipped for attention and projected a stream of swiftly flowing data that told Teleman that a flight of Soviet fighters was patrolling at thirty thousand feet. Teleman flipped a number of switches and got the radar tracking to trace their flight patterns. They were ahead and below nearly 130 miles south when first spotted. He was less than two hundred from the confluence of the Soviet, Mongolian, and Chinese borders and, as he guessed, the planes were merely another border patrol on a dawn sweep. Shortly, he was over the border into Red China, still at 140,000 feet and watching the Tarbagatai Mountains rounding on the horizon.

His target was now three hundred miles distant and Teleman assumed control of the aircraft. He throttled back and began losing altitude swiftly. The flight plan called for two long passes, one at a hundred thousand feet to survey the terrain and the other at forty thousand feet for close-ups. He was feeling extremely uneasy about the low-altitude pass, and the closer he approached to the target area the more uncomfortable he became. When the altimeters indicated one hundred thousand feet, he leveled off and cut his speed back still more to Mach 1.2, until he was barely crawling up on the Sinkiang highlands.

Twenty minutes to contact. The twisted, narrow Tarbagatai Mountain range slid behind and he was over the rugged highlands that edged the Gobi Desert. The rugged land of the Sinkiang plateau sped by as he slanted in. He started a long, seventy-five mile turn that would bring him on to a heading of 212° and into position to begin his search pattern along the border. As a safety precaution Teleman began to crank the radar outward to its full range of sixteen hundred miles and instructed the computer to keep watch and report anything that rose above eighty thousand feet. Then he turned his attention to the ECM console and began to narrow down the counterdetection radar cover to an area less than five miles across. All down the 90° meridian Teleman had maintained a fifty-mile diameter ring, not enough to attract attention at the altitude he had been holding, but enough to prevent accidental detection.

Ten minutes to contact. All detection systems were silent. The low light-level television cameras were showing him apparent one-mile altitude shots along his flight path for ten miles on a side. He could make out no sign of life, no roads or tracks or signs of human habitation. A few minutes before, he had left the desert and scrublands behind as the terrain climbed to eight thousand feet and became grasslands, depending for their meager water supply on the swift rivers flowing down out of the Tien Shan and its foothills. The winter was fierce, but the scouring winds had kept the sloping hillsides relatively free of snow below seven thousand feet. The plateau would rise another two to three thousand feet before cresting and beginning to flow downward toward the Kazakh border seventy miles west.

Fifty miles due east of his present position lay the Chinese city of Urmachi, probably the staging point for Chinese troops fighting in the hinterlands below. Off to the southeast glinted the frozen surface of the Kara Nor that would mark a rough position from which he would make a sharp turn to the northwest and fly up to the first checkpoint to pick up the star-fix coordinates for the border sweep.

As he made the turn the night-light TV cameras blanked for a moment, shifting resolution and iris assemblies as the sun began to brighten the snow-splotched landscape. He could still discern no sign of troop movements, or of life, period. But he knew he would, soon enough.

Now he was less than ten miles inside the Kazakh border, roughly paralleling the line the Soviets were reported to be holding. A swollen river rushing out of the hills, snow covered now, but green in the spring and early summer, slipped tantalizingly past on the ground surveillance screen. The countryside was deserted because of the winter and the war, but in more peaceful and warmer times, Mongolian and Tartar sheepherders shared the valleys, fresh steppe grass, and frequent small rivers from the mountains. In normal times they drove their flocks into the region for the long summer pasturage, peacefully not interfering with one another. Now, he knew, the valleys below were full of radar sites, long-range missile and artillery positions, and troop concentrations of both sides.

A range of pockmarked hills marched across the land that was beginning to fall away into a long valley stretching westward to the border. Abruptly the scene swam as the aircraft navigational sensors locked on to the proper stars and altered the course of the fleeting shadow until it was solidly on the wire. For the next hour the A-17 tacked back and forth across the irregular border, defined only by the series of star-fix coordinates held in magnetic tape.

Teleman had completed the first pass at one hundred thousand feet over the border city of Tahcheng and negotiated the turn-around point some sixty miles north. In manual control again, he was very carefully edging the aircraft down to forty thousand feet, the lowest he had ever flown over enemy territory. He knew that he could be sighted visually by either side and hoped that the lack of radar fixes would be thought due to opposition counter-measures. Just in case, he warmed up the decoy rigs and slapped them on to standby. If radar beams came questing after him, their distinctive pulse patterns could be analyzed. The ECM would then broadcast high-frequency radio signals up and down several bandwidths. This would have the effect of presenting to the radar operator a broken, rapidly flickering signal that hope-fully would be blamed on freak atmospheric conditions.

As the A-17 came over the Irtysh River where it flowed down through a deep gorge cut through the foothills of the Altai Moun-tains, Teleman suddenly glimpsed a small patch of heat on the infrared screen some thirty miles west of the Kazakh border into Sinkiang. A feeling of elation coursed through him. The whole operation might turn out to be easier than he thought. Ending the coded message that Larkin had transmitted from the ship containing his countering orders was the message 'Imperative you procure visual data of war situation.' He had to come back with actual photographs of the fighting for the mission to be successful. Without photos, the impact of the conflict between Red China and the Soviet Union would be lost on the world. The public would tend to interpret it as another smoke screen or propaganda play. The patch of heat detected by the infrared sensors could very well lead to those photographs.

Teleman examined the IR screen carefully. There, in the center of the blacked-out snow-covered rock and scrub-covered walls of the gorge that led toward the border was a barely discernible shade of gray, only slightly lighter than the surround-ing valley. Teleman pulled around in a tight circle, concentrating visual sensors and cameras on the spot. He had earlier cut his speed from Mach 1.2 to sub-sonic when he had dropped below one hundred thousand feet to avoid sonic boom. Now he throttled back even more, running out the variable geometrical wings until they were extended to the fullest to hold his speed at two hundred knots.

The television cameras were displaying the deep valley and he carefully began cranking up the image until he could make out a two-wheel track twisting through the rock and paralleling a tiny stream. Shortly a military vehicle came into sight around and from under a shoulder-like overhanging rock. It moved slowly into the open and began to pick up speed along the track. A minute passed and a second vehicle appeared, and then a third.

Teleman brought the aircraft around on the opposite heading and slowed still further until the fan assemblies engaged and wound up to thirty thousand RPM to provide extra airflow over the wing surfaces to support the aircraft. He was now down to 105 knots. A check of the radar detectors showed nothing more than a routine search patrol nearly eighty miles south, probably Chinese. No scrambled Chinese fighters were recorded. He turned his full attention back to the vehicles again.

The trucks were now moving along the roadway at about forty-five miles an hour, pretty fast for military vehicles on an almost nonexistent road. He cranked the images up to their highest degree of magnification and identified them as Kirov five-ton troop lorries.

Ahead of the trucks Teleman could see that the narrow gorge opened up and climbed steeply to a flattish plain that butted sharply against a series of rocky foothills. The foothills appeared to be their destination. Now he could also see artillery pieces on limbers bouncing along behind each truck. As the trucks reached the spot where the valley began to widen, they had to pass through a narrow defile several hundred yards long. There was no place to turn off the road and, because it snaked through the gap, it would be all but impossible to back out with the artillery pieces. The Chinese must have been waiting for just that moment.

Artillery opened up from somewhere deep in the foothills. The first truck was lucky and ran the ranging gauntlet. Cannon shells, four of them, burst high on either side of the first truck. As it cleared the pass, it sped for the safety of the foothills less than half a mile away. The second truck was not so lucky. It was caught by a fifth artillery shell that arrowed down into the defile and exploded. The truck disintegrated in the explosion, the gas tank and amunition going up in a fierce welter of flame. The third truck skidded to a halt only a short distance behind and was hit almost immediately. For three more minutes a heavy barrage of fire pursued the first truck, but it managed to reach the foothills below, to which the enemy artillery men obviously could not depress their guns. Teleman's cameras faithfully recorded the action on tape.

The entire sequence had taken less than two minutes, but two minutes was too long for Teleman to maintain such a low speed. Someone would be bound to notice. He increased power to bring the aircraft up to five hundred knots and forty thousand feet again as he broke out of the tight orbit and resumed his search along the border. The flight plan called for a shallow zigzag pattern along the border that would carry him fifty-odd miles into enemy territory on the first, high-altitude pass. The second pass would be modified by data from the nonvisual sensors and would concentrate on areas of heavy troop concentrations. One area particularly was read out by the flight-control complex. It indicated modifying data being received from one of the SAMOS series designated Advanced Reconnaissance 7. The satellite system had spotted an unusual degree of infrared activity twenty miles behind Chinese lines in the vicinity of Kuldja on the Ili River. The river flowed through a wide pass and crossed the border fifty miles east of the scrub town, important only as a staging point for whomever could hold it. At the moment it was in the hands of the Chinese.

Its principal danger lay in the fact that it commanded the shallow heights that led gradually to the border and the start of the Kazakh steppe, then out across the flat grasslands. The pass down which the Ili River flowed from the Tien Shan to Lake Balkhash was an arrow aimed directly at the huge Soviet military complex around the Kazakh city of Alma Alta.

The infrared patch that AR-4, satellite AR-7's predecessor, had detected immediately caused its IR and visual light lenses to shift focus. At the optimum moment, recorders were activated and they picked up two images. In its brainless way AR-4 was excited by what it saw. The visual light cameras showed a cluster of trucks and, more important, a special variable called a 210-mm cannon mounted on a massive tracked crawler. As AR-4 had watched, the cannon had spat a shell. The IR cameras saw the flash of fierce gases erupting from the muzzle and immediately the computer tripped a relay that caused the tape to spurt through the reel. The visual light cameras tracked the shell in free flight as the lenses shifted focus quickly to follow the trajectory.

In twelve seconds of flight the shell flew unerringly to detonation. There was no explosion worth mentioning, merely a spreading cloud, recorded by the IR cameras until it cooled and was lost in background scatter. Program 14—designed to watch for nuclear weaponry—noted the disappointing blast and gave way to Program 1, GENERAL SURVEILLANCE.

Program 1 took its time digesting the data—all of three nanoseconds—then scanned rapidly across its disk memory to match this variable against any of eight billion bits of data. It found none. Program 1 reached the end of its rack and automatically tripped Program 99, code named OVERVIEW. Program 99 evaluated the data, found the flight pattern it needed, then instructed Program 1 to include the new datum in its general report. Five minutes later a coded message left AR-4 and was received by a picket ship south of Ceylon. By the time the message came to the attention of the project director on the night shift in Virginia, AR-4 was already eleven minutes away from the site deep in the Tien Shan and over East Pakistan. The task of relaying the instructions from Virginia plus the new information fell to AR-7, traveling a parallel track to AR-4 but 250 miles east and half an orbit behind.

Teleman studied the new data for several seconds, then punched the program tab that recorded the new flight plan segment, modifying the original, and fed it to Flight Control. Immediately, the A-17 lifted for altitude, climbing swiftly on its turbofans to eight thousand feet. If warranted, he would return to complete the original low-level flight after checking out the threatening artillery piece. The 210-mm gun was one of the largest artillery pieces in the world. It was capable of throwing a three-thousand-pound shell a distance of forty-two miles. Originally, a similar artillery piece had been designed by the United States Army in 1953, as a nuclear cannon for tactical uses in the event of a war in Europe. The Soviets had immediately retaliated with their own version. But as short and intermediate-range ballistic missiles improved in size, accuracy, and transportability, the cumbersome gun had been discarded. Obviously the Soviets had discarded at least one of theirs to the Red Chinese, probably in the lates 1950s when everything, at least outwardly, was still sweetness and light between Russia and China. Now the Chinese appeared to be using the cannon against their one-time benefactors. But, as the instructions pointed out, they had not used a nuclear shell—or if they did, it had failed to explode. Teleman's job was to verify the possibility that a nuclear shell might have failed or else find out what they were shooting that required such an effort and such a large caliber weapon.

'Great,' he muttered aloud.

Ten minutes later Teleman passed over the muddy city of Kuldja and the frozen Ili River. He turned inland for a brief moment to bring the aircraft to the head of the pass, and then swung into a tight sub-sonic orbit again. A ground control map flew across the scope matching his ground speed. At the proper moment Teleman began the long, twenty-five-mile swing on to a heading of 353°N and bent to check the surveillance radar. The screen was blank except for scattered blips above him, indicating the presence of high ice-cloud formations. Interested, he shifted to Weather Surveillance and asked for a readout on the ice cover. The panel indicated that it was building quickly to a solid cover above 175,000 feet and gradually extending eastward to cover all of Central Asia. At the moment, it was solid—solid that is to radar, but invisible to the eye—between the Kirghiz SSR-Tadzhik SSR border to the south and the Urals to the east. He instructed Weather Surveillance to continue monitoring the cover and flipped back to the surveillance radar. Teleman then cranked the image outward, extending it to its full 1600-mile diameter. There on the western quadrant, four blips were rising, probably from the base at Alma Alta. The interceptors were well inside the Soviet border and did not appear too interested in anything other than patrolling for Chinese aircraft. They were down on the deck at less than ten thousand feet. East, there was little activity except for what appeared to be cargo aircraft on the Chinese side. He spotted a long line of heavy-cargo planes, escorted by fighters, coming in from China proper.

Teleman checked once more on the four Soviet interceptors, watching for a long moment as they completed the formation and turned north and east. They appeared to be flying sub-sonic —as a border patrol would. But if they turned east still further and crossed the border, they would bear watching. To be on the safe side he fed data to the computer and ordered it to keep tracking. Then he turned his attention back to the ground control map.

He was now almost directly over the location of the cannon emplacement. The new flight plan called for two passes, one at forty thousand feet to survey the countryside and, if he could manage it safely, a second lower pass over the impact area for close-ups. The altitude was left up to him. Teleman looked pained —that was their polite way of telling him to get right down on the deck if he could. To make the fastest possible approach with the least amount of time over the target area, he resumed manual control and fell off fifty miles to the east. He would make a quick pass straight down the valley and pull up hard to eighty thousand feet. The pass should carry him over both the cannon site and the impact site with less than one full minute spent below sixty thousand feet. The second pass he would worry about later.

Teleman made the first run across the target in a straight pass while all of his surveillance equipment—infrared, ultraviolet, topographical laser, and telephoto visual light—ground away. There was little activity on the ground, with the exception of two Red Chinese Mig 21 patrol crafts rising from the vicinity of Ala-Kul to the north. He had nothing to fear from the Chinese interceptors even if he came within visual sighting distance. His speed was more than a match for any armament they carried. The ground control map flew across the screen, a green streak acting as the pointer to the first of the locations.

The sensors picked out the exact location of the 210-mm gun from the satellite coordinates and displayed the area beneath on the scope. The gun emplacement was covered with camouflage netting and he shifted to the IR panel. On the scope he thought he could pick out several trenches and some activity close to the gun itself. Then he was away and past, hoping that all of the sensors combined had been able to pick out a coherent picture. The laser panel was signaling for attention and he switched it up. The laser had spotted a diffuse cloud on the order of two hundred parts per million some thirty miles east. Quickly he reran the instructions from AR-7 until they matched the location.

When the shell from the gun had exploded it had released a cloud. Of what, AR-4 was not equipped to tell. But it was still there after twenty minutes, and spreading slowly, apparently on the prevailing wind. The laser indicated particulate matter as the main composition of the cloud—thin droplets of liquid. That pretty well ruled out an atomic shell, he thought, even if it had failed to explode properly. Teleman paused for a moment, then deciding, he boosted power to the turbofans and swung the wings forward a few degrees and headed quickly for the deck. At a little less than Mach 1 he bore westward toward the cloud, flying up the valley and losing altitude as fast as he could shed it. 'Gas?' he wondered aloud. If the Chinese were using gas, the Soviets might not be so reluctant to initiate a nuclear conflict. In this godforsaken area it could be done fairly safely, that is if they could limit the exchange to the war area and not extend it to each other's cities. The Soviets might be trusted to do that, but not the Chinese. They would have to escalate if they were to remain effective.

The valley seemed outwardly calm in the early morning sunlight that was beginning to touch the snow-covered slopes. But he knew that the snow and convolutions of the land hid masses of troops and weaponry. He knew that the radar operators on both sides of the border must be wondering about the peculiar blank spots in their radar that kept recurring over the war area and along the lengthy border. He was sure that conferences were being held by phone between the radar sites and headquarters areas to decide whether to scramble investigating fighter aircraft. Teleman was reckoning that he would have less than ten minutes more before the first aircraft appeared. It would be dangerous to the project, but probably not fatal to him if he was spotted visually. The A-17 could outclimb and outrun anything either side could throw against him.

As Teleman neared the open plain where the shell had impacted and scattered its mysterious cloud, the lasers indicated that it had spread to cover an area at least twenty miles square. The single shell fired had exploded over the western crest of the last ridge separating the valley from the plains, and the prevailing westerly winds had swept it down and across the plain. Teleman warmed up the Terrain Avoidance Radar for the second pass and settled into the northern end of the wide, bowl-shaped plain for samples. The wing scoop covers slid open and he throttled back until the wings were fully extended and he was flying at less than five hundred miles an hour. He completed a first pass at five hundred feet and saw nothing visually although the flickering display from the monitoring consoles assured him that the sensors were faithfully recording every blade of grass and tree leaf for later analysis.

He swung up in a tight turn over the southern end, dipped the port wing, and lost altitude until he was down on the deck at little over two hundred feet and lumbering along at 140 knots. He turned into a lazy zigzag pattern and put all of the sensors to work and the aircraft on automatic pilot. Teleman rubbed his face and sighed, then picked up the binoculars to search the snow-covered meadows and hillsides beneath while the aircraft went into the rolling jolting pattern calculated by the TAR to maintain an even two-hundred-foot altitude over the undulating land below.

There was plenty of evidence of past battles on the ground: numerous shell holes, trenches, shattered tanks and personnel carriers, and long stretches of churned mud left by maneuvering vehicles. A fierce battle must have swept through the area only yesterday, as several of the destroyed vehicles were still sending up thin columns of smoke from fire-blackened hulks. The snow-fall of the preceding night had spread a thin layer of white over the battle area, but it had not been heavy enough to cover all traces. The overcast sky and the banked, heavy blue clouds to the east suggested another snowfall and fierce winds in a matter of hours, and he thanked the weather control satellite system that had provided the data that had brought him to the battle area before the new snowfall began.

Then, off to the right, at the base of a gentle slope, well hidden by a thicket of aspen, he caught a flicker of movement. Cutting out the autopilot, Teleman continued the zag around until he could make a straight pass. The ungainly 120-foot A-17 pivoted delicately and loped across the plain.

Watching the scope now rather than looking through the glasses, he could see a vehicle resembling a jeep jerk out of a stand of aspen and head erratically into the meadow. As he watched, the jeep struck a patch of thick, churned mud and bounced to a stop, thoroughly mired. The driver struggled to get out, then collapsed backward across the seat. From the padded uniform and hat, he was obviously Chinese.

Teleman cut in the autopilot again and checked the valley floor to the west with the binoculars while the aircraft resumed its interrupted search pattern. He had now been down in the valley at two hundred feet for a minute and a half. *Safe-time* was getting mighty short. Whatever that shell carried, he thought, they did not seem to care whether or not they hit their own troops as well. Then he saw what he had missed on his first and higher pass: a Soviet tank sat astraddle a point where several muddy tracks converged. Its turret gun was pointed in the direction of the hills off Teleman's starboard wing and he could plainly see two mortar emplacements concealed by its bulk. The powerful glasses showed figures clad in green Soviet uniforms, some with white snow coverings, scattered like dropped firewood. The turret hatch on the tank was open and he could see a body, half in, half out. Other troopers lying on the ground were twisted into grotesque postures, some still jerking spasmodically.

Teleman's first thought was of nerve gas. He keyed the tele-photo lenses on the visual cameras to the scene and boosted the image up on the scope, closing on the mortar emplacement while he put the aircraft into a tight orbit at three hundred feet. He swore as he checked the chronometer readout. One more minute and he would have to get out whether he had everything or not. Now he could see the bodies of other soldiers, some in foxholes, some scattered around the meadow as if they had tried to stagger toward the river. The faint footprints in the fresh snow were silhouetted in the dawn sun, indicating unsteady trails. A single trooper lay on his back, arched over the lip of a foxhole, one arm thrown across a pile of mortar shells. His helmet had tumbled back off his head, leaving his face exposed to the dead light of the early sun. Teleman could even see the man's long blond hair stirring in the vagrant breeze that reinforced the prediction of the impending storm. The image of the hair registered sub-consciously. Teleman peered at the face, framed in the scope: it was covered with blood and vomit and the eyes of the man were open, staring directly, it seemed, into the cameras. For a long moment Teleman could not tear his eyes away from the face as the cameras recorded the scene in minute detail. Then he broke the aircraft out of its orbit and dismissed the rest of the flight plan. He had all of the information he needed. Judging from the evidence he had seen so far, the Chinese were using either gas or germ warfare. For some reason, with the image of the dead Russian soldier's face before him, he was betting on bacteriologi-cal agents.

# CHAPTER SIX

TELEMAN wondered how many shells had been fired before the satellite surveillance system had spotted the 210-mm cannon. This one appeared to have been timed for just after dawn; probably so that the Chinese could gain a quick estimate of its effectiveness as well as initial Soviet reaction.

So far, there did not appear to be any. He checked the atmosphere sampling tanks and the lights glowed green, showing that the covers were sealed. Now it would be up to Washington to extract what they could from the samples.

A quick scan of the radar panels indicated that there had been no unusual air activity recorded in the nine minutes he had been below forty thousand feet. But deep in the valley as he had been, his radar was shadowed by the hills to the east. He considered a moment, then pulled the nose up sharply and cut in afterburners. He came out of the shallow valley, clearing the hills like a rocket. In less than thirty seconds he had passed sixty thousand feet and switched the engines to ramjet. The sudden explosion of thrust kicked him back into the acceleration couch. The pressure suit accommodated itself to the change caused by the sudden acceleration while the PCMS adjusted stimulant flows. Off to the east, the surveillance radar had two Chinese Migs spotted, heading for the broad valley. As he climbed, the Chinese pilots, now far below, pulled up sharply, caught by his surprise exit. They chased him upward for a short while, but by the time they reached sixty thousand feet he was leveling off at 120,000. Teleman caught the flicker of air-to-air missiles reaching for him as the Chinese aircraft tried a last frantic measure to bring him down. But there was never a chance. There would be, he knew, some soul-searching at their intelligence headquarters later on—if the pilots were believed. There would certainly be no radar sightings to confirm their story and the *Thoughts of Mao* would provide no sensible answers.

Teleman grinned to himself as the A-17 pulled out of the climb and settled into a search-and-photograph flight mode, then turned to the monitoring console to run through the information the sensors had so far picked up. As the data, reduced to language forms and equations, streamed across the screen, he found more information than he had hoped for. The laser topographical radar had managed to build a thorough map of the war area. Also spotted were several Soviet and Red Chinese missile installations that he suspected were previously unknown to US Intelligence. Near the town of Lepsinsk on the Kazakh SSR side, a cleared site with camouflaged bunkers betrayed a VTOL fighter airdrome. That meant that the Soviets had moved their air operations closer to the border than had been suspected. The vertical takeoff and landing fighters were limited in operating range, but they were Mach 2.1 fighters and could react and be over the selected target or engagement in a lot less time than conventional jet aircraft. By moving them into the area around Lepsinsk, the Soviets could meet the threat of the heavy Chinese airbase at Nordach, located well into the jut of the Sinkiang border, from which they could bring fighter bombers within striking distance of Alma Alta.

The IR sensors had located vehicle weapon parks on both sides of the border, including a number of heavy artillery sites, well dug in and virtually invulnerable to counterartillery attacks. Both sides had prepared well, Teleman thought, and obviously for a number of years. Much of the fighting on the plateau would have to be done by infantry troops supported by aircraft. It was still short of 0800, localtime, only forty minutes after local sunrise. Except for probing patrol actions, the bulk of the day's fighting was probably still to come.

The action earlier in which the two Soviet troop carriers had been knocked out would furnish ample evidence that a shooting was was actually going on. That revelation would make quite a stir in the United Nations, particularly to certain neighboring and nervous countries. The more sophisticated nonvisual sensor data would be pored over eagerly by the attachés of many nations. But the dangerous information, the data that really counted, lay safely in the atmosphere-sampling tanks. Either gas or bacteriological agents, it would make no difference. Either would be enough to bring world condemnation of the Red Chinese, even by nations friendly to her. It was doubtful if their usual pattern of denial would avail them in this instance. The doubt would be there, and there would be calls for an international monitoring team. And the evidence could not be hidden. Teleman was well pleased with the morning's work. And so would Washington be.

Teleman was completing the final leg of the search pattern preparatory to shaping a course northeast for rendezvous. He was flying at eight thousand feet in the vicinity of Lach Rom on the Chu River. The aircraft was on automatic, following the irregular border by star-fix coordinates when Teleman caught a tiny flicker on the trailing edge of the surveillance radar screen. The blip showed at sixty thousand feet near Pezhevalsk, on the Soviet side of the border. As he watched, the blip was read out as an Ilyushin Falcon, closing the four-hundred-mile gap at Mach 2.5. For long seconds he continued to watch, wondering where the Soviet aircraft was going in such a hurry.

The Falcon was the latest Soviet interceptor, capable of Mach 3.2 and carrying an armament consisting of four Mach 4.8 air-to-air missiles that could be armed with small nuclear warheads. The aircraft was only recently being distributed to the Soviet Tactical Air Command as a high-speed, high-altitude interceptor with a ceiling of a little less than 180,000 feet. Its major task was to act as defense against the new, high/low-level Mach 3 penetration bombers of the USAF Strategic Air Command. Teleman had spotted flights several times before over the Soviet Union, but always either on training jaunts or border patrols. None had heretofore been aware of his presence.

This one, though, seemed to be another matter. The Falcon was holding its course on a direct line that would cross his less than a minute after he passed over the border into Soviet territory. Experimentally, he made a small course correction that lengthened his stay in Red Chinese territory. The Falcon changed to match.

For the first time Teleman felt the cold chill of fear that not even the PCMS could cope with. That damned aircraft was waiting for him, he thought. How in the name of all the gods . . . frantically, Teleman lifted the A-17, ramjets flaming, and scrambled to two hundred thousand feet.

The Russian pilot pulled his aircraft up sharply and cut in his afterburners. The long, thousand-foot cone of hot gases showed as a thin ghost image on the radar screen. Teleman began to increase his speed, shoving the throttle control up past Mach 2.5. The intruder was still closing. He checked the ECM unit. It put him at the center of a three-hundred-mile-diameter circle, but still the flickering image came on to meet him at the interception point, now less than two hundred miles ahead. And the Falcon had the advantage of being down-course. That damned ECM unit was working, but still the Soviet aircraft came on. Somehow, the Russian had him visually, Teleman knew.

That left Teleman with only one other move. He switched the surveillance radar to scan to the east—nothing more than scattered Mig patrols on both sides of the border and occasional cargo craft on the Chinese side, all well below forty thousand feet. He quickly checked the Falcon. It was still there and in another few seconds would be in range to fire a salvo of twin missiles. He did not want to chance those. The PCMS, anticipating his decision from the combined inputs of his body setting itself for action and the information coming to it from the surveillance radar, began to increase the flow of amphetamine stimulants. Teleman's actions became a blur as he pulled the A-17 around in a narrow curve to the north-east. The gap between the two aircraft opened as though a knife had slashed through an invisible cord, and the Falcon fell rapidly behind as Teleman streaked for the deserted reaches of Sinkiang. Watching the surveillance radar, he felt a small measure of relief as the Soviet aircraft disappeared from the scope. At least they were not going to take a chance on trying to shoot him down over Chinese territory. They wanted the A-17, or what would be left of it, badly.

As he streaked deeper into Sinkiang, Teleman watched the Falcon. The Soviet aircraft pulled around to the west in a tight turn that was almost a match for his, then straightened out and ran, presumably for its base at Alma Alta.

Teleman found himself very interested in that final maneuver. A number of questions were suddenly occurring to him. Number one: Why did they send only one aircraft? And number two: Why did it return to base so quickly instead of loitering in the vicinity to see if Teleman would try and cross the border again? There was only one way to find out, he decided. Swinging back again toward the border, he increased his speed to Mach 4. Seconds later, as he approached the spot where he had first sighted the Falcon, a second Russian aircraft showed up from the southwest quadrant, the same quadrant from which the first had come barreling in.

Somehow, they were tracking him, Teleman thought. They must have aircraft stacked up low down on the deck where his surveillance radar could not pick them out of the background scatter. He did not wait this time to see how close he could push on to the border, but swung to the east again in the same tight turn.

Again the Falcon turned and headed after the first one to base. A third time he tried it, streaking for the border at less than a thousand feet and Mach 2. The sonic boom below would be enough to cause concussion and alert everyone within fifty miles. But in this deserted desert country he was not concerned about being sighted.

And again the Falcon showed up, cutting his flight path on a diagonal that would have the Falcon meet him as he crossed into Soviet territory. Frustrated, Teleman went into a climbing turn east and at Mach 1.8 headed into Sinkiang.

He was holding an altitude of eighty thousand feet—a comfortable level for the A-17 that made the best use of its fuel capacity. It was now obvious to him that the Soviets had developed some type of sophisticated, visual tracking system that could not only pick him out at great altitudes and distances, but hold him at supersonic speeds as a Falcon closed. A visual tracking system would require a second man in the aircraft; this probably explained the limited stay-time. The increased payload taken up by the observer and the visual tracking equipment would cut well into the cruising range of the Falcon. Although it was designed for long supersonic flight, it could sustain its Mach 4.8 speed only for short durations, for the approach and attack. During the cruise to and from the target, the speed would be well down into the more conventional ranges. But the problem confronting Teleman now was: At what range could they track him? Did they have to have flying patrols in the air, or did they have ground observing stations with much more sensitive equipment than an aircraft could possibly carry? The Soviets could have had plenty of opportunity to observe him while he was orbiting the fire fight involving the trucks, as well as during his pass across the valley where the shell had impacted.

That in turn led him to the next series of questions. Did they know about the A-17? Obviously they did. A visual tracking system sophisticated enough to pick up what amounted to a flyspeck moving at speeds up to Mach 4.5 over even several hundred miles distance would require a substantial outlay of both men and money. And to have set-up in the vicinity of the Soviet-Chinese war zone, they would have had to know that this conflict would bring him on the run. There was nothing the Chinese could put into the sky that would require a visual tracking system. Teleman shook his head. It was all such a pre-posterous chain of events, but then so was the U-2 flight that was shot down over Russia in late 1959, by a missile whose existence was not even suspected by Western intelligence. And so vicious was the pace of missile development that in 1965, up-rated, second-generation versions of those same missiles were provided to the North Vietnamese for use against US fighter-bombers as obsolete Soviet weaponry.

The Soviets could very well have rushed the development of a visual tracking system in much the same way that they and the United States always had when a clear requirement arose. A-17 flights had been going on over Soviet territory for more than a year now, and the increasing appearance of dead spots in radar warning and detection systems would be enough to indicate that something or someone was intruding over Soviet territory with alarming frequency. Even if they had not been particularly worried about intelligence-gathering missions, they would be scared to death that the same ECM systems could be placed in manned bombers or even intercontinental missiles. So the knowledge that the Soviets were on to the A-17 overflights, and on to them with a visual tracking system, was suddenly more important than the information he had gathered from the war zone. The problem was how to get the information back to Washington.

By now he was six hundred miles into the northern reaches of Sinkiang and less than ten minutes from the Mongolian border. Mongolia was still firmly in the Soviet camp, perhaps not firmly enough to have the new Falcons, but it was not worth the risk of finding out. Coming up dead ahead was the faint thread of the Irtysh River. The floor of the desert was as deserted as only the Gobi could be. In this particular area not even Mongolian herdsmen could live. The river, here near its headwaters in the low hills that lay two hundred miles off his starboard wing, was still little more than a muddy stream, not yet purified and strengthened as it would be later on during its 2,500-mile rush to the Arctic Ocean. South, the Gobi cut into the province of Sinkiang, cut a swatch of utter desolation for another five hundred miles before the land began the long climb back to the fertile steppes leading to the Tien Shan, whose eastern flanks began on the far side of the Turfan Depression.

Teleman punched the tabs to the key in the ground control maps of the Tien Shan. When the image centered, he stopped the flow and asked for the altitude overlay, then settled back to study the lofty summits. The Tien Shan was actually the northern extension of the Himalaya chain, reaching north and east for nearly fifteen hundred miles. Next to the Himalayas, the Tien Shan was the longest mountain chain on the Asian continent. The southern slopes on the west rose out of the Pamir Plateau and covered more than four hundred thousand square miles. It was a cinch that the Soviets would not be able to cover the entire range with visual tracking equipment. But he still did not know the altitude range of that equipment. And the Soviets would be expecting him to try and break through somewhere. They must know, or at least suspect, that he had to recross Soviet territory. And he did, he thought ruefully. Normally he would fly out of the fix by crossing China and refueling over either the Bay of Bengal or the China Sea. But not this time. They must have been watching the progress of the blind spots on the radar screens as he crossed Soviet territory, making educated guesses with their computers until they hit upon a familiarity with his flight schedules. He had no support waiting anywhere except in the Barents Sea. The mission was too complex and the secrecy too great to try and stretch it to alternate points. Each flight was carefully made up and very little margin of error allowed. He had no alternate landing bases outside the continental United States. No landings in foreign territory could be allowed. If he had to abort a mission, he was to head for the nearest ocean and bail out.

So this mission, it was back to the Barents Sea or not at all. Teleman decided that the risk of crossing Soviet territory with the information he had so far collected justified the attempt.

As he continued to study the map of the Tien Shan, a plan began to take shape. The range averaged 250 miles wide and the peaks ranged up to 23,620 feet in the Tengri Khan, in the center, to 17,946 in the Bogodo Ula in the east. A good chunk of the range was glaciated or thickly forested. For the most part, the average elevation ran close to twenty thousand feet, and, located as it was on the edge of both the Gobi Desert and the Himalayas, the interior slopes on the southern face would be sparsely inhabited.

Teleman leaned forward and began setting up a flight plan that would carry him directly south of his present position to the vicinity of the Turfan Depression. There he would drop to fifteen thousand feet and wriggle in between the northern flanks of the Altyn Tagh Mountains in the Kun Lun range on the northern reaches of the Himalayas and the Tien Shan. At fifteen thousand feet he would be able carefully to pick his way through the valleys and canyons of the Tien Shan and come out far south of the war zone, thus crossing the border at 49° latitude into Kirghiz SSR. By staying down on the deck through the mountains, it would be impossible for the Soviets to track his progress. Teleman hoped only that by now, six hundred miles into Sinkiang, he was well off their scopes. Seconds later, after checking fuel levels, the computer agreed with the revised flight plan. It would be cutting it fine, he decided, but it could be done without having to touch the fuel reserves. And, as a bonus, it would put him less than ten minutes off the rendezvous schedule he had set up with Larkin.

Thoughtfully, Major Joseph Teleman turned to the never-before-used direct line communication channel to his headquarters, nestled deep in the soft Virginia hills, and began composing the message that would shake one of the most vital, least known, and smallest portions of the United States military establishment.

## CHAPTER SEVEN

THE DEAD, coppery sun dragged itself out of the heaving ocean and hung sullenly against the slate sky. Folsom had never seen a sunrise that boded so ill for the day to come. The sun was merely a not overly bright ball, shrouded in layers of ice. Its light was as dull and washed out as the running seas around and gave no warmth at all, real or imagined, to the scene over which it presided. Folsom stamped his feet on the caked ice of the bridge deck and swore under his breath. The *RFK* was shrouded in a more substantial ice than was the sun. So much more substantial that she was riding noticeably lower in the water. The deck heaters had been running at full power all night and the interior of the hull was unbelievably hot. But even heaters that piped waste heat directly from the nuclear reactor heat exchangers had not been sufficient to cope with an Arctic storm of such magnitude.

The dry-bulb temperature showed only eight degrees below zero, not enough to freeze sea water. But the anemometer, clacking on the masthead like something possessed, gave the answer. Wind speed was averaging close to fifty-seven knots, a Force 11 wind on the Beaufort scale. And below zero, for every mile of wind speed, you add another degree below freezing to the apparent temperature to obtain the true temperature. The true temperature was $-33°$ F. Even swathed from head to foot in his heated Arctic gear and wearing double-insulated and heated boots, Folsom was half frozen. The wind was strong enough to tear the crests off the long swells and fling them back as ice that froze solidly into place the moment it touched the ship.

Ahead of the ship, the wind-whipped swells, with their lashing crests of white water, built in slow succession to inundate the decks as the *RFK* crested wave after wave. Folsom periodically ducked behind the windscreen to escape the cascades of water that poured over the bridge deck—in spite of its being forty feet above the water line—and left the deck plates slippery with sea water and ice.

After fifteen minutes on deck, Folsom was finally driven back inside, where he stood gasping for air in the sudden 105° temperature change. He shed his foul-weather gear and climbed into his high seat. The height of the storm was still to be met in approximately four hours. By then the short Arctic day would be long over and the impenetrable blackness would have closed in. The previous night there had been a sky glow through the scudding clouds, but tonight there would be only the black of the deepest pits of hell. The ice layer had thickened above forty thousand feet and the first tinges of storm clouds bearing the blizzard that always followed a katabatic storm were beginning to appear. Folsom did not like this storm or the way it was progressing. Already it was well on the way to becoming one of the worst ever recorded. With a whole ship he would not have been concerned, but the bow section shore-up job was beginning to show signs of strain. He did not know how many more hours of pounding it would take before seams started to open. And open seams in these seas would be disastrous.

With a long sigh, Folsom heaved himself out of the high seat and left the bridge. As he passed out of the hatch he picked up the flashlight racked beside the coaming and stuck it into his pocket. The bow areas of the ship were deserted. The captain had ordered all but the forward missile rooms and the communication station to shift operations aft.

It took Folsom several minutes to reach the forward compartments. Each hatch had to be unsealed, then resealed again. The closer he moved to the outer hull, the louder became the tympanic roar of metal flexing under great strain. The seas were running so heavily that even below the water line, as he was, the outer plates near the bow were flexing in the wind and swells each time the forefoot lifted above the waves.

Folsom unsealed the last hatch into the ballast spaces between the ship's interior and exterior hulls. The ballast water had all been pumped out forward to raise the bow under its coating of ice and force the stern down farther, where the great engines could maintain a continual purchase on the water. In these winds, even a moment with the four screws out of water could find the battle cruiser being spun wildly by the winds, broadside to the waves. Once allowed to start, even a 16,500-ton battle cruiser could be tumbled over beams end, turned turtle, and sunk.

The ballast tank was ice cold. Traces of water remaining after the pumping had frozen to a smooth glaze on bulkeads and deck. Folsom had to hang on to the metal rungs spaced in even rows along the side and bottom to cross the eight-foot space that separated the two hulls.

The outside of the ballast tanks acted as an integral part of the hull. The tank itself was crisscrossed with steel bracing bars. Folsom stood up gingerly, riding with the slow rise and fall of the ship, and flicked on the flashlight. The strong beam sprang out boldly in the wet air, striking the ice- and water-coated sides of the tank to flash back as sparkles from millions of diamonds. He played the beam along the tank wall until he found the eight-foot-long gash, high up above the water line. Carefully he examined the steel plates that had been welded over the gash, checking for signs of water seepage. He could find no major breaks, and with the ice and dampness it was impossible to spot small leaks.

Folsom stood uncertainly below the welded plates, playing the light around the sides of the tank. He would have felt much better if he dared order the tank flooded to capacity with sea water. Filling the tank would have eased the strain on the welded joints. But it might also put them far enough down into the waves so that they would never recover. Finally, after a long minute of helplessness coupled with frustration, he shrugged and turned back to the hatch, clicking off the light. Folsom carefully dogged the hatch shut and then made his way aft to the engine room, amidships.

Although the *Robert F. Kennedy* displaced 16,500 tons and was nearly seven hundred feet long, she carried a crew of only eighty men. With the ship standing to general quarters in the storm, most of this minimum crew was on duty or else snatching a few hours of restless sleep in the duty bunks scattered around the ship. A powered elevator took Folsom down to G deck and he walked aft another hundred feet, pushed open the engine-room hatch, and stepped into the softly lit, instrument-paneled room. The duty chief nodded to him and came over as he approached the master control panel.

'What's she look like outside, Commander?' Lieutenant Charles Barrows grinned as Folsom slumped down into the extra command seat.

'Rough. The seas are running better than fifty feet right now. How are your engines doing?'

'Better question would be how's the hull doing.'

Folsom grinned. 'I guess it would be at that. I was just up there. So far no sign of any separation and no seepage . . . but, I don't know.'

Barrows nodded slowly. 'How about if I send a couple of boys up to put in some strain gauges, wired to the control room. Shouldn't take more than an hour or so.'

Folsom nodded. 'Good. That's really what I came down here to see about. By the way, how is the overhaul on number three free turbine coming along?'

Barrows turned and reached across the console for a check list and leafed quickly through the pages. 'They are reassembling the bearings now. Should have it all back together and checked out in twelve hours.'

'Twelve hours . . .' Folsom made an elaborate face. 'Way too long. Try and cut that in half.'

Barrows turned a startled face. 'In half! For God's sake, what do you think we are, miracle men?' Nevertheless, he reached for a microphone and roared, 'All right, you half-witted slackers. The Exec wants that number three engine operating in four hours. So get off your tails and move.'

'Six hours . . .' he mumbled.

'It is rather important. We are going to come about at 0400, and if the seas or the winds get any worse, we are going to need all the power we can get. I sure would hate to see this bucket swing into a turn and keep right on going—straight down. Which brings me to the next point. Isn't there anything you can do about the ice on the deck? We are carrying nearly four hundred tons right now and the ship is so damn low she looks like a submarine.'

Barrows scratched his head. 'I sure as hell don't know what it would be. I am squeezing every last calorie of heat out of the reactor now. The cooling system is shut down for the lower decks and I'm saving the reactor cooling system until we do come about. If I switch it off now, the reactor is going to overheat.'

'Okay, I'll leave the details up to you. But the computer shows that if the ice-build-up rate continues steady, we are going to have about a hundred and fourteen more tons of it on the deck by 0300. And that is going to make coming about very, very touchy.'

Barrows tapped his fingers nervously on the console. 'All right, let me see if we can come up with something else that will help the deck heaters out. Forty years ago—they tell me—they never worried much about ice build-up. If the deck heaters couldn't keep up, they just gave a hundred or so sailors safety lines and buckets of ashes and told them to go to it. But what the hell can you do with eighty men, sixty of whom are on duty during general quarters at any one time, and no ashes.' He shook his head. 'Progress. Sometimes it does more to work against you than for you.'

Folsom grinned and left, after extracting a promise to get the number three engine back on line as soon as possible. He went directly up to the bridge and to the computing table. As he climbed into his high seat again, he switched on the navigation course plot and studied the fine red line that had marked their progress since 1900 the previous evening. The red progress line was superimposed on to the projected course and showed every little deviation from the plot. But it was running fourteen miles behind; it was clearly indicated by an angry red circle encompassing the end point of both lines.

He sat at the console, unconsciously tapping a pencil while he tried to figure a way out. Increased speed would apply more pressure to the bow. If they came late to the turn-around point, they would be late to the rendezvous. If they stayed behind—and the computer showed that, given the same conditions, at turn-around time they would be thirty-two miles short—they would not be in the lee of the North Cape. And with the ice building up at an ever-increasing rate, it would be far too risky to attempt the turn in the open seas.

Folsom swiveled to stare out the forward ports. The heavy gray sky formed a low-hanging ceiling barely clearing the mountainous seas. It was now nearly 1100, one hour past sunrise. But the sun, filtering down through thousands of feet of ice and storm cloud, shed very little light to relieve the funeral pall. The wind, throbbing around the ship and even through thick insulation, could be heard clearly above the low-key noises of the bridge. The barometer had dropped to the lowest point that Folsom had ever seen, 28.49 inches of mercury. He knew that the worst of the storm and winds were yet to come. And they were heading directly into the teeth of it—in fact, rushing headlong to meet it.

The anemometer, clacking loudly on the masthead, was still registering a fairly steady wind speed of fifty-seven knots, a Force 11 wind, strong enough to blow the crests off the waves. As waves approach shore, an entirely different set of hydrodynamic principles come into play, and the waves become the more familiar breakers, with crests of rolling white water as they break on the beach. In mid-ocean, waves are usually long swells several hundred feet long, with a rounded bosom rolling to the far-distant shore. When the wind is strong, then the water forming the swell is pushed faster toward the crest so that it overshoots and falls free in a mass of white water. Out there, Folsom could see, the wind was blowing so hard that the water that was pushed over the crest was blown free into long streamers for fifty and sixty feet downwind. He shivered involuntarily before the frozen wastes of the Arctic Ocean.

But daydreaming would not solve his navigational problem, and for the hundredth time he damned the destroyer that had ripped their bow, thereby causing all these problems. With an undamaged bow, neither he nor Larkin would have worried about the effects of the angry seas on the bow. They would have put the ship on to a long, rectangular course until rendezvous time and the hell with the pounding on the bow.

His thinking was interrupted by the appearance on the bridge of Barrows' electronics crew. They politely elbowed him aside to get at the electrical conduits over his console to run temporary lines from the strain gauges in the bow. With nothing else to do for the moment, Folsom wandered around the bridge and the various consoles as unobtrusively as possible, stymied by the mathematics of the situation.

A half hour later he thought he was beginning to see a way out of the problem. The wind speed had increased another three knots and the seas were running to swells nearly sixty feet high. The wind was blowing steadily from the north-northwest quarter, deviating little from 10° north, which was what he had been half hoping for. For the past twenty minutes he had observed little or no deviation either in direction or speed. When he fed the new information into the course computers, it worked out perfectly. By falling off two points from the wind direction, he would bring the *RFK* farther to the west in a shallow arc that would increase the distance toward the Cape lee. Feeling very much like a skipper of a sailing ship, he ordered the course change to take advantage of the wind.

The *RFK* rolled far to starboard as the two rudders inched over in response to the instructions from the bridge. The roll went on through thirty, then forty, then fifty, to fifty-seven degrees. Folsom watched the inclinometer with apprehension, and when the needle began to move back toward vertical, he let out a pent-up breath. Good lord, he thought, if she would go over that far with just a minor change with the wind, how would she handle when it came time to reverse course? He glanced around the bridge and saw that the others on watch were also looking at the inclinometer and were just as apprehensive as he.

At 1200, Larkin came on to the bridge. He nodded to the officer of the watch, signed the log, and came over to Folsom's console.

He turned, before saying anything to Folsom, and said, 'Mr. Peterson, please stay on the bridge for a few minutes. I would like you to relieve me while Mr. Folsom and I go below.'

The second officer nodded and sank back into his high seat and began flipping through ship's status report forms. Folsom unbuckled his seat belt and followed Larkin off the bridge, wondering what the captain had on his mind. Neither said a word until they entered Larkin's quarters.

'Sit down, Pete.' He indicated a comfortable chair against the bulkhead. Folsom took the seat and glanced around at the comfortably appointed room. Larkin had thrown out the regulation Navy furniture as one of his first official acts on assuming command of the *RFK*, in the belief that a new skipper should assume all prerogatives in setting new traditions on a new ship. Certainly, the comfortable living-room-style furniture was much more relaxing than the hard-backed steel and plastic furniture that had been furnished by the shipyard.

He accepted the coffee that Larkin ordered and sat back in the chair to watch his commanding officer pouring his own coffee. Folsom really knew little about Larkin, and he doubted that many men did. Larkin was old Navy, relaxed but steeped in tradition; he probably would have been more at home in the more easygoing Australian or Canadian navies if he were to be judged by his command style. In two years he had yet to hear the captain raise his voice to give an order. And he could not ever remember Larkin having to give an order twice.

But the man kept his own counsel. Never had there been an exchange of personal information between them. What little he knew about Larkin had been gleaned from his service record, to which Folsom, as executive officer, had access, and from talk around the various officers' clubs. The service record had been exceedingly dry, as always, but at the same time was an intriguing document, more from what it had implied rather than described. Folsom knew, for instance, that Larkin had commanded a destroyer during the Vietnam conflict and had been decorated with the Navy Cross for bravery under fire. But it had remained a noncommittal note in a record until he ran into a chance acquaintance in San Francisco who had been communications officer on the cruise for which Larkin earned the decoration.

The story was that Larkin had taken his destroyer to within a hundred yards of fringing reefs off the South Vietnamese coast just below the Demilitarized Zone. He was to lay down point-blank covering fire for a Korean patrol driven back and pinned down on the beach by a superior and well-dug-in North Vietnamese Army unit. Larkin had moved in so close that he had come under intensive mortar fire. The destroyer took three mortar rounds, one directly through the fan tail, which had exploded against the rudder controls, blasting them out of action. In spite of the damage, Larkin had remained on the scene, in fact moving in even closer to bring anti-aircraft guns into broad-side position to lay down a sweeping barrage for twenty minutes while army helicopters moved in to pull the Koreans out. The service record for some reason missed noting the award of the Republic of South Korea Distinguished Service Medal.

Folsom's friend had many other tales of Larkin's skill and bravery, which he was more than happy to relate to Folsom during a long two-fifths-of-gin afternoon and evening. All were in a similar vein. But what stuck most deeply in Folsom's memory was his friend's description of Larkin as an aloof, although quite personable, and lonely man. Exactly Folsom's own conclusion.

Even Larkin's face bore out his manner. It was a face that was at once alive but closed to outsiders. The gray eyes stared out at you from under straight, medium thin brows with a direct stare that forbade anything except the exact truth. Larkin was a tall man, but spare, almost to the point of gauntness in some respects. His face was thin, with the skin stretched tightly across the brow and nose. But the shoulders were broader than would have been expected for a man so tall and lean. There was something about the man, something in the posture, that Folsom could not isolate, that belied the personal aesthetism that really existed. The furniture in the cabin may have been comfortable and pleasantly arranged, but it was certainly not opulent. The color scheme matched the paneled and steel walls, but that was all. The desk, set under the air vent, was clean and neat. A choice selection of books could be seen in the barred rack over the desk and the titles were intriguing, indicating a disciplined mind.

Larkin settled into a chair facing him and balanced his coffee cup on the arm. He glanced at Folsom, who sipped at his coffee and waited. It was characteristic of Larkin, he thought, to un-knowingly make you wait uncomfortably until he started to speak. The gray eyes peering out from the calm face gave the impression that Larkin was measuring your character and strength. It was not intentional, he knew. It was only that Larkin was marshaling his own thoughts.

Larkin cleared his throat. 'I noticed that you made a course correction. Good thinking. These seas are going to get rougher.'

Folsom nodded. 'I had engineering rig up strain gauges on the bow patch. If it starts to weaken, we'll want to know about it in plenty of time.'

Larkin smiled briefly. 'Yes we will at that.' He sat for a moment sipping his coffee. 'I just got word from Virginia that our Russian friends are on to the system.'

Folsom sat up. He really knew very little about the supersecret games they had been playing lately. Between themselves they always used the name Virginia to refer to the agency that directed their actions. Although he did not know really who 'Virginia' was, he could pretty well guess that it meant the forty-two-acre complex in the hills just outside Washington that was Central Intelligence Agency Headquarters. But what was the *game* the Russians were on to?

Larkin pulled a sealed envelope off the desk top and handed it to Folsom. 'Open it.'

Folsom tore the end off and extracted the folded papers. He spread them on his lap and picked up the top sheet. DOD 630-29K. That was one he had not seen before. He looked up questioningly at Larkin, but Larkin was gazing in deep absorption at the design on his coffee cup.

The top sheet was an instruction page for the five that followed. It held one small paragraph that immediately caught Folsom's eye. If he accepted the terms of the attached contract and signed, he would be 'liable to twenty years in a federal prison or $20,000 fine or both if he revealed to any unauthorized person or persons any material or information given to him in connection with that relayed to him by Captain Henly Larkin, USN, Commanding Officer of the battle cruiser U.S.S. *Robert F. Kennedy,* or in any way violated the provisions of the National Defense Act.' The rest of the forms were standard Department of Defense Top Secret Clearance sheets, already filled out and dated the day he had received his Top Secret clearance. Puzzled, Folsom turned the pages until he came to the last. It was a simple, green-colored sheet with a short list of questions and space for his signature and the date. It was headed 'Q' Prime Clearance. He whistled softly. He had heard of the QPC, but never had expected to receive it. Usually, it was a clearance reserved for the President, cabinet officers, and the Joint Chiefs of Staff, to whom there were no secrets. Not even the highest-ranking members of Congress got that one. He looked up.

'Rather surprising, isn't it? But that's how important this project is. Will you sign the form?'

Folsom nodded, and Larkin handed him a pen.

'Then do so,' he said quietly. Folsom scribbled his name and added the date.

'You are now cleared to receive "Q" Prime information,' Larkin said. 'The clearance search was run the day you came aboard, and if something had happened to me while we were on duty you would have found all of the instructions in my safe. The decision as to when to bring you into the project was left up to me. Because I believe that the fewer people who know about this project the safer it will be, I have not done so until now.' He paused to drink slowly.

'Why did you decide now that I should know about it?' Folsom asked much more calmly than he felt.

Larkin waved his hand in a manner to take in the ship and the storm raging outside. 'To date there has been no emergency that has warranted it. But now there is what you might call a proper combination of circumstances. As I said, the Russians are on to our most closely guarded secret since the Manhattan Project. Additionally, the sea is running into one of the worst storms on record and our ship could be in very serious danger. In the next few hours you are going to have to have a full understanding as to why we are not going to be able to do anything more than complete our assigned mission at all costs. And, if we survive the storm, we may have trouble of a kind we have never encountered before except in practice'—Larkin hesitated, letting the tension build—'Soviet submarines may be out to sink us.'

Folsom stared at him, wondering if the old man had not finally succumbed to the pressures of commanding a ship. As if aware of what he was thinking, Larkin grinned and shook his head. 'No, I haven't gone out of my mind.'

He got up and pulled a map from the desk drawer and spread it on the table. It was a map of the northern Eastern hemisphere showing the Soviet Union, Europe, and the Arctic. On it was penciled in red a line paralleling the 90° meridian to the Sinkiang border, then swinging north in a long, curving arc across the Soviet Union to their rendezvous position off the Ryabchi Peninsula of Scandinavia.

'This map shows the flight path of one of our three specially equipped reconnaissance aircraft. The aircraft is capable of speeds in excess of Mach 5 and flight times of . . .'

For a long time Folsom listened to the dry matter-of-fact voice explaining one of the nation's most closely guarded secrets. After the first few minutes he recovered quickly from the astonishment accompanying the discovery of the exact depth and extent of the surveillance missions that the United States had conducted over the past two years and the role he, or the *RFK* to be exact, had played. The deeper Larkin went into the explanation/briefing, the more he understood the almost fanatical secrecy that surrounded the project. Not counting the employees at Lockheed and the Air Force crew at Gillon Advanced Test Site, who never were allowed to know the full story, Larkin told him that there were less than fifty people in the United States who knew about the A-17. Fifty people and possibly the entire Soviet military establishment, Folsom thought ironically. Larkin was the only U.S. military official outside the United States territorial boundaries who knew about the A-17, with the exception of a submarine commander in charge of all relay operations for the entire southern hemisphere.

'And that, Pete, is the whole story, or at least as much as I think it is necessary to tell you at this point.' The old man looked piercingly at him. Folsom met his eyes unwaveringly.

'What are your orders then, sir?'

Larkin rubbed the back of his head and walked over to stand and stare out the porthole. His voice, when he spoke, was low, barely carrying across the ten feet that separated them, hinting all the actual loneliness of command that only the captain of a ship, or perhaps the commander of a Strategic Air Command bomber, could feel. The loneliness in knowing that you had no one to whom you could turn to for advice. 'I wish I knew . . .' He let his voice trail off.

But with the next breath he swung quickly around from the porthole and said firmly, 'For now, we have no choice but to continue to the turn-around point and rendezvous tonight on-station.' He walked briskly back to the desk and handed Folsom another flimsy.

'This is the last message we received after I made the status report an hour ago. It says, quite simply, "Imperative maintain station—Soviets on."'

'Why couldn't we continue to the lee side of the Cape and wait for him there. One hundred and fifty miles shouldn't make that much difference to the pilot,' Folsom continued.

'But it does. We have no way of contacting the aircraft. The pilot must initiate all such contacts with us. Secondly, the radio transmitter that he uses is a VHF-FM set with a range of less than twenty miles, to reduce the chance that hostile ships or aircraft might pick up the transmission. If we aren't where we said we will be, then he is done. He can't contact us and we can't give him his next set of orders. And that set of orders has his next fueling coordinates. Everything possible has been done to lessen the chance of his being discovered by electronic snooping.'

Folsom nodded. 'So if we aren't there, he's as good as dead.' He paused and massaged his weary eyes. They felt as if large boulders of jagged rock were slowly working their way up under the lids. He had been on duty, without sleep, for nearly twenty-four hours, and his mental faculties were beginning to match the syrupy slowness of his body. 'That is one job that I certainly do not want under any circumstances.'

'How would you like the job of having to be in the right place at the right time, everytime,' Larkin asked bleakly. 'You've got it, Pete.'

# CHAPTER EIGHT

THE WELL-DEFINED southern edge of the Turfan Depression cut a sable horizon through the pale gold of the Gobi and the dust-laden sky. To his right, the blue expanse of Bagrach Kol gleamed in the late morning sunlight. The Bagrach Kol had the singular distinction of being the largest and one of two free bodies of water in all the Gobi, and it is salty beyond belief. The other was the almost dry and equally salt-laden Lop Nor Basin. For some minutes now the eastern reaches of the Tien Shan had been in view, and from fifteen thousand feet Teleman could easily make out the dark smudge farther down on the southern horizon that was the Kun Lun range.

He flew steadily due south, leaving the alkaline lake and the pebble desert of the Depression behind. When the Tien Shan were well past his starboard wing, Teleman began the long turn east that would take him down the valleys between the two ranges to cross the Soviet border well south, or so he hoped, of the visual tracking net the Soviets had so hastily thrown up.

Beneath, the land began to rise as the flanks of either mountain chain spread out to form a comfortable supporting base. The ground flowing beneath resembled nothing as much as a flat plate, broken here and there with upthrust rock formations, the edges folding up on themselves and sprinkled with a black pepper of stunted scrub bushes reminiscent of mesquite. As always, he was amazed that deserts look so much alike. Looking at the scene sliding past, he would not have been able to distinguish between the Gobi and stretches of Nevada and New Mexico desert.

The Lop Nor was beginning to appear off his starboard wing as he looped back up from the far end of the turn. This last was a maneuver designed to shake any possible last vestiges of Soviet observation. He hoped that the long swing south would be interpreted as an attempt to fly out over the Himalayas to the Bay of Bengal and the Indian Ocean beyond. It was too bad he could not, he thought regretfully. It would certainly be one hell of a lot easier than the long way around that was still to come.

As Teleman drew abreast of the second salt lake, the Tarim River, flowing down out of the peaks of Karakorum in the western Himalayas to Lop Nor, appeared, a thin crooked line of a river swollen now with the first evidence of the spring thaw. As he crossed the Lop Nor he passed into Chinese Eastern Turkestan.

The countryside below appeared considerably colder between

the ranges. The snow line reached almost to the floor of the new desert that was beginning to appear ahead, the Taklamakan. Pobeda Peak, rising in an almost sheer vertical from the banks of the Tarim on its southern face, reared up, higher by nearly ten thousand feet than the fourteen thousand feet at which he was now flying. It occurred to him that this was the first time he had ever flown *below* a land feature and for some reason it made him uneasy. Possibly, Teleman considered, it was brought on because it put both himself and the A-17 into perspective—a perspective that he lost at the two hundred thousand feet that lent him a minor godhead in which he was unconcerned with human fumblings toward power and gain, and made him content with observation and obscured the need for involvement. For long minutes he flew past the shining expanse of the 24,400-foot peak, gleaming along its crest as the sun inched light over its ridges.

For the next forty minutes he followed the Tarim southwest across the Taklamakan until it struggled up through a wicked series of foothills into the Karakorum. From here, relatively safe and comfortable in the heated/air-conditioned cabin of the silent aircraft, gazing at the twisted rills and cols of the mountains, he could feel the excitement that he knew men like Sir Edmund Hillary and Barry Bishop must have experienced when they stood at the foot of a peak such as Kanchenjunga, or Godwin Austen, or Mount Everest, preparatory to beginning the ascent to the 'roof of the world', a term the Sherpas had given the Himalayas, stretching a thousand miles from the Hindu Kush in the west to the Nan Shan in the east. But at the same time, he could only shake his head and wonder why a man would risk his life in the loneliest arena of the world to climb peaks that had been shrouded in snow and wind since man was little more than a gene spark in some species of reptile.

The Tarim had been left behind now and the Pamir Plateau, thirteen to fifteen thousand feet high, was beginning. Teleman lifted the airplane accordingly, another thousand feet. The two Tibetan cities of Yarkand and Kashgar would be slipping past in a few minutes and he ran a check on all of his antidetection gear. He would pass between the two cities, in reality little more than villages, but villages with large Chinese garrisons. He would be out of sight of both towns, Yarkand to the south and Kashgar well to the north. The only tricky spot would be the narrow dirt highway that ran between the two, and he was counting on the heavy snowfall of the previous night to make it impassable; he would be out of Chinese territory before fighters could be scrambled to intercept, even if they could break through his radar fouling.

As he drew abreast of the city of Kashgar, out of sight to the north, he cleared a ridge and the vista of the Pamir Plateau opened up before him. Ahead, less than five minutes flying time, was the Tadzhik SSR border. The radar net was indicating no hostile aircraft anywhere within the 1,600-mile diameter of its extent, but Teleman was not banking on that. Although the Tien Shan range, rising yet another nine thousand feet above his flight level, formed a perfect barrier to questing radio impulses, the entire Soviet and Chinese air forces combined could have hidden behind the wall of rock and he would never know it. It was times like these, he thought resignedly, that made him regret the excessive caution that would not allow him to interrogate the satellite system at will for fear of detection. Especially now, when the Soviets appeared to know about the project anyway. Because of the surrounding mountains, his radar could show him only dependable information on a very narrow cone leading directly up the valley to the border. In very short order, he knew, he would find out just how smart he had been.

Teleman came out of the sheltering arms of the two mountain chains fighting for altitude. At 150,000 feet he leveled off and took a good look around. He had narrowed his counterdetection radar to a circle two miles in diameter—no sense in advertising his presence. Teleman took a look at the weather gear and found the friendly ice cloud bank still stretched above him. Below, the plains of Turkestan were beginning to open up and he could just make out the hairline of the mighty Amu Dar Ya that tumbled and roared from the Hindu Kush to the Aral Sea a thousand miles northwest. The area over which he had just passed had been the fabled lands of the Kyber Pass and British soldiery of Kipling's tales. But for Teleman there would be no glorious charge of British lancers to rescue him at the last possible moment. All he had was himself and the A-17 to depend on.

A sudden flurry of the computer tapes and there on the screen, closing in from the north, was a Falcon. This time the Soviet pilot had been caught napping. Teleman was ahead of rather than behind him. It was going to be a stern chase, he thought without humor as he flicked the series of switches that fired the ramjets and scrambled to 200,000 feet. The intruder dropped behind momentarily, then increased power and began to close up. As the A-17's speed increased, the PCMS reacted accordingly, infusing Teleman with a calculated mix of hallucinogenic and barbiturate drugs. Within seconds Teleman was no longer thinking of the aircraft as a collection of metal and plastic components, but as an extension of himself. Actually, he did not feel on a conscious level that he had become the aircraft; it simply did not occur to him that there was any distinction. He *was* a part of the aircraft.

That bastard is gonna catch me, he thought in surprise. The contact readout chattered noisily to itself and showed less than forty minutes needed for missile range to be achieved. Teleman paused, finger on the throttle lever. It occurred to him that the Falcon could not maintain that speed and altitude for more than a few more minutes. Even as he was thinking, his body was reacting and lifting the A-17 to 225,000 feet and Mach 4.5. Simultaneously, the trailing Falcon slewed off and fell below, angling down and north to the nearest air base, while a second came streaking up from just ahead of the last Soviet aircraft's position. The chase was now shaping up into a gigantic chess match. They were going to run him down and if they failed at that, they would chase him into an area where fate, resembling a Falcon with a loaded and ready missile, would knock him out of the sky.

Teleman's mind was working furiously, weighing various possibilities, while he tried to sort out the various loopholes in each that would allow him to beat the odds stacking up against him. He could continue to climb to maximum altitude and speed, cutting into his remaining fuel load (already shaved to the danger point by the long flight into Tibet), to and maybe below the poundage needed to achieve rendezvous; or he could try and outfox his energetic pursuers. He checked the computers to see how much longer he dared defer the decision: ten minutes.

He was now flying at 225,000 feet at Mach 4.5 and heading due west across the southernmost part of the Soviet Union. Teleman made a small correction for the rendezvous pattern he had set up. Immediately the Falcon followed suit. He flew on, keeping a wary eye on the plane below. After five minutes, the second Falcon began to drop down in a long glide to its base, and then made an extended turn to the north, dropping lower all the time. At once, a third Falcon came roaring up to take position, still well behind, but having gained nearly twelve miles on his predecessor. The contact readout did a quick readjustment and flipped up the 'comforting' news that it would now require only eight minutes before missile range could be achieved, and two minutes left to make his decision. After that, he would be committed to a stern chase across Russia.

This third intruder seemed a little more impatient than the first two, Teleman thought, watching him close in faster. Probably wanted to hog the glory of bringing down the *Americanski spion Samolot*. Teleman grinned. Only four hundred miles separated the two craft now, and Teleman considered it time to take some positive action.

'Enough of this fooling around,' he muttered aloud, his voice sounding depressingly empty in the silence of the cockpit. Teleman went to work with the decoy missile setups, programing a new flight pattern into the computer. The computer would have to take care of the cubs, he thought. He was going to be too busy shortly to draw a decent breath. Teleman was about to give the Soviet detection systems a thorough workout. He knew that the observer would be busy with the optical tracking gear, but the pilot would have time to operate the semi-automated radar gear they would still carry. He doubted that they would remove all of that, as it would at least provide the approximate area in which to search. Obviously, the optical gear had a range of at least four hundred miles since that was the distance at which they had picked him up as he came out of the mountains. At five hundred miles, with his own ECM now narrowed to a mile in diameter, he would be only a hole in the sky to the Falcon radar. But he could really give them a red herring to play with.

Teleman chuckled. A red herring for Reds. Quite appropriate.

He began to flick the ECM switch controlling the antiradar gear on and off in a haphazard pattern, hopefully making the Soviet pilot think that his own radar gear was breaking through the electromagnetic interference the American gear was causing. At the same time he put the A-17 into a steep downward curve south and continued around into a tighter and tighter spiral, all the while keeping a close watch on the digital counter clicking off the closure rate to missile range. On the radar scope, the Russian pilot smoothly followed suit, never hesitating once. The flickering image of the A-17 must have been clearly visible on the radar scope. Teleman followed the course of the Falcon, waiting patiently. He was counting on the natural impatience, coupled with anxiety over losing the target, that he knew the Russian pilot must now be feeling. He had just begun the third spiral when it happened. He saw the Falcon clearly increase speed and go into a tighter and faster curving descent than the A-17. It was so impetuous that he did not even need the readout to tell him that the Russian had moved, moved to catch him within missile range by turning faster and steeper. Teleman waited a moment longer to be sure the Russian was committed.

He straightened the turn abruptly and pulled the nose up quickly. The ECM was in full operation again and, as he started into the climb, the A-17 released a ghost-image missile that, traveling at his speed, began to pull away from the aircraft into the same spiral course that he had been flying. The violent turn that the Falcon had made in an effort to catch him inside should have lost the A-17 to the visual observer. The ghost image, a small, ramjet-powered affair, was further complicating matters by producing the same signal that simulated the mother A-17. Teleman could see the pattern plainly on his own radar screen as it pulled farther and farther away. After the two were separated by several miles, the computer, following Teleman's instructions, began to turn the ghost away from the spiraling descent into a straight run south, as if running from the Soviet aircraft.

Teleman hoped, hoped so hard it was almost a prayer, that there was a terrific argument going on between the pilot and observer on board the Falcon. If this bird was going to hold true to pattern, he had about another five minutes or so to go before he would have to drop out and turn the chase over to the next in line.

Teleman wondered at the organization they must have to be able to figure out what he was up to: return the Falcons from their rotating picket duty nearly fifteen hundred miles northeast, land and refuel them, and put them back into the air less than two hours later, strung out in a perfect line to intercept him as he came sneaking across the border.

Then he stopped cold. Or else they had one hell of a lot more of these specially rebuilt Falcons than he had counted on. So far, he had faced four, and that meant they must be supported by at least twelve more if the pickets were to be effective. Since they would not know for sure where he would try to cross, the Soviets would have to keep at least thirty-six modified Falcons on the ready line. One set of twelve on station, twelve on their way from the base to the line, and twelve on the ground being serviced and fueled. 'Ye gods,' he muttered.

Now it was beinning to look as if his long shot was going to pay off. The following Falcon began to come around on a course halfway between Teleman and the ghost so that he could keep an eye on both until he decided which was the real intruder. He was being a little more cautious than Teleman had planned on. The gap between him and the ghost had widened to 160 miles and he instructed the computer to pour it on. Instantly, the ghost leaped ahead at close to Mach 5 and the range began to open. By now, the crew of the Falcon must be desperate. He checked his altitude and leveled off at 180,000 feet to watch for further developments.

As he waited, a fourth Falcon appeared on the scope, screaming for altitude. The third began to drop back and finally, after a few seconds, turned sharply into a bank and began spiraling down. Overshot his fuel, Teleman thought grimly. He hoped their escape capsule was in good operating condition. The fourth Falcon moved up fast, but still was far below the altitude at which the third had fallen out. This was exactly the situation Teleman had been hoping for. He ran for the ice layer. The crystalline structure of the high altitude cloud was so tenuous as to be almost nonexistent, in fact it was detectable only by instruments, but still thick enough to reflect radar waves. He did not have to worry about radar sighting, but the thin haze the cloud cast would also make optical tracking that much more difficult in the strong, late morning sunlight. Seconds later he began the second phase of his plan by falling off slowly southward.

It was rare to see an ice cloud layer of this extent much above ninety thousand feet, although scattered and shredded bits of ice could always be found at this altitude. The effects of the Arctic storm, Teleman thought, even 3,600 miles south. Anyway, it was here and he was going to make darned good use of it. Safely into the nebulous ice layer, he settled back to the long chase that would lead him north and west across the Asian landmass.

His radar screens indicated that the Falcon was still tracking the ghost by radar. The readout indicated that they would close up enough within four minutes to spot it as a phony on the visual apparatus. And when that happened, all hell was going to break loose. And sure enough, after four long minutes, in which Teleman widened the gap between the A-17 and the pursuing Falcon by nearly five hundred miles, he spotted the Soviet craft coming around in a tight half turn. Obviously they had discovered the ghost for what it was and were now running back to the projected path of the last visual sighting. When they got there, they would find him nowhere in sight—he hoped.

Sure enough, here came the reinforcements. Four more Falcons were rising fast along the path where they had last sighted him. As unobtrusively as possible, he fell off even farther south. Now that the Reds were lost in the dust, he was free for the moment to cope with other problems. Right now he was safely out of range of the visual gear. In fact, by dropping off south, he was now falling behind the fourth and rearmost Falcon. He was pretty sure the Soviets would figure that he would pull a trick like this and would right now be using all of the radar at their disposal to try and spot the blind area, now less than a mile wide, that his ECM gear was causing. That would explain the systematic spacing of the four Falcons, each two hundred miles apart. In addition, they might shortly be using their mid-continental radar line, jacked around south to search for him. It was time to increase the ECM before they did pick him up.

As Teleman reached for the ECM gear panel, he caught a flicker of light on the radar screen as one of the Falcons changed course. The digital readout chattered quickly. Too late, he groaned inwardly. Either one of the aircraft or the ground stations had picked him up. The Falcon was heading directly for him.

Working quickly, he extended the counterdetection range to its full sixteen-hundred-mile range. It seemed to have no effect on the approaching Falcon. He could not spot a single indication of wavering or uncertainty. Swearing softly, Teleman checked the fuel-load readouts. Mach 4.5 was the limit unless he wanted to crash somewhere in Poland or France, out of fuel. The contact-point readout now gave him six minutes before the Falcon reached the missile range. He checked his location quickly and found that he was south of the ancient capital of the Mongolian Khan Timur-i-leng, the city of Samarkand, less than three hundred miles from the Afghan border.

Would the Soviets hesitate to cross the border, as they had north over Sinkiang? There was only one way to find out, he thought grimly, and dropped into a steep turn south, sliding down in a long glide that would bring him across the border at 140,000 feet. It was a desperate gamble, but one that had to be taken.

The next six minutes passed slowly. Teleman fled south for the border pursued by the Falcons, slowly gaining ground by their relay tactics. As the chase lengthened, Teleman began to observe the flight characteristics of the other pursuing aircraft. His radar showed two other bandits wheeling into the flight line from the north. He could imagine them strung out in a long line, in both directions, all the way to the air base at Alma Alta. Of the two on his radar beside the immediate pursuer, one was heading back. The sudden flurry of activity involving the four Falcons when they thought they had lost him obviously had not exhausted them. Then on the horizon Teleman spotted the Amu Dar Ya, the river that formed the northeastern border, separating the Soviet Union from Afghanistan.

The radar screen showed the second following Falcon almost within range, and indicated that Teleman would cross the border with seconds to spare. As if realizing that he was losing his prey, the Soviet pilot fired a salvo of missiles. Teleman watched the two rockets spurt ahead of the aircraft and begin to close in on him with deadly silence. As soon as the missiles were away, the Falcon throttled back and dropped swiftly down in a sharp turn, trying desperately to conserve fuel for the impossible run back to the Alma Alta base eight hundred miles north.

The missiles fell far short, not a serious hazard after all. Teleman bent wearily forward and programed the ECM to respread the sixteen-hundred-mile safety net around the A-17. The remaining three Soviet Falcons had pulled around to the north as he crossed the border, and climbing swiftly up to his altitude was a single replacement with which the Soviets would probably try and keep him in sight. But it would be a hopeless task, Teleman knew. He now had a pretty good idea of the effective range of their visual tracking gear. Five hundred miles seemed to be the ultimate limit and accurate tracking could be performed properly only at less than four hundred miles. Accordingly, Teleman pulled into a long arc to the southwest that would bring him out of range in less than twelve minutes, and throttled back to Mach 1.9.

Two problems, both serious, still faced him. One was how to repenetrate the Soviet Union in order to make the rendezvous point on time; the second was his dwindling fuel load. Both problems were interdependent.

After fifteen minutes of intense work with the computer, Teleman sat back and studied the results. Keeping him company the entire while was the lone Falcon, six hundred miles north and safely inside his own border. Teleman was sure he was out of sight of the Soviet aircraft. He had to be in order for this new course to work.

The computers, taking all the variables into account, including the fact that it was very possible for the Soviets to again pick him up deeper into the Soviet Union, had drawn a flight path that would keep him outside the boundaries of the Soviet Union until he reached the vicinity of the Caspian Sea. He would re-enter the Soviet Union from northern Iran, skirting the southern edge of the Caspian at two hundred thousand feet. He would use a full ECM range of sixteen hundred miles, as the Soviet border radar net would be on alert and it would be impossible to escape their notice anyway. It was very likely that, if they could have visual tracking systems for aircraft, then they could also have ground stations to perform the same job over a wider range and with greater accuracy. But radar disruption of sixteen-hundred-mile diameter should make it impossible for the radar net to provide enough of a course approximation to the visual tracking stations to aid in spotting him in the three minutes or so that he would be within range.

Teleman fell off slowly, deeper into Afghan territory, always paralleling his original line of flight, keeping the Russian plane on the edges of his radar screen while slowly leaving him behind. The one-sided chase continued due west now, until he had left the torn earth of the Hindu Kush far behind and below lay the rugged Plateau of Iran. Every ten minutes, regular as clockwork, he watched another Falcon spiral up to take his station on the other side of the border.

The A-17 was on full automatic now and Teleman was merely a passenger. At a certain point the aircraft banked steeply to the south, then steadied in response to a small correction in the flight plan. After half an hour of this blind run and chase, his companion, now six hundred miles behind him, overstayed his ten-minute pattern. Teleman bent to the radar screen, watching to see what would happen. A minute passed, then a second and a third. In the fourth minute the Falcon slid off one wing and dropped quickly into a long glide northwest. Teleman checked his maps. The air base at Ashkhabad on the Soviet side of the Turkman SSR-Afghanistan border was now within range. Operations had probably been shifted accordingly, Teleman thought.

He turned his attention to the ground control map rolling out on the screen. His flight path was marked by a triangular bar reaching to the black horizon line. The flight path was superimposed on an actual view of the terrain below. Off his starboard wing was the Iranian city of Meshed and he knew that the Iranians had a large radar complex north of the city, watching the Russian border. His crossing point would be almost directly over the city of Babol, two hundred miles northeast of Tehran.

After this little bit of unscheduled horseplay, his fuel load was going to be cut mighty fine to get him to rendezvous. He would have to reduce speed severely and yet he still had to get there on time. He was certain that Larkin, from what little he knew of his contact man, could be depended on, gale or no gale. He had not received any weather reports on conditions between Greenland and Novaya Zemlya since he started his run south from the Arctic. To avoid the least possibility of detection, all but two monitoring channels were shut down automatically during the mission portion of any flight over Communist territory. The Soviets were known to monitor the Advanced SAMOS satellite system by ground and shipboard stations in an effort to break the codes used. The only weather information he could receive, then, was from the military weather satellites directly overhead, and they reported on local conditions only. Satellite-to-satellite transmissions were too easily monitored and traced to allow him to interrogate at will. Teleman could therefore only guess at weather conditions in the Arctic, and if the ice clouds that overlay most of Asia were any indication, he had to conclude that they were extremely bad.

Once more he had the computer review the flight plan for him. In twelve minutes he would be crossing the border into Soviet territory. Teleman was well aware that, if he had missed anything while setting up the course, the flight plan would end with him and the A-17 scattered across miles of steppe, rather than orbiting the *Robert F. Kennedy* prior to refueling for home.

After crossing the border, the flight path would take him over the southern end of the Caspian Sea to the Caucasus Mountains and across the Sea of Azov, then over the bend in the Dnieper

River to bypass Kiev, and out across the Ukraine to Poland. Over the Ukraine, he had a choice to make. Depending on local weather conditions and any indications of Soviet fighter activity, he could, if he had to, drop farther south into the Czechoslovakia-Hungary region and run for West Germany and the North Sea. That alternative was his last-ditch escape attempt if they tried to intercept him over continental Russia. If not, he would make for Poland and the Baltic Sea and up across the Scandinavian Peninsula. That route would put him at the rendezvous point with ten minutes of fuel left, much more preferable than ditching in the Barents Sea. He could do the last in seven hours by holding his speed to Mach 1.5, his most economical cruising speed.

Ahead now was the Soviet border, and it was time to crank out the radar counterdetection gear. A circle of interference sixteen hundred miles across would keep them busy for a long time, hunting for him with that damned visual gear.

## CHAPTER NINE

LARKIN was on watch, strapped securely into his high seat, when Folsom stumbled through the hatchway on to the bridge. Larkin nodded a greeting without taking his eyes from the violent seas visible through the revolving screen. Truly mountainous waves were building, even here in the lee of the cliffs forming the sea edge of the North Cape. Folsom, peering out through the spinning circle of glass that kept the ice and sleet from completely shrouding the bridge windows, was shocked to see just how high and rough they had become in the two hours he had been off bridge duty. In the engine room, where he had been assisting with the overhaul for the last hour, the motion of the ship had been rough, rougher than he had ever experienced that far down in the hull of any ship. But the spread of tortured wave and glooming sky through the glass was beyond belief. Folsom estimated the waves to be rising nearly eighty feet. The anemometer showed wind speed gusting to 105 knots. The sweep of horizon, broken only by the faintly visible headlands of the Cape to the extreme west, was filled with masses of cyclonic cloud that intermittently obscured frost-sharp stars, glistening momentarily overhead whenever the ship, cresting a wave, rose out of the dense spray fog. The wind-riven clouds, still low on the horizon, were bearing down savagely. In less than two hours the U.S.S. *Robert F. Kennedy* would reel under the impact of the storm's major onslaught.

Since early morning Folsom had been aware of a mild tension building in the pit of his stomach. Now staring through the spinning disk of glass, it threatened to choke him. He swallowed and reswallowed as inconspicuously as possible. He had been through bad gales before, but never one of such fury or with a damaged ship. For the hundredth time since the strain gauges had been installed, he leaned over to study the dials. All four gauges, their leads attached to the insides of the patch and to the hull plates, showed periodic flex that he knew would be loosening the welding beads. Earlier he had sent a crew into the hull tank to reweld the plates flush against the tank, but they had been unable to finish more than three strengthening bars before the mounting vibration of the hull plates against the hammering of wind and wave made further work impossible.

Folsom turned away from the dials and noticed Larkin's face as he stared into the wind- and wave-filled night. The narrow face was strangely lit by the soft bridge lights, causing the angles and planes of the skull to set in rigid patterns. The face betrayed not the first sign of emotion. In spite of the intensity of the angry sea, Larkin sat comfortably in the high seat, arms folded across his chest, studying the small cone of night visible through the madly whirling screen.

Folsom's musings were interrupted by the radioman. Startled, he turned to find the rating standing at his shoulder. Folsom glanced at the sailor's face and was not surprised to see the small light of controlled fear deep in the man's eyes. He knew the same flicker of light must also be in his. Hurriedly he took the message and turned away. 'Ye gods,' he said softly. 'Here it comes.'

Larkin turned his head to look at him, then accepted the message Folsom handed to him. He read it through without comment, then passed it back to Folsom.

'It does look like we are in for it. Gale force winds of 125 to 130 knots expected in the next three hours, decreasing to 90 to 110 knots for the following eight hours. Ouch.'

Larkin bent forward to read the strain gauges. 'How much time before we reach the turn-around point?'

Folsom glanced at his watch. 'About ninety minutes, sir.'

Larkin rubbed his face absently, and then stared at his hand as if expecting to find the answer there. When he did not, he grunted and looked up at Folsom.

'Stress is building far too rapidly on the bow section to suit me. I think it's time we came about. We can loiter somewhat on the way back to make it come out right, can't we?'

'Yes, sir.'

'In that case, prepare to come about, Mr. Folsom.'

Folsom nodded and made for the plotting table, the ball of

fear in his stomach growing larger and tighter at the same time. He had to force himself to keep his voice steady as he ordered the general quarters alarm sounded through the ship, then made the announcement. He had just finished and was putting the microphone back into its clip when the ship's intercom buzzer sounded. He flicked the switch on. 'Bridge here.'

'Mr. Folsom, Rigsby here. We got real trouble in the hull tank. Those damned welders . . . the whole patch is weakening fast.'

Folsom spun around. One of the needles on the strain-gauge dial was jerking madly. Almost at the same time, the other gauge started to follow.

'Captain,' he spat out, and flipped the volume up a bit so that Larkin could hear.

'Go on, Rigsby.'

'The main forward structural member is cracked—right along-side the weld. I'm getting a trickle of water right now near the top of the patch.'

'Is there anything that can be done?' Larkin asked.

'Yes, sir. Flood the tank.' The tinny reproduction of the intercom barely concealed the nervousness of the man's voice. Folsom could imagine him all alone in the immensity of the tank, knowing that the interior hatch was secured and that it would take forty seconds to get it open. If the patch should go, he would be crushed to death by tons of freezing water pouring into the tank. That same water would also pull the *RFK* down farther by the bow until the first wave that broke would send her straight to the bottom. Folsom could feel the knot of fear rising into his throat, threatening to erupt into endless screams. The figures on the scratch pad, which he had scribbled from the strain-gauge dials, dissolved into a meaningless jumble, and the console reeled for a moment before he clenched the side of the plotting table and gripped until his knuckles went dead white. He fought with his body to control the panic as he watched the wind indicator flicker wildly with the first of the gusts that would quickly grow to a full 125-knot gale. Flashes of thought broke through his guard . . . the sudden wrenching snap as the bow broke loose under the pounding and the bulkheads . . . never designed to withstand the pressures of the naked, angry sea . . . giving way one by one . . . the *RFK* settling deeper into the waves . . . the Arctic seas pounding and smashing through the bulkheads . . . the ship buckling against the impact . . . plunging bow downward. . . .

'We're shoring up the patch and the structural member with braces, but they won't hold up long.'

'All right then, do what you can and keep me informed.' Larkin's voice was calm in the midst of Folsom's own mental storm. 'But as soon as you get the braces installed, I want you and the crew out of there. Do you understand?'

'Yes, sir, but if we stay, or one of us anyway, we'll have time to warn you and get out.'

'No,' Larkin said sharply. 'You could not give me any more than a minute or so warning. The strain gauges will provide that. As soon as you are finished with the bracing, get out and report aft to the repair station. Is that understood?'

Larkin's matter-of-fact analysis of the situation and Rigsby's almost suicidal offer to remain behind in the hull tank to provide the ship with a few seconds extra warning began to calm Folsom. He had never experienced this kind of paralysing fear before, but he knew, as did every man who faces danger in situations over which he has little control, that eventually he would meet this shattering fear at least once before he died. He had seen men suddenly grow rigid before going into battle, or divers just before making a deep dive, veterans who had been through many engagements. It happened, and there was nothing you could do about it except hope that you could handle the situation when it did happen. He reached down and picked up the pencil that had dropped from his nerveless fingers and pressed it slowly on to the pad, willing his muscles to move again, to continue to draw the numbers indicating the course change required and the time they would have to lose at reduced speed to bring them to the rendezvous point on time.

Larkin flicked off the intercom and turned to Folsom. His voice was strong and full of command. 'Mr. Folsom, get me an exact position fix, as close as you can. Then run the new course through the computer and alert the crew that we are coming about. Keep them at general quarters until we have straightened out on the new course . . . and make sure that Rigsby and the rest are out of that hull tank. Give them five minutes more. I'm going below for my foul-weather gear. You will take the conn while I am outside, but follow my directions.'

'Outside!' Folsom exploded. 'Captain, you can't go out there!'

Larkin grinned. 'Watch me. How else do you think we are going to get her around? You can't see worth a damn through that screen. This ship is going to have to be steered around those waves like a tin can. That means we come about as we crest a wave—and only the right wave at that—and complete the turn before we hit the bottom of the trough or else we will roll over and go right to the bottom.'

Folsom took a deep breath. 'Captain, you will freeze to death before we can come about.'

'Not if you hurry about it.'

Larkin turned away and hurried down to his cabin for his

foul-weather gear. When he returned to the bridge a few minutes later, Folsom was just finishing his instructions to the helmsman. He looked up as Larkin came on to the bridge, zipping up his jacket. A marine came hurrying up with a nylon safety line and clipped one end to the harness already around Larkin's chest.

'Listen for my count. As we come up the wave I'll start counting backward from ten. When I get to one, be ready to put the helm over hard . . . and better keep the turbine engines idling up to speed as well. We'll have plenty of need of an extra kick.' Folsom nodded and Larkin turned away, jamming the helmet down over his head.

He snapped the throat mike into place, tested it quickly, then pulled down the faceplate and left through the emergency hatch. Once outside, still in the lee of the bridge, he checked the microphone again, then buckled his safety straps to the railing. With the safety line trailing behind, he was now about as safe as he could possibly be . . . until the first good wave decided to wash him overboard. Against the power of those tons of water the line would snap; or, if it held, would probably cut him in half.

The plates of the catway leading around the top of the bridge structure were caked solid with ice. That ice, washed constantly by spray, was slippery underfoot, and he moved carefully to keep his footing. As he came out of the lee of the deckhouse, Larkin grunted in surprise as the wind cut through the nylon and electrically heated layers of foam padding as if they did not exist. Almost immediately his fingers and toes went numb. The temperature close to $-20°$, when combined with the 110-knot wind, gave a chill index of $-98°$. Unprotected, he would not last more than a minute before his heart stopped beating. As Larkin moved out on to the forward position of the weather deck, the wind pulled and plucked at him to send his feet sweeping away. He crashed against the steel wall of the deckhouse with stunning force, and for several minutes was unable to clear his head enough to get to his feet.

The forty-foot journey from the deck hatch, up the narrow ladder, and around the curve of the bridge was made, an inch at a time, on hands and knees. The wind was a solid wall of force through which he had to tunnel, and finally he was reduced to using his hands to pull himself from stanchion to stanchion along the railing. The stanchions were set every six feet, just beyond the grasp of his extended arm. He had to wait between each stanchion, arms stretched wide to hold the stanchion and the edge of the catway, resting, readying himself for the lunge to the next. Then, when he grasped it, he had to pull himself painfully up to the frozen metal and reach for the next. His task was made even harder by the fact that each stanchion supported a wedge of ice nearly two feet long to windward. His gloves froze to the ice and he had to pull them loose each time. If he lost a glove, he would also lose a hand. An uncovered hand would freeze into uselessness in less than two minutes. And Larkin needed the use of both hands to make any progress at all.

Larkin stretched out full length on the ice-coated deck to reduce the amount of his body exposed to the wind. The wind was like a solid hammer of steel pounding away in rhythmic gusts, thumping him into the ice, and then, as it got under his body and lifted him clear of the deck, flinging him back against the safety line. The struggle soon became concentrated into forcing his hand out to grasp the next stanchion and pull himself along the deck. He had thirty-five more feet to go to reach the center of the catway.

The strain on Larkin's shoulders was causing the muscles to scream in protest each time he reached for the next stanchion. Then it happened.

Between the fourth and fifth stanchion, his hand slipped off the ice-coated tube. The wind reached, slamming him back against the harness, and the line fouled. Another gust of wind caught him and almost pulled him through the railing before he got the straps cleared. Then the petulant wind smashed him back, cracking his leg viciously against the bridge plating as if it were alive and frustrated by the puny efforts of this unbearable, unnoticeable insect. For a minute Larkin lay crumpled against the bulkhead while the pain in his leg slowly subsided. Then by sheer strength of will he pulled himself to the next stanchion.

After twenty minutes he had managed to get as close to the center of the bridge as he could.

So much ice, he thought. He would never have believed it. Every square inch of the ship above the water line was coated with several feet of ice that glistened here and there in the bridge lights. The forward part of the deck was covered with mounds of ice that obscured bollards and lines and winches. No wonder the *RFK* was riding so low. If he *had* filled that hull tank the extra tonnage of water in the bow would have brought her so low in the water that they would have been swamped in short order. Although the *RFK* was no submarine, she could ride low for a long while. But eventually the weight of the steadily accumulating ice would send her to the bottom as surely as if the patch had opened.

Larkin rested against the railing with his arms wrapped around the icy stanchion. After a minute or so he regained enough strength to ask for the searchlights. Two powerful beams of light lanced out, swirling around to light the forepeak before disappearing into the twilight gray. Highlights of green and white foam were snatched from the waves and flung back at him by the wind.

Larkin pulled himself to his knees and wedged his body between two close-set stanchions. Standing on his knees, he tried to peer ahead into the deep twilight gloom of the Arctic storm as water and ice smashed back at him from the knife-edged prow. He found that he could keep the faceplate of his electrically heated helmet and suit free of ice with his gloves, but the sea and sky were so close to the same shades of greenish gray that it was almost impossible to tell which was which. After a while he began to make sense of the scene. The waves, he found, were silhouetted in the searchlight as the ship climbed towards their crests. He timed several, counting the seconds—one thousand . . . two thousand . . . three thousand—until he had gained a rough average of the time it took the *RFK* to climb, pause at the crest, then rocket down the far side into the deep trough. The motion of the ship was far too irregular to judge the size and height of the waves because of the tremendous forces being applied laterally to the ship by the wind blowing from only two points off the port bow.

He crouched, waiting, his arms wrapped around the railing. The water streamed back, soaking him thoroughly in spite of the waterproof clothing. The wind drove into his trouser legs between the sealed boot tops and cuffs, down his neck and beneath the helmet, disregarding the faceplate as if it did not exist. He waited, already half frozen, trying desperately to stay awake in the intense cold.

A towering roller built up in front of the ship. The bow followed, lifting toward the crest at an impossible angle, and Larkin started his count. He reached one, just as the ship crested, teetered for a moment. Now, he thought, just . . . 'Now!' he screamed into the microphone and felt the ship vibrate through its shroud of ice as full power was fed from its nuclear engines to the spinning propeller shafts. The ship tilted and started its headlong rush for the trough.

# CHAPTER TEN

FOR A curious moment Larkin was aware only of the beams of the twin searchlights probing into the depths of the trough, immeasurably distant. The stark, white light caught and held the peculiar green-blue color of the frigid Arctic waters. With an effort he wrenched his eyes away and strained through the gloom to the next wave, not quite a quarter of a mile away. Light flashes from the searchlights danced in front of his eyes, obscuring the express-train speed of approach. In spite of the pounding, the cold, the spray, and the near panic, he found he was still counting smoothly.

'Now, hard to port, all engines emergency full.' Again his voice was a near scream. In spite of the violence of the wind on the crest, the ship shuddered along its stem as the nuclear engines were supplemented by the six gas turbine engines spewing thirty thousand shp apiece in less than eight seconds from idle. The cruiser, which had begun to swing from the wind, stopped as suddenly as though it had hit a brick wall. The engines drove her deep down below the crest, and momentarily out of the full force of the wind. The *RFK* slewed to port, its stern snapping around as the rudders came hard over. As she reached the trough she was broadside to the next mountainous wave.

Larkin groaned in agony. That damned ice, he cursed. The vast tonnage of ice had slowed her, pressed her too deep into the water for the engines to cope. And the next wave was already towering above her and would roll her like a stick. The ship heeled, farther and farther over, until Larkin gave up hope. A deluge of water washed him under, burying him completely. Then the great battle cruiser broke free; shaking her head like an angry terrier, she righted herself and shed water in torrents. She came up with a bone in her teeth as she surged around to point in the opposite direction. The following wave rolled under and lifted her high into the wind. The ship skidded down into another trough, her bow smashing deeply into the water. For a heart-sickening moment, Larkin thought again she would never surface, but once more the bow knifed up, and she shed water. The next wave was easier, as the engines were cut back to one third. And finally she ran before the wind, moving with an easy rolling motion through the towering waves.

Larkin hung exhausted and freezing as the ship straightened and lifted more easily into the next wave, now chasing water to the crest. Water was no longer breaking over her bow in a steady stream, but came instead in fitful spurts. Larkin felt two hands go under his arms and he was lifted to his feet. The forward portion of the bridge on which he stood was now in the lee of the wind as the storm pounded in from directly astern.

Half supported, he stumbled across the deck and into the heat and glare of the bridge. After the intense cold, the 72° temperature of the interior was almost intolerable. He slumped into the seat and Folsom pulled off his helmet and boots. It was Bridges who had come out on to the deck for him, and now he stripped off his mask and gloves and fetched a cup of hot coffee. Larkin gulped it down as fast as the scalding liquid would allow.

Folsom walked easily across the bridge to where Larkin was seated clutching his coffee. He stopped and grinned down at the captain.

'Aren't you the iron sailor,' he chuckled in a low voice. Larkin smiled back.

'I thought I was before I went out there. Now I'm not so sure.'

Folsom bent to read the dials on the strain gauges. 'Well, at least that's one worry gone. At this rate we could keep on for the next ten years.'

'Good. In that case, I'm going below for some sleep. Call me in two hours.'

'I'll call you when we hit the rendezvous point, not before.' Larkin glanced up, startled.

'Not before, I said.'

The captain stood up, trying valiantly to square his shoulders. 'That's mutiny, I think, Mr. Folsom,' he said in mock anger.

'Yeah, I know. Now get below, before I call a marine to escort you.'

Folsom watched fondly as Larkin went below to his quarters, then he turned and went back to the plotting table. He studied the map and the course he had laid out to the rendezvous point for a long while, then he went to stand before the screen. He reached down and flicked on the searchlights and swiveled them around to scan the sea on both sides of the bow. Clean circles of light were cut into the mountainous waves by the two million candlepower lights, which picked green out of the freezing Arctic waters and gleamed off white crests now blowing in the same direction as the *RFK*. He concentrated on the motion of the ship under his feet and found that she was moving in a rhythmic dance in time to the roll of the waves under her keel. Darkness had fallen in all of its intensity. The frozen air glistened with a million scattered stars, the very crispness of their light indicating the depth of the cold. Low on the southern horizon was the storm bank, spun out from the leading edge of the storm. Folsom knew that the seas would be at their worst in that area. But they could run on into the sheltering lee of the Soviet coast, safe in the knowledge that no Russian ship or aircraft could put out to look for them, nor would submarines be cruising near enough to the storm-racked surface to spot them electronically. By the time the storm abated enough for the Russian Navy to resume regular patrols, they should be putting into the Clyde, their intermediate base before sailing for Newport Naval Base, Rhode Island.

Folsom turned away from the screen and started his regular watch tour of the various consoles, checking on the condition of the ship. He was still worried about the deck heaters. Even with the extra heat being piped up from the reactor cooling system, they still were not coping with the ice. Perhaps, now that they were running before the waves, they would not be taking aboard as much spray, not unless the wind veered, anyway. And to judge by the satellite photos of the storm center, if they maintained present speed and heading they would sail into a radial arm of wind within two hours. Then they would be taking the wind and spray across the bow quarter as well as one hell of a cross chop from the waves as the wind tried to push incalculable gallons of sea water from their already set path. It was going to be one hell of an afternoon.

Two hours later Folsom was ready to modify his judgment as to what kind of afternoon it would be, but modify it downward. He turned away from the ship's intercom. Barrows, the engineering officer, had every right to be extremely unhappy with Folsom, but his voice had been steady enough, with no hint that he did indeed blame the executive officer. Barrows had just finished reporting that the main condenser system had frozen solid. It had been Folsom's order to use the major part of the reactor heat to feed the deck heaters. This meant that the heat normally used to maintain the condenser system at an even 36°F had to be channeled into the deck heaters and the reactor crew had to vary the power output to control the condenser system by hand. When Larkin had called for full emergency power from all engines, an overload had been thrown on to the condensers. The temperature had dropped quickly while the reactor worked at full power, until, when the engines had been cut back to one third, the temperature in the condensers stood at 33° F. The reactor crew had gone furiously to work to try and bring the temperatures back up to a safe 36° F, but in the succeeding two hours the system had oscillated widely, and, finally, the first seed crystal of ice had formed in the outside banks.

Even rechanneling all heat being fed to the decks had not been enough to stave off the rapid icing. Five minutes later the webbing of pipe was full of half-frozen slush. Barrows had closed down the main system and shifted to the auxiliary condensers. If needed, he could go directly to sea water, but the resulting corrosion would mean a major overhaul for the system and two months in drydock to complete the job.

Damn it all, Folsom swore to himself. Why now of all times? This whole blasted cruise seemed to be jinxed. First the collision, then the storm, and now the condenser system. What in the name of the God was next? Barrows estimated that he would need at least three to four hours to thaw and flush out the condensers. In the meantime the auxiliary banks could handle slightly less than eight knots speed. That in itself would put them nearly forty minutes behind on the rendezvous.

He snapped on the intercom and punched the code for engineering viciously. 'Chuck, use the auxiliaries. If you can't get the main condensers thawed in three hours, we'll have to use the boost engines to make up forty minutes.'

'Right, sir. I've got a crew checking them over right now. How does the deck ice look?'

'Just a minute.'

Folsom turned and pressed against the glass. The decks showed up clearly in the searchlights. The glare from the ice was strong, but not so strong that he could not make out the forward winch boom lying horizontal on the deck where it had been lashed. It was covered by ice that barely showed a mound. The boom, when horizontal, lay three feet above the deck.

'Still too damn thick for me,' he said into the intercom. 'But that'll have to wait. Use all the reactor heat you need to get those condensers thawed!'

Teleman lay relaxed in the acceleration couch, letting the liquid pulsing of the aircraft flow placidly through his body. The PCMS was bringing him slowly out of a two-hour nap, a much-needed nap that, while it would not completely restore him, would bring his body systems to the point where the proper dosages of amphetamines could keep him awake and completely aware. He eased the couch forward into a semi-sitting position and lazily scanned the ground control monitor currently displaying the Pomeranian coastline of Poland 180,000 feet below. Even at this distance he could see specks of white dancing on the surface of the Baltic Sea as it rolled and thrashed to the commands of the storm front beginning to reach across northern Europe.

In Hamburg, less than three hundred miles west, it would be colder than the gates of hell a thousand years before the fires were lit, he thought. It always seemed that the bottom had fallen out of the thermometer when one of these Arctic storms came sweeping out of the Baltic into Germany. He recalled with fondness the two years he had spent with the Defense Intelligence Agency in Europe. He had toured Europe from the Baltic to the Mediterranean and Belgium to Rumania—all but Scandinavia, with the exception of Denmark. He had never crossed the Kattegat. For some reason he had kept putting off Norway and Sweden and Finland, meaning to cross the channel, but never quite making it. He shrugged in a half stretch to ease cramping muscles and shook himself out of his reverie. One of these days he would go back, and Scandinavia would be first on his list.

By now he could make out the southern coast of Sweden lying beyond Bornholm Island. The cloud cover was closing in quickly below and the northern end of the Baltic Sea had turned slate

gray. Patches of cloud to the west were beginning to glow red
in the waning twilight.

Teleman was heading directly north across the Baltic toward
the Gulf of Bothnia. He would fly up the length of the gulf,
then over the curve of the Scandinavian Peninsula where Sweden
joined Finland. By following the twenty-fifth meridian due north,
in less than two hours he would enter Norwegian airspace north
of Finland. Then, twenty minutes flying time later, he would
rendezvous with the *Robert F. Kennedy* off the North Cape,
completing a twelve-thousand-mile round trip, dump his information, and head home.

'And a damn good thing, too,' Teleman said aloud to hear his
own voice. Rendezvous was still some 2,500 miles away and the
gauge needles for his main tanks were already well into the
empty zone. Shortly he would have to switch to the reserve tanks
with their two-thousand-mile additional range. By that time, he
figured on his knee pad, he should be somewhere in the vicinity
of the Finnish coast. He was also going to come on to the
rendezvous point nearly thirty minutes late. Teleman wondered
how the ship was going to take that. He hope to hell that they
would have a refueler standing by. The flight plans he had been
given hours ago called for him to swing west and rendezvous
with the tanker over Iceland. At this rate he would be lucky to
make the Cape.

Directly below, he caught a fading glimpse of Gotland sliding
through the clouds. The cloud cover was closing down fast and
he wondered idly whether or not he would be able to see the
lights of Stockholm as he passed over the city.

The run into and across the Soviet Union had not been disastrous after all. It appeared that he had lost his tail over Iran,
since the last Falcon had dropped down at the end of its ten-
minute run and none had come up to take its place. Perhaps they
were figuring that they had scared him badly enough when he
fell off into Afghanistan and had decided to opt for the Indian
Ocean. He sincerely hoped so. He had flown the tightrope between Tehran and the radar base at Gurgan, and then out over
the Caspian Sea without being spotted. East of Baku he almost
had heart failure when a blip showed up suddenly on his screen
and the readout put it at 150 miles distant. It had turned out to be
nothing more than a fragment of the same ice cloud he had used
for cover, but even so it was several minutes before the adrenaline
stopped playing hockey in his bloodstream. Teleman was sure
that he had nearly blown out the PCMS unit.

Once past Baku, with its intensive radar net, he had made
a long, sweeping turn west to cross the Russian SSR between
Makhachkala and Kizlyar on the Caspian coast. The long flight

across the Ukraine to Poland had been accomplished while he slept without so much as a radar bogie to disturb his dreamless exhaustion. He was about done in and he knew it, and the PCMS knew it. He had had to program specific orders into the computer or else it would promptly have dropped him back off to sleep once more.

With the end of the mission less than two hours away, and that comfortable hospital bed in California only five and a half hours off, he felt he could afford to lose the extra sleep.

Teleman could not explain why, but he had rather an uneasy feeling about the next two hours. The escape from the Soviet trap had been just a little too pat; that last Falcon had given up a bit too easily for all the effort it and the others had expended. He had a hunch, and in this business, he had found, you played your hunches.

The ground control map showed him the narrows of the Gulf of Bothnia. The infrared gear was displaying sharply detailed pictures of the Finnish towns of Kikkola, Jacobstad, and Nykarleby and the Swedish town of Umea opposite. He knew that both the Swedes and Finns had small military garrisons well hidden nearby and the Swedes had a squadron of aging Hawk antiaircraft missiles, but nothing to worry him. Both concentrated the bulk of their military establishments to the north in concert with the Norwegians to meet the threat of the Soviet armies heavily invested in the Kola Peninsula north of Finland and east of Norway.

The ground control map was beginning to describe the northern coast of the gulf when a small blip appeared on the forward edge of his radar screens, coming south from the direction of Finland and on an intercepting flight path. Quickly he checked his systems and carefully increased the ECM range.

The image grew swiftly, closing on him at near his own speed, but still a hundred thousand feet below. At first he thought it might be one of the Concorde polar flights, but the recognition pattern was all wrong and the approaching craft too small. Puzzled, he reached out and upped the ECM range even more; then he realized that he had made a fatal mistake. The approaching aircraft had to be a Soviet Falcon. By increasing the range of the ECM, he had advertised his own presence as thoroughly as if he had radioed Moscow his exact position. Teleman banked suddenly to starboard, then straightened abruptly and ran for 220,000 feet.

The Falcon maintained course for a moment, then suddenly doubled its speed and rocketed upward. Both the IR and radar screens showed the long ionization trail of the afterburner.

Teleman held for a few minutes, watching the other plane. The Soviet pilot was out to get him once and for all, and Teleman

knew it. As if to prove it, the interceptor did not waver but bored
steadily on, closing the four-hundred-mile range in seconds. Desperately, Teleman slammed the nose down and blasted the ramjets to full thrust. He shot away beneath the Russian and pulled
up sharply behind, wishing mightily for at least a 20-mm cannon,
and preferably a wing pod full of heat-seeking missiles. As he
came up behind, he straightened out, running for the Arctic. His
only hope was to stay as far away from the Russian as possible
and outlast him.

Teleman had gained a few miles by pulling beneath and behind
the Soviet pilot. But even as he was pulling away, the Russian,
without a wasted second, had begun to climb into a loop. Now
Teleman watched him spiral into a loop so tight that it should
either have killed the pilot or torn the wings off the plane or both.
At the top of the climb the Russian did a vicious wingover and
arrowed down after him.

Now Teleman realized that he had been underestimating the
Soviets' desperation. Not only did they want very much to bring
him down, but they were willing to violate any territory since he
had escaped their trap in Asia. It should all have been amply clear
to him in view of the magnitude of effort they had expended in
shifting the Falcons around to run him down over Tashkent. His
overtaxed mind finally saw what he should have realized earlier,
what the Soviets had already figured out. There was no chance
of the aerial fight being recorded on radar. Only the Falcon would
be seen. The Russians could either ignore any protests that might
be forthcoming from the Finns or Swedes or pass it off with an
apology and explanation that the Soviet pilot had merely strayed
while on a test flight of a new aircraft. His peculiar antics could
be explained as part of the test-flight regime. Teleman himself
would be invisible from the ground and there were thousands
of square miles of forest-covered mountains to hide the wreckage
of the A-17 from everyone but Russian search parties.

The radar panels were showing the Falcon rapidly approaching
from the rear. Teleman had just enough fuel left to reach the
rendezvous point and loiter for perhaps five minutes waiting for
the tanker. Unless he could shake this bastard, he thought grimly,
he would never make even Norway. It all depended now on who
could outlast whom. The Soviet pilot must be running low on
fuel as well. He had made his initial approach at Mach 2.5 and
followed that up with a series of bursts to Mach 4. Figure twenty
minutes' flying time from Leningrad or thereabouts—maybe he
could lose him yet.

Teleman decided fast. He put the A-17 into a shallow climb and
rocketed to 175,000 feet at Mach 3.7. His pursuer dwindled for a
moment and then came on again, afterburners flaming a long trail

of ionized gas on Teleman's radar screen. He was watching his fuel readout now as closely as he monitored the radar. He was going to have to cut the fuel load fine, yet leave enough to permit him to at least reach the ship. He had to be within radio range to transmit. If the refueling tanker was there, great; if not, it would be a short swim in those water temperatures. Teleman had had no illusions about coming out of this mission alive from the moment he recognized the Soviet aircraft over the Baltic. But the information had to be gotten back. Not that the mission was so vitally important, in fact it was probably only someone's bright idea— we have the aircraft in that vicinity, let him go take a look. What was important was the fact that the Soviets had developed an optical tracking system that ignored the ECM efforts. The next A-17 flight was due to go out in a little less than seven hours from now. If it went, the Soviets would be waiting for it.

The Russian interceptor had caught up quickly, apparently throttling back as he came up on target. Teleman sheered violently off his starboard wing, but the Russian flier had anticipated him and came around smoothly, still locked on to Teleman's tail.

They were deep into Finnish territory now and the Russian had cut the distance to less than a mile. Teleman could not understand why he did not fire. Those damned missiles the Falcon carried had appeared to have a range of nearly two hundred miles and were optically controlled from the interceptor. Teleman twisted and turned, trying to lose his remorseless pursuer. But the Russian, with laughable ease, remained locked on to his tail.

Teleman suddenly dropped his speed, cutting his engines back to idle, and dropped both landing flaps and gear. They were nearly useless in the almost nonexistent air of 175,000 feet, but every miniscule bit of drag would help. For an uncertain moment the A-17 slowed relative to the Falcon. The pilot, surprised by this unexpected maneuver, streaked past him. This brief relief in the unbearable tension caused Teleman to laugh wildly; then, regaining some measure of control, he slewed violently to the right, again falling off his starboard wing and down. He was once again behind the Russian and he meant to make the best of it. In fatal desperation, he arrowed straight down, running flat out for the cloud cover at twenty thousand feet. Ahead of him the radar showed the Falcon dropping into a full-powered dive as he pulled out of a sharp right turn and followed Teleman down.

Carefully, Teleman eased the power up, keeping the nose pointed down as sharply as he dared. The wings were fully retracted against the fuselage and he was little more than a powered dart, struggling to keep the A-17 from entering a spin mode that would finish him against some mountainside in Finland. The Russian, clawing into a shallower dive, began rapidly catching up again. In agony, Teleman watched the digital readout on the radar panel as the margin narrowed. It was clear that within seconds the Russian would make it to the cloud cover ahead of Teleman, there to use the three- or four-second lead to unleash the two deadly missiles nestling in the fuselage.

Teleman ground his teeth in frustration and shoved the throttle forward to its stop. At the same time he slammed the wings forward for maximum lift and lit off the ramjets with a bang. The A-17 shuddered under the giant hand of acceleration, but the magnificent aircraft rose to the challenge. Through the red acceleration haze Teleman saw the altitude indicator strain upward. The PCMS audio and visual alarms clattered and clanked wildly as they fought to keep Teleman from blacking out. The acceleration indicator read out 12 G's as the A-17 started into a climb.

Teleman ignored everything except the altitude indicator and the throttle. Gradually he was pulling up short in relation to the Soviet. He had caught him by surprise again. At sixty thousand feet Teleman leveled out. The Russian was still well behind, nearly eight miles, and still climbing for altitude. With the A-17 leveled out and the engines in the turbojet mode with afterburners, Teleman streaked for the North Cape at Mach 4.

But the Soviet Falcon was not through. This was the last chance and both pilots knew it. Neither had anything to lose. Teleman judged the Soviet pilot had passed his point-of-no-return when he went into the dive after him. Now he was rapidly closing the gap in one last desperate try. And there was nothing remaining that Teleman could do about it. He now had barely enough fuel to make the rendezvous point. Even if the tanker was waiting, he doubted whether enough flying time remained to complete refueling.

The Soviet pilot was pulling out all stops. He closed on Teleman at Mach 4.5, boring straight in, then lifting abruptly to pounce from above. As he neared, his guns opened up. He kept his thumb down on the firing button and walked a stream of tracers across the A-17. Where were the missiles? Teleman screamed silently. Twisting his head to glance back through the rear observation slit, Teleman could see the sheet of tracers marching toward him. The aircraft rocked violently as at least one cannon shell smashed through his starboard wing without exploding. Then the Falcon slipped below to come streaking up from beneath. Teleman sheered away but the Russian remained locked on.

He slammed the A-17 from side to side, nursing every last bit of speed he could from the engines. For seconds both aircraft twisted and wrenched through the frozen air with tracers from the Falcon's cannon probing around the A-17. Like a wounded

snake, they thrashed through the Finnish skies. A second burst
chewed into the tail structure. The A-17 fluttered like a wounded
bird and went out of control. The Falcon edged up, cannons
waiting for the optimum moment, the Russian pilot waiting
hungrily, with the patience of death, for the A-17 to line up cross-
wise in his gunsights, waiting to place the last burst. Then Teleman knew why there had been no missile. Because of their bulk
and weight the missiles had been removed and replaced with
electric cannons, to save fuel and add speed. Now both pilots were
waiting for the inexorable closing of their flight paths. The milliseconds turned into minutes for both as they approached the
invisible spot in the sky that would nebulously mark Teleman's
grave.

The Falcon fluttered, arced up slightly, and fell off, arrowing
down until lost in the clouds below. The Soviet pilot had waited
perhaps a second too long.


CHAPTER ELEVEN

TELEMAN watched the black dot of the Falcon on his radar screen
disappearing into the black night until the Russian aircraft vanished into the carpet of cloud. Beneath were the heavily forested
northern reaches of the Kjolen Mountains and the empty taiga
surrounding the Ounus River, an area inhabited only by Lapps
who still followed the migrations of their reindeer herds. Unless
the Finns had picked up the final moments of the Falcon on their
own radar, it could be years before the wreckage was found.

Teleman stared at the screen, sick with exhaustion and despair.
The Russian crew's suicide had been for nothing. The gamble,
their fuel load against his, coupled with their ability to knock
him out of the sky, had been lost. Now both were dead. Teleman
knew that, if they had managed to eject, they could never have
survived the buffeting of the gale and its sub-zero fury. He examined the fuel gauge. There were eight hundred pounds of the
liquid hydrogen fuel remaining in the reserve tanks, another fifteen minutes' flying time. If the commanding officer of the battle
cruiser was as intelligent and resourceful as he had shown himself to be in the past, there would be a tanker waiting at the
rendezvous point. He might be able to make it after all . . .
unless more trouble showed up.

Teleman extended his radar fully and waited. The silver-green
screen was empty—so far. But it was doubtful if the Soviets would
depend only upon one aircraft to complete the job. They rarely
played gambles or depended on half measures, and the depth of

the system they had erected against him in Asia was more than proof of that.

All of a sudden the A-17 rolled out of control and pitched over into a dive. Teleman's head snapped back hard against the head-rest. The A-17 began to spin wildly. A tremendous banging sounded aft in the fuselage and, twisting around, Teleman saw the starboard rudder assembly through the rear observation slit flap madly. Terrified, he slammed the throttle forward and ran out the landing flaps for the second time. The A-17 was still roll-ing, down through seventy, sixty-five, sixty, fifty-five, fifty thousand feet before she began to slow. Carefully, his body now under full control of the PCMS, he began to increase power, running the wings forward again. Abruptly the pounding ceased and the A-17 began to bring its nose up into a level attitude.

For the next ten minutes Teleman fought furiously with the controls to maintain the damaged A-17 in some semblance of level flight. He had cut the speed back to sub-sonic and managed to fight his way to eighty thousand feet where, hopefully, the thinner air would lessen the drag on the twisted metal of the tail section. The aircraft still had a tendency to twist into an uncontrollable wingover that would drag him down into the rolling clouds of the storm-filled night below. The computer-controlled linkages aft through the fuselage had been damaged beyond the ability of the alternate circuitry to compensate. The rudder controls were next to useless and he was forced to depend on ailerons and landing flaps for lateral control.

In spite of all he could do, Teleman was slowly losing altitude. The altimeter was circling down through seventy thousand feet with a steadiness that was almost terrifying in its deadliness. The encounter with the Falcon had taken place over the Finnish coast of the Baltic Sea and stretched into the wide margin of mountain separating Sweden from the Norwegian Sea. The Russian had crashed somewhere in Finland, and Teleman hoped to God that the Russians would have a mighty hard time explaining what an advanced Soviet interceptor with empty cannons was doing in Finland—if the Finns ever found it. And if he wasn't careful, he thought humorlessly, the Americans would be doing the same kind of explaining about him, only in spades when the Finns got a look at his equipment.

From the feel of one of the engines, he was beginning to wonder if a stray cannon shell or perhaps a piece of ricocheting metal had not blasted loose a couple of compressor blades. He was beginning to lose power in number two. A moment later his theory was confirmed when a shattering vibration wracked the aircraft. His hand darted to the cutoff switch and abruptly the

racket vanished. At the same time the other engine whined up to
power to carry the increased load.

Teleman rubbed his aching head and tried to think clearly. The
baleful eye of the PCMS warning light glowed at him in exasperation, warning that he was overextending himself. Big news. He
could certainly feel it. His head ached abominably from the
overdose of drugs he had been absorbing in the past few hours as
well as from the lack of any real sleep. He swore at the light and
dialed an increased dosage of amphetamines. He hardly felt the
new dose.

'If I get out of this mess,' he muttered aloud, 'I am going
to need at least three months in the hospital to get washed
out.'

Talking to himself was something he rarely did. This time it
made him feel a little better. For the last twenty minutes he had
been telling himself that he was not going to make it, at least in
one piece. But, obviously, his subconscious had refused to accept
that.

He considered the computer for a moment, then began to feed
in coordinates and switched the monitoring gear to add information on the aircraft's condition and fuel load. The answer that
came out seconds later was worse than he expected.

He was still nine hundred miles from the coast of the North
Cape and twelve hundred short of the rendezvous point. By
throttling back the remaining engine and staying sub-sonic, he
could just about make it to the Cape—which was sure as hell a lot
better than going down in the Barents Sea, all things considered.

As he thought about it, a germ of an idea began to take shape.
Teleman forced himself to lean back in the couch and relax. He
was so tensed up and worn out from the last several hours of flying hide-and-seek that unless he eased off he never would bring
the idea into the open.

Trying to think like the Soviet commander responsible for bag-
ging the *Americanski spion*, he knew that he would have only the
reports from the downed aircraft to go on. And he doubted
whether the Russian pilot had been close enough to get much of
a reading on the damage his cannon fire had done. The entire
sequence had taken less than two minutes, and any time the
Soviet crewman would have been close enough for a detailed look
would have been limited to a few seconds. And the last burst
fired had come while the Russian was diving past and beneath.

So, not knowing the extent of any possible damage, they would
reckon him to continue on his present course, perhaps varying a
few degrees in either direction to throw them off. They would
suspect, although they had no way of knowing for sure, that his
fuel was running low. How low, they could only guess. And they

would know that he was either heading for a rendezvous some-where north of Norway or else for a sub-polar route to the States. Following that most logical line of reasoning, they knew he could outrun any pursuing Soviet interceptors. The last thing in the world they would expect would be a reduction in speed. Or would they? In any event it was his only chance. Fortunately, their optical tracking gear would be useless until they broke out of the storm. As it stood now, then, he could make the coast—that is if nothing else went wrong, if no more Russian aircraft appeared, and if nothing else fell off the aircraft.

Surely the Russian pilot had been sending back a play-by-play description of the one-sided dogfight. The Soviets must know that their boy crashed and that the A-17 was still in the air when last seen. And with only one path open, straight north, they ought to be able to field enough aircraft to knock him down. About now, he thought grimly, one of those Russian copies of the old Steer-man biplane ought to be good enough for that job.

Teleman flipped the warm-up switches on the transmitters. This new development was going to force him to break the strict radio silence always maintained on overflights. To get the infor-mation to the *RFK* he was going to have to transmit over normal and open commercial channels. The whole secrecy bit was blown anyway, and there remained no need to preserve what faint modicum of secrecy remained. The Soviets could and would monitor all they wanted. The codes were supposed to be 'break-proof', and in any event they could certainly be changed after this disastrous mission.

Stiffly, he leaned forward to examine the cloud cover below. The UV Doppler gear gave him a reading of twenty-two thousand feet on the cloud tops. If he ducked down and into the upper reaches of the cloud cover, with his ECM gear he just might be able to elude Soviet aircraft long enough to reach the Cape. What he would do then, he would figure out when he got there. One problem at a time for now.

Very carefully, Teleman eased the nose down into a shallow glide that would help to stretch the fuel. He eased the engine speed back until he was flying at 450 knots and anxiously scanned the sky with the search radar. So far so good. As he dropped lower the half moon illuminated the soft bosoms of cloud with a pearlish light. In spite of the hundred-mile-an-hour winds that he knew must be raging lower down, the surface of the cover appeared untroubled. The A-17 dropped lower still and the softness began to give way to scudding rags of cloud that did not look so peaceful after all.

At thirty thousand feet he caught the first faint whisper of the wind and marveled at the power of this storm that sent the thin molecules of air whispering along at even this altitude. It wasn't until he was down a thousand feet into the cloud cover that he felt he had eluded, at least for the time being, pursuit by Soviet fighter aircraft eager to finish him off. Now, if the cover would only last until North Cape.

The winds within the clouds were not as bad as he had expected them to be. In spite of the jolting, the A-17 seemed to be taking the ill-use without immediate danger of coming apart. The tail section, according to his instrumentation, was pretty badly chewed. The skin covering was torn, but the thin titanium was holding together quite well. He still had no control over the rudder assembly, but was able to compensate with wing surfaces and landing flaps.

For the first time in half an hour he was able to sit back and begin to think carefully about what evasive action he might take if jumped again. He wished desperately that he could take the chance of snatching a few moments' sleep before the ordeal of the ejection and landing took place. But he did not dare. After the volume of drugs he had absorbed, he knew that, in spite of everything the PCMS could do, he would not be able to wake quickly enough to deal with split-second emergencies.

The A-17 stumbled on through the wrack of shielding cloud toward the North Cape of Norway. Somewhere ahead, Soviet aircraft searched the Finnish and Norwegian skies with optical and electronic detection gear for any traces of Teleman. Soviet picket aircraft and ships joined ground stations monitoring the entire spread of communications bands Teleman would be likely to use in transmitting his information. In his office at the Lenin Air Base outsid Leningrad, the Soviet commander of the search mission fumed at his helplessness. Somewhere in the Barents or Greenland sea a picket ship was waiting for the American aircraft. Submarine or surface ship, it would make no difference to the aircraft and ships he could put on to the task of finding the intruder aircraft at its rendezvous point. But the storm negated his best efforts. No surface ship could put successfully to sea until the seas moderated. Aircraft could not penetrate the storm beneath the cloud layer. Instead he was forced to string fighters out in a long line with no guarantee that the American would fly obligingly up the gauntlet. The American pilot had bested the Soviets once along the Afghan border. It was the sheerest luck that they had spotted the trailing fringe of his ECM net as he turned north over Poland. Luck like that could not happen twice, damn it!

## CHAPTER TWELVE

FOLSOM stared pensively out the starboard port, watching the storm-thrashed waves towering on either side of the ship. Only rarely now did they break over the bow to come dashing down the length of the ice-smooth deck. He became aware that Larkin had come on to the bridge and had moved over to stand behind him.

'The seas seem to be easing somewhat.'

'Yes, sir. We aren't taking such a pounding now. The repair crew has managed to re-weld the cover plates in the bow section and rig a couple of beams to help hold it in place. I don't think we'll have any more trouble, from that quarter at least.'

'Then there are small things to be grateful for.' Larkin smiled. 'You have managed quite well, Mr. Folsom. I must say that I am proud of both you and the crew.' Larkin delivered this rare compliment in a matter-of-fact voice, but Folsom was deeply touched by it.

'Thank you, sir. Although you might want to modify that when you hear about the condensers.'

Larkin chuckled. 'Expecting a rocket were you? I read the report when I came up. Don't worry about it. As you know, man does not always triumph over machinery,' he quoted solemnly. 'There was nothing else you could have done. And I think the auxiliary condensers can handle the cooling system for now.'

He paused and stared out at the waves. 'What have you decided about using the boost engines?'

'Well, uh, nothing really, at least at the moment. I didn't think . . .'

'Come now, you are the executive officer. You probably know this ship and her engines better than I do. Do you think she could handle seas like this under emergency power?'

Folsom hesitated a moment before answering. 'Yes, I think maybe she could,' he said thoughtfully. 'Ordinarily I would suggest that we go farther under the lee of the Cape. We might find easier waters there. The only thing that worries me is whether or not the hydrofoils could stand the pounding. In and out of the water so much . . . shorter seas would be a lot easier on the struts.'

Larkin rubbed his mouth and chin. 'Go in closer to the coast . . . I don't really know. Most of the charts for this area are not accurate. This coast hasn't really been thoroughly re-charted since the Germans did it in 1941. The coastal shelf is full of reefs. . . . How close in would you want to go?'

'At least five miles.'

'Five miles!' Larkin exclaimed. 'That puts us inside Norwegian waters.'

Folsom nodded. 'I know, sir, but anything less would do us no good. That's why I don't think we should try. The Norwegians probably wouldn't raise a fuss if they spotted us. But, if for some reason they did, the investigating board would have to examine our logs and there would be no way of concealing the fact that we did violate Norwegian waters without permission.

'We can gain a few extra knots by coupling the boost engines to the main drive shafts anyway.'

Larkin nodded assent and turned away to cross to his high seat. He sat down and scanned the readout dials that presented the status of every vital portion of the ship. Both Larkin's and Folsom's panels—identical in every way—were to the *Robert F. Kennedy* what Teleman's PCMS console had been to the A-17.

'All right, Mr. Folsom,' he said finally, 'let's play it that way.'

The *Robert F. Kennedy* came to the rendezvous position like an icy ghost. Every external fitting that faced the sea and wind was covered to a depth of three feet with gray, rock-hard ice. Long rills ran along the length of the weather deck, covering every shroud and stay and the lower reaches of the single antenna mast protruding from the superstructure. Only the upper, working portion of each antenna was clear due to its own independent electric heater. The *RFK* was streamlined like no other ship had ever needed to be. Instead of the block-like superstructure characteristic of modern destroyers and cruisers, the *RFK*'s bridge was built in a V and sloped aft. Her fore and after decks were free of the usual cannon turrets and other protuberances and the weather deck ran smooth from bow to stern in a gentle line except for the superstructure. At the same time, the sides of the deck curved, from a center line formed by a ten-foot walkway, downward to meet the hull. But now the ship resembled nothing as much as a child's plastic toy boat covered with ice.

Larkin ordered the ship into a station-keeping pattern and reduced speed to eight knots, only enough to maintain steerage-way in the heavy seas. The *RFK* came about to fight the seas around a four-mile rectangle, with the legs into and running from the waves.

On the bridge, Folsom glanced warily at Larkin, standing before his console, his eyes glued to the radio operator's hunched back as he sat ears straining under the earphones to catch the slightest whisper of sound over the VHF-FM frequency. Folsom knew Larkin was extremely worried. Knowing the full story and the knife-edge schedules the reconnaissance aircraft had to keep to, he was worried as well. Minutes before they had received a transmission from the refueling tanker, maintaining his assigned rendezvous position two hundred miles to the west. Everything was waiting, the stage set for the final scene. But where was the leading actor? Larkin shifted his weight from one foot to another. Imperceptibly at first, the motion of the ship was becoming rougher as she turned into a crosswind run. Larkin noted it with a sharp glance at the gyroscopic-driven indicator and immediately turned back to face the radio operator.

Teleman was less than four hundred miles from the North Cape when he decided that perhaps he had pushed his luck as far as it would go. His fuel readouts were showing barely enough left to reach rendezvous, but the single, remaining engine was certainly not acting like there was. Twice, within the space of two minutes, the engine had coughed like an old man on a cold winter morning and then resumed its steady drone. Teleman had never experienced a fuel shortage in the A-17 and he was at a loss as to how to diagnose the malady.

He was still maintaining a steady twenty-two thousand feet deep in the top layers of the Arctic storm. So far he had not been spotted by the searching Russian aircraft, but the radar screen was showing them strung out like pickets in a fence. They were putting out quite a bit of effort to greet him, he thought, but it was one honor that he would be happy to do without.

Teleman ran a correction bug-hunter program through the computer directed at the fuel readouts. Nothing showed up and he tried to relax, telling himself that if anything had been wrong the computers would have spotted it. He had almost convinced himself when the engine shuddered again. This time the unevenness persisted, the engine's RPM's dropping quicky until he thought he was going into a flame-out condition. At twenty-one thousand RPM, they caught again and the compressor came back up to the proper rev level. If he was running low on fuel, he figured, it was probably due to the increased drag from the damaged tail section. He had been checking on it steadily for the past hour, watching larger and larger chunks peel loose. Added to the fuel problem, he was now worrying about how much longer the entire aft fuselage was going to hold together. Of all places he did not want to eject, he could think of few that ran second to the top of Norway in the middle of an Arctic storm. If he was lucky, a wandering Lap might find his body, perfectly preserved in its thick coat of ice, several years hence.

Leaning back as comfortably in the acceleration couch as he could after six straight days, he stared at the instrument panel and the various displays trying to decide how soon to raise *RFK* to transmit his information. He was so tired that the various displays and panels full of readout dials and verniers refused to focus into concrete entities. Instead they were all running together into a fuzzy, jumbled mass of softly glowing colors. He was so tired that he knew if he closed his eyes not even the last trumpet would be loud enough to wake him.

When the engine failed a fourth time and the RPM's fell and kept on falling, he decided, enough, and threw the radio transmitter switches.

'Target One, Target One, acknowledge.'

The communicator buzzed on Larkin's console. He snapped it on with an impatient motion and acknowledged sharply.

'Captain, this is the communications room. We are receiving an in-clear radio message from identity Beatle—'

'What the hell?' Larkin roared. 'Did you say Beatle?'

'Yes, sir, he's coming in on 110 Mc. and his voice is funny . . . kind of slow and broken.'

'All right . . .' Larkin was thinking fast. Obviously something had gone wrong. The recon aircraft was already fourteen minutes late and now he was transmitting over an open channel, in-clear. 'All right,' he repeated. 'Pipe him up here and acknowledge.'

Almost instantly, the bridge speakers burst into life with a rumble of static.

'Target One, Target One, acknowledge.'

Much longer, Teleman thought, and it would not matter. Already he could see several radar blips that he knew to be radio monitoring aircraft beginning to form a triangulation pattern.

'Target One, Target One, come in you blasted idiots. What the hell do . . . you think is going on up here?'

Teleman followed with a long string of profanity. If nothing else, that should convince them that he was an American.

'Identify yourself.' The message was short and in the clear.

'Target One, Target One, stop playing games. This is Beatle!'

The eleven men on the bridge swiveled almost as one to stare in surprise at their captain. In a year and a half of these mysterious missions around the world this was the first time that anyone except Larkin had heard the hushed voice that came in at periodic intervals. The marine guard started forward, hesitated, as if not knowing what to do. Then training took over and he strode over to Larkin's desk. Larkin ignored him. He was now concentrating on the speaker and his communications officer acknowledging the call. The bridge operator had still not recovered from the unexpected shock and sat staring at his captain with a quizzical look on his face. Folsom moved to stand behind Larkin, he too ignoring the flustered marine.

'Quit horsing around down . . . there, I'm . . . in . . .'

'Target One here, Target One here, status quickly.' Larkin's voice was tight, the strain evident. He knew as well as did Folsom that this could be a Russian trick to draw them out, to establish radio fix down which a salvo of missiles could streak at any moment. The radar operator came to suddenly and with a half-choked shout swung back to his screens.

'Bandit . . . jumped over . . . Finland. Tail . . . surface badly shot up . . . losing altitude . . . fuel almost gone . . . bandits waiting . . . stand by for transmission . . . this channel.'

'Beatle wait until within usual procedural range. Repeat, wait until within usual procedural range.'

'No good . . . cannot last that long.'

Teleman stopped, breathing deeply with the effort. The warm, comforting hands of sleep were again closing around him. He had to shake his head several times before he could focus his thoughts enough to even wonder why the PCMS was not compensating.

Then he saw why. The single-minded computer feedback systems were convinced that he was jeopardizing the mission. The flashing MISSION ABORT sign was flickering at him. If he had not over-ridden the controls earlier, the computer would probably have disregarded the threat of the Soviet fighters and decided whether or not to run for home at top speed or trigger off the destruct bomb carefully packed away in the center of the aircraft.

Now he was becoming aware that his heart was beating like a trip hammer. His vision had closed to a narrow tunnel that encompassed only the instrument panel. How much more of this total body-system abuse he could take before his heart quit or he had a stroke he did not know. He knew only that he must get the message through to the *RFK* that the Russians had the optical tracking system.

'Target One, do not interrupt . . . prepare to receive . . . transmission. Bandits are on to . . . ball game . . . all in transmission . . .'

'No,' Larkin shouted. 'We have a tanker on the way. He can reach you in less than fifteen minutes.'

If he could have, Teleman would have laughed. In fifteen minutes he could very well be dead, from several causes, not the least of which were Soviet interceptors.

'On my mark . . . five seconds to transmit . . . five . . . four . . . three . . . two . . . one . . . transmit.'

Over the radio Teleman could hear the squeal of tape decks spinning madly as twenty-six hours of constant speed recording on sixty-eight channels was transmitted. Then he leaned back exhausted. His job was done. The strain of the mission and the almost constant skirmishing with Soviet interceptors in the last eight hours, with only a few minutes sleep at a time, and the overload of drugs in his system caused a stultifying lethargy that was interrupted only by his heart rate. His portion of the task was indeed finished. And so was he. It had been twenty hours since he had more than a few snatched hours of drug-induced light sleep, with the rest of the time occupied in intense mental and physical concentration, again prompted by drugs.

The A-17 began to fall off and he brought it back with difficulty. The tail section was beginning to vibrate badly again as he lost altitude into the storm, threatening to come loose somewhere aft of the cockpit at any moment. The engine coughed once more and resumed its dull steady murmur. The emergency reserve tank levels were pushing well into the danger zone now.

'Can you hold for tanker?' Larkin asked again. The familiar voice was high pitched over the radio, rumbling faintly with storm-induced static.

Teleman brought himself upright with difficulty. 'No . . . fuel almost gone . . . not even reach you . . . sorry about clear message . . . no difference . . . bandits on to everything . . . so don't worry . . .'

Teleman stopped abruptly. He was beginning to ramble and every second he continued to talk brought the Russians that much closer. 'Approximately ten minutes . . . flight left . . . losing altitude . . . down on . . . coast . . . destroy . . . plane.'

'You can't,' Larkin almost shouted. 'Try and make it . . .' Then he realized the futility of what he had been going to say. At five hundred miles an hour, that meant almost forty minutes or more to the ship, and with only ten minutes of fuel left— idiotic, he told himself savagely.

Teleman's voice came again, weaker and weaker as he talked: 'I'll come in low . . . over coast . . . eject . . . plane . . . destroy.'

Larkin, standing on the warmly lit bridge of the *RFK*, could picture the lonely man in the cockpit of his damaged aircraft. He would be going slowly through the motions of setting the timer on the self-destruct charge. As soon as he ejected, it would begin to count off three minutes. If Teleman did not eject within five minutes of setting the timer, it would go off anyway, with enough force to blow tiny pieces of the aircraft over a five-mile area. Larkin figured quickly on a scratch pad, glancing from the Doppler distance readout to the radar operator, shaking his head.

'Target One here. We are getting a position fix on you and

will track you down. I'll bring the ship in and pick you up as soon as the storm subsides enough to get a helicopter or boat in.'

Even as Larkin spoke the radio operator handed him a decoded note, which he read through and then handed to Folsom to read.

'The hell . . . you will . . .' Teleman muttered. 'Get . . . those tapes back.'

'Sorry, I've just been directed to pick you up. Obviously they are going to want to hear about the bandits and fast. All over-flights have been suspended until they can talk to you.'

Teleman was now down to ten thousand feet. He glanced at the ground control panel to see the storm-thrashed tundra and forest sliding by below. He laughed bitterly. 'If . . . I get . . . out . . . this . . . be . . . miracle. Goodbye.'

There was a sudden silence as Teleman's voice disappeared. Only the hollow hissing of static marked the open channel. Feeling strangely empty, Larkin strode to the radar console and, resting a hand to support himself against the violent motion of the ship on the back of the operator's chair, watched the screen intently. Coordinates were fed directly into the radar equipment from the communications room, but the operator, listening to the flow of words and numbers, made minute final changes in frequency, pitch, and direction.

Abruptly, he swore and sat back. 'Hell, that does it. We've hit a dead area . . . it must be almost two hundred miles wide.'

'Easy now,' Larkin said. He leaned over to point to the white patch of light obscuring a large part of the screen. 'Narrow your scope down to encompass this patch. That's the ECM equipment he carries. He will show up in a moment.'

The operator could not resist a muffled expletive. Ten minutes passed slowly while the white blue continued to fill the radar screen. Finally the radar operator muttered, 'What the devil kind of equipment does he carry for God's sake . . . sir,' he added.

'Better that you do not know any more right now,' Larkin chided gently. 'Just keep your eye on that . . .'

As he spoke, the obscuring patch of light disappeared, and there, toward the center of the screen, was an intense white dot, flickering in and out of scale with a steady pulsation. It appeared to be nearly two hundred miles southwest of them, which would put it somewhere close to the coast of the North Cape. At least Larkin hoped it would. It would be all too easy in this miserable storm to miss the coast and drop into the ocean. The ejection capsule was designed to stay afloat in water, but he doubted very much that it could withstand for long a storm as intense as this.

'Get a damned accurate fix on that blip,' he snapped. Then Larkin swung around to the plotting table. 'Mr. Folsom, set a course for the coast and make as much speed as you can.'

Moments later the great ship came around in a short, half circle that leaned her far to port like a sloop in a high wind. Tons of water flew from under her heel and piled up behind in a tattered rooster's tail as the nuclear engines jumped to flank speed and she straightened out abruptly and settled into the waves. She resembled nothing as much as a motor torpedo boat, rather than a 16,500-ton battle cruiser, as she fought her way south toward the Cape, ignoring the waves piling before her bow. Low in the water as she was from the immense tonnage of ice, Folsom managed to crank twenty-three knots from the engines while a worried engineering crew watched the instruments below. Finally, Barrows could stand it no longer. He reached over and flicked on his intercom, dialed the bridge and demanded the executive officer. When Folsom answered, he wasted no time on preliminaries.

'Mr. Folsom, if we don't cut back, we won't have any auxiliary condensers left either. They can't take the load from flank speed much longer.'

'Then make do,' Folsom said grimly.

Barrows, unaware of the events on the bridge, stared at the intercom in disbelief. Then he shook his head. 'In that case, *Mr. Folsom,*' he said acidly, 'I suggest we shift to the boost engines for one quarter power output.'

Without waiting for an answer from the bridge, he flicked off the intercom and swung around to his waiting crew and began snapping orders. Within four minutes the boost gas turbine engines were coupled to the main drive shafts and the last of the explosive starter cartridges were echoing in the narrow steel cavern of the engine room. Barrows watched as great gas turbines, now on line, whined up to peak RPM, then he began trimming them back until the ship was running steady under the combined thrust of five of the six power plants.

Teleman shut off the radio and sat staring at this last link with safety. Then he turned to the radar panel. From the activity it was showing, he had finally been spotted. At least three blips were closing fast, but not fast enough. They were still at least three hundred miles away and the eight minutes it would take them to get within cannon range would be more than enough for what he had to do now. Even if they carried visually guided air-to-air rockets they would be useless in the depths of the storm clouds.

He pulled the plastic-coated check list from the clip on the rim of his seat. Twelve items were listed, a matter of a few seconds. He pressed the destruct button and closed the spring-loaded clip over it to hold it firmly down. Once the ejection sequence began, the spring clip would be released, and three minutes later one hundred pounds of strategically placed deta-sheet explosive would shred the aircraft beyond reassembly. Then he removed his soft, cloth flight helmet and slipped on the hard plastic headgear and plugged the oxygen lines into the ejection module supply.

When the list was finished, Teleman hunched forward and studied the ground control map. He was still a little more than a hundred miles from the North Cape and the ground unrolling below was all tundra. He did not, under any circumstances, want to go down in that. In his condition even a few minutes without shelter on the open, windswept tundra would be enough to kill him. According to the computer display describing the North Cape area, he could expect to cross a band of highlands that would end the tundra, about ten miles from the coast. On the far slopes, leading down to the cliff-barred coastline facing the Barents Sea, an open forest of fir should furnish the shelter he would need.

Teleman began to take the wounded A-17 down deeper into the storm. According to the *RFK* he should break out of the cloud cover, *after* he ejected, around two thousand feet. He did not particularly like the idea of having to bail out blind, but it was certainly preferable to hanging around until the Russians showed up. He hoped that his heading for the deck was causing the Soviet pilots as much consternation as it was him. But, then, they would have orders to get him at any cost. As long as he kept the ECM going, they would not be able to get a fix on him. If he could get down to about three thousand feet before he had to eject, then he would be low enough for the ejection capsule to be shielded against the ground.

The minutes passed slowly while the A-17 wobbled on. The engine was cutting in and out steadily now and Teleman knew it must be draining the tanks right down to the last dregs. The North Cape was now clearly outlined by the IR panel as a white ragged line against the dark gray of the warmer water off the coast. The ground control map, with its simulation of the terrain below, was too gross to show any helpful details. The IR was all he had to go on. The ejection was going to be mighty tricky, he thought. He would have to time it so that he would land well back of the cliffs rather than in the water, yet not far enough back so that he could not walk to the beach to meet the boat. With these high winds now almost off the Beaufort scale, Larkin was quite optimistic if he expected to get a helicopter in to pick him up. It would take days before the winds abated enough for the helicopter to make it off the deck, let alone land over the strong updrafts that would be blowing off the cliffs.

He watched closely as the aircraft passed slowly over the cliffs, its speed now below 250 knots. Neither the visual nor the IR scopes told him much at all. The temperature was too low, too bone-chilling, for much warm detail to show among the granite surfaces of the coast. From the IR display there appeared to be no beach at all, but whether this was from the action of high waves he could not tell. If there was no beach he was going to have a devil of a time getting off those cliffs. They would not be able to get a boat in and he knew damned well that he could never survive three days. With these happy alternatives facing him, Teleman brought the A-17 around in a long turn that would bring him in a circle back over the cliffs. As he began his second pass over the coast he dropped the A-17 still lower until he was only fifteen hundred feet above the cliffs. Visually, he was totally blind. His instruments told him only that there was a solid surface below. Whether it was thickly forested or a mass of jumbled boulders he had no way of telling, but time was running out too fast to worry about that. Teleman wiggled his feet into the stirrups and shoved the control column into its locked position. His last act as pilot of the aircraft he had flown for the past three years was to arm the bomb that would destroy it completely.

As he did so, the computers took over total control of the aircraft. He saw the red, flashing DESTRUCT light come on just as the metal shields slid down between him and the instrument panel. The two halves of the flattened hemisphere joined together with a solid *thunk* and the blowers switched on with a high-pitched whine. Teleman settled himself securely into the acceleration couch as it adjusted to a semireclining position. He took a secure grip of the handholds and drew a deep breath, just as the bottom of the A-17 exploded away and the ejection capsule was jettisoned downward. As he fell he could see the distorted bottom of the fuselage pass over him. The capsule began to tumble end over end in the high winds, but not before he saw the lightened plane, huge and sleek in the dead light, bound up, corkscrew, and then recover as the autopilot caught hold of the control surfaces.

Teleman did not see the aircraft bore on into the Barents Sea, where five miles off the coast it erupted into a burst of white flame and plummeted into the icy seas. Pieces of wreckage were blown in every direction, much of it burning fiercely as it hissed into the waves.

The ejection capsule smashed upward, jerking Teleman cruelly against the restraining belts. Through the observation slit Teleman could see the orange and white parachute pop open wide.

The ejection capsule bounced several more times, then settled down to a steady swaying. Inside, Teleman was powerless to control the descent or landing area, in fact helpless to do little more than lie there while the capsule was swung and jostled at the mercy of the winds. From fifteen hundred feet it should not have taken more than two minutes to make the descent. Instead it took eight—eight minutes of endless swinging, and Teleman had no idea in which direction.

When the capsule did land it hit with such force that it ruptured the inflated air pods beneath. The wind caught at the parachute and began to drag the capsule. The automatic chute release did not go off as it should have. As he grabbed for the manual release Teleman had a confused impression of trees and rocks rolling past the observation slit. Teleman yanked several times on the manual release before it finally gave and the capsule rolled free and came to rest with a grinding sound that presaged the blast of wet snow and air that barreled in.

Teleman tore the straps loose and wiggled around in the seat to peer at a foot-long gash in the metal beneath his feet. The capsule had stopped against some obstruction, so that it was canted over at a steep angle. The close confines of the interior gave him little room to move about, but he managed to reach the emergency pack strapped beneath the seat and haul out the sleeping bag, cursing fluently under his breath. He got the sleeping bag jammed into the hole and at once the shrieking sound of the wind died away to a thin whistle. Teleman struggled back into the couch, breathing hard.

The amp meter showed a full charge in the batteries that should be good for several hours of steady heat output, providing he ran nothing else at the same time. The interior temperature was already down to twenty-two degrees above freezing, and unless he wanted to freeze to death while he slept he had to bring it back up. Forcing his fuzzy mind to work, he did a rough calculation on how long it would take the *RFK* to reach the coast. As near as he could tell, he could not be farther than five miles from the cliffs, probably three hours hiking in this miserable storm. He felt the best the *RFK* could make in the seas that he had glimpsed briefly from the air was about twenty knots, this close to the Cape. At two-hundred-odd miles that would be at least ten to eleven hours.

Teleman knew that he had to get some sleep, no matter what happened. His heart was thudding painfully again and his eyes refused to focus. Hell, he thought, he would make it six hours of sleep. They would wait for him.

Painfully, he brought his arm up and fumbled with the alarm on his wristwatch, setting it for six hours. The last thing he remembered was trying to peer out of the narrow slit to see what the terrain was like. The roar of the wind in the trees and the delicate shuddering of the capsule knocked him out as effectively as a blackjack.

## CHAPTER THIRTEEN

THE STORM crested a few hours after Larkin turned the ship to run before the heavy seas crashing down on the battered, ice-shrouded shape with winds of gale force as it ran toward the coast at twenty-three knots. Teleman's call had come just after she had reached the rendezvous point. As soon as Teleman had bailed out, the radar operator had done his best to track the ejection capsule as it plummeted into the thick forest edging the coastal cliffs. They now had the pilot's location pinpointed to within a mile and were running for the location as fast as they dared in the heavy seas.

Larkin motioned Folsom over to his console and handed him a flimsy that had just come in. 'Another little missive from our bosses. In spite of our health, we must put forth our ultimate effort,' he said dryly.

Folsom grinned and took the flimsy. It was as Larkin had said, minus the sarcasm of course: they were to expend every effort to assure the safety of the pilot. In short, get him before the Russians did.

'They seem to be forgetting that the Norwegians might have something to say. Allies or no, I should think they wouldn't take too kindly to such operations off their coasts, or in their coastal waters, for that matter.'

'I agree. And I would also guess that if Washington had informed Oslo, they would have told us so.'

Folsom nodded, then glanced at the chronometer. 'About four hours yet and we should be off the point where he came down.' Already, Folsom noted, both he and Larkin had begun referring to the unknown pilot as a personal acquaintance.

Larkin got up stiffly and walked over to the forward ports. 'In effect, those orders say to bring him back at any cost,' he said half aloud. 'At least we appear to have the weather on our side. It is doubtful if the Soviets will send surface ships out searching after him, or aircraft either for that matter. But submarines are definitely in this year and the sub pens at Murmansk are only ten high-speed hours away.'

Folsom joined him at the ports, both staring out into the sky that was beginning to lighten with a gray dawn that only made the seas and the cold that much more oppressive. 'Well, it at least is going to give us a chance to test our own ECM gear under what you might call semicombat conditions. To this point, I hope, they do not know that we are out here. Or rather,' he amended, 'they don't know who and where we are. It's very likely that they picked up part of the transmission and so they will know that somebody must be out here to pick it up.'

Larkin nodded agreement with his analysis. 'And it will be very important that we keep it that way.'

'What about those?' Folsom indicated the silent tape console with its full reels of data from the aircraft.

'I am sending those at 0800—direct—and through double-scrambled circuits. It may be that the whole ball game is over in terms of these missions. What his mission was this time I don't have the faintest idea. But the Soviets know that the pilot picked up whatever he was after. So we have to get to him before they do.'

'So we go get him,' Folsom said simply.

'That's right.'

Teleman opened his eyes. A gray, washed-out light stared at him. The sound of the wind roaring through trees was louder than ever and the rocking of the capsule was more pronounced than he remembered. An insistent shrilling filled the capsule and it was several moments before he could wake himself enough to realize that it was his wrist alarm. Teleman shut it off with a fretful twist and lay back on the couch. Weariness that was almost pain flowed through his body, flooding down his arms and legs with heaviness. Flashes of light obscured his vision and the control board before him swam unevenly with the residual effects of the lysergic drugs. The batteries were just about dead and the intense cold was beginning to work its way inside. In addition to the tiredness, he was stiff and aching in every joint, both from the cold and the cramped position in which he had been lying. Finally, his head ached abominably.

When at last he managed to sit up, the first thing he did was to remove his helmet. With the pressure of the heavy plastic and leather gone, his head felt curiously lighter, but at the same time ached even more. Teleman groaned and rubbed his temples. After five minutes more of half sleep, half wakefulness, he managed to get himself moving.

He worked the acceleration couch into a sitting position with a great deal of pulling and swearing only to find that he could not get at the lockers where the survival gear was stored without getting completely out of the ejection capsule. Peering through the view port, he was not sure that he liked that idea at all.

The narrow slit showed thick forest. He must have come down

through the trees, which accounted for the terrific pounding he had taken. The snow was more than a foot deep, with deeper drifts piled up around parts of trees and brush. The branches of the trees danced wildly in the wind. Snow blown up from the surface mingled with the snowfall to create an obscuring ground blizzard composed more of ice particles than snow. Nevertheless, unless he wanted to freeze to death here, there was no help for it—he had to leave the capsule to get the gear out of the lockers.

Teleman slipped his helmet back on and fought with the hatch release until it popped open. He half fell, half climbed out into the bitter cold that immediately bent him double and made him gasp for air. The intense cold, close to twenty below zero, snatched the warm air from his lungs and for several minutes he struggled to regain his breath, breathing air warmed by cupped hands.

Once outside, it was easier to pull the seat all the way forward and open the lockers. The bundles he drew out were tightly packed and opened easily. He pulled them around the side of the battered capsule and beneath the overhanging branches of a thick fir. Here, out of the wind, he opened the first and checked its contents, carefully piling the equipment he did not need back into the bag.

Teleman found a .22-caliber pistol, which, after a moment's hesitation, he tucked into the waistband of his trousers. VERY pistol, field glasses, small but complete first-aid kit, rations, extra socks, gloves and boots, all went into the pile that he would take with him. He shed his lightweight flight jacket while shivering uncontrollably and pulled a set of Arctic pants and parka over his flight pants and bare skin. Over his boots went a pair of Arctic vacuum boots. Finally, he pulled the hood of the parka over his head and tied it securely beneath his chin.

Teleman managed to get the compass and, after a moment's indecision, a tube of Benzedrine tablets into the pocket of his parka. He did not want anything to do with them at the moment, but they might come in handy in an emergency. His metabolism was so low after the long flight and the steady diet of drugs that it would be disastrous to use them now. But he might need them later, he thought. If there was a later.

With a pack of rations, he crawled back into the comparative shelter of the capsule. While he ate the cardboard-flavored ration he tried to figure out where he was. After choking down half the bar, he rewrapped the half-eaten pack and shoved it into a pocket. He glanced at his watch: now six hours and twenty minutes since he had radioed the *RFK*. They ought to be coming on to station shortly, so it was time he got going.

Teleman climbed out of the capsule again and walked around to pick up the pack he had made up from the survival kit. The rest of the gear he shoved into the capsule, then closed and latched the hatch.

Set into the middle of the door was a small, spring-closed flap. Teleman opened this and dialed the switch to three minutes. Then he turned and, in an awkward, stumbling gait, ran for the trees.

The thermite bomb exploded. Teleman, watching from a safe distance, saw the flames run in streamers up and down the capsule before fusing into a single sheet. In minutes the capsule was reduced to a shapeless, hissing mass in the steady snowfall. Teleman crouched at the base of a large pine until he was satisfied that the capsule had been completely destroyed. His last link with the aircraft, in which he had spent what he considered the most important years of his life was severed. Now, cut off from the stabilizing effect of his semi-computer-controlled aircraft and thrown on to his own, he was confused and uncertain, and the drug residues only increased the intensity of his anxieties.

For a moment he felt as if the complexity of the situation was going to overwhelm him. The windblown snow swirling about him narrowed his world to a tiny circle. Into this world, he huddled against the base of the tree and buried his head in his arms, trying to shut out its effects.

The roar of a jet aircraft, hidden in the clouds, but low enough to be clearly heard over the wind, shocked him into consciousness. He sprang up, head cocked to one side, listening. He could hear the fading scream of tortured air as the sound went toward the coast.

Teleman stooped down to gather up a handful of snow and rub it on his face. The Soviets had tried three times to kill him. They had succeeded in unhorsing him, so to speak, but he was not down yet, at least in any but the descriptive sense.

The pilot, with grim determination, shouldered his pack and, following his compass, set off due north to the cliffs of the North Cape.

Larkin chafing at the delay, paced the bridge, back and forth from meteorological gear to helm, making short sorties on to the deck to judge the condition of the storm. Larkin would never admit it to anyone, but he trusted his own innate weather sense more than all the meteorological gear in the world. That the gale was subsiding, he was now certain. And as swiftly as they begin, katabatic storms, by their very nature, are short-lived, but while living are possibly the most dangerous storms of their kind. The aftermath would still be thoroughly dangerous, and the blizzard it would bring would be both a help and a hindrance. It would at least keep the Soviet surface craft snug in port since the high seas would continue to run for quite some time yet, subsiding slowly over a matter of days, even after the winds had blown themselves out. Larkin was worrying about the pounding the bow was again taking as they plunged toward the Cape at high speed. Each time the forefoot smashed into a wave, the shock could be felt through the entire ship.

The engineers, still at work in the bow cofferdam, were complaining more and more frequently, and finally Larkin ordered the tank evacuated. The bow plates and patches had been restored earlier. Everything that could be done had been.

At 0500 the heavy seas began to abate. The temperatures rose above the freezing mark and the heavy snow turned to sleet. It poured down in buckets, ending Larkin's tension-induced deck watch for the time being. In two hours the deck heaters were able to clear away most of the accumulation of ice. The wind, still blowing Force 9, in combination with the heavy seas, peeled and ripped the remainder of the ice away in great chunks, and the ship slowly became more responsive to the helm as she rode higher.

The cruiser beat its way southwest, now a gray shape slipping through the snow and rain and running seas, rolling thirty degrees to either side in the mountainous waves as it sought the shorter waters of the coastal shelf and the tiny indentation in the cliffs that was as close to the downed pilot as she could get.

Teleman had been trudging north for an hour when the wind died abruptly. One minute he had been leaning directly into the forty-mile-an-hour winds, struggling against the solid hand that barred his way, and the next he was standing beneath the trees wrapped in the eerie silence that heavy winds leave when they depart. He glanced up at the swollen cloud cover, lowering over the barely seen tops of the trees. With the disappearance of the wind, the snowfall began to thicken, and in a few moments he could barely see trees less than ten feet away.

He strained forward, listening for the boom of waves against the cliffs, but heard only the peculiar whisper of snow falling through the fir trees. A few moments later Teleman resumed his slow pace. The snow beneath the trees was almost mid-calf deep, but dry and powdery, and he had little trouble plowing through it. What bothered him most was the cold. He knew the temperature must be at least thirty below zero. The emergency kit had not included a face mask and Teleman rubbed his cheeks continually with his gloved hands to maintain circulation. The thin scarf tied across his mouth had crusted with ice from his exhaled breath and was practically useless.

The exertion of walking and fighting the wind was pure torture. Muscles and nerve endings screamed at the agony of movement after so many hours of physical inactivity. Teleman knew he was weak beyond belief, and the deep cold biting into his body was taking a dangerous toll on his already overloaded metabolic system. Earlier, he had briefly considered using the radio and trying to contact the ship to give them an exact position fix. Then he could hole up in the lightweight tent in his pack until they got to him. The only trouble was that it would give the Russians an exact fix at the same time. A couple of bombers and a saturation bombing run on the area would take care of him once and for all. The fact that the Soviets had tried to shoot him down three times had more than convinced him they were playing for keeps. If they could not have him, they did not want the Americans to get him back either. He had seen too much of their optical tracking system. Since no hint of the system had come out of the Soviet Union from Western intelligence operatives, he surmised that it was one of their most closely guarded secrets. The United States was too far ahead of the Soviets in electronics for radar and other sensor countermeasures for the Russians to compete effectively. The important computer, transistor, and circuitry technologies had been developed to a very high degree in the United States while the Russians were not concerned with the miniaturization and microminiaturization techniques that required advanced circuitry and electronic concepts.

All of this passed through Teleman's exhausted mind in a very abstracted form. Yet he was well aware of every detail, every ramification. For two years his life had depended on his ECM gear. The optical tracking system was obviously the mainstay of Soviet hopes against an invasion force of supersonic and hypersonic aircraft. Teleman knew enough about the system to enable the American intelligence and scientific communities to analyse and develop optical countermeasures. The race would be evened up again. The Soviets wanted him badly, but would kill him if there was no other way to shut him up—all of this coincidentally with their war on the Sino-Soviet border.

Teleman rubbed his ears vigorously with both gloved hands, cap tucked under one arm, and sighed. It was going to be rough on his ears, but there was no hope for it. He had to be able to hear aircraft coming enough in advance to duck under the closest tree. If he did not and was spotted, he could expect the aircraft to make an immediate pass over the area with rockets, napalm, bombs, cannon, or whatever devilish weaponry it carried, and that would be the end. He shifted the pack to a more comfortable position and started slogging forward once more.

Even though the wind had died, the going was not that much

easier. The forest thickened quickly with dense stands of frozen pine. The ground, in spite of the intense cold, had become soggy underfoot, almost on the verge of muskeg, and after nearly an hour more of walking he had covered little more than a mile. Teleman had never seen such forest this far north of the Arctic Circle. He decided that it must be due to the last-gasp effects of the Gulf Stream Current as it finally dissipated off the North Cape. He recalled that in Alaska, in the foothills of the Brooks Range nearly two hundred miles north of the Arctic Circle, there were similar fir forests.

Then, strangely enough, the pines thinned rapidly, almost in a matter of yards, it seemed. The forest gave way to scattered brush and glacial boulders. Even though the ground was rough, full of snow-covered and treacherous rills, Teleman found it easier walking than the thick forest. But on the verge of exhaustion as he was, it hardly made a difference. Even so, he hesitated on the edge of the last stand of trees.

He could see almost a hundred yards ahead now through the driving snow. The compass still showed him to be on course, but the open ground ahead would provide no cover from searching Soviet aircraft. Against that expanse of ice-cold white, on an IR screen he would stand out like a neon sign in a desert. Nor could he hope to burrow far enough into the snow to escape detection.

Finally, after several minutes of almost incoherent self-debate, which to his surprise he found he was conducting aloud with himself, in a weary fit of exasperation, he shook his head and started forward. To hell with it, he thought. If they were going to find him, they were going to find him and that was that. If he did not make the coast shortly he was going to die anyway. Almost imperceptibly at first the ground beneath his feet began to climb. The snow, slowly turning to sleet that drummed down on to him, plastering his hair against his head, which he had forgotten to re-cover with his hood, obscured his vision—vision that now was almost useless as his brain refused to sort and display images properly. The half snow, half sleet was melting and beginning to trickle down his ebony face and seep beneath his collar.

Teleman stumbled in one of the rills; he had stepped on to what appeared to be a solid surface. He foot had gone through the thin crust of ice and his leg jarred down stiffly, pitching him forward. For minutes he lay half stunned until some inner instinct lifted him up and sent him stumbling forward again. It was several minutes later that he realized he had fallen.

After that his head seemed to clear a little. Teleman felt the wetness of his scalp and raised the hood. Ahead he could see a fairly large stand of bush, which appeared similar to cottonwoods.

Almost without thinking he veered, and a moment later threw himself down beneath the outspread branches and rolled in as close to the base of the bush as he could.

He had never seen such godforsaken country. The sleet and snow swept across the almost barren muskeg with an ululating keening. The gray sky pressed down thickly and the galling snow lent additional oppression to the landscape. The entire scene reminded him of Dante's description of the tenth circle of hell, so unreal and remote from earth it seemed. The predominate color was gray: gray sky, gray snow, gray rocks, gray trees, and he was the doomed soul, doomed to wander forever in this gray hell searching for the stream of Lethe. Teleman shivered at his morbid thoughts. He could feel what little heat remained in his body quickly dissipating. He knew that he had to get up and keep moving or else he would very quickly freeze to death. But soft tendrils of sleep were curling around his eyes, forcing them closed. With a quivering effort, he forced them open again and struggled to his feet. He faced the snow and rising wind and went on.

Now, as the sleet stopped and the snow fell thicker, blotting away every trace of detail in the barren landscape, he was moving on a treadmill in the middle of white nothingness. For hours it seemed to Teleman, he struggled onward as the wind rose higher, until he was again facing a thirty-knot wind. With vicious suddenness, the wind would quarter, driving him far off course. He no longer knew whether he was moving north. He had dropped the compass sometime back and now had nothing against which to check his direction. Far down in the depths of his conscious mind, he knew that, as long as he kept walking in the direction with which the terrain rose, eventually he would come to the coastal cliffs. Whether or not he would last that long never occurred to him now. Only his survival training was driving him forward, forcing him to plod forward rather than drop in his tracks to freeze to death.

The trees were totally gone, as was the brush. Dimly he knew that he was struggling to climb a steep hill. By now Teleman was nearly asleep, only his subconscious operating his body. He neither knew nor cared where he was or what he was doing except on the dimmest conscious level. But still he went on. climbing the hill that stretched away before him, apparently forever.

Suddenly the wind died for a moment and the snow swirled away as if a curtain had been drawn. Teleman was standing on the lower lip of a hill, which in actuality was the back side of the cliffs leading to the coastal waters. Then the wind came again and the snow fell harder around him. Teleman went to his knees and began to crawl forward, blindly, until he had worked his way to the top and the forward edge, which was sheltered from the wind and where the snow fell more thinly than it had before. There was no place for the wind to whirl snow from the drifts to add to the blizzard. He could see, far below, the pounding sea—the waves tall and cold green, smashing into the jagged baseline of the cliffs less than thirty feet away. The waves swept in from the sea in tremendous combers that, as they approached the cliffs, curled up, drawing a paler line at the fold and collapsing against the restraining wall of rock with a shattering roar. Teleman saw that there was no beach. If there had ever been, it had surely been washed away under the onslaught of the waves. The snow was now so heavy that he could see no more than a few hundred feet out to sea.

After a few minutes more, the wind slicing in from the sea with the keenness of a razor forced him back from the cliff edge. Teleman carefully backed away and then moved along paralleling the crest until he found a depression surrounded by two large boulders, which offered some protection against the wind.

Teleman huddled into the lee of the rocks and shrugged off the pack. He sat on his heels, leaning back against the rock, and let the weariness that was exhaustion flow through him. If he could only stay awake long enough to contact the ship, he thought. If the Russians did not pick up the transmission, if the ship was there, if they could get a boat in, if they could beat the Soviets to him . . . *if* . . . then he would have made it. In spite of his tiredness, he grinned weakly before pulling the pack over and digging through it for the radio. Those were some pretty large *ifs*.

The lightweight unit was almost too much for the meager remains of his strength. Teleman pulled the radio to him and leaned it against a rock. His numbed hands refused to curl around the tip to the antenna for an endless time before he managed to pull it out.

'Target One, do you read me? Target One, do you read me?'

The dials were softly illuminated and the power light was glowing red. His watched showed nearly thirty minutes past the time the ship should have come into radio range. The radio had both military and VHF-FM side bands. The VHF was for short-range line-of-sight work, not much more than fifteen miles. The military side band gave the transceiver a range of nearly two hundred miles. He used the VHF-FM band, hoping that the Soviets would not be monitoring within that range. Somewhere out there the ship should be standing less than five miles off the coast, waiting for his call.

'Target One, Target One, do you read me? Do you read me?'

The small radio sputtered with a faint static composed of low rumblings overlain with a high-pitched hissing. Teleman wondered momentarily where the hissing was coming from. The transceiver employed transistors and printed circuitry, not vacuum tubes.

Kneeling in the soft, powdery snow, Teleman tried again and again to raise the ship. In the nine hours since he had last had communication with the *RFK* innumerable things could have happened. Soviet aircraft or submarines could have found her . . . could have attacked . . . sent her to bottom . . . could have . . . hit seas too much . . . where the hell was . . . damned ship . . . could not last . . . much . . .

Teleman had lost all feeling in his feet and hands and was forced to use his clenched fist to work the transmit switch. Over and over he repeated his monotonous call, his voice becoming weaker and weaker until he was barely whispering into the microphone. He huddled on his knees, back against a sheltering rock, drifting hypnotically with the falling snow, whispering over and over again his call signal as the snow began to cover him with a soft, warm blanket. The will to stay awake was gone. He no longer even thought about the importance of staying awake. After a while he became aware that he had stopped calling. The radio was there in front of him, half covered with snow. He wanted to move closer, check the settings, but somehow he could not. It was as if he were paralysed.

Still kneeling, half bent over the radio, his mouth half open, he decided to rest a moment then try again. Almost without volition, his eyes closed and the warm softness of sleep began to infuse his body.

He pulled them open with a jerk, for a moment clear-headed and wide awake. The radio was spitting and crackling at him. He stared, then with an effort that, literally, almost killed him, reached out his frozen hand and pushed the receive switch. The answer drew his conscious mind back from the brink of the killing sleep and summoned his will and strength to go on a few minutes longer, drew it up from some dark recess of his body.

'Beatle, this is Target One, Beatle this is Target One, do you read me? Do you read me?' The voice on the other end of the tight radio beam could not conceal the anxiety beneath the calm exterior of the professional radio operator's voice.

'Target One?' he managed to croak, not knowing whether his voice was loud enough to be heard.

The radio operator's voice, almost lost in the storm of strange-sounding static, came over the tiny speaker again:

'Leave your transmitter on, we are getting a position fix.'

For a long time Teleman digested the message, trying to force his leaden mind to understand. Then he pushed the transmitter switch to position identification and a second transmitter built into the radio began sending out a tight VHF beam that the ship would ride in.

A voice that Teleman recognized as belonging to Larkin broke in. 'We are standing off the coast about a mile from where you appear to be. Can you fire a flare to pinpoint your position?'

Teleman stared vacantly at the radio. Larkin tried again. 'Can you fire a flare to pinpoint your position?'

The radio operator pressed his earphones to his head, then turned the gain up another notch.

'Is he still there?' Larkin asked.

'I think so, sir, the transceiver is still on position fix and—'

The radio operator was interrupted by Teleman's faint voice. 'Will shoot . . . flare . . .'

Teleman pulled the pack to him and fumbled through the contents. His hands were so cold they refused to work, and in an agony of frustration he dumped the canvas bag, scattering the contents. Crawling painfully forward, he got to his knees again and scrabbled through the snow for the VERY pistol. After a few moments his fingers encountered the leather holster and he drew it toward him. He sat back against the rock and, using both hands, wedged the grip between his knees. Then he pushed the restraining clip forward and pulled the breech open. With his teeth he pulled a cartridge out of the bandolier fastened to the holster, transferred it to his hands, then into the pistol.

Teleman sat back, exhausted by his efforts. For a minute he sat, gathering strength. Then he hunched himself around until he was pointing in the direction of the sea and tilted the barrel of the pistol up to a steep angle. He forced two fingers through the trigger guard until the pistol went off. The flare arched up and quickly lost itself in the falling snow. Five seconds later Teleman saw the flare explode as a bright flash of light that began slowly to drift down. Even through the snow he could trace its crazy undulations as the tiny parachute was shaken and thrown from side to side by the wind. It landed in the snow not fifty feet away and Teleman stared stupidly at it as it sputtered and hissed to extinction.

As he sat watching the flare he heard Larkin's voice calling over the far-away transmitter saying that the flare had been seen. He nodded his head in reply and, as the last of the flare died away, slipped into unconsciousness, still staring at the spot where it had landed.

## CHAPTER FOURTEEN

FIVE MINUTES LATER and Teleman would have seen the *Robert F. Kennedy* moving majestically through the thirty-foot waves less than a mile offshore, rolling and pitching certainly, but less than would have been expected with a conventionally designed ship. Her rounded deck, almost flush with the water, gave the appearance of a half-submerged submarine as she slipped through the waves. Her deep wing-back bridge, canted aft, seemed to flow smoothly into the rear deck and thence into the sea, with no perceptible change in structure.

Above, the leaden sky glowered down on equally leaden seas. Larkin, standing on the narrow catwalk from which hours before he had fought to turn the ship from the rampaging sea, raised his face to feel the thick, wet flakes filtering down and grimaced as they melted on his upturned face. Both he and Folsom had come out on to the catwalk for a few moments of privacy while they discussed various means to reach the downed pilot.

'I have never seen the temperature rise so quickly after an Arctic storm,' he said. 'If this keeps up, we'll have rain in another hour.'

Folsom's face was clouded with worry as he surveyed the sky, the seas, and the dimly seen cliffs to port.

'I only wish I knew what the hell it meant,' Larkin growled.

The battle cruiser was maneuvering off the cliffs at less than six knots. The waves, marching in rank down from the Great Barrier two hundred miles to the north, first were lifted by the narrow continental shelf then flung forward across three miles of shallows until they smashed into the base of the cliffs on the Norwegian North Cape—the first obstacle in two hundred miles. The waves pounded into the rock as if attempting to smash it from their path, as though an entire continent did not lie behind. As the waves recoiled from the shock against the stone, they curled under themselves and swarmed back out into the depths, creating a maze of undertows and crosscurrents that could easily be disastrous to a landing party. This close to land the winds had dropped into the mid-forties, but their velocity, coupled with the roll and pitch of the ship, was far too high to permit the launching of the helicopter the *RFK* carried.

Now, less than a mile off the cliffs, this was as close as Larkin dared bring the great ship. Radar examination of the coastline indicated sheer rock sloping steeply to the sea. The point of land opposite was a fierce line of rock wall. The waves piling up in thirty-foot breakers indicated that little of no beach existed.

Larkin was now debating whether to try farther down the coast or attempt the certain suicide of the helicopter. The pilot had volunteered, but Larkin, knowing that it was a measure that could only be tried as a last solution, had rejected the offer.

He sighed deeply and pulled his hood tighter against the icy wind. 'Mr. Folsom, take her down the coast at eight knots until we find a spot to land.'

Folsom nodded. 'How far do you want to go?'

'Not over two miles. If we find nothing we'll try the coast to the west.' He shook his head doubtfully. 'I don't know though, the charts show nothing but cliffs for the next ten miles in either direction. If we don't get to that pilot soon, we may as well not even bother.'

Folsom nodded and picked up the microphone to order the course change and get the lookouts out on to the bridge deck.

The ragged coastline slid by with inexorable slowness. The battle cruiser moved along the line of breakers marking the cliffs while snow fell intermittently but heavily enough to obscure visibility much of the time. The cliffs, sixty to a hundred feet high, were steep columns of rock that seemed to rise directly from the sea, and nowhere along their length could the searching seamen find any trace of beach, however small, that would permit a landing. After fifteen minutes Larkin reluctantly ordered the *RFK* brought about. The great ship now quickened its pace for the run up to the west. Time was growing short. Larkin knew Teleman would be on his last reserves of strength. Unless they got to him shortly, he would, in his weakened condition, die in a matter of hours.

The landing place, the only one they found, was a tiny beach less than a hundred yards wide and so shallow that the heavy seas washed perilously close to the base of the cliffs. From what Folsom could see between the crash of each wave, the beach, such as it was, was covered with heavy gravel and sloped upward steeply to the cliffs. A shallow cut led up, to disappear around a chimney of rock, but presumably pointed to the top, ninety feet up. It would be a rugged climb, Folsom knew, and a bad one in the winds which would surely be sweeping up the cut turning it into a wind tunnel. But it was the only feasible landing place they had found so far. And unless they moved farther west, down the coast another twenty miles to where the cliffs began to peter out, it was the only one they were going to find.

'Pete, what do you think? Can a boat be gotten in?'

Folsom searched the narrow beach again with his glasses before replying. 'I think so, Captain. If the waves are timed right, I think it could be done. Getting back out again will be the trick.'

Larkin turned his own glasses on the beach. 'If you can get in and find the pilot, you could wait it out in the boat until we can get a helicopter in.'

'Me, Captain?'

Larkin lowered the glasses and turned to Folsom, his face completely serious. 'Yep—surprise. I would like you to lead the landing party. You *know* how important it is that the pilot be gotten out.'

Folsom nodded silently, turning his eyes away from Larkin to stare at the distant line of cliffs. Larkin's voice contained all the explanation needed. He was indeed aware of the importance, the vital importance. 'In that case, I would like to take an armed party, just to be on the safe side.'

'Of course. Anything you need?' Larkin paused, considering his executive officer for a moment. 'What do you think, Pete?' he asked softly.

'I guess I can only give it a try,' Folsom said with a grin that he did not feel.

The lifeboat that rested on the aft deck was certainly odd in contrast to the sleekness of the *RFK*. It was a flattened sphere twelve feet in diameter, its bottom resting on a flaring, truncated cone skirt. Made of fiberglass, it was painted international orange. Folsom had always had cause to shake his head every time he saw the lifeboat above decks; strange-looking as it was, he knew it was the safest possible design that had yet evolved. There were no open areas to fill with water in heavy seas. You entered the boat through one of three hatches near the top and let yourself down into a roomy interior lined with bunks. In the center was a closed-off electrical heating unit, powered either with a wind-driven generator or a fuel cell. The thing was literally unsinkable. The flaring skirt around the base provided stability in seas running to forty-foot waves or better.

Folsom gathered his two-man party around him to receive their last instructions from Larkin, who shook hands briefly with each man, and then they climbed aboard and sealed the hatches. Larkin stood back as the winches eased the boat off the deck and over the side. As it slid slowly down into the waves, through the upper rim of ports, Folsom and his crew could see the hull of the *RFK* towering over them. The waves caught at the lifeboat before Folsom got the engine started and slammed them into the side of the battle cruiser with bruising force.

Folsom picked himself up from the deck and started the engine, cursing all the while. Once the engine caught and the boat got underway, he was able to concentrate on keeping the spherical lifeboat, amazingly stable in heavy seas, pointed in the direction of the cliffs that appeared every now and then through the waves.

As they neared the breakers, Folsom idled the engines and pressed his face against the tempered glass of the port. He wished mightily that he could open one of the top hatches to steer, but he knew that one heavy wave pushing them under momentarily would swamp the lifeboat. Except for quick glimpses he caught whenever the lifeboat rode up a wave far enough for him to see over the mountainous seas piling up ahead, he was surrounded by ever-moving walls of water.

Folsom felt the boat ride up again, and ahead, through the glass, was the line of cliffs, startlingly close. This was it, he thought, and gunned the engines. The boat paused at the crest of the breaker as the propellers fought to exercise their command over the tumbling masses of water. But it was not enough. As the boat began to slide down the forward edge of the wave, a mean crosscurrent caught the skirt and spun it around. The men inside felt the boat slam hard against the shingle. Folsom glanced back in time to see the following wave towering over them before the boat was engulfed by foaming white water that lifted and tossed it high into the air. The three-ton boat, flung as if it were a child's toy, smashed down hard on the rocks. A second and a third wave kicked, then rolled the lifeboat farther up on to the beach.

It was several minutes before Folsom could extricate himself from the mass of equipment on the deck where he had been thrown. He slumped down on to one of the padded seats lining the interior and rubbed his temples with both hands, then stirred one of the prone figures at his feet.

'Come on, up, up! Do you want to lie there all day?'

The answer was somewhat muffled, but very much in the affirmative. Shortly they were all three moving around with nothing more than bruises to show for the wild ride. Folsom was exceedingly grateful that the *RFK* carried the new Life Sphere lifeboats. The same ride in the old, open whaler type would certainly have drowned them all.

He crawled out of the top hatch and slid down to the beach. The boat was canted over at a drunken angle and the flaring skirt around the base had been twisted and torn loose from its welds by the wild careen across the beach. Several deep gashes had been ripped in the outer fiberglass hull, but none penetrated the interior hull. What caused the sinking feeling in the pit of Folsom's stomach was the sight of the snapped and bent propeller shafts and the hopelessly mangled rudders.

Folsom examined the damage while the other two clambered out and joined him on the beach. Both grunted at the damage.

'I would say that boat is just about finished.'

Folsom agreed. 'But there's no help for that. Let's get the equipment unloaded and get going. We'll have to wait until later to worry about the boat.' While the others went to work, Folsom made a report by radio to Larkin. He did not minimize the importance of the loss of the lifeboat but neither did he dwell on it. Larkin promised to get a second lifeboat in as soon as they were able to return to the beach with the pilot. His report finished, the three men began moving out along the coast to the east. A fast but difficult climb brought them to the top of the cliffs. They wasted no time but immediately struck out east. All they had to go on to find the downed pilot was a radio fix that could be off by as much as a quarter of a mile in any direction.

In the long hours during which the U.S.S. *Robert F. Kennedy* maneuvered off the Norwegian North Cape, the storm passed on to the northeast where it would gradually lose force as it began to curl north toward the polar icecap once more. As the storm center moved deeper into the Barents Sea toward Novaya Zemlya, the high winds in the vicinity of the Cape began to lose strength, until, an hour after Folsom and his party had landed, they were blowing at a steady forty knots. As the winds died, however, the snow fell thicker and thicker and the temperature dropped rapidly, bringing what Larkin had most feared—intense cold. The waves, still roused by the passage of the fierce winds across two hundred miles of ocean from the southern edge of the Arctic ice pack, continued to run high, beating themselves to death in a final rush of breakers and white water, smashing away at the same cliffs that had defied them for millions of years.

Folsom, marching along the top of the cliffs, could see the tremendous breakers rushing on to the thread of beach through the swirling snow. The cold had already deepened to twenty below zero and he had ordered the others to don face masks for protection from frostbite. In spite of their Navy-issue Arctic gear, all three were numb to the bone.

Fortunately, Folsom thought to himself, the cliffs above the narrow beach were fairly smooth. There were no deep crevices or caves into which the pilot could have crawled that would take them hours to search out.

The landing party stumbled across Teleman almost by accident thirty minutes later. Chief Petty Officer Beauregard McPherson found him still half crouched in a kneeling position facing the frozen radio. Folsom went to his knees beside the still figure, ripping off one of his gloves to check for pulse. He found one, slow and fluttery, but a pulse. Another half hour, or even less, would have done it, he knew.

Folsom stood up and looked around. Half a mile away he could make out the thin first line of trees through which Teleman had struggled to reach the cliffs. With the pilot half carried, half dragged between them they trotted toward the dubious shelter of the trees. They pushed their way deep into the snow-laden firs until the wind was hardly more than a fitful breeze eddying the falling snow into swirls of white. Even above the soft, steady roar of the wind through the pine tops, they could hear the crash of the breakers against the cliffs.

In less than five minutes they had the nylon mountain tent rigged and the heater going. Folsom quickly stripped the sodden flying clothes from Teleman and got him zipped into a chemically heated sleeping bag. Over this, he pulled still another sleeping bag. As the tent warmed quickly from the primus stove, Folsom anxiously watched the face of the unconscious pilot. The features had the pinched, waxy look that comes from the first stages of frostbite—or from death by freezing. Even though he had been sheltered by the rocks from the wind and if Larkin had been correct in his interpretation of the pilot's physical condition after a six-day mission, then the man was close to exhaustion. Hiking through these trees would only have worsened that condition, badly. Larkin had cautioned him about using any drugs on the pilot. There was no way for them to know how his system would react to further drugs if he was deep into exhaustion. Folsom was helpless, then. There was nothing he could do except keep him warm and wait until he regained consciousness, and then get as much solid food into him as the pilot could take. His own body would have to do all the work. Folsom was amazed that the human body could take such abuse and still manage to function.

After the self-supported tent was securely rigged and their gear squared away, Folsom dug the radio out of his pack and extended the aerial. When he threw the transmit switch, he heard a weird rumble of static and hissing that overpowered any transmissions for a moment. Then suddenly it cleared.

Larkin was on the other end moments later and Folsom made his report, forgetting quickly about the unusual static.

He described the desperate state that Teleman was in and his fears that he might not regain consciousness even in the warmth of the tent. 'Besides,' he finished, 'right now, I think that if we tried to move our man the trek back to the beach would probably kill him. The temperature is dropping very fast up here.'

Larkin's voice contained undertones of worry. 'I agree that you ought to stay put until you see how he is. I should have known that the false rise in temperature would lead to an even deeper drop. Katabatic storms often end this way. You can probably expect the temperature to drop at least another twenty degrees in the next twenty-four hours.'

'Ye gods, another twenty degrees!' Folsom exclaimed.

'That's right . . . but at least it will bring an end to the winds.'

'Yeah, thanks for small favors,' Folsom murmured.

'I'm afraid we are going to have to stand farther out to sea until these waves let up.'

'I was afraid that the seas were going to force you out farther,' Folsom replied.

For a moment there was silence as the two men tried to think of what to say next. Larkin continued to stare through the forward ports at the heavy snow thrashing past as the battle cruiser moved through the waves at eight knots. Folsom, hunching over the radio, listened to the wind's keening beyond the tent walls and felt the loneliness of being cut off from help in the face of the enemy. The other two caught the mood and silence enveloped the tent until Folsom said, 'Well, it looks like we are stuck here awhile. I'll set two-hour radio watches for routine checks.'

'Fine. We'll keep you informed. Out.'

Several minutes later the tent flaps parted and Folsom crawled out and stood up. The wind moaned through the treetops with force enough to whip the powdery snow into twirling gusts. Vaguely he had in mind a short hike for a good look at the area, but the snow, falling heavily, and the wind, backing and filling through the trees, had created a ground blizzard. He changed his mind. It would be too easy to become confused and lost in the closely pressing trees. Instead, he rounded the tent and headed for the line of cliffs half a mile distant.

The snow overlay provided treacherous footing among the frozen grass hummocks of the tundra. The powdery snow had not settled and frozen enough to provide firm footing as yet. He wondered just how far the muskeg extended. If for some reason they had to run for it, it would be bad enough with three healthy, rested men, but damned near impossible with the exhausted pilot. Less than a hundred feet from the tent he stopped and decided not to go any farther. The wind had freshened slightly and in a few minutes time the snowfall had almost doubled. He had seen this happen before and knew that for the next few hours they were in for a heavy blizzard. As he turned back, retracing his dimly seen footsteps quickly before they were covered by the falling and drifting snow, he thought of the heavy blizzard with gratitude. The Russians, should a capture party be landed, would not be able to move either. Once back in the tent, he organized the watches, checked on the sleeping Teleman, then settled into his own sleeping bag and was asleep in seconds.

\*          \*          \*

The snow continued to fall heavily during the long night. Folsom had taken the second radio watch but the *RFK* reported nothing new. The ship's detector systems had so far uncovered no trace of movement in the vicinity of the North Cape: land, sea, or air. They had been, however, monitoring radio traffic and Larkin gave him an abstracted report. The Russians were seriously considering attempting the rescue or capture, depending on how you looked at it, of the downed pilot. Other than that, most of the transmissions had been in a new code which the ship's computers had as yet been unable to break. The transmissions had been recorded and relayed to Virginia, but so far they had had no word on what they contained. Folsom signed off with an uneasy feeling that something big was brewing. He only hoped that they would have some warning before it happened.

The close-woven mesh of the nylon tent fabric was covered with snow. Even without the snow, the mesh did not allow much in the way of air circulation. The outside temperature had dropped to 35° F as the wind had all but disappeared, but inside the tent it had become stifling. When they had opened a tent flap, the warm air had immediately rushed out into the night, leaving the inside of the tent as cold as the outside. The three men had tried to keep the tent free of snow, but the blizzard was so heavy that it was almost useless to climb into parkas and boots and work for twenty minutes to brush away the snow. Folsom, lying in his sleeping bag after his second watch, was restless and wide awake. He groaned and rolled over, trying to ignore the closeness of the air, thinking longingly for the very first time of the mind-deadening desk job he had left in the Navy Department to serve aboard the *RFK*.

## CHAPTER FIFTEEN

LARKIN, too, was lying awake in his bunk, but for different reasons. His mind was churning with the possibilities for action. Larkin was trying to examine the situation from the standpoint of the Soviet war room, which must, from somewhere, be directing the 'rescue' operations. He had, as had many other military commanders before him, found it of great value to put himself in the enemy commander's place and as dispassionately as possible work out the tactic needed to destroy the enemy. This particular situation was a little bit different from others he had encountered in the past. This time he was sure that the enemy commander did not know the *RFK* existed. They might suspect that somehow, some American forces had gotten to the downed pilot, but they would not know the nature of these forces—which was a damned good thing, he thought grimly. Three men, armed with rifles, cut off from further support, in the middle of the North Cape, was not much of an opposing force to worry about.

They had made radar contacts with several, presumably Russian, aircraft throughout most of the afternoon and evening. All seemed to be orbiting the North Cape area where the pilot had gone down. None had ventured out to sea, a sign that Larkin interpreted as meaning the ship was undetected. Larkin was not worried about the ship. She was more than a match for anything the Soviets could throw in against her. But the Soviets would move twice as fast if they knew the *RFK* was nearby.

As long as the blizzard lasted, he was safe from visual detection. His own electromagnetic counterdetection gear would protect him from electronic snooping; so Larkin held the position of the reserve queen on the chessboard, the deciding factor of the game.

The buzzer on the intercom over his bunk interrupted his musings. He reached a hand and flipped the switch. 'Larkin here.'

'Sorry to disturb you, sir,' came the unruffled voice, 'but sonar shows a blip, unidentified and approaching subsurface from the northeast.'

'Be right up,' Larkin snapped and sat up, rubbing his face with his hands. He had not had any decent sleep for more than twenty-four hours now and it was beginning to tell on him. He stumbled across to the lavatory and washed his face with hot water and soap, then rinsed with cold. With the cold water still running, he held his wrists under the stream until they were all but numb, then toweled his face and arms vigorously. This helped to refresh him for the moment. Wishing that he had time for a shower, he pulled on trousers and shirt, knotted a tie quickly, tugged on his turtleneck sweater, and, picking up his cap, left for the bridge.

Three minutes later he was peering at the heavy seas through the ports, bracing himself against the railing. 'All right, kill the lights.'

The tortured scene of thrashing white water and intense snow disappeared abruptly as the powerful searchlights winked out. Larkin turned from the screen and made his way to his console, where he strapped himself in. The marine guard, doubling as steward, brought him coffee.

'Let's have a status report,' he said into the microphone. 'First the radar.'

'We have identified the sub as Russian, possibly Anatov class, presumably nuclear powered. She is a hunter-killer-type from her hull and, if Anatov class, used for long-range coastal patrolling. Her present position is 32.76 degrees by 74.34 degrees, moving at fourteen knots, east by northeast. We are projecting a landing point now at eighteen miles southeast of where Mr. Folsom landed. ETA at four hours and fifty-six minutes at present course and speed.'

'Very well, put it on the board.'

Above the consoles against the after bulkhead a large screen lit up with a holographic map projection of the North Cape and its interlocking chain of islands and fjords, modified by sonar and radar information. The shallow coast and underwater shelf were clearly outlined for three miles out to sea. As Larkin watched, a star-shaped locator blazed up over the landing-party camp and a smaller pointer marked the location of the wrecked lifeboat.

Farther east Larkin could see the long red trail culminating in a boat-shaped target point that was the Russian submarine heading into Porsangerfjord. A yellow dotted line extended ahead and was now resting on a shallow beach where the cliffs began to straggle down into a steep shelf. Twelve miles west and five south was the Norwegian town of Kjelvik, scarcely more than a fishing village of some two hundred inhabitants and a small Norwegian Coast Guard base. The fjord waters were frozen solid just north of the town and the Russians would have little trouble crossing.

Larkin shifted his gaze to the western coast showing on the map and found the extensive naval air base north of Rolfsö, first constructed by the Nazis in World War II as their northernmost air base for use against the Allied convoys making the dangerous run to Murmansk. From this same base the German Condor bombers had been able to bring the convoys under attack almost from the time they left Iceland. The Norwegians had taken the base over following the war and it now was their main defense post against a northern attack by the Russians. Even though tensions had eased considerably in recent years the base was still manned and in ready condition as a NATO installation. He knew that the twelve-inch radar-controlled guns first installed by the Nazis could cover anything within a radius of seventeen miles. They were backed up by intermediate-range surface-to-air and surface-to-surface missiles. Larkin knew that he had better not involve the Norwegians unless absolutely necessary. His orders were strict: to pick up the pilot at any cost; avoid alerting the Norwegians; avoid a pitched battle or any contact at all with the Soviets.

Larkin sighed heavily and sat back in the chair. The heavy red line marking the path of the submarine had moved another half inch and he sighed again. 'Another complication.'

'Pardon, sir?'

'Nothing, just talking to myself. . . . What do you make of it, Mister?'

The radar man hesitated only a moment. 'From the radar, she's running half submerged with only her conning tower out. She's hugging the coast and heading for a point fifteen miles from where Mr. Folsom landed. There is only one place she could have come from, sir—the sub pens at Murmansk.'

'Why not from out at sea, riding out the storm below the surface?'

'Wouldn't make sense, sir. In order to be safe from the coastal ridges and rocks outside of the Murmansk channel, she would have had to stand at least forty miles off the coast. A surface ship would be safe enough anywhere along the Russian coast, but a submarine would need at least sixty feet over her sail in these seas and that means at least a hundred and twenty feet of water for maneuvering room. The coast around Murmansk, in fact in any of these fjord areas, does not run much over eighty feet. So she had to come from the sub pens. It would take her at least eight hours at her present cruising speed of fourteen knots to get here.'

'That makes a good bit of sense,' Larkin agreed. 'I think you may be right. If so, then we should not have to worry about any other Russian subs sneaking up on us from the northern waters for a while. If they are going to come, they will come in from Murmansk.'

Larkin sat back a moment and stared at the map. The rugged coast of the North Cape stretched away to the southeast before it turned sharply south into both Porsangerfjord and Laksefjord, wide deep chasms that would furnish protection for the submarine when it surfaced. It would also put them eighteen miles down the coast from where Folsom had landed. The submarine's apparent track indicated they were heading for the northern end of Porsangerfjord, where they would have the additional protection of the point. The map showed the ground in this area of the North Cape rising quickly from sea level to eight hundred feet, but gradually enough so that there would be a decent beach, partially sheltered from both the sea and the winds, with more than enough protection to land a small boat.

Larkin made his decision. 'Mr. Bridges, lay a course for a point where we can keep an eye on both the submarine when she goes under the lee and Mr. Folsom's party. Then have the crew stand to general quarters.'

'Aye, aye, sir,' Bridges replied. He motioned to the communications officer and strode quickly to the plotting table. As he went over the lighted board, the GQ klaxon began its strident rasping throughout the ship. Almost immediately the control board began to wink from red to green as each station reported in.

The U.S.S. *Robert F. Kennedy* came around on a course that would bring them to bear directly on the submarine and settled into the waves. Larkin himself took the conn and rapidly closed the gap between the two vessels. So far it appeared that the submarine had not seen the *RFK*, and Larkin doubted that, with her more limited equipment, they would be able to break through the ECM shield around the battle cruiser. They would be having troubles enough to spare much time for surveillance in any event.

Larkin stood in as close as he dared until only fifty miles separated the two ships. His own detection equipment was excellent and there was no sense pushing his luck. For twenty minutes they watched the submarine as it changed course to run in under the lee of the Porsangerfjord, much as Larkin had expected. He was sure from the way the submarine was being handled that the Russian commander knew these waters well. Fjords are tricky places to take a submarine into. The complex currents between the narrow walls and the convolutions of the rock sides and bottom create a maze of conflicting sonar reports so that the underwater gear becomes almost useless for anything other than short-range work. The Russian commander was clearly over-running his sonar and Larkin wondered how many times the Russian had done this before. It made sense when he thought about it. This section of the Cape was practically deserted, with the exception of a few fishing villages. The only military installation on this end of the Cape was the coast guard base, placed there to protect the fishing fleet, not to conduct coastal surveillance. Other than that, there was only the Norwegian-manned NATO base on the far side of the Cape.

To neutralize the NATO base if war should occur, a head-on attack would be suicidal. But a sufficiently large force in regiment strength, complete with vehicles, could be landed in Porsangerfjord and strike overland to take the base from the rear. With the NATO base in their hands the Soviet sub fleet would have free access to the Barents and Norwegian seas, and from there could move into the North Atlantic with little or no opposition.

Approximately twenty minutes went by before the radar operator called Larkin's attention to the radar scope again and interpreted the puzzle of dots in the growing pattern on the screen.

'It looks like they are surfacing, sir. More of the sail is out of the water and the decks are coming into view.' A few moments later he said, 'Now she's heaving to . . . about two miles off the beach, I make it, sir.'

'Probably doesn't dare go in any closer. In those seas I don't know as I blame him,' Larkin commented.

'Even inside the fjord, she must be rolling through forty degrees. I pity her crew,' Bridges murmured over Larkin's shoulder as he watched the screen.

Larkin nodded. 'They will have a devil of a time getting a boat off the deck and manned. That's one operation I would like to see. It would do you good as well, Mr. Bridges. Those new-fangled life spheres don't call for much of a knack in launching. Swing her over the side and cut her loose. Couldn't sink one if you tried.'

Bridges made a skeptical noise and Larkin grinned.

'According to the charts, there is a small cove directly in from where the sub is lying,' Bridges pointed out. 'But there sure isn't any shelter there. It faces north, into the winds.'

'Even so, they might get the boat in . . . but, I sure wouldn't want to be in it.'

On the screen a small shape detached itself from the bulk of the submarine and headed toward the shore. As soon as the boat was away the sub began to submerge.

'I have engine noises, very faintly, sir,' said the sonar operator.

'At fifty miles?' Larkin asked incredulously.

'Yes, sir. It might be due to the temperature of the water. I've had it happen before, although never this far away from the source.'

'I'll be damned. What do they seem to be doing now?'

The sonar operator pressed the phones tightly to his head. 'As . . . as near as I can tell . . . they have just submerged, probably to periscope depth to watch the lifeboat. They don't seem to be going anywhere.'

'Keep a sharp sonar watch. All engines to stop. Switch to silent running.' Larkin shifted restlessly in his high seat. 'If we can hear them, they just may be able to pick us up as well.' The quiet murmuring died throughout the ship as the mechanical gear shut down.

'They might have picked us up already over the noise of their own engines, even though it isn't likely,' Bridges said as he moved to Folsom's console and strapped himself in. His hands played quickly over the keys and the various panels came alive. Then he ran a quick status check of the ship and its gear before changing over to monitoring the radar and sonar consoles. Deep in the hull, the main sonar and radar rooms, located at opposite ends of the ship for safety, were also keeping a sharp watch, under the direction of the chief petty officer. Certain isolated points might have escaped the human operators, but nothing that appeared to be out of bounds passed the attention of the giant process computer that overmonitored the entire system.

'Just at periscope depth, sir. They don't seem to be aware of us. I would guess that the changes in the water layers carrying their engine noise is just a fluke. I doubt if it works both ways. And we may lose it anytime,' he pointed out.

Larkin nodded. 'That may be so, but there is no harm in being careful. I would guess that they haven't picked us up either. We at least are in international waters. Even so, if they had picked us up they would be getting ready for a fight. In fact, their missiles would probably already be on the way.'

It took the Russian lifeboat over an hour to negotiate the two miles of angry sea to the cove, and once under the lee of the cliffs it disappeared from their radar, lost in the mass of signal noise reflecting from the rock. From the radar it was impossible to tell whether he boat had made it in, and the propeller noises from the tiny engine were completely lost over the fifty-mile distance in spite of the reflecting layers of water that had temporarily expanded the senses of the ship.

Larkin touched the switch to the main radio room. 'Put your sweep on the speaker system, please.'

A moment later the speakers on the bridge burst into life. Larkin grimaced at a noise that sounded like someone using a cat's tail to play a musical saw. The radio operator was running up and down the bandwidth with the tuner. A small computer unit monitored and controlled the process, hunting until it picked up a definite signal. For three minutes the noise continued until the wearing howl was broken by a loud whistle, then a Russian voice transmitting a series of call letters broke over. This was followed by another voice spewing a choppy flow of Russian. The tranmission was over quickly, to be replaced by the normal static of an unused frequency.

Almost at the same time, the radio operator was back on the speaker. 'We have it all taped, sir.'

'Good, get it off immediately with a top priority rating. I want an answer in five minutes, sooner if possible.'

'Aye, aye, sir.'

Larkin got up and walked over to the plotting table, swaying with the motion of the ship. He stared down at the map, then picked up the pair of dividers from their holder and began to measure off the distances between Folsom and the Russians. He walked the dividers carefully over the distance and found that he did not like the story they had to tell. Less than twenty-two miles separated the two groups—twenty-two miles that the Russians would not waste any time at all in covering. The only thing in Folsom's favor so far was the fact that the Russians did not know exactly where the ship was. But, even so, in spite of the storm and difficult terrain, the Russians would find them within twenty-four hours. He did not know exactly how many troops had been landed, but he was ready to lay odds that they would split up, one party marching along the top of the cliffs where they could search the coastline below while the other moved inland a mile or so. The beach party could not fail to spot the wrecked lifeboat. Once they had that, it would be only a matter of time until they found the camp.

Larkin turned back to his console and dialed the weather channel, although he already knew what it would say. But then one could always hope. So it was no surprise when he found that both the Greenland and Iceland weather stations were still predicting another thirty-six to forty-eight hours of heavy seas and high winds along the Norwegian coast. They expected the winds to begin dropping in about twenty-four hours, but at sea they would remain strong enough to preclude launching the helicopter.

'Damn, damn,' he muttered to himself. Folsom was really in for it now. He returned to the plotting table and bent over the map and with the dividers measured out the distance to the Norwegian Coast Guard Station and then to the NATO base. The distance to the coast guard station was shorter by eight miles, but the route would take them directly into the arms of the Soviets. The only refuge, then, was the Norwegian-manned NATO base, twenty-six miles from where Folsom had pitched the camp—that or the interior of the Cape area, and Larkin doubted whether the pilot would survive for long there.

'Radio room to bridge, we have the translation.'

'Go ahead,' Larkin ordered.

' "Shore party calling ST-101, shore party calling ST-101.' This was repeated six times, sir. Then, 'We have landed without injuries. Lifeboat is badly damaged. Will begin search immediately. Radio contact will be re-established hourly on this frequency." End of message. There was no reply from the ship, sir. They used a standard band, short-range radio at 120 kc.'

'Very good. Establish a continuous monitoring watch as of now. Feed everything you pick up to Virginia, top priority, after running it through the computers for translation. I want Virginia's literal translation as a check.'

'Aye, sir.'

Larkin turned to Bridges, still seated at Folsom's console. 'Well, Mr. Bridges, we are off. Contact Mr. Folsom and tell him what has happened. Tell him I will call him again at'—he looked at his watch—'0600 with instructions . . . ah, amend that to suggestions. In the meantime, they are to get all the sleep they can. Also, they are not to call us except in an emergency. No sense in letting their position be pinpointed.'

'Aye, sir.' Bridges turned to the radio operator as Larkin went below for some badly needed rest.

Teleman came slowly awake to the sound of a hushed voice. For several minutes, still drugged with exhaustion, he lay in the sleeping bag, scarcely aware that he was awake. A darkness, half dispersed by a light source that he could not see, drew a curving line directly above his eyes. For a minute he thought he was back in the aircraft, looking down on the earth from two hundred thousand feet, seeing the bisecting dawn line. The lighted portion of whatever it was above/below him, he could not tell which, was a darkish blue color, the same as the earth from altitude at dawn. The other half was dead black and the bisecting line itself was fuzzy, shading through a spectrum of bluish gray from light to dark.

The voice puzzled him, but as yet he was not able to turn his head, for some perverse reason. Gradually he became aware that he was stripped to the skin and covered with some kind of heavy, heated material. Then he remembered the intense cold, the cold and the wind.

He mustered the will to turn his head. For a moment the scene refused to focus and vertigo gripped him, spinning him end over end. Gradually the picture before him steadied and he slowly began to make out details. The first was the fabric line of a sleeping bag. Beyond, the hunched backs of two other men bending over something hidden by their bodies. Various pieces of gear were stacked around the walls of the tent. The lantern casting the dim light was suspended from the center of the tent, a heavy flashlight, giving off a steady light.

Both men were unaware that he was watching and wondering who they were and where he was. Then in a rush the memories came back as that part of his brain cleared with an almost physical jolt. He remembered the aircraft, the long flight across Asia, the desperate running from the Russian interceptors, the ejection over the North Cape. The last thing he remembered was a hissing flare landing nearby.

As the fuzziness evaporated, Teleman began to realize that he had been picked up by somebody. But Russians, Americans, or Norwegians? He turned his head again to see the man whose back was nearest him nod two or three times, then reach out to part the tent flaps. Immediately a gust of wind danced in, bringing whirling snow with it.

'As far as we know right now, they sent only one boatload, maybe twenty men in the landing party.' The voice that came over the radio was almost lost in the sound of the wind battering the tent.

'Any idea how long it will take them to get here?'

Teleman felt a flood of relief pour through him. At least they spoke English. They must have come from the rendezvous ship, he thought.

The tiny radio voice came again. 'The MTI radar shows the coastal cliffs in that area as quite low and sloping back into what the map indicates as a level plain. I don't see them waiting until the storm lets up. They are east of you by twenty-two miles.'

'Well, assuming that the terrain isn't much different from what we've seen here, I'd say it would take them nearly twenty-four hours to get this far. I'd also guess that they don't know exactly where the pilot went down, or else they might have tried a landing farther up the coast.'

'That may be. But of course if they had wanted to avoid detection as much as possible they would have landed in Porsangerfjord. It's the only sheltered spot along the entire coast all the way to the naval base.'

'Well, unless the weather changes drastically, I'll go along with your estimate of twenty-four hours. They have an awful lot of searching along the way to do in the meantime.'

'Yeah. I just hope we are reading the situation right and that they somehow did not track our boy by radar or somesuch. I'd look mighty foolish if they came marching in several hours from now, not even winded.'

He glanced around and saw Teleman staring at him. Folsom's eyes widened in surprise and he waved a hand in greeting. Teleman continued to stare at him, too tired and fuzzy to do more. Folsom finished the report quickly and signed off. Then he crawled back to the sleeping bag in which Teleman lay.

'How do you feel?' he asked as he reached into the sleeping bag for Teleman's arm to take his pulse. In contrast to the rapid, fluttery 166 beats per minute that he had exhibited several hours ago, his pulse had now slowed to 93, above normal, but probably due to the drug residues remaining in his system.

'Beat,' Teleman said weakly.

'Other than that?'

'Nothing. I think I could . . . sleep for a week.'

Folsom grinned at him. 'Yeah, I bet you could.' He looked around at the sailor still folding up the radio and called him over.

'I want you to meet one of your helpmates. This character has an itchy trigger finger, or at least he thinks he does,' Folsom amended, grinning. 'He's our chief gunnery officer—an empty title as we have no guns except for a one-inch popper for salutes. We stole him from the SEALS just for jobs like this. His name, and this you won't believe, is Beauregard Hubert McPherson, which probably accounts for the majority of his fierceness,' Folsom added.

McPherson grinned sheepishly and said, 'Hello,' his big, warm hand all but engulfing Teleman's.

Teleman looked up into the large, round face hanging over him like a second moon and smiled feebly, but did not find the strength to reply. Folsom saw that he was still exhausted and he and McPherson backed off.

'Okay, get some more sleep. We'll make the rest of the introductions later.'

Teleman nodded once and then was sound asleep. The two sailors looked down at the sleeping form and both shook their heads at the same time. 'I'll bet that guy has really been through hell,' McPherson murmured.

Folsom was silent a moment, then: 'Yeah, and I bet he'll go through more before we are out of this.'


## CHAPTER SIXTEEN

BEAUREGARD HUBERT MCPHERSON, Chief Petty Officer, United States Navy, and former member of the SEALS, the naval version of the U.S. Army Special Forces, shifted the AR-18 carbine to his left hand and with his right eased himself down into the slippery defile leading to the beach. Half sliding, half climbing, he went down through the thick snow from rock to rock until he reached the beach. Once there, he did not hesitate, but turned east and began loping down the beach in an easy, ground-covering jog. The snow, whipped by the wind into swirling curtains, was heavier along the water's edge than it had been above the cliffs, which was just what he wanted. Not only would the thick snow shield him from anyone approaching, but it would also serve to cover his tracks completely, something he could not depend on the drifting snow to do above the cliffs.

He pushed on steadily for two hours, often having to climb over rock piles washed into weird position by eons of waves and Arctic storms. Once he had to reclimb the cliffs when the beach, often little more than a narrow thread, ran out. As he trotted he kept a sharp lookout toward the sea, even though the snow was so heavy that visibility was zero after fifty feet at best. But McPherson was a careful man. He had fought with the SEALS in Vietnam five years before raiding into the delta in small parties to perform kidnapings and assassinations of leading Viet Cong terrorists. They brought the same type of terror to the Viet Cong that the VC had used so successfully against the South Vietnamese. After

Vietnam had come assignments in Thailand and Cambodia, and, finally, the famous raid into China to rescue the crew of a United States Intelligence ship captured on the high seas.

McPherson, in short, was an expert on survival under the worst possible conditions and had proven it time and time again. A SEAL had been assigned to the U.S.S. *Robert F. Kennedy* at the request of the Secretary of the Navy, who had been far-sighted enough to realize that a SEAL's talents might be needed at some future date. The pilots of the A-17 recon aircraft were the most valuable commodity in the world. Standing orders to the *RFK*, the Remote Mission Control Point as she was known by the twenty or so men privy to her actual missions, were to get back the pilot of a downed aircraft at all costs, although McPherson was not one of those few who knew the exact nature of the missions that Teleman performed.

But even so, he continued down the beach at an easy run, heading for a point of land some eight miles west of Varangerfjord, which he and Folsom had estimated the Russians would reach by 1100. It was 1030 now, and he still had approximately two miles to go.

The wind was blowing in fiercely from the sea, driving the snow in ragged gusts, when McPherson found the point. High up on the cliffs and folded in among a series of chimneys and crags, McPherson found a cleft that was hidden from sight above and below, yet would afford him a clear view up and down the beach —or at least it would have if the snow had not been so heavy. As it was, his effective seeing distance was almost nil at times.

But it was all McPherson needed. Directly below, the beach described a narrow, inward-turning arc. A small barrier of rocks, piled up by countless generations of waves, drew a dam from the base of the cliffs to the water. To negotiate the dam, a man would either have to climb up and over, which would leave him fully exposed for several minutes while he did so, or else work part way up the cliffs over a series of icy ledges. His hiding place afforded a view along the rim. The rock peaked at this point so that McPherson had a clear field of fire downhill, enabling him to control the terrain within rifleshot inland.

As he sat in his well-shielded cubbyhole, he reviewed Folsom's orders. The object of this little jaunt was to delay the advancing Russians as much as possible. By attacking them here, nearly eleven miles from the camp, then retreating as fast as possible, Folsom hoped to fool the Russians into thinking that they faced a sizable party. If it worked, the Russians already on the beach would call for reinforcements and, if everything went as it should, wait until they were landed.

Even if the Russians did not wait for the reinforcements,

McPherson could make the eleven miles directly back to the camp in under half the time it would take the Russians, as they would be traveling more slowly, fearful of ambush. Teleman needed all the time for sleep that they could gain for him. For the run for the Norwegian base he was going to require every bit of strength he had. So, in fact, were they all.

After nearly an hour of waiting, a flicker of movement on the beach caught McPherson's eye. The wind, blowing laconically for the past few minutes, decided at that moment to freshen; and as the snow parted, he caught sight of three men dressed in Arctic gear, advancing toward his position, still several hundred yards away as yet. Carefully, McPherson edged first his parka hood, then his forehead over the edge of the cliff until his eyes were level with the ground. At first he saw nothing, but when he did he rather wished he had not. There was indeed a second party hiking along the top of the cliffs. There were five men, spread out in a line reaching from the edge, three hundred yards inland. The wide separation between each man was going to make it hard to keep track of them all once they dropped into the snow for cover.

McPherson shifted his attention to the three men approaching along the beach. His eyes narrowed as he studied the situation. The wind was blowing hard enough so that it should effectively cover the sound of his firing from the men along the top of the cliffs.

By not revealing his position to the party advancing along the cliff tops, he might be able to damage the beach group and then get away before they could alert the others to flank him from the top. McPherson laid the carbine on the rock and sighted in on a featureless bundle of parka and boots trailing the main group on the beach by several yards. With luck he could knock him out and shift to the leadman before they realized they were being shot at. McPherson drew a deep breath and steadied the sights, then another movement caught his eye. One man was walking along the top with what appeared to be a portable radio. He was close enough to hear the report and perhaps see the muzzle flash if McPherson fired. But he was also near enough to the edge so that he could be fired upon without the rest of the topside party noticing right away.

McPherson lifted his carbine and laid it on the shoulder of rock in front of him. He snapped the safety off and squinted down the barrel through the sights until the Russian was centered exactly. Slowly he opened both eyes and, as the man came into range, waited until he had approached to one hundred yards and slowly squeezed the trigger. The snap of the .222 cartridge was lost in the wind and snow. McPherson glanced hurriedly around to see if the others in the party on the cliffs had noticed. Apparently they had not. The soldier, shot squarely through the chest, had dropped, then slid down into a crevice. But his rifle had fallen out of his hands and slithered down on to the beach, fifty feet in front of the advancing troops. One of them scurried ahead and bent to pick it up. His shout of surprise carried clearly to McPherson and, with a sigh, he shifted the rifle to cover the men on the beach as they dropped flat and wormed quickly under cover.

McPherson watched while the officer in charge ran up and examined the rifle. He stepped back quickly to examine the top of the cliff, then reached for his radio. McPherson dropped him with one shot, then followed up with a raking blast that drove the others deeper into cover.

He poked his head up for a quick look at the cliff party still approaching and unaware. A rifle shot splattered the rock above his head, and then a ragged fusillade splashed snow and ice around him. He returned the fire briefly, more to make them pull their heads in than to do any damage. At this range and in the heavy snowfall there was little likelihood of them hitting him, and his only chance lay in carefully selecting his targets, one by one. He did so and was rewarded by a thin cry and the sight of a body toppling out of the line of rocks. The volume of fire at his position increased. The Russians were quickly, but very gingerly, working their way closer to the shelter of the dam. Once they reached that point, he knew, it would be time to leave.

He opened up again with short bursts at the fleeting glimpses of uniforms below. The wind had increased sharply and, instead of working for him, was now beginning to work against him. Suddenly a flare burst almost directly over his position. McPherson forgot about the beach party and flung himself up to sight on the members of the cliff-top party, momentarily transfixed by the flare. Before they could move he pulled the trigger and swung the muzzle, traversing the line of tiny figures. At the first report they dropped into the snow, but McPherson kept up the fire steadily for several seconds. Then he sprang out of the cleft and charged inland at a diagonal, leading away from the cliffs into the trees. He had a good lead and in his white snowsuit made an imposible target to follow. Quick rounds of desultory fire followed, but none hit close enough to be seen. In less than a minute he reached the trees, slowed to a trot, and continued for half a mile until he reached an open glade.

The open area was several hundred feet across, large enough for the wind to have full play. As a result the surface toward the center was a smooth expanse of unbroken snow, while the southern end was drifted high. He thrashed out into the glade, making as deep a trail as he could. At the first line of drifts he threw himself down and kicked and thrashed for a moment, then stood up to survey his work. Even at the rate the snow was drifting this would remain for at least an hour. Satisfied, he carefully retraced his steps back to the trees on the same side of the clearing that he had entered and backtracked for several yards. A low-hanging branch gave him the opportunity to swing up and out of his trail and head deeper into the forest at a wide angle from the track he had made going in.

Certain that he had both sidetracked the Russians and done as much damage as he could for now, McPherson trotted to the edge of the forest and, once out into the open, made for the edge of the cliffs and the comparative easy going of the wind-swept rock. A couple of hours spent floundering around in the deep snow and woods should tire the Russians enough to delay them by at least four to six hours. Smiling happily to himself, he ran steadily on.

## CHAPTER SEVENTEEN

WHEN Teleman awoke for the second time, the period of disorientation was immeasurably shorter. In fact, after the dimly remembered cold and wind on the cliffs, the stark, blue walls of the tent, with the litter of survival gear and Arctic clothing, seemed almost comforting. Across the tent, cleaning one of the carbines, knelt the man who had introduced himself as the ship's executive officer, Lieutenant Commander Peter Folsom. A second sailor, the one who had been asleep next to him before, worked over a pair of makeshift snowshoes. He was a small, almost rat-faced young man, Teleman thought, and he was instantly sorry for the comparison. He hated snap judgments, but was forever making them and usually regretting it later. Teleman grimaced and shifted his head for a better look. Unconscious of the scrutiny, the other worked on, face screwed up in his effort to twist the webbing strings of the netting tighter over the frame. He had a pile of dishwater blond hair that could only be described as unruly, trite though the description was. It was his hands that Teleman noted almost at once. They had long, tapering fingers, but unlike most thin hands these were at once powerful and sensitive. The sailor looked up from his work and a pleased smile crossed his face.

'Hey, boss, I think our partner in crime is awake.'

Folsom looked away from the rifle and grinned as well. 'So he is. How are you feeling this time around?'

Teleman pushed a hand out of the sleeping bag and rubbed his forehead. 'Other than the damndest headache you ever heard of, all right, I guess.'

'Feel like you're up to some traveling?'

'Traveling!' Teleman struggled into a sitting position. The effort left him dizzy and weak. Folsom got up swiftly and crossed the tent, grabbing up a pack as he came. He helped Teleman to sit up and shoved the pack behind his back for support.

In the sitting position, Teleman could see that the sailor he had been introduced to earlier, McPherson, was now against the other wall, wrapped in a sleeping bag.

'What about this traveling? Out to the ship, maybe?'

The grin disappeared from Folsom's face to be replaced with a worried frown. 'I'm afraid not. The seas are too rough to launch the helicopter and our lifeboat got smashed up as we came in. Now the waves are too high to launch another with even a hope of reaching the beach in one piece. So it seems we are pretty well cut off from the ship.'

Teleman absorbed this for a moment. 'Then what's the next step?'

'That's where the traveling comes in. There is a Norwegian-NATO naval air base about twenty-five miles down the coast. We are going to have to head for it.'

'You mean we have to walk twenty-five miles?' Teleman was astounded. He doubted right now if he could walk twenty-five steps, let alone twenty-five miles, and said so.

Folsom gave him a wan smile. 'I know how you feel, or at least I think I do. I am not sure that any of us can do it. The weather out there is like nothing you have ever seen before, worse even than when you landed yesterday.'

The executive officer smiled at the surprise on Teleman's face. 'Yeah, early yesterday in fact. You've been out for the twenty-four hours since we found you.'

'Good God, I had no idea . . .'

'Don't feel bad about it. You were in pretty rough shape when we picked you up. Another few minutes out there and we would have had to chip you out of a block of ice.'

Folsom turned. 'Julie, wake Mac up. We got some talking to do, then we had better make tracks.'

Folsom stretched across the mound of gear and pulled another pack to him. While McPherson went through the motions of waking up, Folsom rummaged through the contents of the pack and came out with a zippered, waterproof plastic map case. He selected one and spread it out next to Teleman's sleeping bag while the other two gathered around. McPherson crawled up on his knees, scratching his heavy black beard. He smiled shyly again at Teleman and stuck out a hand. 'Glad to see you awake again, sir.'

'This joker here,' Folsom said, indicating the other sailor, 'the one you haven't been formally introduced to, is Chief Warrant Officer Julian Gadsen. He's another free-loader. His speciality is driving the captain's launch—and eating.'

Gadsen chuckled and reached a hand through the maze of shoulders and shook Teleman's hand. Teleman discovered that at least part of his first impression had been right. Gadsen's hands were indeed strong. Obviously Gadsen was something other than what Folsom suggested—a seagoing taxi driver.

'I didn't get a chance to tell you before because you dropped off to sleep again, but we're all three from the U.S.S. *Robert F. Kennedy.*'

Immediately, Teleman glanced sharply at Folsom.

'Now wait,' Folsom said, 'I'm aware of what's going on. These two aren't, but at this point in the situation we are all in, you don't have to worry. Both are cleared about as high as you can go. You have to be to get assigned to the *RFK.*'

Teleman thought about it a moment. 'Okay,' he said tightly, 'maybe you are right for now. I'm in no position to bargain at the moment. But let's just stay away from that area right now.'

Folsom nodded. He could see that Gadsen and McPherson were doing their best to maintain noncommittal smiles. He knew that security procedures do funny things to people, particularly when they are not privy to the secrets being discussed. Innuendoes or oblique references always create hostilities no matter how much you realize the need for security and secrecy in military or defense affairs. He only hoped that Teleman wasn't going to turn out to be a son of a bitch on such a minor matter—at least at the moment.

Teleman was well aware of what Folsom was thinking. He could see by the withdrawn expressions that maybe he had overstepped a little. He was about to say something to ease the situation when the thought suddenly occurred to him that he really did not know who these people were. The idea that they could be Soviet agents acting out a part was half rejected in his mind as being overly dramatic, when angrily he pushed the modifying thought down. It was not too farfetched. It was not any more farfetched than his flying a supersecret aircraft at one to two hundred thousand feet over the continent of Asia for five and six days at a time, or that they should shoot him down and on, of all places, the North Cape of Norway. He studied the three men gathered around him and for a moment found himself ready to listen for traces of a Russian accent. That did it. He burst out laughing.

The three sailors were taken by surprise. 'Now what the hell are you laughing about?' Gadsen demanded.

Teleman laughed even harder. 'You . . . wouldn't believe . . . it if I . . . I told you,' he choked out at last. Then he went into throes of hysterical laughter. Gadsen and Folsom exchanged glances, then Julie leaned forward and slapped him sharply, once, then twice. The second slap brought Teleman around and he stopped, shut his eyes, and sank back down into the sleeping bag. In seconds he was sound asleep.

'Well, I'll be damned,' Folsom said.

'You probably are anyway, chief,' Gadsen snorted. 'That was a classic case of nervous release. God, what that poor guy must have been through lately. Judging from his reaction, he must have been close to a complete nervous collapse. Now he'll probably sleep for an hour or two, then when he wakes up he'll be all right.'

'Julie'—Folsom clapped him on the shoulder—'even if you never finished medical school, you are a definite comfort to have around. Come on you two,' he said, shaking his head, 'let's get this junk ready to go.'

*This* time, as Teleman slept, he dreamed that he was back in the A-17, being pursued by a series of Falcons. As each aircraft rose to replace the one ahead it closed quickly and fired a missile. The ice-sharp clarity of the Asian terrain unreeling before him shifted with the watery changes of dreams, but somehow the mass of the Himalayas to his right never varied, either in view or intensity. He was passing so close to the bulk of the mountain flanks that he could clearly see a Mongolian sheepherder, mounted on a wiry pony, waving to him. As he watched the man, the A-17 came to hang opposite, so close that the wing tip, fully extended, seemed to brush along the Mongolian's cap. The sheepherder glanced back along the way Teleman had come, and turning himself, Teleman could see through the solid wall of the cockpit the entire valley spread out below. Close behind were two Falcons, so close that rockets emerging in slow motion from the pods on either side of the aircraft's nose were already visible.

Both he and the sheepherder turned at the same moment to stare directly at one another. The Mongolian began to wave at the following aircraft, his face suffused with the agony of help-lessness. Teleman turned again, and this time the rockets had traveled half the distance and grown in size until they were as wide as freight cars. They traveled in three sets of pairs and seemed to reach out to encompass him. The Mongolian was still waving desperately at his wings. Sitting in the pilot's couch, face pressed against the glassite of the view port, Teleman could not understand why the A-17 was not moving. The sound of the engines thundered in his ears, yet the aircraft would not budge.

The Mongolian vaulted from his horse and ran forward to grasp the extended wing and, with a mighty heave, wrenched it backward. Then Teleman understood. With a last glance back at the rockets reaching out hungry hands for the tail section of the A-17, he threw the switch that swung the wings back. The aircraft vaulted forward, instantly leaving the now smiling face of the sheepherder disappearing in the distance. The crazy patchwork of the dream began to flow backward into a smooth whirlpool that suddenly sprang high and Teleman was sitting both upright and awake.

Folsom sprang up, startled by Teleman's sudden movement. 'Ye gods, you startled me.'

Teleman looked around for a moment, not quite sure what was reality and what was dream. 'Where are my clothes?' he asked thickly.

Gadsen picked up a pack and crawled over to Teleman's sleeping bag. 'The clothes you arrived in are not the kind you want to wear when hiking in the Arctic, my boy.' He opened the pack and pulled out a pair of wide-mesh nylon underwear, lined ski pants, a loose nylon sweater, and a quilted dacron parka and hood and pushed them toward Teleman.

'Put these on. I think you'll find them quite a bit warmer than a flight suit.'

'Yes, and hurry too. We were just about to wake you.'

Teleman did as he was told, fumblingly at first as his tired brain sorted out fact from dream fiction. Some of the iron weariness had left him after his long sleep. But not enough, he thought. His body was still sluggish, although he knew he would lose some of that once out into the cold fresh air. But he knew damned well that he would never be able to walk twenty-five miles . . . why did they have to walk twenty-five miles anyway? He could not remember at first, then gradually, as the cobwebs cleared away, he remembered snatches of conversation they had had earlier. Teleman pulled the parka over his head, found his .22 revolver on top of his pack, and surreptitiously tucked it inside. Then, with the boots in his hand, crawled over to where the other three were clustered around a map.

'Our Red friends,' Folsom started without preamble as soon as Teleman joined the circle, 'appear to want to welcome us to the land of the midnight sun.' In spite of the flippancy of his words, his voice was grim.

'We were informed about twelve hours ago that a suspected Russian submarine had landed a party of eighteen men about twenty-two miles southeast of here in Porsangerfjord. Then the sub withdrew a few miles and submerged. The landing party headed westward, apparently searching for you,' he said glancing up at Teleman.

Teleman shook his head in confusion. 'How the hell would they know where I was?'

Folsom grinned wryly. 'I suppose if we could track you down by radar they could too.'

'But that's impossible. The ejection capsule carries its own ECM gear. They would never have been able to track me.'

'Could be,' Folsom admitted, 'but somehow they are on to you. Maybe they just figured that you would have bailed out somewhere along the coast and as a last-ditch measure sent out the landing party in the hopes of picking you up.

'Be that as it may, *they are* out looking for you. Three hours ago Mac, here, got back from a little delaying action. He waylaid the party about twelve miles down the beach, shot them up a little, then led them off into the forest. He estimates we gained about six hours while they sort themselves out of the trees enough to realize they have been tricked. When they figure that out, they will head west gain, even faster.'

'Do you think they know exactly where we are?'

'I don't think so. If they did, they would have come straight here. As it is, Mac says they have one group down on the beach and the other along the top of the cliffs.'

'Well if that's it,' Teleman said with a deep sigh, 'then there isn't much to worry about. I landed about five miles into the trees. The capsule contains a self-destruct mechanism that literally reduces the thing to a lump of metal. If it's still snowing, it ought to be pretty well covered up by now. How far back from the cliffs are *we*?'

'Wait a minute,' Folsom said quickly. 'It's not that simple. We are about a mile back from the beach. And we could move the tent farther south if I thought it would do any good. But our lifeboat is still on the beach. And the damned thing weighs about three tons. There is no way to move it, short of using explosives, which we haven't got. So the Russians are going to find us if we stay around.'

'Now there is a problem there, isn't there?' said McPherson, peering through the tent flap. In spite of himself, Teleman shivered in the icy touch of the Arctic wind.

'It looks as though the wind will be kicking up the sea pretty badly by now. You can even hear the waves smacking into the cliffs. On top of which, the snow is so thick that you can't see your hand in front of your face. That rules out the helicopter on two counts. . . . So we walk.'

'Walk?' Teleman repeated weakly.

'Walk. All the way to the Norwegian naval base, or at least as far in that direction as we can to stay ahead of the Russians. We walk until the helicopter can get in to pick us up or we reach the base.'

Gadsen, who had been studying the map, looked up. 'Commander, you've studied this place pretty thoroughly, just what kind of a base is it?'

'It's now a combination radar and naval station. Pretty heavily defended and with some outmoded coastal artillery left by the Nazis, but supplemented with Hawk missiles. Our Ruski friends won't risk outright aggression to get Teleman back—at least I hope they won't—and if they do the Norwegians know how to use both the missiles and the artillery.'

'Well why in hell don't we call them up and ask them to send us some help? They must have Sno-cats or something like that.'

Folsom looked pained for a moment. 'Come on, you know the answer to that as well as I do. The old man says no. And that is that.'

Teleman glanced away, slightly ashamed. He knew why the 'old man' said no. And he knew that Folsom was practising a slight deception. The old man was not the commanding officer of the *RFK*, but his own boss sitting warm and comfortable somewhere in the Virginia foothills. They could not ask, except as a last resort, for help from the Norwegians because he was not supposed to be in Norway. The United States had no authorization from the Norwegian Government for overflights. And the only way to avoid embarrassing questions and strained relations was not to let the Norwegians know that he was in Norway. So they would have to start walking toward the base in the hope that something would happen—either the weather would moderate or else they would be able to get some other kind of aircraft to pick up the party. If all else failed, they would have to walk in on the Norwegians. The problem at the moment was to stay far enough ahead of the Russians to keep from being captured.

Teleman's head ached with the intensity of tightening thumb screws. In addition to being weary beyond reason, his vision was hazy and full of wild afterimages resulting from the microtraces of lysergic acid remaining in his system. As he sat across from the executive officer he was positive that ample precautions had been taken to ensure that he would not be captured by the Russians. But which of the three sailors had orders to kill him if capture appeared imminent?

Was it Folsom? he wondered. Folsom knew too many details,

knew the vital importance of his missions—details that could not be gained by conjecture alone. If not Folsom, which of the other two? McPherson, if what Folsom had told him was true, had hiked eleven miles one way to waylay the Russians. A former member of the SEALS, he would know all about assassination. But, on the other hand, he knew nothing about the other—what was his name?—Gadsen. Maybe the question he had raised about the Norwegians sending help was only a blind to allay any suspicion that he, Teleman, might have.

God, maybe they were all three in on it. They could be waiting to see how things would work out before they moved. He would just have to wait and see, he decided. But Teleman knew one thing: nobody was going to put a bullet in his back, not after all that he had been through. If he was going to die, then it was going to be from a Russian bullet.

Teleman unconsciously sank back a little farther against the gear. His face took on for the briefest of moments the haunted look of a hunted animal. His eyes were narrow and glittering in the uncertain light and the skin of his face drew into a drum tightness. If one of the three sailors had been watching, what he would have seen in Teleman's face might have prevented a portion of tragedy.

Folsom interrupted Teleman's thoughts as he spread out a more localized map of the North Cape and pointed to a small indentation on the western side of the deep gash cut in the coastline by the Porsangerfjord. 'This is the point where they landed. In this weather it will take them almost a day to travel far enough to reach the lifeboat. Now that Mac has had a crack at them, we can safely assume that we've gained another six to eight hours while they chase themselves through the boondocks after the phony trail he left behind. But we have now used up nearly four hours of that time. So, all in all, we are probably still five hours ahead of them, until they get far enough along the coast to spot the lifeboat.

'Now,' he said, staring speculatively at Teleman, 'the Russians probably had a darn good idea where you were. But until Mac hit them they probably had no idea you had any help at all. We can expect them to be confused for a while, wondering how many others are waiting in ambush along the way. I think we can consider the *RFK* as a hole card—although whether a joker or an ace is hard to tell at this point.'

'You know, Pete,' Gadsen interrupted, 'if we do get into enough of a bind that we do have to call the Norwegians for help, that damned sub could very well be monitoring for just such a transmission. If that happens, they will probably just move in and shell the hell out of us. They must be carrying some kind of deck gun or surface-to-surface rockets.'

'Yeah, I thought of that too. If we do have to call on the Norwegians, it will be up to the captain to decide whether he wants to open fire on the sub or not. If he does, there will be no way of hiding the fact. Talk about conditions for an international incident, whew!'

'Kind of in a bind ain't we, then?'

'Precisely, so let's *git*. Here's our destination,' he said, pointing again to the base, marked on the map in red. 'We had better move out of these trees and on to the cliffs. It will be rougher going, but we can follow the coastline for a while. About here it turns into tundra, which should be swept pretty free of any deep snow.' He indicated a point about six miles down the coast. 'There, I expect, it'll be a toss-up whether or not the tundra is passable. If so, we go across. If not, we follow the coast.'

Teleman leaned closer to examine the chart. It showed an irregular jut of land that bulged around the tundra for a distance of nearly thirteen miles. The contour lines on the chart indicated that the bulge was composed mainly of steep crags and shelving granite, leading to a sharp drop of fifty feet or so to the water. Once past this bulge, the land flattened again to narrow beach and even narrower pine- and scrub-covered terrain fronting the tundra.

'Pray for the tundra,' he murmured. 'That climb around the point will be hell.'

'There is one other possibility,' Folsom said thoughtfully. 'I had thought of heading south to Kistrand at the head of Porsangerfjord. The only trouble with that is this range of hills, just about here. They rise to a little over a thousand feet in less than the two miles between us and the town. And the only pass or anything resembling a pass leads west, and then south for a total distance of thirty-five miles. According to the map, the pass is at eight hundred feet. Teleman could never make it.

'So then, the only choice we have is to go west toward the naval station at Tanafjord. If the weather breaks, the ship will be able to reach us with the helicopter on the way.'

Teleman nodded acquiescence. 'All right. If it turns out that somebody has to carry me, don't say I didn't warn you. Either carry me or shoot me,' he added, looking sharply from face to face. He thought he saw a faint tinge of surprise in Folsom's eyes, but he could not be sure. It did not make any difference, he thought. He must watch all three of them closely now.

Folsom smiled. 'All right, we've been warned. But don't worry about it. Even if we do have to carry you, we will get you back, one way or another.'

The executive officer stood up. 'Okay. We head out in five minutes. Julie, pass out those snowshoes.'

Gadsen got up and pulled out four pairs of make-shift snow-shoes from under the pile of gear on his side of the tent and passed them out.

'Sorry about the pack frames,' he apologized, 'but I figured sore shoulders were better than tired legs.'

The snowshoes were made from aluminium bracing taken from the Himalaya mountain packs. Gadsen had straightened the frames and bent them into rough circular shapes, then used nylon line for webbing and the rough bootstraps. They were clumsy, but would serve to keep the wearer on top of, rather than floundering knee-deep in, the snow.

While Teleman pulled on a pair of insulated boots over two pairs of heavy wool socks and one pair of felt underboots, McPherson and Folsom loaded the gear and sleeping bags into the packs. Then he pulled his dacron parka tighter and zipped it close to his throat, pulling the hood up and tying it tightly. Around his neck went a six-inch flap that snapped in back, covering chin and throat. Folsom handed him a face mask, which he snapped to the throat flap and along the rim of the hood.

'I feel like a man from Mars,' he muttered through the muffling fabric. The others looked much the same.

'The very best Arctic gear the U.S. Navy has, Major.' McPherson laughed. 'Once we get outside, you'll wonder why the damned clothing couldn't be warmer. Me, I intend to write a letter to Naval Supplies when I get back, telling them just what I think of this stuff.'

Folsom looked Teleman over carefully. 'How do you feel now?'

'To be truthful, pretty weak. But I think I can make it.'

Folsom undid a pocket flap on his pack and pulled out an aluminium tube. 'Try a couple of these, Benzedrine. They'll pick you up.'

'Yeah, I know. But I'll wait awhile.' Teleman wondered if Folsom had any idea what effect that Benzedrine would have on him. 'No sense exhausting myself too early.'

Folsom nodded. 'Yeah, I guess you're right.' He turned and quickly looked over the other two. 'All right, let's move out.'

They broke camp quickly, each man carrying a carbine, canteen, and thirty-pound pack, with the exception of Teleman. He insisted that he carry at least his own carbine and the tent. Reluctantly, McPherson gave it to him. The tent folded into a compact package weighing less than ten pounds, but even so McPherson knew that in his weakened condition the extra ten pounds would soon begin to weigh on Teleman like ten thousand.

Folsom took the lead. Head down, and with the queer shuffling gait that snowshoes force, he struck out through the scrub forest toward the cliffs at a steep diagonal. The snow was deep and the wind whistling through the trees swept at them from every direction, dumping snow from the laden branches on to the four men trudging below. Folsom led them around the deepest drifts, sticking to the open areas as much as possible so that the drifting snow would thoroughly cover their tracks.

It took them an hour to walk out of the trees and reach the cliffs. An hour of tense shuffling on the round snowshoes that cramped muscles unknown to Teleman until then. The width of the snowshoes forced him to walk with his legs farther apart than he was used to, and shortly the muscles on the inside of his thighs were screaming for relief. And the dense underbrush made the walking that much harder. Bushes, half hidden in the snow, caught at the rims and webbing of the shoes. Within the first hour Teleman had fallen twice.

As soon as they stepped from the tree line, the full force of the wind caught them squarely. Snow, swirled up into a ground blizzard, stung at their eyes and any exposed skin surface, finding its way inside snow masks, around the elastic wrist and ankle bands and between hood and parkas with an insidiousness that was almost human.

It had been Folsom's intention to strike west along the rim of the cliffs as long as they lasted, but the ground blizzard, whirled into a fog of ice crystals, made travel along the cliff tops too hazardous. It would have been very easy to walk over the edge before realizing it. McPherson led them back away from the cliffs for fifty yards and, bent into the rising wind, they moved parallel to the line of cliffs, using their meager lee for what shelter that could provide from the gale-force wind.

Within the second hour the wind rose to what Folsom judged was fifty miles an hour. It had also backed several points until it was blowing from almost due north. The wind carried the scent of the icy wastes from the Great Barrier, less than two hundred miles north, bringing with it the same fierce temperatures and flying ice spicules that scoured the ice of the polar cap into tortured shapes. Folsom traveled now with the compass constantly in his hand, fighting to keep them on a course leading generally westward. But the proximity of the north magnetic pole made it all but useless for more than general direction keeping.

As the wind increased, so did the labor involved in walking. The snow had drifted to three and four feet deep in some places, and where it hadn't drifted at all it stood at least two feet deep. The snowshoes were of some help in keeping them above the crust, but the extra work of adjusting their gait to the peculiarities of the webbed shoes made Folsom wonder if they were not just trading one exhaustion for another. The only thing that seemed to be in their favor was that the top of the cliffs was fairly level, sloping gently downhill to the south. Folsom was under no illusions that the Russians would stop to wait out the storm. They would assume that their quarry was also taking every advantage the storm offered. Once they found the damaged life-boat but no sign of a camp, it would not take them long to con-clude that they were heading for the Norwegian naval base. The only hope the Russians would then have would be to cut them off before they gained the naval installation. And Folsom knew damned well that, if they did call for help, either the submarine or Soviet aircraft would arrive in quick order to shell the hell out of them. With these thoughts to keep him company, Folsom grimly forced them on through the Arctic desert.

For Teleman the hours passed endlessly in a haze of pain as tired muscles and joints protested every movement. The cold was more than insidious. In his weakened condition it was waiting to kill him if just once he let down his guard. His only hope was to keep moving, forcing his body to make optimum use of the slender reserves twenty-four hours of sleep had rebuilt. What would hap-pen when these reserves were exhausted he knew very well. At one time Teleman had voraciously read everything he could find on Arctic and Antarctic exploration. He knew, for instance, that in spite of the tremendous will to live that had infected Scott and his crew in the Antarctic, it had been impossible for them to travel that last eleven miles to the supply cache that had literally meant life or death. And now he understood why. He was fast reaching that point where it becomes impossible for the body to put out that last ounce of strength, that last bit of will that forces dying muscles to one more movement. The intense cold of the Arctic activated the body's main defense system against cold, involuntary shivering, but it also killed after a few hours. Shivering is an in-voluntary or autonomous muscle movement that cannot be con-trolled consciously. And it takes energy to shiver, and a prolonged bout at last saps all reserves. Then the body dies because there is simply no more heat to power the machine.

Teleman was shivering, shivering violently. He had never been so cold in his life. And in spite of the Arctic clothing and the heavy parka, the cold cut as if they were merely tissue. The first touches of frost had long since begun to reach through the insu-lated soles of his boots. By now, after four hours of walking, his feet were completely numb. He hated to think of what was going to happen when his feet and hands began to thaw . . . if they ever did.

From then on he stumbled constantly, half supported by the

giant McPherson, whose strength seemed endless. Through the snow mask Teleman could feel the skin of his face grow numb, then contract in the cold as if it were trying to pull his skull apart. Feebly he rubbed his cheeks and nose with gloved hands, and the pain of even this faint bit of returning circulation was fantastic.

As they traveled farther across the rough crags of the rear cliff tops, clambering over rock outcroppings to slide painfully down the snow- and ice-slick far sides, Teleman marveled, with the part of his mind that was still conscious, at the strength that McPherson was exhibing. Even now as Folsom and Gadsen were beginning to slow, their movements becoming more and more unsteady as they fought against the exhausting wind and cold, McPherson still half carried him, still showed no signs of weariness.

After the sixth hour Folsom began to call five-minute halts every half hour or so, but after the morning and the brief brightening of the five to ten minutes of clouded sunlight at noon, they rested standing. No one dared sit or lie as the cold deepened and their exhaustion grew. Once down, they knew they would never be able to get up again. Finally even McPherson dared not rest for more than a few moments.

By late afternoon they had entered another branch of the forest, this one clutching the coast. The pounding of the surf was violent in the almost still crystal air. The wind had suddenly died away to a light breeze and the continuing heavy snowfall did little to muffle the crash of waves against unyielding stone. The trees, stunted and twisted by years of storm, were widely spaced and unchoked with the undergrowth that had marked the inland forest. But the trees, forced to grow lower, made up for the lack of brush with low-hanging branches pregnant with fresh snow.

At 1600 that afternoon the wind had stopped completely. The tired party of four men came to a stop. For the last hour Teleman had been traveling in a semi-daze, barely conscious. But now even he was revived momentarily. Folsom peeled back his face mask and hood and the others followed suit. He turned his head in a slow circle, searching for any trace of breeze. The air was silent, barely moving. The intense cold seemed even more pressing now in spite of a lack of wind to stir it across their exposed faces. The wind-scattered trees of the stunted forest were immobile, drooping even lower with the steadily accumulating snow.

The small party began to stumble forward again, reeling under the load of their weariness and the heavy, depressing atmosphere that had descended with the cessation of the wind. Even McPherson was growing exhausted. His gait grew less and less steady. Teleman exerted a tremendous effort and managed to walk upright by himself for a few moments before the snowshoes caused him to stumble. From then on each of the three sailors took turns supporting him.

A muffled crack sounded somewhere behind them. Instantly they were on the ground, searching for cover in the meager waste. For long moments they lay, all thoughts of their wearinss forgotten. Folsom shifted his carbine and peered over the barrel, trying to penetrate the snow-filled landscape, then after a moment he got shakily to his feet, laughing softly.

'Come on you deadbeats. Up and at 'em.' He helped Teleman up as another sharp rifle report was heard.

'Trees,' he explained shortly. 'The cold is beginning to crack the damned trees.'

By 1800 they reached the edge of the tundra. The jut of the coast pulled away to the north at this point, heading into a region of higher ground which the line of cliffs rode in lazy undulations of crags and clefts. McPherson edged out into the beginning of the tundra plain and knelt to brush the accumulated snow from the frozen dirt and rotting vegetation that overlay the hard surface of never-melting ice. After a few moments he motioned the others out.

Folsom, Gadsen, and Teleman followed him out to where he was staring at the darkness that obscured the way ahead. Behind them a three-quarter moon was beginning to break through the rack of clouds, its pale gold light lending a warm tint to the ghostly, wasted landscape. Teleman reversed his carbine and sank to his knees, leaning on the gun for support. He had been profoundly grateful when the wind had died; at these temperatures snow froze into solid crystals of ice, tiny particles that, whipped by the wind, worked their way between snow mask and hood and glove and cuff. After hours of exposure Teleman felt as if his wrists and neck were ringed by crusts of burning ice. His gratitude had been short-lived, however. As the wind had died the cold had deepened, until now he guessed it was close to forty below zero.

Folsom dropped down beside him. 'How are you feeling?'

When Teleman, too tired to speak, only nodded, he grinned in sympathy. 'We've covered about thirteen miles so far. I think it's going to be a little easier from here on in. The map shows this tundra stretching almost to the base. At least we can get rid of these damnable snowshoes.'

Teleman nodded again, barely aware of what Folsom said. His mind was wrapped in a warm haze that not even the bitter cold of the Arctic could penetrate. Folsom's words meant nothing to him . . . he was suspended in a sort of limbo through which he floated not caring what happened to him. But when Folsom's arms went under his to help him to his feet, the haze failed and he was suddenly back in the hell of cold and wilderness. Gadsen cut the thongs that held the snowshoes on, then collected the four pairs and tied them on to his pack. He said nothing and neither did the others. Each man was conserving every last bit of energy he possessed with all the avidity of a miser. Each knew that to expend even the tiniest fraction could mean the difference between reaching the base and freezing to death within sight of it.

The four men struggled on, pushing as far into the tundra as possible before stopping for the night. Teleman continued to move mechanically in the semi-daze that had overtaken him earlier, but the rest had refreshed him somewhat and he was now able to stumble forward by himself. He had long ceased to feel the cold as such, to feel it as anything but an iron pain clamped down upon his entire body. His heart, he was dimly aware, was beating at the same trip-hammer rate that had alarmed him during the final moments of flight. Every movement was sluggish in the extreme, and he no longer thought about the damage being done to his body by the impossible stress being placed on it by the intense cold and bone-breaking task of hiking twenty-five miles through sub-zero cold. He longed for the warm hospital bed and the intensive care that normally followed each flight. Instead he moved in a world of his own, in which the glimmering moon and the pale stars beginning to show as the clouds were slowly torn to pieces by the aftermath of the storm were a blur overhead. He had even stopped concentrating on placing one foot in front of the other. His subconscious had now taken over the task of moving his legs in proper rotation. He was only hours from death and he no longer cared.

## CHAPTER EIGHTEEN

LARKIN paced slowly back and forth before the insulated windows fronting the dimly lit bridge, apparently oblivious to the scene around him. At eight consoles, eight technicians sat hunched before the banks of instruments. The atmosphere was heavy with depression. Nothing had been heard from the shore party for nearly twelve hours. During that time the shadowy Soviet submarine had moved slowly out of the Porsangerfjord and rounded the point to slip carefully down the northern coast of the island at a depth of sixty feet.

The *RFK*, standing twenty miles offshore, had long since run out of the freakish water-layer conditions that had expanded her sonar range earlier in the day. In fact, reverse conditions were now in effect. The *RFK*'s sonar gear had an operational echo-ranging capability of thirty-eight miles under optimum conditions.

Now she was able to pick up firm signals only at a maximum of twenty-two miles. Beyond that the decreasing signal-to-noise ratio wiped away any traces of the target.

In spite of the trouble with the sonar gear, they had been able to follow as the submarine had moved twice from the south-eastern end of the island in Porsangerfjord to its mouth on the western side, then out into the Barents Sea to proceed slowly down the coast as if searching out a landing site. They passed the point of beach where the American party had landed, and continued down the coast. At first Larkin had thought, as the submarine had come to a stop to lay off the coast with only the sail showing, that they were examining the terrain. Now he was not so sure. The sub had remained surfaced for twenty minutes, long enough to have launched a raft. If indeed a second party had gone ashore they would logically have landed several hours travel up the coast from where Folsom and his men were. Larkin had no firm idea of just how fast and far they had traveled, but his last radio contact with Folsom, several hours after they started out, had put him a mile west of where the sub came to a stop. By the time the submarine had arrived off the coast in the late afternoon, Folsom would certainly have moved several miles farther west. Evidently the Soviet commander had misjudged the Americans' rate of progress.

His face betraying none of the anxiety he felt, Larkin continued his pacing back and forth across the bridge, stopping now and then to examine a scope over a technician's shoulder. If ever there had been a hand-picked crew aboard any United States Navy ship, the small complement of eighty men aboard the highly automated *RFK* were it. Every man had been personally requested by Larkin, many from personal knowledge of their capabilities and the rest from service records. They were the best there was, he knew. And he had drilled them mercilessly into an operational team in which every man knew exactly what was expected of him—the basis of proper and workable military discipline.

It was not, however, the crew's reaction to the tense situation facing them—or their future performance—that he was worried about. Each and every crew member was aware that the Russian submarine they were stalking could easily be carrying nuclear missiles. And at a few miles, even if their missile defenses were quick enough to destroy incoming weaponry, any nuclear explosion could be fatal to the ship's crew. No, Larkin was not worried about the crew. They knew what they faced, and had known since the day they agreed to sign on—that this possibility was more likely to come to pass on the *RFK* than on any other operational ship of the Navy. For a moment the grim humor of the situation relaxed Larkin's mind. The ship, the most advanced in any navy in the world, the one always earmarked for just such clandestine operations as played tag with nuclear destruction, had been named for a man whose overriding concern was the nuclear disarmament of the world. Larkin shook his head and turned to face the line of windows.

The cold seas were running savagely; there was no relief for his introspective mood from that quarter. Larkin swung himself into the high seat before his own console.

The meteorological officer two consoles away tore off a Xerox and reached over to hand it him. Larkin took it with some misgivings. But it was only the quarter-hourly weather report indicating moderating seas for the next thirty-six hours. He turned again toward the window.

The seas, this close on to the coast, were no longer breaking over the bow in huge runnels of water, but the waves were still running forty feet or better. The lingering half light of the short midwinter day was still bright enough to show the grayish-green colour of the half-frozen surface as it billowed up into sharp-edged mountains only to be struck broadside by violent winds that sheered off the crests, as neatly as would a razor, in long foamy streamers. The seas might be in the process of moderating, but here on the Norwegian north coast, exposed to the full force of the dying gale, actual conditions were showing little support for such optimistic predictions.

As he continued to gaze out of the ports, his mind turned to the supplementary orders that had come in over the private channel minutes earlier. The gist of the orders was that Larkin was empowered to notify the Norwegian Government and request their assistance if the situation got out of hand too rapidly for long-distance consultation. If that was not forthcoming, then he was instructed to ask for asylum for the pilot and his three crewmen. He was not, and the not was underlined, allowed to do so except in the most extreme emergency.

But it was the last paragraph of the message that added a few more gray hairs to his head. The message stated that he was to use all powers of persuasion at his disposal to rescue the pilot if the Norwegians should prove to be uncooperative—as they had every right to be, he thought. It was utter nonsense for the State Department *not* to notify the Norwegian Government as soon as possible. Not only could they render valuable assistance, but for God's sake, it was *their* country and they were allies.

He might have his orders to bring Teleman out with all of the force at his disposal, but he was damn sure that no copy of any such message existed in Washington. Washington, if caught, would merely claim that it was a transmitting error or that Larkin had exceeded his authority. In any event, if he had to act pursuant to those orders, the entire wrath of both governments would fall on him like a ton of bricks. His naval career would be at an end. And, if he did not act in accordance with the orders, he would be either secretly court-martialed or shunted out of the Navy. It had happened before, he knew. And Larkin could count at least fifteen qualified naval officers waiting to step into his shoes.

It was no wonder that Larkin got out of the high seat and resumed his pacing. A lesser man would have gone screaming off the bridge in frustration.

It was nearly 2100 before Folsom called a halt for the night. During the last few hours they had straggled into a line over a mile long. McPherson, still the strongest of the party, had taken up the tail-end position to act as rear guard and to make sure no one was left behind in the snow-filled wastes. Teleman was only a few paces ahead of him.

Folsom had chosen the campsite on the basis of time rather than location. The tundra stretched for miles in all directions, flat and unbroken except for two miles north, where one could barely make out the faint line of cliffs against the night sky. As he waited for the others to catch up, he felt as if he were standing in the middle of a flat dinner plate whose white lack-of-color under the three-quarter moon and cloud-free sky reflected enough light to hurt his eyes after the deep gloom of the past day. If the snow had not been fresh Folsom knew there would have been virtually no light reflection from the surface. Ice crystals would have tended to absorb light and reflect only a little at random. He had witnessed this phenomenon before while aboard a destroyer standing off the Great Ice Barrier in the depths of winter. The icy surface had reflected virtually no light unless it was coated by fresh snow.

Gadsen staggered—literally staggered—up and sank down in the snow a few feet away. He sat, knees drawn up and head down, for several minutes before regaining breath enough to speak coherently. Folsom, glancing down the trail of disturbed snow they had left, could see McPherson and Teleman approaching, still more than a hundred yards away.

'God, if you hadn't . . . stopped . . . I would have collapsed . . . in another few feet.' Gadsen managed to force out between ragged gasps for air.

Painfully, Folsom shrugged out of his pack and let it fall with a solid thump to the frozen ground. His voice when he spoke was as weary as Gadsen's, reflecting none of the lightheartedness of the words. 'Courage me boy, only another nine miles to go.'

'Courage hell . . . the only thing that keeps me going . . . is the Russians . . .'

'Yeah,' Folsom said, nodding. 'I just hope to hell that they are as bushed as we are.' He watched the approaching pair and saw one fall heavily. The other bent over and slowly helped him to his feet.

'Come on, Julie. Can you make another few yards? I don't think those two can.'

Gadsen nodded, got up, and followed Folsom back to where McPherson had stopped to wait as he saw them returning. By the time Folsom and Gadsen had reached him, he had already unpacked the tent and was in the process of rigging the light-weight metal frame. Teleman half sat, half sprawled on the snow, watching him work with dull eyes.

While Gadsen helped McPherson with the tent, Folsom came over and knelt beside the exhausted pilot.

'How do you feel?'

'Yuck.'

'That's what I figured.' Folsom peeled Teleman's mask off and studied the graying face while he fumbled with his own mask. The pilot's face was drawn and white and covered with yellowish cold blisters. Teleman had been shivering ever since the after-noon rest stop. Folsom had noticed it earlier, but there was abso-lutely nothing he could do about it, even though he knew the combination of shivering and difficult exercise of hiking across the uneven, snow-covered tundra had completely worn the man out. But he had not dared stop earlier. So far they had seen no sign of the Russians pursuing them and he wanted to keep it that way as long as possible.

Folsom helped Teleman up and into the tent. He did not wait for Gadsen to pump up the stove and get it going, but hustled Teleman into a sleeping bag fully clothed, between the last of the chemical heating pads.

After a few minutes of steady pumping and priming Gadsen got the stove going, and shortly the temperature had risen to the freezing mark inside the tent. Gadsen adjusted the flame to keep it at that temperature and laid four ration packs on the cover to warm.

'If this cold gets any worse,' McPherson said a few minutes later as the four men ate, 'it's going to be the roughest last few miles you ever saw.'

'I've been thinking about that all afternoon,' Folsom said. He laid the empty ration pack down and stretched out on his sleep-ing bag, using his pack for a back support.

The ration pack dropped from Teleman's hands. He was too weak to hold it any longer. It fell softly on to the folds of the sleeping bag and for the moment no one noticed. He was barely awake now, struggling to keep his eyes open long enough to listen to the conversation. He had never been so tired in his life. Circulation was beginning to return to his feet and hands and the pain was as unbearable, as he had feared it would be. In spite of the agony he felt that, if he once closed his eyes, he would sleep forever. To stay awake he massaged the tender skin of his face.

'The Russians will be desperate to catch us by now. They will have found the lifesphere ten hours ago at the least. And the lifesphere will tell them that we came from a ship, an American ship at that. What they will want to know at this point is whether or not the Norwegians are involved. But you can damn well bet that they will be searching with everything they have to locate the ship.' Folsom stopped for a moment to think.

'I feel sure,' he continued, 'that even if they think some Americans have gotten ashore to find Teleman here—especially after Mac shot the hell out of them—they are not going to be scared off by the possibility of a pitched battle. In fact, I would even be willing to bet that they are figuring just as we are—that we don't dare get the Norwegians involved at this point. So, if anything, the Russians are going to move faster and harder.'

Folsom stopped to examine the three haggard faces peering at him in the dim light of the stove. Bone-breaking fatigue was on their faces, Teleman's especially. The hike under normal circumstances would have been nothing to these men, but the intense cold, Teleman's deteriorating condition, the wind, deep snow, and exceedingly dry cold all combined to sap strength at a magnified rate. His own legs and feet were screaming with returning circulation and fatigue. It was only with the greatest difficulty that he was able to still his shaking hands.

Earlier in the afternoon a thought had occurred to him, a possibility that should have been amply clear to him earlier. He was extremely angry with himself for not having thought of it before. The only excuse he could make was the cold, the cold that sapped every last bit of strength, that required the utmost concentration just to place one foot in front of the other, the cold that required of you that no outside considerations interfere with this concentration because, if they did, you would find yourself slowly freezing to death, prone in the snow, without any awareness of having stopped moving minutes before. He was apprehensive about releasing this bombshell. Not only was endurance at the bottommost point for the three men facing him, but so was morale. It would not take much at this point for them to give up and climb into their sleeping bags. If this happened the Russians would certainly find them in a few hours at the most.

'Whether or not the Soviets will travel all night,' he said slowly, choosing his words carefully at first . . . then Folsom realized that he need not be careful, that these were not men to give up so easily after having come so far. If that had been the case they would have done so hours before. . . . He began again. 'I did not think of this until a few hours ago, but the submarine . . . there will be no need for it to stay in the Porsangerfjord. In fact, it will probably put out to sea to keep pace with the search party.'

The other three continued to watch him, flickers of apprehension growing in their faces.

'When the search party finds that we left without waiting for them, they will probably inform the submarine, which will then break all speed records moving down the coast to drop off another party, well ahead of us. It will be quite plain to them where we are heading. They can read a map as well as we, and they will know that we sure as hell are not going to head inland to Kistrand. If they do drop another party, then they've got us in a vise.'

The other three reacted with varying degrees of anger or disgust, mostly directed at themselves for not having seen this possibility before. Teleman was awake now, the pain and fatigue of his screaming muscles forgotten for the moment.

'Okay, what do we do then?' Gadsen asked.

Folsom rubbed both hands across his face, massaging his weary eyes and wishing to God he had never left the Pentagon. 'Well, first we all need sleep. So we take four hours out. That means we stop six hours and everyone but Teleman will stand a two-hour watch. Teleman is out, he needs all the sleep he can get.'

He ignored Teleman's angry but feeble protest and continued. 'Two hours each on watch will give us four hours of sleep. I'll take the first watch, Mac, you take the second and Julie the last.' They nodded in agreement.

'What about tomorrow?' McPherson asked. 'If we stop tonight, the Russians are going to be breathing down our necks.'

'I agree,' Folsom replied. 'But I don't see what else we can do. We all need rest too badly to move on any farther tonight. I don't think it will do us any good to turn inland and try and approach the Norwegian base from the south. They will probably be watching for just such a move. I would guess the submarine will drop the second party as close to the base as they dare and work them back toward the first group. So about the only option left us is to make tracks for the base as fast as possible and hope to God that somehow we will miss the second party.'

'How about letting the *RFK* know?'

'No good. If we use the radio they'll pick us up and pinpoint our location right down to the last meter. I can't conceive of them not keeping a watch on the possible frequencies that we might use. All we can do is wait until they find us before calling for help. The captain should be able to figure some way to give us covering fire . . . if not, then he can contact the Norwegians for help.'

The four sat in silence for several minutes before Gadsen commented, 'I sure as hell wouldn't give a plug nickel for our chances.'

'Don't quit yet,' Folsom warned. 'We still have a couple of things in our favor. Number one, they have to move a lot more carefully than we do. They never know when Mac is going to open on them again, or even the Norwegians for that matter. They are in unfriendly territory. We, at least, can be assured of asylum in Norway. They can't.

'Number two, they don't know where we are, at least exactly where we are. And they don't know that the ship is standing off the coast . . . at least I hope they don't.'

The silence descended again, unbroken even by the roaring wind that had been their constant companion for so long. The silence was thick, thick and heavy with the threat of their total exhaustion and potential capture.

Teleman settled down into the sleeping bag and pushed his thawing feet against the chemical warming pad. In spite of his utter exhaustion, his mind was churning with the implications of Folsom's words. They did *not* have much chance. That much was clear to a blind idiot. There was still nine miles to go to the Norwegian base, nine more miles that would take them all day tomorrow in their steadily degenerating condition. He knew that he could not make it and he doubted very much if the others would be able to either. The temperature was dropping fast, and six miles over the frozen, knee-high tufts of tundra grass in forty-below weather was too much to expect of any man.

His mind began turning insidiously back to the thoughts that had nagged at him during the endless day. Which of the three men had the orders to kill him?

Teleman groaned inwardly. He was certain that one of them would try to kill him, but which one. He could not watch all three at once. McPherson had the training and the skill, that he knew. He had also been very solicitous of him all day, almost carrying him since noon. But Gadsen—he had not learned very much about the man at all. Except for a few wise comments on their predicament during the day, he had not spoken much. . . . In the middle of his self-created maze of danger, Teleman's brain blanked and he was deeply asleep.

'Well, we can only wait and see what the new day brings,' Gadsen sighed.

Folsom pulled on his face mask and gloves. 'Yeah, I guess so.' What else was there to say? he thought.

He slammed a new clip into his carbine and shoved extras into a pocket. 'Night-night.' He grinned and pulled the face mask tight, then pushed through the tent flaps and crawled outside.

The cold air hit him with the force of a truck, sucking the warm air from his body. Still on his knees, he curled into a tight ball, coughing into his fur-lined mittens, breathing slowly to avoid frosting his lungs. In a few moments the spasm passed and he straightened out, his face still buried in his gloves while he breathed carefully to regain his breath. Even through the fur and nylon parka, the touch of the air was like hot iron. He stood up and began beating his arms together. We have to walk nine more miles through this, he thought, and he knew that they would never be able to make it, no matter what the circumstances were, no matter what the prize, up to and including life itself. It was an impossible task.

But deep inside he knew that they would do it or die trying. Just as the Russians would catch them or die trying. And he also knew that the Russians would not be waiting out the night in a tent—they would be using the night.

The harsh moon was a quarter of the way up in the sky. Its light falling on the freshly snow-covered ground gave him visibility almost to the horizon in every direction. The wind had died away completely, and in the frigid, still air his breath froze instantly, wreathing his head in a clammy fog if he stopped too long in one spot. The moon highlighted the tundra, with the hummocks of grass standing out in bold relief. Folsom had never dreamed it could be so cold. He had never experienced anything like this before.

The stars burned in the sky in spite of the moonlight, and the air was so cold and dry that he could detect no trace of ring around the moon. As if to form a backdrop for the unearthly beauty of the moon, the aurora had sprung into the northern sky, shimmering curtains of color that fluctuated and flowed in the gentle breeze of the electron stream arising eight minutes away in the sun's corona. At any other time he would have been entranced with the shifting tapestry of color and form, but not tonight.

He moved slowly away from the tent, walking carefully around the tufts of frozen grass as they had been doing since entering the tundra. Not one of them could afford a twisted ankle now. Folsom stopped to peer around. He could see nothing on the waste of frozen terrain in any direction. At this point he knew that they were about seven miles from the sea. But in the crystal air the fury of the sea against the cliffs was faintly audible.

At a thousand yards distance from the tent Folsom turned and
began to move in a circle, with the tent as the center point. He
would leave tracks in the snow, tracks that the Russians could not
miss, but it didn't matter. Tomorrow the Russians would find the
campsite anyway.

There were two directions from which the Soviets could
approach: east or west. The main party would come from the
west. Although Folsom did not make the mistake of discounting
them, he was fairly certain that this group, after travelling for
almost a day longer than themselves, would be as exhausted. It
was the group from the east, the expected second landing party,
that he was worried about. They would be fresh.

Folsom concentrated his attention then on the east and the
west. After forty minutes of plodding around the mile-long circle,
it became a question of whether he could last the remaining hour
and twenty minutes. Even with the most intense concentration
and violent shivering and the continual plodding, he had to fight
desperately the sleep that would steal quietly into his mind. Sleep
that made him the same promises of warmth that it had made to
Teleman all day, sleep and the warmth that his body craved now
more than anything in life.

Folsom strove to shake off the exhaustion that was wearing him
down, reaching at his eyelids with sandpapery fingers, and forced
himself to keep plodding. Somewhere in the back of his mind, as
he trudged through the endless circle under the erratic northern
lights filling the sky with trembling curtains of fire, somewhere
deep, almost below the conscious level, something was wrong, but
his mind was too hazy, too sticky and numb, to pinpoint the sense
of wrongness. Vaguely he realized that the missing factor was important, but the longer he walked, the more time that passed,
the farther away the vagrant thought slipped. Now it was beyond
his capability to muster the necessary energy to concentrate, and
soon it had slipped completely from him.

On a sweep to the north, half asleep and mumbling to himself, McPherson came up behind and laid a hand on his shoulder.
Folsom felt the big man's hand grasp at his parka and automatically swung around, the butt of his carbine whipping through a
vicious arc at the other's unseen midsection. Only Folsom's tired
reflexes saved McPherson from a solid clout in the belly. Mc-
Pherson caught the rifle in one huge paw and stopped it, then
gave Folsom a gentle shove toward the tent and watched him
stumble away before he too began the chase around the endless
circle.

Teleman was at the bottom of a long shaft. Above, the velvet-
black sides of the hole spiraled up to an undefined blob of half

light, a formless nothing. His mind refused to work, refused to coordinate sensory impressions, was mired in a haze of quicksand. He fell sharply . . .

Teleman sat up in the darkened tent and waited for the shapeless blurs of darkness to form into patterns that represented walls of the tent and pieces of gear scattered about.

The hoarfrost from their breathing was growing thick on the nylon walls. The suddenness of awakening had disoriented him for several panicky minutes before he realized that huddled next to him in sleeping bags were both McPherson and Folsom, and Gadsen's sleeping bag was empty. That told him that it was the last watch before they would move on again. After the few hours of sleep, his mind and senses were preternaturally sharp. He did not realize that this was due to almost complete exhaustion and that it would melt away after the smallest exertion, leaving him again a semiconscious drone.

He got quietly out of his sleeping bag and fished out the chemical heating pads. Of the three that Falsom had put in with him, only one retained any heat at all. He tucked it underneath his parka against his chest and picked up his carbine, a ration pack, and face mask and moved quietly to the tent flap.

When he poked his head out through the tent flaps, the mask, still heated from the tiny stove, warmed the air passing into his lungs to a breathable temperature. The combination of aurora borealis and moonlight illuminated the surrounding tundra with midevening intensity. After a moment he caught sight of Gadsen coming up from far to the east. The sailor was walking slowly, stopping every now and then to search the horizon carefully through the field glasses.

Teleman squirmed through the flaps and in a crouching run started south. After two hundred yards he flung himself flat in the snow and wriggled around to see if Gadsen had spotted him running from the tent. Gadsen had not and was now coming around the far side of the tent, almost a mile away from where he lay. Teleman decided to stay put until Gadsen had completed that part of the circle and started around again to the east. In his white parka he would be invisible at half the distance. So he lay unmoving in the snow, watching as the distant figure traveled farther around in his wide orbit.

What chain of reasoning had prompted him to leave his companions and strike out on his own he did not quite understand. He realized that he was carrying extremely vital information on the American state-of-the-art in electronic countermeasures, aircraft and engine design and sensor technology. He also knew that this information locked away in his brain could easily be unlocked by the Soviets, and, therefore, he was much too valuable to let himself fall into their hands. Folsom, McPherson, Gadsen—all, or one, meant to kill him. Only that factor was ice clear in his drug-crazed mind.

What Teleman had endured in the past seventy-two hours might easily have killed a lesser man. Instead of recovering in the special-care unit of a military hospital, he was staggering around the North Cape of Norway in the midst of the century's worst Arctic storm. His body still contained microresidues of the various psychic and physical energizers and, without the compensating PCMS, was on the verge of a complete nervous breakdown. The momentary hysteria hours before, which had sent him into a shallow coma that Folsom and Gadsen had mistaken for sleep, had been the beginning. The deepening cold endured since then was affecting the action of the drug residues, changing and catalyzing their effects to an extent never before tested. As a result Teleman's mind burned with the steady intensity of an arc lamp. As he lay in the snow his mind was busy collating drug-affected impressions, misunderstood facts, and skewed extrapolations, all of which only served to reinforce his conviction that those helping him were actually his assassins. Forgotten was the intense effort, at the risk of their own lives, that had already been expended to aid him.

As Gadsen disappeared around the far side of the tent, Teleman got shakily to his feet and began to run at little more than a half trot due south. He had no firm plan in mind for his escape. The sudden awakening minutes before had brought only the galvanizing need for escape. Somewhere deep in his mind was the idea of heading south for several miles, then turning east into a shallow arc that would bring him to the naval base from the southeast at an angle great enough to pass unseen by Folsom and the others. If they had already arrived at the base he would simply denounce them as his would-be killers and claim asylum.

Teleman trotted on for several more minutes under the wavering streamers of electrons decorating the sky. The weird light made seeing difficult and twice he tripped and fell headlong. The third time he fell he found that he could not immediately get up. Stunned more by the lack of movement in his legs than by the force of the fall, Teleman lay prone, able to move only his head. The few minutes of running had taken him well away from the vicinity of the tent. He lay now in a blank white desert where the only movement was the aurora borealis dancing solemnly overhead. After several minutes during which the cold penetrated his furs with ice-fingers, he was able to get to his knees and, using the carbine as a crutch, pull himself to his feet.

Teleman staggered forward again at a shuffle, leaning heavily on the carbine. But to his mind's eye he was running as swiftly as an arrow. Only a few more hours, he thought happily to himself, and he would reach the naval station—well ahead of the others. Once there, he would tell them all that had happened in the past two days, tell them that both Americans and Russians had violated their territory. Maybe they would even let him go along when they went out to round up the intruders.

Now he was strong and fresh again. The territory unreeled beneath his feet as he bounded over the snow. On the horizon was the low bulk of the naval base and the slender stems of gun barrels thrusting out toward the sea. He was so close, he thought, that he could stop and rest awhile, for there was no sense in arriving so out of breath that he could not tell his story. He stopped and sank down in the snow. Only a few minutes rest and then he would finish the last half mile. The brilliantly lit base area was now clearly visible, even if it was a few feet above the ground. That would make no difference. He could jump that high. Funny, these Norwegians, that they should paint the buildings and the compound a bright green. It was a naval base . . . it should be blue. . . .

Folsom came completely awake the instant Gadsen burst through the tent flaps.

'Off to the west, about a dozen men . . . a mile out.'

Folsom was already shrugging into his parka as McPherson grabbed up his pack and twisted to wake Teleman.

'Goddamn,' he bellowed.

Folsom swung around and stared at the empty sleeping bag. 'For Christ's sake, where the hell has he gone?' he roared.

Gadsen popped his head outside and then back in again. 'Wherever it is, we ain't got much time to look for him. It's going to take those bastards about ten minutes to get here.'

Folsom stood stock-still in the center of the tent, his mind churning furiously as he tried to decide what had to be done next. 'All right, leave everything here but the carbines and ammunition. Outside and keep low so they can't see us.'

The three men crawled quickly outside into the bitter air and huddled close to the ground. Folsom pulled the binoculars to his eyes and examined the approaching Russians. There were six men spread out into a skirmish line almost half a mile long, both ends beginning to curl to flank the tent. Quickly he swept the horizon north and then south. Turning to the east, he scanned the snow carefully to the horizon, but saw no sign of any second party closing from that direction.

In the meantime McPherson had been searching the snow around the tent. He raised an arm and motioned the others to join him, then pointed at a line of tracks leading south.

'I'll lay odds that's our boy.'

'Okay, south is as good a direction as any now. We go get him,' Folsom ordered, his angry voice gritting through clenched teeth. 'What the hell do you suppose got into him anyway?'

Neither Gadsen nor McPherson replied, and in moments, hunching low to the ground, they were running south along the line of tracks. McPherson had unslung his pack and was dragging it after him in a vain effort to wipe away the trail they were leaving.

If anything, the temperature had fallen even lower in the past five hours. As the men ran they left long streamers of frozen breath hanging in the crystal air. Above them the multicolored aurora borealis glimmered and writhed across the northern sky and Folsom again felt the strange, nagging sensation that he had forgotten some vital point. But as his body began to tire after the insufficient three hours of sleep, he found himself concentrating to the exclusion of all else, on running.

They stopped after ten minutes and threw themselves prone in the snow to rest and check on the Soviets. Through the glasses Folsom could see that the Russian troops were less than a hundred yards from the tent. The northern and southern ends of the line had circled until the tent was in the center. They were lying prone in the snow while two soldiers were crawling up to the tent. Folsom rolled over on his back and waited for his ragged breathing to smooth. In the ten minutes the three had been running they had covered perhaps one mile at a half trot, half run. All three were severely winded, but at least, Folsom thought, they had put enough distance between themselves and the tent so that they could now go on without being spotted in the fitful light.

'How far do you think Teleman managed to get?' he asked McPherson.

'I doubt if he could have gone much farther. I'm surprised we haven't found him yet. He was in pretty bad shape when we stopped. We'll be lucky to find him alive,' McPherson finished bleakly.

Folsom swore savagely. 'The old man will have my head if we don't.'

Gadsen, looking miserable, rubbed his face with gloved hands. 'I don't see how the hell he could have gotten out of that tent without me seeing him,' he muttered.

'Hell, how were you to know that he would take off? You weren't watching him. You were watching for the Russians. If there is any fault here at all, it's mine. We should probably have rigged up something to wake us . . .' Folsom shook his head. The 'what-if' line of excuse-making was a waste of energy. He stood up and took a last look at the Russians through the glasses, then swept the east once more. The two scouts had almost reached the tent. He knew it could not take them much longer to find out that their quarry had flown the coop. Whether they would automatically assume that the Americans had left ahead of them or would discover their tracks was a toss-up. In either case he wanted to get as far away as possible. Nothing had shown on the eastern horizon yet, but somewhere out there another Russian party was approaching. He wished to God he could get in touch with Larkin. Suddenly he felt completely inadequate to cope with the situation.

'Come on, let's go,' he said quietly, starting south again along the parallel set of tracks that Teleman had left.

Teleman's tracks were becoming more and more irregular as they trudged on. Shortly they came upon the spot where their quarry had first fallen. The depression in the snow, almost invisible in the uncertain light, showed that he had fallen cleanly and gotten up again without hesitation. Not daring to pause, the three sailors pushed on. Now the pace that Folsom had set was beginning to wear heavily. Their breath was coming in gasps of exhaustion, their half run, half trot beginning to flag. When they reached the second indentation in the fresh snow surface Folsom waved them to a halt. Gasping for breath and leaning heavily on their carbines, they knelt in the snow. Finally, after a few minutes, McPherson dragged himself forward a few yards and came back with Teleman's insulated canteen. The three looked at one another and with the same thought were up and running at once. Within the next few hundred yards they found his carbine, the lightweight pack, and finally the spot where he had fallen the third time.

Folsom looked around wildly but the horizon ahead was bare. In the past few minutes the aurora borealis had grown in intensity, but its wild gyrations made visibility even poorer. All three were gasping hoarsely for breath, barely this side of collapse themselves. But not once did they stop to consider their own bodies. The thought uppermost in their minds was: If they were this bad off, how much worse was Teleman? With a hoarse command from Folsom, they started forward again.

By now they had come three miles from the tent. The tent and the Russians were lost in the gloom on the northern horizon. For the first time since he had landed on the North Cape, Folsom began to hope for a resurgence in the high winds that had buffeted them all through the day, or better yet, another blizzard. Given either to wipe out the last traces of their trail and they might win yet. But the cloudless sky offered the hope of neither.

They were running again, running with the desperation of exhausted men who must run to save their lives and that of a comrade. Under the eerily lighted sky they raced on across the snow-covered expanse of the tundra plain in pursuit of the staggering track of the delirious pilot.

Once they stopped for a brief rest and Folsom searched the horizon with the binoculars. There was no sign of pursuit in any direction. But he knew that condition would not last. Then they were off again, to stop almost immediately. Gadsen had seen it first, a lump of rags huddled into the snow.

Complete and utter silence had descended over the vast reaches of the North Cape. Along the shore the storm-raised combers continued to pound against the rock with monotonous regularity. But inland nothing moved on the plain of snow. It was as if the cold had frozen even the air into immobility. Folsom knelt down by Teleman's body and turned him over slowly. He pushed back the neck flap, pulled off one of his own gloves and felt for a heart beat.

'I'll be damned. He's still alive,' he said wonderingly.

'You're kidding,' Gadsen said, dropping down beside him. 'How the hell could he be?'

Folsom shook his head and rebuttoned Teleman's neck flap. 'You've got me. Now, how do we get him out of here?'

McPherson shrugged out of his pack and reslung his rifle. 'I'll carry him.'


## CHAPTER NINETEEN

THE STRIDENT SOUNDS of the battle alarm echoed through the ship. No practice situation now; each crew member understood full that this was the real thing. Lieutenant Commander Bridges, strapped into the seat of the executive officer's console, watched the battle lights flick from amber to green as each station reported in. A hard knot of both fear and excitement was building in his stomach as the track of the submarine, relayed to his console from the large bridge display, began to move steadily towards the battle cruiser.

'All stations manned and ready, sir,' he reported, as the last light, the security room, turned green.

'Thank you, Mr. Bridges,' Larkin said calmly. 'Bring her round on a course of 070° and ten knots, rig for silent running. All ECM to on.'

Bridges punched the heading into the computer console and stabbed down the ECM gear switch. The computer control net within the ship allowed either the captain or the executive officer to control the ship during battle stations, thus avoiding the

NORTH CAPE285

delays encountered in relaying orders through the helmsman and then to the engine room. Larkin still preferred to sit aloof on his high seat and give orders, leaving it to the executive officer to handle the ship. No provisions had been made for controlling the ship from any other location, nor was there need. In nuclear sea warfare there is no such item on the shipwright's bill of materials as armor plate. And conventional weapons were of no value against the U.S.S. *Robert F. Kennedy*, as she was well protected by her speed, defensive weaponry, and ECM gear. A direct hit on the bridge would not matter. A hit with nuclear weapons within 500 yards would destroy her utterly. Within one mile, a direct hit would probably kill the entire ship's complement with radiation.

Larkin had not moved his eyes from the holographic map display since the Russian submarine had turned toward them and begun to run out to sea, directly away from North Cape Island, where it had lain since early that afternoon. Since 1500 the *RFK* had tried in vain to maintain a radar and sonar watch on the submarine, but its proximity to the rock walls of the cliffs edging the island had created a maze of conflicting signals.

All during the long afternoon and evening, the feeling that the Russians had indeed landed a second party had grown. Now, with the submarine moving for a third time, it could mean either that the Soviet commander had realized his mistake and was moving to land a third party ashore between Folsom and the naval base, or that the *RFK* had been spotted. Long, agonizing minutes passed with the speed of a glacier's tread as the submarine increased its speed to twenty-two knots on a course that would bring an intercept in less than an hour.

Finally, after twenty minutes, the submarine came about to a course paralleling the west coast. Larkin let loose a sigh of relief that was lost in similar sounds from the other eight men on the bridge. The submarine was still unaware of their presence. But an even greater dilemma now presented itself to Larkin. His theory, that the submarine was moving down the coast to drop the third shore party as close to the unsuspecting naval base as it dared, from which they would then work their way back to meet Folsom, was confirmed.

He knew that he could trust Folsom to avoid capture as far as possible. But Folsom was surrounded and probably not even aware of it. As he weighed the possibilities, the choices became clear to him.

As captain of the U.S.S. *Robert F. Kennedy*, and responsible not only for the safety of the ship but his own shore party and the downed pilot, Larkin indeed had a choice to make: reveal his position to the submarine and engage, or wait until the third shore party was dropped and move in to destroy the submarine and save his own landing party with whatever fire support he could provide. The first choice was the more logical, but its danger lay in the fact that the Soviets had already expended a great effort to capture Teleman, and it was more than likely that the submarine would turn and fight rather than run. If that happened, it could very well be the start of, if not a third world war, then a major freeze in East-West relations, which could be even more disastrous in the long run. A third possibility, that Teleman would be captured and taken aboard the submarine, which would then be sunk, to Larkin's credit, never even suggested itself.

Larkin, very uncharacteristically, had sent off a blistering message to Virginia with instructions to relay to Washington and the White House Position Room for immediate action. The message had laid down in no uncertain terms exactly what would happen if the submarine was allowed to disgorge its human freight. Minutes ago a terse message had come in over the direct channel ordering him to wait for orders.

Now he sat at the command console, the power and weaponry of an entire World War II Navy at his command rolled into one single ship, and he was powerless. All he could do was shadow the submarine at a distance of eighty miles. It was now obvious to Larkin that the submarine commander was heading for a sheltered spot on the western coast of the North Cape to drop a third landing party. The Soviet skipper was obviously going to attempt to take advantage of the bad sea conditions as cover for his landing party above the Norwegian naval base. If he did so, all hope for Folsom and his party outrunning the other two parties was gone. They would fall right into the arms of this third party.

Larkin was caught in a quandary and his helplessness showed in the steady drumming of his fingers on the console panel. He decided to wait. The submarine was now moving around the lee of the North Cape and into the weather side, fully exposed to the wind and waves that screamed down from the Great Barrier across two hundred miles of open sea. It was just possible that the submarine would not be able to spot a location where a third shore party could be landed.

The U.S.S. *Robert F. Kennedy* dug into the waves as Larkin ordered her speed increased to fifteen knots. She burrowed into the high waves and thrust forward, white water breaking around her bow as she swept on, running for position off the mouth of the fjord.

'Hold his head up a little higher . . . he'll choke if . . .'

Teleman did choke as the steaming hot tea dribbled in equal

portions down his chin and throat. He coughed weakly, tried to sit up, and found he could not.

'I'll be damned,' he heard someone say. 'I never thought he'd wake up again.'

He managed to open his eyes, focus on the face above, but it was a moment or two before he recognized Folsom beneath the beard and cold blisters. He lay back exhausted until a heavy voice, speaking a guttural language, brought him bolt upright, mind clear and sharp for the first time in two days. In back of Folsom was a parka-clad figure holding a rifle loosely but ready on the back of Folsom's head. Beyond the Russian soldier were several more, all crowded into the tent, heads bent together as they talked. Every few moments one of them would look over at him, a smile of victory on his face.

He found Gadsen and McPherson, both cramped against the tent wall with their hands and feet bound securely. Only Folsom was unfettered, and the Russian guard never took the rifle off the back of his head.

'How the hell . . .' he began.

Folsom gave a brief smile. 'You decided to . . .'                    ...

That was as far as he got. The Russian jabbed him in the back with the rifle and motioned him away from Teleman. Then he called out a phrase in Russian to the group of men.

One of them, stooping in the low tent, came over to where Teleman was sitting and grabbed his wrist. Angrily, Teleman shook his hand loose and pushed the man away. The guard stepped in close with the rifle, shoving it into Teleman's face, forcing him back against the rolled-up sleeping bag.

'You goddamned idiot, get that thing out of my face before I take it away from you and bend it over your head.'

The Russian did not understand English, but the intent of Teleman's words was clear. His smile grew wider and he moved in closer, snapping off the safety at the same time. A harsh word from the man Teleman had pushed away stopped him and he backed up, still wearing the grin that plainly invited Teleman to try and back up his outburst.

Teleman saw that, like Folsom, the Russians were heavily bearded an their faces all bore traces of frostbite and the chapping effects of the dry, bitter air. This must have been the first party, he thought, the group that had been chasing them for nearly three days. He wondered how they had managed to take them unaware in the tent. He glanced over at Folsom, but the exhausted executive officer was sitting with his forehead resting on drawn-up knees, almost asleep.

'You are the pilot of the American spy airplane?' the Russian asked in accented but perfectly understandable English.

'What kind of airplane?' Teleman mimicked the accent.

'You are stubborn. However, that will not last. For now, are you feeling all right?'

Teleman ignored him and slumped back down on the sleeping bag and closed his eyes. 'Get lost,' he said wearily.

The Russian gave the guard instructions in Russian and Teleman caught the words *chyornii chelovek*, and knew they referred to him. The guard nodded and backed away to sit down against the wall of the tent, rifle in his hands, relaxed but ready.

Behind his shut eyelids Teleman's mind worked furiously. Flashes of memory having to do with running across the tundra kept passing through his mind, but he could not decide if they had to do with the long day's hike or were somewhere in between. He kept recalling green buildings on the horizon, but ascribed these to dreams. He still had vivid memories of the dream involving the Mongolian sheepherder. As Teleman got himself under control and began to think clearly again, he realized that for the past forty-eight hours he had been fighting off the effects of lingering traces of lysergic acid and amphetamines. Even without the drug effects, the long periods of the desperate flight across the North Cape should have been forgotten as they occurred. This would have been normal for any man as exhausted as he was. But not to be able to remember more than highly colored and wavering details as seen through a glass partly obscured with flowing water, Teleman knew was not normal. Then with a shock he realized that he could remember nothing at all since one of the late afternoon rest stops. He could recall no more than hazy snatches of a warm sleeping bag and Folsom's voice laying out the guard-duty pattern.

Teleman concentrated on what Folsom had said, trying to bring back a little of what remained . . . he had awakened to see Folsom and McPherson rolled into their sleeping bags. Gadsen had been on guard duty and he remembered that he had crept away from the tent. The entire sequence of events suddenly was clear to him. He had been convinced that the three Americans were plotting to kill him, to keep him from falling into Russian hands. He had crept away from the tent to run south with the idea of reaching the Norwegian naval base. He recalled the bitter cold . . . falling . . . and after that, nothing, until he had awakened a few minutes ago as Folsom forced the hot tea down his throat.

He opened his eyes, sick with the realization that Folsom, Gadsen, and McPherson had been captured because they had come after him rather than save their own skins by abandoning a madman and making a run for the Norwegians. Now the four were exhausted, their last hope completely gone. Five Russians

were in the tent and, as he glanced about, the tent flap parted
and a sixth entered.

He closed his eyes again. He was to blame for their being
captured. It had been a foolish stunt to try and run for it alone.
It had been a stupid reaction to believe that the three sailors
who were risking their freedom, their very lives for him, would
try to kill him. That this reaction was due to the traces of the
drugs still left in his system, coupled with exhaustion and intense
cold, did not occur to Teleman. He knew only that he was to
blame.

'Hey, Commie, come over here.' Teleman struggled up into a
sitting position again, sneering at the guard who swung the rifle
to cover him.

The English-speaking Russian approached and Teleman
motioned toward the guard. 'Tell that fool to put that thing away
before he shoots himself.'

The Russian ignored him; his face bore no traces of humor at
Teleman's attempted levity. 'What do you want?'

'I want to know what happens next.'

The Russian turned away and Teleman grabbed his sleeve.
The Russian swung around and hit him squarely across the
face.

'Keep your hands to yourself,' he said through clenched lips.
'You or your friends killed two of my men. I do not like that. If
I did not have such orders, I would kill you all and have done
with it.'

Teleman rubbed his face where the other had struck him. 'Did
it ever occur to you that your own pilots tried, and almost
succeeded, to kill me?'

'Of course. You are a spy,' the other hissed and left him.

So that's that, Teleman thought. No information is going to
come out of that one. Of course he knew what was going to happen
now. Very soon there would be more Russians, and then a long
walk to the coast and the waiting submarine. Then back to Murmansk at high speed where an MVD cellar and an intelligence
squad would be waiting to question him. Oh, very carefully of
course. There would be no actual physical torture, but Teleman
knew what successive hours of sleeplessness could do, particularly
in his condition. And after they had taken blood samples and
found the drug traces in his system, they would know just what
chemicals and combinations of interrogation to use. He would
never know just what he would sign in a matter of hours. Nor,
for the purposes the Russians had in mind, would he need to
know. With a signed confession and careful edited television
tapes to play to the world, it would make little or no difference
what he said or did. His capture and subsequent confession would

not offset the black mark the Russians were going to take over the war in Sinkiang, but the information they would extract from him would make the trouble more than worthwhile. Then it would be years before the United States would be able to develop a new surveillance system of such magnitude—the completion of the Super SAMOS system was still five years away.

Damn it all, he thought bitterly, he had really blown it now.

Teleman lay back against the sleeping bag and closed his eyes, trying to shut out the knowledge of what the coming hours would bring, not only for himself, but for Folsom, McPherson, and Gadsen. He knew they would receive the same kind of treatment. The capture of three American sailors would only be the icing on the propaganda cake. For the Russians it would be a double victory. Not only would they have the pilot of the most advanced aircraft the United States had ever built, but three crew members of the most advanced naval ship—all for practically free.

Teleman shifted uncomfortably, and as he did so his hand brushed something hard beneath his parka. His breath caught in his throat. Very carefully, as casually as he could, he moved his hand away. The Russians had not searched him. Of course not, he thought, he had been almost dead when they found him. They would have been in too much of a hurry to get him back to the tent. And, in failing to search him, they had missed the .22 caliber survival pistol he had pushed into the waistband of his trousers when he had dressed for the start of the long race. Probably not even Folsom was aware that he had the pistol. It had remained tucked inside the folds of fur and nylon where even he had forgotten about it.

For several seconds he did not move a muscle, as his mind raced to find a way to capitalize on the possession of the revolver. One .22 caliber, nine-shot revolver against a 7.65 mm Soviet service rifle and five other assorted weapons. In the semidarkness of the tent could the guard determine its puny size? If he could, would it make a difference? Would he guess at the power of the magnum charges? Could he, Teleman, cover him in time to prevent an outcry that would alert the others? Too many questions, too damn many, but then, it was their only chance.

Teleman settled himself as if falling asleep and cracked his eyelids only far enough to watch the guard. Obviously the man was as weary as they. Although he still sat upright, the rifle now rested across his lap and his eyes were half closed. Even so, Teleman could see that they glanced steadily around the tent, watching, aware of every move being made.

Teleman felt the deep gulfs of sleep tugging at him again. The tent had warmed considerably from the heat of packed bodies and the small stove. The folded sleeping bag made an excessively comfortable bed, and he had to continue the portrayal of the exhausted pilot in order not to arouse their suspicions. Teleman knew that it was now a race to see if the Russian would relax his vigil before he, himself, fell asleep.

Five minutes passed, then ten minutes. Teleman concentrated so hard on staying awake that his eyes watered, blurring his vision. He turned his head ever so slightly to the left and felt a sharp disappointment. Folsom would be of no immediate help. Although he had not been tied, he was sound asleep, and Teleman was certain that it would take something akin to the last trumpet to wake him.

But he was wrong. Folsom groaned and started to turn over. In the process he half sat up and so was facing directly across the tent from the guard. Immediately the Russian came to his knees, raising the rifle, pointing it directly at Folsom. This was the opening that Teleman had been waiting for.

The guard leaned forward to prod Folsom and his shoulder momentarily obscured his view of Teleman. Quickly, yet carefully, Teleman reached beneath his parka and pulled the revolver from his waistband. Before the guard had settled back, glaring at Folsom, Teleman had dropped his arm back to his side, hiding the pistol under a fold of his parka. Out of the corner of his eye he could see Folsom half sit forward, rubbing his forehead where the guard's rifle muzzle had jabbed him.

Every second counted now, literally counted, Teleman knew. The five Russians in the front of the tent were still deeply engrossed in their conversation and nearly all had their backs to him. The guard was still watching Folsom. In a moment he would settle back across from Teleman.

Teleman raised his hand and arm until the pistol was lying across his chest, muzzle pointing directly at the Russian's heart. The guard, rifle still aiming at Folsom, turned and Teleman watched with satisfaction as his face took on a comical look of surprise. Very carefully Teleman pointed with his left hand, motioning for the guard to keep silent. Then he kicked Folsom.

For a minute Folsom did not respond, and Teleman felt sweat break out on his forehead in fear that the executive officer had fallen asleep again. He did not dare take his eyes off the guard, who any moment now would recover from his surprise. Teleman motioned savagely for him to raise the rifle toward the tent roof and kicked Folsom squarely in the knee. This time he jumped.

The entire scenario unfolded as a slow-motion dream. Each action was drawn out to a nervous breaking point and Teleman was almost convinced that the Russian would blur into motion and pluck the pistol from his unresponsive fingers. Then Folsom was moving out of the line of the muzzle and extracting the rifle from the dazed guard.

Folsom glanced at Teleman from his kneeling position and shook his head in wonderment. Feeling very aged and decrepit, Teleman got to his knees, then both Teleman and Folsom faced the five Russians in the front of the tent.

'The first one who makes the slightest move gets shot,' Folsom intoned solemnly.

They stiffened as one man and swung around. The same shock suffused the five faces as had colored the face of the guard. Finally the one who spoke English managed to stammer out a confused question. His answer was the roar of the heavy military rifle tearing a hole in the tent flap. Folsom said nothing more, merely glared over the rifle barrel, his meaning intently clear in the acrid cordite fumes filling the tent.

Satisfied that they were thoroughly cowed, Teleman crawled around behind Folsom and went to work on the lengths of nylon cord binding Gadsen and McPherson.

'All right, if you are all ready let's move out.' Folsom finished a quick survey of the tent and motioned toward the tent flap. He turned once and grinned back at the miserable and bound Soviet troopers as Teleman, Gadsen, and McPherson, shouldering a large bundle, pushed past him and out into the cold. 'Have fun boys. We'll send the Norwegians back for you. *Strasvechi!*'

'Oh . . . that means "Hello", Pete,' Gadsen chortled.

'Oh, yeah . . . how 'bout that?'

Still grinning, he followed the others out and they turned south-westerly. The Russians had been stripped of their clothes down to long underwear and socks. Their clothes were in the bundle McPherson was carrying. Without clothes, these six Soviet troopers would be unable to chase them farther. Five minutes exposure in the bitter, sub-zero weather would kill them if they tried. Instead, they were left with an ample supply of fuel, at least enough to last until the Norwegians or their own comrades could rescue them from their predicament.

The four men, heightened with the excitement, almost, but not quite, looked forward to the remaining miles of the trek across the tundra and down through the edging cliffs that would bring them to the Norwegian naval base. Even the fact that Folsom had added an extra three miles to the trek to take them far south of the anticipated second party did little to dim their spirits. In a matter of five or six hours at most they would be trudging into the safe hands of the Norwegians. The warmth of that reception they would worry about when the time came.

The worst that could happen would be internment—preferable under any conditions to the MVD cellars in Murmansk.

Although still exhausted by the three days and more of exposure to the Arctic storm, the several hours of forced rest had done much to revive them. Teleman was completely clear-headed, though still experiencing brief periods of dizziness and disorientation from the remaining drug residues. Even so, he was confident that he would make it through. What shape he would be in he did not know, or even much care any more. Just to make it through, that would be enough now.

Folsom set an easy yet steady pace. The four men moved along under the brightening aurora borealis. They were strung out in a line one hundred yards long, Folsom leading off, Gadsen second, followed by Teleman and McPherson, with his bundle of clothing, acting as rear guard.

McPherson, as he strode along carefully watching Teleman, smiled to himself every once in a while, recalling the scene in the tent. The first he remembered after falling asleep in the over-heated tent was Teleman sawing away at his, McPherson's, bonds with the guard's knife. It had taken him several moments to awaken enough to realize what was happening. The Russian troopers had been lined up in front of the tent and ordered to lean precariously forward with legs and arms spread and hands on the tent wall, which provided a not-too-firm support. Folsom had watched every move with the heavy Russian army rifle cocked and ready as the Russians stripped under his watchful eye. Gadsen, cradling a Russian submachine gun, had joined him, making pointed comments in Polish, which some of the Russians understood.

McPherson shook his head. First he runs away and manages to get us all captured because we were so intent on trying to bring him around that the Russians just walked up on us, then he pulls a pistol and we all walk away.

'Hey, Major,' he yelled ahead to the stiff figure.

Teleman turned his head to glance at the burly sailor.

'Hey, Major, when you get tired of this airplane nonsense, I'll get you into the SEALS—if you promise to lay off the acid!'

It was close to four hours of very nearly steady travel before the party reached the first indications of the cliffs leading down to the Norwegian base, still two miles distant around the headland. The going had been both easier and faster than they had expected. So far they had seen no sign of the supposed pursuing forces and Folsom had about decided that any threat of a third party had been pure imagination. The Soviets could not carry unlimited manpower aboard the submarine. In any event they had swung nearly three miles south of their former line of march and so had probably avoided them.

Folsom called a halt and hunkered down to wait while each man trudged up. During the long march the line had gradually lengthened until Teleman and McPherson were half a mile behind. Teleman was still walking under his own steam, but the set, agonized look on his face was an eloquent indication of his physical condition. McPherson had discarded the bundle of winter clothes three miles south and west of the tent, pitching them behind one of the hummocks of tundra grass growing in the otherwise desolate plain of snow and ice.

While he waited, Folsom scanned the area ahead with the binoculars, knowing that the roughest part of the journey still lay ahead. Seen through the field glasses, the tundra in front of them appeared little different from what lay behind unless one noted the low ridges and hummocks that marked the edge of the coastal cliffs. How high, and how rugged they would be to negotiate, he had no idea. He only hoped that they would not prove impassable. The edge of the cliffs were, he judged, now less than a mile ahead. He swept the glasses to the north, but the terrain was bare of any movement or sign of life.

As the others drifted up he hunkered down on his heels and waited. The continuous walking through the savage, sub-zero cold was fast reducing them to walking ghosts. The euphoria that had infused them on leaving the tent had long since evaporated during the gruelling hike. Folsom knew that the stick figures in their flapping Arctic gear clustering around him were close to the very last extreme of physical effort. If any of them felt the way he did . . . and Teleman for one was in even worse condition . . .

Briefly he described the route ahead. All knew that the only information about the cliffs came from the topographical map he carried in his pocket. How reliable it was, they did not know. Curiously enough, their lives might depend in the next few hours on some remote German cartographer of the defunct Third Reich Wermacht. The map had originally been drawn for the Nazi Occupation forces in Norway.

Teleman groaned and got to his feet, swinging his arms. 'Hell man, I don't care how hard it's going to be, let's just get it over with. If I spend much more time in the great outdoors, all you'll have left to carry back will be a solid block of ice.'

Folsom nodded and stood up. 'Okay with me too. But don't say I didn't warn you.'

The small party struck out toward the fringing hummocks. After a few hundred yards the hummocks began to turn into slab-sided hills as they emerged in the deceptive light. Shortly

the party had reached the base of the first line of hills and began
the steep climb to the top. Before they had gained half the
distance Folsom ordered a halt while they tied themselves in line
with a length of nylon rope. In their weakened condition a
misstep resulting in a fall would take the individual all the way
back down. And they did not have strength to waste reclimbing
hills. It took the four men twenty minutes of climbing to reach
the gently rolling crest, less than four hundred feet above the
level of the plain. Folsom untied the rope from his waist and
walked forward to where the downward slope began and pulled
the field glasses from beneath his parka.

Standing on the crest of the hill, he could make out the sheen
of the fjord waters below. Between the hill on which he stood
and the final line of cliffs leading down to the fjord were a series
of rugged and broken hillocks and cols of bare rock, resembling
the snaggle-toothed mouth of some mythical Scandinavian giant
wrenched up from the fringing rock.

Disappointment crashed down on Folsom. They would have
at least another hour of rugged climbing before they could reach
the fjord. And then there still remained the hike to the Norwegian
naval base, out of sight around a headland a mile or so north. So
damn close . . . so damn close . . .                                    ,

Folsom turned away from the depressing scene and trudged
back to where the others waited and sank down beside them.

'There's a stiff climb ahead,' he said bitterly. 'Another hour of
climbing before we hit the cliffs.' He picked up his carbine and
fiddled with the stock.

After a moment of silence, McPherson stood up and took the
glasses to search the horizon to the east and north. The four-
hundred-foot height of the hill gave him a wide scope of vision.
In the uncertain light he almost thought he had spotted their
tent far to the north and east, but when he tried to find it again,
he failed. Finally he swung around restlessly and went back to the
far side of the hill. The spectral figures of Folsom, Teleman, and
Gadsen joined him as he went past.

Folsom accepted the glasses again and, after another moment's
hesitation, trudged to the rim of the hogback and lay down full
length in the snow. The expanse of frosted rock stretched away
below him, resembling the familiar waves of the Arctic storm,
each crest of rock capped with a dusting of snow. He rewarmed
the eyepieces in his hands. Directly below, the hillside sloped
away at a gentle angle until it met a sharp drop of some forty
or so feet to a shelf of granite, a man's height below that. From
there the slope was gentle for a half mile until it rose abruptly
to a sheer rock wall that, from this distance anyway, offered little
hope of hand- or foot-holds. He shifted slowly south, finding

nothing that would indicate an easier way, then north. After several minutes he located a shelf that seemed to have been slashed out of the rock wall, forming a small pass that cut through at mid-height. From what he could see of the other side, there were no impassable obstacles.

He rolled over and sat up. 'I think maybe there is a way to at least get through that rock wall down there.'

Teleman nodded painfully and shifted the burden of the Russian carbine he had been carrying since leaving the tent. So far he had successfully resisted McPherson's attempts to exchange it for his own lighter AR-18. Teleman shifted the carbine on its sling around his neck and shoulder and nodded. 'After having come so far, it would be a shame to quit now.'

McPherson nodded.

'I guess that makes it unanimous then,' Gadsen said. 'Let's move out.'

Once again Folsom watched the motley crew of scarecrows assemble and rope themselves together. On the verge of exhaustion, as he himself was, he marveled at the deep reserves in Teleman that enabled the man to go on.

They headed down the slope with the shuffling gait of tired men, each fighting to retain his foothold in the hard-packed snow of the windward side. At the foot of the hogback they halted while McPherson hauled a longer rope out of his pack and fastened one end into fixed loop.

'You first, Commander?'

Folsom nodded and slipped the noose over his head and down under his shoulders. He backed off a ways and tested the firmness of the knot by pulling against McPherson, then swung carefully over the edge of the steep slope and half slid, half climbed down until he was just above the vertical drop to the shelf. He glanced up at McPherson and waved one hand for slack and disappeared abruptly over the edge. He reappeared a moment later, standing on the ledge and slipped the noose off. McPherson pulled it up and motioned Gadsen to go next. Gadsen followed Folsom down, and, in minutes, McPherson was hauling it up for Teleman.

'Feel up to it, Major?'

'There's only one way down . . .'

'Yeah, there is at that. Look, just take it easy. I'll pay out the rope. You just hang on for the ride. The commander will help you down that last bit.'

Teleman nodded. 'How are you going to get down?'

'Just tell the others to stand clear. I'll be right behind you.' He grinned.

Teleman smiled back at him. 'Thanks for your help, Beau. I couldn't have made it this far without you.'

Teleman grasped his arm, then started down the slope. A few feet away he slipped, and McPherson hauled back on the rope to keep him from tumbling. The stretch with Teleman was the hardest of all for McPherson, who had to maintain a steady tension of the line to keep him from going over the edge of the drop-off.

His strength, as prodigious as it was, was nearly exhausted by the past days' efforts. Teleman, all but dangling on the end of the rope, realized this and scrabbled hard with his boots for a foothold in the wind-packed snow. Finally he managed to kick through the crust and dig the toe of a boot in and bring himself to a halt. Teleman waved weakly up to McPherson to wait and gratefully felt the cutting edge of the rope slack off. He knew that both of them needed a moment's rest.

With his left boot he kicked a second toehold in the snow and lowered himself the length of his drawn-up knee and kicked a third hole with the right boot. Then he rested a moment and peered over his shoulder to see how near the drop-off was. Still twenty feet or so to go. Teleman lowered himself again and clutched at the first toehold with his gloved hand. Now he was able to work his way down carefully, saving McPherson the effort of fending his 172-pound weight. Shortly he felt empty space beneath his boot, then a moment later Gadsen had reached up and caught his foot. The rope slacked enough to give him room and he waved Gadsen away and dropped the last eight feet into the banked snow at the foot of the wall. The rope followed him down like a snake and he got shakily to his feet and backed away from the wall, motioning Gadsen and Folsom to do the same.

'The man says watch out . . .'

At the same time he caught sight of McPherson scrabbling down the slope on his seat, legs extended to break his speed, an idiot grin affixed to his face. He slowed slightly above the drop-off, then shot over to land relaxed in the trained parachutist's roll, legs bent and a roll-over on to the left hip. McPherson got to his feet, brushing away the snow, still grinning.

'Most fun I've had since I started this cruise.'

'Crazy idiot, you could have busted your neck in three places.' Folsom grinned and waved at the other two. 'Come on, let's tackle the next phase of this endless jaunt.'

The next mile was an easy slope downhill leading to what Folsom had optimistically termed the *pass* through the rock wall that now stretched above them. Close-up the wall did not appear as formidable as it had through the glasses, but still the pass offered an easier and less strenuous climb.

The faint touches of wind that had begun to spring up again on the plain were stronger among the rock formations. The weirdness of the tiny valley was accentuated by the aurora borealis, which, at the same time, made seeing so difficult that Folsom had been forced to an easier pace than he would otherwise have chosen. Even so, they had covered the mile to the pass quickly enough. The pass was a natural path leading up, twisting through the rock until it disappeared around a curve several hundred feet away. For a moment Folsom hesitated to start forward. The narrow way was an ideal ambush site. Ridiculous, he thought, there was no way in the world that the Russians could have selected this particular place to lie in wait. . . . Folsom snorted and started the climb.

## CHAPTER TWENTY

FOLSOM had been partially right. The pass, such as it was, had been clear through the rock barrier barring their way to the narrow ledges that marked the beginning of the steep slopes leading down to the fjord. The Russians spotted them as they were midway in their descent.

The four had reached the top of the pass and rested for a few minutes before going on. On the narrow ledges between the top of the pass and the edge of the cliffs they were buffeted again by the stiffening winds blowing in from the sea. After a brief examination of the cliffs Folsom was surprised with the apparent ease with which they could make the descent. Although steep, the cliff face—sheltered from the generations of wind in the deep fjord, which had worn the seaward-facing rock smooth—was broken and channeled enough to present an almost ladder-like descent of its 160 feet. They began the climb down to the beach with some faint degree of optimism.

It was Gadsen who first heard the faint rifle report and saw the spurt of rock indicating where the bullet had struck. His warning shout thrust them under an overhang into the cover of the wall itself, from which they tried to spot the Soviets on the cliff top. The overhang was invisible from above and prevented a clear shot from the top of the cliffs. It had been pure luck that someone, overeager perhaps, had fired too soon. In any event, the four Americans were safe for the moment.

But only for a moment. There were several alternate ways leading down from the cliff edge and the Soviets could flank them easily and within minutes. While the overhang furnished cover from above, there was nothing to use as shelter against fire coming from either side. The four men knew that they had to move and move fast.

'Down that way, through the cleft,' Folsom shouted over the wind gusting through the rock crannies. 'One at a time. Mac, lead off. When you reach the cleft, give us covering fire.'

McPherson nodded, crawled to the edge of the overhang, and peered carefully upward. Nothing moved on the cliff tops, above or on either side. He looked down and spent a few seconds examining the route he would follow. Then, satisfied, he came to his feet and plunged downward to a narrow shelf, ran lightly along it for several feet, and vaulted over a boulder into the shelter of a slot in the rock wall. A single shot snapped after him, but no spurt of rock indicated where the bullet had struck. McPherson waved a hand over the top of the boulder to show that he was all right. A moment later Teleman saw the muzzle of his carbine appear and he nudged Gadsen.

'Let's get set,' he muttered.

'You first, Major,' Folsom said tightly, 'and don't stop. Just go!'

Teleman nodded.

McPherson popped up and fired a fast burst, then ducked back down again to scramble to the far end of the slab-shaped rock A fusilade of rifle fire danced off the rock where he had been. McPherson waited for it to die away and jumped up to fire again, a long burst this time that raked across the top of the cliff. Teleman scrambled forward at the same time. As he dropped on to the ledge he thought he heard a faint scream, but the sound whirled away on the wind, almost instantaneously. It sounded as if it had come from above, but he couldn't be sure. He shuttled along the ledge awkwardly, wondering if it had come from McPherson, until he heard Mac's carbine stuttering again, and he concentrated on his running.

The ledge was less than eighteen inches wide and the footing treacherous with scattered rock and shale. As he neared the end he slipped and fell forward on to the boulder with stunning force. His head glanced off the rock and exploded with pain. Feebly cursing, he dragged himself over, almost directly beneath McPherson's carbine, and slid down the other side. Seconds later Gadsen fell over on top of him and Folsom followed in a dive that just missed the tangle of arms and legs.

McPherson crouched down beside them. 'Everybody get here in one piece?'

Teleman sat up, massaging his forehead, and his hand came away coated with blood. So what else is new, he thought with resignation.

'Julie, check that cut,' Folsom snapped. 'Mac, what's the situation?'

'About seven of them, I think. One was going over the edge

when I hit him. He got hung up on that spur or rock there,' he finished.

Folsom pulled the binoculars from beneath his parka and turned them on the cliff tops. In the brightening light of mid-day he could make out a green-clad arm draped over the same outthrust of rock McPherson had pointed out. Nothing more. The cliff top was bare.

'Okay, you convinced them to keep their heads down anyway. I think we have enough cover, if we move fast and stay close to the rock, to make it down to the beach. We should be able to reach that headland before they hit the beach.'

He turned to Teleman and squatted down beside him, where Gadsen was wrapping a piece of cloth around Teleman's fore-head. The make-shift bandage was already stained bright red, but the blood was congealing quickly in the cold.

Folsom had caught a glimpse of the cut before Gadsen had gone to work on it. An ugly gash across the bend of the forehead on the right side, almost three inches long. The fall on the rock had laid the skin open to the whitish bone.

'That cut is going to leave a nasty scar,' he murmured as Gad-sen tied the bandage tight and sawed off the ends with his sheath knife.

'Big deal,' Teleman muttered.

Folsom backed into the shelter on the cleft, stood up, and care-fully edged forward until he could just see over the boulder. The sun was just edging above the horizon as they went over the top. Now the line of the cliff was back-lit with what to his night-adjusted eyes appeared as full daylight. Down in the cleft, where the sun would not reach until at least May, he knew that it was still pitch dark. He was counting on the gloom in the south-westward-facing cliff to provide as much shelter as the rock.

He watched for a full minute before he caught sight of some-one moving on the top. As he watched, the figure crawled cauti-ously to the edge and peered over. Folsom motioned to McPher-son to raise his carbine. Mac joined him quickly and as Folsom fired a snap shot Mac followed up with a burst. The figure rolled back. Whether or not they had hit him was impossible to tell. Folsom watched for another minute to see if he would try again. McPherson nudged his arm and pointed to the left of where the figure had appeared. A soldier, almost invisible in his green uniform as he slid over the edge into the gloom, caught Fol-som's eye. He nodded to McPherson and together they poured bursts of fire at the figure. But they were too late. The trooper had made it into shelter.

'All right,' Folsom called softly. 'Let's get out of here before they start tossing grenades down.'

McPherson led the way down the cleft, and singly, they made a dash out of the cleft into the shelter of another overhang. No shots were fired after them. The way down would have been no trouble to rested men, but in their exhausted condition the journey was another nightmare of snow-covered rocks and icy sheathing. They moved from cover to cover, never daring to pause for rest as they slipped and slid and climbed down and around the cliff face. Near the base they encountered a sloping pile of rubble that eased the steep descent somewhat, but threw in their path another obstacle of large boulders and chunks of fluted rock that had to be circumnavigated and wriggled through rather than climbed over.

Twenty minutes later they were on the pebbled beach. In spite of their desperate need to go on, Folsom called a rest halt. Teleman sprawled out on his back, barely conscious of the biting cold and snow that lay thickly in the shelter of the fjord. The soft lapping of the waves against the shore less than a hundred yards away belied the fury of the storm, whose final traces they were still experiencing. Teleman lay, gasping for breath. Above him, he realized for the first time that the sky was brightening quickly. The gap of space between the narrow walls was changing to velvet blue and the stars were disappearing from sight. The wavering aurora borealis had all but evaporated in the sunlight, weak as it was. This was the first sunlight he remembered seeing since several hours before he had ejected, and for some reason it felt good. The steadily increasing light gave him a measure of badly needed hope. He sat up. 'Commander,' he croaked, 'I don't even know your first name.'

Folsom rolled over on his side and grinned lopsidedly. 'Hell, you don't do you? It's Pete . . .' And he stuck out his hand.

'Glad to meet you . . . hell of a place for it though.'

Then he remembered: 'How about the radio. Since everyone knows where we are now, maybe you should tell the ship.'

'Yeah . . . Julie, break out the radio and see if you can raise the ship. If not, then the Norwegians. We're gonna need some help, man, and fast."

Gadsen pulled the transceiver out of his pack and, as they started down the beach in a half walk, half trot, began to fiddle with the dials.

'Hell of a note if the Russians get us two miles from the Norwegian base.'

'Don't worry, Major, soon as we round that headland, orders or no orders, I'm going to fire every damn flare I got.'

The low profile of the headlands rose starkly out of the sea off the portside of the U.S.S. *Robert F. Kennedy* as the battle cruiser

ran past the eastern entrance to the fjord. The cruel gray waters
of the Barents Sea were still running heavily and even from two
miles out the bridge crew could make out the dash of spray
rising from the fringing rocks. The fjord was dangerously narrow
for any ship the size of the *RFK*, even one as well equipped
with underwater navigational aids as she was. Only cutters called
at the Norwegian naval air base through the fjord. Larger ships
unloaded, when they had to, in the deep-water port on the Norwegian Sea side and supplies were trucked five miles to the base
on the all-weather road. But for the most part, resupply was
accomplished by aircraft.

At sea the winds were still running an average of thirty-seven
knots, as Larkin had known they would be. Now he sat helplessly,
eight line-of-sight nautical miles away from the shore-based Norwegian help, and he was still powerless to do anything to request
their aid. In addition, they had long since lost the submarine as
it had entered the fjord. He was, however, very certain that the
sub was still deep within the rock walls, and that it was going to
get a very nasty surprise when it tried to leave. But for the
moment there was little or nothing that he could do.

Daylight had come with a vengeance. The aurora borealis had
been driven away by the low-hanging but brilliant sun as it
edged farther across the narrow band of sky for its brief two-
hour appearance. The uncertain light of the aurora borealis had
been almost worse than no light at all. Its constant flickering and
dim glow made firm visual sightings impossible. In spite of this
handicap, Larkin had managed to sketch the outline of the
fjord's mouth on a pad to fix the details in his mind and had
marked in the rough position of both ships. The radar provided
an approximate outline of the fjord walls for a distance of three
miles into the meandering canyon and indicated just enough
room to swing the ship almost on the axis point of her keel. The
sonar confirmed the chart depth markings. There would be
sufficient room beneath her keel. Larkin tapped the pencil on the
pad and made his decision.

'Mr. Bridges, lay a course into the fjord six thousand yards up
from the mouth. We'll swing about and sit there until we see
how things are going to shape up.'

Bridges acknowledged the orders and picked up the microphone to the engine room. Slowly the *RFK* got under weigh
and, at eight knots, began to edge her way carefully into the
mouth of the fjord. Larkin got up from his console and shrugged
into his parka, picked up a pair of binoculars, and went out on to
the catwalk. The night, with the stiff wind, was bitterly cold. He
dialed the proper lenses into place and began to search the fjord
mouth from side to side.

On the eastern flank of the steep rock walls plummeting almost straight down, a cluster of needle-sharp rocks reared up jaggedly from the sea bottom. The glasses showed waves dashing themselves furiously, but in vain, at this miniature bastion. Plumes of spray were probably topping sixty feet, he thought to himself. Those rocks might present a hazard if they possessed an underwater ridge jutting away into the mouth.

The western entrance was clear, at least of visible obstructions. At least two hundred feet separated the nearest possible approach for any underwater ridge extending from the eastern flank from the western walls, which were not quite as sheer in their drop to the water. There was barely enough room to take the battle cruiser through, but it could be done—if done carefully. Beyond the entrance there were only a few indications on the chart that suggested small islands. Once past the entrance, Larkin knew that he would be able to take the battle cruiser anywhere that the submarine could go. He did not trust the map, but he did trust the ability of the Soviet commander.

Twenty minutes later the *Robert F. Kennedy* was gently nosing her way past the entrance. The sonar gear showed an unexpected two hundred feet beneath her keel, even more than normal for Scandinavian fjords on exposed ocean coasts. Bridges was the conn and Larkin, with a microphone conveniently at hand, had again joined the lookouts on the catwalk. The slopes of the fjord slipping past were completely deserted, as they usually were. Only a fool would venture into this hellish terrain in these weather conditions—or even at midsummer for that matter. Not one sign of vegetation marred the granite structure of the walls. In sheltered recesses patches of snow could be seen, and occasionally long sheets of ice reaching from some unseen crevice stretched in a long icicle to the water. The walls on the eastern side were patently unscalable. Larkin knew that, unless the steepness and height of the cliffs grew less the deeper they penetrated, Folsom and his party could very well find themselves stuck on the cliff tops until the helicopter could be launched.

Larkin was heartened somewhat by the fact that the pitch and chop of the ship were lessening inside the fjord. The winds, obstructed by the narrow entrance, were rapidly diminishing in power and it was possible that the helicopter could be launched in a few hours. But for the moment the winds were blowing Force 6, between twenty-five and thirty-one miles per hour, and the waves running to five and six feet in a strange eddy of currents and crosscurrents deflected from the underwater walls. Time—Larkin needed time now more than anything else. What he was going to do when they spotted the submarine, he did not yet know. So far, past the entrance, he had been hugging the steep eastern wall, knowing that he would be invisible to the submarine's sonar as the reflections from the underwater walls scrambled.

The microphone whistled at him.

'Captain, we have a sonar contact, possibly the submarine.'

'Bearing?'

'Dead ahead sir, on the western side. They are not using any ECM at all, so they must not suspect we are around. Range is five thousand yards.'

Larkin thought for a moment. 'Thank you.' He keyed the bridge channel. 'Mr. Bridges, all engines stop. Run a check on the ship status.'

'Aye, sir.'

Larkin turned back to the railing and stared down the fjord. A shallow bend in the fjord wall blocked his view of the submarine less than three miles away. The sonar had picked up the submarine under an outthrust of the wall that did not extend more than a few feet below the water line. With the ship's engines halted, the vicious rocking of the ship became more pronounced in the heavy chop. He watched the eastern wall, gauging to himself the speed at which they were being swept on to the knife-sharp ledges. It was faster than he expected. There was no possibility that they could maintain their position without running the engines. And if they did that, it would be only a matter of time before the submarine picked them up. Anchoring was out of the question. He needed mobility, instantaneous mobility. He could have that by standing outside the entrance and keeping an eye on what the submarine was doing.

For the first time since taking command of the *RFK*, Larkin cursed the fact that she possessed no more than the 1·5-inch salute gun. With a four-inch cannon, or even an anti-aircraft gun, he would have merely steamed around the curve, leveled the cannons, and called for a surrender. With the submarine facing away from them and riding on the surface, he could have blown her out of the water if she resisted.

He almost hammered the railing in a measure of frustration. How in hell could he bring that damned submarine to terms? A boat party was out of the question . . . or was it? Ever since Teleman had been shot down, Larkin had been aching for a chance to take some kind of direct action. Five thousand yards. They could be on that damned submarine before they knew what was happening. If the hatches were closed, as they would be in this chop, a couple of charges of gelignite would take care of that. Lookouts could be dealt with. His mind raced furiously as he forced himself to remain calm. He would need the whaleboat, eight men, carbines, gelignite charges. . . .

'Mr. Bridges, assemble an armed boat party.'

Ten minutes later Larkin sat in the stern sheets of the whale-boat with the tiller under his arm as they pulled away from the almost flush afterdeck. Feeling somewhat like Horatio Hornblower, he had buckled a revolver belt around his waist and stuck a flare pistol in his pocket. On his signal Bridges would bring the *RFK* around the headland and run down on the sub-marine. Unless a second flare was fired, his orders were to run the submarine under. Larkin and Bridges both knew that this was absolutely the last resort in case the armed attack by the nine men failed. The battle cruiser bows, cutting into the hull of the sub-marine, would crumple to the first main bulkhead if that happened. But in any event the submarine would be sitting on the bottom of the fjord. It would then be Bridges' obligation to see that the same thing did not happen to the *RFK*.

Behind him Larkin could hear the coughing of a second whale-boat starting up. Ten men were in that party and they would continue down the fjord to find Folsom's party and render what-ever assistance they could. It was probably a futile effort at best, but at least they had done everything they could. Larkin had sent a message direct to Virginia by satellite relay detailing his plans, but had not waited for a reply. Those short-sighted idiots would probably countermand his decisions.

Larkin took the whaleboat in as close to the narrow beach as he dared before turning parallel. The depth of the fjord made it pos-sible for him to come within twenty yards of the rocky beach. Ahead, the jutting headland that screened the two ships from each other stood out boldly in the weak sunlight. Larkin could have wished for darkness, but he suspected that to wait for the remain-ing hour of daylight to pass could very well be too late. By the time they rounded the headland and came within a thousand yards of the ship, he judged that the sun would be dipping close enough to the horizon so that darkness would be almost complete within the fjord.

As the whaleboat puttered on with the muted roar of its muffled forty-horsepower engine, Larkin felt his own excitement reflecting back from the armed party. Each sat, staring forward, backs stiff with tension and hands firmly clasped around weapons. The gelignite charges were in two packs resting on the floorboards. One of the sailors had his foot resting on the top of the packs and a cord fastening both together looped around his wrist. Larkin reached down and picked his carbine up and ejected the clip, checked it, and then slammed it home. The sharp snap made the sailors jump. Larkin grinned at them and settled back against the thwart, portraying a relaxation he was far from feeling.

He swung the tiller over, turning the bows to pass as close to the headland as possible, and looked back. The sunlight filtering down through the canyon was beginning to wane, but the bows-on silhouette of the *RFK* was sharply etched against the crack of blue-gray sky.

The boat ran on, cutting around the final curve of the rock out-thrust, and cautiously Larkin edged even closer to the rock wall. The noise of the engine was faint, but he wondered if the soft whoosh of the steady wind would be enough to conceal it from the lookouts that would surely be stationed on the sub's bridge.

Before they cleared the final jut of rock, Larkin idled the engine down and let the boat drift, slipping the gears into reverse but keeping the clutch depressed. The whaleboat continued under its own momentum, and there against the far shore was the sail of the submarine. The bows were pointing in toward the eastern side and she seemed to be anchored in the middle of the fjord, although Larkin knew that no skipper in his right mind would anchor under these conditions. Then he heard the muffled chugging of engines. She was using her engines to keep station. Larkin was flabbergasted. She was *not* nuclear powered. Those were diesel engines.

What a lucky break, he thought. If they cut directly across the fjord and approached from the stern the chances of being spotted by the lookouts, who would be watching the eastern cliffs, were remote. And he could make speed. The noise of the submarine's own engines would cover the whaleboat's.

'Watch them very carefully. We're going in.'

Larkin shifted back into forward and let the clutch out in one smooth motion. He pulled the throttle out and felt the reassuring feel of the boat as it leaped ahead. Five minutes. That's all he needed. Five minutes.

He almost got it. They were fifty feet from the submarine's stern when they were spotted. Larkin kept the throttle out until the last moment, as two sailors from the lookout stations came running aft to see who they were. One called out something questioning in Russian that sounded like *Norski*.

'*Ja, Norski*,' he shouted back, promptly exhausting his Norwegian vocabulary. He cut the engine and called softly to his men, 'When I yell go . . . do so. But no shooting unless you have to.'

As they pulled up to the stern a figure appeared on the bridge, took one look, and ducked back out of sight. Larkin could almost hear him frantically calling the bridge.

A line was thrown to the two Russian sailors, who caught it and pulled in. While they were occupied with the rope, Larkin bellowed, '*Go*.'

His own men poured out of the whaleboat and on to the sloping stern to the surprise of the two Russians, who dropped the rope and reached for their slung rifles. They never had a chance. It seemed that half a dozen carbine butts hit all at once. They dropped without a sound.

Larkin leaped on to the stern and immediately felt a vibration run through the ship as the beat of the engines deepened at the same time.

'Get those charges set!' From forward and the bridge simultaneously came the sound of hatches slamming shut.

'Peterson, you and Johnson take the aft hatch. Orlowski and Brone get a charge against that ballast tank, where it joins the hull five feet for'ard the hatch. Move!'

As the men jumped on to the decking with the demolition charges, Larkin could feel the submarine begin to move. He knew that it would take less than thirty seconds to get up enough weigh and ballast to get the decks under water.

He yelled at the remaining four men and ran for the sail and bolted up the ladder. The bridge was clear, all hatches battened down.

'Two of you up on the lookout. The rest, get around the sides, out of sight.'

Larkin backed away rapidly. He knew that when the charges went off somebody was going to come out of that hatch, and they would probably come out shooting. He waved the two men now on the catwalk to watch the forward hatch.

'Anybody comes out, open up.'

He glanced around quickly and swung back down over the side to see how the demolition parties were coming. Both were running for the bridge, the ignition wires trailing out behind them to the charges taped against the hatch and ballast tank.

Larkin hopped back on to the bridge and shouted down to fire the charges. Already the after portion of the deck was under water and forward, waves were curling up around the forepeak.

The explosives went off with a resounding clang. The submarine shuddered along its length and the engines changed beat as he heard the high-pitched whoosh of compressed air blowing ballast from the tanks.

Larkin yanked the VERY pistol from his belt and fired the flare straight up into the rapidly darkening sky. The flare arced up to three hundred feet and burst with a beautiful display of red flame. In less than two minutes the *RFK* should burst around the head-land.

He broke open the pistol, ejected the second flare, and rammed a new one home. Larkin had estimated that it would take the *RFK* six minutes or so to reach the submarine. He had managed to stop the submarine; now could he capture it before the *RFK* smashed it to the bottom under her forefoot?

He leaned over the coaming once more and shouted down. 'Peterson, you and Johnson get back to the boat and be ready to take us off. Orlowski, you and Brone cover that aft hatch, just in case.'

He swung around in time to hear the squeal of the hatch being opened, and drew his pistol with his right hand. He waved the others back around the curve of the bridge. The hatch cracked open, held a moment, then pushed farther up. Larkin knelt down, almost in back of the hatch, and waited. From where he knelt, he was out of sight. A head appeared, looked around, and, seeing no one, pushed the hatch back until the lift engaged and it clicked back. Larkin leaned forward and pressed the pistol muzzle into the temple of the emerging sailor.

Larkin had never seen anyone turn white so fast, and in spite of the tension he grinned.

'*Strasvechi, tovarish—Americanski.*' Then in English, 'Do you speak English?'

Very carefully the head wobbled back and forth in what Larkin took for a negative answer. The sailor, with the .445 Navy Colt pressed against his temple, looked ready to faint.

'*Nyet,*' he managed to force out.

Above his head, Larkin heard two carbines firing.

'What's going on?' he demanded sharply.

'Trying to get out of the forward hatch, sir. We fired a couple of bursts across the deck and they changed their minds.'

'Good, keep 'em scared.'

Larkin risked a quick look at his watch. Four minutes to go. 'Any sign of the ship?' he yelled.

'No, sir . . . wait, aye, sir, just rounding the headland now.'

'Anybody down there speak English?' Larkin called through the hatch.

After a moment, a voice answered, 'Yes.'

Larkin tapped the sailor on the head with the pistol butt. 'Down, buddy. . . . All right, get up here fast.'

A minor commotion was created in the narrow hatchway as the reprieved sailor scrambled down past the other climbing up. Another minute was wasted while he did so.

Larkin waved his pistol and an officer climbed out to stare around in shock. The Russian was dressed only in shipboard uniform and gasped as he felt the cold. He immediately huddled against the canvas windbreak that had been rigged on the bridge.

'My name is Larkin, commanding officer of the battle cruiser *Robert F. Kennedy*, United States Navy. You are now a prisoner of war and your ship a prize of war.' Larkin knew that this was not true since no state of war had been declared, but he was depending on the shock value of the statement to unbalance the Russian even more.

The Russian glanced around and saw the others with leveled carbines, gulped once, and swung back to stare at Larkin, who was casually slinging his carbine over his shoulder.

'I . . . I . . . I am Ptior Shafesky Rasnikov, Lieutenant Commander . . .' He broke down and finished up lamely, 'Executive Officer . . . what are you—'

'Cut it,' Larkin grated harshly. 'You have just two minutes left to surrender this ship. Look out there.'

The Russian officer followed Larkin's pointing finger and saw the *RFK* running at full speed for the submarine, less than 1500 yards off. His eyes, as they turned back to Larkin, were round with surprise.

Larkin waved the flare gun in his left hand. 'Two minutes. If I don't fire a flare before then, she'll run you under.'

It took a full half minute for Rasnikov to digest what Larkin had just said, and then he swung around and grabbed the bridge microphone and shouted a stream of incomprehensible Russian. The sounds that emerged from the speaker were just as incomprehensible, but seconds later Larkin heard feet scrabbling on the ladder. He jumped to the hatch and pulled it loose, but Rasnikov screamed at him to stop.

'The Captain . . .' he explained weakly.

A slim figure jumped from the hatch, brushed past Larkin, and leaned across the railing to peer at the approaching *RFK*.

The *RFK* had come to within two hundred yards and every detail behind the ports of the lighted bridge was plainly visible. The curling bow wave served to accentuate the sharpness of the prow, aimed directly for the submarine's bridge.

The Russian captain stiffened, and turned slowly to face Larkin. As they stood there examining each other, Larkin sensed the shock that he knew must come with the knowledge of a ship lost. He thought that perhaps he must have come close to this same feeling the day he had run in under the North Vietnamese coastal guns and taken that hit in the fantail.

Slowly the Russian nodded and turned his palms outward. He said something in Russian and the executive officer translated.

'We surrender,' he said quietly. Larkin looked sharply at the Russian officer. He was certain that the captain had said *I*. The *we* surrender was indicative to Larkin of both discipline and ability. He nodded with approval and raised the VERY pistol and fired the second flare.

Twenty minutes later Larkin was climbing the netting thrown

over the side of the *RFK*. Behind him, on the deck and bridge of
the submarine, *RFK* crew members were herding the Russian
crew up on deck and filing down into the submarine. As he
regained the deck he looked down the fjord, then back at the
Russian captain clambering up after him. Suddenly he jerked his
eyes back to the fjord. There against the sky a red flare was climbing. Seconds later it was followed by a third and then a fourth.
Forgetting about the Russians, he ran for the bridge.

As he came through the hatch Bridges swung around on him.
'Captain, flares at 8563 yards down the fjord. Our recognition
signal—one long, two short. We had part of a radio transmission
a minute ago. They need fire support.'

Larkin did not hesitate. 'Answer fast. Plot the range and get me
an open channel to Virginia.' Seconds later he was explaining
quickly the capture of the Russian ship and advising official contact with the Norwegians before he had to contact them.


## CHAPTER TWENTY-ONE

A SICK FEELING of despair settled over Folsom as Gadsen
struggled with the radio to raise the ship. Each time he flicked
the switch over to receive, a steady stream of hissing poured from
the speaker.

'Damn it all, it's no use,' Gadsen said bitterly. 'The aurora is
blanking everything out.'

The problem that had been nagging at Folsom throughout the
night and into the early morning hours now burst upon him. It
had been the intensity of the northern lights, the aurora borealis.
The stream of electrons pouring into the magnetic field of the
earth from the sun was probably causing a world-wide disruption
of radio transmission—at least for all communications depending
upon ionospheric bounce. For all practical purposes, under the
onslaught of the solar storm, there was no ionosphere right now.

'Any chance of getting through at all?'

Gadsen settled his carbine on his shoulder, slung the radio set
around his neck, and began to play with the transmit switch,
flicking it back and forth in code pattern. 'Maybe we can stir up
some interest in a code,' he muttered.

The jerky gait over the rocky beach of the fjord did not help
Gadsen any and twice he stumbled as he concentrated on the
radio. After a few minutes he switched to receive.

'Nothing,' he said over the hiss of static. 'Damned thing is
useless for now.'

Darkness was falling swiftly now. Only a few brief glimpses

of light were visible over the top of the eastern wall. Folsom glanced back and saw Teleman stumbling along, half carried by McPherson. There was nothing yet visible of the pursuing Russians and they had almost reached the headland. They had gained at least five hundred yards, but Folsom knew that, as soon as the Russians reached the beach, they would come on with twice the speed his people were able to make.

Grimly he concentrated on reaching the mass of rock that would furnish them a small measure of cover, perhaps enough for the last mile to the Norwegian naval base. He only hoped to God that flares would attract attention in time for the Norwegians to get a boat across the fjord to pick them up. Maybe, just maybe, the Russians would not pass the headlands. But he doubted it. With the wind blowing straight down the fjord they could hold a major gun battle, complete with artillery, within sight of the Norwegians and not be heard. Again he looked back the way they had come and this time saw that Teleman had fallen and McPherson was wearily trying to get him up.

'Go on, Julie . . . the headland . . .'

Folsom ran back to where Teleman was still on the ground. As he came up, McPherson had stooped down and was trying to lift him in a shoulder carry. But Mac had pushed himself too far. Even this last effort was too much for the giant reserve of strength he had inherited from his Scotch ancestry.

Folsom slid to a stop, panting too heavily to speak. Teleman opened his eyes and saw Folsom bending over him.

'Seems I see you from . . . this position . . . quite a . . . bit . . .'

Folsom grinned in spite of himself and rummaged in the pocket of the parka and came up with the aluminium tube of Benzedrine tablets. Teleman stared at them, then nodded. 'Yeah . . .'

Folsom willed his shaking hands steady as he uncapped the tube and poured out two tablets each for Teleman, McPherson, and himself. Mac unstoppered his canteen and they choked the pills down.

Teleman sank back down. 'You may deliver a dead pilot, but at least you'll deliver a pilot,' he whispered.

Folsom smiled, feeling very small and weak in the face of the endurance and courage the man on the ground in front of him had shown. 'You'll be alive, or none of us will be.'

Mac got ponderously to his feet and bent and helped Teleman up. Already, in their weakened condition, they were beginning to feel the effects of the pills. To Teleman the vile taste of the half-chewed capsules was the first real indication of returning sensation he had felt in hours of trudging through the sub-zero cold. The taste of the capsules also increased his thirst, but as the effects of the pills heightened the taste was soon forgotten.

As his mind cleared he felt a measure of strength returning. The misty edge of unconsciousness began to recede somewhat and, like the others, he began to run in a jerky half trot. Shortly, as they approached the mass of rock that marked the headland, he lost all sense of weariness. He knew it would not last long. His only hope was to hang on until he could obtain medical care, before his heart burst from the overload. He put aside all thoughts of what might happen and concentrated on moving ahead as fast as possible while he could.

As they caught up with Gadsen, Folsom handed him two pills and without a word they trotted on.

They passed the headlands and came out on to a long, straight stretch that disappeared around a sharp curve in the fjord, three miles north. Folsom cursed violently and yanked the map out. The beach to the headland was accurately marked, but the area beyond showed no long stretch of beach, merely a short bend to the east and then the naval base on the western side of the fjord. Folsom threw his head back and breathed deeply through his mouth, fighting to control a futile anger. The damnable chart had been wrong, wrong all across the island. This time it was so wrong it would kill them.

They could never clear the three miles of beach before the Russians overtook them. They did not have the strength. Goddamn it all, he swore savagely to himself, we could have stayed in the tent and gone peacefully back to Murmansk and saved all this trouble.

The effects of the Benzedrine tablets still held them, but Gadsen, Teleman, and McPherson stood in a stupefied circle around Folsom waiting for his decision. He recalled what he had told Teleman only minutes before—'You'll be alive, or none of us will be.'

'Come on. Let's go.'

Darkness had fallen completely and their old comrade the aurora borealis was again triumphant in the night sky to light their way. They had covered nearly a mile when the sound of a rolling explosion reached them. As one man, they came to a halt, ears straining forward. No other sound came, merely the echoes of the boom.

Folsom did not wait. He grabbed the VERY pistol and fired a flare straight up. Then they broke into a run. Folsom fired a second and a third in their recognition signal. It could have been the Russian submarine he knew, and then again it could have been the Norwegians, or even the *RFK*. In any event, it no longer mattered. Twice more, at four-minute intervals, Folsom fired flares in patterns, and each time, as they ran, their eyes fastened on the line of cliffs to the north.

On the fifth volley an answering pattern ascended into the night sky, low over the cliffs, two short and one long intervals. If they had had the breath, they would have cheered. Instead, they ran even faster, though the effects of the Benzedrine tablets were beginning to wear off.

Ten minutes later the first bullets kicked up sand and pebbles beneath their feet. Without breaking stride, Gadsen swung the radio up and frantically began to call their ID in the hope that, somehow, he could punch through.

'Down,' Folsom yelled.

The open beach offered no shelter of any kind. Their only hope now was to hold the Russians at a distance where their bodies, lying prone, would offer an almost impossible target. McPherson hit the ground in a firing position, the sling of his carbine already wrapped around his forearm in manual-approved fashion. Carefully he selected his targets and snapped off shots. The distance was too far for rapid fire; it would only waste the remaining ammunition already pretty well exhausted by the two previous actions. Folsom and Teleman followed suit, and at least had the satisfaction of seeing the approaching Russians drop to the beach, although whether from strikes or for cover they had no way of telling.

Folsom rolled half over, 'Any luck with that damned radio?'

'Nothing.'

He reached under his parka and extracted the flare pistol. He had two cartridges left. Just as he brought the pistol into firing position, Gadsen's voice screamed excitedly:

'I got 'em, for a moment, Commander.'

'Fox Baker, read you loud . . . under fire . . . do you need support?'

Gadsen twirled the gain to maximum, and there, on the rock-strewn beach of a deserted Norwegian fjord, Folsom, Teleman, McPherson, and Gadsen heard the most beautiful sound of their lives to date—the flat tones of the ship's radio operator.

'. . . flare . . . pinpoint . . . your . . .' The rest was lost in the roar of static. Seconds later Folsom fired the next-to-last flare and all three watched as the thin trail of red formed the stalk of a blossoming rose. As it faded Folsom fired the last for good measure.

'Now, run like hell,' he roared.

The four men ran as they had never run before. They pounded down the rocky beach, skirting along the water's edge where the footing was firm. The breath whistled in their lungs as they ran, ran with the desperation of life itself. Behind them the Russians were running also, no longer firing, but running to overtake them. In spite of efforts that came with an impetus from their innermost beings, the Americans were losing ground. The pursuing Russians, fresher by many days of sleep, were less than two hundred yards behind when the first salvo of rockets screamed in to explode across the beach and out into the fjord. Almost immediately a second salvo followed twenty yards to the rear of the first, and then a third and fourth salvo, each moving back on the Russian troops, who broke and ran for the cover of the cliffs. It seemed almost as if the fire control officer on board the *RFK* could see his target. A rain, a curtain of fire exploded behind them, the concussions hammering at their bodies while the air filled with the continual roar of exploding missiles.

They ran on, Teleman straining every last ounce of energy he possessed to keep up. Then, as suddenly as it began, the fire died away, and behind them they could see the stick figures of the Russians up and running after them again. The rock walls of the cliffs had furnished sufficient protection from the missile fire and they came on unharmed.

Teleman suddenly became aware that bullets were kicking up the beach around them again. He flattened, threw a glance over his shoulder, but Gadsen was past and running back before he could stop him. Teleman saw Julie's slight figure go to one knee, heard the sharp crack as he began firing rapidly. The lead figure screamed, threw up his hands, and tumbled headlong. Bullets smacked around Gadsen with curious popping noises, but he continued to fire coolly, the crack, crack, crack of his AR-18 abnormally loud in the cold air.

Folsom yelled at Teleman to run and he, himself, turned, his rifle blazing toward the Russians. Teleman heard the faint *plat* of the bullet that struck Gadsen and knocked him backward across the beach. As if at a great distance, he heard someone ask if Gadsen was dead and realized that is was his own voice. Folsom screamed at him, but he saw from the angular position of Julie's body, where it lay at the water's edge, that he was dead.

Nothing exploded inside his brain, no galvanizing fury flung him at the Russians. Instead a cold fury at the entire foolish system that was responsible for this man's death took hold of him. He cocked the Russian submachine gun he was carrying and walked back down the beach, away from Julie's body. The submachine gun kicked in his hands and he saw the line of Russians hesitate, then scatter to the right and left. He tripped over a rock and fell headlong. He put his head down on the cold snow and knew that he would never run another step from where he lay. His frustration came out a harsh scream. Folsom and McPherson dropped down beside him and began firing at the zigzagging figures that, in spite of the barrage, seemed to pass through untouched.

McPherson emptied a clip at the approaching Russians and rammed a new one home. Carefully he picked his targets as Folsom kept up a continual line of fire to keep the approaching soldiers off balance. McPherson sighted carefully and fired and watched as the soldier in his sights disappeared, his rifle flying from his hands. Then a bullet struck him in the cheek and tore through his shoulder.

Without thinking, Teleman threw away his empty Russian submachine gun and scrabbled for McPherson's carbine. He fired twelve shots, closely spaced, but very carefully, and thought he hit one.

The answering fire was striking ever closer now. The Russians were less than a hundred yards away and still they came on, four left, crouching low and running swiftly forward, firing as they came. These were no sailors, Folsom realized, but trained soldiers, probably marines.

A bullet kicked stone chips and snow in Teleman's face, forcing him to jerk his head away. He rubbed viciously at his eyes to clear them and swung back, but the Russians had turned and were running back to the south.

Teleman, stunned, rolled to see Folsom staring after the Russians. Then they heard the heavy, staccato bark of automatic weapons behind them. Both turned to see blue-jacketed sailors pouring from a beached whaleboat. Disbelieving, Teleman got to his knees as sailors rushed past them after the fleeing Russians. Then he and Folsom began to laugh, both with great tearing gasps that were almost sobs. They were still laughing when the chief petty officer ran up to be confronted with the spectacle of his executive officer alternately laughing and sobbing, his arms around a gaunt scarecrow of a man with a bandaged head.

## *Author's Note*

THE NORTH CAPE of Norway is perhaps at once the most beautiful and the most savage of lands on this planet. In summer it becomes a rendezvous point for devotees of the midnight sun who come as tourists to view the endless daylight of midsummer from this northernmost point on the Scandinavian Peninsula. But in winter the Cape is deserted of all but the fishermen and their families who occupy its handful of fishing villages. Only they are able to survive the rigors of its sub-zero cold and the Arctic storms that rage down from the Great Barrier two hundred miles north.

In these days of developing international maturity, which are more often expressed through individuals rather than their governments, no part of the world, no matter how isolated or desolate, is free from the complications of national competition for that hegemony called national security.

I wish to thank certain people for their cheerful assistance with this book. First of all, Susan my wife, for her unflagging encouragement and devotion to the typing and editing chores; then to Lieutenant Colonel Robert Gillon of the United States Marine Corp, a seventy-three-mission fighter pilot veteran of Vietnam for reading the manuscript and advising on and correcting the technical aspects; to Olin Witthoft, my good friend and capable representative of United Aircrafts' Pratt & Whitney Aircraft Division, who spent many hours with me working out the technical details of the A-17 aircraft; and to John Shell, Ph.D. and associate director of the Institute of Pharmaceutical Chemistry, for his analysis of the effects of the amphetamine and lysergic acid families of drugs under conditions of physical exhaustion and sub-zero temperatures. And, finally, for assistance in coming to know and describe properly the North Cape area and its weather, both the Royal Norwegian Government and the United States Navy.

J. POYER

# THE HAWSER
# PIRATES

Oswald Wynd

'The Hawser Pirates' is published by
Cassell and Co. Ltd.

## The Author

Oswald Wynd was born in 1913 in Tokyo where his parents worked for an American mission. He joined the army on the outbreak of war and was attached to an Indian Army Brigade on the east coast of the Malayan Peninsula. He was a Japanese P.O.W. for three and a half years and received a Mention in Despatches for work done as an interpreter for prisoners. Oswald Wynd has written a number of books including the Doubleday $20,000 prize novel of 1947 and *Walk Softly, Men Praying* (Cassell 1967) and he now writes for a living at his Scottish coastal home in Crail, Fife.

To Nicholas Flower

# PROLOGUE

BERT WHELAN turned away from the helipad and went down a flight of iron stairs to the lower deck. At the foot of these he shouted after the radio operator: 'Who is it wants me?'

The answer was shouted back.

'Tug. On radio telephone.'

'What's wrong now?'

The radio man didn't either know or care. He disappeared through a door, leaving it open behind him. Bert's feet clanged on the metal gangway. Ahead, through thick, wave-resistant glass, he could just see the tug's flat, elongated stern deck, with the tow-cable stretching back from a winch for six hundred yards to a Y-join connection from the rig's corner turrets.

The radio man had gone back to a control panel. He was lighting a cigarette. A tin tray beside him, a tobacco company's issue to pubs, was full of stubs. He didn't look at the rig's navigational officer. Most of the time the crew on this two-acre floating monstrosity contrived not to look at their navigational officer. He was there because the new regulations required his presence as a safety precaution. Bert knew perfectly well that no one on the rig thought he contributed much towards their safety. Privately he agreed with them.

On a flat table built in against another thick glass window was a telephone left off the hooks. There was also a chair and Bert sat in it. He put out a hand.

'Rig calling *Saturn*. Whelan here. What is it?'

'Hang on. I'll get the Captain.'

The voice was casual. Whatever discipline was maintained on the tug it wasn't the kind that Bert had been accustomed to in twenty years of holding a Master's ticket. He waited, thinking again of those twenty years, three as Third Officer, eleven as Second, and the last six as First Mate. But never a command. He woke in the night sometimes to damn the Benson Line for their rationalization, for the switch from ten thousand tonners to much larger and fewer bulk carriers, something that had played hell with promotion prospects in the company. In the London offices they called the new ships bottoms, which was about what they were, floating tanks, automated for both navigation and cargo handling. At an annual general meeting the Chairman of Benson's had talked about a satisfactory re-absorption rate of redundant personnel. Bert had been one of the sacked who had been re-absorbed . . . on to an oil rig.

'Captain Underson here.'

It was a flat, clipped voice, on the quiet side, almost totally

without any identification mark of accent. If this tugboater with
his slightly foreign sounding name had actually been born and
raised somewhere in Britain, experience of serving all over the
world had sandpapered away traces of origin. In Australia, New
York, or Galveston, no one would have any excuse to call him a
Limey.

The *Saturn*'s Master and the rig's navigational officer had never
actually met, the nearest they had come to it being a scene with
loud hailers in which Underson had been a compact, small-
seeming figure using an amplifier from the tug's tower platform,
and giving orders. Queries from the rig he contrived not to answer
himself.

Bert cleared his throat. 'If you're calling me to say there's a
Force Six brewing, I get the weather reports, too. We had Force
Seven at the backside of Harris and we're through the Pentland
Firth now. So what?'

'I'm casting tow,' Underson said.

'You mean something's gone wrong with your hawser?'

'No. We're leaving you.'

For a moment Bert just stared through the glass.

'And what am I supposed to say to that?'

'I don't know. I expect a number of people will say quite a lot.
I can't help that. This is an emergency.'

'What's an emergency, for God's sake?'

'You'll get it all from your radio man if he's been listening.
A forty-thousand-ton tanker with a full load from the Gulf of
Mexico to Grangemouth drifting straight towards the Old Man
of Hoy and the two-hundred-feet cliffs behind it. Engine failure.'

'How does that affect us?'

'I'm going to that ship.'

'Like hell you are! The rig manager will have something to
say about this.'

'I'm sure. I rang to tell you to put down your anchors. Our
fathom reading says twenty-two. You'll be all right.'

'We'll be *what*? We're a hundred and fifty miles from exploration area!'

'I know. I also know that if the *Mary Worth* goes on those
rocks it'll be another *Torrey Canyon,* with the biggest oil slick
yet seen heading straight for Scotland. Not to mention what'll
happen to her crew. I'm certainly the nearest tug. Probably by
five hundred miles.'

'So we just put down anchors and wait for you?'

'Yes. Why not?'

'I'll tell you why not! Because you're under contract to take
us from the Clyde to a point in the North Sea where we begin
operations. And I'll tell you something else, Underson. I know

what you're getting paid for this job. It's twenty-five thousand quid.'

'The gossip gets around, doesn't it?'

'It'll be more than gossip if you dump us! You'll never get another rig tow anywhere!'

'I don't really like this work.'

'Now you listen to me . . .'

'I have been for some minutes. I'd prefer it if you didn't shout into your mouthpiece.'

'God! I can see what you're after. Engine failure! If you get that ship to port the salvage award . . .'

'We won't go into that. My motives are humanitarian.'

'Says the man laughing!'

'I'm not laughing. If it's blowing Eight when we get there we'll have quite a time with the *Mary Worth*. I'll have to pull her through the Pentland Firth to Kirkwall. When I've done that we'll rejoin you.'

'You'll find a Dutch tug out in front taking us on to exploration point one. And a breach of contract suit slapped down on your company. Not for twenty-five thousand, either. You'll be putting this rig in jeopardy. That's a matter of millions. How are your owners going to like that?'

'The very thought of their reaction puts grey in my hair '

'If you think you can be funny about this . . .'

Bert turned to the radio operator.

'Get the rig manager. Quick!'

'I heard that,' Underson said. 'I've had enough shouting for one afternoon.'

'Believe me, the shouting's only started. It'll be to London next. There's going to be a big roaring.'

'I'm sure. I'll sign off, Whelan. Consider this as a test of the rig under minor stress conditions. You've got as good a hold for your anchors as you'll have off Peterhead. Once you're out there Force Ten will be routine. Not to mention hurricane strength as a recurring possibility. So if your anchors don't hold or you lose stability with Six you'd better claim on the builders. I'm winching in tow-cable now. In ten minutes you'll be on your own.'

'Wait . . . !'

The line went dead. Bert Whelan, staring through the window in front of him, saw froth at the *Saturn*'s stern. The tow-cable slackened, then went into the sea. He sat with his hands flat out on the deal table, aware of his anger as part of the rig's tensions. He wasn't really identified with these, just trapped in them.

The *Discovery* was one of the biggest of her kind ever built, two acres designed to carry a three thousand ton drilling load, this mounted on submerged ballast tanks to give the artificial

island stability enough to continue operations under gale conditions. She had cost six million to build, the order for her placed
as part of the pretty wild gamble that tertiary rock off the northeastern Scottish coast held oil. A great deal of the world's oil has
been found in tertiary rock, but also, there is a great deal of
tertiary rock in which there is no oil, a fact that made company
executives assigned to the *Discovery* project tend to wake up to
attacks of migraine.

Top brass, when really nervous, keeps moving. Even with the
rig at sea there was no escaping those executives; they used the
helipad like a bus stop, with almost continual chopper noise
announcing the arrival of the third Vice-President from Dallas,
or representatives of the builders, or the manager of the London
office, or a mixture of all three. The rig's scratch crew played
poker and the important visitors all ignored the navigational
officer who was really unnecessary, simply put there as a result of
threatened government legislation, with the authority to drop
anchors when told to, and pull them up again when ordered.

'You wanted me, Whelan?'

Bert turned. The rig manager had arrived on board yesterday
when they were just off Dunnet Head and he looked as though
he had plans to spend this evening with his wife in an Aberdeen
hotel, all at company expense via helicopter taxi. He was a big
man, wearing a duffel coat and white crash helmet. He had been
in oil for twenty-five years, boring for it in Mexico, Texas and
Borneo before present policy lunacies forced him out on to water.
He didn't like working over water, or the current odds against
success, and a new set of stress wrinkles kept his expression dialled
to near permanent rage.

The radio operator edged past the rig manager and went to
a chair. He sat with his back turned and lit a cigarette, neutral
and calm. Bert's anger had now quite gone. He had the feeling
of having wasted much of his life in indignations from which
others had profited. In a normal voice he explained what had
happened, while the man in the doorway stood hunched, hands
shoved down into his pockets. When he finally spoke it was to
the radio operator.

'Get shore relay. I want London on R.T. Now!'

He turned back to Bert. 'Whelan, have you any idea what
delays cost the company when the rig is manned and operational?'

'No.'

'Seven pounds a minute. Over ten thousand a day. It's a pity
you weren't able to tell our tug captain that. It might have made
him think again. What are the chances of his answering our call?'

'Poor. He's signed off.'

'A loud hailer, then? He's near enough.'

'You could try,' Bert said.

The rig manager stared. 'I like your determination, Whelan.' He went out. Bert sat on, listening to the radio operator chatting with the relay station, neither party in any hurry over a rush call. Through thick plate glass he could just hear the whine of the tug's electric winches at the job of reeling in tow-cable.

The *Saturn* was eighteen hundred tons gross and the diesels packed into that steel hull had practically enough horsepower to pull an up-ended Empire State Building across the Atlantic unaided. She was only two years out from the Bremen shipyard who had built her for British owners; the tug registered in London, and operated on a free-lance basis throughout the oceans of the world under a marine upstart who thought he was God, called Mark Underson.

Tugs used to come into the world looking as though they expected to be unloved, hoping to get by with nothing more than an aggressive truculence. But there is a new breed. The *Saturn* wasn't squat and she didn't have a dumpy funnel behind a sentry box wheel-house, featuring instead twin sixty-foot towers that rose, tapering slightly inwards, just aft of her bridge. Between these, high up, was slung a fire-fighting platform which also served as a searchlight mounting. One of the towers took off engine exhaust, the other provided internal steel ladder access to the platform, as well as storage for the hose pipes. There was also another feature Bert had looked at often, though never seen in use, a flat midships deck carrying two boats which could be swung out to reveal a properly marked helipad. Throughout the entire long tow the *Saturn* had worn those boats tucked inboard like a wide-hipped virgin holding her thighs together tight, resisting any outside interference. The tug ignored the helicopter comings and goings over on the rig. You could talk to her by a number of methods, but only talk.

Now she wasn't even accepting talk, only listening and watching. Her radar reflector revolved at a low, almost indolent 20 r.p.m., an extra eye not needed on a day with visibility at twelve. Bert sat on, half hypnotized, seeing that whipped foam putting a topping on low waves without crests, thinking about the tug's advanced technological equipment which probably included computer controlled course setting and automatic coffee dispensers. Those bastards had it all ways, together with a take-home pay that would put winch operators, after bonus payments, into the executive earning bracket. Twenty-five thousand quid for a tow that was a fill-in job between the really lucrative deals! And they were now off after one of these, shivering in anticipation from altered engine revs, ending the boredom of a five-knot haul. Over there on the *Saturn*'s bridge her captain was probably laughing.

# CHAPTER ONE

THE *Semirande* rolled on the great Atlantic swells, her fat belly thrust deep in the water, not moving over the sea so much as held solidly in it, subject to every detail of turbulence and responding with a personal contribution from deep sunk, thrusting propellers.

'Like being in bed with a good woman,' Jules told himself, as he had many times before. All the crew had heard that one, too often.

The Captain had his hands on the rail, body rigid to the ship's movement, as though his feet were riveted to the decking. It had taken him long enough to get where he now was, in command of his tug, years of crawling up and down the coasts of France and the Low Countries, towing strings of bloody barges. He had been doing that when Hitler came and went on doing it, working for old Henri Plentin, a collaborationist if there ever was one. Though the old fox had escaped the label.

Jules Dartan spat into the Atlantic. In early autumn you could still smell ice up in these waters, ice in the form of vast, uncharted islands floating at the centre of a defensive screen of fog. It wasn't quite fog tonight, but the haze was there and would thicken. With radar you were supposed to be secure against the ice mountains, adequately warned, but somehow Jules had never been able to trust that little screen with the rotation through it, keeping the feeling that like all instruments it could fail, suddenly landing you in one of those panics which young sailors these days didn't even consider, of ice right there only two ship lengths ahead, the mass of it even on the blackest nights having a kind of light of its own, a soft glowing. Jules could remember these times from a boyhood in trawlers, the ring of the engine-room telegraph, that shouted order for full speed astern, the ship trembling its way back from danger while all the time in everyone's mind was the thought of long, submerged, greenish tentacles groping with dagger claws to tear through a double bottom.

He turned, seeming almost to unanchor himself from the narrow strip of boarded deck. His eyes focused on a brass plaque by a door in the bulkhead and under an iron-barred, thick-glassed oyster. This said that the *Semirande* had been built by the Duprez Bergac yard at St Nazaire and launched in 1961. It did not say that at the time of her commissioning the tug, of 1,270 gross tons, with diesels of 4,800 horse-power, had been the largest and most powerful of her kind afloat, France's bid via the

Plentin Company to challenge Dutch, American and Greek interests in the area of deep-sea salvage. It did not say, either, that she had been almost two-thirds paid for by government subsidy which old Henri Plentin had somehow wangled through deputies under his control. The gamble had been successful enough to make the major Dutch company offer considerably in excess of the builder's price a full five years later just to bring the *Semirande* under the Netherlands flag and eliminate her as a rival. But the *Semirande* had continued to sail under the Tricolour.

He pulled back the door and warm air from the chartroom smacked him in the face, much too warm air. Periodically Jules issued orders for the heating to be reduced, and it was for a day or two, then crept up again to something equivalent to a Paris luxury hotel in January, warm enough for tropical pot plants. He stood inhaling the strong smell of paint being blistered off hot pipes to which was added the usual reminders of the cook's gastronomic failures which somehow got into the ventilating system for circulation to all decks. On the *Semirande* you weren't allowed to forget the day's meals even after your stomach had managed to digest them.

Jules went through the chartroom and out on to the bridge. Tourin, the Second Mate, and the helmsman, were both peering through glass at the pitch-dark night as though hypnotized by their efforts to see something. Tourin was a Breton, twenty-eight years of age, who thought it was time he was made a First, though nobody else did.

'There could be ice about,' Jules said.

The Second's head turned. 'Nothing on radar.'

It was difficult not to react to that. If this boy had seen a berg it would be on film. Useless to try and explain how it felt to be just under a towering mass from which a chunk the size of a four-storey building could suddenly detach itself to crash into the sea, causing minor tidal waves and a cloud spray liberally laced with knife splinters of frozen salt water.

Jules went back into the chartroom, found his pipe, went on into a passage and down steep stairs to his cabin. He didn't bother to switch on a light, groping for a bottle of cognac in a top drawer, then getting his tooth glass from its holder by the basin. He went next door and knocked.

Berand hadn't quite finished hiding something.

'One day they're going to catch you at it!' Jules roared.

The First Mate said nothing. He reached under a crumpled blanket beside him on the berth and pulled out a round embroidery frame. On stretched canvas a design was half-finished. He found his silks and started to work again.

'We're having a drink,' Jules said.

'I'm on watch in an hour.'

'To hell with it. The ship's been put on automatic pilot and the radar's our eyes. So Tourin tells me. You know, Berand, I can't like that boy. Never been able to. Why?'

'He doesn't like himself.'

'And you? Do you like yourself?'

Berand shoved in a needle and pulled it out again.

'Moderately.'

Jules braced against a roll.

'Moderately! I'll give you a moderate brandy, eh?'

'That's the way I like it. With water.'

Jules balanced two glasses in the bottom of the handbasin, poured dollops in both, carefully propped the bottle against a bulkhead, and added water to one drink. He put a glass on a shelf near the Mate and held the other, sitting down on the bunk. For a moment he stared at embroidery.

'You know, Berand, you're an awful old hen. I don't know why I've put up with you all these years.'

'I'm your audience and your nurse.'

'My what? Did you say *nurse*?'

'Sure.'

The needle went in and out.

'So you think you look after me, eh? How?'

'I get you out of fights and brothels.'

Jules thought for a moment, then said: 'By God, you do.'

'At your age it's time the fights stopped. I don't know whether you've noticed, but you haven't been coming out of them too well recently.'

'Who says?'

Berand reached for his glass, took a small sip, then put it back on the shelf. 'I was thinking of Rotterdam,' he said.

Jules stared at the floor.

'That pup Underson.'

'That pup only gave up his plan to put you in hospital when he realized you were old enough to be his father.'

Jules emptied his tumbler, stood, and poured more into the glass. 'I'm not old enough to be Underson's father. Anyway, he shouldn't have left his wife in a place like that.'

'It was in a café. And we all have to leave our wives alone at times.'

'You know what I mean, Berand. She didn't look like anyone's wife.'

'She looked like a perfectly nice girl to me. Maybe your eyesight isn't what it was.'

'Damn you! Stop trying to get at me. Anyway, you know nothing about women.'

'I've been married to one for twenty-seven years.'

'I meant whores.'

'I see a good deal of them, too. When I'm collecting you.'

Jules began to laugh. He leaned back against a locker. Berand looked up, then returned his eyes to needlework.

'Well, aren't you going to ask me what's funny?'

'No.'

Jules came over and sat on the bunk again.

'That time in Dakar. The two girls. We couldn't make 'em understand you wouldn't. No French. Fresh from a tribe or something. I had to take 'em both. Remember?'

'I also remember that I took the *Semirande* to sea. It was two days before you came up on the bridge.'

'Something I ate.'

'Prostration.'

'That's a bloody lie!'

Jules leaned forward, elbows on knees, glass in two fists, staring at worn carpet. 'Maybe I take up knitting,' he said. 'We'd make a great pair. Hiding our hobbies in case any of the boys saw us.'

There was silence from Berand. He pulled up his silks and selected a new one, threading the needle with swift, practised skill. Jules looked at him.

'Is Celeste so good for you that you can wait? Always?'

'You know the answer to that.'

'You're a funny kind of Frenchman.'

'Maybe.'

'You remember Luci, Berand?'

'Naturally. Poor woman.'

'Why the hell do you say that?'

'She was married to you.'

'She was no good to me!'

'She was frightened of you for nearly a quarter of a century.'

Jules glared. 'Why do I sit here next to you when you say things like that? Why do I treat you as a friend? I tell you, Luci . . .'

'Can't you leave her alone, even now?'

'She was always running to the priest.'

'Probably felt she had to do duty for both of you.'

'She's left me with two kids, hasn't she? To look after.'

'They're doing all right.'

'I never thought my son would become a civil servant. A bloody civil servant. That was Luci's doing. She didn't want him near the sea. By God, he's never even wet his feet in it. Sits in a Paris office with hair a barber curls every week. As for Simone, whenever I'm around she looks like she's about to put a clothes-peg on her nose so she won't smell me.'

'Well, you don't wash as often as you might. And there's usually brandy on your breath.'

'I make the money for her to spend, don't I? That's all they want from me. By God, there's going to be one helluva fight when I'm shovelled under. Simone and Jacques dividing the spoils. Everything in two heaps exactly equal. Weighed and measured. They'll probably split the aspidistra.'

Berand liked that. He laughed. It pleased Jules to have his jokes appreciated.

There was a shouting from beyond the door.

'Captain Dartan? Captain Dartan?'

Jules got up. 'I'm here.'

Berand hid the embroidery. Jules sat on the blanket over it. Ginole, the radio operator, stood in the doorway. He was from Toulon, his accent a deliberate affront to the whole of northern France. Ginole rubbed a nose that remained permanently greasy in a face that mostly suffered from dry skin. He was a man who seemed more conscious of his nose than anything else in life, except perhaps the assorted sets he operated.

'Tanker in trouble.'

All Ginole's messages were in telegraphese.

'Eh? Where?'

'Eight-fifty west. Off Orkneys.'

'Who is she?'

'*Mary Worth*. Houston Oils. Registered Panama. Forty thousand.'

'One of their smaller ones,' Jules said. 'Where for?'

'Grangemouth. Full load.'

'Has she called for assistance?'

'No. Message to owners. Partial engine failure.'

'What's the weather like in the area?'

'Six going Seven. Northerly.'

Up at the Orkneys this probably meant wind force increasing to Nine or over.

'Any talk from other tugs?'

Ginole shook his head.

There could still be rivals within reasonable range of the tanker. Salvage skippers are almost as fond of the solitary silence as Trappist monks. Jules was thinking particularly of the *Marie Grooter*, based on Milford Haven. The tanker's call to owners might be enough to have her heading north now at speed. The Dutch came out on long shots and Jules had come up against the *Grooter* before and lost. A repeat would be bad for his name in the business.

The Netherlands tug was about the *Semirande*'s age, the deposed queen of the Hoofstanger fleet assigned to the waters around Britain, thought good enough for them. She could do eighteen knots when pushed, and was equipped as a fire-fighter. In the modern sense the *Semirande* was not. Once he'd had a tow-line on a bulk carrier when fire broke out aft, and it had been the Dutchman who put the fire out, not the tow-tug. That had meant shared salvage on a three-one basis, the one being the *Semirande*. Old Henri Plentin had not been at all pleased.

'You can go,' Jules said. 'Radio silence from us.'

There was a flick of surprise in Ginole's eyes. He shut the door.

'He'll be clacking to the rest of the crew that we're going to the tanker,' Jules said.

'Naturally.'

'It can't be more than three-fifty miles. We could be there tomorrow afternoon. Do we go?'

'You know I don't offer opinions in these matters.'

'The perfect Mate. Who could be a skipper himself if he only had more guts.'

'What, and leave you? When we're so happy together?'

Jules grunted. He stood.

'It's the *Grooter* I'm thinking of. If she comes out she could make it some time tomorrow night. Unless she happens to be cruising in the north Irish Sea. Then she could beat us. What are you sitting there brooding about? Celeste waiting for you in Brest?'

'In a way.'

'I'm sick of damn tows. I want some action. And a decent award.'

'This could be your chance.'

'You're a great help! All you want to do is get on with that sewing. What happens to those things when they're finished?'

'Celeste finds them useful as wedding presents.'

Jules opened the door. One hand carried the tumbler nipped in against the neck of the cognac bottle. 'I'm going to have a look at the charts. You don't think this is a good idea, do you?'

Berand lifted his head. 'We're due a refit.'

'Ach, to hell with that! The boys will be with me . . . if they smell money.'

Jules Dartan stood out on the open wing of the *Semirande's* bridge. He wore his peaked cap, a duffle coat with the hood muffled up at the back of his neck, and binoculars hanging on a strap. Magnification wasn't much help, it just showed distant waves looking exactly like the ones near the ship. Under sun screened by thin cloud the sea had taken on a purple tone, huge mounds of water like clouded wine jelly topped off with mock cream. There was a smell of ice in the north wind. His hands in felt-lined gloves were cold. His spirits had been subjected to a temperature drop, too. Hatred of these frigid seas was a legacy from a time in trawlers as an apprentice on Arctic fish hunts. He had sailed under a skipper with the flair that brings in big catches, a man celebrated for the risks he took, and after thirty-five years Jules still had sharp edged memories of those voyages, the long plodding approaches to the grounds, up the Channel into the North Sea, past a Scottish coast that always seemed to look steel grey, then Orkneys and Shetlands, finally the Faroes, that last human outpost before the area of endless January night.

Up there they had been only fifty miles from a sister ship which had rolled over under black ice and gone down, her last message only three words. Jules's skipper had heard those words but continued to press on north into the dark, while his crew swore, sweating on freezing, slippery decks to bring in the trawl. As the holds filled the little ship's sluggishness increased on those climbs up the sides of invisible water mountains and down again into their valleys. Wind had brought an unbelievably frigid bitterness and an endless roaring through which the voices of men shouting penetrated as thin, desperate shrieks.

Fatigue had never pushed away a boy's fear. Jules had taken terror to his bunk and lain with it, conscious for hours of a black ocean's conspiracy to kill, of that endless battering at a thin hull he could touch with his hand. Condensation put drops of water on rusted rivets within inches of his nose, and he had stared at them, his head turned from light that never went out, smelling men's bodies and his own terror. Dreams had sometimes offered nightmares of death, one of a plunge down a narrow, circular funnel suddenly opened in the sea, a boy dropping, lost forever, into a round well with no bottom. Shouts had usually woken him from that one, angry voices bellowing, and he had curled his body into a ball under the temporary womb of blankets.

Tourin shouted from the wheel-house door.

'Ship on radar, sir!'

Jules didn't turn at once. He used glasses in a bid to confirm the screen's evidence, but the sea stayed empty, horizon hidden by streaming spray. Then, like a sceptic priest who doesn't really believe in the ritual he is about to perform, he went into the wheel-house.

The Second had chosen the middle range scale, 15,000 yards, and the skipper, as if displeased with a television picture, reached out for the swept gain control that increases distant echoes and reduces sea clutter. He made out the bright spot of light just to the starboard of the heading marker. It was big enough to be the tanker. He searched for a smaller spot that could mean another vessel in attendance, but there wasn't one. Jules set up the comparison unit which allowed the radar plan position indicator to be superimposed on the navigational chart, studying the result.

The blob was almost certainly the *Mary Worth* and he put her seven and a half sea miles to the north-east. The coast of Orkney Mainland was just faintly visible as a continuous background line which should mean that the tanker was something like three miles off Marwick Head, apparently stationary, holding her own against the seas but making no way, or very little. Her captain had obviously decided against risking his ship on reduced power in the frenzied currents of the Pentland Firth, hoping to ride out the storm on her one functioning engine. If gale force increased, as it now looked like doing, he would be driven back slowly on to the massive cliff walls of north-west Hoy.

Of all the damn stupid places in which to ride out a storm this beat anything Jules had seen. Why the hell hadn't the idiot turned his ship before the weather really deteriorated and crept back out into the open Atlantic where he would probably have been safe enough?

Ginole came out from the chartroom with another spoken telegram. 'Hebrides Gale Force Eight.'

Jules turned his head. 'Break radio silence. Tell them who we are.'

The radio operator was back in under ten minutes.

'No answer,' he said.

'Aren't they talking at all?'

'In company code. To New York.'

'Well, keep at them. The've had that gale warning. Her master will have to make up his mind damn soon.'

The wheel-house was as hot as a farm kitchen after a baking. Jules took another look at the screen, then went back out on to the bridge wing. Water bullets stung his cheeks. He buttoned up the duffle coat and stood balancing against the movement, conscious of a change in it, a new speed in the lift to the crest of waves and the drop away. The seas were getting larger and coming closer together, with deeper troughs, the tempo of the storm increasing. Wind from the north had disciplined the ocean, regimenting the waves, and these rolled, no longer sloppily crested in foam, but heavily about their business farther south, en route somewhere fast with no casual crumpling along their peaks. Jules knew that wind force was mounting and could easily reach Ten. And the ease off, when it came, would still be offering grim hazards to any tow, a turmoil of heaving water the long postscript to fury.

Spray screens lifted and dropped around the *Semirande*. The gaps between these gave glimpses of rollers to an uncertain horizon. Jules knew perfectly well that there was no need for him to be out on the open bridge ship-spotting, at least while they were still at this distance from the tanker. A screen had told them where the *Mary Worth* lay and for the next hour of their approach this was all that was needed. Still, he wanted to see that hull with his own eyes as soon as possible. He wouldn't have liked now to do without any of his contemporary navigational aids but at the same time kept up the old rituals, sometimes to a point which made his crew suspect him of being round the bend, as when he put a man up in the *Semirande's* bows to take lead and line soundings in shallows while the bridge depth finder was churning out scientifically accurate readings.

Jules's binoculars settled on a range. He braced his feet apart and swayed his body to keep glasses steady, seeing what appeared to be a huge sea developing a sudden upthrust along its crest. This turned into a ship's forepeak, with bow pointed towards a lead overcast at an angle almost suggesting a final stern plunge to death.

Spray shot up again. In the next clearance the *Mary Worth's* aft deck-housing was on a lift, and looked huge, a five-storey block precariously perched on a ship's poop, white paintwork bright. A wallowing tanker looks half a submersible and this one's long midship section remained hidden by wave and blown spume, the bow coming up, then disappearing as the apartment house swung high, but with nothing in between except occasional hints of stubby derrick masts.

The *Semirande* must by now have been spotted from the tanker's bridge, and whatever official policy towards an attendant tug might be, the crew over there would be feeling considerable relief. Jules was pretty certain that it was only a matter of time until the *Mary Worth* was forced to acknowledge her need for help. On that one engine it didn't look as though she was even holding to the north.

It was certainly no moment in which to feel triumph, getting a line on the tanker was going to be hell and mightn't be possible for a very long time. But he was here, first on the scene, and also the only tug likely to show up in this remote corner of the Atlantic, the challenge his and maybe a fat prize, too.

Most sailors believe in luck. Jules had known runs of both good and bad, and now had a feeling a spell of the good had started. Luck had put him at reasonable distance from the *Mary Worth* when her signal went out, just as it had been behind his decision to take the great north circle home to Brest, via the Irish Sea, from a tow to St John's, Newfoundland.

He focused the glasses again. Some fluke levelling out of swells had lifted the tanker on almost even keel, both bow and galleon stern visible with, across her flat belly, a foaming cataract of water. Suddenly, and directly beyond that submerged well-deck, another ship lifted into view. At once Jules recognized it as a tug, and before it was out of sight again could name it from twin towers.

That damned radar! It didn't show two ships when one was behind the other. The *Saturn* was here, a hyena already waiting by the stricken. He put one gloved hand over the rail and shouted into the wind, from wild anger.

'Sacred name of the Mother of God!'

## CHAPTER TWO

CAPTAIN LOUIS ENDICOTT was a family man, his home base a five-bedroom house in East Orange, New Jersey. He had two more years to serve before an excellent pension from the Panamanian shipping subsidiary to a New York based parent company and had been moving easily enough towards an unblemished finish leading to retirement in the Florida sunshine. Privately he regarded himself as one of the sea's favourite sons. The fact that his ships had all been non-accident prone had seemed almost a fixed pattern that was going to see him through, something in his horoscope. The nearest he had ever come to a hurricane was its tail, with the sting gone, and he seemed always to get clear of Latin American ports just before the shooting started. Even the notorious bad spot of the Pentland Firth on this run had only been modestly turbulent during the *Mary Worth's* passages and he had begun to think it had earned an undeserved reputation. No one had ever called the Captain 'lucky Louis', but he hung that identity label around his own neck, a secret joy. He couldn't now really believe what Ziekmann was saying.

'I tell you, we'll be a god-damned hulk. Just that. And it can happen any time.'

'Chief, you said . . .'

'Okay, I said, I said! Now I say something different. Look, we're having the guts shaken out of us down there. Every time that one damn functioning prop comes out the water it's like the big California fault had finally slipped. You can't expect my boys to work in this. Man, you can't hold a power tool. I can't even keep my teeth in.'

The tanker underlined his point. Her prop came out. Everything loose in the cabin danced. Vibration had fireproof partitioning screeching. From deep in the ship's bowels there was a grating like flywheels failing to mesh because of missing cogs.

'How do you like that?' Ziekmann shouted. 'If you feel this much up in the penthouse what the hell do you think we get? I'll tell you! The boys say her spine is going. I'm no deck officer, but I'd swear it's gone Nine outside. My turbine's just not going to stand up. So call in those tugs while we still got power to help 'em. Believe me, Captain, if you wait until we're just a big lump on the sea they're going to have one helluva job. Don't you realize we won't be able to keep this great can into the wind? Seen those waves out there? How's it going to be with them hitting us broadside?'

'We're still holding under our own power, Ziekmann.'

'Oh, God, listen to him! Tell me, Captain, have you ever been on a ship with dead propulsion? In a sea?'

'No.'

'Well, I have. Pacific typhoon. On an old kettle bringing men Stateside from Korea. I was a kid and I came damn near the screaming horrors. I'm not so sure I wouldn't again. I still want to live. Look, have you thought about where we are? That's the Pentland Firth down there at our backside. The most stinking, god-awful piece of water on this globe outside of Cape Horn. When the waves reach sixty feet with those currents there just isn't anything like it.'

'Which is why I kept out of there,' Endicott said.

'Oh, sure. You kept out. Only not far enough. We've now got Hoy to contend with, solid rock cliffs a couple of hundred feet high just waiting. And deep water right up to them too. So you're taken right in to be bashed to hell. Call in a tug!'

'I give the orders on this ship, Chief.'

Ziekmann rose. The jerk of a roll pitched him across the cabin to a bulkhead. He put out his arms and pushed himself away from it like a swimmer turning in a pool.

'You give the orders,' he said. 'Mind if I use the radio to send some last thoughts to my old Ma in Philly?'

He went out. Endicott sat on at the desk. He knew he should be on the bridge, but had to be alone to think this through. Most of what he had to think about was the owners. He began to do this with a sudden, swelling bitterness. An outside chance had suddenly trapped him. If that engine had gone 100 miles back on their course they could have run with the storm, on quarter-power, riding it out. Here the quarter-power that might save Ziekmann's one functioning turbine wasn't enough for holding and with that power they would slide back slowly towards Hoy. And even with the remaining engine full out he knew that he wouldn't be given the power to turn the *Mary Worth* and fight her through those seas, broadside on to them. They had to hold north.

In a desk drawer were the last coded instructions from a sky-scraper head office, informing the Master of the *Mary Worth* that he was to make every effort to deal with his situation without calling for assistance. The message included a veiled rebuke for sending that first signal in clear. They didn't know in New York that the message had brought two tugs on the scene. They wouldn't like that piece of news at all.

Endicott pulled the sheet out and read it again, his eyes stuck to a rider clause saying that the ultimate decision was left to him. That was always put in, like a threat.

The ultimate decision was the crux. The choice was his all right, and some choice. He could play safe and ask for immediate help, or gamble on the wind dropping and a chance of getting the tanker to port unaided. Salvage, or no salvage, in fact. Endicott knew only too well what tends to happen to the career of a skipper who has forced his owners into an awards court. The chances are he loses command of the salvaged ship and doesn't get another. Retirement is accelerated at reduced pension. And if he does get to Florida it's wearing a big label that everyone can read. He reads it himself for the rest of his days, together with his wife and kids.

A bloody two years, that was all it had to be. Lucky Louis!

He stood, feeling the push up under his feet as the *Mary Worth*'s stern swung high on a wave. He waited for the jarring. It didn't come. The ship creaked, but there was no protest from an overworked turbine. Down in her belly two engines were silent, side by side.

Jules lay on his bunk surrounded by rattles from drawers, chests and cabinets. Usually he could turn on sleep from a switch in his brain but the wiring for this seemed to have fused. In a locker a loose coat-hanger was in regular collision with the panelling, staggered morse, waited for. From somewhere on the stairs Ginole started to make a dismal hymn out of the Captain's name.

'I'm in my cabin!' Jules bellowed.

The radio operator stood in the doorway rubbing his nose.

'May Day from the *Mary Worth,* sir. Total engine failure.'

Jules banged booted feet on the deck. His heart went into a series of extra loud beats.

'When did the call go out?'

'Seventeen-thirty-seven.'

The electric clock said seventeen-forty-one.

'Any acknowledgement?'

'Scottish shore station. And *Saturn.*'

'What did *Saturn* say?'

'Standing by to assist.'

'Standing by? Nothing about Lloyd's open form?'

'No.'

Jules, and many another tug skipper, had on occasion used the Lloyd's open form as a kind of blackmail, and not too gentle blackmail, either. Accept or else. It is the only contractual agreement between tug and ship asking for assistance that is recognized in an awards court. Once agreed to it is binding on both parties and the demand for that acceptance is usually a pretty bad moment on board a vessel in distress. If Underson hadn't played that card yet it meant that he wasn't—as he had seemed to be—ignoring the opposition, and this did something for Jules's slipping ego. In these circumstances Underson was as good as admitting that the tow belonged to the tug which got its line on the tanker first, which was the normal procedure, though not all skippers stuck to it by any means. Jules had been at salvage competitions where, from the moment of its arrival, one tug had assumed that there could be no other winner. The Hoofstanger ships tended to this approach, and damn them for it. But here was Underson being a little gent, and also not in any obvious rush to dash in and get to work. Maybe these seas frightened him, even on that electronic marvel of his, which was a nice, warming thought.

For some reason Jules remembered again a scene in a Rotterdam restaurant, a pretty girl alone at a table and a sailor in his first hour on shore woman-hunting who suddenly gets the feeling he is going to strike it lucky tonight. And whatever Berand said that blonde piece *had* smiled at him. Practically the whore's welcome. She hadn't screamed when he sat down, either. The screaming had come from Underson sounding like a jungle cat with its night's meal threatened by a sudden intruder. It hadn't been much of a fight, either. The girl had stopped it. The little bitch was last seen laughing.

Ginole was patiently waiting. Jules snapped up his head.

'Signal Master *Semirande* to Master *Mary Worth*. Preparing to put line aboard. Got that?'

'Yes, sir.'

'Let me know if there's any talk between the tanker and the *Saturn*. Tape it if there is.'

Jules picked up his cap and followed Ginole out of the cabin. It was Berand's watch. The Mate stood close up to the bridge glass, peering through it, holding on with both hands to a rail. He looked like a nervous passenger who hasn't begun to find his sea-legs. It was incredible that this man could take the wheel and put a ship easily through the wildest sea. It was a gift granted to an improbable recipient. Jules had seen him nose the

*Semirande* into a pilotless harbour visited for the first time as though he had been born on a boat in that bay. The Mate could read a chart like a musician sheet-music, getting the feel of it at once.

Dark hadn't quite closed down, delayed by a rent in overcast which allowed through an eerie terminal pallor. This touched wave peaks to the end of vision but left their troughs dark. There were lights on the *Mary Worth,* her dynamos still functioning, a party glow at every port and window. The *Saturn* was now about a mile ahead of the tanker, bow into the seas.

'Look at that,' Berand said, as Jules came up beside him.

The *Mary Worth* had gone out of rudder control and was being pushed around to the west by wind and sea. Her bow lifted, but faltered from no power drive. A wave crest hung, then tipped forward to crumple down over the forepeak, obliterating it, smashing beyond to the low well-deck, sweeping along this for a frontal attack on the stern superstructure. Spray went fifty feet above the bridge and the squat funnel. The tanker staggered through a broken wave into the trough beyond, sinking almost out of sight, then surging up broadside on to the next huge sea. Deck-housing rose like a skyscraper pushed from below and the ship broke through a new crest stern first, as though the accommodation block had its own buoyancy and could survive whatever happened to the rest of that pounded hull. Then wind smacked into exposed superstructure and the *Mary Worth* keeled over so far to port that her starboard boats were visible. She seemed to go down the far side of a wave with her port quarter tucked in against its flank. Jules watched the short radio mast and funnel come upright again down in a trough. He felt pity for the crew over there.

A speaker crackled in the chartroom.

'Ginole here. *Mary Worth* signal to *Saturn*. Am completely out of control. Request be taken in tow. *Saturn* return signal. Will put line on you as soon as conditions permit.'

Jules switched off pity. That tanker was as good as commissioning the *Saturn*, and never mind the Lloyd's form. They'd taken a look at what was on offer in the way of tugs and chosen the newest model. Well, if Underson was going to just hang around waiting for conditions to improve maybe it was time he learned some lessons in this business.

Jules went over to the intercom and punched a button connecting him with the radio cabin.

'Ginole? Captain here. Signal to *Mary Worth* from *Semirande*. We are coming in now to put line on you. Stand by to receive it. Go on sending that until they acknowledge.'

\*     \*     \*

Ziekmann sat on his berth, feet propped against the roll board, back on the bulkhead. When the *Mary Worth* sank over to port the blood rushed towards the Chief's head. This didn't make him feel sick, just angrier. He had left the engine-room because the only thing he could possibly find to do down there was lurch about kicking his diesels. He was trying to get sense out of the transistor clamped between his knees but all it would give him was snatches of German which had been good talk to his ancestors, but not to him. The French beams all seemed to be warming up with music for a listener's wild night out in Paris. Where were the Scottish? At after eighteen hundred they ought to be on the air somewhere.

Then he found them, a composed voice telling five million people there had been another strike at their one car factory and that a conservative politician had made a long speech in Inverness, proceeding to the road accident figures for the month and topping everything off with a human interest story about a golfer who had narrowly escaped being struck by a thunderbolt which had actually killed a cow instead. To Ziekmann it sounded more like national sedation than the news. Then the announcer cleared his throat.

'Word has just reached us that the forty thousand ton Panamanian tanker, the *Mary Worth*, with a full load of crude oil from Galveston to Grangemouth refineries, has sent out a distress signal reporting total engine failure. Earlier the tanker had radioed her owners that an explosion had reduced her to half-power and that she meant to ride out a northerly gale to the north-west of Orkney Mainland. Since then, however, the weather in the area has deteriorated and it is now reported from Cape Wrath to be gusting Force Nine. In so far as can be ascertained the tanker is completely adrift only some seven miles north of the cliff-bound coast of Hoy, towards which huge seas appear to be sweeping her. An R.A.F. Shackleton from Kinloss has just taken off for the scene equipped with flares and other life-saving gear should this be needed. The nearest radio relay reports that two sea-going salvage tugs, as yet unnamed, have already arrived on the scene and are standing by. We will be interrupting later programmes with further bulletins as more news comes in. Meanwhile we are taking you over to Captain Colley, in Glasgow, for an expert's view of the situation.'

An expert's view ought to be interesting. Even worth taping for a playback later to the Captain, who was probably too busy doing damn all up there on the bridge to listen to the radio. Ziekmann rolled off the bunk with some difficulty, found his recorder, switched it on, and brought the transistor over to it, sitting on the deck by both.

Captain Colley had a good opinion of himself as a marine expert and had to be prodded back from making this plain by an interviewer at the other end of a phone line.

'Would you say, Captain, that this could be another *Torrey Canyon?*'

'Well, yes and no. You see, this tanker isn't just going to be run up on rocks and held there, breaking up slowly. If the drift continues she'll be smashed against cliffs and break up in no time at all.'

'Which means her oil will be in the water quickly?'

'It certainly does. No question at all of dealing with that oil at leisure this time. It could all be out of the tanker an hour after she hits, coming straight down on the north Scottish coast.'

'What about the tanker's crew? A pick-up by helicopter?'

'In a Force Nine gale? A helicopter is going to have a job to keep from being blown straight out of the sky, let alone trying to pick men up from a pitching deck. This is one of those times when the job can't be done from the air.'

'So everything depends on the tugs?'

'Absolutely. And they're going to have one devil of a job. Getting a line on board in these conditions can be nearly impossible. Then there's the tow if they do. You've got a massive dead weight of cargo and hull to pull against a howling gale. The strain on any kind of cable under these conditions is terrific, with the yawing about. I've seen them snap like sewing-machine cotton. And remember they'll be having to do all this under flares. That's tricky at the best of times.'

'If the tanker isn't taken in tow is there any chance of her being able to miss Hoy into the Pentland Firth?'

'Difficult to answer. I've got my charts here. Looking at them I'd say it depends on a number of factors. The currents are not favourable. And we can take it that with the engines out there will be no power steering. A ship of that size on manual won't be able to get much rudder reaction in those seas. I should think she's taking the waves broadside on right now. And if that's so she'll be driven along, out of control, with water breaking over her all the way. Sizing things up, with a dead north wind, I wouldn't give her one chance in ten of clearing into the Firth.'

'How long do you give her before she hits Hoy?'

'That's not easy to say offhand. Too much is involved. The wind could drop. Or increase to ten. It seems dicey one way or the other at the moment. And then we've got to remember she's a loaded ship, heavy in the water, setting up her own resistance even to hard driven seas.'

'Can you explain that more fully?'

'Let me think. Yes, well imagine an empty barrel floating on the waves, right on top of them. It has very little resistance and is taken shorewards fast. But have that barrel three-quarters full, semi-submerged in the seas, and you'll see it won't be swept along nearly so fast. There's resistance in depth to the superficial movement even when there are very big waves. If you're watching that barrel you'll see the seas run past it. It takes its own time to the shore.'

'So you'd give the tanker hours yet?'

'Oh, yes, certainly.'

'In your view, Captain Colley, should some kind of emergency be declared now? Perhaps even at government level?'

'Well, it's a crisis situation. If the tugs aren't able to establish a tow we'll have something even worse than a shipwreck with loss of crew life. We've got to think about that cargo. I believe that planes should be readying now to burn that oil off the water the moment it appears.'

'You mean . . . after the wreck?'

'Yes.'

'And what about the men on board?'

'The poor devils won't be alive by that time. Not one of them. Not on that coast. At full tide, which will be soon after midnight, the force of the waves will be incredible. No ship could stand up to them when it is held against a wall of rock, and a tanker is the most vulnerable of all. She'll break her back, then tear in two. The stern superstructure will go. A bit like someone attacking a piano with a sledgehammer. The best you can say is that it won't be a drawn out business.'

The radio left disaster and passed on to Scottish dance music. Ziekmann said: 'Christ!' and switched off both the recorder and the set. But he was going to take the tape up to the bridge. It would be a pleasure to watch that soft-assed sailor's face as he listened to the playback.

Jules wiped the back of a hand across his face. He had always hated oilskins, they stank and impeded movement. Inside them he felt like something on a poster appeal for a marine charity. He shared the bridge wing with Tourin who was manning the rocket gun, the Second's identity snuffed out by a sou'wester, just chin and a piece of nose showing. Tourin was half-crouched behind the railing and the mortar mounted on it, like a man wanting to get down to prayer but handicapped by rheumatic knees. It was obvious he wasn't enjoying his assignment much. Every time spray came over he bobbed his head.

A plane had brought in parachute flares; light from these was long lasting, illumining huge circles of ocean. Under wind noise a drone of engines was an intermittent bee-buzzing, though

the plane itself remained invisible in the overcast, well above
light sent down. The air was full of chattering voices, too, plenty
of advice being offered, but Jules didn't want to hear any of it
and had ordered Ginole to keep radio silence meantime. The
tanker continued to ignore the *Semirande*.

'Sir?' Tourin was practically shouting.

'Well?'

'What range do you think we'll get from the rocket into this
wind?'

Jules simply didn't know. In moderate conditions this rocket
had thrown its cylinder into the wind to something over three
hundred yards but in severe gale the average was about two
hundred. Jules certainly didn't want to take the *Semirande* to
within two hundred yards of that tanker.

'Probably a blow back,' he bellowed.

Tourin's hunch over said that it was no time to be funny. A
moment later the sou'wester moved again.

'Why don't we come downwind on her?'

'Because I don't want these seas on my arse.'

'The *Saturn*'s going to have them that way.'

'From what I can see the *Saturn*'s doing sweet f.a. Underson's
a bloody show-off. He's putting on an act for the tanker. I hope
they're enjoying it.'

The *Mary Worth* was now taking every third or fourth sea
over her stern funnel; not just spray, solid water rising in geysers
up her starboard deck-house wall, then arching over to sluice
down the entire superstructure. Her forty degree rolls showed
that starboard davits had all been stripped of their boats. The
port side still had one left but a second had been torn away to
hang by bow lines. This boat kept swinging out, then back in
again, to smash more windows on a lower shelter deck and buckle
more plates. Three times little clumps of men had appeared
clinging to rope lines in a bid to saw through a wire cable and
let that lifeboat fall away. They hadn't succeeded. During lulls
in wind noise the sound of solid water hitting the tanker travelled
over to the *Semirande*, a deep, reverberating thud. When the
ship's bows came up and that elongated, oil-pregnant belly had
to take the strain, there was a dismal stress groaning from her keel.

A new flare exploded. Someone else was certainly seeing to
the lighting, which was a help. Jules lifted binoculars and looked
aft. The bulk of Hoy was now within the fringe area of the
illuminations and the sight of those cliffs must be breeding
terror over on the tanker. From this distance spray seemed to be
feathering the cliffs but Jules knew, and so did the Master of the
*Mary Worth*, that those broken waves were shooting water up
for four hundred feet.

Wind sliced off a crest to test out oilskins on the *Semirande*.
Tourin ducked in time. Jules stood with iced salt water streaming
down his face and then working its way as cold damp to a string
vest. He went into the wheel-house which was still cosy.

Berand had taken over from the helmsman. He now looked like
a croupier at a down at the heel casino, not hopeful but intent.

'I want to close to within three hundred yards,' Jules said.
'Think you can do it? And hold it?'

'It's your suicide.'

'What do you mean?'

'Forty thousand tons plus load coming down on us when
we're in a trough.'

'Not under her, man. Aft. We'll fire back cross wind.'

'You planning on a stern tow?'

'Yes. Any objections?'

Berand said nothing.

Jules went out into the whitened night again. The Mate
probably wouldn't have made much of a career in the Navy,
but he was none the less destroyer commander material . . . if
you didn't look at him. Under those embroiderer's hands the
*Semirande* somehow contrived to go light and precise to the
helm. The tug had been simply holding into the seas, sometimes
with engines in reverse, but now she came about with a spurt
of power, up on to the foreslopes of a wave. They began to run
along the upper heights of that sea like a tank going over rough
country under cover from the enemy, Berand keeping his listing
ship up on a mound of water which swept them south as they
drove east. Somehow twin screws held their bite right to the
unavoidable moment when the crest, in a kind of petulance, lost
patience and toppled over.

Jules grabbed for a handhold. Tourin went down on his knees
behind the railing bulkhead, his arms around a stanchion. Solid
water hit. Jules lost grip and was slammed back against the
wheel-house. For seconds Tourin was out of sight. He reappeared,
still crouched down, surrounded by a frothing shambles of foam
that reached up to Jules's calves. Boxes of rocket lines were afloat.
For minutes vibration was teeth-jarring. Then, very slowly, the
tug rolled over on to a down slope, scuppers streaming, her bow
swinging around into the wind again.

Berand had done exactly what was required of him. The *Mary
Worth* was now to port of the *Semirande*, her stern quarters vast.
These went into a lift and Jules saw motionless, dripping propellers and a huge rudder that didn't move either. Except for
those lights she looked like a derelict hulk. They didn't seem
to be bothering about that suspended lifeboat any more, probably

past caring. It was battering steadily to widen the entrance to a cave opened in steel plates. Lucky for them that the hole wasn't to starboard, which would have meant more water through a breach than pumps could have coped with. Jules had seen a small passenger liner die like that, from a smashed door at accommodation level through which the seas had flooded.

Berand was back to holding position again. On each summit spray rose about the *Semirande*. The attendant plane was now hoarding its flares and suddenly the *Saturn* sent up one from her tower platform. This pinpointed the new position she had taken up only some five hundred yards to the north of the tanker.

Jules stared. God, she looked efficient, practically a revolutionary design. The old snub bow effect had been eliminated by a built-up forepeak from which a short, flat deck led back to a windowless lower deck bulkhead suggesting something on a guided-missile cruiser. Above this the bridge was all glass, entirely enclosed, no wings at all, no need for oilskins. The *Saturn* had been built to deal with everything except crane lifts from the sea bed and even the Hoofstangers had paid her the compliment of copying some of her features for the new keels they were laying down. Underson had over nine thousand horsepower to play with, computers for course setting, plus every conceivable type of electronic equipment that could be packed into her air-conditioned control centre.

Jules felt a flat envy. A ship like that would add a new dimension to an experienced man's skills. She oughtn't to be commanded by a boy. With Berand beside him on that bridge he could throw a real scare right into the middle of Hoofstanger complacency. Old Plentin, of course, wouldn't put down the money needed for such a ship. He had moaned enough about the *Semirande*'s price, and building costs had nearly doubled since her launching. That new tug he was going to add to his fleet wasn't even on the drawing-board.

Jules shouted to Tourin above wind noise. 'Have a practice shot.'
'At this range?'
'We won't expect miracles. Try aiming between the tanker and the Englishman. You might just catch the right drift back.'
'I'll need a flare.'
'You can have it.'

The *Saturn* obliged again. She seemed to have plenty and no worries about keeping down operating costs. In so far as Jules could see she wasn't making any use herself of that light sent up.

Tourin worked in slow motion, with frozen fingers, sliding the rocket shell into its mortar casing, checking the lead line to its coil box. The *Saturn*'s flare lost its first brilliance and Jules turned into the wheel-house to get a replacement. The *Semirande* went into a lift as the *Saturn* sank. Tourin fired just as Jules came out on the wing again.

Watching the flight of that rocket was like trying to follow a golf drive on a television screen subject to summer interference, but in half a minute the result was obvious enough, the lead wire went straight down into the sea from the rail of the bridge over-hang. Tourin might have been fishing for mackerel.

'I'll put up a flare,' Jules shouted. 'Angle her up more this time. You're playing for range. And we've got to see the damn thing.'

They saw the second rocket all the way. It didn't get too far, climbing straight up to a wind squall which flipped the shell over and re-directed it towards the sea aft of the *Semirande*. There was a second fishing line from the bridge.

'I can't do a thing at this range.'

It wasn't the range that was the trouble. Jules suppressed an itch to have a go himself.

'Try again. There's enough light.'

Tourin's third shot was an improvement, the rocket going into the sea almost directly astern of the tanker and only about a hundred yards from her.

'You're getting it,' the Captain said like an indulgent papa.

'But what the hell's the good? Even if I get one on there's no one over there to secure. There hasn't been a man out on these decks in the last hour. They're just not noticing us.'

'They will.'

Jules went back into the wheel-house.

'Some fine shooting,' Berand said.

'The Second would like you to tuck us in under that can's rudder. Will you?'

'No.'

'I thought not. This as close as you'll risk?'

'Yes.'

'You think too much about your happy home life in Brest.'

'I'm waiting for you to show us how a rocket ought to be fired.'

'It's the *Saturn*'s turn.'

'Then we'll see something.'

'You know, I don't think so. Not unless they have a new type rocket fitted with a homing device.'

'It's downwind for them.'

'But the wind is starting to do odd things.'

Jules didn't take out a new flare. He heard the plane engine again, and thought about the possibility of a film camera up there, which was a shade disturbing. A salvage operation ought to be allowed a certain privacy, without a permanent record of the action that could later be shown to an awards court.

The last flare had died but there was still some light. Part of this came from the glow over on the *Mary Worth,* but there was also a glittering at the horizon. The moon shone down on that distant sea from the sawn-off edge of cloud formations.

Jules was certain that the wind was losing punch and there was change on the water, a slight ironing out, crests no longer peaked, but rounded off, with the gaps between waves widening and their troughs shallowing up. Underson might have been waiting for something prophesied by his computers.

Brightness blossomed above the *Saturn.* The rocket she put up glistened on a nice clean course towards the tanker. It made three-quarters of the distance before wind snapped back on to the alert. A shining torpedo, that had looked gyro-controlled, suddenly turned west and took a long, slow plunge into the Atlantic. Under the same flare they had two more tries and the last one came down, like Tourin's, only a hundred yards short of the *Mary Worth.*

The Second, sou'wester pushed up from his face, had been watching intently. He seemed to have caught the competitive spirit. At the same time he didn't enjoy having the Captain close beside him in the role of weapons training officer. He said, with a certain sharpness: 'Like a shot yourself, sir?'

'All right. You put up the flare.'

'The *Saturn* seems to be thinking about a bow tow.'

'I don't give a damn what they're thinking. Underson won't have a clue anyway. He'll be issuing orders straight from a salvage manual.'

The moment he said that Jules regretted it. Tourin's mouth had gone tight. He was praying right then to his patron saint, if he had one, that the skipper would make one almighty bollocks of that first shot.

A lift showed a wind frenzy pockmarking the higher slopes of waves. Gusting meant lulls, too. Jules saw the *Mary Worth* caught by the squall, her bow being swung around almost to south-west, which suddenly presented most of her port quarter as a target area. He fired.

The trajectory was all right, a beautiful high arc, but not too high. He stood waiting for interference from a gust. Tourin was doing the same thing. Then the Second called out, half-bitter, half-triumphant for the home team.

'My God! She's going to make it. Over the well-deck!'

The well-deck was precisely where Jules had not intended his line to fall.

The dimmed-out bridge of the *Mary Worth* was just an observation platform, it had lost all other function. One of the starboard windows had been smashed and, when a vast sea slammed in, water poured through like a drain being flushed, swirling inches deep before it cleared by a direct access stair down to A deck. One of these cataracts had smacked into the Mate on his way up. He was now lying in his bunk with a broken leg which Goldberg, the Second, was trying to set.

There was still lighting from emergency dynamos, but heating had gone, and currents of icy air swept through the ship. A new sound had been added to an endless creaking and the roar of sea, doors banging. A hundred doors seemed to have burst their locks, to batter back and forth on wracked hinges. The galley, four decks below, had been abandoned by her two cooks who couldn't even make coffee. A debris of pots and pans clanged and clattered in every roll.

The bridge had become a congregation point, men drifting up to watch the sea since there was no longer anything else for them to do, mostly Ziekmann's oilers. The Captain suspected that the Chief had told them to come. Louis Endicott hadn't ordered them off. They stood about holding on to anything available and a few were sitting on the deck. One tow-headed boy had his head forward on his knees. When water surged around his buttocks, freezing cold, he didn't even lift his head.

Orders were sterile as issued. Three times Louis had sent the Bos'n and a detail out to get rid of that lifeboat, but they had come back, soaked under oilskins, to report failure. Louis didn't think they had tried very hard. He couldn't really blame them. He was conscious of a curious, almost psychic, connection between the ship's loss of power and his own, as if he was the brain still living and recording in a completely paralysed body. It wasn't fear he felt, just a frozen helplessness, like something in a dream, watching the puppet figure of the ship's Master maintaining dignity and caricaturing calm.

Louis turned at a shout. Goldberg was careening across the bridge, grabbing for handholds.

'How's Johnson?'

The Second shook his head. 'Not so good. He's had morphine. We set the leg. Don't know if we got it right. He needs a doctor, Captain.'

'We'll soon be able to call in a helicopter.'

Goldberg stared. 'Think so?'

'Wind's dropping. Marked change in barometric pressure.'

Louis observed his own confidence. It was commendable. Somehow he wished that tow-head would look up and believe. Goldberg wasn't believing either. He was looking south, through salt-smeared glass.

'Frenchman seems to be up to something. New flare.'

The Captain didn't even glance to port.

'We need the bigger tug. She has the power. I'll go down and see Johnson. You're on watch.'

'Yes, sir.'

It was something to do. Louis climbed a hill towards the stairs but not a head turned. Those who were looking at anything were watching the sea, the television stare, living framed there, everything else meaningless. The flight down-tilted as he got to it, becoming a ledged drop, and he hung on, waiting.

The Mate's door wasn't banging. Louis turned a handle. The cabin retained an immunity to the nightmare beyond; it still belonged to the man in the berth. Johnson was beneath a heap of blankets which had some kind of cage support at leg level. He was half-propped up against pillows, and shivering. His eyes had the brightness of fever.

'We'll have to fix up visiting hours,' he said.

Louis smiled, holding on to a locker with one hand, shutting the door with the other. 'How are you, Bill?'

'Like someone who's just been patched up by the Marx brothers. Where did Goldberg get the idea he was bonesetter?'

'Someone had to try.'

'I'd rather have had the cook. You know something, Louis? I'm going to be a cripple for the remaining hours of my life.'

The Captain talked about helicopters again, while bright eyes watched him.

'Forgive my teeth chattering,' the Mate said. 'I'm cold, but it's also shock. The kind they give you oxygen for. We don't stock it. And that's my fault. Sit down. You look liable to go flat on your face. What's she hitting now, forty degrees?'

'Sometimes.'

'I'd guess a lot of the time. What's Ziekmann been doing since he played you that tape of the news?'

'Keeping out of my way.'

'The bastard.'

Louis held on to the back of an anchored chair and changed the subject. 'Is the morphine helping?'

'If it could be worse without I don't want that. Those tugs still trying to get a line on us?'

'Yes.'

'Louis, you're looking tired. Not scared, just tired. And there's something I want to say right now. If we get out of this it's sure to be straight over to those briefcase-carrying shits in New York. Right?'

'Probably.'

'Okay. I'm with you. Right there. You're not going to become one of those Captains who has his Mate piss on him at the inquiry. Nor your Second, either. I'll fix Goldberg, that is if I live after what he's done to me. What I mean is, you did the only thing any man could have done in the circumstances.

'That's not true,' Louis said.

'God damn it, it's never true! But it's what you say at an inquiry. And if man after man of us gets up with the same piece those bastards can't touch us.'

'Ziekmann won't get up with that piece. He wanted me to call in a tug while we still had power.'

'Louis, you were obeying the owners. Staving off salvage. And who listens to an oiler, anyway? When it comes to my testimony I'll jump on Ziekmann's head. Who landed us in this? His goddamned engines. That's going to stick out a mile and he knows it. Did he say they were needing an overhaul? Or sail under any kind of protest about the state of those turbines? Did you ever hear him say they were knocking, or anything? I was sure back in the Gulf there was a vibration increase. I said so. Ziekmann took off like I'd raped his woman. He's nuts.'

The *Mary Worth* went into a deep roll to port. Louis felt his feet going from under him and crouched over the chair back. Johnson, grimacing with pain, braced himself back against pillows from both hands on the roll board. They waited for recovery point, a jerk before the swing up again.

'Christ! She's going!'

The jerk came. The deck lifted. Johnson was ashamed of having cried out. He closed his eyes.

'That's about the worst yet,' Louis said.

He saw sweat on the Mate's forehead, but the man was still shivering. 'I guess I'm not myself. It's lying here.'

'I know. I'd better get up top. See you.' At the door he turned. 'And thanks, Bill. Thanks a lot.'

The Mate didn't want to be left. He was trying to keep this from showing. Louis closed the door, pulling it hard for a lock click.

Ziekmann was coming upstairs from B deck, almost on hands and knees. He looked up and saw the Captain.

'The Frenchies! They've got a line over us. Lying on the welldeck. Clean across. What the hell you guys been up to on the bridge that you didn't see it? If you don't believe me you can look out my cabin port to the well-deck. It's there, I tell you!'

Louis stared. His voice was harsh, loud above the creaking. 'What good does a line over the well-deck do us?'

'Eh?'

'You expect me to order out a party to take that thing for'ard. Along a gangway that's awash, with half its railing gone?'

'What? You mean you're not even going to try to secure?'

'Ziekmann, for God's sake use your head! While these seas are running the only line we can secure is for a stern tow. Which means over our upper decks somewhere. If you've got any suggestions how I get that Frenchman's line up over five decks of superstructure to a stern achoring I'm listening.'

'We could drop a rope down. Tie the line to it and pull it up.'

'Do you know what you're saying? That would have to be done from open deck above the bridge. And there's nothing to hold on to up there. Further it has a curve. About every ten minutes a wave breaks over.'

'A man could climb out on some sort of climber's rope.'

'Want to volunteer?' Louis asked.

A wave slammed in. The *Mary Worth* lurched, moaning. Banging doors sounded like a revolver battle. Din from the galley was a riot mob going mad. Down the stairs, from the bridge-deck, came another cascade of water, sloshing over the shoes of two men on its way to a lower level. Ziekmann watched it go.

'The reserve pumps'll be packing up any time,' he said.

'You haven't answered my question, Chief?'

Ziekmann turned.

'Okay, I'll do it. Just to show up you deck bastards.'

Jules regarded that line over the tanker's well-deck as another write-off. He had tried five follow-up shots under two flares, missing with all of them. They were nearer misses than Tourin's, but there wasn't a great deal of consolation in that. Over on the *Saturn* Underson was saving flares, watching and doing nothing. He was probably waiting for the storm to ease. This was happening but Jules couldn't see improved conditions for a tow in the hours ahead. Almost certainly cyclonic gusting would replace Force Nine north, squalls coming in from half the angles of the compass. You'd never know just how you were going to be hit, which would make things worse for rocket firing, not better. The sea, too, could have new games to play, wind and current setting up wave collisions under conditions of general turbulence to make you regret an earlier, almost orderly, succession of spaced swells. The *Mary Worth*'s drift towards Hoy might be slowed down, but it wouldn't be stopped. Unless she was pulled away from those cliffs she could still strike before dawn.

'Captain, they're putting a light down on the well-deck.'

'What?'

'Hanging it out one of the front bridge windows. It looks like they're going to try to take our line for'ard.'

Jules stared. Then he swung through the wheel-house and chartroom to the radio cabin. Ginole was wearing headphones.

'Anything from the tanker?'

'No, sir.'

The man seemed to be eating biscuits, on iron rations.

'Well, get them and find out what the hell's happening over there. They're going for our line.'

On the open bridge Jules lifted glasses. The *Mary Worth's* lights created a dazzle effect. He could see no sign of men on her boat-deck. The tanker went into a surge up a wave and the suspended lifeboat flashed white as it swung out, then back again. The tanker was still being pounded by seas on one quarter and that hammer on the other.

Jules let binoculars drop on their strap and went to a hooded searchlight, pulling off the canvas cover. He swung the big lamp down on its mountings and switched on. White glare bounced from the foreslopes of a wave, then lifted, groping over water to the tanker's hull, finding this but losing it again almost at once as the *Semirande* went into a trough. Focusing was hit or miss. Jules stood with legs braced, trying to get the beam on to upper deck and funnel. He got the lifeboat first. This had lost shape, rounded into something almost like a demolition contractor's iron ball, and the hole it had torn in the plating and glass was at least ten feet across, covering two decks. It seemed incredible that the steel davit cable hadn't snapped.

The *Semirande* rose and her searchlight hit upper deck and funnel. Jules saw what he was looking for. He shouted for Tourin to take over the beam.

'A man on top of the bridge. Must be roped. Suicide if he isn't. Try to keep the light for'ard of the funnel.'

Tourin played about getting range. Jules lowered glasses to the well-deck. Two men were out on that suspended gangway from stern deck-house to bows, but just on it, ready to get back behind a bulkhead door when a sea was shipped.

The Second proved better at holding the light steady than the Captain. The beam showed a figure sprawled out at the start of a streamlined curve of deck over the bridge. He looked as though he had dropped from a height on to pavement, spreadeagled. A water geyser reared up from the starboard and came down on him. The *Mary Worth* streamed. The men on the gangway had gone, but that figure high on unprotected plating was still there, though his position had altered. He was tethered back to a funnel stanchion like a goat to a stake, the seas could shift him, but not sweep him overboard. Whoever he was, he had guts.

'Captain, I think they've tied our line on to a rope.'

Jules lowered glasses. Light dropped with them. He still couldn't see any rope hanging from above the bridge, but the lead wire from the *Semirande* glistened. It was being pulled up.

Ginole shouted from the wheel-house door.

'*Mary Worth* on R.T. for *Semirande*.'

Jules didn't move. 'I'll be there in a minute.'

He didn't turn until the arc light suspended from the tanker's bridge went out. Ginole was waiting with the receiver held out. 'Her Captain.'

Jules cleared his throat. He was still taking his time. His English was slow and careful.

'Master *Semirande* here. You wish me? Over.'

'Captain Endicott, *Mary Worth*. We have secured your line. With some difficulty.'

'So?'

'Hello, are you reading me?'

'Yes, I read you, Captain Endicott. But many signals from us have no acknowledgement.'

'I'm sorry about that. I was in contact with the *Saturn* for a long time before you showed up.'

'Indeed? We intercept no signal.'

'Captain, we were using R.T. I didn't even know you were on the way to us.'

'What is the situation now? You accept our tow when secured?'

'Yes.'

'Lloyd's open form?'

'Oh, God, yes!'

'Very well. You will keep this line open to us, Captain.'

Jules put down the receiver. Ginole said: 'Got them, have we?'

'So it would seem.'

Jules's voice was quiet. But when he was outside the radio cabin, and had pulled shut the door, he leaned back against it for a moment before going to the bridge.

From the wheel-house door he shouted to Tourin.

'They accept our tow. We'll be sending the whip across soon. Get aft and prepare the hawser.'

Jules came to stand by the Mate. Tourin passed behind them without saying anything and went below.

'What will you be buying Celeste this time? A fur coat? You ought to be able to get her a good one.'

Berand said nothing. He moved the wheel two points. Jules laughed.

## CHAPTER THREE

TOURIN worked his way aft, relying more on handholds than his feet. Scuppers along the *Semirande*'s flat stern-deck couldn't drain away all the water coming aboard and at each roll miniature tidal waves rushed from port to starboard, then back again. The tug, usually fairly dry for her type, was now awash. Under the restraint of her tow she was taking a pounding from chopped seas. Spray streamed across her, stinging and ice cold. Periodically the engine beat broke for an easing of the hawser as the *Mary Worth* went into one of her heavier lifts. They were making no more than three knots, but this due west, out into the Atlantic away from Hoy and the Pentland Firth. In daylight and improving conditions they meant to come back again, for the tow around the north of Scotland.

Tourin spat over the rail. The sea in retaliation came on board and he nearly lost handhold, while water sucked at his boots and poured in over their tops. He hung on, thinking about prize money and how his girl would react to the news of his cut. She would want marriage. He didn't.

The *Semirande* rose and scuppers almost cleared her. Tourin let go and slithered down to a stern in unpleasantly close proximity to a churning sea. A searchlight from the bridge, beamed back, showed him a foaming wake with the hawser going to stern above it. The fat rope yawed back and forth on smooth steel which allowed it play beyond revolving bollards and the winches. He could see no sign of wear to the strands. It might, however, be a good idea to let it out a bit in an hour or so.

A gust smacked into the tug. For all her squat lines she keeled over. The *Mary Worth* was going to do a lot more than that. Engine heat broke again. Tourin made for shelter and reached it as water came down, like a spill from a giant's bucket. He waited until there was a clearance, then pushed open a bulkhead door and stepped over the sill, into heat. In the passage creaking was louder than the sound of diesels. He swayed along, both hands out, and went into the galley.

The cook was nodding on a fold-down seat, with chilblained fingers folded across his stomach. A heavy-bottomed kettle steamed on the oil range. Tourin fumbled about making himself a mug of powdered coffee which he drank straight because he couldn't be bothered to mix up powdered milk or find a can.

'Oh, it's you,' the cook said.

'That's right. When's breakfast?'

'In three hours.'

'Don't you ever get to your bunk?'

'Not so often. Heard about the new tug?'

'What?'

The cook nodded, his hands still holding in his guts.

'*Marie Grooter*,' he said. 'I'm just back from the bridge. Coming up from the sou'east, she is. Fast. You can just see her lights. But they'd picked her out on radar. Those Hoofstanger buggers.'

'We've the laugh on them. A long trip for nothing.'

'They never make long trips for nothing.'

The cook was a failed café proprietor and tended to pessimism. 'How's the old man taking it?'

'Doesn't seem to worry him.'

Suddenly it worried Tourin. He had been spending prize money on a new Fiat. He put down the mug. The cook lifted a hand and wiped his mouth with the palm.

'When our hawser goes we'll see some real action from those Hoofstangers,' he said. 'Flashy stuff. They'll move right in to kiss that tanker's arse. They'll show us. Put a line on her by hand or something.'

'Our hawser isn't going to go.'

'Says you.'

The tug jolted, like a train shunting. Pots rattled. A cupboard door flew open. The cook looked up but took no action.

'How long do you think a piece of rope is going to stand up to that?' he asked.

'Is Berand still at the wheel?'

'No. It's the old man. Can't you feel it?'

Tourin went out. He went along to the tiny cabin he shared with the Second Engineer. Lecren was lying out along the upper berth dressed for the tropics in a pair of blue jeans and no shirt. He had been reading a girlie magazine but this was lying on his chest while he stared at a naked bulb, as though to hypnotize himself to sleep.

'You fellows really have it rough, don't you?' he said, as Tourin started to peel off wet clothing.

'That's right. And we don't clock-punch like you.'

'We don't clock-punch. The Chief lives in his hole. He wouldn't come out for meals if he could help it. And he's in a helluva state now. What this is doing to the engines. He thinks what's wrong with the world is that the young don't love their engines enough. You know what I think is wrong with the world?'

'No,' Tourin said, without interest.

'Too many damn old men in it.'

Tourin felt his shirt with his hands and decided that it had better come off, too. The cabin, about the size of a railway sleeping compartment, began to smell strongly of the male animal. It always did, but more so at some times than others. He opened a drawer and there was a heavy whiff of oiled wool put away damp. He took a couple of steps to heating pipes, pushed Lecren's washing to one side, making room for his own things. He draped these, then threw oilskins out into the passage to leave room for manoeuvre meantime.

He got on with the engineer all right. It was a good thing they did, though the moment the tug docked they went their own ways.

Lecren had a steady in Brest who took him to her bed at once and more or less kept him there until sailing time again. He'd probably have married the girl if she hadn't had a husband already, so he was the lodger. It was a great thing for a sailor to meet up with a travelling man's wife, and so far the two men's spells at home didn't seem to have overlapped. It mightn't have mattered much if they had. She was a good cook too, Lecren said.

Tourin found dry trousers, pulled them on and tucked in his shirt. He lifted his arms to get a sweater over his head just as his feet were jerked away. He pitched forward towards the heating pipes.

Tourin lifted his head, slowly. He was on the deck, flat out on his back. He remembered at once that he hadn't fallen that way, which meant that someone had turned him over. Lecren's bunk was empty. He became conscious of vibration increasing as the tug went into a lift. A sound came from down the passage, bubbling sobs that mounted almost to a scream, then lapsed to a whimper. Tourin pulled himself up, his head pounding. Wobbly on his feet, he didn't probe for a bump on his skull, it wasn't a moment for arm lifting.

He managed to walk by using bulkheads, first in the cabin, then out in the passage. He wanted to be sick. Lecren came out of the galley.

'You okay then?'

'What the hell happened?'

'The hawser went. We must have been in a trough. With that engine thrust we went through the next wave instead of over it. I didn't think we were coming up.'

'Who was that howling?'

'Cook got a kettle of boiling water over his feet.'

'Help me into these oilskins. I'm going up top.'

'You look green. Better lie down!'

'Help me into them!'

The nausea stayed with Tourin on the companion stairs. It was in his mind, too. No prize money. No damn prize money! The hawser wouldn't have gone with Berand at the wheel. It was the old man's doing, so bloody sure of himself.

Tourin turned into the radio cabin without knocking. Ginole didn't like this. He cleared one ear by lifting a phone.

'Well?'

'What are you getting from the tanker?'

'Damn all. Where have you been? I heard them shouting for you.'

'Out cold. So we can't find out from the tanker where the hawser break was?'

'Berand winched it in. It was half-way. Not friction with metal at all.'

'Is the *Mary Worth* not talking to anyone?'

'The Dutchman. Coming up fast.'

'They're playing the field, are they?'

'Seems like it.'

'I hate their guts,' Tourin said.

Ginole laughed. He slipped the cover over his free ear. It was dismissal.

On the bridge Berand was standing beside the old man, who had the wheel. If there had been a post-mortem this was over. It was impossible to tell whether there was tension between them. Berand had gone into action straight from his berth, wearing a long sweater down to his hips over striped pyjamas. He looked like a suburban householder who has been burglar-hunting with a poker. Neither appeared to notice the arrival of the Second. Since he was dressed for it, and couldn't risk words anyway, Tourin went straight out on to the starboard wing, opening and closing the sliding door. The moment wind hit him nausea surged again. He put both hands on the aft rail and was sick over it, his body trembling and his skin suddenly greasy with sweat. He remembered a child being sick, wanting attention and petting, someone to hold his forehead while he suffered. But no one had come to do that. Which was the bloody history of his life, no one giving a damn.

His eyes were watering as he looked aft. There was no mistaking the *Marie Grooter*. Cloud had broken enough to allow through diluted moonlight but the Dutchman wasn't content with this. He believed in advertising and had switched on everything he had, including a big deck arc of the kind homebound seiners use when gutting fish on board. The illuminations showed a middle-aged tug with a beamy spread and squat funnel. Her foremast, though, seemed to bring her up to date with a shimmer of screens for electronic and listening devices, so many of these she almost suggested a Russian spy trawler. There was no hint of stabilizers in the way she whacked through waves, as determined as an ice-breaker, rolling to unpleasant degrees and sending up explosions of spray.

Tourin stared, impressed. A wet ship, certainly, wetter than the *Semirande* by a long way; nobody's home from home, that tub, but she had something he recognized at once. It was the Dutch signature, worn by their salvage craft for at least half a century, an almost insolent announcement that there was no type of sea disaster they hadn't been up against at least twenty times before and that they arrived on all trouble scenes totally ready to cope. Every Dutch tug seemed to move around the globe displaying this confident statement like a pennant. And most non-Dutch skippers and crews hated them for it.

The *Grooter* still had one light in reserve and this came on suddenly, a bright ray over the water which was totally useless from that distance, its function purely psychological, the marine equivalent of a fanfare of trumpets.

Tourin began to feel better. You had to acknowledge a good act when you saw it. He wondered how many jobs the *Grooter* had pulled off as a direct result of one of these circus entrances. She was hours behind her rivals, but simply used this fact to come on like the big star of the night after the intermission. And there wasn't any doubt about it, the other acts had gone stale; the *Semirande*, her time of triumph sadly over, was back to square one again, holding at 500 yards from the *Mary Worth*. The *Saturn* was keeping to about seven hundred to the north of the tanker. Underson had apparently been certain the *Semirande*'s hawser would go in these seas and had trailed a tow west into open Atlantic. The only real change in the situation was that the cliffs of Hoy were now fifteen miles east and invisible over the horizon. And the plane had gone home for good. From the point of view of outsiders a crisis was over and the midnight news on the radio had reported, in two lines, that the tanker was under tow. The announcer had sounded almost disappointed, as though he knew he was letting down a few million listeners who had waited up in slippers by their dying fires for another thrilling instalment before shuffling off to their electrically warmed beds. Tourin wished he could show some of those comfortable bastards this post-Force Nine sea. He cleared sickness phlegm from his throat and spat towards a big wave.

At six feet two and three-quarters Tom MacDonald was too big for a tug and knew it. He went around conscious of the deck only inches from the top of his head and was forever bending through doors and down stair wells. He would have been stooped in his thirties if it hadn't been for the special dorsal muscles exercises in his P.T. bible, *Yoga, the Way to True Strength*.

He kept carrot-red hair shorter than fur of the same tint which covered much of the rest of him, this colouring a throwback to Scottish ancestry, though his people had been Londoners for generations. The only thing he really remembered about three or four visits to Scotland was a wrestling match in Leith in which The Man from Outer Space had thrown Mighty Ben Lomond clean out of the ring into the fifth row of the audience. That night had really been something. It hadn't been faked either, it couldn't have been, Ben Lomond broke his jaw.

The *Saturn*'s bridge was the only place on the ship that offered almost enough room for a wrestler. With huge windows going down to within inches of the deck it somehow suggested a big sunroom tacked on to a cramped bungalow. On your watch you could get in quite a bit of exercise walking up and down behind the helmsman. MacDonald had worked it out as a hundred and five times port to starboard and back to the mile, though the most he had ever achieved non-stop without duty pauses had been four miles, this during a four-knot tow in calm weather, and with Ackroyd as his helmsman.

Ackroyd was there now, his job to keep the *Saturn* bow into the wind which still remained generally northerly, and did this with moderate efficiency, shipping more water than MacDonald would have done himself at the helm, but not much more. The man had been at sea for twenty-two years and had stayed a deck-hand through all that time in the simple pattern of getting drunk the moment he hit port and keeping that way until it was sailing time again. Once his ship cast off he became a total abstainer, even from the beer ration, taciturn and reliable, good company for no one.

A ceiling speaker offered static crackles, the R.T. left open and piped through from the radio cabin for any messages that might go out over it. But the *Grooter*, after establishing liaison with the tanker, had gone back to silence.

A buzzer sounded. MacDonald went over to the communications panel. 'Mate here.'

'I wanted the Skipper.' It was Ginnis, the Second, up on the tower.

'He pushed off about forty minutes ago.'

'To his cabin?'

'I dunno. You can ring through and see.'

'What are your orders?'

'To hold at about seven hundred. Which we're doing as you can see. I watched the *Grooter* come up aft for a while but I got tired of that. Now I'm looking up towards the Arctic circle.'

'You sound fed up, Tom.'

'How are you enjoying the breezes up there?'

'It's frigid. What I'm wondering is why we aren't moving in for some more rocket tries before the *Grooter* takes over?'

'I haven't the answer,' the Mate said.

Ginnis hung up, but two minutes later he was back again.

'You know where I found the Skipper? He's in the engine-room with the Chief. It was the Chief I talked to. The Skipper couldn't come to the mike. There was a sound like a power tool, Tom.'

'They'll be working on our secret weapon. Mark One will be coming up any minute now.'

'I don't think this is funny.'

'Do you hear me laughing?'

MacDonald switched off. Almost at once the ceiling speaker coughed into a kind of English.

'This is Scherner, *Marie Grooter* calling Master *Mary Worth.*'

The tanker acknowledged on what seemed to be very low power, a voice with a squeak in it and when the Captain came on he sounded like a very old man with a death wish. Scherner's reaction was to bellow and he reached decibels that fuzzed reception.

'Now, Captain, you listen. I got to have bow party. They got to be up there to get my line. Understand?'

The ghost over on the *Mary Worth* didn't like the suggestion, pointing out that a section of the catwalk his men would have to use to the bows had been washed away and the well-deck was still taking a great deal of water over it.

'What you say? Seas too high? Listen, what you scared of? Some water, eh? Well, I tell you we get bloody wet here. We don't hide inside no glasshouse like the Englishmen.'

MacDonald went rigid.

'Captain Endicott, I don't do no stern tows, see? We don't get you to port by no bloody stern tow.'

That was one for the *Semirande,* which meant that the *Grooter's* big ears up on a masthead had been listening for a long time.

'When I see your men on bows I come to put line on you. Get that?'

Endicott capitulated and signed off. MacDonald went in close to one of the long windows and closed his hands over the grip bar bisecting it, again looking towards the Arctic circle.

'The Friesland bastard,' he said.

'But a good skipper.'

MacDonald swung around. Mark Underson was standing at the starboard end of the bridge, looking aft. He could move about on the *Saturn* like this, suddenly arriving, not seen in transit.

It had something to do with the compact size of the man. Now he stood balanced, not needing a handhold, the dim-out blurring his profile. MacDonald moved over.

'I was thinking about poor sods out on that catwalk.'

What Underson said showed he was thinking about salvage techniques. His heart didn't bleed easily.

'Scherner's right about a stern tow. Can't be done in these seas. Do you think I'd have followed the *Semirande* and her prize out here if I hadn't been damn sure her hawser would go? And if we'd got our line over her back there at Hoy I'd have made them secure forward, whatever Endicott had to say about that. Dartan was wrong. He knows it now.'

'You're not worried about the *Grooter* taking the prize from both of us?'

'Yes, I'm worried about it. But Scherner has one big fault. He's too keen. He tends to fall over his own feet.'

The Skipper ought to know his Dutchmen, he'd been with the Hoofstanger company for years, though this was a phase in his career he rarely talked about. MacDonald had wondered why. It could be that the Hoofstangers hadn't thought enough of their English recruit to promote him. He'd stayed a Second all his time with them.

'Oughtn't we to try and get a line over before the *Grooter's* in action?'

'So you've been talking to Ginnis? Tom, I know what the crew is thinking. But there are times when what your crew thinks and what makes sense are two different things. And this is one of the times.'

'You know what you're doing,' MacDonald said.

Underson laughed. 'I don't detect any confident ring in your voice. Like my assessment?'

'Yes.'

'Scherner's going to put on an act. It's his nature. Gazelle leaps across the tanker's bows. Pretty, if you like marine acrobatics. But these don't provide the best conditions for a man aiming a rocket gun.'

'So what do we do?'

'Gamble that even with the *Grooter* threatening we have a little more time in which to let the sea go down and wind drop.'

Once again the tanker put an arc light out of a bridge window, shining this down on the catwalk. Three men came out on to it.

'Give me your glasses,' Underson said.

He looked through them. MacDonald could see figures hesitating, waiting for scuppers to clear a sea that boiled just under them. These boys would be about as happy over their orders to get for'ard as a dawn patrol sent into no-man's-land.

'You'd think they'd build those cans with a covered passage to the forepeak,' MacDonald said.

'It would cut down on tank space.'

The *Grooter* switched off a searchlight and used a flare. This showed her positioned over beyond the tanker, about parallel to the *Semirande*. She was surrounded on a wave slope by froth from her props. The *Mary Worth* went into a lift which hid both the tugs, following this with a roll to port that put the men on the catwalk out of sight, too. The *Saturn's* rise showed the bow party at the gap.

'They're going to make it,' MacDonald said.

The Skipper said nothing. He got as tightly bound on his nerves sometimes as a clockwork motor twisted too hard by its key. MacDonald kept quiet through the next ten minutes, even when he saw the first man climbing the forepeak ladder, then the second, then the third.

'I can't see. He had to ask, 'Are they roping themselves on up there?'

'Yes.'

Scherner would be feeling pleased, even though a lot more water smashed over the tanker's bows on to that platform than was spilling across the low well-deck.

On her third flare the *Grooter* moved, hidden except for her masthead, by the *Mary Worth*'s hull. When MacDonald really saw her again she was horribly close to the tanker's bows, practically under them on the crumbling crest of a swell, shooting up water like a New York fireboat. The Dutchman sank into a trough on the *Saturn*'s side of the *Mary Worth*, only her funnel and mast showing, but these indicating that she was going into a quick turn to the south again. She came into view stern-first to the *Saturn*, propellers churning.

Scherner came on the air, shouting for the tanker's captain.

'Endicott? What the hell your men doing, eh? I get my line right over you. I see it. You in walkie-talkie contact your bow party?'

'Yes. I've just been on to them. They say they couldn't see anything with all that spray you put up. And a wave took our Third right to the rail. It's rough up there, Captain Scherner.'

'Rough? What your bloody Third Officer become sailor for, eh? To keep dry? Listen, we work like god damn here. You tell 'em get off their backsides and secure my line, see?'

'Hang on a minute, I'll get on to the bows.'

The speaker crackled as though from tension generated and then Endicott came on the air again. 'Captain Scherner? My Third is sure the line was never over the bows.'

'What? Your Third on his stomach saying his prayers, maybe? You tell him work now, pray later. You want I talk to him?'

'No!'

'Okay. I come in again, see. Now!'

The *Saturn* offered a wave-top view for most of the *Grooter*'s second run across the tanker's bows under a new flare. But Scherner's luck was out. A geyser of water shot up between him and the *Mary Worth* which was menacing enough to make a Dutch helmsman sheer off and roll over a sea well clear of sharp steel bows. But a rocket must have been fired from beyond a crest for Scherner's yells tested a speaker again.

'Those *haut ver dammer* bloody fools! Endicott! My line is on your bows again. Until she slides away. No one does nothing!'

The voice from the tanker was much louder, as though her captain had taken to howling, too.

'How the hell could you expect them to do anything? They took tons of water up there. We've lost contact.'

'You mean your Third lose his walkie-talkie?'

'Probably.'

'Captain, you know what I think? You don't want no tow. You want to ride home by yourself. Okay, have a good trip.'

'Scherner! Listen to me! If you stopped that bow jumping and aimed your rocket over the well-deck just aft of the fore-peak there might be a chance to secure.'

'Hear, hear,' Mark Underson said.

But Scherner had the last word.

'Over, Captain Endicott. And bloody out!'

'What now?' MacDonald asked.

'A pause for schnapps. I'm going down to the engine-room. And don't look at me like that, Tom. I have a project on with the Chief. It isn't a chess game. You could call it a gadget. But pre-electronic.'

Berand was at the wheel. He had replaced pyjama bottoms with trousers, but was still in the shapeless handknit sweater. Jules went to a window behind the binnacle box.

'I can't see the bow party.'

'Taking cover behind winch machinery,' Berand said. 'And who would blame them?'

'Wind dropping?'

'In force, yes. But it's coming in from every direction except due south. Which will be hell for rocket-firing. Are you still trying for a line on the tanker?'

Jules swung around. 'What the hell's the matter with you, Berand? Of course we're putting a line on her.'

'No need to shout. You're not the only one whose nerves are twitching. When?'

'Now.'

'For a stern tow?'

'No!'

'If you're asking me to do a Scherner in front of that big can's bows I'm going to my bunk now.'

'We're not bow jumping. Just getting in closer. Towards her forepeak. As close as you'll take her.'

The Mate reached for the engine-room pipe and ordered full astern. In half a minute the *Semirande* started to shiver. Then she clamped on the foreslopes of a wave to travel south with it, as though bowing herself out backwards from an audience with a personage. Moments later Berand asked for half-ahead and there was bow spray again.

Jules went out on the starboard wing, sliding shut the wheel-house door behind him, but conscious of the Mate in there behind him wearing his 'the old man's been at the bottle again' expression. All right he had gone below for a run off and stayed ten minutes to have a cognac. This was his damn ship and he was answerable to no one on her. *No* one! He wanted to shout that out, but Berand would have heard.

The Mate had been right about the wind, though; it was going to make rocket-firing a lottery, with skill not really coming into it. Where the hell was Tourin? In his bunk, probably, snoring. They were a lot of clock-punchers these days, who would go off duty to the bell on a sinking ship. God knew what the world would be like in twenty years when that lot came into authority. They were always bleating about what they had inherited from their parents, but it would be damn interesting to be around to see what they handed on to their sons. Longer hair and longer beards, probably. Or there could be a reaction, everyone going around bald, showing the chins they hadn't got.

Berand had brought the *Semirande* in parallel to the *Grooter* and then manœuvred around her stern, and the two tugs suddenly seemed to be sharing the same turbulence, a weird double act, running lights and lit ports swinging up and down together. The Dutchman, a solo turn if there ever was one, resented this. A searchlight came on, blasting Jules and the ship behind him in whiteness. A loud hailer scraped a voice through the sea's roaring.

'Where the hell you think you go? Get to hell out of my way.'

Jules didn't turn his head. He was suddenly remembering a day in Rotterdam, two years ago it must be now, with the *Semirande* coming into the crowded harbour with a string of barges behind her. Old Henri had thought of this as something to put against a lull in deep-sea work, money earning, and much better than giving one of his crews a couple of weeks shore leave. The word about their cargo of compressed fertilizer for the bulb fields of Holland must have got about and the Hoofstanger skippers were waiting on their ships and in the cafés. The *Marie Grooter*, not then on English station, had been anchored. Scherner had used his loud hailer then, too, bellowing across three hundred yards: 'So you're towing shit these days?'

For the first time in his life Jules had wanted to ram another ship. He was near to the feeling again.

'I tell you . . . get off my course, *Semirande*. I go to the bows now. They don't want no tow from you. What you use for hawser, eh? String?'

Jules kept his eyes on the tanker. A moment later the *Grooter* used her siren, four sharp screeches. The spotlight went off. A foam blanket from the Dutchman's screws reflected the glow of her lights.

Tourin came out on the wing to show that he hadn't been in his bunk. 'She's going to cut right across our bows, sir!'

'Let him.'

Scherner had apparently taken over the helm himself. He was the kind of man who wouldn't delegate, leaping about doing everyone's job, and some of them not too well. He pushed his ship over the swell shared with the *Semirande*, angled on it, clearing a rival's bow by not more than twenty yards. As she broke through a crest spray came sheeting back and Jules ducked, but still rose dripping. He counted ten and set the young a good example by saying not one word.

Berand had taken no evasive action. He topped the wave as he had intended to. The *Mary Worth* was dead ahead and for once almost on even keel, her aft quarter looking like a resort hotel at the height of the season.

All those lights suddenly changed colour, first with an almost explosive flash of orange. This faded to gas-light yellow, staying at that for half a minute. Then there was blackout, as though from a master switch.

'My God! Was she on emergency dynamos, sir?'

'Yes.'

Jules went to the searchlight, thinking that a beam on the tanker's bridge might bring some cheer at least, but the *Grooter* got in ahead of him with a flare. For a moment he saw this as a simple act of kindness, then noticed a churned wake over to port. Scherner had issued his orders for a run-in, and the Almighty and Dutch skippers never re-think an order. Endicott, trying to cope in sudden dark with a total breakdown in his communications system, except for walkie-talkie, was to come to attention and concentrate on what the *Grooter* was up to. The same was expected of those men cut off up there on the forepeak who couldn't even talk to their own bridge any more. There was no doubt that Scherner had his talents, but imagination wasn't one of them.

Berand had sensibly reacted to a new situation by stopping a slow approach towards the tanker, putting the *Semirande* on reverse engines, to hold at about three hundred yards. Jules, who had been going into the wheel-house to order this, stayed where he was and watched.

This time the *Grooter* didn't come quite so close to those meat chopper bows, but near enough, and Jules saw the flash of a rocket. He did not see men up in the tanker's bows leaping around

to secure a line. No doubt the Dutchman was again packing the
air with his comment on that.

The *Grooter* went behind the *Mary Worth*'s hull and disappeared except for a wildly waving masthead which indicated
that she was coming around in an astonishingly sharp turn. It
seemed probable that she was wagging her stern like a cat that
has just missed a bird.

'Never give up, do they?' Tourin said.

'No. He's got that tattooed on his chest.'

Jules went to the wheel-house door.

'Take her in when you're ready, Berand. Tourin, tell Ginole
to try and get on to Endicott with a walkie-talkie. I want the
Captain to know we're going to put a line over her well-deck
just aft of the forepeak. Then get back and handle the flare for
me. I want light for this shot.'

The *Saturn* provided light from her tower platform.

'More target practice,' Jules announced. 'We won't hang
around watching that.'

'Maybe we ought to,' Berand said.

'Why?'

'They've just released something. It's not a rocket.'

Jules turned back on to the wing again. He stood staring north.
The *Saturn* was in view beyond the tanker's well-deck and far
enough back from the *Mary Worth* for those towers to stay in
sight even when she was in a trough. Something white was drifting
from that high platform. At first it looked like a paper napkin
snatched from a picnic. Then it dipped, showing itself as oblong
and rigid. A thermal caught the thing and shot it up for almost
two hundred feet above the tug. It had two long, fluttering tails.

'What in hell's name . . . ?'

Berand's voice came out of the wheel-house.

'Never fly a kite, Jules?'

'Eh? My God, you're right. Has Underson gone mad?'

'Want me to close now for your shot?'

'No! We'll wait.'

The *Grooter* was interested, too. She used her searchlight,
angling this up. As the flare faded the spot caught the kite and
managed to hold on to it. Jules remembered a war. He half
expected to hear *ack ack* fire.

'Berand! He can't believe he's going to get his line over that
way.'

'Why not?'

'It's lunatic.'

'I wonder? You can do a lot with a kite. Even in gusting like
this. Mistakes don't matter too much. You correct them.'

The kite started a plunge, tails fluttering, towards the sea. It was jerked back towards the *Saturn*'s platform and recovered, surging up again, that check line spinning out. Scherner's spot lost target. The *Saturn* put up another flare.

'Well, I'm damned,' Jules said.

It didn't matter to the handler that the platform he stood on was pitching about, he didn't have to take aim. A spate of squalls came in from the north, taking the kite high and speeding it on a straight line towards the tanker.

Scherner reacted to that favourable gusting from his position beyond the *Mary Worth* and fired a rocket. The shell glistened on its direct arc for seconds, then went west, with the kite. The kite was pulled back towards the *Saturn*, the rocket went in the sea. 'Scherner's getting rattled!' Jules shouted.

'How do you feel? Want me to move in now?'

'No. Wait till the kite's in the drink.'

'The handler knows his job.'

'A stunt like this can't work, Berand!'

'Why not? Technology isn't everything.'

'A kite? A bloody kite! Underson'll be laughed out of the business.'

'Not if he gets the tow.'

The *Grooter*'s spot gave up attempting to follow a flight, the ray dropping to sea level and lying there as though exhausted. The *Saturn* used a new flare. The kite was all of 800 feet up and coming in high above the *Mary Worth*. Suddenly a flashing sword lifted off the sea and swung around towards the *Saturn*, finding first her bows, then slashing up towards the platform, managing to hold on it.

'The dirty bastard!' Tourin shouted. 'He's trying to dazzle them!'

'Whose side are you on?' Jules snarled.

The *Saturn* had a stronger searchlight than the *Grooter*. This came on from a height advantage and moved across the water like a bleach stain. It found the Dutch tug's plates, climbing them to explode 10,000 candle-power against wheel-house windows. The night was well lit. The kite sailed on.

Jules watched through binoculars. He saw the drop. This was fast, like a bird shot down. The kite hit the sea between the *Mary Worth* and the *Semirande*, a white patch on a wave crest, then lost in a trough, apparently sunk. A line from the *Saturn* lay neatly across the tanker's well-deck catwalk, only a matter of feet from the ladder up to the forepeak. A man stood up from behind a winch, seemed to be releasing himself from a rope, then made for the ladder. The *Saturn* assisted him with her beam. The *Grooter*'s beam sank on to waves and died.

Jules walked into the wheel-house. He stood there.

Berand said, 'I'm waiting for orders.'

'Brest.'

'You're not hanging on for dawn?'

'No.'

Berand lifted the engine tube.

'Half-astern. Jules, I've just remembered hearing before we left for Newfoundland that the *Saturn* had landed an oil rig tow. From the Clyde around Scotland.'

'So what?'

'That's why she was here so quickly. From somewhere in the North Sea. It may be that she hadn't finished that tow. Just left it.'

'What?'

'It's the sort of thing Underson might do. We could check.'

'How?'

'Scottish radio relay would put us in the picture. It's worth a try.'

'You mean . . . that rig could be anchored? Just waiting?'

'Yes. .Waiting for us. There mightn't have been time for another Hoofstanger to get up from Holland, even if one of their ships was free.'

'God! You could be right. I'll see Ginole. Berand, you use your head now and then. I'll say that.'

'Someone has to on this tub.'


## CHAPTER FOUR

JESSIE LAWTON brought the Daimler Majestic automatic down to thirty for a restricted area. The car was one of the few things in life that continued to frighten her. It was a nearly perfect car, a long mass of maroon lacquer, but too big, too powerful, often giving her the feeling it was going to slip out of control and become a lethal projectile. Whenever Jessie read about the risk of one man being able to punch the one button that would lead to nuclear holocaust she thought of all those knobs on her car fascia, some of which she had never touched because she didn't know what they were for and didn't want to learn.

Her first car had been a seven horse-power Austin, with canvas hood. Back in the thirties she had handled that little box in a positively dashing manner, pushing it up sometimes to a death-defying forty-five, enjoying the vibration and the jolts from its cart springing. In that immediate post-flapper era, with the depression deep all around her, Jessie had been a firm-jawed, serious girl in her late twenties with objective clearly fixed ahead of her, these being to survive the general misery and if possible grow rich.

Even then she had been a career woman, and not bad at it either, earning the remarkably large salary for her sex of £350 a year, which had been enough to pay for a five-roomed flat in Edinburgh's dull but respectable Marchmont area, plus maintaining a hungry mother who lived with her, plus the baby Austin. Her income was also enough for a fortnight's holiday every year in London where she stayed in a near-luxury hotel for twelve shillings a night, bed and breakfast. Once there had been a wildly extravagant week-end in Paris with a girl friend. Both had travelled in Harris tweed suits from the Fifty Shilling Tailors, and both had got sore feet from French pavements, but no propositions from young French males.

The Daimler went whispering past Edinburgh's Zoo, moving on to the slight descent which gave a wide view of the city. She glanced at this, almost startled to notice that the old dominance of the castle on its rock was now diminished by a glass tower that glowed a faintly gangrenous blue from its striplighting. There were other towers like it on the skyline, but for this latest construction she had a particular responsibility. Thirty per cent of the finance which had pushed it up had come from her pocket. Until this moment, however, she hadn't realized that the positioning of the new building on its ex-slum site amounted, from one of the main roads into the city, almost to a sneer at the old Edinburgh so rapidly dying all around it. Her sudden slight embarrassment wasn't really personal but came from her role as Vice-Chairman of the Historic Edinburgh Protection Association which had been formed to save Scotland's capital from being ruined by contemporary architectural monstrosities. The cause was already lost and Jessie decided that it was time to resign office. And since the great expansion of her activities outside the city the organization was no longer of any real use to her, though at one time, particularly in her husband's day, it had frequently given clear leads to the profitable property deals on which the Lawton fortune had been founded.

At Murrayfield she turned south, relieved to be out of the traffic stream, choosing her own private and devious route to the Morningside area in which she lived. The by-ways took a long time but peace of mind was worth it, and she arrived home without incident.

Jessie rarely looked at the house in which she lived. It didn't, in fact, bear looking at, a nineteenth-century rock pile set in an austered garden of trimmed grass and trees that were butcher-pruned every five years. The house had come to her, along with the Daimler, as part of the inheritance from Arthur Lawton, her late husband, and both were due respect because of this. She got out of one portion of her legacy and went into another.

Not a sound greeted her in the front hall, which was spacious and chilly. The house had automatic heating, but in late autumn this was not yet on for sensible reasons of economy. The kitchen, however, was warm enough from the monster solid-fuel cooker which one of her two dailies stoked before leaving. Jessie filled a kettle and put it on a hot-plate, found a tin of pilchards and opened this, set out china, sliced some bread, and got milk and butter from the refrigerator. The electric clock said six fifteen and she checked a diamond-studded timepiece on her wrist against this. It was too late for the Scottish radio news and she didn't want any of the chatter that followed this. She would eat and go to bed early with the financial sections of three London papers.

The phone rang. Jessie went to the extension on a dresser and gave her number, not her name, having found that to admit identity is to expose yourself, quite often to charity appeals and more than once to a threatening voice telling her that unless she put £1,000 in crisp new notes under a stump in Blackford park she would be carved up. Threats never frightened her and she certainly had better things to do with her money than put it under tree stumps.

'Chessie? Chessie, are you there?'

She felt the usual twitch of resentment against the man's irrepressible familiarity and didn't try to keep the stiffness out of her voice.

'Oh, it's you, Mr Lazzari.'

'Sure it is. And where you been the last three days, then? I am phoning and phoning.'

'What about?'

'What about, she asks. Don't you read no papers?'

'Mr Lazzari . . . !'

'Or listen to the radio, maybe? You don't hear a thing, eh? What is there up in Scotland, no news at all?'

'Will you kindly come to the point!'

'Okay. We're in big trouble, Chessie. So big you don't credit it. Not unless you read the papers or listen to the radio. Where you been?'

'In the Highlands.'

'Eh? And what is the Highlands, please?'

'The Highlands of Scotland, man!'

'Where there are no telephones, no radios, no newspapers?'

'There are all these things if you have time for them. It so happened that I didn't have the time.'

'Then what you do?'

'I don't see that it's any concern of yours. But if you must know, I was dealing with a crisis in my new motel at Aviemore.'

'Oh, I get it. So it's business? I should have guessed.'

'It was very much business,' Jessie snapped. 'The cook, the barman, the housekeeper and seven maids all walked out. Just at the start of the season.'

'Season? Is this a season?'

'Skiing, Mr Lazzari.'

'God! What I don't know, it's terrible. And of Scotland I know nothing.'

'What did you ring up about?'

He told her in his own way, and taking his time. She could see him gesticulating with a free hand as his voice got louder and louder.

Lazzari gave the impression that he did most of his living in sleek London restaurants. He claimed to be Lebanese from Beirut, but could have been almost anything from anywhere. A few years in England had enabled the man to find all the ropes that interested him and to learn how to pull them. His speciality was arranging speculative investment in high yield projects, especially those so placed that at least a proportion of the income from them could be stashed abroad to avoid British taxation.

Jessie accepted Lazzari for what he was, his appearance on the London scene to her mind a direct consequence of the restrictive trading legislation which continued to pour out of government offices. His role was to soften the pain of this for a select few, and he did it very well. She disliked his insufferable familiarity but had learned that you couldn't put him in his place, he didn't seem to have one.

'So you see, Chessie, what it is, eh? The bloody soup.'

'Not quite, Mr Lazzari.'

'Oh? Up there in Scotland you keep calm, is it? Me, I don't stay calm. Not one little bit. I don't like this. I don't like quarter of a million pound lawsuits from big oil companies. Slapped on our *little* company. If we have to pay, then what? You tell me. What happens to Anglo-European Salvage? I tell you this, Chessie, I never like that name too much. It smells big, okay. But what's the use of smelling big when you only got one boat?'

'Ship,' Jessie corrected.

'Eh?'

'It's not a boat, man. Boats are things you row.'

'That's right. Go on about nothing. How about the lawsuit?'

'It's a bluff,' Jessie said.

'And how are you knowing that?'

'If they really had any intention of suing us for breach of contract they wouldn't be mentioning sums like a quarter of a million. Their lawyers would see they didn't. Fifty thousand and I'd be worried. Quarter of a million and I'm not. I'd say that where we'll hit trouble is when we try to claim more towage fee than that original five thousand down payment. Then they may throw the book at us. But that's all we have to worry about.'

'What you know about the oil business, Chessie?'

'It suffers from hysteria. We're seeing one of the attacks. But it will pass. Mr Lazzari, in the circumstances you've just outlined the humanitarian factor comes into things. Strongly.'

'I don't get you? What's a humanitarian factor?'

'The *Saturn* dropped her rig tow in order to save lives.'

She heard him take a deep breath.

'Who you try to kid with that one?'

'Not you. But it's the way it can be made to look. And when the oil executives cool down a little they'll realize this. If they don't their legal side will spell it out to them. The last thing any oil company wants is to be made into a kind of ogre in a court of law. They get a lot of bad publicity for ruthlessness as it is.'

There was almost half a minute of silence on the wire. It might have been from respect.

'Chessie, you're a bloomin' miracle. That's what I say the first time we meet . . . that woman's a bloomin' miracle.'

'Thank you.'

'But I think you're crazy! All right, oil is mad business. But they think big money all the time. I'm still scared. And Sir Richard is twice as scared as me. You should see him, it's terrible. He keeps ringing, where are you, what the hell's happening, all that. His shouting gives me a real headache.'

'Sir Richard is only a name on our notepaper.'

Suddenly Lazzari laughed. 'Go on, you tell him that!'

'I will if it becomes necessary. Has our baronet made any positive suggestions?'

'Sure. We got to sack Underson. Right now.'

'Clear thinking. What then?'

'We make the Mate captain.'

'And order him to put Underson in irons, I suppose? Pending a company inquiry?'

'I don't know where we put Underson. But he's sacked.'

'No, he isn't. Perhaps I'd better see Sir Richard. At an informal company meeting tomorrow. I'll get the last flight down tonight, you can always get a seat on that. I'll be at the Mayfair Hotel if you should want me at any time before eight fifteen.'

'You mean eight fifteen in the morning? How should I want anyone then? I'm asleep.'

'Not tomorrow. You'd better be there, Lazzari. Nine sharp in the offices. Fix it up with our baronet and the accountant, will you?'

'You think I can get Sir Richard into London for nine in the morning?'

'On second thoughts, perhaps not. But I can. I'll telephone him myself.'

Mrs Jessie Lawton claimed her minimum rate single room at the Mayfair Hotel shortly before two in the morning. She breakfasted at seven off a trolley by courtesy of night service, porridge, bacon and eggs, plus three cups of coffee and by eight fifteen was in a taxi for the City, allowing plenty of time for traffic holdups. She was wearing what she regarded as her London uniform, a dark grey flannel suit with skirt coming well below the knees, a toning beret over pepper and salt hair, a plain white blouse with a high neck, three diamond rings and a diamond cluster with heavy carat central stones. Diamonds were the only personal possession she cared to acquire, she liked their glitter, what it stood for, and the way the value of the gems kept easy pace with inflation. On the seat beside her was a short mink coat bought ten years earlier, together with an alligator handbag, also vintage, which matched square cut, low-heeled shoes.

She looked what she was, a period piece, but expensively period. Taxi drivers, taking one glance at her, didn't expect large tips and didn't get them.

She was the first in the inner of the two rooms which Anglo-European rented in a building scheduled for demolition. Furnishings were bleak in the extreme, a large desk, filing cabinets, and four modern chairs mounted on chromium pedestals. Above a dead grate hung one picture, this new and shining, of the *Saturn* as she had been on her trials, a foaming bow wave and glistening paint.

Jessie sat down, found an economy-sized tipped cigarette in her handbag, and lit it. She was no longer a heavy smoker, having been told by her doctor that it was only a matter of time until the female lung cancer rate caught up with the male, and her rationing was strict, nothing until well after breakfast, and at the maximum ten a day. That seemed to minimize the tar intake risk. Her mother had lived to be eighty-six and Jessie felt that her own incentives to last at least as long were considerably stronger.

Voices in the outer office suggested that another director had arrived. Lazzari came straight through.

'Chessie, my love! Welcome again to London.'

She looked at him. He was wearing Middle Eastern city clothes, a striped suit with a too bright blue tone, a floral waistcoat, and an ochre tie with the knot hidden by his chins. His skin shone, particularly damp where it folded over itself. Black hair glittered with brilliantine. His teeth, all his own except where supported by gold, flashed. He held out both hands. Jessie took neither. It occurred to her that this man, in the London of twenty years

372 THE HAWSER PIRATES

ago, perhaps even ten, would have stood no chance whatsoever except in Soho. But he had arrived at the right time.

'So? You are not so happy this morning?'

'I'm fine, thank you. No sign of Sir Richard yet?'

'I think he has coronary soon. You should see him yesterday.'

'It's today I'm interested in. Has there been any contact between this office and the *Saturn* since it took the tanker in tow?'

'I don't know. I find out from Perkins.'

'I thought you were supposed to keep in daily touch with this place?'

On the way to the door he lifted both hands, palms uppermost. 'Chessie, you know me. I got a lot of stoves cooking all the time. Sure, I'm company secretary. But does that mean I come in every day and sit here? What you think I am, eh?'

'I could make a number of pretty sharp guesses.'

He grinned and went out, leaving Jessie with the irritating feeling that she would never be able to handle this man, and she was used to handling her contacts. In his own way Lazzari had won round after round with her and looked like continuing to do so. He came back again and shut the door.

'Perkins says no message in, out. And I forget . . . our accountant isn't to come. In bed with flu. Chinese, Indian, I don't know. One day there is coming a terrible flu like the black plague. Worse than atomics. We all get it. Finish.'

'The germ will die of cold just south of the Scottish border.'

Lazzari flung himself into one of the pedestal chairs.

'Chessie, you kill me! You know you really do. I wake up at night laughing after we have been meeting.'

She found the thought of this man waking up to laugh at her disturbing. To her knowledge she had never affected anyone else in this way before. Arthur hadn't found her in the least humorous. The really active bond in their marriage had been a deeply shared interest in property development, to which had later been added the quite exciting gamble of running deep-sea trawlers out of Aberdeen.

A voice in the outer office announced a new arrival. Lazzari, who had been testing his chair for comfort angles, sat up straight, but their co-director didn't at once join them, taking time out in his crowded day to be affable to Perkins.

Sir Richard Clanmer's commercial success was, in Jessie's opinion, largely accidental. As the junior director of a private London banking house he had, years before, visited Australia and while out there had somehow stumbled on information about the unexploited mineral potential in the sub-continent. The bank had acted on this news and invested. Suddenly it had been bonanza. Sir Richard's personal stock in the company skyrocketed.

Overnight he was established as something of a wizard at tracking down likely new fields for investment, and just at this point his bank joined in the great unit trust scramble, producing a vast new subsidiary of growth units, income units, security units, and crowning all with the new issue of something that no one else had thought of up to that time . . . adventure units.

These were designed for the investor who had never been fortunate with horses or football pools, but was still convinced that if he could just find the right field his luck would change. The customer was promised all the thrills of a flutter but at the same time told that his gamble would be under the control of one of the best financial brains in London . . . Sir Richard. It had turned out that there were an astonishing number of people only too ready to rob their post-office savings of the minimal entrance money of £100 just to have a go.

Jessie suspected that being the head of Adventure Units had kept Sir Richard off normal sleep for the last year and a half. He put up an impressive bluff, but still bore the marks of a man who feels that his tomorrows, whenever he took time to consider them, looked terrible. They looked terrible to Jessie, too. She had a great deal of experience in adventure speculation and knew only too well what it demanded in the way of a cool head, an instinct which told you when to cut losses and run, plus a readiness to be totally ruthless when this was called for, as it often was. In her estimation Sir Richard lacked all these qualities, bringing to his task the kind of caution that was going to cripple him. As a name in the City the man was of use to her at the moment, but whenever the signs appeared that his dark days were looming . . . she gave him three more years at the outside . . . it was her plan to unload him fast.

The door opened. Sir Richard was still in his thirties, but somewhat portly already, with the kind of pale, fine hair that gets starved off a scalp early on, the surviving vestiges fluffed out over prominent ears. He said good morning to Jessie, then glanced at Lazzari with poorly concealed distaste. He took some time deciding which of the two remaining chairs he would use, sat and sighed.

'This is all a most unfortunate business. Disastrous, in fact.'

'Nothing of the kind,' Jessie said.

Sir Richard stared. 'Really, Mrs Lawton? Perhaps you'll explain what you mean by that?'

Jessie did. It took her three minutes. She used fingers to tick off her points. The head of Adventure Units seemed fascinated by the flashing.

'If this is *not* a crisis, Mrs Lawton, what would you call it?'

'A flurry.'

'You can really mean that? A flurry? This is all the importance you give to a wilful breach of contract with one of the most powerful oil companies in the world? Which could crush us like a gnat?'

'Let's not get things out of proportion, Sir Richard. The rig hasn't been damaged in any way. It ought to be under tow again soon, if it isn't already.'

Sir Richard leaned forward. He seemed suddenly almost pleased with himself.

'Oh, so you haven't heard? It *is* under tow again. Very much so. By a French tug and a Dutch one. The French tug couldn't handle things on its own, apparently. So they're sharing. And sharing the money, too. What should have been our money.'

Jessie looked at Lazzari. 'Did you know about this?'

'No.'

'Why not?'

'Chessie, I must go to Paris yesterday.'

She controlled anger. Sir Richard had taken control and he liked that. He began to sound pompous again.

'I got in touch with my adviser on shipping matters last night and he made our situation plain, Mrs Lawton. Very plain indeed. The most we can hope for from an awards court is part salvage for the tanker tow. The Frenchman gets the other part for pulling her away from danger. Our share could be less than his. In fact they're going to do very nicely, part of the tanker award, and part of our fee for the rig tow. I'd say that the Frenchman has come off easily the best.'

'This time.'

'You're still defending Underson?'

'His record doesn't need defending.'

'I am not interested in his record! What concerns me is his totally irresponsible conduct in this case. We simply cannot afford to have our tug operated by a man who is prepared to throw all caution to the winds.'

'You have to do just that quite often in salvage.'

'Indeed? And where will we be in one year's time if we keep on this captain who tears up contracts?'

'Showing an improvement on this year's nineteen per cent gross profit on capital investment. How many of your other holdings do better?'

'That is *not* the point, Mrs Lawton!'

'It is to me, as principal shareholder. I built that ship for the big profits. You don't get these in towing. The skipper I need has to be a gambler. And I have no intention of turning on him, or letting anyone else do it, simply because one of his gambles didn't quite come off.'

'In other words the man can do exactly what he damn well pleases?'

'Within reason, yes. For as long as I have confidence in him. I also own trawlers, Sir Richard. In many ways it's a similar business. If I tried to keep a rein on my trawler skippers I'd be a fool. Because they're independent men, like Underson. They operate from experience and instinct. Instinct is more important. It tells them where the fish are. And they go after them, in winter into the dark. There has been a lot of howling down here in London about forcing trawler skippers to keep in radio contact all the time. But the plain fact is that they'll never do this because talk on the air would give away a fish find to rivals.'

'Are you trying to excuse Underson for not answering messages from his owners?'

'We haven't been sending him any.'

Sir Richard inspected the ceiling, as though thinking that the room needed re-decorating, which it did.

As a matter of fact *I* have, Mrs Lawton.'

'I don't understand?'

'It's simple enough. I put through radio telephone calls to the *Saturn* from my office. And each time the wireless fellow on the ship acknowledged the call but said the Captain was not available.'

Jessie's anger was cold. 'You didn't consider this was exceeding your authority as a minority shareholder?'

'Dammit, I *am* on the board. And you weren't available. I got hold of some charwoman at your house. Why the devil don't you have a secretary on duty up there in Edinburgh when you're away?'

'You haven't answered my question, Sir Richard!'

'And you haven't answered mine! The situation was at crisis point. You had gone off somewhere. The accountant here was ill. I knew perfectly well that Mr Lazzari would do nothing without your authority. Someone had to do something.'

'What were you going to say to Underson?'

'Ask him what the hell he was up to! And I did find out one thing . . . that man has complete contempt for the authority we represent.'

'I don't like your use of "we".'

Sir Richard took a deep breath. He stirred in his chair.

'If you don't like my use of it in these circumstances then I think I must ask you to accept my resignation from the board.'

'Certainly.'

He was astonished. And after that first reaction Jessie was sure she saw something else, fear, as though he realized suddenly that directorships weren't something in God's gift to the privileged, but could be snatched away at speed, even by a woman. He recovered quickly.

'I hope you realize, Mrs Lawton, that this will mean the withdrawal of Adventure Unit funds from Anglo-European?'

'Of course. I'll take up those holdings myself.'

Sir Richard used dignity. He was trained in it and made an almost elegant withdrawal, slightly pained, but there was no shouting and no rudeness. From the door he bowed to Jessie, ignoring Lazzari. This time, however, he didn't linger in the outer office to be affable to the clerk. The door to the passage shut with a bang.

Lazzari got up and went over to a grimy window.

'You can find this money, Chessie?'

'Not without selling something I don't intend to.'

'So?'

'I'm counting on you to raise it.'

He swung around.

'It's not so damn easy!'

'What? To Luke Lazzari?'

He lifted both hands.

'Listen to me. Sure I can get money. But I got a reputation to keep, see? People trust my judgement. I put their money into something that's no good and I get the chopper. What I'm thinking is that Sir Richard quits us talking. With a big mouth. He doesn't like the way Anglo-European is being run, so he walks out. He won't stand for contract breaking, he'll say. And they listen to him in the City. They don't like it neither.'

Jessie smiled.

'Don't worry too much, Mr Lazzari. I may live in Scotland, but I know how the City reacts. Sir Richard isn't going to be talking about us. For one very good reason. Our company offers a better return than any of the other holdings in those ridiculous units of his. They offer adventure, remember? That's a big return at a certain permitted risk. If there's too much risk he lands in trouble, but if he plays safe with small takings he isn't doing his job. The poor man. He has a lot to think about. I'd say he'll take a few days off to do it, then get in touch with me in Edinburgh. When he does that I'll allow him to think he's being firm.'

'What the hell you mean by that?'

'That I'll do exactly what I want with Anglo-European and let him know this, but at the same time I won't be rude about it. He has no inkling of it as yet, but I'm counting on Adventure Units to help finance a new tug we'll be building. I'll be calling on your sources too, of course.'

'My God! You make another boat?'

'I wish you wouldn't call them *boats*. But I am in due course making another, as you put it. And Sir Richard will still be with us to help find the money.'

'Maybe you don't keep him. He's plenty mad.'

'So am I. But we'll both cool down. And the next time we're in touch I'll be able to give Sir Richard the assurance he wants, that there will be no contract breaking in future. When the *Saturn* undertakes a tow she will finish that tow.'

'So after all you fix Underson?'

'It's not the word I would have chosen. The Captain and I will reach an understanding. I defended him to Sir Richard and would again, but I won't pretend I'm happy about this tanker business. I'm going to have a meeting with Underson as soon as he has brought in his tow.'

'You want I should be with you?'

'Thank you, Mr Lazzari, but I think not. Now I suggest we go out for a cup of coffee. There's time for it before I collect my suitcase for my flight home.'

# CHAPTER FIVE

MARK UNDERSON lay along the settee in his cabin, his feet propped up on a built-in chest of drawers. He was listening to a record player. He had never kept a journal, just bought discs. A cupboard held the music from his worlds, Chinese jazz, syncopated screeching of Indian sopranos, a sound of *gamelans* from Java, a rare recording of an aborigine stick band acquired in Darwin, and another of Dyak male voices in North Borneo. The records from Europe were a mixed bag, the one on the turntable Greig's *Solveig's Song*.

The singing contained everything he remembered about Bergen. His trawler had put in there with engine trouble on Mark's first voyage to the Arctic, a refrigerated cargo of fish threatened by that delay and everyone, particularly the Skipper, out of temper. They were in port for three days in a town that, though geared for sailors, seemed to have no interest in foreign ones. It had been high summer and perfect weather, the days so long that night was no more than a brief recess from sunshine. The little city had somehow suggested a sealed off immunity to the rest of the world, concerned in its own affairs, aseptically clean and apparently terribly righteous. There was damn all to do. This mightn't have mattered if the girls hadn't been so beautiful.

Mark had walked streets thronged with splendid blondes, all wearing thin dresses that came out of cupboards only for a few weeks in the year. To a man just in from cold, empty seas and as usual randy from abstinence, it had all at first sight seemed like an offering of Valhalla to the brave warrior. But in fact those days had provided just about the satisfaction of a candy shop to a diabetic, none of the bright packages were to be touched, let alone unwrapped. In his bunk at night his mind had played over a long video tape in full technicolor of Botticelli girls swaying through the clear white evening light of their setting, laughing and chattering as they went, but apparently a virgin chorus.

There had been one particular girl who worked in a café, tall, deliciously fair, and with a surprising, rich contralto voice. She practised her English on him but if she had heard of sex wasn't admitting it. She told him about her boy friend, a deck officer with the Jenson Line on their Far East run, met up with only every couple of years or so on his home leaves but for whom, presumably, all that splendid ice would one day melt. Meantime she wouldn't go out with anyone else; that wasn't the way things were done in Bergen, you waited.

On his last evening, more than slightly drunk, Mark had gone to an open-air concert and at it heard the music of these people, sound lifting against an almost melodramatic background of steep hillsides that resisted night shadow. A singer with the kind of physique that didn't come into his dreams, but still with a voice like the café girl's, had sung *Solveig's Song*, sending the sombre, deliberate notes of apparently deep-frozen love up and up to challenge the distant crying of sheep. Next morning, just before sailing, Mark had bought the disc.

These days *Solveig's Song* had somehow got mixed up with Alice, who was tall and fair and swayed slightly as she walked in a summer dress through the exhaust fumes of Hyde Park. He had never told her about Bergen as though, for all its innocence, that time was part of all those other times a man does not confess to his wife. And Alice was remarkably incurious. She had never once asked how he had made out for women in those years which had taken him all over the world. She had no questions at all, even about thirty months in Singapore just before they met, when he had come nearest to settled domesticity with a half-Thai, half-Chinese girl called Lin who had no breasts, but was tidy, willing, and careful with the money he gave her. It had been quite painful to leave Lin and she had wept at the parting, but with tears you knew would dry up before your ship was over the horizon. Actually, he had been surprised to get two postcards from her and had returned money beyond that final and not ungenerous settlement. He didn't often think about her now, or wonder what she was doing. And anyway, he knew.

*Solveig's Song*, through which Alice walked, came to an end and clicked off. Mark stretched and yawned. A tow that is going all right, and in reasonable weather, he found a bore. You feel

your ship held by that blundering weight behind it, with routine
on board gone dull. Even the meals were at their worst, cook
losing inspiration when he couldn't see a bonus coming up.

The buzzer on the communications panel went. Mark got up
and walked over to the little wire-covered mouth. He pushed a
button.

'Collins, sir. The tanker's come back on the air.'

'Since when?'

'I don't know. I listened at four hours. She wasn't sending
then. There was nothing this morning. Then at fourteen hundred
she signalled New York.'

'Why didn't you tell me?'

'There didn't seem much point. It was in code. And I was
waiting to see if New York sent back. That's just come in. Also
in their code.'

'Have you been trying to break it?'

'Yes, sir.'

'What are the chances?'

'It may take time. If they're using an ordinary commercial
variation it should be easy enough. But if it's computer devised
I really need a computer to crack it.'

'What about the one in the chartroom?'

'It can't be adapted to this problem.'

'I'll have to report that to the owners. We want another
fifty thousand quid to buy a code-breaker.'

That didn't earn a laugh.

'Look, Collins, I've got a pretty strong hunch that it could be
important to us to know what New York is saying to the *Mary
Worth*. Really try to get that code, will you?'

'Yes, sir.'

It was like asking a jigsaw maniac to get to work on another
puzzle, only in this case the man's hobby was so vital to the
*Saturn*'s interests that if Mark had been asked to choose between
the Chief or Collins he'd have plumped for his radioman. The
brutal truth was that with automatic bridge control of engines
you could make do with almost anyone down below, but a code-
breaker was a gift from the gods to a salvage tug.

The wall clock said fifteen twenty-eight and a typewritten
note pinned on the bulletin board announced a captain's
inspection of ship at 15.30 hours. In precisely one and a half
minutes a knock on the door would be the Bos'n reporting for
duty with a red note-book and a stub pencil.

Mark did these inspections at least once a week, the notice a
warning to tidy up for them. He went around the *Saturn* with
as sharp an eye as a Victorian housekeeper checking up on the
maids. The ceremonies weren't popular with the crew, but he

didn't give a damn. He put on his cap in front of a mirror, getting the right angle, which was a fractional list of the peak to port. The knock came.

'Ready for inspection, sir!'

A check of the ship took more than three-quarters of an hour. All the A deck cabins were reasonably tidy, except the Chief's which never was. The only one at home in the officer accommodation was Ginnis who had been listening to a transistor and reading a paperback. He rose, wearing a polite smile which said he thought this near naval patter was a lot of bloody nonsense.

On B deck Mark took his time, and in the gallery even had a look at aluminium pots, but when he came to a steel door in a bulkhead crossing the ship, inspection was over and the Bos'n dismissed. The *Saturn*'s Captain entered the engine-room as a visitor only, and as long as this was made quite plain could count on a reasonable welcome.

Parker turned as a metal door clanged, but the Chief apparently heard nothing above the beat of that vast pulse he spent his life checking. He stood at a panel which recorded for the engine-room staff what the bridge had ordered through automatic control, looking as though he would like to attack it with a hatchet. Mark paused, as usual half-awed by the sight of twin diesels, each capable of developing 4,725 horse-power, plus the reserve which was the Chief's secret and one he meant to take to the grave. In spite of air-conditioning there was a heavy smell of heated oil. Everything was surgically clean. Over at a long work bench the tools were racked, each polished before being put back into place. Even more than most ships' engine-rooms this was a temple, the reason for the tug's existence, needing nearly a third of the hull for housing at B deck level and going down another deck to mountings just above the bilges. Under the grille on which Mark stood was a huge area of lit mystery into which he had rarely penetrated, and didn't really want to. It wasn't good to be reminded of how dependent the upper deck was on a priesthood dedicated to the service of these monsters.

The Chief turned.

'Well, Captain!' He could pitch his voice in a different octave from that rumbling of turbines. 'Inspection, eh? Did you find any unemptied chamberpots?'

Mark shook his head. He didn't smile.

'Neat, tidy, and clean, that's what we are,' the Chief said. 'In fact you're blessed with a keen crew. Fortunate man. Sorry I can't offer you a cup of tea, but there is never any service at all for some time before and after these solemn ceremonies of yours. Would you like some ice water?'

Mark made his escape via the hawser store under the stern-deck. Here the great coils waited on fixed bollards like sewing-cotton on a machine. There was a smell of tar and paint, and a marked vibration increase from the shafts. He went up an iron ladder and through a hatch on to the low stern-deck.

The air bit into his lungs. The sun was trying to shine though it wasn't able to do much about brightening up the Aberdeenshire coastline, which looked as it usually did, a grey bulwark against the North Sea. Gulls were in attendance, almost as many as for a trawler, probably hoping that the cook would have a failure to flush overboard. The trouble was he usually served them. The birds had been messy about their droppings.

Mark refused to dwell on the thought of a rig now in the process of being towed, somewhere over that stern horizon, towards its semi-permanent anchorage, pulled by Scherner and Dartan in unholy alliance who were making do with the leavings. In this case the leavings were going to be better than the prize and Jessie would have something to say about that. Well, to hell with it.

He looked without affection at the *Mary Worth*. The fat-bellied old bitch was wallowing along at the end of a hawser with her slubbery cargo still intact below decks, ready for discharge at Grangemouth. After she had been lightened she'd probably be taken somewhere else for repairs, Leith or Newcastle, but coastal tugs could have that job. The *Saturn* wasn't waiting. He wanted back to Hull and from there to Alice.

Mark didn't know whether he accepted the idea of telepathy but was still certain that if Alice and he kept a time check they'd come up with a startling pattern of coincidence, an overlapping of minutes when each was acutely conscious of the other. He might, of course, be imagining her response from a wish to believe in it and a need to have their marriage something more than the two months out of twelve he managed to spend with her. She had a hell of a life, really, waiting. He was no longer sure that he had any right to count on the compensations, the nice flat, money in the bank, her own car, and Harrods round the corner. She'd had a job at first, but this had meant that she couldn't just get on a plane and fly to wherever he was in Europe, Rotterdam, or Lisbon or somewhere in the sun along the Mediterranean. Now she just waited. He didn't really know how she occupied the waiting time, and it wasn't something she talked about much. There were references to visits to her sister who had a house in Tring, and three kids plus an engineer husband, or meetings with girl friends in town. Men weren't mentioned. But there were plenty of men available to a Solveig walking through the park.

There was a point in his thinking about Alice that Mark

never allowed himself to go beyond. A red light came on, the signal to turn to something else. He switched to flying a kite.

It had been a bright idea in the circumstances and should go down in tug history, but the trouble was he hadn't chosen his moment too well and the story had a belly-laugh ending. He could hear them telling it in Rotterdam bars . . . 'so the silly bugger finishes up with this tow that's worth a lot less to him than the one he chucked.' A good many rounds of drinks would be bought on that one, particularly in Holland where the extrovert boys' idea of a good joke was someone getting kicked in the balls.

Rotterdam was always a test. You sailed into it an immediate object of specialist interest, particularly if you were in the running for a prestige reputation as the *Saturn* was. Here the current kings of salvage met up for bols and some eye gouging, and you were rated by what you had done in the last six months. Further, if there was a story they could pin to you, you'd wear it like a tail for the rest of your life. Mark knew that as sure as hell he was going to be that kite boy until he was fifty and the most he could hope to do was eliminate the bellow of laughter when the nickname was produced. This meant a systematic kicking in of a few teeth in salvage operations over the next few years, and he didn't flinch from the prospect.

Mark went back to his cabin. It was policy not to appear on the bridge too often during one of MacDonald's watches. Though he didn't know it yet the Mate was being groomed to take over command of the *Saturn* when Jessie Lawton finally got around to building the new Anglo-European tug, which would then go to the fleet commodore, who would be Captain Underson. The plans were all there on paper, including blueprints, though there were now going to be a few changes made on these, including a couple of open wings to the bridge from which a rocket could be fired. A glass house was cosy, and towers gave you a fine view, but rocket-aiming was still essential in this business, which meant the right platform from which to discharge them. That was not sixty feet up in the air.

He was glad to have this point to put to the old girl, something to add body to an interview that was going to have its thin, tight areas. Owners have the shortest memories of all backers, the vagaries of sea commerce seeming to produce a high degree of sensitivity to profits. And Jessie had been born with a special line in this sensitivity. She was Scotland's gift to contemporary fiscal realism.

Mark knew he was afraid of her, though he was certain he had never let this show. He opened a can of beer and had just sat down with it when the buzzer got him up again.

'Collins, sir. I've broken the code.'

'Good man!'

'And there have been two signals, one from the tanker to New York. The other's a reply. I'm de-coding it at the moment.'

'I'll come up.'

Collins was looking pleased with himself. He had a right to be.

'That was damn quick. I saw you working at this for days.'

'Well, I was lucky. It's just an ordinary commercial variant. I've seen *Times* crosswords harder to do. You'd think a big oil company would protect themselves with a computer-selected pattern. This is like going on using one of those old safes you can open with a bent hairpin. But I've often noticed that with the Yanks. There's all this gas about their technocratic superiority and then in one small sector of their operations you find them using stone-age techniques. It's as if their efficiency consultants had gone home tired.'

There were moments when Collins made Mark conscious of a generation gap. He was in one of them. He spread the first signal out on top of a locker.

HEWOIL NEW YORK FROM CAPTAIN MARY WORTH STOP EMERGENCY POWER BREAKDOWN UNABLE SIGNAL STOP PRESENT POSITION NORTH SEA LONG WEST TWO LAT FIFTY-SEVEN STOP UNDER TOW ANGLO-EUROPEAN TUG SATURN PROCEEDING GRANGEMOUTH FOR OIL DISCHARGE STOP SERIOUS STORM DAMAGE STOP COMPLETE ENGINE BREAKDOWN TEMPORARY SEA REPAIRS IMPOSSIBLE STOP WILL REQUIRE FURTHER TOW TO AVAILABLE DRYDOCK AFTER GRANGEMOUTH STOP INSTRUCT WHETHER RETAIN SATURN SERVICES FOR THIS STOP ENDICOTT.

Endicott was wondering about keeping the *Saturn* on for a coastal tow, was he? It was incredible how little most captains knew about salvage specialization, probably because they didn't want to know. Tugs were a dirty word and having to use one a skipper's nightmare. At the same time you'd have thought that the master of a tanker would have realized that hiring the *Saturn* for an empty hull tow from Grangemouth to a drydock was like expecting a surgeon to take over post-operative nursing as well as the carving. And at his professional fees. Hewoil wouldn't like the bill much.

'Here you are, sir.'

Collins swivelled his chair around and sat with a straight back as though he wanted to watch the Skipper's reaction to the latest from New York. Mark took the sheet.

CAPTAIN MARY WORTH FROM HEWOIL EXECUTIVE BRANCH STOP

COMPANY TANKER FELICITY WORTH COMPLETING OIL DISCHARGE
GRANGEMOUTH STOP SHE WILL SAIL APPROXIMATELY SEVEN HOURS
TO RENDEZVOUS YOUR CORRECTED POSITION DITTO FIFTEEN
HUNDRED HOURS STOP VITAL YOU TERMINATE TOW WITH SATURN
IMMEDIATELY STOP SUGGEST STATE PARTIAL ENGINE REPAIR
COMPLETED READY PROCEED UNDER OWN POWER STOP FELICITY
WORTH WILL TOW YOU NEWCASTLE WHERE DISCHARGE OIL IS
BEING ARRANGED PRIOR TO DRYDOCK STOP BREAK TOW BEFORE
COMMUNICATING DECISION TO SATURN STOP HEWOIL.

Mark looked at Collins.

'The lesson for today, brethren,' he said, 'is that when you
think you've smelt a collection of bastards you were probably
right.'

'What can you do about this, sir?'

'Quite a lot. If we move fast.'

'Want me to get the tanker on R.T.'

'I certainly don't. Just go on listening. Take recordings if they
got on R.T. and file everything that comes in on that code, or
any other way. If Endicott isn't a complete shit he'll ask New
York for a clarification. Not that it's needed, just for a stall. The
message screams loud enough. I'll take this last signal with me,
you can transcribe another. Oh, and don't be startled if you hear
my voice coming over the tanker's R.T.'

'What?'

Mark closed the door. He went through the chartroom.

'Tom! Emergency!'

MacDonald turned.

'Engines half-astern,' Mark ordered. 'Pay out another hundred
yards of tow-cable. Then bring her round due north.'

'Are we cutting tow?'

'No. Trying to prevent them from doing it. I haven't time to
explain. You'll get it all from the radio cabin.'

Mark punched engine-room on the communications panel.

'Parker here.'

'Captain. I want the Chief.'

Wigham took his time, he always did. He said that anything
worth doing was worth doing slow and sure. He even walked
that way.

'Chief? You're going to lose Parker to a boarding party.'

'I don't think I heard you right, Captain?'

'You heard me. I'm taking Parker and Ackroyd and the three
of us are climbing on to the tanker.'

'And may I ask what's happening?'

'Lawyers might call it an act of piracy on the high seas. I call
it a hawser inspection. I want Parker to join me on the tower

platform in two minutes. Tell him to bring a small knapsack with razor and toothbrush. We may be staying the night. You'll have to nurse those engines without your Second.'

Mark turned. The Mate was staring at him.

'*Can* you do this?' he asked.

'I don't know till I try. Ackroyd off duty?'

'Yes.'

'Well, rout him out and get him topside. Then take the *Saturn* back to the tanker. We'll need fenders over. I want you to nuzzle right in to the *Mary Worth*'s bows, on our port. We go down a rope ladder from the tower fire-door on to her forepeak hangover. If you're careful you shouldn't scrape any paint. As soon as we're on her you pull away, pick up the hawser slack and pretend nothing has happened. If there are voices from the tanker's bridge you do nothing about it. Until you hear mine from over there. I hope you do, too. Not gunfire.'

MacDonald was silent for a moment.

'Skipper, I have a Colt four five.'

Mark grinned.

'So you've finally confessed? Did you really think you'd kept that a big secret on a little ship? Thanks, but no. An armed hawser inspection wouldn't look at all good at an inquiry. Best to be British about this. After all, we're dealing with nationals of a friendly country which holds us in contempt. You're in command here. If the Chief won't do what you tell him put the man in irons in the hawser locker. I've always wanted to see how we'd get on without any engine-room crew at all. Only don't tell him I said that.'

Mark went to his cabin. It didn't take him long to find what he needed. In a sock drawer was a half-bottle of whisky. He left the socks and took the whisky. American ships, even Panamanian-American, had a dreadful tendency to be dry.

Parker was on the tower ladder ahead of him.

'The Mate brief you?' Mark shouted up.

The Second Engineer looked down.

'No, Captain, I knocked on Collins's door.'

'Your role,' Mark said, as he climbed, 'is to inspect an engine-room so that you'll be in a position to say before a court, if it comes to that, there wasn't a hope in hell of the *Mary Worth* being able to move under her own power.'

'I get it.'

'There may be considerable opposition.'

'I get that, too,' Neil Parker said from the landing gallery.

Mark pulled himself up by the guard rail.

'Get this door open. We won't eject the platform. Don't need it. Just a ladder. Where's Ackroyd?'

'Probably looking for the latest copy of *Breezy Stories*. He never goes anywhere without one of those things.'

Mark left Parker to unclamp the portside door which opened over a sheer drop to the sea. He went out on to the platform. The *Saturn* had now almost closed the distance back to the tanker and her manœuvre must have been causing a lot of interest, if that was all. He heard Parker shouting to Ackroyd to bring up a rope ladder.

MacDonald made a neat job of that near docking alongside a moving object. The tanker was lifting up and down in the choppy seas and managing a roll as well. The tug, bow on to the wind, moved less, but there was still plenty of opportunity for a nasty crunch leading to dented plates on both ships. It was a moment when automatic engine control was worth its cost, whatever the Chief thought about that. The Mate could nudge in close to the *Mary Worth* able to count on a quick reaction if he decided to jump back again, the twin controllable pitch propellers giving bite almost at once. The real risk was the incalculable factor of metal magnetism, something like lust happening between two hulls, sucking them together. Against this fenders wouldn't be able to act as padding because contact point would be between foredeck overhang and the *Saturn*'s tower. It would have been easier to come alongside the tanker at her well-deck, but this would have meant a long climb down the rope ladder and Mark wanted his advance to be from the hawser anchoring.

'Ladder over, sir.'

Inside the tower Parker and Ackroyd pressed against a curve of bulkhead to let Mark past. He held on to a grip bar and looked down. Turbulence between two hulls was already a tide race and a man falling into that would be sucked under the *Saturn*'s screws for shredding.

'I shouldn't have detailed you two,' Mark said. 'It ought to have been a call for heroic volunteers.'

Parker laughed. Ackroyd did not.

Mark went backwards into space. By the time he was eight rungs down his weight was making a pendulum of the ladder, swinging this out and then back, against the tower. The lower he went the harder those jolts. Parker peered down.

'Watch your hands on this thing,' Mark said. 'Easy to lose fingers.'

'Don't look now, sir. But there's a party coming along the catwalk to repel boarders.'

Mark did look. It was quite a party, six of them, travelling fast, and carrying an aluminium ladder for gap bridging.

'Parker! Tell me when to jump!'

'Go down at least three more rungs.'

Mark did that. There was a swing out from the tower.

'Now!'

It wasn't easy to let go. He landed on all fours beyond the railing on metal deck, glad to be there. Parker was half-way down the ladder. Mark went to the rail.

'When I grab your legs, let go!'

'Right.'

Mark went back and down, pulling Parker with him. The engineer got to his feet again quickly and retrieved Ackroyd by the same technique. Mark saw MacDonald watching from behind bridge glass and gave him the thumbs up. Almost at once the *Saturn* put up a splatter of froth from reversed screws.

'Ackroyd, you're to stay here by the hawser anchoring. It is my order that no one is to touch it. To break tow they're going to have to use force against you. I'm not asking you to fight all-comers, but if it comes to a showdown I want you to be seen to be overpowered. We have witnesses on the *Saturn*. Get the idea?'

Ackroyd got the idea and didn't like it. He hadn't signed on for this kind of active service, and his face said so. He managed a nod but couldn't find a word with which to acknowledge a perfectly lousy order, or it wasn't a word you could use to the Skipper.

'We'll meet them on the gangway, Parker.'

The confrontation took place just forward of the gap over which there was now a ladder. The last man had crossed this just as Mark and the engineer reached the catwalk. But they didn't get very far along it, halted by a figure in blue winter serge with an officer's cap, standing with his arms out to the railings on either side. He was dark-browed and blue-jawed, sent forward to deal with a Limey invasion, which he meant to do. His support team had been well chosen, too. They all looked as though they had wrecked a few bars in their time.

'You guys just walk on to any god-damn ship whenever you feel like it?'

'When that ship is my responsibility under a Lloyd's form, yes.'

'So that's your cover?'

'All that's needed. I'm Captain Underson. This is my Second Engineer, Mr Parker. Who are you?'

'Goldberg's the name. Second Mate.'

'Mr Goldberg, will you please take me to Captain Endicott?'

'Like fuck I will.'

'In that case I'll find him myself.'

'You going back on your little tugboat, mister. So whistle it in again.'

'The *Saturn* has resumed tow.'

'Is that what she's doing?'

'Mr Goldberg, I'd like a word with you in private. Come forward with me.'

Mark didn't wait for the man's reaction, he took a few paces along to the steps up to the forepeak. Then he turned. The Mate was still standing with his arms out to railings.

'You needn't worry about Mr Parker rushing your men,' Mark called out.

That got a laugh from the team. For a moment Goldberg hesitated, then shrugged and let go the railings. He sauntered up the catwalk.

'Well?'

Mark kept his voice low.

'It may interest you, Second, that my radio officer broke your company code some time ago. We have a little file on that interchange between this ship and New York. All properly documented for use. Maybe you'll see how that changes the position?'

The dark face showed nothing. 'Why the hell should it?'

'I'll tell you. With that file we can screw your company in any court. Good and proper.'

'Big talk.'

'Fact. You proposed allowing the *Mary Worth* to sit as a derelict hulk on a main shipping route in a crowded sea. Your engines can't be fixed and you know it.'

'She's no derelict. She's manned.'

'But without power. And your lighting is on emergency. Which means it could go again. The wind's dropping, Mr Goldberg. At this time of year in these parts that almost certainly means fog by dark. And you were proposing to wait through long hours of darkness for your sister ship. Straddling a shipping lane. A marine hazard, in fact, not properly notified as such. That's what I mean when I say I can screw you in any court. And if you touch that hawser that's exactly what's going to happen. Are you beginning to get the picture?'

'We got a right to wait for our own ship!'

'If you really believe that you're a bloody fool. And New York will tell you so just as soon as they understand the new developments. So you see I've some things to talk to your Captain about. And I'm going to see him. If you or any of that hand-picked gang back there so much as lift a hand to stop Mr Parker and me from going aft there'll be an assault charge slapped on you for trying to prevent us from carrying out our duties under tow agreement. Get it?'

Goldberg got it all right. He had nothing more to say, but his eyes were black with anger.

## CHAPTER SIX

LOUIS ENDICOTT looked past Underson towards a bulkhead on which was a grouping of four photographs. The largest was of his wife, with the kids under her, all as they had been fifteen years ago when he was first made captain. At the bottom was a blown-up family snap showing them out in the front yard smiling against strong sunlight. They all seemed to have their eyes shut, in a kind of happy prayer, offering thanks for what they had been given in life, the two-bathroomed Dutch colonial, the Buick you could just see parked outside the garage, a good provider properly centred who hadn't even begun to grow bald from stress, and Tomboy, the setter bitch they'd had in those days offering tail and hindquarters to the camera. Endicott had never up-dated these pictures, perhaps because what they had once said still held.

That is, until two days ago. Now, suddenly, their interest was historical.

He was conscious of himself as a man living within his luck for all his active life, confident because this was such a modest issue. He might have been one of those the Fates left alone and even permitted a pretty good ration of mercies, since all he had really indented for was an unpretentious security. But the Fates had, after all, got around to his case, pulling it out from back files like tax assessors long held up over their dealings with the big operators, but getting that backlog clear finally, able to turn attention to the smaller fry.

The day-cabin was back to norm, tidied and once again stable. There was even ice water in a Thermos jug. Underson had taken the offered chair and the tension which had been sharp when he first came in was beginning to ease. The tug captain looked both relaxed and sure of himself.

'I don't want to make this sound like an interrogation,' he said. 'But there is a contractual agreement between us. And things that need explaining because of this.'

'Such as?'

'Well, you've just said you didn't order your Second forward to keep me off this ship. Mr Goldberg acted on his own initiative?'

'He did. In the normal course of his duties as officer of the watch. I wasn't available on the bridge, nor was I in this cabin. I'd gone to see the First Officer.'

'Where your Second couldn't find you?'

'Presumably not, since he didn't.'

'Captain Endicott, I suggest he didn't try very hard.'

'You can suggest what you like. I don't see how it concerns you?'

'It concerns me because Goldberg made it quite plain he had come forward to throw me off the *Mary Worth*, not to find out why I was on board.'

'In that case he exceeded his authority and I'll tell him so.'

'He's still listening to you?'

Endicott sat up very straight. 'What do you mean by that?'

'I've just come from seeing Chief Engineer Ziekmann. It wasn't easy to get my man down into your engine-room. Quite a shouting match. Your name came into it.'

'So?'

'I'd be a fool, Captain Endicott, if I didn't sense some kind of crisis on this ship, with you and your incapacitated First on the one side, and Ziekmann and most of the rest of the crew on the other.'

'What god-damned nonsense!'

'Is it nonsense that Ziekmann has been something of a hero since he got that line aft for securing?'

'There may be something in that.'

'I'd say there's a helluva lot in it. The Chief says you dared him to do it and he took your dare.'

'Ziekmann doesn't always watch his mouth.'

'Captain Endicott, I get the impression that your Chief now thinks he is running this ship. And with the crew behind him.'

'You can get any impressions you like. And a damn lot of good they'll do you!'

Louis Endicott reached out for the Thermos jug. He poured himself a glass of ice water. His hand was steady but his heart thumped. This was the start to a long series of questionings leading up to a terminal one with the company executive Vice-President. Well, damn the lot of them- They'd put him down in the end, of course, but he was beginning to feel that luck going doesn't have to mean that pride gets whipped away, too. You can hang on to that and have it look back at you most mornings from a shaving mirror.

'Captain, this accident to the First took place at the height of the storm?'

'That's right.'

'So you've really had no practical help from the man since then? Though you went to see him a good deal.'

'What is this getting at?'

'You went to see your Mate because he was your only real ally on this ship. And when I boarded you were down with him talking over that pretty curious message from your owners. It's my belief that while you were in conference your radio man leaked

that signal to Goldberg, who passed it on to Ziekmann. And
when Goldberg saw my tug coming back it was the Chief he got
on to at speed, not you. There's almost a smell of mutiny about
it.'

'You can smell anything you like!'

'I'll withdraw mutiny and say a pretty serious breakdown in
ship's discipline as a direct result of stress conditions.'

'How am I supposed to react to that?' Endicott asked. 'Let the
tears flow?'

The tug skipper grinned. He had the teeth of a year-old dog
with bones in its diet, very white and very sharp looking.

'You won't let me be on your side, will you? And I'm trying.
Captain, you're holding some cards again, whether you realize it
or not. Thanks to a man on the *Saturn* who breaks codes as a
morning setting-up exercise. You can't possibly carry out company orders and cast tow because that's going to release all hell on
brass hats if you do. When New York knows I'm in the picture
there will be hot lines to lawyers, and no cheering news from
those specialists, either. Your company has committed a boo-boo.
Even the best organized ones do every now and then, for which
skippers should be truly thankful. It gives us a chance to serve
the dirt instead of always being on the receiving end. Are you
with me?'

'No.'

'All right, I'll spell it out. I don't think you're to blame because
your crew got out of hand. Maybe you should have kicked Ziekmann back down into his cave early on, but there's still time.
And I'd like you to know that I'm ready to fly to New York to
testify on your behalf. About that signal from owners.'

'Your idea is that I blackmail my company?'

Underson laughed.

'Find a prettier word if you want to. But why bother? If you
play things right you'll emerge from any inquiry pure lily white.
The way I see it, if you move in now with both fists you can win
ten straight rounds without even getting breathless.'

'Why should you want to help me like this?'

Underson stood, then went round his chair and leaned forward on it, from his hands.

'Maybe I didn't like your Chief's language. Also, have you ever
met a skipper who loved owners? I'll get back to the *Saturn* before
dark sets in. But I can be at the other end of an R.T. connection
any time you'd like a friendly chat.'

'Which means you want progress reports?'

'Well, they'd be a nice gesture, in view of my interest.'

Underson grinned again, and left the cabin.

Louis Endicott sat perfectly still for all of two minutes. Then he got up and walked over to the bulkhead grouping of photographs, staring at Grace as she had been fifteen years ago. She could still look like that when she was happy. She had a kid's delight in surprises, especially really good ones. Fleet commodore?

He took a deep breath. The old man feeling had gone. He went back to the desk and flicked a switch on the office type intercom.

'Radio cabin? Captain here. Is that Hatfield?'

'Yes, sir.'

'If a personal signal to me ever does any wandering on this ship again you'll get an air ticket Stateside from the next port of call. You'll be out of the company and blacklisted for sea service. Get that?'

After a moment a voice said: 'Yes, sir.'

'Okay. Signal to head office, New York. Signal begins: Tow tug has key to company code and received your last message in full. Stop. Tug captain has protested tow casting by powerless hulk in shipping lane major breach maritime practice. Stop. I agree. Stop. Am disregarding your order as transmission error. Stop. Confirm this error immediate. Stop. Am proceeding as agreed Lloyd's form with engines out of commission under *Saturn* tow. Grangemouth. Stop. Cancel rendezvous Felicity Worth. Stop. Signed Endicott. Give me a read back, Hatfield.'

The Captain listened carefully, then he asked:

'What time is it in New York?'

'Just after twelve hundred hours, sir.'

That was pleasing. It seemed pretty certain that quite a team in head office would be lunching off anti-acid pills and not much else. Endicott flicked out the radio cabin and flicked in the engine-room.

'Captain here. Who's that?'

'Third Engineer.'

'I didn't hear your "sir". I'm waiting for it!'

'Ah . . . sir.'

'Tell the Chief he's to come to me in my day-cabin. Now. That's an order!'

Jessie Lawton's experience of Grangemouth was negative. She had seen it often enough from the main Edinburgh-Stirling road, but at a distance; by day a science fiction mass of refinery towers, at night even more so. It had been a place to by-pass, oil an industry in which she had no stake and therefore no informed interest. Now she approached the new city that has grown up in the last fifteen years with a feeling almost of intrusion, the huge Daimler somehow making her too conspicuous. And certainly her car, at a sedate fifty-five, was being sneered at by a constant stream of little tin boxes. These flipped their rumps as they passed. Jessie accelerated to sixty-five, gripping the wheel, but the boxes continued to cut in far too close to a long maroon bonnet. Several times she was tempted to use her horn.

New factories started to flank the road, a considerable proportion of them, as she knew well, financed by American capital. It could almost be said that the town ahead of her was a direct by-product of dollar investment, and certainly the place had an alien feel, humming, and made contemporary by a perpetual threat hanging over it of a vast petro-chemical explosion. The Daimler's filter was beginning to allow through a reek from tainted air.

Jessie hadn't a clue how to get to the docks, which meant parking the car somewhere, probably against a forbidden kerb with traffic wardens waiting to pounce, while she asked the way, and it was likely that she'd had to go through this ordeal a few times before destination. Her incompetence behind a wheel was a continuous, secret shame, like a pointer to old age. The obvious solution, a chauffeur, had been ruled out on two counts, first economy, second admission of defeat.

Ahead, walking along a grass verge, was a man with a greyhound on a lead. Jessie braked and pressed a button. The passenger seat window dropped.

'I wonder if you could tell me the way to the docks?'

A face looked in at her, broad, young and healthy. A hand came up and plucked out a cigarette.

'What's that again?'

'The oil docks. I don't know Grangemouth.'

'Oh, aye. Well, let's see. You go on to the first roundabout and bear left. Then to the next traffic lights . . . look, lady, you're going to have a helluva job.'

'I'm afraid I am.'

'I'll jest pop in and show ye. That's best.'

'But I couldn't . . .'

'Och, I'm daeing nuthin'. Bess'll go in the back. She's fine in cars. Gets aboot in them enough. To the tracks, ye see. We was just oot a walk. These beasts take a helluva lot o' exercising.'

'This won't be taking you out of your way?'

'I havenae got a way, I'm telling ye. Just killin' time. Here, Bess.'

He opened the rear door, settled his bitch, then got in beside Jessie. 'Off ye go then. This is a nice job. Cost a packet.'

'Too big for me.'

'Aye, maybe. Director's special, eh?'

Jessie changed the subject. It seemed odd that the man was

walking his dog at this hour. She never hesitated over putting the direct question when curious. 'You're off work at the moment?'

Her guide laughed. 'Aye you could say that.' He lit a new cigarette from the stub. 'Left now. Carry on doon tae the lights. The name's MacPherson.'

'This is very kind of you, Mr MacPherson. I'm hopeless in strange towns.'

'What you wantin' at the docks?'

'The tug *Saturn*. She came in last night.'

'Aye, ah ken. I saw her doin' it. Yon's quite a wee ship. If it wusnae in the water ye'd think it was frae ooter space. That light's still green. Left sharp. Carry on till I tell ye.'

Jessie went round the corner.

'Are you unemployed, Mr MacPherson?'

'Aye. Unemployed and unemployable. That's what they ca' me.' He laughed.

'But . . . that's ridiculous! An able-bodied man like you?'

'What's ridiculous aboot it? Why should I work mah guts oot for the bosses, eh? I mean to say, what good does it dae ye?'

'It could earn you a decent living!'

'We manage fine.'

'On unemployment benefit?'

'Hell, no. Social Security. It's what they used to ca' National Assistance, but it's been upgraded wi' a bit o' new dignity. And I can tell you, if you work it right, it makes the dole a mug's game.'

Jessie desperately wanted another look at her guide but didn't dare take her eyes from the traffic. She had never been a direct employer of labour, except for some contact with trawler crews, and had little experience of what in her youth had been called the working classes. It seemed time she learned something about them.

'Are you saying that you do better out of this National Assistance than you would from Unemployment Benefit?'

'Aye, if you work it right, like I said. Take the next fork left. Mind you, it wants a bit o' practice.'

'In what way?'

'Well, you got to know the ropes. You get the sack, see. The Labour Exchange phones your boss and he says yer no damn good and so the Exchange says you won't work you don't get the dole. Mind you, before you get here maybe you have to get chucked oot o' three jobs they find for ye. But in the end yer chucked oot the Exchange, tae. So you go along to Security and tell 'em the rent's going up, and you've twa kids, and the wife can't work wi' her bad knee. They fix you up all right. You do better than the dole by a few quid, that's for sure.'

Jessie just missed a parked van.

'But . . . what a way to live, Mr MacPherson!'

'What's wrang wi' it? We do okay. And mah Ruthie's lucky. Twa, three quid frae the bingo most weeks. It'll be the golden scoop one of these days, sure thing. And I run Bess back there. She's paid off fine.'

'You're a young man. You mean to go on like this all your life?'

He laughed. 'Sure. And I hope it's a long one.'

Jessie elected silence, accepting guidance without comment. MacPherson seemed an old friend of the man at the dock gates and no questions were asked. The car bumped softly over rail lines, past cranes and looming sheds. Without help she would never have reached target, but gratitude was smothered by a sense of outrage. The dreadful thing was that MacPherson simply couldn't be got at, unassailable in what seemed to her a total shamelessness. This in itself was a direct mockery of ancient Scots dogmas about industry and frugality. What she was up against suddenly was an unnerving rejection of the formulas for living which had been her faith. And there was nothing you could do about it. He was certainly no candidate for any kind of conversion. Sack this man and he just went along to Security, laughing.

'You'd best park there, Missus. I'd lock her up if I was you. These bloody sailors, they'll pinch anything.'

Jessie jerked on the handbrake. 'How are you going to get back?'

'Walk. It's nae matter where I exercise Bess so long as she gets it. We're doon here often. The *Saturn*'s over beyond that roof there, even if ye canna see it.'

He got out and let his bitch free. Jessie locked all the doors. Now that she was able to look at the man she somehow didn't want to, conscious of his amiable lack of interest in her and her affairs, never a question from his side. He gave no opening for a sharp lecture on how forty years of conscientious work could see him driving his own Daimler. He didn't want a Daimler. She fumbled with the catch on her bag.

'I'm most grateful to you, Mr MacPherson . . .'

'Aye, well you can keep yer bag shut. I'm no wantin' a tip, thank you. Here, Bess, come on. Cheerio, Missus.'

Jessie watched them go. She had the feeling, though she couldn't isolate a reason for this, that she had just been subjected to the worst possible prelude to a meeting with Mark Underson. That man strolling away with his greyhound running back and forth along the dockside had undermined the verities of a lifetime packed with unwasted minutes. It was absurd that the briefest of casual contacts should result in this state of mind, but she couldn't shake herself into any semblance of normal briskness.

Jessie needed a cigarette and broke a rule about never smoking out of doors, groping in her bag for a case, then bending over in the shelter of the car to work the lighter.

The country couldn't survive a generation of MacPhersons, it simply couldn't! And it was appalling to think that the numbers of men like him were probably swelling day by day, almost as if they were nature's answer to automation. Social Security! She knew about these things, of course, but had never conceived of a life deliberately planned, and with cunning, in the use of them. Arthur would have been as scandalized as she was. He had believed in a basic pool of unemployed to keep the economy firm, but that pool became quite useless as a stabilizing factor if the men in it didn't want jobs when these became available.

The gas lighter kept blowing out. She humped herself over it, then straightened to see a man coming towards her from the corner of the shed, almost at a run. He was wearing a cap and dark blue double-breasted jacket. To her astonishment he stopped at a few paces and saluted.

'Thomson, Ma'am. Bos'n.'

Jessie stared.

'What? Oh, of course. Ah . . . how do you do, Mr Thomson. You've come to take me to the ship? That's very kind of you.'

She was conscious of the cigarette. It struck the wrong note.

'We had a man at the dock gates, Ma'am. But he phoned in that you drove right past him.'

'Really? I'm sorry. Actually, I had a guide. I picked him up. He was most helpful.'

Quite the wrong thing to say. The Bos'n's expression made this plain. She knew she ought to be grateful to Underson for his consideration, but at the same time there was no need for all this ceremony.

'I don't think you should leave your car here, Ma'am.'

'Please don't call me "Ma'am". I'm not royalty.'

'Very good, Mrs Lawton. It's quite a walk to the ship. You can get a car right up to the gangway. Would you like me to drive you?'

'No! Oh, well . . .'

She must get over this ridiculous feeling of being rattled. And the Bos'n was only trying to be kind. She gave him the keys and managed a smile. For a moment Jessie was quite certain he was going to bow her into the back seat, but she would have none of this.

The Bos'n drove the car with caution, as though deeply aware of what it had cost. In fact it was ten years old and Jessie's garage man had told her that she couldn't expect much on a trade-in, only hirers for weddings would be interested in an old job of this size. He had suggested the figure of £250 as generous, which had made her decide to keep it for some years yet.

They moved slowly around the end of a shed. The *Saturn* was a long way down the quayside, moored in against it. Jessie had approved the design of the ship and been over her a few times but from this angle she looked completely strange. MacPherson had called her a thing from outer space, and he really wasn't so far off from the truth. She decided suddenly that the *Saturn* lacked that something which most docked ships manage to convey at once, a feeling of mystery, of secrets retained during a brief resting from an endless and often grim endeavour against the sea. Trawlers suggest this, smelly and gull-attended, but muscular from contest. This vessel was as neatly efficient and as contemptuous of the world beyond as a barman in a fashionable hotel. She had recently taken a beating from heavy seas, but there was no sign of this, her paintwork glistening. No face looked down from the shining windows of the bridge, the car's approach was probably being watched on radar, for that disc up on one of her towers was certainly rotating, which seemed a deplorable waste of power while she was tied up.

Underson had borrowed from somewhere what looked like a liner's gangway, perfectly enormous, this sloping up to the boat-deck. There was a sailor on duty at the foot of it. She was being mocked with pomp. Jessie felt a flush rising to her cheeks.

The sailor came forward to open her door. It was the moment for a brass band on deck to strike up, but the *Saturn*'s Master hadn't appparently as yet got around to training one.

He was waiting for her at the top of the gangway, wearing his cap and double-breasted dark blue. Though not perhaps quite average height for a man he looked handsome enough in uniform, blue eyes under jet eyebrows, and a white smile.

'Welcome on board, Mrs Lawton.'

Jessie peered down between the boats.

'What? Don't I have to inspect a guard of honour?'

Underson laughed. 'I'll remember next time. Will you come this way, please? I thought we'd be more comfortable in my cabin.'

The stateroom was surprisingly spacious for a tug, a bunk with drawers beneath, and a settee covered in easy-wash black plastic. There was a large desk directly under one of the clamped portholes and an extra chair. In front of the settee was the unnautical touch of a glass-topped table chained to the deck. There was no obvious personal possessions lying about, certainly no hint of clothes and the mock panelled bulkheads were bare. A door to a bathroom was just open giving a glimpse of the blue tiling and fixtures, which had surprised Jessie on an earlier inspection, a feature certainly not in the specifications. She could only suppose that the builders had some luxury plumbing left over from work on a liner and had decided to use it.

He withdrew, firmly shutting the cabin door, leaving the blue bathroom to issue its own invitation, which Jessie accepted. In front of the mirror she took off her beret and puffed up hair which had once, before her shingle period, been worn in braided earphones, and now again carried a suggestion of these in a side fullness breaking the otherwise straight lines to a bun on her neck. The light, designed for a man's shaving, was brutal, but she was used to facing the truth about her looks. Her figure had always been reasonable, rather shapely legs, and not too much excess weight around the middle, but her face had presented what a lavender-overalled lassie in a London beauty salon had once called 'Madam's little problems'. It had been Arthur who had persuaded her to visit that establishment, four sessions during a ten-day business trip, but Jessie hadn't quite learned the trick of shading out a firm, square jaw-line by the use of toned powders. She still had untouched the complete beauty kit brought back to Scotland, her make-up drill kept to a little Woolworth powder plus a touch of lipstick in the bright colour tones of the Clara Bow era.

When Underson returned she was sitting in a corner of the settee feeling considerably freshened up, with MacPherson at last put in his proper place, which was right outside her current problems. The Captain carried the coffee tray himself and set this down on the glass-topped table. He took the armchair. He was attentive, offering biscuits, which Jessie refused. It was no time to be chewing.

'Captain, why didn't you answer company signals?'

'I'd had no contact before with this baronet. There seemed no reason for his interference.'

'Sir Richard is a member of the board. In my absence he was perfectly justified in what he did.'

'He's your deputy, then? I hadn't been informed of that.'

'I haven't a deputy. But I was away for a few days and couldn't be located. The finance side of this business is not your affair, Captain, but it is very much mine. You probably know that Adventure Unit holdings in our company are not large and you probably think they're not too important. But you'd be wrong there. Sir Richard is on the board for reasons other than the money he brought with him. If he leaves others might want their money out, too.'

Jessie was feeling slightly like a Sunday School teacher dealing with a nine-year-old sceptic.

'I'd have thought, Mrs Lawton, that with Lazzari's special

investment inducements you could get all the money you wanted at any time.'

That was a shock. It had never occurred to Jessie that Underson would have made it his business to find out how Lazzari arranged finance. But she couldn't risk probing the Captain's comment to find out just how much he knew, the only thing to do was ignore it.

'In the City a breach of contract is about the worst sin there is,' she said, not looking into those blue eyes. 'Anglo-European just can't risk wearing that tag. Sir Richard doesn't know too much about the tug business and what he does makes him nervous. I've tried to explain to him the way we operate and I've defended your going to the *Mary Worth*. It was a gamble that didn't quite come off. We're going to lose money as a result, quite a lot of it. Sir Richard is looking at that as well as the contract breach with the oil company. *And* the threat of a lawsuit resulting.'

'Do you believe the rig company will sue?'

'In the circumstances, no.'

'Then we can put that bogey to one side. What I've done is fail to pull off a piece of salvage that would have been splendid publicity for the *Saturn* and the company, not to mention a fat bonus in all our pockets. I'm sorry about that. It happens. It will happen again. So will the bonus earning successes.'

'You don't need to tell me that.'

'I was beginning to think I did, Mrs Lawton. And while we're on the *Mary Worth* I've a funny feeling you've one or two questions stowed away about how I conducted the operation. Right?'

He was trying to force the pace. Jessie decided to meet this. She met his gaze. 'You were first at the tanker. By some time. Why did you just stand by until the other tugs came up?'

He grinned. 'A showman needs his audience. Other ships, planes.'

'Is that your answer?'

'No. We were at the fringe of an Arctic hurricane. It had been going for days. The weather reports didn't suggest an early ease up, but I was sure it was coming. Also I knew that until these seas went down at least a little, hawsers to the *Mary Worth* wouldn't hold. The *Semirande* managed a much longer tow than I thought she would. We had hours in hand until the tanker was at real risk and I decided to wait for improved conditions. These came. Admittedly too late for the big prize. We don't wear the victor's laurel, which I can see makes things a bit difficult for you with Sir Richard. It's my guess, though, that if this had been a crowning ceremony our baronet would have been ready to put his business ethics into cold storage.'

That was **true** enough. Jessie found her bag and started to look through it. Underson took a cigarette box off the table and snapped it open. 'Have one of these. Duty free. Illegal when we're tied up in a British port, of course.'

Jessie had forgotten what luxury tobacco tasted like.

'More coffee?'

'No, thank you.'

'Then let's get on with the post-mortem.'

'That's not what I've come for, Captain. I'm here to discuss company policy. For the future.'

He looked interested. 'You plan changes?'

'Yes.'

The Captain sat back in his chair. He appeared relaxed except for his hands which seemed to want to live a life of their own. She remembered that he had recently given up smoking.

'I don't need to stress again that we can't afford the reputation of being contract breakers,' Jessie said. 'At the same time salvage bids of the *Mary Worth* kind are a vital part of our business. We have to strike some kind of a mean. I'd say that circumstances have to be very exceptional indeed before you break tow as you did with the rig.'

'I see. I'm pulling a load under a sound income yielding contract and no other tugs in the area when a forty-thousand-ton passenger liner is badly damaged in collision with a freighter. But that's not exceptional enough so I signal . . . "sorry, busy, can't help".'

Jessie refused to be rattled.

'I'd say a clear case when you do go to the liner. If you can safely leave your tow.'

'You mean to print a company manual for my guidance? What to do when?'

'No. You'll consult us direct whenever there is a major decision to be made, as in the case of the *Mary Worth*.'

'Like hell I will!'

'Captain don't jump to conclusions! My ideas involve reorganization at our end, too. I realize that in an emergency you must have an immediate reply to any signal you send. The situation in which Sir Richard took the initiative must not happen again. I mean to see that it can't.'

'You're coating the pill, Mrs Lawton. But I still don't like the taste. I'm to work at one end of a long rope which has the other tied to your rocking chair.'

'We're not trying to curb you! Only insisting as owners that we're kept in the picture.'

'Tell me something. Has Sir Richard insisted on this as a condition for keeping his money in Anglo-European?'

'I told him he could take his money out if he didn't like the way the company was being run! *I'm* insisting on this arrangement.'

'Then you can work it all out with a new captain. He may be a bit hard to find. MacDonald isn't quite ready. You might lose money under him for a couple of years, though after that things should pick up.'

There was almost a full minute's silence in the cabin. Underson was staring at her Jessie kept her voice calm.

'Are you seriously suggesting you'd resign over this?'

'Without notice. Sue for breach of contract if you like. I'd rather enjoy defending myself. It might interest the press. Look, Mrs Lawton, these days a captain has about the same authority as an ambassador. Which is damn little. Modern communications have reduced ambassadors and captains to stooge roles. I see the trend and the reasons for it. But I still mean to resist it for myself.'

'The Hoofstanger skippers keep in continual contact with head office!'

'To *tell* head office what they're going to do, not to ask permission to do it. Not the top boys anyway. And that's the group I mean to join. Mrs Lawton, the *Mary Worth* is now emptying her guts not very far from us simply because I took the kind of action which wouldn't have been any use if I'd taken time off to consult head office. And if I hadn't done what I did we'd have been taking a very much smaller towing fee than we're going to. Also, I don't think I'd have got your permission. Not to play pirates.'

'To do *what*?'

'I'll tell you about it.'

Jessie listened with the feeling of nerves tightening all over her body. Behind what Underson said was a statement of intent, that this was how he meant to operate the *Saturn* while he had command, and if the owner didn't like it she knew what she could do. She had brought the wrong tactics to this meeting, money power talking to a tug skipper of only two years standing who still had his reputation to make. The last thing she had expected was an ultimatum. It wouldn't be withdrawn, and she had never given in to one in her life.

'You know what I found over there on the tanker, Mrs Lawton? An owner-haunted captain. Not a happy breed. I don't intend to join them.'

'I've asked nothing unreasonable of you.'

'You've asked for an owner's boy. I'll tell you something . . . MacDonald may play it that way while he's finding his feet. But he won't go on doing it. He's no more the type than I am.'

'You think you'd get another ship?'

'In time.'

'Not in British service.'

He grinned at her. 'You'd see to that, would you? I believe it.
All right, I'll go abroad. The Germans are coming up fast with
new tugs. After all, they built this one.'

'Do you think they wouldn't demand owner control?'

'Well, there's always the Swedes. Or the Greeks. And I've
heard rumours that the Plentin company is planning expansion.
They won't get salvage skippers from amongst those barge towers
of their coastal services. You know, it's really a seller's market for
captains on the deep-sea side. There just aren't enough of us.
You wouldn't have employed me in the first place if there had
been a better qualified man available. I'll always be grateful to
you for giving me the initial experience. Two years as skipper of
the *Saturn,* which I left to better myself.'

There was a noise like a muted door buzzer. Underson went
to the communications panel. 'Captain here. What is it?'

Jessie heard the answer clearly enough.

'Collins, sir. A personal signal to you has just come in. Confidential. Do you want me to read it?'

'No! I'll come to the radio cabin.' He turned. 'You'll excuse
me? I shouldn't be long.'

Jessie sat staring at the door. Her arms and legs felt heavy, as
though circulation to them had been impaired in some way. She
didn't want to move, particularly she didn't want to think, but
she had to. Astrology had never interested her, yet there was no
doubt that some days were ill-omened for the conduct of her
affairs. And a bad start in the morning tended to lead through
to a dismal finish.

The plain fact was that she had been out-manoeuvred from
the very first by someone she had seriously underestimated.
Underson was astonishingly sure of himself for a man who hadn't
even been Mate in his last job, just an out-of-work Second when
Lazzari found him. Then she knew this wasn't a fair assessment
of the Captain's background, which certainly had its interesting
chapters.

She had refreshed her memory about these last night from a
file. Underson's grandfather had been Danish, an immigrant to
Newcastle, his father a marine draughtsman killed in World
War II. His mother had married again, an Australian, and they
had taken the boy to Melbourne. He reappeared in Europe as
an apprentice with the Blue Funnel Line, leaving them for two
years in Arctic trawlers out of Hull. After that he had joined
the Ben Line on their Far Eastern run and had been Third
Officer when he got his Master's ticket. An aunt in Newcastle
left him something in the region of £10,000, quite a windfall,
but he hadn't wasted it, remembering about the money to be

made in fishing if you were lucky. He had bought a piece in a privately owned trawler again out of Hull and sailed in her as Mate for three good seasons which, according to Lazzari, had seen him with his capital trebled when he sold out and left fishing.

At this stage Underson had been something rather unusual, a young sailor with considerable capital behind him. Perhaps as a result of this, and not having to worry, he had elbowed his way into one of the tightest closed shops in the world, the Dutch salvage business, getting a last-minute fill-in job with the famous Hoofstanger Company on a tug that was about to be sent to the Far East to operate out of Singapore. He had stayed the full two-year term with this ship in the Orient and returned with her. The Hoofstangers had not promoted him, which might have been the reason why he left them. Certainly, when Lazzari tried to get some information on Underson from the Dutch company they had flatly refused to say anything.

One thing was very plain from all this. Underson had packed his bags and just walked out quite a few times in his career. Financial independence, or something very near to it, put him where he could tell almost anyone to go to hell and mean it. He set his own value on himself and if other people wouldn't accept that assessment that was their loss, not his.

The trouble, as Jessie knew well, was that it *would* be her loss. The right replacement was going to be incredibly difficult to find, and she didn't believe it could be MacDonald. She needed a skipper with flair and Underson was already showing clear signs that he would develop a high degree of this.

'Sorry to have kept you waiting,' he said politely. 'Won't you have another cigarette?'

Jessie shook her head.

'And what plans have you for the *Saturn* after she's back in Hull, Mrs Lawton? Anything lined up?'

It was like an inquiry from a stranger who really isn't very interested.

'Mr Lazzari is in Belgium now about a tender for a dredger tow from Antwerp to Umtulu Pulundi in Gutongo.'

'Oh, God! *That* place.'

'You know it?'

'I was there once with the Hoofstangers. That was enough. Incidentally, won't the Dutch be after this tow?'

'They're committed at the moment with all but their stationed tugs. Mr Lazzari seems confident.'

'Could mean that no one wants to go near Gutongo. I hope you're leaving plenty of time for *Saturn* shore leave?'

'There should be a week before sailing for Antwerp.'

'Not enough! I promised a fortnight.'

'On whose authority?'

'Mine. We're due it, as you know well. It would be a pity if you tried to operate this ship like the Plentins do the *Semirande*, totting up lost income for every day she's tied up.'

'That's a most offensive remark, Captain!'

He smiled. 'Sorry, We're not hitting it off today, are we? Odd. I've always felt we understood each other. It seems we've been wrong. Perhaps you'd be interested in this. It's my confidential signal.'

He handed over a sheet with typed capitals. Jessie could read the words without her glasses.

TO CAPTAIN MARK UNDERSON, MASTER TUG SATURN, GRANGE-MOUTH, SCOTLAND STOP CONFIDENTIAL STOP RETIRAL VACANCY ON TUG MARIE GROOTER IN TWO MONTHS FROM TODAY STOP YOU ARE OFFERED THIS COMMAND STOP TERMS CONTRACT TO BE ARRANGED IMPROVEMENT YOUR PRESENT AGREEMENT STOP REQUEST YOU COME ROTTERDAM EARLIEST FOR DISCUSSION STOP SIGNED HANS HOOFSTANGER.

Underson started to talk before she had finished reading, as though chivalrously giving her the chance to recover composure.

'I was surprised that Scherner is nearing sixty, but he must be. It's an inflexible rule that all Hoofstanger skippers retire then. No extensions however well you may be doing. And it must be admitted he hasn't done badly. Of course they pay remarkable pensions. It helps to buy loyalty from an early age, knowing that's ahead. You retire on two-thirds of your terminal take-home.'

Jessie's thought was that if the Hoofstangers were out to get her before Anglo-European became anything like a threat to them, they had set about it in the right way. In their shoes this was precisely what she would have done.

Underson was sitting down again.

'Have you replied to this?'

He nodded.

'An acceptance?'

'No. A stall. I said I'd let them know after I'd had two weeks holiday in Bermuda with my wife. If they don't like that they needn't come back on the theme again, but I think they will. It seems that my former big brothers have gone on watching me.'

Jessie was suddenly coldly in control. 'Have you had any other evidence that they were doing that?'

He nodded again.

'A year ago they offered me First Mate on one of their newest, with the first command that came along after. Probably they had the *Grooter* in mind then.'

'She's a very old ship compared with the *Saturn*.'

'Sure. But I wouldn't stay on her. The Hoofstanger fleet offers a big field for play now. And more building. I think they really want me back in the field. Apparently not put off at all by my near miss with the *Mary Worth*. Good kite flying. It was, too; I handled that thing myself. Of course I speak Dutch pretty well, which eliminates any problems there. Also, they may be beginning to feel that the *Saturn* is a challenge to them in her way.'

'Which she won't be with you gone from her bridge, Captain Underson?'

'I didn't say that.'

'You meant it!'

He smiled. 'I'm going to miss MacDonald. The others, too, of course. But you get used to working with your First. Maybe he could take a crash course in Dutch?'

Jessie stood.

'Perhaps you could let me know by telephone when you have officially handed over to Mr MacDonald?'

'I'd rather take the *Saturn* back to Hull before I leave her.'

'Which would give you time to offer all the crew jobs with Hoofstanger?'

'They wouldn't dream of authorizing that. Their selection board is as tough as an Atomic Energy Authority's. Much vetting. No, it will just be a sail down to our home port with some sad leave takings at the end. And time for a few more chess games with the Chief.'

'I'm surprised that you have these areas of sentiment, Captain Underson.'

'I'm a very sentimental man. I'll see you down to your car.'


## CHAPTER SEVEN

MARK had ignored the national speed limit out on a motorway and he wasn't respecting traffic regulations in a surprisingly quiet three a.m. London, either. He pushed a blue M.G. sports saloon hard around corners and didn't stop for amber lights, jumping through a few red ones. The car went down deserted canyons of shopping streets just ahead of its own exhaust sonic boom, the tyres shallowing glistening puddles, sending sheets of spray towards bright yellow kerb lines. Bodywork was mud spattered, wipers on overtime.

The M.G. escaped from its own echo in the Bayswater Road, jerking left into the park, past bare, dripping trees beyond which water showed a faint reflection of city lighting held down by overcast. He hit seventy-three crossing this oasis of mock country, but at the turn into Kensington High Street braked down hard, the sober citizen again in his own particular suburbia.

It cost money to claim this as your part of town. He saw the seven-storey block holding his shore-base some time before he reached it, the newness shining out. It had a façade of balconies, and its amenities offered practically everything including space for one car per flat in an underground garage. Alice's Mini had that space; Mark had to find his own parking, and it was minutes before he was able to do this. He locked the car, wondering if he'd find it vandal marked later, and started the walk home.

His feet made no noise along empty pavements. In a near white raincoat he moved like a ghost with a purpose, empty-handed, past walled-away sleepers. No lights showed from windows in his own block as he turned towards a glass-walled entrance area. This offered a discreet glowing, like the illumination by a bank vault. A key put him on soft carpeting in a lobby featuring a long box of evergreen exotics which weren't plastic and seemed to do well enough under their private, bogus sun.

He walked towards the lifts. The indicator above one of them went red suddenly, and he stopped, staring at it. The arrow started swinging down . . . seven . . six . . . five . . . very slowly. They were slow lifts.

Seven was penthouse level. Alice and he had one of three flats up there. Mark had passed the time of day with a neighbour, a blue-rinse elderly dame who wore her diamonds to Harrods round the corner. He had an impression of the husband, moustache and bristle haircut, the angry look of a well-heeled retired general who found the world these days full of young men who ought to be forced to have their hair cut and made to drill for at least ten hours weekly. The other flat housed a company promoter and his wife, both middle-aged, who looked as if the struggle to get up to the top floor had worn them out. Mark had never spoken to either.

The red light went out. The doors opened. The man who emerged from the cage gave Mark a look and then couldn't have cared less. He was somewhere in his thirties, tall, no City type, expensive country suiting with the trousers probably still hung from his shoulders on elastic webbing. Both his shoes and his manner were custom built. What was strange he ignored. After that one glance he ignored Mark, though he didn't at once leave the building, pausing by a shadowy mirror to do something to his tie. He seemed unhappy about the knot, and fiddled with it. Then he took out a handkerchief, pressing the white linen against his lips, checking this for stain.

Mark thought how he would kill him, a right and a left into the stomach, followed by a right again just below the heart. That great tower would fall.

The man turned suddenly and went quickly over carpeting to the glass door, through this, and out on to the pavement. He was in a hurry now, back in routine again after an experience outside it, late for something, possibly his wife's bed. Mark closed his eyes and held them shut for seconds. The red spots were still there. He turned slowly towards a bright box welcoming the sailor home with fluorescent lighting.

The lift scarcely seemed to be moving. In New York you'd be up seventy floors in the time it took this one to climb seven, but finally he was released on to wool pile twice as thick as at lobby level. He saw the three doors and took out the key which fitted one of them, putting this in the lock carefully, making the half-turn left, then right again, which broke through elaborate security. The hall beyond was dark. He shut the door without the faintest click and stood in the warm still blackness listening. He moved towards the main bedroom, not reaching for a light switch, waiting outside it for all of a minute, not hearing a sound.

In the narrow cupboard that had been labelled a single bedroom he took off the raincoat and dropped it on the floor. He did the same with his jacket. The curtains hadn't been pulled and a low red sky advertised that London never really sleeps, only pretends to. He dropped on his stomach along the divan. The cover had a musty smell.

God! The one thing a sailor should never do is marry.

Out in Kensington High Street car brakes shrieked.

'Mark! What on earth . . . ?'

She had her hand up to the switch. She seemed tall standing there, wearing a nylon nightdress. He could see her body through it. Long fair hair was down on her shoulders, she always wore it straight, there was never any need for curlers, so she couldn't suddenly screw on to her head those badges of wifely innocence.

'When did you come?'

A good question, probably troubling her.

'Mark, for God's sake say something! Are you ill??'

'No.'

'But . . . why didn't you phone?'

That was what he usually did, in fact always had done, as soon as the *Saturn* docked. He knew now he'd been a man not wanting to run the risk of a surprise. Well, he'd run that risk tonight.

'There's something wrong,' she said.

He sat up, a coward again. He couldn't complete the scene, couldn't round it out.

'I had a long drive from Hull. Exhausted. Roads greasy. I thought I wouldn't . . .'

'Oh, *darling*!'

Her hand dropped from the switch. She might have been holding on for support.

'You came in here not to wake me? Do you think . . .'

He looked at her.

'. . . after all these weeks, when you come home, I want consideration? Oh, Mark!'

He looked at his feet.

'You haven't even taken off your shoes,' she said.

His slippers might have been warming by a radiator.

'I can't get it,' she said. 'Creeping in. Not waking me. Don't you know I always want to be wakened? By you.'

She held out both hands, but didn't come any closer, didn't try to touch him. She wasn't going to do that until the right moment. Alice had always shown a great deal of technical expertise. It had surprised him when they were first married, but then she hadn't claimed to be a virgin. None of them did these days.

'Come on,' she said. 'Our room. I'll let you sleep. If you find you really want to.'

Her hand was a probing mouse, researching his skin. Nibbling fingers worked lower but he wasn't beginning to get the right reaction. For one thing she was ahead of any reasonable schedule, for another he was thinking about postscripts to sex.

With Lin there had never been any. Her duty done she had lain as immobile as a bamboo pole, cool on a tropic mattress, available for use again if required, but meantime snatching at sleep as though it was the only really valuable thing, its complete permanency the happy end of the living process. Lin had woken from sleep as though at once conscious of fear, totally still, her eyes wide, forcing herself slowly to face up to the consequences of being awake. He didn't flatter himself that she had ever escaped from her terrors with him, in a way they had been increased by what he gave, the temporary security with the time limit, the imitation domesticity from which she went to market with her basket, buying food for the man who had bought her. In a sense the girl had known with him things that were outside her norm, and that she was frightened to lose again. But that was all of it. There was no question of love, no potential of pain from it, or the endless guessing about what really was going on behind the words and movements and laughter of another.

The mouse gave up its investigations. .

'Sleepy, darling?'

'Not really.'

'Mark, why did you do that . . . creeping in? Not opening this door?'

'I told you. I was worn out.'

'You haven't been acting like it since.'

'You're a great reviver.'

She put lips to his shoulder.

'Love me?'

'You know the answer.'

'Then why be so tied up? You're all knots.'

'The cure is seven slow, deep breaths.'

She punched him, then kept her hands to herself, as though she thought it was his turn to take over the warming-up exercises. In fact it was, but he couldn't. All he could do was lie there thinking that on the *Saturn* he had made himself a nice phantasy to live with, one that could be invoked any time when he had twenty minutes off from more extrovert activities. Twenty minutes for *Solveig's Song* and bringing into operation their private telepathic communication. How big a bloody fool could a man get?

Then she surprised him.

'On your ship do you think about me?'

'Yes.'

'Often?'

'Yes.'

'I think about you, too. Wondering what you're doing. Mark, if anything happened to you I'd . . .'

She couldn't find the right word. He didn't try to help, he couldn't find it either. She pushed her body against his side.

'Don't you know how I feel about you? Don't you?'

'I like to think I do.'

'But don't I show you? Don't I?'

She was worried about something. Her hand came back, a forefinger teasing around his right nipple.

'Mark, do you often have sex dreams at sea?'

'Every night. It's the high protein diet.'

He felt rather than heard her giggle.

'And is it always me?'

'Always.'

That was a lie, but she seemed to like it. She came right over on to him, slowly, a journey of lips to his lips, and before the end of her mouth's travels he was ready.

London was awake, still under the red reflection of night lighting, but committed to a day, rumbling, the wide road below the flats dedicated again to the pompous industry of heavy lorries. Mark was conscious of being totally isolated from the area of his authority, not so much oppressed by the city now round him as knowing himself without any confirmed tracks across it which could give a man the illusion of an acceptable identity in terms of place. They were all fooling themselves, of course, the city allows no one any identity. A few might seem to have emerged from the mass, conspicuous above it, but they were still just names in a vast book waiting to be erased to make room for another name. Still, if you had your regular path through the echoing, a pub where the bar-girl knew you, a shop that used your name, it gave a kind of conviction to the daily movement. In London he had no path, no pub, no shop, just this rented flat in which Alice said she waited, and a fast car to take him away again, back to the sea. It was only in London that he became introspective, dreading this like an expected recurrence of chronic disease.

Alice turned over in the wide bed and struck him from her sleep, quite hard just below the triceps, muttering something. She was quite a dreamer and had, at times, long conversations from the subconscious that sounded like a question and answer game, immensely important to her, if meaningless to a listener. Probably under an anaesthetic she would tell all, but the surgeons wouldn't permit an audience.

He eased himself away from her and out of the bed. Halfway to the door he almost fell over his trousers, reaching down for these and with a sailor's almost instinctive prudery about total nakedness pulling them on, though the flat was very warm. He went to the kitchen in bare feet, clicking the switch. Fluorescent lighting took its seconds before revealing what had been advertised as Californian fittings. These had got away from the operating theatre look, homey with Formica pretending to be aged oak, the deep freezer even having ye olde hinges. But there was a reminder of the chartroom computer when he switched on the cooker, a red electric eye glaring at him, a warning that he couldn't boil a kettle unnoticed.

He was sitting at the table drinking tea out of Crown Derby when the door opened. Alice hadn't bothered to put on the nightgown. 'You keep sneaking away,' she said. 'I think you're frightened of me.'

'I need refreshment. Have a cup?'

'That's our best china, you nit!'

She sat down on a stool, put her elbows on the table and yawned. He got up, found another cup, and poured.

'Ciggy.'

He had quite a hunt for the pack, then gave her a light. She looked up. 'How long are you home for this time?'

'At least two weeks.'

It was too soon to tell her the truth.

'Lovely,' she said. 'Gorgeous two weeks. At the end of my life, when it's all totted up, and if I live to be eighty, I'll have had about a year of you in our bed.'

'You're forgetting my retirement.'

'We'll be old.'

They drank tea to that. He put his elbows on the table, too, thinking what good breasts she had, which didn't slump much even when she was humped over.

'I hate this god-damned flat,' she said.

'You chose it.'

'I did not! You took me round to a selection of places you thought suitable. And it was obvious you liked this one. It was the most expensive.'

She didn't often have the *tristesse*, but it seemed to have hit her this time.

'I don't know anyone in this whole building, do you know that?'

'Have you tried to?'

'I've looked at them. Old fossils. Dead from the neck down and the ears up. The trouble is I see myself growing like that. Screened by your money. And as the years tick away. You know what I did last week? I went to Sotheby's and suddenly found myself bidding for a perfectly hideous piece of Dresden, a little tower supported by pink cupids with a fruit dish on top. I stopped at ninety but it went to a hundred and seventy-three. I might have got it.'

'Where's all this leading?'

'I want out of here before being so handy for Harrods gets me. Not to mention my hairdresser and meeting friends for calorie-watching lunches.'

'Any ideas where you'd go?'

'If I'm not to take a job again, yes. The country.'

He stared. 'You?'

He had a picture of her sitting naked in a converted farm kitchen somewhere while the yokel who did the heavy digging peered in through leaded windows, licking his lips.

'The country is something not unknown to me, Mark. I lived in it until I was seventeen.'

'Sure. Your father the Rector. Caps touched in the village and you innocence on a bicycle.'

'What the hell do you mean by that?'

'That you won't find it again. In a few short years the picture has been painted over.'

'How do you know?'

'Because I get about quite a bit in the M.G. The Rectory orchard is a caravan park these days, with all the happy villagers making money out of the week-enders. That's what you'll find for a hundred miles in any direction from here.'

'I might go a hundred and fifty.' She reached out for the pack, took another cigarette, and lit it. 'But as a matter of fact I've found something very much nearer than that. In Buckinghamshire.'

'What? I thought the whole county had been set aside for a new overflow town?'

'Not by Stewkley.'

'Where's that?'

'Quite near my sister's at Tring.'

'It's never seemed to me that Bob and Mary had exactly the ideal set-up at Tring.'

'Mark, this isn't like that. A little Georgian cottage. It has an acre. And it's not near any main road. Mary and I came on it quite by accident. And the next day I took Bob over. You know how he is about dry rot and so on.'

'An expert,' Mark agreed.

Alice didn't notice. 'He says it's structurally sound. Though there are things to be done.'

'Like a couple of bathrooms, and the kitchen, and a new roof. Not to mention a permanent electric pump to keep down the water level in the cellar.'

'It's on rising ground.'

'My God, Alice, are you really sold on this?'

'Yes.'

'But what would you *do* there?'

'There's years of work. I'd be busy all the time. And I'll be near Mary. You can drive all the way on back roads. Bob says he'll help with the garden. I want half in fruit trees.'

'You sit there stark naked with a damn dream!'

'Do you mind me being stark naked?'

'Well, it's not very country.'

She looked at him.

'You hate this, don't you? It's right outside the Underson plan for a wife. Who has the best of everything, living in an air-conditioned hat-box while her man scours the seas for sinking ships. Well, maybe you have the good life as a marine scavenger, but I don't. I sit up here on this roof waiting to hear about your latest triumph off Pernambuco, or whatever.'

He stood up. 'What do you think I'm sweating my guts out as a scavenger for, since you call me that?'

She smiled. 'You own sweet self. You love it. When you're about to go back to the *Saturn* your face takes on a different look. The man returning to his kingdom. Oh, you try not to seem too eager, and the bedding me has been all right, but you're still twitching for that ship. You can't help it. You're God there, aren't you? Everyone bows.'

'On a tug? You're crazy!'

'In their way they bow. I've seen them at it often enough. But on shore nobody calls you "sir". In Bucks, though, we might train them to in the village, who knows? Great excitement at the post-office because the Captain is coming home.'

He stared down. 'You can be a real bitch!'

'It's about time you found out, isn't it?'

She shoved her arms out over the table and then dropped her head on to them. He saw the curve of her back like a child's, the spine's seemingly fragile vertebrae. She looked vulnerable, her body a statement of this, thin arms, small wrists, fingers clenched on both hands. She wasn't wearing his rings.

He thought of the man in the country suiting checking his lips for staining. There weren't many cottages in Bucks just lying empty waiting to be discovered these days. Even the rumour of one brought agents and hordes of would-be commuters. The dream home was near her sister's and who else? Had a tall man found it for her, part of his manor?

He walked across the kitchen.

'Mark! Don't go away!'

'I need some sleep.'

He went down the corridor to the small room with the musty bedcover. The door had a lock, but he didn't turn the key, lying down, half-expecting her to come there again, but she didn't. He told himself that he did need some sleep, he damn well did need it.

He didn't get any. London grew noisier and grey light came from the window into the expensive square footage of the little room. On the *Saturn* he fell into his bunk and just went out, the switch to unconsciousness completely automatic.

At eight he got up and went into the second bathroom for a shower, emerging to the sound of the radio playing in the kitchen. He went back into the cubbyhole where his clothes were, finding slacks and a nylon pullover he didn't remember seeing before. He had everything he needed in this place, but none of it was familiar. The slip-ons felt stiff and new on his feet.

Alice was at the electric cooker, in a long housecoat, her hair combed and her eyes carefully made up. She turned and smiled. 'Fry up,' she said. 'Nothing like some solid feeding for an emotional hangover. I hope you got your sleep?'

'No.'

'Oh, darling. Sit down and pour yourself some coffee. This won't be a minute. One of the things I'm looking forward to in the country is a kitchen filled with cooking smells. This damn thing has a vent that sucks everything away. We're deodorized out of this world. Never a stink in the penthouse.'

He sat and stared at her back. The radio was on pop. Everything pointed to a bright new day except Mark's feelings and the weather. It was still gloomy outside and there were raindrops running down the window.

'There you are now,' Alice said, putting a plate in front of him. 'Processed pig and national eggs.'

There was a healthy portion for her, too.

'Thinking of keeping hens, are you?'

'No, you get your eggs from the post-office. Lovely deep brown ones. From non-battery birds. Oh hell, the toast.'

Alice always made excellent coffee. She kept a battered tin percolator for the job, probably an heirloom from the Rectory, into which went water and an impulsive heap of grounds plus some salt, the contraption then put on a hot-plate to bubble for twenty minutes. It was enough to make the purist blench, but what came out of the spout was rich and dark and life-giving.

'Darling, I simply forgot to tell you. What do you think we've got suddenly in this nirvana for God's rich anointed? You won't believe it. A fully qualified tart.'

He had been swallowing a piece of not quite adequately chewed bacon and had to reach for his cup to send this on its way.

'The company promoter moved out suddenly, which was a relief. I hated meeting his wife in the life. Even worse than meeting Lady Battle of the Bulge. But Gwendoline is marvellous.'

'What did you say?'

'Georgeous name, isn't it? Rolls on the tongue. I'm sure I've seen her on the covers of *Woman's Life* but not for a while. That was before she went out for the really big money. Obviously she's pulling it in. We chat. You know how slow the lift is, it gives quite a lot of time, really. I've always meant to ask her in for a drink, but it's a bit awkward. I mean, one doesn't know their hours, when she sleeps, and so on. It's all done madly discreetly, of course. You simply never see the men. Nothing to cause offence, even to Penthouse B. No wild parties in C. Nothing like that. It's sweet of me to tell you really, but then if the sailor phones up to say he's met an old buddy from Singapore and will be late I won't have far to look, will I? Why are you staring?'

Mark reached for a piece of toast and buttered it carefully. He felt on the verge of nausea. She filled his cup again.

'Two weeks,' she said. 'What are your holiday plans?'

'We're flying to Bermuda. Renting a pink villa by a white beach. It comes complete with staff. You don't have to lift a finger.'

'Oh, Mark! It'll cost the earth!'

He could look at her then. 'That troubles you?'

'Well, it's a super idea. Absolutely. But . . .'

'You'd rather spend your money on a new roof?'

She smiled. 'Something like that. I know I had the gripes last night. I was a bitch. You said it. But I . . .'

'Yes?'

'The bitchery isn't chronic yet. It can be cured. It won't be if I stay here.'

'Simple as that?'

'Probably it isn't. But it's what I feel. Mark, look at it this way. Living here is just wasting your money. We're pouring it out, for what? I could live in the cottage and run the car and do the place up just for what you pay a landlord to have this address. And I don't give a damn about the address. Do *you*, really?'

'I suppose not.'

'Well then, why go on here? Let's pack our tents like the company promoter and re-plan our budget. It's a good business address for Gwendoline, of course, and maybe she has a girl friend. Imagine General and Lady Bulge outflanked! It's delicious. Mark, will you come down with me today to Bucks? In the rain? Or is that too awful of me?'

'I'll come.'

'Darling, it'll be marvellous. I'll have my cottage, and I can still come to any port you want. There are kennels half a mile away for the dog.'

'We're having a dog?'

'A Great Dane, to scare away intruders. Phosphorus on his jaws at night. And when I've got the lawn replanted I may even do the conventional thing for the sailor's wife.'

'What's that?'

'Swell with your child.'

He sat very still.

'Well? Don't you want that?'

'Yes.'

'You'll be surprised at how much we both want the same things when we get all this tidied away. And I'll stop being jealous of the *Saturn*.'

'You can stop that now. I don't have her.'

'What?'

'Mrs Lawton sacked me in Grangemouth.'

She stared. 'My God! And we were flying to Bermuda!'

'I meant to tell you on a white beach. I thought it'd be easier.'

'Oh, Mark, you damn fool!'

'I guess so.'

'But . . . what does this mean? You're not giving up the sea?'

'No. I'm going to the Dutch again.'

'An offer?'

'Good one. Probably more money coming in. Certainly not less.'
Alice was silent for seconds. 'But you hate it,' she said.
'Yes, I hate it.'
'Oh, Mark, I've been horrible to you. That's why you came home like that. You were . . .'
'No!'
'I could kill myself. Whining away.'
She came round the table and put an arm over his shoulders.
'Don't get the wrong idea,' he said. 'I don't love her as a ship.'
'You liar.'
'She's just a tin box.'
'You god-damned liar!'
She kissed the top of his head. After a moment she said: 'You go back to her again? You don't mean you've left her for good?'
'Yes. They'll send on my gear. I packed it.'
'I'll go up to Scotland and kick that old bitch's teeth in.'
'She'd just get a new set off National Health.'
Alice crouched down beside his stool.
'How could she do this to you?'
'It's a question of confidence.'
'She said she'd lost that in you?'
'More or less.'
'Mark, you have a foul temper. And you're stubborn. And you can also be a block of very cold ice.'
'All those things.'
'Get the man to put that in writing for future use. By me. I will *not* see you hurt!'
'I'm not hurt.'
'You're bleeding. How much money have we got?'
'Enough to live in your cottage, even with inflation.'
'Well?'
'No.'
'I thought not. Anyway, you'd mess up my plans. I wouldn't know where to put you when the plumbers were in. What I'm trying to say is, couldn't a way be found to patch up things with that old cow?'
'We served each other ultimatums. She doesn't like them, and I don't either.'
'I can just see it,' Alice said. 'What do your men on the *Saturn* think about all this?'
'Nobody burst into tears. Actually, they were sleeping when I left the ship.'
'You just sneaked away?'
'You might say that.'
Alice stood and started to walk up and down, her arms folded over her breasts. 'I feel sick,' she said.

He could sympathize with the feeling, though his own nausea had gone. He sat with simple, almost totally unnerving shame, like a small boy caught at what he has been taught is mortal sin. He wondered whether Alice, if she knew what had kept pushing to the front of his mind for a sizeable chunk of the night, could ever put that estimate of her to one side and carry on as before. He certainly wasn't going to try the experiment of telling all. If she ever took a lover it would be his fault, not something stemming from loneliness or boredom, either. And she wouldn't be sly about it.

'I'd better shave,' he said.

He was conscious of her watching him go. In the second bathroom, behind the mirror, he found a large bottle of male perfume. It wasn't disguised as an after-shave lotion, but said frankly: 'Musk, the male scent.' An hour ago that bottle would have frozen him solid in suspicion. He took it along to the kitchen.

'Who the hell's been using my bathroom?'

Alice turned down the volume of the nine o'clock news on the portable. She pulled out the glass stopper.

'Bob. He smells like that these days. They got a baby-sitter a couple of weeks ago and came up for a theatre and the night. You don't fancy it?'

'No.'

'I don't either. We'll take it back to him today. You know what the weather report is for the immediate future?'

'Changeable, with snow, sleet and ice in most districts.'

'That's right. Perfect time for house buying. Owners are ashamed of their hideous-looking property. And at this time of year everyone is made pretty conscious of the horrors of long-distance commuting. We'll knock a thousand off their price.'

'And what is their price?'

'I was wondering when you were going to get around to asking that.'

'Well?'

'Six thousand five hundred.'

'What? For no roof?'

'It *has* a roof. Bob says it's a good one. Cornish slates, or something.'

'I bet mounted on the borings of the death-watch beetle through all the timbers. I'm beginning to see why the place hasn't been snapped up.'

'Mark, if you really hate the idea . . .'

He kissed her.

'I love it. It'll be a new bond between us. When I'm battling a hurricane with a tow I'll be able to think of you hard at it, too, putting buckets under those drips in the east wing. And have you checked garden soil for eel-worm? They say if eel-worms are really established it takes fifty years to get rid of them.'

'Bastard!'

The radio announcer had come to the end of his bad news and was giving a summary of earlier detail just in case his listeners had started to cheer up. He cut through this, his words up an octave.

'We have just learned that the Norwegian liner *Sogne Fjord* has been in collision in the North Sea. She is reported badly holed, with engines out of action. Two fishing boats operating in the Dogger Bank area are going to her assistance. There is no information about the other vessel involved and no word of casualties.'

Mark went to an extension phone on a counter. Over his shoulder he said: 'Where's that big atlas I got you?'

'I'll find it.'

He lifted the handset and dialled.

'Get me Hull. Not a code number. A ship tied up with a land line from the dock. The tug *Saturn*. Got that? Speed it. Emergency.'

Alice came back into the kitchen. She said quietly:

'You want me to find you the North Sea area?'

'Yes.'

She slid the open book on to the surface beside him. He stared at it while he waited. The connection took all of a minute.

'Bridge, tug *Saturn*. Second Officer Ginnis.'

'I thought you'd be Mate now?'

'Is that . . . ?'

'Underson. In London. Are you on to this *Sogne Fjord* business?'

'Yes, sir. But there isn't a lot we can do about it.'

'What? From Hull you've got a head start on everybody!'

'But MacDonald went ashore this morning just an hour ago. To drive to his aunt who lives in the Lake District. Unless he hears on car radio there's nothing we can do. How can I get in touch with him?'

'What about the rest of the crew?'

'Parker's away. And so is Ackroyd.'

'But the Chief's with you?'

'Yes.'

'Then sail. And don't ask on whose authority. I know I haven't got any. But take her out, Ginnis. Belt up there. This could be a clean, sweet job. Tell Collins to get his ears flapping. He told me coming down he'd broken the new code the Hoofstangers are using. That means he can find out what ship they're sending up. They won't be on silence yet.'

'We already know, sir. It's the *Grooter*.'

'What? Impossible! She'll be in the Irish Sea on her way back to base.'

'No. She stood by the rig; they weren't too happy about their positioning. The *Semirande* went back to Brest but the *Grooter* stayed. Then she was ordered to call at Rotterdam on her way back to station. She was coming south when this happened. Now she's going to the *Sogne*. We can't position her, but she may be nearer to the Norwegian than we are.'

'So you were going to sit on your arses in dock and let the Hoofstangers have this? Ginnis, that's no bloody way to operate a tug.'

'MacDonald . . .'

'To hell with MacDonald. Get out there! And you're going to have a supercargo. I'll join you.'

'What? You . . .'

'Our unused helipad, remember? Due for a christening.'

'My God!'

'He helps those who help themselves. You'll get a signal from the bird when to swing out those boats. And, Ginnis, don't let the Chief bully you about his engines. The speed is full ahead all the way. I ought to be with you before you make contact with the *Sogne*. We'll find your position from radio reports. Now get the *Saturn* awake!'

He hung up. Alice was staring at him. 'Can you do this?' she asked.

'No.' He went to the table and poured himself some coffee. 'And further, the Hoofstangers are going to love having the man they've just offered a career showing up to help the opposition. They're out to get Jessie before she becomes any kind of a threat. That's really why they rolled out all those bright prospects to me. It's not that they think I'm a boy wonder. They could have found a perfectly good replacement for Scherner in their own ranks. They must have at least six seasoned Mates who would qualify.'

'So?'

He smiled at her. 'So it's the moment for a little wifely advice about how we've got to start being prudent and consider our own vital interests.'

'When you start being prudent, Mark, I don't want you.'


## CHAPTER EIGHT

MARK had flown in helicopters before, but nothing like this model. It was used for aerial photography, a two seater, the cabin almost entirely Perspex, which gave the feel of being inside a large, airborne electric light bulb. Visibility was total and unnerving. Also, the machine wasn't meant for this type of work and had a limited range. They had flown up the coast to Newcastle, refuelled, then gone straight out over the sea towards the Dogger Bank. The pilot thought he had enough in the tank for the round trip if their fix on the *Sogne* was the right one.

Alice had found the helicopter. Her last job had been production assistant to a film company and she'd had dealings with a firm specializing in support services for movie making. They had three helicopters for hire with pilot, and the cheapest cost a lot. If Jessie declined to pay the bill, as seemed almost certain, Mark would be telling his broker to sell a block of shares.

The sea was five hundred feet below. A Force Three wind had dispersed fog and a watery sun put a faint shadow of their craft on to steel blue waves. The heating inside the globe wasn't up to much and Mark's feet were ice blocks.

The pilot chewed gum. His age was difficult to assess, somewhere in his thirties, perhaps. He wore a peaked golfing cap and hadn't bothered to shave. Life had bored him for a good many years. He sat watching the horizon most of the time, noise shutting him away in a separate compartment as effectively as the glass screen behind the chauffeur in a Rolls. Suddenly he shouted:

'Be over target area in about five minutes.'

Mark could see nothing on the sea, but the horizon was still hazed, cutting down visibility to eight miles even from their elevation. He reached over and switched on the R.T., picking up the mike.

'P.X.27 calling salvage tug *Saturn*. Come in if you read me. P.X.27 calling *Saturn*.'

Collins's voice was loud even through engine roar.

'*Saturn* is reading you P.X.27. Over.'

'Check your position with the bridge.'

'Have just done. Was expecting you. We're square on fifty-five east two, heading due north.'

'In sight of the *Sogne*?'

'Not yet. Her fix puts her twelve north. Visibility seven. Maybe twenty minutes. Are you coming in?'

'Soon. Having a look round first. I'll call back if there's any error in the *Sogne*'s fix. Otherwise not. Tell the bridge to clear the landing pad. Any sound of the Dutch on R.T. to the *Sogne*?'

'Not so far. They used radio an hour ago. They were then twenty-nine north of the *Sogne*.'

The *Grooter* could do eighteen when pushed, and Scherner would be pushing her, which probably put the Dutchman now about eleven miles from the crippled ship to the *Saturn*'s twelve. But the *Saturn* had at least a couple of knots more speed. It looked like being a photo finish. Mark signed off and then sat back, suddenly remembering about the *Grooter*'s skipper playing it dirty with searchlights off Hoy. Scherner had also, at one time or another, had plenty to say about the *Saturn*'s helipad.

'There's your Norwegian,' the pilot said.

She was a few points to port, a snow-white ship, only a couple of years off the ways, her superstructure entirely of aluminium, this permitting the kind of built-up heap of deck-housing on a relatively shallow draft hull which, in an all-steel ship, would have seen her capsizing in the first real sea. Mark knew that she was not, in fact, top-heavy, but she still looked it, offering passenger accommodation for 400 in a gross tonnage of under 5,000, plus a considerable cargo space. This he had found out from the company's London agent, together with the fact that she wasn't heavily booked on a winter trip, only fifty-seven fare payers on board.

As they got closer the *Sogne*'s list to port was obvious but not as bad as Mark had been expecting. She ought to be an easy enough tow provided movement through the water didn't start crumpling bulkheads. If that happened things could get very tricky, as they might, too, if weather conditions worsened. A straight haul to Newcastle was the answer, and not at more than three knots. The fishing boats, which the radio news had reported as going to the *Sogne*'s assistance, had apparently pushed off again, there was no sign of them. In fact, in a relatively calm sea, there was no feel of panic in the situation, but that didn't mean that the tow wouldn't yield nice returns from an awards court.

'Want me to do a run over her?'

Mark nodded. 'Then get me back to *Saturn*.'

They came in from the small liner's starboard side, and on that approach the Norwegian looked like a piece of new kitchen equipment in shiny white enamel. There wasn't a mark on her. Figures were visible out on the bridge wing but the sight of a 'copter didn't appear to cause much excitement. They had probably had plenty of air visitors.

The pilot passed over the *Sogne* and then turned his machine. Mark saw port damage, almost amidships: an ugly ulcer in the vessel's white skin, with black gangrene setting in around the edges. That tear began just below the first line of her portholes, widening down towards her plimsol and with the unpleasant suggestion of a sea cave below water. Her propulsion was towards the stern, as the positioning of her one funnel indicated, which meant that the engine-room had just missed penetration, but one bulkhead had gone, causing enough flooding to shut down power. Her pumps were on emergency. Discharge vents showed that these were still hard at it, and the ship wasn't any-

thing like as deep in the water as might have been expected from
that gash. It seemed to Mark highly probable that she had cross
deck as well as vertical watertight bulkheading. The big mystery
was how the ship which had been responsible for that rip in another's plates could have just sailed away into the fog, reporting
nothing, particularly when her own damage must have been
extensive. Even the underwater bulbous bows being featured on
a lot of the new bulk carriers couldn't have made that hole low
in a hull without at the same time smashing in her own forepeak.
Mark had some questions and no answers.

'That must be the boat your radio man was talking about,' the
pilot shouted.

The 'copter had been on hover. The pilot now swung his
machine around to save Mark from having to swivel his neck.
The *Grooter* was coming out of a haze wall, wearing all her usual
badges of competence, like a Rover Scout who has passed all the
tests. Mark's feeling weren't mixed as he looked at the ship he
might have commanded, he didn't like her. He was certain he
never could.

The globe rose and turned south again at 700, clearing the
*Sogne*. There was no sign of the *Saturn* coming out of another
haze wall. Mark began to have the tug skipper's nightmare; her
engines had conked out under the load of extra revs asked of
them at maximum speed and the ship was about to become the
most contemptible of all things afloat, a salvage vessel requiring a
tow to port. It was three minutes before he saw her, and with a
healthy bow wave, and breathed again. Her boats were slung out.

'Where the hell's this pad?' the pilot asked.

'Behind her towers.'

'Doesn't look room enough for a Monday wash. You used it
before?'

'No.'

'Gawd. So I'm the guinea-pig?'

'There isn't much of a sea running.'

'Okay, you put her down.'

The 'copter came in like a dragon-fly to a large bloom, sniffing
first to see if the nectar was going to make a landing worth it.
From 300 those bright painted circles looked like an under-sized
archery target on which a bull's eye was improbable. Mark put
the question that was in his mind.

'Think you can make it?'

'I once landed on a stony Greek hillside during an earthquake.'

'You mean the 'quake was on?'

'That's right. All the production unit flat on their faces. Like
they'd just heard my passenger was the company president
straight from Hollywood checking up on what was happening to

his three million dollars. After touch-down I was nearly rocked into the valley. I took off pretty quick. Like I'll do today.'

'No.'

'Eh?'

'I want you to wait.'

'That's no part of the agreement.'

'You carry my line to the *Sogne*.'

'I'll do *what*? Think again, Captain.'

'You'll only be on board for half an hour or so. Time for a cup of coffee.'

'Time to get my plugs salted up.'

'Would two tenners interest you?'

'Not for two seconds. You're asking me to do part of your work.'

'I'm asking you to drop a lead line on to the Norwegian, that's all. On your way home.'

'Look, Captain, I'm beginning to get the picture. It's a Western. And the baddies are winning. They're that other tug we saw. I don't know how you people usually get your ropes on to a wreck, but it's quicker by 'copter. My price is a hundred.'

'I don't have that kind of money on me.'

'You ought to travel with more for current expenses. I'll take your personal cheque marked to bearer.'

The dragon-fly flapped its long tail in the Force Three, hovering.

'Fifty,' Mark said.

'For that you can do your own rope slinging. I don't know what you get out of all this if you win, but I'll bet plenty. All I'm asking for is drinks money. I'm a thirsty man. You can see it in my nose.'

'Seventy-five.'

'You used to dealing with Arabs, or something? I've told you the price. Personal cheque one hundred.'

'Damn you!'

'Last time I saw a priest he said I already was. Didn't even bother to suggest a penance.'

'All right, a hundred.'

'Make it out now, we've plenty of time.'

Mark found his wallet. The pilot held the machine remarkably steady so that the writing wouldn't get blurred. He took the cheque with his left hand, blew on it, then tucked it away in a pocket of his jerkin.

Down on the *Saturn* the entire crew seemed to be taking up positions from which to view the big spectacular, but Mark noticed a certain caution exercised in the stances chosen, as though with a view to quick cover in event of an explosion. Ginnis was just outside the door on to the boat-deck and behind him, tucked back into the passage, were faces. One or two hardy spirits had risked the dubious protection offered by davits. On the high gallery between the towers two figures appeared. One was the Chief. To Mark's knowledge the man had only climbed that ladder on four occasions and he claimed that each trip had taken a month off his life. Nothing but an expectation of the worst would have forced him up those rungs.

'Okay, here we go,' the pilot said.

Rotor noise increased and its downthrust seemed to cause some distress to the audience, but the actual landing was an anti-climax, so easy. They hung at six feet, between the slung-out boats, then went down on to plating during an up heave of the deck, bang on top of the red spot bull's eye.

The pilot cut engine. 'Now you know you can do it,' he said. 'Do I get a rum issue?'

'This isn't the Navy.'

'Whisky'll do.'

Mark unlocked a curve of plastic and dropped to the deck, practically into the new Mate's arms. Ginnis's welcome seemed sincere enough, as though he had been feeling the strain of temporary command.

'The *Grooter*'s beating us,' Mark said. 'We've got a lead line coil of more than a thousand yards, haven't we?'

'Yes, sir.'

'Well, get that ready to spin out. The 'copter's taking it up for us when we get near enough.'

'And after my refreshment,' the pilot said, sliding down from the cabin.

'He's an alcoholic. Cook!'

'Sir?'

'Coffee for our guest. And there should still be a bottle of whisky in my cabin. I left it for the new captain. See to that, will you?'

'Sir.'

'Ginnis, when you have the line ready, join me on the bridge.'

Faces in the passage were welcoming enough, but there was a certain restraint, too; everyone being nice about a comeback performance which no one really believed was going to have a very long run. Mark went up stairs hating Jessie Lawton for taking his ship away from him. He walked through the chart-room and out on to the glassed-in porch. The helmsman turned his head.

'Glad to see there's someone still on duty,' Mark said. 'I was expecting to find total computer control.'

The man grinned. 'Fine you're back, sir.'

'Thanks. What's our speed?'

'Twenty-one and a half.'

Automatic control was at full ahead. Mark thought about asking the Chief to surrender that extra knot or two he kept in reserve, but knew it would be no use.

The *Sogne Fjord* was dead ahead, still not taking up nearly enough space on the seascape, but contriving to hide the *Grooter* which was certainly boiling at her from the north. Mark went to the communications panel.

'Collins? Underson here.'

'Saw you come in, Captain.'

'The radioman sticks to his post under all circumstances. And drowns with his earphones on.'

'Not this one.'

'I want the R.T. left open, switched through to the bridge speaker. To pick up the sweet music of Scherner's howls. Has he done any talking in the last minutes?'

'No.'

'He will. And let's hope he wastes plenty of time over the open form ritual. What can you tell me about the *Sogne*? She looks like she'd been holed by a mine not a ship.'

'Latest theory is the nose of a submarine.'

'Eh?'

'There was no explosion. Nothing on radar right up until the moment of impact, which was tremendous. The *Sogne* reckon they were pushed sideways by something big. It could be a sub surfaced just there with a lot of forward thrust on her and some kind of black-out on her feelers. It can happen.'

'But don't they know by now? Hasn't the sub reported?'

'No, not a peep. No one thinks it sank without a trace, either. Just that it was Russian . . . probably nuclear. And very publicity shy. Probably bound home now for repairs. Maybe with a leak in her atomic shielding, which could happen too easily after a big bang. It's one of the things those boys have to live with, and better them than me. If there's anything on radio I'll put it through to the speaker, too.'

'Do that.'

Mark went to the windows. The surface of the North Sea didn't look attractive. Her black depths, in a damaged sub, was his idea of hell. Like most sailors the very thought of undersea work appalled him. A Hoofstanger salvage master on one of their wreck raisers made a packet and was king pin on the ship equipped for his operations, but Mark had never contemplated training for that big money specialization. The last thing he wanted to do was sit in a diving bell 600 feet down working electric claws through two inch port-hole glass, or to perform solo wearing a pressure suit amongst the eyeless fishes of the eternal dark. It wasn't his idea of the good life.

Someone came out of the chartroom, and Mark turned, expecting Ginnis. It was the Chief, following his stomach and wheezing. He was wearing his usual grey, zip-up boiler suit decorated with a few picturesque oil splashes and his face had an even higher colour than usual. He had been christened Alfred James Wigham, but like the other name for God, this was never used. He was Chief, or 'sir', and some other things as well. He moved with a portly dignity suggesting an overfed cleric, but for all his weight the man had a remarkable sense of balance and could come down a pitching passage in the *Saturn* with the decorum of a man leading an ecclesiastical procession, his engines providing the organ voluntary. Why he was in tugs no one had ever found out, he was certainly qualified for higher things, such as presiding over a liner's propulsion. He had a wife in Tooting whom he rarely saw but with whom he was apparently content and a couple of teenage daughters with whom he was not. Mark had been totally surprised to find that he was only forty-six, he looked a well preserved sixty-five. His language was as saintly as his appearance, totally untainted by profanity, something unusual in his calling, but, for all that, what he said commanded immediate attention, it came from the stomach, rich and melodious.

'I don't see why,' he said, coming slowly over the deck, 'if we must have those towers we can't have a lift in one?'

'Nice to see you again,' Mark said.

'Is it? Why did you go off like that?'

'Hiding my grief.'

The Chief came and stood up against one of the windows, but he didn't hold on to the bar provided. 'What's this performance?' he asked. 'One in the eye for our lady in Edinburgh?'

'Something like that.'

'Then let's hope it's successful. You'll make your situation worse if it isn't.'

'I know.'

'In view of the way things are, do we go on calling you "sir"?'

'Just like you never have.'

He ignored that, peering at the *Sogne*.

'I'm told the *Grooter* is going to beat us again.'

'There wouldn't have been any danger of that if you'd produced those extra knots you hoard.'

'We are at maximum speed.'

Mark didn't call him a liar.

'I found that last chess gambit on the way to Hull quite interesting,' the Chief said. 'You would have lost, of course. It was wild. The game is not one for the intuitive approach.'

'You ought to try playing with the computer.'

The Chief was not amused. It was surprising, with his assistant left on shore, that he was prepared to stay away from his engines for so long. He must be very curious about something. Mark didn't believe this had anything to do with getting a line on the Norwegian.

'MacDonald is not ready to command this ship,' the Chief announced.

Mark was startled. He turned his head, but the Chief continued to stare at the Sogne, which was now the most important thing in a frame.

'Has he had much of a try-out, seeing he's only had command while the Saturn was tied up?'

'He's an excellent Mate,' the Chief said. 'And ought to stay one to get more experience.'

'We've all got to take the jump some time.'

'When ready. Don't get me wrong. I like MacDonald. As Mate. He's part of the balance of this ship. And that's important, whether you realize it or not. I have left ships because the balance was wrong.'

'Chief, you're sounding like a bishop.'

He took no notice.

'I've been giving this matter some thought. And I've come to a decision. If Mrs Lawton insists on replacing you then she'll have to replace me, too.'

'What?'

'You can use that against her if you like.'

He walked away, nodding to Ginnis who came past him. The Second looked back over his shoulder.

'What's the Chief doing up here, sir?'

Mark didn't answer. He swung around again to look at the Sogne Fjord. 'I wish to hell we could see the Grooter. He can't be closing yet or he'd be gabbing his head off.'

'Maybe he's keeping quiet because he knows we're here.'

'I don't think so. Collins has kept the radio silence since being on the R.T. to me. Is the 'copter ready for take-off?'

'Yes, sir, line's attached.'

'And what are the odds in the below decks mess-room?'

Ginnis seemed embarrassed. 'Two to one against.'

'Better than I was expecting. Put ten bob on for me, will you? Saturn to win.'

A Dutch voice came out of the speaker using Low Country English to ask a Norwegian if he was prepared to play by Lloyd's rules. The Sogne replied in better English that they hadn't much alternative in view of the fact that water was gaining on the pumps, and was the Marie Grooter prepared to give immediate pump assistance from her own auxiliaries? The *Grooter* was, and the *Sogne* was to stand by for a line over her bows. The *Saturn* still had just over a mile to go, considerably more than the thousand yards of her longest wire coil.

Mark was sure now that the *Grooter* had not picked up any of the *Saturn's* earlier signals and the radar screens on two tugs were both showing only the large blob of the liner. His nerves were doing their old trick, which was a tightening of their network from a large clockwork key that was being slowly turned at the top of his spinal column, just at skull base. He could practically hear the clicking. It would end in a racking headache that aspirin and whisky couldn't cure. Sometimes he wondered if he was suited to this life. He was tension prone, but there was no doubt a mental response to sudden pressures, a flipping on to over-drive.

'Ginnis! Spin our lead line off its drum. Attach the end to a float. Then get the 'copter off.'

'Sorry, sir. I don't think I understand?'

'All the *Grooter* is going to see is our line being dropped on the *Sogne's* bows by the 'copter. They can't see we're not attached to the other end of it. What the Norwegian sees doesn't matter. We pick up the float when we reach it. But our line's over there first.'

'My God, yes!'

'Get moving. I'm staying here. As soon as you've got the float on us again I'll take her for'ard of the *Sogne* to tow position. And don't muff the pick-up. The *Grooter's* almost certainly going to come around to see what's happening this side of the *Sogne*. If they get on to this they're going to be plenty mad.'

When Ginnis had gone Mark walked up and down the bridge behind the helmsman. These were not moments in which to be a recent convert to non-smoking. He wished he had compromised and kept his pipes. It seemed a long time before the 'copter's engines came on, noise an assault on the ears even under cover. The bridge offered no view at all of the stern boat-deck and he saw nothing of the ascent until it had reached 100 feet. At 300 the pilot jerked his craft forward towards the Norwegian and the trailing wire came into view. The red marker-buoy appeared moments later, skipping across low wave tops towards the *Sogne*.

The pilot gave value for extortion. He brought his bird down again to about fifty feet, concealing his flight towards that white hull from the Dutchman on the other side of it. Then, when he appeared to be only yards from the *Sogne's* superstructure, he put on all brakes and hung on hover, still low over the water. After a rest the 'copter went into a crab-like sideways movement towards the liner's bows, but the moment he had got past the

superstructure to the well-deck the chopper zoomed again to all
of 150, hanging over the *Sogne*'s forepeak, clearly to winch down
the line, not just drop it. Crewmen came running to retrieve it.
On R.T. Scherner sounded choleric.

'*Marie Grooter* to other tug. You damn get out! This my tow!
They accept Lloyd's form from me, see? You get out! Acknowledge!'

Collins's voice cut in. 'Do we acknowledge, sir?'

Mark went over to the communications panel and flicked a
switch. 'No!' he said.

'Do you want to go on hearing him?'

'Yes.'

The *Saturn* had 500 yards to the red, dancing buoy. The Norwegians had secured. The 'copter went up like an express lift to
500 and then, as though the rest of the party didn't interest him,
the pilot made off west. Scherner began to sound like an operatic
baritone who has lost pitch and doesn't know how to get back on
it again for the rest of the aria. Though decidedly florid-sounding
Dutch oaths came bellows in English to be acknowledged. Then
the tug Skipper had a go at the Norwegian Captain who had
shown himself to be a reserved man, not easily rattled. His words
came over precise and neat, bullets into Scherner's hopes.

'I accept open form with the first tug to put a line on me. That
is correct.'

If the *Sogne*'s Master had noticed a dancing red buoy he wasn't
admitting it. He had probably looked up a salvage manual and
noted the *Saturn*'s considerably superior horsepower, not to
mention her pump capacity. Also, the 'copter operations might
have impressed him as an efficient use of contemporary techniques. Mark began to grin.

'Bear on the buoy,' he said to the helmsman. 'When you get it
pump the thing along our plates.'

'Sir. Do we cut speed?'

'No!'

A moment later Mark said: 'I'm going aft.'

He hadn't meant to, but the next scene was going to be played
on the *Saturn*'s stern-deck and suddenly he had to be there.

The Second was at the ready by the low rail with a boat-hook.
He had the Bos'n and a seaman stationed as reserves further aft,
also with hooks, in case he missed.

'Ginnis! I'll take over. You're on the bridge. Hold speed.'

He didn't want to go. That was too bad. It would also be too
bad if the Skipper missed the buoy. A muff on Mark's part would
be poker interval talk for months.

'Pearson, I want you for'ard of me, up there. Your job is to
smash the buoy in against our plates, and then to try to get

your hook round the lead line if you can. I'll go for the ring lift. Bos'n, if I miss it's yours. We're damn well not going to have to come round again.'

There was an audience on the boat-deck. Mark shouted at them. 'You up there! Keep your eyes peeled for the *Grooter*. She may be coming round the Norwegian's bows. The moment you see her yell. Any sign of her mast over the *Sogne*'s well-deck?'

'No, sir.'

'Well, watch for it.'

'The buoy's coming now, sir!'

Mark and his fishing party leaned over the stern-deck bulwark, feet braced out, boat-hooks down. The red buoy was coming at them like a scooter clearing traffic. The line from the *Sogne* was well under water, with too much slack in it to anchor the float. There was a risk that the bow wave, sweeping out from the tug, would bounce the buoy away from them. Mark had the sick feeling that Ginnis or the helmsman wouldn't allow for this and counter by a sudden sharp swing of the *Saturn* to port, but it was too late to do anything, he was totally cut off from bridge control.

Vibration altered slightly. The *Saturn* dipped into a port roll from a swing of her bows. The wave from the stem broke, and in its breaking carried the buoy in a trough straight for the tug's plates. Ginnis knew what he was doing all right.

Pearson's boat-hook went down for the smash and grab, managed the smash, but missed the line. The ring presented itself as a target for Mark's hook, then rolled away. The Bos'n's boat-hook came forward to smack the ring round again. Mark connected, his hook through. For a moment he just held the buoy against the stream along the tug's plates, then began the pull up.

'Nice team work,' he said.

There was a shout from the boat-deck.

'*Grooter* coming round the Norwegian's *stern*.'

Mark didn't look up.

'Help me get this damn thing on deck. Quick!'

They weren't quick enough. By the time that outsize top coated with glare paint was balanced on the bulwark railing the *Grooter* was in full view, her bow and her bridge towards *Saturn*. Scherner would be peering through binoculars.

'Secure the line as soon as we've got a bit more slack,' Mark ordered. Then he ran for the iron ladder to the boat-deck.

On the stairs to the bridge he felt the *Saturn* go into a starboard turn roll, this deep enough to make him grab for a handrail. Ginnis had taken the wheel himself, putting the tug over to nor'east in the direction of her tow position in front of the *Sogne Fjord*. Already the secured lead line, tightening on a drum, was lifting from the sea. Mark went to a port window.

The *Grooter* had started to put up a bow wave, pulling away from the lee of the *Sogne*, turning to what for moments looked like collision course with the *Saturn*, then swinging to port from this. It took Mark half a minute to see what the game was. Scherner was making for a place on 700 yards of rising lead line which would let him nose his bows just under this. He would put one of his crew up on the *Grooter*'s forepeak with a wire-cutter. As simple as that!

'Ginnis! Get back to the stern. Slacken off the line as far as it'll go on the bollard. Quick! He's going to cut our connection if he can. If we can get that wire under water again it'll stop him. He won't dare risk his props!'

Ginnis ran. Mark took the wheel and spun it. The *Saturn*'s bows came round to due east, putting the two tugs on almost parallel course, the *Grooter* racing for a wire that was beginning to travel away from her in an arc, but still high, no sign of a droop.

Mark shouted to the helmsman. 'Take over! Hold this course.'

He went to the port corner of the bridge and watched the *Grooter*. The Dutchman's bows were almost on the lead line when suddenly it dropped, hitting wave tops with a whip of foam, then disappearing. The *Grooter* went into a dramatic full astern that boiled the sea behind her. Mark put out his hands for a railing he rarely used and hung on. Up under his skull small hammers were at work, chipping away. He remembered saying to Ginnis on the phone from London that this could turn out a clean, sweet job.

'Hard to port,' he ordered. 'Head for tow position for'ard of the Norwegian.'

The *Grooter* appeared to have gone on stand by but her Skipper came back on the air via R.T. to the *Sogne*'s Captain. What he said wasn't outstandingly coherent, but certain things came through all right, amongst them the fact that he meant to report both the *Saturn* and the Norwegian. It wasn't specified to whom. The main idea seemed to be that his loss of the tow constituted a major breach of salvage ethics. In so far as Mark knew no one had ever written a textbook on the subject, though it would certainly be a handy work of reference for any tug's chartroom.

'Underson?' That was a howl. 'Come in if you read me!'

Mark made no move to come in.

'I tell you something, Underson. I get you! I get you sure!'

Scherner couldn't be in the picture about his company's offer to an ex-Anglo-European skipper. And if word of this ever reached him, it might prove fatal.

'I'll be back before we take up tow,' Mark said.

He went through the chartroom to the radio cabin. Collins was looking like a man who really finds his work enjoyable.

'I hope Scherner's roars haven't blown out any of your printed circuits?'

'We still seem to be functioning, Captain. Is that the finish with the *Grooter*?'

'I think we can say she's out of play. Though I'm not sending the hawser over until I'm quite sure. And we'll keep a sharp look-out meantime for their frogmen equipped with limpet mines. Get me the *Sogne*'s Master on R.T., will you? It's about time we established diplomatic relations. And I'd like to send a personal signal by radio. To Captain Scherner.'

'I'll get that off while your on R.T. Message?'

'It's not long. Just . . . "Happy retirement", signed Underson.'

The phone rang. Jessie picked up the receiver.

'I have your shore relay connection now, caller, shall I put you through?'

'Please.'

She waited.

'Radio Officer, tug *Saturn*.'

'Mrs Lawton here. Is everything going all right, Mr Collins?'

For a moment it seemed as though she had lost the link up.

'Oh . . . yes . . . Mrs Lawton.'

'I heard on the ten o'clock news last night. My first thought was to call you at once. Then I realized the tow might be having its problems, especially at night, and that it would be better to wait until today. If everything is going reasonably could you put me through to Captain MacDonald?'

'What?'

'I said . . . may I speak to the Captain?'

'Well . . .' The man sounded as if he had a breathing problem. 'He's . . . down in his cabin.'

'Having a well-earned rest?'

'Yes. I guess so. Just hold on a minute.'

There was a wait, then Collins's voice.

'You're through to the Captain now.'

Jessie cleared her throat.

'Mrs Lawton here. I was just explaining to Collins that I didn't try to get in touch with you during the earlier stages of the tow. For obvious reasons. But that didn't mean I wasn't most excited about what I read and heard. There's been a good deal of publicity. Of course it's a passenger liner, which always interests the press. And the *Saturn* has been mentioned by name several times. I had a phone call this morning from my co-director, Sir Richard Pierce Clanmer. He was absolutely delighted. And so am

I. All I really want to say is that I can't imagine a better start than this to your command of the *Saturn*, Captain.'

'Probably MacDonald could, Mrs. Lawton. Chances are he's having lunch with his auntie in the Lake District at the moment.'

Jessie closed her eyes. The voice was unmistakable. Words were hard to come by. It took her half a minute to find any.

'I thought . . . you'd left the ship?'

'I had. I came back again.'

'From where?'

'London. By helicopter. I was able to join *Saturn* in time for action. As you say, it's been quite good.'

'MacDonald . . . ?'

'Off on leave. Surely he told you he was going?'

Jessie said nothing.

'He couldn't be located.' Underson's voice was smooth. 'I decided to resume command. Temporarily, of course. I'll leave the *Saturn* again at Newcastle. MacDonald can join her there. And thanks for the congratulations. I'll pass them on to the rest of the crew. It's nice to feel that the owners are sharing our happiness at a time like this. Especially Sir Richard.'

After a moment Jessie said: 'You . . . hired a helicopter?'

'That's right. You can use my bonus share to pay for it. I won't claim. And you now know that the pad can be used. Mind you, I don't think I'd like to risk it in a heavy sea. But normal conditions and it's a piece of cake. It was good of you to call.'

He hung up.

There was a rap at the door, then this opened cautiously. One of the dailies peered around. Jessie's anger, still smouldering, flared again.

'If you want into a room, Mrs Milton, *come* into it. The tea tray's over there.'

'It's not the tray, Mrs Lawton. You've got a visitor.'

Jessie couldn't think who it might be. Her social life had declined almost to the point of disappearing since Arthur's death and hadn't been particularly exciting while he was alive.

'Who?'

'I didn't catch the name. I put her in the drawing-room. It's a bit cold, so I put on the electric fire. I hope that was all right?'

It would be a collector for charity, not the kind with a tin can, but wearing a mink jacket and expecting a cheque. They were always the hardest to get rid of.

Jessie put out her cigarette and went down the hall. For years the drawing-room had been dusted and left, the only life in it now two bars of an electric fire and a girl. The girl had long fair hair and was still wearing a wool coat, standing facing the glow, reaching down to it with her hands.

'Yes?'

The girl turned. She was pretty. These days Jessie could never put an age to anyone under thirty.

'I'm sorry,' she said. 'It's freezing outside. I hadn't realized Scotland was so much colder. I'm Alice Underson, Mark's wife.'

Jessie went stiff. It was a moment before she remembered the civilities.

'Oh, yes? Would you like to sit down, Mrs Underson.' She paused, then forced herself on. 'If you'd like a cup of tea my help is still here.'

The girl shook her head. 'No, thanks. Perhaps a drink? Whisky?'

'I don't keep whisky. Though there's some brandy in the kitchen.'

Alice Underson smiled. The effort was obvious.

'We'll skip the drink. You don't mind my smoking in here?'

'Not at all. But I think perhaps we'd be more comfortable in my study.'

In view of the background to this visit Jessie thought she was behaving with creditable civility.

Without the wool coat, and in a large wing chair, Mark Underson's wife was mostly leg in patterned stockings. Very good legs, but a lot of them. She must be nearly as tall as her husband.

'I'm meeting Mark in Newcastle tomorrow when his tow arrives. I thought I'd come by Edinburgh.'

'An odd route,' Jessie said, from behind her large desk.

'I wanted to see you about Mark. You knew he was on the *Saturn*?'

'Yes.'

'He rang me up in London only an hour before I left to fly up here.'

'And suggested you see me?'

'Oh, no.'

She twisted a ring. It was certainly a large diamond but Jessie would have needed a closer look to make anything like an assessment of quality.

'Actually,' the girl said, 'he'll go through the roof when he hears what I've done. I belong to the wife compartment. Not supposed to stray. Though he's always expected to come home suddenly to find me in bed with another man. But he wouldn't dream I could do something like this.'

She smiled, inviting a response. Jessie stayed in her frigid reserve. She found it difficult to come to any terms with a generation which talked as easily about sex as a head cold.

'Mrs Lawton, I'm here simply to ask . . . must you do this to Mark?'

'I don't know what you mean?'

'Look, I had a bumpy flight. Don't let's fence. In a way I'm a neutral in all this. A girl doesn't love something that keeps a man away from her for nine months in the year. Especially if she really wants that man, and I do. I make do with playthings, Mrs Lawton. I'm getting a house in the country now. I'm going to play with that. I'd like Mark to live in it with me, but not the way he'd be if he has to. You could call this putting down all my cards, one after the other. And you sit with your hand in to your chest.'

Jessie had actually had her hands folded in her lap. She unfolded them. 'I still don't begin to understand.'

'Terribly simple. I want Mark the way he is. And if this means getting away from me for most of the time, I still want him. It's a difficult proposition to sell to anyone else, I know. Doesn't seem to make sense these days. But there it is. And what's happening with the *Saturn* is just slaying him. All that stuff about going to the Dutch . . . did you believe it?'

'Yes.'

'But you can't now. Not since this Norwegian thing?'

'Why not?'

'But didn't he tell you? He was up against that Dutch tug . . . the *Marie* something or other. The one they offered him.'

'The *Marie Grooter*? The news never mentioned her.'

'Well, she was there. I can tell you that, because Mark told me in a long phone call from the ship. They practically had a naval engagement to get the tow. So that's his new job with these Hoofstanger people right out of the window. Not that he ever had any intention of going to them. He left London for the *Saturn* knowing the Dutch tug was on the way to the liner. In so far as I can ever understand his motives at least one of them this time was to thumb his nose at the ship he might have got. He didn't want her or any other Hoofstanger tug.'

Jessie sat perfectly still. The faces of the young seemed to her remarkably expressionless and Alice Underson, if she was under stress, certainly wasn't showing this. The only sign that might be interpreted as nervousness was the way she kept lifting a hand to push the curtains of fair hair.

'Mrs Lawton, Mark knows perfectly well that the Dutch only made him that offer to get at you.'

'Are you suggesting that he thumbed his nose at them, as you put it, on my behalf?'

'No. That was all for himself. The big gesture. He loves the *Saturn*. And believe me a wife knows what a man's love is. There have been times recently when I thought the only thing for me was to walk out on the bastard.' The girl smiled. 'How's that for an emotional appeal, woman to woman? I think it's pretty good. But you're a hard sell.'

'What do you expect to get from me?'

'The idea was a compromise peace. Is that so impossible? You give a little, Mark gives a little. I'll see that he does. And what the hell is it all about anyway? Why have you got into this jam, both of you? You want him, don't you? Don't you want him as skipper of your tug?'

'Under certain conditions.'

'O God! Let's hear them.'

Jessie looked at the wall opposite as she stated her terms, conscious that the girl was watching her. Alice Underson's comment came quickly enough.

'Mark plays it your way or he doesn't play at all.'

'If you care to put it like that.'

'I'm putting it like the facts. You want him to take this dredger tow to Africa under some guarantee he gets his load there without going off on any sudden wild tries for fame and fortune.'

'It isn't the gambles I object to, it's their timing.'

'The Norwegian thing was the right idea?'

'Certainly. We weren't committed anywhere else. Your husband knows the position perfectly well.'

'Oh, sure, he knows. But he's been hit in his male pride. Its their second most delicate organ. And then there's the fact that he's always hated owners.'

Jessie stiffened in an unstable chair, which creaked.

'How interesting!'

'Actually, I think he hates you a lot less than the others he's worked for. Mrs Lawton, do you ever smile?'

Jessie was taken aback. She could find no immediate answer to a very simple question and was aware, as she had been with this girl's husband, of the initiative stolen from her by a kind of verbal sleight of hand. Also, she was being challenged to take offence.

'Why not a cooling-off period?' Alice Underson suggested. 'The thing they're talking about for strikes. Time for a re-think.'

'You mean while your husband continues to command the *Saturn*?'

'Yes. Mark goes off on this Africa tow promising to be a good boy and radioing home office every day. Actually, I think he'll be glad of the rest. After all, he's just shown you what he can do. A nice peaceful cruise would probably suit him. And his crew, too. Warm sunshine after a British winter. On this voyage they don't even have private thoughts without telling you about them.

Then when they get back there's a round table conference over tea and biscuits.'

'To do what?'

'Re-think policy in a more friendly give and take atmosphere.'

'The policy is fixed.'

'All right! But pretend you're re-thinking it, for God's sake!'

'You'd make a clever mediator, Mrs Underson, if you took it up professionally.'

'All I say to that is whatever they're paid, it isn't enough. Will you do it?'

Jessie looked at a blotter for a minute, then lifted her head. 'Yes.'

The girl seemed astonished.

'Whew! You never know when you're winning, do you? Now all I've got to do is explain to Mark tomorrow morning why I came here in the first place. That's going to take some doing. And I won't even have a decent night's sleep before it. The train I've booked a seat on gets me to Newcastle at two a.m. I hope they've got padded benches in the station waiting-room.'

Jessie was surprised at the relief she felt. In the flood of it she became almost social. 'You travel to your husband's ports a good deal, don't you, Mrs Underson?'

'Sure. It keeps him away from whores. Or that's the theory. But I'm not joining him down in central Africa. If you want to do me a small kindness you can fix it so his ship has a quick turn around.'

'I'll do what I can about that,' Jessie said, and smiled.

Alice Underson stared. She got up suddenly. 'I'll leave you to your work. Thanks for not throwing me out.'

Jessie took a deep breath. 'Might I suggest we have dinner together?'

The girl had a quick look around the room. She wanted to escape. But she was Mark Underson's wife, with no more than a mention in his file, which now seemed an oversight. She obviously liked alcohol and its influence loosened tongues. That might be very useful indeed.

'There's an excellent restaurant in the hotel by your station,' Jessie said.

'Well . . . ?'

'We could go now. After all, it's the cocktail hour.'

There was no doubt that the girl reacted well to the suggestion of something to drink. Jessie was brisk. 'I'll ring for a taxi.'

'Isn't the car outside yours?'

'We won't use it tonight.'

'You don't drink and drive?'

'That is correct,' Jessie said.

## CHAPTER NINE

WHEN HE HAD to have dealings with a rat, Henri Plentin preferred to do this in the privacy of his chateau, usually after dark. He looked at the one opposite him.

'I was a little surprised that your company's agent had to come to me from London,' he said. 'Why is this? I understood that headquarters were in Monte Carlo?'

'It is a matter of policy, Monsieur Plentin.'

The man's French was passable, suggesting one of the lost North African provinces.

'An extraordinary arrangement. But perhaps necessary as a precaution? Some of what you do is illegal?'

'No, M'sieur.'

'But skirts the law?'

The man was fractionally too long over his answer.

'I wouldn't say that.'

Henri Plentin laughed. 'Some might. However, no matter. We're none of us saints. It was perhaps explained to you why I need your company's services?'

'We never ask for explanations.'

'I see. Few of your customers would volunteer them? Well, I will. It is not my plan to start a revolution in France. The country suits me very well as it is. And my needs are modest. To deal with a situation that is too common in our time, alas. We have rubber interests in the upper reaches of the Congo River. The area is officially pacified after the troubles of some years ago, but in fact is not. We don't get and can't expect army protection, which means that if we are to continue to function we must arm ourselves, and also have it known locally that this has been done. You can imagine the situation?'

'But perfectly.'

Henri Plentin took a sip from his glass of dry white Alsace.

'How do you deliver your . . . ah . . . goods?'

'In crates labelled agricultural machinery, or anything the purchaser wishes to have stamped on them. They are steel-bound to discourage curiosity.'

'And of modest size?'

'Almost any size you specify, M'sieur.'

'I had in mind five metres by three, with a depth of perhaps another three?'

The man made a note.

'Certainly. When there is any possibility of customs inspection we pack in special bottoms, with the top of the crate free for more normal trade goods. This naturally requires a certain additional depth.'

'How delicately you put that! But I shan't need your special crates. My interests have their own river transport and it ought to be possible to arrange a rendezvous with a tramp steamer just off the coast. It is only a small matter, after all. I had in mind perhaps two hundred and fifty automatic rifles.'

'Czech, American or Israeli, M'sieur?'

'Which is the cheapest?'

'The Czech.'

'And what about your second-hand department? Surely you have one?'

'We can only supply a Czech used rifle.'

'I'm sure that would serve the purpose very nicely. You can let me have the appropriate ammunition, of course?'

'At any time. With your order, or separately.'

'And delivery dates?'

'Within four days of agreement anywhere in central Europe.'

'I am not signing for this order.'

'We don't operate with contracts, M'sieur. Your cheque on a Swiss bank is all that is required. Payable to a numbered account.'

Henri Plentin smiled. 'What would we all do without the Swiss, eh? The spiritual home for gentlemen's agreements in a world that has such need of these. Oh, there is one thing more. Grenades. I understand they are most effective amongst rubber trees. As a noise deterrent as much as anything. I shall want quite a number. You can supply them?'

'Any amount.'

'I think perhaps five thousand. I suppose these can't be supplied from your second-hand department?'

'No, M'sieur. We have to manufacture. We do this in three grades; large, medium and small.'

'The small. And I shall have to ask to see your price lists shortly.'

'We have no printed list. But I can quote you on any item.'

'Dear me, racing inflation as in most businesses. Not even worth printing a price list.'

The salesman had his head bent over his notes. He said, without looking up: 'I'd suggest a hundred rounds per rifle. That will be twenty-five thousand rounds of ammunition.'

'Oh, come! I'm not about to declare war. All we're interested in is frightening terrorists, not killing them. Make it ten thousand rounds. Even that sounds excessive. Delivery will be to a bonded warehouse at Amiens, Courege et Tatre, Rue de Cinque 9. Approximate delivery time to be notified to a man Souffron there. You've got all that?'

'Yes, M'sieur,' the salesman said, writing.

'There will be no further contact with us about this matter. That is understood?'

'Completely. You wouldn't consider adding a few British Brens to your order, Monsieur Plentin? There are World War II surplus, but maintained in immaculate order.'

'You seem determined to commit me to a campaign, young man. When all that interests me is moderate security where there are no police to provide this. How much are your Brens?'

'Two hundred and fifty American dollars.'

'Certainly not cheap. But then the price for antiques is rocketing.'

'They'd be useful things for your estate managers to have under their personal supervision. As a reserve.'

'Hm. Four. No, make it six.'

'Very good.'

'I'd be fascinated to know what your profit margins are on all this. Quite fascinated.'

The salesman had no comment.

'It's so odd, isn't it?' the old man said. 'In an age when your product might be regarded as a basic need, there is this odium attached to dealing in it. In my younger days you'd have been called a merchant of death. Hysterical nonsense, of course.'

The salesman stayed busy with his notes.

'Our time, too, has a positive obsession over the idea of respectability. Which is directly associated with the rate of dividend return. Any company which declared anything over fifteen per cent would immediately be investigated by government commission of some sort. I suppose this bars you from a regular market quotation?'

'We are not a public company, M'sieur.'

'How wise. We also prefer to capitalize ourselves whenever possible.'

The salesman checked the total of a column again, then tore off a sheet and bent forward to slide this over the desk.

'I have converted the dollar price for the Brens to Swiss francs, M'sieur. That is the total.'

Henri Plentin put on his spectacles.

'Merciful saints! Costs for new equipment are certainly going to swamp profits this year. What if I tried to bargain?'

'You would force me to point out that this is a seller's market.'

'I could ask for other quotations. There is, I believe, an excellent firm in Florida. And we have the dollars available.'

'On an average they ask thirty per cent more than we do.'

'And your rivals in Europe?'

'Back street traders. Who offer no guarantees of quality.'

'It would appear that you have a Plentin cornered.'

The old man opened a drawer, pulled out one cheque book, put this back, and after groping about produced another. For a moment or two he seemed to be studying the stubs. Then he asked: 'I make it out to . . . ?'

'Account M.X.393, Banque de Sursee, Basle.'

This particular rat was efficient. It might be worth having him investigated, indeed, perhaps unwise not to. At the top of the stub he wrote . . . 'Check . . . Luke Lazzari.'

The Brest offices of Plentin Cie, were in a converted private house in a part of the city where the streets are so steep the pavement keeps breaking out into steps. Jules Dartan was puffing a little.

He paused on the concreted strip of terrace to get his breath back, with a tremendous view of the harbour in front of him, and a clacking of typewriters behind. Already the Captain was beginning to feel the resentment he usually took away from this place, of being a cipher, representing little more to these people who ran his life . . . or most of it . . . than the flag they stuck on a map to show where the *Semirande* was. The Plentins were great stickers on of flags, like desk generals, and one of the downstairs rooms had a whole wall given over to the world, the Plentin vessels marked with blue labels carrying their names. Land-based interests, which didn't have to be moved about, had green buttons. There were a great many of these.

Jules turned and went through a glass door, expecting to get about the rating of the head gardener at the old man's chateau back in the country, and this was exactly what he did get, the girl receptionist producing a minimal politeness for an oaf from the sea, at the same time making it fairly plain she wished the company would work out some other way of contacting their slightly smelly skippers. Jules glared, thinking that the skinny bitch wouldn't begin to make a decent lay, and pitying the man who got trapped into signing for her.

'Captain! How good to see you.'

Jules turned.

The further a Plentin was from the ultimate authority the more affable he tended to be, and Claude was not only a long way from the throne, but, as the terminal product of the old man's second marriage, didn't have a hope in hell of really getting any nearer to it. Ahead of him were six brothers, all of them in the business and all of them healthy. The Plentins bred on the principle that the more there were of them the better it was for France.

'I've just come down from Father. He'll be free in a few

minutes. We might have a cup of coffee meantime. Now . . .
where can we go?'

His own office was probably a converted coal shed.

'I know! The map room.'

The receptionist had a protest. 'M. Gaston Plentin will be
wanting the map room very soon.'

Claude swung around. 'Eh? Well, that's all right. We won't
be in there for long. See about coffee, will you?'

'I'll tell your secretary.'

Jules noted the contempt behind that, Claude must have a
helluva life in this place.

Winter sunshine poured into the map room. The world was
still there, with its flags and buttons. There was also a long table
with ten chairs around it, these covered in green plush. Claude
pulled out two.

'Do sit down, Captain. The *Semirande* has been doing very
well recently, hasn't she?'

The tug might have been a provincial music hall artiste who
has suddenly broken into the Paris circuit with an imitation of
Piaf.

'I hope your father thinks so.'

'I'm sure he does. We were all talking about you just the
other day. Maybe your ears were burning?'

He was a nice boy, probably because he had no real future.
Jules found himself wishing he had brought Berand along for
this interview, but the Mate was already with his Celeste and
her cooking. Berand's simple patterns didn't include interview-
ing owners. He was not a man going places, he'd arrived where
he wanted to be.

'Your crew will all be looking forward to some leave?' Claude
suggested.

'They've all gone like bullets to where they usually go, yes.'

The young Plentin's smile seemed fixed.

'And you, Captain?'

Jules shrugged. Suddenly he felt sorry for himself. 'Who knows?
For a widower with grown children, what is there?'

Claude had no suggestions. He stood.

'I wonder what's happened to that coffee? My secretary isn't
very good at these things. But there should be some wine somewhere. Would you prefer that?'

He began to open cupboards. One stayed shut.

'They've locked it,' Claude said, embarrassed.

Jules wondered what he would do with this one at sea. Push
him overboard, probably. The Plentins could well be on the
point of doing just that.

The door opened; it wasn't coffee, but Gaston. He was number three in his generation, and already a driving force in the company, dapper, almost a man about town until you had a good look at his face which was no-nonsense pure Plentin.

'Oh, it's you,' he said to his brother. 'How are you, Dartan? I'm afraid I'm going to be needing this place in a few minutes.' He stared at the cork-backed world. 'Hello! Claude seems to have left you still out at sea.'

Gaston plucked the *Semirande*'s flag from the Channel and anchored it in Brest. His brother looked miserable.

'That's better. You should attend to this thing. It's your job.'

'I was going to!'

'That's never an adequate answer. I'm sorry to drive you out of here, Dartan, but I'm sure my father's secretary will look after you until he's ready. Claude . . . a word.'

Jules went through the door as he was expected to, but stood just beyond it, near enough to pick up the whispers. The receptionist suspected he was doing that. He didn't give a damn.

'Claude, you've seen Father this morning?'

'I'm just down from his office.'

'What's his mood?'

'Very good.'

'Well, that's something. But it won't last.'

'What's happened?'

'All our Gironde haulier drivers have come out on strike. It's that damn company I didn't want us to take on at all. If I had my way we'd touch nothing in the Bordeaux area.'

'What are you going to do?'

'It's what Father's going to do that worries me. Go on, take the Captain up.'

Jules was left in charge of old Henri's secretary of twenty years' standing and allowed to sit on a sofa while she ignored him. The woman had red hair and wore a pink twinset which gave her the look of a plump prawn dipped in the chef's special mustard sauce. Add a bit of green garnish somewhere to whet the appetite and still no man could possibly want her. The older he grew the more women he encountered whom he would, in no circumstances, take to a bed. A youth's taste is catholic and experimental, but the man in his prime looks for all the signs he has learned not to disregard. Since landing the warning notices had been all that he had seen. He was too old for the girls and their mothers unnerved him. It was a difficult period for a man's sex life. Perhaps he ought to try Paris again, and see his son at the same time.

A voice barked on the intercom. The prawn answered.

'Yes, sir. He's here.' She looked at Jules. 'You can go in now. Knock once.'

He knocked once.

Henri Plentin had a fat folder open on the desk in front of him. Jules knew that it was the *Semirande* file, with copies of all recent signals to and from the tug.

'Ah, Dartan. Sit down. That chair. Pull it in a bit. Well, you seem to have been active.'

From the old man this was high praise. It at once set the tone of the interview, to fair. Often during these sessions Jules had felt like a schoolboy kept late by an angry headmaster. But now the owner asked only a few questions, all reasonable, and gave the impression that with the pointers to profits he didn't care too much about the answers. In under ten minutes the file was closed, and Henri Plentin put one hand on the cover, like a clergyman after a reading from the Holy Book. But he didn't then pronounce a benediction.

'I'm having the *Semirande* on station for the next few months, Dartan. Down in the Cape Verde Islands.'

Jules reacted like a man under psychiatric therapy experiencing his first electric shock treatment. He sat bolt upright in the chair. Henri Plentin observed the patient's response with something like satisfaction.

'Think I'm out of my mind, eh?'

On the face of it that was the only thing *to* think. Jules had been twice to the Cape Verdes. They lie in the South Atlantic, far south, forgotten by God and the Portuguese who own them. Half are practically without water and all subject to arid winds blowing sand over from Africa. During one of Jules's visits there had been no rain for three years and this had resulted in an unpublicized famine.

'Know the place?' Henri Plentin asked.

Jules nodded. 'I was there a long time ago. After leaving trawlers. I was still an apprentice, on a coal burner. We put in to St Vincent for bunkering.'

'So?'

'Well, there's no bunkering these days. And I shouldn't think many ships put in.'

This news didn't seem to trouble the old man at all.

'You'll be based on St Vincent.'

The files in Jules's brain produced an aged, yellowing print of an island in a steaming sea, a treeless lump of extinct volcano into which everything needed for man's survival had to be imported. As a play centre for off-duty sailors its amenities had been nil, and he had heard no rumours of improvements since. Weird enough places are developed for tourism these days but it seemed highly improbable that this had happened to the Cape Verdes. They were certainly in the tropics, but tended to shrouding mists, with an endemic flux of the bowels which wouldn't much appeal to the international beautiful people.

'It's only for a limited period, Dartan. You'll be on special assignment. I wanted something reasonably near Europe, but still out of the way.' He paused. 'The time has come for a very close look at our salvage operations. A very close look indeed.'

For years Jules had been half-expecting to hear these very words, and as a lead into the announcement of shut-down in one area of the Plentin enterprises. The *Semirande*, unsuitable for the company's coastal towing services, would be sold to the Greeks and Captain Dartan, senior captain, would then be offered for his last years at sea the command of some old tub on the Low Countries barge haul.

'We're expanding in deep-sea salvage,' Henri Plentin said. 'In quite a big way.'

Jules needed a really deep breath, but didn't take it.

'What I'm telling you is in strict confidence. In so far as the rest of your crew is concerned St Vincent is a station on strategic new shipping routes by the Cape. That's all you need tell them meantime, at least for the voyage down there. Of course what we're up to will get out sooner or later, but I'm guarding the element of surprise as much as possible. I want to come into this new phase as quietly as we can. We're up against two major problems. First, new ships; second, crews to man them. No need to tell you that salvage needs specialized training. Well, we'll get the men and train them. I've feelers out in a number of directions. The new bulk carriers are reducing crew needs. Plenty of potential material for us is becoming redundant. We can pick and choose. The process has already started. Our selections will be flown out to you for training. That's what the *Semirande* is going to be for the next few months. A training ship. You'll be the principal of a college. What do you think of that?'

Jules didn't think much of it. He said nothing. The old man's flow continued.

'Crew material can be flown out to you. There's an air service from the Canaries. My idea is perhaps a month's intensive training and then a turn-over to a new lot. You seem to be brooding over something, Dartan. What is it?'

'The new ships, sir.'

'What about them?'

'Well, it's not going to be easy to buy tugs on the open market without everyone in salvage knowing about it almost at once. We watch each other.'

Henri Plentin smiled.

'Don't you think I know that? But I'll wager that people like the Hoofstangers haven't been watching closely enough this time. I've already got two new tugs. In America. From the Grumand company. Both based on the Pacific coast when I bought them. Seven thousand horse-power and only three years old but already due for replacement. The Grumands need even bigger powered jobs for their specialist tows of the huge new rigs. Had you heard of this sale?'

'No, sir.'

'Nor has anyone else. I'm having those tugs extensively re-fitted at Kure in Japan. By-passed my own St Nazaire yard to keep security. They'll be ready for re-commissioning in four months. You'll have one, Berand the other. The pair of you will fly to Japan when the time comes with scratch crews to take them over. What do you say to that?'

Jules was feeling slightly dazed, but he remembered one thing. 'The *Semirande* is due for a re-fit, sir. You don't mean us to leave for St Vincent without this?'

'No. St Nazaire is waiting for you. It'll be a quick job. You'll recall what crew you need to take your ship over there, sailing tomorrow. Berand's ready for a command of his own, isn't he?'

'He's been ready for a long time.'

Jules looked out of the window. He could just see the masts of a tanker. Somewhere in the city down there Berand, happily unaware of promotion seeking him out, was making merry with his legal spouse.

'I want your opinion on Tourin, Captain. He has his master's ticket. Under the new arrangements the *Semirande* will be our oldest ship in salvage, put mostly on long hauls. Is Tourin ready to command her?'

'No.'

'Eh? Why not?'

'He doesn't trust himself. Until he learns to, crews won't trust him.'

Henri Plentin wasn't accustomed to having unqualified opinions thrust at him by one of his skippers. For seconds his face threatened storm, but he said, mildly enough:

'Responsibility isn't what the man needs?'

'I wouldn't count on it.'

The old man stood and began to walk up and down the office. Jules, sitting quietly, began to feel the first stirrings of something he had never expected to experience in this room, a sense of power. He was being consulted. He represented specialized experience which Plentin Cie. simply couldn't do without in this sudden expansion. The company's new need offered him positive authority. He had only to reach out and take it. Jules Dartan was going to be commodore of a fleet.

'I'm not stopping with the Grumand tugs, Captain. My idea

was that we make our challenge with four ships, including the *Semirande*. Which means buying one more some time in the near future. I'm looking round. Any ideas?'

Jules thought for a moment.

'If the *Saturn* ever came on the market she'd be a good buy.'

Henri Plentin stopped pacing. He swung around to stare. 'Fancy her, do you? Well, that's interesting. Very. And one never knows in this business. Tugs are always changing hands. I might have a try for you, eh? That Scots woman has always run her one ship on a shoe-string. From what I hear it's getting a bit frayed. Might snap at any time.'

## CHAPTER TEN

MORE THAN TWO WEEKS of a five-knot tow had convinced Mark Underson that there is nothing uglier than a dredger, not even one of the new vast rigs with heavy legs lifted, or the half of a 200,000 ton tanker being hauled for an electric mating to the other half built 3,000 miles away. A rusting tramp with scrap jammed into her holds for the last journey to a breaker's yard isn't a pretty sight either, but it has its own pathos, and a tug-man can look at the poor, wallowing old bitch who has outlived her marine usefulness with something near to pity. But no one, probably not even a dredgerman, could look for long at a dredger without wanting to spit.

Most of them at least pretended to be ships, with their own propulsion, and often a reasonable turn of speed from engines capable of being switched to power the chain buckets. But the Republic of Gutongo had decided to keep down overheads by dispensing with the crew needed to work their dredger as a vessel, and this one was engined only for silt lifting, helpless to move herself. It was destined for service on the Gutongo River, pushed to new sites for slime lifting by harbour tugs, and so hadn't been built as a ship at all, just a steel raft for floating machinery, with no hint of a tapered bow. Shallow draft made her a relatively easy but very wet tow, and in preparation for this her grab buckets and deck winches had all been coated against salt damage with shiny white plastic. In the dark this glistened, and gave that heap the look of an iceberg.

During the passage through the Bay of Biscay the nameless monster had thrashed around at the end of her hawser like a mechanical elephant run amok, and for two days, to ease the strain, speed had been cut to three knots. Even though the haul was 500 yards astern Mark often had the thought, especially at night, that the thing might at any time take on some grotesque initiative of its own and come lumbering down to overlay them.

The dredger was technically seaworthy, of course; it had to be; but nothing about the lift of that squared-off front-end on to a wave gave the men on the towing craft any conviction of this at all. Those delegated for hawser watching shifts aboard her went to the job looking like patients about to undergo major surgery, particularly after one pair, marooned back there for three days by weather, had come aboard the *Saturn* again apparently suffering from shock, with horror stories about the raft's movement. Ginnis, the Second, who had been one of them, said you needed centrifugal space training to survive, and rations ought to be tubed for squeezing into the mouth. He claimed a chipped front tooth from trying to drink out of a Thermos, and total insomnia for seventy-two hours.

They had come very near to skipping this tow altogether, dredger delivery delayed by two weeks, and while the *Saturn* waited to cross to Antwerp a chance had come up to take a moth-balled destroyer from Dartmouth to Taiwan, where the warship was to be broken up. Mark had been all for the job to the Far East but Jessie had suddenly received cash compensation from Belgium for holding her tug in readiness, which had put paid to her Captain's bids to get out of the Gutongo project. However, their trials with the dredger seemed over for the time being and for the last four days the raft had come along behind them as easily as a big caravan on a motorway. The sea was glassy, the barometer set fair, and local forecasts promised continued high pressure.

Mark hung over a rail on the boat-deck. There was no moon but the stars seemed the size of eggs. The *Saturn*'s movement stirred up its own breeze, and it was cool enough to make a man linger beyond air-conditioning. The day hadn't been bad either, in spite of the heat, marked by the sudden appearance of a troupe of dolphins, the gay fish, who are prepared at any time to put on a tireless callisthenic display in which there is scarcely a repeated stunt. They had kept clear of the dredger, as though they didn't like the look of it either, though this could have been because they realized their major audience was up front.

The dolphins had gone now, demanding full sun for their act, possibly spending the dark lying on their backs snoring, ready to roll over again at dawn to come after convoy at twenty-five knots. Or maybe the night was devoted to plankton-munching. Mark leaned out and wondered if there was ever a sailor who didn't love these fish of good omen, who were also the ocean's brightest children.

The sea in these latitudes had a different smell, vapours drawn from it by hard sun still apparently continuing an upward drift in the dark, touching the skin and lips in passing with a feather that was warm and salty. He stared down at the mass of little lights ignited in the water by the disturbance of their passage, the phosphorescence fanning out astern in the shape of a huge arrowhead pointing at the tug, with another blunter arrow aft of the dredger, markers indicating their course. In war-time that might have been a hazard, ships in tropic waters betrayed to enemy aircraft by a weird glowing from which they couldn't escape.

'Oh, there you are, sir.'

Starshine gave Collins the look of a hungry ascetic.

'Who has sent us an urgent signal?' Mark asked, and yawned.

'No one. I thought it was time we got off our daily message to Mrs Lawton.'

'Oh, Lord, I'd forgotten.'

'Maybe we could skip it this time?'

'No, I promised contact every twenty-four hours. What's happened today?'

'Nothing.' Collins said, as though no emergencies made him wonder what he was doing with his life.

'How about the dolphins? Tell them we sighted a school but none of them asked for assistance and we're continuing tow.'

'Are you serious, sir?'

'Yes, something has to make the old girl laugh sometime.'

'I don't think it would be that signal.'

'It doesn't make you laugh?'

'No.'

'All right. Curb me. Report continuing course, *Saturn*.'

'Very good, sir. Oh, I was on the bridge. They have a ship on radar. Due north behind us, just at the horizon. I tried contact by radio. No acknowledgement.'

'That wasn't civil.'

'Their man may be off,' Collins said, with contempt. 'You get that with tramps. I'll go on trying.'

'Does it really matter? They'll see us.'

'I like knowing what's around, sir.'

'You're quite right. I get lazy. It's this climate. Put me ashore in a hot country and I'd be a bottle-a-day man in no time. Can't you feel my grip on the *Saturn* slipping?'

'Not yet, sir. I'll get that signal off.'

'Send one to my wife, too, will you? Message . . . Thinking about a house with plumbers in it, and the men on the roof. But especially about the supervisor. Signed Mark. Can you remember that?'

He did an immaculate, toneless repeat, then slid away towards a companion ladder.

Mark took a deep breath and looked at the sea again. A star had come down to the horizon, a lusty star with a red tinge, and it somehow put him in mind of lips searching for other lips, and finding them, and the slower in coming urgency of a known love in which there is nothing frenzied, just the build-up through tested stages. A man should never want anything else, but get him half-drunk in a port and he does. Alice knew. She never asked any questions.

He thought about her going to Jessie Lawton. When they had both got over his anger she had told him about what had happened and at the same time contrived not to tell him exactly what had been said. This wasn't because she didn't remember, she remembered every word, but preferred to serve these sieved. The interview had come over pasteurized by a kind of sweetness he didn't believe in for one minute, even if the old girl had taken her out to dinner afterwards. A tape recording of the meeting would have been interesting. It had kept him his ship and he ought to be thankful. In a way he was, but he had enjoyed the war, too, the ultimatums, the irrevocable decisions, all resolved by a hen party. What they thought about it on the *Saturn*, God knew. The Chief's curiosity was persistent, it even came out over chess, as though the old bastard thought that peace had somehow been declared too easily for the Skipper. And maybe it had, maybe it couldn't last. There was in Jessie Lawton a steel core of will which she was driven to use against other wills, even when these weren't really a match for her, but made of baser metal subject to softening. Mark knew that he would never really be at peace with Jessie because she wouldn't be with him. They would both be watching, he the owner, she the means to her ends. The old girl didn't come near to warming his heart at all, and never would, probably because early in life she'd had a transplant for an imperishable plastic pump.

The horizon-kissing star had turned into a ship and after watching her for minutes Mark decided she was coming fast, at a guess sixteen, which said not a tramp. Her lights, staying low in the water, said not a passenger liner, nor a bulk carrier, nor a tanker. She could be a corvette, and if that was the case it would account for the no talking. The navies of the world only talked when they felt like it, and some of them didn't feel like it very often. There had been a time, and Mark was able to remember it well enough, when your location on the world's seas had been a fair guide to the craft you encountered, at least for the smaller ships, and you could guess with some accuracy what flag they sailed under. But not any longer. These waters between the Canaries and the Cape Verdes—except for established traffic lanes through them—should have been the preserve of the Spanish or the Portuguese, but the chances now were that the craft on a course that would take it starboard of the tow was something else, Soviet from the Baltic on unspecified business, or a detachment from the U.S. Med. fleet out looking for a downed telecommunications satellite that hadn't burned up on re-entry and just might be still afloat, or Mao Chinese on a long-distance snoop, or even the newly formed Gutonguese Navy out testing its first purchase with a scratch crew of junketing drunks. Any damn thing, in fact. You never knew what you were up against and wise policy was to mind your own business without too much curiosity.

Collins, of course, would stay curious; it was a kind of occupational disease, but the Skipper was going to his bunk in a nice air-conditioned state room to dream about sitting out in his newly acquired English garden in a British heatwave when the thermometer can zoom as high as seventy-two Fahrenheit. He hoped that the girl serving him tea under a magnolia tree that rarely bloomed in its alien setting would be Alice, but the trouble about dreams was that it could just as well be Lin, and he would wake up feeling faithless.

He took a last look at the dredger. It was there, with riding lights still functioning, and presumably the two watchmen—one of whom was MacDonald—taking their rest. The plastic caps on the bucket step-ladder shone in starlight like teeth on a new denture. It would be a happy moment when they finally unhooked that contraption up the Gutongo River and left it forever. Forty years from now some atomic powered tug would drag the thing back to Belgium for scrap.

Mark walked over the now properly christened helipad and was received into an artificial coolness that for seconds felt clammy. There were men on the *Saturn* who claimed that the washed air gave them head colds, and the Chief was one of these, apparently positively regretting the oil-pungent, sweaty wombs that were the engine-rooms of earlier days. Secretly he probably wished he had been born back in the age of coal firing, watching his perspiration-drenched stokers shovelling fuel into red-hot furnaces. Men were men in those days, even if they didn't live long.

'Captain! This could be important.'

Mark looked up the stairs. It was Collins again.

'You've just had a quasar signal from outer space?'

'That ship has altered course to evade us.'

'Why do you use the word evade?'

'Because they've turned due west suddenly. And they've been talking in code. French.'

'You don't know whose code?'

'No, sir.'

'Have you been identifying us?'

'Yes.'

'Tried R.T.?'

'They don't read me.'

Mark climbed the stairs. 'Let's go out on the bridge,' he said.

Night glasses seemed to fuse the lights and blur the distant ship's outline. But she was still travelling at some speed, now just inside the rim of the horizon and on a straight course for Cuba 3,000 miles away, which opened up all kinds of exciting possibilities. Mark experienced no quickening of pulse, but he was beginning to become interested.

'We can hardly give chase without dropping tow. Which would be a bit hard on poor MacDonald. And anyway, I'd have to ask permission from Edinburgh.'

Collins said nothing. Mark wasn't sleepy any longer. He stood at stern view windows staring like a tourist at something the guide books say is interesting. That ship didn't appear to want to be identified, and yet it had broken silence to talk home. For instructions? Maybe her Skipper was as hog-tied by owners as the *Saturn*'s. It wasn't a free ocean any more, you spent most of your time on it talking to people in offices.

'Let's feed available data into the computer,' Mark said, 'and see what comes out. Not much of a mast, running lights somewhere about eighteen feet above water, port-hole lights below that, but only one row of them, these amidships and for'ard. Certainly midship engines. I get the feel, too, of a long, low stern quarter, though that's guessing. Supposing we don't bother programming our robot, he uses a lot of electricity. As an untrained ship spotter what's the answer you'd come up with, Collins?'

'A tug.'

'Confirmed. A French tug being furtive. Have there been any calls on the air in the last week or so that could have brought a tug down to these parts on spec and at speed?'

'Not that I heard.'

'If you didn't hear them, there haven't been any.'

'They might be on their way to a pick-up.'

'But where? Before they decided to run from us they were on a course almost due south. And there's only the Verdes down there. Have we any information about anything disabled down in those islands?'

'No. And I've been monitoring Hoofstanger signals. They're certainly not on to anything down this way.'

'Collins, get back to your sets and fill the night air with voices.'

'Yes sir.'

He sounded happy again. Ginnis came over from the other corner of the bridge where he seemed to have been hiding, perhaps because he didn't like radio cabin inspired excitements during his watch.

'Do you think it's the competition, Captain?'

'What would they be competing for? Who wants to steal anyone else's dredger? For two cents I'd give it to them. I'm going down to get into pyjamas but if that ship alters course again buzz me.'

Mark took a ration of whisky to his bunk and sat reading a news magazine, but wasn't really able to concentrate on those pre-cooked, packaged items, just brooded over an article which seemed to be suggesting that before too long crack surgeons would almost catch up on Dr Frankenstein with an eighty per cent spare-parts man who would live long enough to glorify modern science via a series of press and television interviews. Mark's reaction to this was pretty old-fashioned, his feeling being that when one of his vital organs went the rest of him would prefer to go with it.

He sipped whisky remembering what the previous issue of the magazine had told him, that every time he got drunk 10,000 irreplaceable cells died in his brain. After that piece of cheering news he had nearly set the ship's computer to work figuring out how many million units of dead tissue he was carrying about up there, but had been frightened off by what the machine might say. Anyway, he was consciously cutting down on alcohol intake, not to please Alice, she didn't seem worried, but because he had decided that in this business he needed urgently what might be left of his wits.

Where the hell was that other tug going? There would have been no mystery, or not nearly such a big one, if the *Saturn* and her tow were using one of the recognized shipping lanes, but they weren't. To avoid any risk of creating traffic problems on the main routes to the Cape and African ports, course south of the Canaries had been set fifty miles west through what should have been a more or less empty waste of South Atlantic. And certainly on this section of their journey they had sighted no other vessels until tonight, which made the erratic behaviour of the one in vision highly curious.

The buzzer signal went. Mark groaned and got up.

'Captain? That ship has changed course again. Due south at ten miles west.'

Mark found slip-ons and the Paisley silk dressing-gown Alice had given him to use on board. He had never worn it to the bridge before, but Ginnis didn't seem at all shocked. He handed over night glasses.

'Still keeping her distance?'

'Yes. Never been any closer.'

'I wonder what our biggest flare would show?'

Five minutes later it showed a profile that didn't need checking in the International Salvage Union's handbook. The *Semirande* had never had a sister ship, and there could be no doubt at all. Her reaction to exposure by light was interesting, she altered course to west again, and appeared to be planning an exit over the horizon. Mark went through to the radio cabin.

'Is your R.T. line open?'

'Yes, sir, I've been calling them.'

Mark took the handpiece. 'Captain Underson, *Saturn*, to Captain Dartan, *Semirande*. Come in if you read me. Over.'

The air stayed silent.

'Switch off, Collins. Do you know their radio man?'

'I met him once in Rotterdam. Ginole's the name.'

'Any chance he works a forty-hour week?'

'No. He'll be listening.'

One of the brotherhood of the curious. It laid them open for sweated labour, though things were changing here, too, and some of the Hoofstangers on station now carried three operators working a round the clock shift system. It would come at sea, too, increasing overheads, and Collins would hate the sharing when it did.

'I'll call over once again,' Mark said. 'If they don't answer I'll tell you to switch off. But leave the line open. I want them to eavesdrop.'

The second call in was unacknowledged. Mark swore and ordered Collins off the air.

'I'm going to signal London,' he said. 'In code. Sighting made tonight—get the exact time and our position from the bridge—of Plentin company's tug *Semirande* on due south course. The *Semirande* attempted to avoid recognition and took evasive action. It would be interesting to know why. Suggest investigation your end to find out what her mission in this area. Please notify us when information available. Signed, Underson. You've got all that?'

Mark signalled with his hand and Collins cut the R.T. line out.

'I've got a feeling that will put them on the air to the owners again. You've never broken the Plentin code?'

'No. It never seemed worthwhile.'

'You didn't take down the *Semirande*'s earlier signals out?'

'No.'

'Well, see that you do the next one. The French shouldn't bother you if you broke the Hoofstanger's Dutch. I've got a dictionary if you need it.'

'You mean you want this as soon as possible?'
'I thought you liked working late?'
Collins looked sour.

Jules Dartan knew he had been a fool. He should have gone
to see Berand the moment they sighted the other tug and its tow,
or at least when the *Saturn* started pushing out those identification calls. This chance meeting at sea had been a shock, the
statistical odds against it enormous, but still the kind of thing that
happens fairly often. And, of course, both tugs had their separate
reasons for staying clear of normal trade routes; it wasn't really
so surprising they had chosen the same course south, far enough
from the lanes to be safe, but still not making a wide detour. It
had been a mistake, too, to send off that signal to the owners, it
had helped identify them and sparked off *Saturn*'s curiosity.
Ginole was as good as saying this now.

'They're after signal text, sir. For code-breaking.'
'I don't understand?'
'Line left open no accident. Planned. We send out signal, they
take it down. Operator breaks it.'
'Breaks our code?'
'Easy. No good. Always thought so.'
'You think we should keep silence, Ginole?'
'Yes.'
'Oh, God, I don't know!'

It was not an admission a captain should ever make. The taste
of brandy was in Jules's mouth and in his stomach a sourness
from the wine with his last meal. The brandy had been taken
in the worst way, too, alone in his cabin, sitting forward on his
bunk, glaring at a bulkhead. Berand had loose bowels and was
lying up for a rest cure, off all duties.

It had been a mistake to change course the first time and a
worse one to do it again. Like bloody panic over something.
And all for what? Merely that old Henri Plentin had said they
were to get to St Vincent unnoticed.

'Why let company know, sir?'
'What?'
'About *Saturn*'s flare?'
'They'd learn about it from the log.'
'Not written up yet.'

Jules felt a flush rise from his neck.

'I've kept my voyage records straight, Ginole. No omissions
and no false entries.'

The radio operator shrugged. He spun the revolving chair,
giving the Skipper his back.

'I'll think about that signal,' Jules said. He went out.

The trouble was he didn't want to think about it, he wanted someone else to. The ship got out of trim when Berand abdicated from his role like this. He got belly trouble because he didn't drink enough. He held a brandy like one of those old hens in a pavement café breaking her temperance rules on a monthly visit to the big city. He didn't drink the stuff, he sipped it. You needed alcohol to help you digest your food.

Jules went downstairs. He stood for a considerable time in front of a mahogany door fitted with ventilation slats. Then he made a scraping noise with one finger on a panel.

'Come in.'

The electric fan whined from its wall bracket. Berand was lying like an effigy on a stone coffin, his hands folded in resignation across a rioting stomach. He was certainly white, but he was always pasty.

'How are you?'

'About the same.'

'Why in hell's name don't you take something? What you need is a good purge, do you know that?'

'Heaven forbid! What was that white light a while back? A flare, surely?'

The man would miss nothing, even when dying. And he'd be working on a piece of his damn sewing until twenty minutes from the end. Berand turned his head.

'Well, Jules?'

'You're right. It was a flare. From the *Saturn*. Identifying us. And a lot of good may it do them. I didn't even know she was down here.'

'I did.'

'You would.'

'You could read the movement records, too.'

'Oh, sure, sure. If I didn't have all those government forms to read. And fill in. All right, I should have known she was in these parts. I should have known about every ship operating within a couple of hundred miles. Even when the bloody *Flying Dutchman* was due to make another appearance!'

'Jules, shut the door and sit down.'

'I didn't come to bother you . . .'

'Shut the door!'

'All right, all right. You're so excitable, Berand.'

'God give me strength!'

Jules glared. 'If you knew the *Saturn* was down here on a tow why didn't you tell me?'

'It's a big ocean. I thought she might be hugging the African coast. Why did you alter course a couple of times?'

'It seemed best not to get too close.'

'You mean you let them see you weren't wanting to be identified?'

'Yes, *First*!'

'That was bright. You've been on the brandy.'

Jules didn't take the seat which folded down from a bulk-head; he stood back against a tiny washbasin. The waste pipe put out a gurgling echo of engine noise. He thought about what it was going to be like to command a ship in which this whey-faced invalid was not Mate. In old Henri's office the future had seemed rose-tinted. Now it was beginning to make him decidedly uneasy.

'Berand, do you know where the *Saturn*'s going with that dredger?'

'Yes. Gutongo.'

'Eh? Isn't that the place where the Plentins used to be big? With a mine or something?'

Berand nodded.

'Copper. But it was nationalized by the Republic. In so far as I know it was a grab without compensation of any kind. A nasty blow to the Plentin pocket as well as pride.'

'What's one mine to them?' Jules asked from his new near directorial status in the company's salvage interests.

'Just a capital asset that by my guess must have returned to them each year about a hundred times what this ship does. They were hurt when they lost it all right. Oh, God!'

'What's the matter?'

'Gripes.'

Jules stood for quite some time looking down at the Mate. 'Berand, what do you honestly think about this tug expansion? You've never really said.'

'My personal reaction, you mean? It's fear.'

'Why?'

'Maybe because I'm like a cat, I don't approve of upset. I've been cosy. It looks now as though I never will be again. I've been lying here thinking about what it's going to be like flying out to Japan to take over a ship I've never seen with a scratch crew I know nothing about. To a man like me the answer is hell. It would have been a real kindness not to have told me about it until nearer the time.'

'You know damn well I tell you everything.'

'Yes.'

Jules shuffled his feet.

'I'm not so sure I'm as keen on the idea as I was.'

'Really? I thought you'd already ordered your commodore's cap?'

'If old Henri is laying out all that money he's going to expect his new ships to start earning fast.'

'How right you are. We'll all be suffering from executive strain in no time.'

'I wish you wouldn't try to be funny about this, Berand!'

'The alternative is to weep for happy times lost. And what good does that do you? You can give me a glass of water. Run the tap. It comes rusty for at least half a minute. Tank cleaning was something they missed on that so-called re-fit.'

A circular saw was busy halving his skull. Mark opened his eyes, then rolled off the bunk and swayed across the cabin. He punched a button.

'What is it?'

'MacDonald from the tow, sir. He's on walkie-talkie. Wants you. Will you take it on the bridge set?'

'Yes.'

Mark went into the bathroom, rinsed his mouth and spat. The quiet life on a tow, up before the dolphins to see the dawn every morning. He took time to put on shirt and trousers.

Ginnis was bleary eyed from sleep on the chartroom settee, a privilege granted to the officer of the watch doing double duty. The helmsman looked only semi-conscious. The sea was flat, pearl grey, waiting for the first sun before it began to steam. The *Saturn* seemed to have no motion at all, beyond vibration. Mark picked up the box.

'Underson here.'

'Captain, it's been a funny night.'

'You woke me up to tell me that?'

'I don't mean flares and the *Semirande*.'

'Recognized her, did you? Is the raft starting to break up?'

'No. But I think we've got a cargo on here. Without bills of lading.'

'Where? She hasn't got a hold.'

'She's got buckets.'

Mark blinked. There was a smell of coffee sneaking up into the bridge.

'What's in the buckets?'

'I haven't looked. The plastic's like iron. Until last night everything on here clanked. The least movement and it does. But there wasn't that movement, just the hawser jolt sometimes. That set up this clinking.'

'I'm not following you too well, MacDonald. It's probably the time of day. You think there's something inside those buckets?'

'Sure of it. I thought about spare tools, but there's nothing on the indent. We've got all the maker's instruction books for operation, diagrams, that kind of thing. No hint of anything that would be loose in a bucket. It's a metallic sound.'

'What do you want me to do; authorize you to slit one of those plastic covers?'

'That was my idea.'

'Have we got any way of sealing it again if it turns out to be a wrench?'

'Heat, maybe. I'm sure the Chief can come up with something.'

'Okay, open her up. Though what can you send to Africa in a dredger that Africa wants?'

'Perhaps I'll be able to tell you in half an hour.'

Mark looked at a grey sea that was developing shiny streaks through a matt surface, like a cauldron of jam just coming to the boil. He went down two decks in search of coffee.

Cordell turned from his electric stove. Like most cooks on small ships he was a professional failure at something else, and this large, slack man had only reached corporal in army catering by the end of a long service engagement. About once a month, after the kind of food that starts mutinies, Mark swore the Cordell would be replaced the next time they were in Hull, and it was always at this point that the man decided he had gone too far, immediately swinging into one of his near top cuisine cycles, practically reaching marine *cordon bleu*. Gourmet meals came up from a galley filled with baritone song and oddly enough this phase often occurred during the most appalling weather conditions, with the tug heaving about in a Force Eight. Cordell was undoubtedly a moderate manic depressive, which is not the kind of nature that fits comfortably into confined tug patterns, but he still had a place on board that went beyond his cooking: he was ship's bookie. To sack him might do a damage to the social patterns on the *Saturn* that would be worse for morale than periodic indigestion. It was an admin. problem for which Mark hadn't found any solution and didn't really expect to.

Food hadn't been particularly good recently, or noticeably bad. Things could go either way. Cordell's morning face said this.

'I'm looking for some coffee to wake me up.'

'Okay, Captain. I've had everybody already. The Chief's wanting his breakfast.'

'A bit early, surely?' Mark said gently.

'That's what I said. All those yobs asking for a forty-hour week ought to get a cook's job at sea. They'd learn somethin'.'

Cordell poured rich, dark treacle. Even tinned milk didn't spoil the flavour. Mark sipped, then issued a morale booster.

'There's no coffee anywhere as good as yours. Even my wife's.'

Cordell considered the tribute.

'I could do you a fry-up quick, Captain?'

'No thanks. I'll wait.'

The walkie-talkie was on a settee in the chartroom, switched on and crackling. Mark sat down beside it, staring at the computer. No one had asked the thing any questions recently and it looked sulky, a wasted asset. The machines would win in the end, serviced by other machines built for the job, and man's brains, with the incentive to function removed, would atrophy. It might take a few hundred years but it would happen. Other parts of man would wither, too, which was going to solve the population explosion, and there'd be no need to colonize Mars. Though probably the machines would want to move up there.

Collins was in the doorway watching him.

'The *Semirande* hasn't risen to bait, sir.'

'What?'

'They've been keeping radio silence. No message in French code or anything else. I'll go on listening.'

'Well, it was a good try.'

Collins didn't seem to think so. Probably it was unethical to try to fool another radio operator, against their professional code.

'MacDonald calling Captain Underson. Over.'

'Underson here. Well?'

The Mate paused for effect.

'Bren guns.'

After a moment Mark said: 'I won't ask if you're sure.'

'I've still got the packing grease on my hands. Only two in the one bucket, but with ammo. Can't say off hand how many rounds. The filler is some kind of foam. It should have prevented the rattling but that one barrel worked through to tap out its message against the bucket.'

'Lucky for us.'

'Maybe. I've been checking the number of buckets. Thirty-eight. But only half on the climb up the ladder ramp. Pretty safe to assume the under ones don't have anything inside. They'd have been too hard to pack.'

'That leaves nineteen that probably do have something?'

'That's right. Want me to go on opening?'

'Yes. I'm coming back for a look.'

'Do that, Captain. Over and out.'

Mark stood. There was no way to keep this from the crew and not much point in trying to. Ginnis turned. He was beginning to need his electric razor.

'We're heaving to,' Mark said.

'I heard you say, sir, you were going back.'

'That's right. The dredger seems to be a supply ship for an African revolution. And since we're heading for Gutongo that's where trouble is scheduled. Revolutionaries probably sitting waiting for us.'

'Good God! But the dredger's for the Government?'

'I don't think the arms are. And we're not even being paid danger money.'

Could Jessie have taken the danger money to help with those overheads that kept spiralling?

The dredger's steel deck was as hot as a stove top. Sun made the sea polished brass, and air had no movement through it, a dead vacuum in which the temperature had been dialled up to ninety-eight. The *Saturn* lay at 200 yards, her engines cut, her hull almost hidden by shimmer glare. The dolphins hadn't shown up this morning, perhaps kept away by a rival act, eleven basking sharks whose huge dorsal fins, seen through rising vapour, seemed re-shaped into the squared conning towers of atomic submarines; a whole wolf pack of submarines slowly circling at a distance.

MacDonald had been operating with a pair of wire cutters and by the sixth bucket had become almost casual about the whole thing, making first a plunge incision through the tough plastic, then carving a line back from which synthetic protective skin was folded to each side. He was sweating like a vet at major cow surgery.

'This bloody ramp gets hotter the higher you go,' he shouted. 'How many more do you want opened?'

'What's in that one?'

The Mate groped around inside his Caesarean and hauled out, with some difficulty, a rifle. He turned over the butt, looking for markings.

'Czech. And I wouldn't like to be issued with this one if I was going to a war.'

'Old is it?'

'Museum stuff. Like the Brens.'

'But unlike the grenades. Come on down, Tom. We know all we need to.'

The Mate shoved the gun back under plastic. He straightened, hanging on to a bucket edge by one heavily muscled arm, squinting out over the sea. In swimming trunks and canvas shoes he was a hirsute red Tarzan apparently looking for Jane.

There was no doubt that MacDonald was feeling better about life than he had for some time. That visit to the Lake District had resulted in a sharp selling of his stock on board *Saturn*. This was grossly unfair, but there had still been that selling, and he knew it. However, he seemed to have a good fairy who only let him suffer for so long. This morning would send his stock right up again. He had demonstrated clearly that he deserved executive rating. Mark was glad for the man, and a personal triumph was going to make him a lot easier to live with.

'Whew!' MacDonald said, using his hands to get perspiration

out of his eyes, then wiping palms on a permanent undershirt.
'I'm going in that water.'

'It's hot and won't cool you.'

'I don't care.'

'They say basking sharks don't fancy us, but I don't believe it.'

'They're a long way off.'

He went down by the painter from the *Saturn*'s boat, keeping
hold of this while he splashed in, dipped his head and splashed
up again via a hand lift on the dredger's deck. He cultivated
those beautiful muscles with a steel spring exerciser plus press-
ups and Yoga had taught him how to revolve his abdomen like
a Marrakesh belly dancer, which was one way to ward off that
scourge of sailors, constipation. Dripping he was still a splendid
figure of a man.

'What are you going to do about all this?'

'I'm certainly not taking our non-manifest cargo to Gutongo.'

'So?'

'We make for the nearest port. Somewhere in the Verdes, I'd
say. Where I can get on a telephone line to our owners. I don't
fancy ship's radio at the moment. There could be listening ears
and my faith in codes is crumbling.'

'You know what I'd do with this load of death?'

'Tell me, Tom.'

'Dump it. Every damn bit. Then carry on with tow.'

'My first reaction, too. But I've had second thoughts. Your
discovery of this stuff just might be a trump card. I don't begin
to know what the game is yet, but we may be able to find out.
Meantime we take the greatest possible care of all this.'

Mark turned and went up the ramp to the third bucket, reaching down through the split covering and fumbling in a carrier
into which the contents had been packed as carefully as eggs. He
looked at the grenade for a moment, then pulled the pin, counting five before he hurled it as far as he could over the sea. There
was a white flash, then a roar.

'All primed and ready for the war to start,' Mark called out.

'Man! Look at those sharks go! They think it's been declared.'

## CHAPTER ELEVEN

THE PHONE SHRIEKED. Jessie jerked as though a stray voltage
from the electric blanket had stabbed her. She got a light on. The
travelling clock said minutes after three a.m. She hauled the
handset over her pillow.

'Is that 031-220-9189?'

From her good cheer the operator seemed to like night duty. Jessie accepted those digits as identification, as always hating to do this.

'I have a personal call for Mrs Jessie Lawton. Is she available?'
'Speaking.'
'It's from Lisbon. Charges reversed.'
'Charges *what*? I don't know anyone in Lisbon.'
The operator thought that any attempt to haggle with post office services was vulgar. 'There is no need to accept the call, Madam, if you don't want to.'
'Oh, all right, I accept.'
Lisbon! Even with the cheap night rates ...
'Go ahead now, caller,' the sweet voice said from exchange.
The caller, with someone else paying, didn't come through. After a two-minute silence of respect to international phone networks the operator said that they seemed to have lost Lisbon, but would ring back as soon as they found it again. Jessie asked how long that was likely to be but the line was dead.

There was no point in putting out the light and trying to sleep, and it would be equally stupid to sit brooding about who could possibly be wanting her from Portugal. She did what the favourite poet of her youth had told her to, and didn't waste the unforgiving minute, putting on spectacles and pulling over one of the work files brought up from the study. It was a report on her trawlers out of Aberdeen and five minutes' reading pricked away all mental sluggishness.

Profits were markedly down. Prices after fish landings were all right but overheads were mounting, takings not keeping pace with costs. There was a kind of commercial madness in the air these days which made Arthur's most active period, the forties and fifties, seem a century away, an era totally lost to changing standards as well as techniques. Jessie couldn't think of a single dogma from her late husband's business creed which was valid now. Current interest rates, by themselves, mocked the very fundamentals of his beliefs, and his shade's exhortations to watch her step became less and less relevant.

The ghostly advice wasn't, in fact, relevant at all. In our time the fool watches his step and stays poor, the wise gamble wildly and get rich. It was as simple as that. You chose something that twenty years ago would have seemed an investment lunacy, backed it with all you were worth, and if your luck was in you could be drawing a sixty per cent return on capital within the year.

Jessie had learned this from bitter experience. She had been offered, through a broker whose judgement she respected, a third share in a pop group known as *The Kilties*. It had seemed an extremely bad joke at the time, especially after she had watched the four horrors on television. The idea was to back the group in the music trade with £50,000 worth of all-out promotion and publicity, with the backers' return to be fifty per cent of the gross take in perpetuity. Jessie had declined the opportunity. *The Kilties* had now had eleven top-of-the-pops in two years and were laden with golden discs. Their current price for a public appearance was £5,000. The broker who had personally bought a big piece in them had decided to retire at forty-seven and was building himself a nineteen-roomed villa on Spain's sunshine coast.

Arthur would simply not have understood a contemporary investment opportunity of this kind; Jessie wasn't sure she did herself, but it happened, and the moral seemed to be that a careful diversification of your interests is a dissipation of assets. What you want to do is make a pool of everything and gamble.

If she sold her seven trawlers and put all her eggs in the salvage basket she would be gambling all right. A sister ship to the *Saturn* was going to cost a million and a quarter at contemporary prices. Of this she must put up at least £750,000 herself in order to make quite certain she stayed Chairman of Anglo-European. That would leave her with a reserve of only about a million and a half in other resources, which was not much better than petty cash to the big ones in the business she was setting out to challenge. Since Arthur's death she had been able to treble the estate he had left, but wasn't particularly proud of the achievement; she was still rated a minor operator by the City of London.

For moments Jessie indulged the phantasy of thinking about what she could do with ten million. Twenty would be about right, but even with ten she would have the freedom and scope to challenge all comers in the field of her choice. And the Hoofstangers, for one, wouldn't be able to dismiss her as a fringe irritation.

The phone rang. Jessie re-identified herself and immediately after that a very well-known voice came in loud and clear.

'Mrs. Lawton? Captain Underson.'

She treated herself to a slow, deep breath.

'You chose an odd hour to get in touch, Captain.'

'Sorry if this call woke you. I booked it at quarter to ten. I've been waiting ever since.'

'Ship to shore radio must be getting a lot of trade. Is this being relayed from Africa?'

'No. It's coming by cable from St Vincent in the Cape Verde Islands. Via Lisbon. The air in any form didn't seem to me to offer adequate security. So I waited until we got here. It's a very personal call.'

Jessie sat bolt upright. 'You waited to get *where*?'

'The Cape Verdes.'

'I presume you have a splendid reason once again for being hundreds of miles off your course to Gutongo?'

'I do. A couple of days ago we found our dredger is carrying twenty buckets of small arms and ammunition, plus grenades.

'*What?* Buckets?'

'Yes. The dredger scoops. They have plastic covers. Make excellent containers. Someone thought it all out most carefully. Our cargo ought to be about enough for a couple of days' sharp fighting. That's long enough for an African revolution in a place like Gutongo.'

'My God!'

'You sound as startled as I was, Mrs Lawton.'

'How did you expect me to sound?'

'I wasn't sure.'

'Just what do you mean by that?'

'We'll skip any thoughts I may have had. You're as shocked and horrified as I am.'

A wind had risen, hitting a corner of the stone house on a direct line from the Pentland Hills. Lazzari couldn't have done this on his own? He wouldn't have dared!

She knew she ought to probe the Captain's stray thoughts, but decided quickly that it was policy not to.

'Those things are still on the dredger?'

'Oh, yes. Back under their plastic covers. Sealed up again.'

'You didn't think of dumping it all?'

'Interesting you should say that. My Mate wanted me to. But I had the feeling it might be a good idea to have the evidence available. Just in case you wanted to conduct some investigations. Within our company.'

'*Our* company?'

'Yes. Lazzari. He got us this tow. He is also an agent for International Equipment Services, registered in Monte Carlo. It markets the kind of hardware we found on the dredger. I see a connection. Don't you?'

Jessie said nothing. Mark's voice went hard.

'Mrs Lawton, this shipment wasn't ordered by the Gutonguese Government. They don't need to smuggle in the arms they need, not even to save shipping charges. According to the gossip I've already heard in St Vincent they're getting all their military equipment from the Chinese at cut prices. This suggests that the stuff in the dredger is for the opposition. If you're organizing the overthrow of a tight little dictatorship your big problem is getting what you need to do it past the security wall. The classic case for the situation was Troy. This time the horse is a dredger. And we're the suckers pulling it. Are you following me?'

Jessie was, very closely.

'Maybe I should point out what this could have done to the *Saturn* and her crew, in case you haven't jumped to it. We couldn't have proved our innocence if that cargo had been discovered by the Gutonguese. At the trial we'd have been labelled neo-colonial spies and saboteurs. I understand that in most parts of Africa that leads to the death sentence these days. Certainly for the Captain. I might have been saved at the last minute from execution as a result of appeals from the United Nations or somewhere. But thirty years in an African jail isn't much of a future. Perhaps you think I'm being melodramatic?'

Jessie wished that she could. Her hands were trembling. Underson seemed to lose control. He didn't shout, but the explosive violence suddenly behind his words was frightening.

'I'm going to find the bastards who put these arms on the dredger! And my only lead to them is Lazzari!'

'That's not reason talking, Captain!'

'No? Look, Mrs Lawton. Your co-director is also an arms salesman. You've known for a while that I was in the picture there. Lazzari arranged this tow. Further, he got you a payment for holding the *Saturn* when the dredger wasn't ready. Looks like someone was keen our ship take that job, doesn't it? I still can't work out why it had to be us. On the face of it any tug would have done. But this is something I mean to shake out of your company director, too.'

'You haven't a shred of evidence against him!'

'Maybe it's circumstantial, but to me it screams. And there's one thing I can check. I'm bringing back a grenade in my hand luggage. It's stamped. I'm pretty certain that under pressure Lazzari will be able to identify it. I catch a flight to the Canaries in a few hours. The connections aren't too good and it'll be twelve hours before I'm Lazzari-hunting in London. But I thought you'd want to know that I'll be there.'

'Captain! Let me handle this!'

'It's not really woman's work, Mrs Lawton. Lazzari strikes me as the kind you have to beat the truth out of.'

'I have my own methods!'

'Maybe. I'm still not terribly impressed with company efficiency at your end. I've been strict about sending the signals you wanted. But when I ask for information from our London office there's no answer.'

'I simply don't know what you mean?'

'I asked London to find out what the Plentin tug *Semirande* was doing down in these waters.'

'The *Semirande*? In the Cape Verde Islands?'

'Yes. You know nothing about my signal?'

'No.'

'I thought you got everything from the *Saturn* sent up to you?'

'I do. I talked to Lazzari on the phone yesterday. He made no mention of this.'

'Now that's interesting. You don't think he's keeping things from you?'

Jessie felt an increase in heart rate. 'I have the *Saturn* file here. I'll check it again. Tell me about the *Semirande* while I do.'

'She overhauled us the night before MacDonald discovered the cache. Behaved like crazy. Skipping around the horizon, and when we arrived here it was to find her anchored, as settled-looking as a hen on eggs. The shore gen is that this is now her station. Can you imagine that? The one Plentin sea-going tug stationed in the Cape Verdes. It looks like the head of the business has finally gone senile. I wouldn't station a row-boat down here. Is my signal in that file?'

'No.'

'Your clerk in London lost it, maybe. Or Lazzari decided it wasn't important enough to send on.'

'Captain, I'll be on the first plane to London. *I'll* see Lazzari.'

'Tell him he can run where he likes, I'll catch up with him.'

'I want you to leave Lazzari to me for the time being.'

'Oh, no. I'll be on that plane to the Canaries.'

'I'm not going to order you to stay by your ship, Captain Underson. But I ask you to.'

'Really?'

'I want to handle this in my own way. And I'll phone you when I've seen the man. Some time this evening. Could I get you at that number?'

'If I took a room here, yes. It's an hotel. But if I miss today's flight I mayn't get another for long enough.'

'I'm asking you to leave this to me!'

There was silence for half a minute.

'All right. I'll leave round one to you. But if I don't think it has been effective round two is coming up. And you can let Lazzari know that.'

'I will. What's your number?'

'St Vincent 784.'

Jessie wrote it down. 'I'll use the night lines,' she said. 'Probably between ten and eleven.'

'We'll hope for a quicker connection.'

'Are you keeping a watch on the dredger?'

'Very much so. Armed. With borrowed equipment. No one will have a chance to inspect those buckets.'

'What's your excuse for being in St Vincent?'

'Turbine trouble. We don't need shore assistance for repairs, not that we'd get it if we did. And our story has been accepted all right. It's a relaxed atmosphere. Though I'd be fascinated to know what they thought over on the *Semirande* when they saw us come sailing in to their base of operations. Okay, over to you until tonight. Goodbye now.'

Jessie moved very slowly to put the handset back on its base. She heard the wind again. There were cigarettes on the bedside table and she lit one. Somewhere at the back of her mind was a feeling that the Plentins had interests in Gutongo. She couldn't remember what these were, but she would find out today, before she saw Lazzari.

Mark didn't at once leave the airless little telephone cubicle, standing to stare at the wall graffiti. Ardent lovers had expressed with pencil on plaster what had been in their minds but couldn't be said over a wire. Some of the artwork had been ineffectively whitewashed over, either by the hotel management or the local league for decency.

He had been able to frighten Jessie Lawton. It was quite an achievement. The timing, of course, had been good, that call from here not actually taking the five hours he had claimed, but twenty-five minutes to a first near miss. The line break had been bad luck, but even with its shock tactics in the early morning appeared to have worked. She would go to London and jump on Lazzari's neck good and hard, which wouldn't do the man any harm, even if he was innocent.

Mark had his doubts still about the evidence pointing towards the company secretary. It was a long shot that ought to be fired in cold fury. Better hers than his. Anyway he didn't really have cold fury available, it was too hot down here for that kind of emotional intensity.

The hotel manager was still in his office, with his feet up on the desk. It was twenty-two minutes to four in the morning but he was lighting a new cigar.

'Everything fine then?' he asked.

'As fine as it can be when you have to tell an owner about turbine trouble.'

'Sure. Too bad. Still you can make holiday, yes?'

Mr Luigi de Walters claimed to be a hundred per cent English from Bermondsey, which his grandfather had left to establish a coaling station in St Vincent. It seemed improbable that his grandfather had left London with that 'de' in front of his name, but there had been other family changes, too, including a considerable darkening of skin. Mr de Walters's voice had lost all trace of Cockney for a trace of Lisbon to which had been added tonal influences from the African continent. It was a pleasant voice, relaxed. The whole of St Vincent was relaxed, out of history since the end of the steam age, and apparently quite pleased to have little to do with the atomic one.

'Sit down then,' Mr de Walters suggested.

'Don't you ever go to bed in this place?'

'Sure. When it's siesta. Night's cooler for staying awake.'

'I must owe you about half a bottle already.'

'Duty free.'

'How come?'

'Don't ask no questions. Just drink. Real Scotch malt. I only drink malt. It don't heat the blood so much.'

'I think I'd better book one of your rooms to siesta in. I'll be using that phone.'

'Sure. No trouble. I got twenty-three empty. That's all of them.'

Mark sat down and looked round the office. It was a pretty good specimen of international jerry building, so much per square foot and a third of the price graft. A thin coating of plaster over hard-board had as many lines through it as a wicked old man's face. The London Palace Hotel had the feel of something in Majorca, a rush job for tourists who were being booked in even before the waste pipes had been connected. Only here there were no tourists. Mark sipped whisky and asked his host about that.

In so far as life troubled Mr de Walters at all the hotel was the source of his distresses. It had been built as a result of much publicity, in Portugal, about development in the Cape Verdes; a landing field to be built for super jets and a great campaign of advertising in the *New Yorker* and *Holiday* about the latest thing in getaway places. If Tahiti could do it why not the Cape Verdes? The answer seemed to be that Tahiti just has more to sell. The promotional campaign had somehow never got started and the only solid memorial to that five-year-old big talk was the London Palace.

The hotel didn't quite have the Hilton feel, though there were two penthouse rooms on the third floor if you didn't mind the slight inconvenience of a flight of stairs to the bathroom. Water was certainly a snag, the shortage acute on St Vincent, which meant taps working twice a day for two hours. There was consider-ably more liquid in the bar than anywhere else in the building.

But it all had a charm that was felt at once. It was naïve. You noticed the little things, like the one pot of geraniums by the front door. Also, the manager had an imported English dog, a setter, which slept in the lobby twenty-four hours a day, appar-ently dreaming of home. Then there was Mrs de Walters, a dark Rubens beauty with heavy eyebrows who had once seen a talking picture in which the leading lady wore one of those blouses that keeps slipping off a shoulder, resulting in heavy breathing from the leading man, and others. She was receptionist, barmaid, and apparently cook, but still with plenty of energy left over for sex. The manager explained that she was his second wife, the first Mrs de Walters having borne her husband nine children and then departed this life, possibly not sorry. Her replacement had all the rewards, as so often happens.

'How is London these days?' Mr de Walters asked, suddenly veering away from the hotel business.

'Being evacuated by all who can get out,' Mark said.

The manager leaned forward. He had been over in 1948, a wild boy, his memory richly stocked with experiences in Lyons Corner House, Piccadilly, and the Windmill Theatre. This went on until four twenty-three when he heaved himself up, with a sigh for youth lost.

'I think something to eat, eh?'

'At this time?'

'Sure. I get my wife to cook. Maybe we eat on the terrace. It's more cool.'

The view outside was in its way remarkable, a vista of dark volcanic rock and polished water. The harbour was huge, a crater which had blown a hole in one side to let the sea in. The sea had life and some movement, but everything else was dead, the land mass a jagged relic from a distant and disturbed geological period. A perfect anchorage had brought the coaling station and a need for service facilities the people.

Mark looked at the *Semirande*. Except for her riding lights she was blacked out. Almost a mile away the *Saturn* suggested a mini-liner, her bridge glass showing a faint glow and all the deck oysters on, wasting Jessie's electricity. She was lying close in to the dredger, ready to growl at intruders.

The meal which arrived certainly wasn't breakfast, goat stew seasoned with chillies together with a red wine from the Canaries which the natives there had refused to drink. Also, Mrs de Walters wasn't in a breakfast mood at all, moonlight did something to her, and though she didn't actually join them she served and hung about, quite often over the table. She was the kind of presence who really needs gypsy music in support plus a real taste for the outsize on the part of her audience. Deodorants apparently hadn't reached St Vincent.

After serving coffee the lady stayed away, obviously having decided that Mark was only half a man. With the pot was a bottle from which de Walters poured a clear, pale liquid he described as brandy, though it certainly wasn't that, nearer pure spirit and a local product, made from sugar cane on one of the other islands that could grow things. It might have been designed to put an approaching new day into an even odder perspective than marijuana and Mark signed off after two sips. But it was obviously the manager's tipple. It made him politically minded.

Politics in a hot climate tend to be nine parts talk to one part no action against the reigning military dictatorship and though de Walters had some nasty things to say about Mother Portugal who had let down the tourist industry he wouldn't have put one of them into a letter to the papers. Mark was interested to find out that the Cape Verdes had a bogey uniting the scattered islands, and this was Africa, with particular emphasis on Gutongo only 450 miles away. It was felt generally that the volcanic upheavals which had created their homeland really should have taken place half-way over towards South America. As things stood geographically quite a case could be made in the United Nations for incorporating the Verdes, as off-shore islands, in one of the new democratic fatherlands on the continent. Clearly the strongest racial strain here was African, but in spite of this the natives didn't want to have anything to do with their blood brothers once removed.

De Walters became most vehement. He wasn't, he said, speaking as an ex-Englishman in this matter, but as a Cape Verdian who would fight to the death any African dictator who dared set foot on this sacred soil.

'We will resist to the last man and the last bullet.'

'Is anyone thinking of invading you?'

'What he says and what he thinks are different.'

'Who?'

'General Makeke. The ruler of Gutongo. He is called "Our Father". It is blasphemy!' De Walters put down his glass to cross himself. 'We are Atlantis!' he announced.

Mark was winded. But the explanation seemed logical enough. When that fabled lost continent sank beneath the Atlantic a range of hills, mostly volcanos, at its southern tip remained above water, and these were the Verdes. Looking out at that view gave one the feeling that if this was so then Atlantis really couldn't have been all that myth has made it and perhaps it's better that it went.

'Makeke! Hah!' De Walters made the gesture of slashing his forefinger across his throat.

'Is that what you'd like to do to him?'

'Others will do it. Soon. I can even maybe tell you the name. The Foreign Minister. Pierre Wawatamba. He is a French black. You know, always in Paris. He brings back white girls for secretaries. He is a young bull and Makeke is an old bull. They fight. It has to be.'

'Would Wawatamba be any less of a threat to you?'

De Walters lifted his hands, palms upwards.

'Who can say? All you can be sure of is trouble coming.'

Mark was almost saddened, the Verdes had seemed immune, totally out of the world's news. It was depressing to find them, too, involved in the contemporary norm of trouble coming. In his experience there are only two types of place these days, trouble coming and trouble arrived. There's no escape. The lone yachtsman who sails for a nice quiet island in the South Seas is dead certain to anchor right in the middle of an Upu Upu independence from big bully Tawongi uprising. The only way to get really away from it all is to be on a tug in the mid-Atlantic during storm Force Ten and even there owners are liable to ring up any time to find out how you're handling their investment. You might just as well stay home and hope that the rioting students damage the other side of your street.

At dawn the dinner party broke up, presumably because it would soon be time for the siestas to start. Mark made his way down to the jetty and started the motor in the *Saturn*'s boat. The swamped crater was now brooding under first light, but the rocks around it were still black. He thought about Wawatamba over in Gutongo who was a young bull on the verge of inevitable conflict with the old bull Makeke.

No one seemed to notice him coming aboard. He left the boat drifting at the end of its painter and went to his cabin. On the glass table was a folded sheet, a signal from London, but unsigned.

CAPTAIN UNDERSON SATURN STOP MESSAGE RECEIVED STOP INVESTIGATION SHOWS TUG NAMED EN ROUTE SOUTH AMERICA TOW CONTRACT STOP

Lazzari *was* acting on his own initiative, and pushing out lies.

## CHAPTER TWELVE

THE SECOND came down from the bridge at the end of the dullest duty on a ship, a watch in harbour. Some skippers didn't insist on these, but Dartan did, and technically they were on standby for emergency. Between decks on the *Semirande* felt like inside a tin oven which has had the primus under it pumped up hard. Dead engines made no difference, nor did fans going in all cabins. The Verdes were supposed to offer a lot of mist and cloud but so far the sun had appeared every morning as a red ball that rocketed temperatures with its climb. The eyes got no rest from glare by turning to land where there was no green, and by noon even the town seemed to have been scorched into a brown stain.

It was a great town, too; you could eat in it, nothing else. The authority was Lecren who had been ashore after dark for intensive research. He said that all the girls were locked up at seven behind grilles. The young didn't appear to swing too much, the Bishop didn't approve of swinging and he was the real power in the islands. People were still afraid of hell, which probably wasn't surprising in a place that could have been its vestibule.

The Captain's door was open. Tourin looked in. Jules Dartan was sitting on the bunk in his underpants. The old were pretty disgusting with their shirts and the Skipper was no exception. His muscles were going stringy, and a roll of fat around his middle looked like an inflated life preserver. Sweat trickled down from his armpits and glistened on his chest. He was leaning forward with a tooth-glass in one hand. The brandy bottle was on the deck.

'Tourin! Has Berand taken over the watch?'

'Yes, sir.'

'What about those shore leave men? Isn't the boat due back?'

'Any time now.'

'How many are off?'

'Seven. But three of them got extended leave.'

'What the hell to do? Who gave them that? You?'

'No, sir. The Mate.'

'Do they all know I want no contact of any kind with the *Saturn*'s crew?'

'They were told. Lecren says the *Saturn*'s men aren't coming ashore. Maybe they prefer that air-conditioning they've got.'

'Nonsense! Sailors'll come ashore. And we're not meeting up with them in cafés when they do. Were you thinking of taking the boat back yourself?'

'Yes, sir.'

'Well, I'd better come with you. Keep an eye on things. I'll get dressed. Tell me when the boat's alongside.'

In spite of the heat Tourin shut his cabin door. He said loudly: 'Hell and bugger!'

Jules Dartan had both his elbows on the table, leaning forward over it. The old man had been making good use of his escape from the Mate. His speech was starting to slur.

'You want to know what your trouble is, boy? You want to know?'

Tourin did not. He had abandoned polite deference to the Captain about an hour earlier.

'You haven't got punch, that's what it is. You know this, when you're on watch you're always looking at yourself on watch. Get it?'

Tourin nodded.

'I'm telling you for your own good. Because there could be a day when I might be recommending you for a job up. Get that? A job up.'

Tourin felt like asking where the hell a job up landed you with the Plentin Company, but kept quiet and looked at the barmaid. Any time she stopped shaving she could grow a respectable moustache. She was also in danger of losing something big at any moment from the slack catchment-area of her neckline. This wouldn't exactly make the evening, but it would be a diversion in a town that didn't have many of these to offer, at least not to sailors.

'When you're on watch, Tourin, see yourself as skipper. Don't look over your shoulder. Don't think about the Mate or me watching. It's your command. Pretend we're dead or something.'

It wasn't ever easy to pretend that Jules Dartan was dead. He was the kind who make their living presence felt, in one way or another. The Skipper got up suddenly, took a moment over balance, then moved off towards the bar with two glasses and a knee sway that came from whisky on top of brandy and no food for some hours. His voice filled the bar with English that suggested a day tripper from Dieppe doing a try-out on the natives of Folkestone.

'So, Rosita, how go it, eh?'

The barmaid smiled, but it was pretty clear she liked her men younger and soberer, a dark glance travelling past the Captain towards the bar's only other customer. Tourin decided that there is a marked difference between wanting a woman and desperately wanting one, and that he hadn't moved into that second phase yet.

'The *Saturn* sailors, Rosita. They are coming to this place?

The woman shrugged. This covered what had been the exposed shoulder and bared the other. She poured two whiskies with a fine contempt for measures and shoved them over with a bottle of soda. Then she picked up a cloth and began rubbing the counter, contriving to move along down it out of range of the Captain's paw which had been making advances towards her bare arm. She looked at Tourin as she travelled. The message was simple, promising a memorable three-quarters of an hour just as soon as he could shake the old fool. Tourin lifted his hands palm upwards to indicate his present unavailability, not cancelling the booking, just asking for a later reservation. There would be many other nights in St Vincent, his need could so easily become urgent, and this might well be the best there was on offer in this town. It was curious that Lecren, who seemed to be quartering the island and concentrating on specific areas each time ashore, hadn't stumbled on this home from home. He was the sort who should have appealed to the barmaid, too; boyish, wearing lightly a sweet innocence that the mature woman longs to snatch away. Of course, Lecren could have been and gone. Away from that settled domesticity in Brest he was a restless hunter, and greedy, too.

Jules Dartan came back to the table with the glasses. He sat down and at once picked up the already exhausted theme of leadership qualities. It was a long-playing record and Tourin wished he could break the disc. He began to have new sympathy for Berand who usually had the job of trailing the Skipper and listening to him. Or maybe he didn't listen. If the Captain could see himself now, the image of the leader, slopping back whisky and drooling on about how to achieve the great heights of a tug command, it might sober him up. All bars ought to be mirrored from floor to ceiling just so that patrons could see themselves disintegrating. It should work wonders for the cause of temperance.

Rosita came out from behind her altar and set about polishing tables, finally reaching the only one in use. She wiped around their glasses, then leaned forward, coming between the two men, but only interested in one of them.

'I'd rather have you in bed than a Dutch bolster,' Jules said, pinching her bottom.

She swung around and delivered an open-handed right to the Skipper's jaw. The smack of this was loud, but Dartan didn't even flinch, he made a grab at her. She flipped away with the buxom grace of a Spanish dancer.

'Her husband must be past caring,' Jules said. 'I'll bet every man on the island's laid her.'

It was clear Rosita did not understand French. She went back to the bar, humming. It looked for a moment as though the incident had switched the Captain from what was needed for command to sex, which might have been more interesting. But suddenly Dartan elected silence, sitting slumped in his chair, staring at his glass, not even bothering to lift it. From somewhere in the hotel came the distant whining of an accordion. It might be the manager they had seen coming in, past a dog, turning to music for consolation.

Tourin sipped his whisky. He'd had too much himself and knew it. He was coming near to the stage of sorrow, when he saw the sailor's life as this, nothing more, sitting in a bar during rationed shore leave with the choice of finding a woman or staying with a bottle. It was the gay life all right. People who worked in the same office for twenty years envied the man of the sea his wild freedom, port after port with different bars and different girls.

'I think maybe we ought to get a meal, Captain. You can eat here.'

'What?'

'Food. We both need some.'

Jules stirred. He jerked his head, shaking himself back into authority.

'No. Going to look for our crew. Don't want 'em . . . mixing with *Saturn* men.'

'Why not, sir?'

'Eh? I told you. Bunch of spies.'

The Captain might think he had hit this theme before, but he hadn't.

'Spying on us, you mean?'

'Sure.'

'Have we anything to hide?'

'We . . . we're on a mission.'

'I thought we were on a new station?'

'In this bloody place? Hell, no. We stay here a while. Do the job. Clear off.'

'And the *Saturn*'s curious about our job?'

'Followed us in, didn't she?'

Tourin was even more interested.

'You mean . . . after we passed them at sea?'

'Yes.'

'Is that why you altered course? You didn't want to be recognized?'

Jules nodded. He frowned, as though a recollection disturbed him.

'What about their engine trouble, Captain?'

'Hell! Did you hear those engines as they came in? Turbine gone? Nothing wrong with them. Could sail now if they wanted to. But they're sitting here. Watching us.'

'Surely they've got to deliver that dredger sometime?'

'Doesn't matter when. Watching us more important.'

Another customer came through the arch from the lobby. Tourin had seen the man twice before. It was Mark Underson. He walked over to the bar. Rosita put up a hand and fluffed out her hair.

The *Saturn*'s Captain looked over at the occupied table. Jules became aware of something happening behind him and turned his head. The two men stared at each other. There was no greeting. Underson ordered a small whisky.

'How about that meal, sir?'

Jules didn't seem to have heard. He put his palms flat on the table and pushed himself up. He did a slow about turn and began to move, with a hurricane roll, towards the bar counter. He docked a few feet along from Underson but took his time about a tie-up, just holding on tight for seconds. Then he straightened.

'We are meeting again, Captain Underson.'

'So we are. And in an out-of-the-way corner.'

Underson didn't smile. No one was smiling, not even Rosita. She had suddenly become the wife of the proprietor, aware that a situation was developing which could easily result in damage to the fitments.

'I am hearing you are with engine trouble?'

Underson nodded. 'That's right. Fortunately we can fix it ourselves. Though I'm worried about the delay in delivering our tow. How would you like to take the dredger on to Gutongo for us?'

Jules took both hands away from the bar counter. He seemed almost sobered up.

'God damn! What you mean by that, eh? What you mean?'

'I was just offering you another shared tow, Captain Dartan. You seem to be free just now. And it's not far to Gutongo. A nice little first job from your new station.'

'Listen to me, you boy with big head. I don't share nothing with you ever! I don't take your tows! I don't even take your woman next time I see her.'

Underson didn't move. His voice stayed quiet.

'If you weren't a drunk you'd be lying on the floor.'

'I drunk? I show you . . .' Tourin moved fast but he didn't manage to get between the two men. A voice from the door did that.

'Jules!'

Dartan's lurch forward was arrested. He put out one hand to steady himself. Berand didn't appear to hurry from the archway. 'It's your watch on the ship,' he said.

'Eh?'

'You heard me. We go now.'

'This man . . .'

'We go now, Jules. Tourin! Take his other arm.'

Mark Underson didn't turn to watch that exit. Rosita broke a tableau of frozen attention, reaching for the whisky bottle.

'Make it a large one.'

There was silence while she poured. Mark took his glass to a table and sat down, back to the bar. He didn't see Berand's return until the *Semirande*'s Mate was standing alongside.

'Captain Underson. I must offer an apology.'

'None is called for. From you.'

'On behalf of another, then. He has taken too much to drink.'

'That was obvious. I made allowances. But if we meet again when he's sober the chances are I won't respect his venerable years.'

'I would ask you perhaps to understand.'

'What?'

'He is under some distress of the mind.'

'Like to tell me about it?'

'I cannot.'

'I see. But perhaps you'll be able to explain why the *Semirande*, which appears to be doing nothing, won't continue to Gutongo with my tow?'

'Is that why you say to Jules?'

'Yes. A fair enough offer, I'd have thought. Shared fee. I wonder why he resented it?'

The Mate didn't answer at once.

'We are on station for emergency here. A tow is not our business now.'

Mark smiled. 'I admit I'd be in a distressed state, too, if my ship had been assigned to station here. Owners can do mad things at times. But I'd have put up a fight about it in company offices. These can be more useful than fights in pubs.'

The Mate wanted away. He took refuge in formality.

'I have expressed regrets. If this is not acceptable, I am sorry.' He turned and went off for escort duty. Mark watched the man's back, with no feeling that his anger had started to cool.

Jessie Lawton had never consciously admitted to a sadistic streak. She wasn't prone to self-analysis, believing that the successful watch others, not themselves. In her experience the self-watchers were invariably commercial failures, those who have made it far too busy for any such nonsense.

Now, however, she didn't deny herself the very real pleasure of having Luke Sharkif Lazzari exactly where she wanted him, which was in a chair opposite to hers in a London hotel bedroom, the man almost green with terror. The door was locked and the key to it in her handbag.

He had taken some finding, in Paris for the day, arriving back on an early evening flight, located at Heathrow Airport, conveyed into the city by private hire, and now in her presence for nearly an hour, suddenly a little man whose balloon of a world had been pricked. He had shouted and wept, wailed and tried a final round of shouts, but was back to near tears again.

'Chessie, I did not know! I swear. You got to believe me.'

There was no reason at all why she should believe him. To do so would require an almost wild leap of faith. Further, there was nothing in the man's history which would make anyone of sense contemplate such a jump. He was what she had always known him to be, a man who had spent his life skating on thin ice that could have dropped him into jail at any time, and it now appeared had on more than one occasion. His offence lay not in this, but that he had dared to conduct his operations on the assumption that she was to a considerable degree a fool. It was not an assumption she could forgive easily, and she had no intention of doing so. What she did mean to do was use him.

'Mr Lazzari, you admit to having sold Henri Plentin a quantity of arms some time ago. You have also just admitted, after half an hour of pressure, that your business with the Plentins didn't end there. They hired you as a commercial spy and your role was to give them information about what happened at Anglo-European board meetings.'

'Chessie, not *hired*! I am blackmailed. When he finds out I am in jail in Algeria he can make me be sent away from England. From France, too. Forever! I don't have any more permit to be here. I am ruined!'

'That, at least, is the truth.'

Jessie found a cigarette. She took her time about lighting it. The silence in the room was ominous. Lazzari tried to find a place, walls, furniture, curtains, on which his eyes could rest with something like comfort. But he failed. They continued to roll, seeming incapable of any kind of fixed focus, their contact with his inquisitor fleeting, as though there was something about a woman sitting in terrible composure which positively seared his retinae.

'My God, you don't listen to me! You don't hear what I say. Sure, I sell him guns. You know I do this business. So you also know, too, I am agent for placing money from that business in companies here. You know damn well where the money comes from for your company!'

She said nothing.

'Okay, you can keep quiet! But you *know*. And when have you said: "Don't do this, Lazzari"? "It's bad for a respectable firm, Lazzari"? I tell you what you are, Chinese monkey, three in a row. You don't hear anything, nor see something, nor speak.'

Jessie blew out smoke.

'I suppose you'll be able to pick up again in Beirut,' she said quietly. 'Where you left off some years ago? Or have you a special reason for not wanting to go home. The Lebanese police, perhaps?'

His eyes focused then, in a stare. His rally had been brief and served him not at all. What it had done was drive this woman farther towards a position from which she would be implacable.

'Chessie, *please*! All I say is I don't know about the dredger. Not one little thing. I don't know what Plentin does with the guns he buys from me. He tell me nothing. He don't use me to fix up the Antwerp tow, I tell you that. It's just ordinary business.'

'How about the signal you sent to *Saturn* saying that the *Semirande* was on its way to South America?'

'I do it, yes. Plentin make me. But this is all I do for him.'

'What you mean is it's all you had time to do before you were caught. Though I'm sure he's now in possession of photostats of all our recent business. Is that so?'

Lazzari managed to hold his eyes down to the carpet.

'The commercial spy is vermin,' Jessie said.

'Okay, you call me this. What I say is I do not lie to you now. It's no good. You find out truth anyway.'

The tribute softened her slightly. Lazzari just might have come to the end of his deceits, from terror and exhaustion if nothing else. And if the Plentins had been involved in the shipment of arms on the dredger it was something they could arrange easily enough without using this man. In fact the more she thought about it the more improbable it seemed that Henri Plentin would use him as anything more than a petty spy. It had been a grave tactical error to allow Lazzari to get to the centre of Anglo-European. The Plentins would be laughing at her for a fool. She didn't like the thought.

The phone rang. It was her booked call to the Cape Verde Islands. 'Is that you, Captain?'

'Yes, Mrs Lawton.'

'I have Mr Lazzari with me now.'

'How is the little bastard?'

'In a confessional mood.'

Lazzari was rubbing his chin as though he had just discovered he needed a shave.

'I hope you've given him my message? And I still mean it!'

'I'm sure. Actually, Mr Lazzari is not responsible for the arms being on the dredger. He's convinced me of that. Though it seems highly probable he was the salesman.'

'I was right! Who did he sell them to?'

'The Plentins.'

It was a moment before Underson said, 'You're sure about this?'

'No, I can't be sure. The evidence is incomplete. However, I think it will pile up. I have here a list of the items involved in Mr Lazzari's last sale and delivered to the Plentins. I'll read it slowly and you might take it down to see if it tallies with the contents you found in the buckets. You won't have the inventory with you?'

'I know roughly what was in the buckets we opened.'

'Six Bren guns,' Jessie said.

'We found them.'

Lazzari was squirming in his chair.

'Five thousand hand grenades.'

'Our estimate was three. But there could be another two buckets full.'

'Two hundred and fifty Czech rifles.'

'About right, I'd say. Ours were Czech. How was the stuff got on the dredger? Lazzari doesn't know?'

'That's so.'

'You believe him?'

'I believe it's unlikely that the Plentins would use him for the operation. Why should they? I'm sure they have more reliable operators. Mr Lazzari was blackmailed by the Plentins into serving as a commercial spy against us. Fortunately, the damage appears to be minimal.'

'What are you going to do?'

'Nothing precipitate. I'm considering the matter. There are several courses open to me. We don't know yet why the Plentins were sending arms into Gutongo, or to whom.'

'I can give you a very near guess.'

'What?'

'From talk here. There could be a revolution any time over there in the Republic. The man likely to be behind it is one Pierre Wawatamba, the present foreign minister. He goes to France a lot. Has many friends there apparently. Could be the Plentins are amongst them.'

Jessie controlled an impulse to tell Underson what she had found out in the morning about the Plentins' copper interests in Gutongo. The Captain knew quite enough to be going on with.

'Wait a moment, please,' she said, putting a hand over the mouthpiece. 'Mr Lazzari, I want you to go into the bathroom. Turn on all the taps. In both the basin and the tubs. Shut the door and wait in there until I call you.'

'Chessie, what is this . . . ?'

'Do what I say!'

He went, with an almost painful slowness, feet dragging. The door shut. In a moment there was the sound of water.

'I wanted Mr Lazzari out of earshot,' Jessie said into the mouthpiece. 'He is now. I don't think he's going to get a chance in the next few days to contact his new employers in Brest, but you never know. He's a slippery fish. I want to arrange some kind of code with you.'

'And I want to know what you're up to.'

'I can't tell you that since I don't know myself yet. But if I try an experiment that is beginning to form as a possibility you'll get a signal to the *Saturn* as to whether or not it has been a success. Some simple phrase should do very well. How about . . . the fruit is rotten?'

'Appropriate.'

'When you get that signal, Captain, you will dump everything in those buckets, leaving nothing at all, not even one grenade.'

'You mean into the harbour here?'

'No. At sea. You'll sail tonight for Gutongo. To deliver the dredger.'

'Are you letting the Plentins get away with . . .'

'Don't be so suspicious, Captain! I'm certainly not doing that. Very far from it. If my plans don't work out as I had hoped you'll get another signal, to turn north and come back to Europe. Bringing the dredger with you. And all those arms still in their buckets. Is that clear?'

'I'm not with you at all!'

'At this stage it's better that you shouldn't be.'

'Now, listen! We found that stuff. If we hadn't you'd have lost your crew and probably your ship . . .'

'I'm well aware of my debt to you and your crew in this matter, Captain. I think you'll find me not ungrateful. But I never go into detail about plans that are not completely formed. As soon as I can I'll put you in the picture. Meantime you'll proceed to sea with your tow. Your turbines have been repaired and you are completing a contractual agreement.'

'Mrs Lawton, I will *not* be put off in this way!'

'You have no choice in the matter. You have my order to sail. See that you carry that order out at once. Goodnight, Captain.'

'Wait . . . !'

She hung up. She hadn't told him where she was. It seemed improbable that the hotel operator had done this.

'Mr Lazzari, you can come out now.'

He came out, followed by a great cloud of steam, looking like a man at a damp end to his active life.

Berand's role as officer of the watch on overtime was nominal. He had brought out a pillow and blanket for mattress and was lying on deck-boards. There were no stars, night had lifted haze from the sea and encased the island in it like a huge sheet of cooking foil. Heat was now pressurized, contained and concentrated, slow cooking flesh in its own juices.

Earlier he had written his usual weekly message to Celeste, on a picture card. She preferred them to letters, much reading a chore to her, and cards, particularly highly coloured ones, could be arranged in decorative patterns that proclaimed her status in life, of a wife who had to do a lot of waiting, perhaps, but was none the less sure of her man, certain that he would come back to her from his travels bringing no disturbing surprises with him, just another piece of embroidery. Celeste was neither imaginative nor particularly intelligent, her feel for living more instinctive than anything, she knew her role as a woman and fulfilled it without apparently being conscious of any discontents at all.

They had lived in the same small apartment for twenty-five years with never any talk of a move. Even changes in their domestic arrangements made her uneasy until she got used to them, she hadn't wanted the washing machine he had bought her, it wasn't necessary, she had managed fine without it. That machine hadn't really settled in to become part of her weekly patterns for years.

They didn't own the car they could easily have afforded, Celeste refusing even to contemplate the idea of learning to drive, defending her position by stories of terrible road accidents. She was still pretty, and looked ten years younger than her age, but would no more have thought of taking a lover than she would of neglecting her nightly prayer.

Berand knew that it was always the same prayer, evolved long ago as a reliable formula, more or less reminding the Almighty that it was His job to keep everything as it was and not serve any unpleasantnesses to His humble. If she had a theology at all it was that God took particular notice of the greedy, serving them out the chastisements they deserved. This made her highly suspicious of all status symbols, like washing machines, a car, and a bungalow standing in its own grounds.

He felt strayed from Celeste in this heat, physically and in his mind, aware that its intensity would have frightened her and perhaps fractionally frightened of it himself because of this. He did not really like his journeys into areas beyond her possible comprehension, as though these threatened what they had together. Mentally he had always gone his own way, but when with her concealed this as much as possible, not wanting to draw any lines under a separate identity. What he loved in his wife was her simplicity and a sweetness from it that was not saccharine. In a way this was what he loved in Jules, too, though there was no issue of sweetness from that bellowing fool. Jules was simple in his unhappiness.

There isn't a great deal you can do for a man who has no idea what he really wants from life and so is given to repeated and rowdy demonstrations against it, except, of course, to see that he gets enough sleep after one of the riots. What judgement Jules had, and as a sailor this was considerable, tended to be clouded by vanity. It had been almost pathetic to meet him in a Brest café after that last interview with Henri Plentin, Jules the new fleet commodore, a long phantasy about himself suddenly apparently confirmed, a man in his fifties belatedly making it big. He'd shown no perspective at all on what had happened or on himself and immediately after swearing an oath of total secrecy had poured out the story. Or most of the story. There were indications now that he hadn't told quite all, these from a slight gloom that had set in after the *Semirande* sailed and increased as they travelled south.

The more something troubled Jules the more confident he became that he was simply showing nothing at all, putting up an effective front. 'A distress of mind.' That phrase had somehow just slipped out to the *Saturn*'s Captain, not really meant when used, but seen now as appropriate enough. In some way that tug anchored over there had become important to Jules Dartan, almost a symbol. Of his conscience? There was certainly a kind of haunting. Berand remembered that almost ridiculous panic when the *Saturn* had been sighted at sea, only partially accounted for by old Plentin's order, and on the day when he had seen the other tug come sailing into this flooded volcano Jules had come very near to doing a Hamlet facing his father's ghost. Something had been said in a Brest office which Jules had preferred to keep out of his account, deciding to sweep it under the carpet. But whatever it was had legs and kept creeping out again, each time bigger than before.

There was a stumbling noise inside the wheel-house. Berand sat up. The sliding door was open. Jules came lumbering through it out on to the wing, continuing straight on to the bridge hang-over. He had a particular walk during his recovery phases, as though he didn't quite dare to lift his feet. It wasn't much better than a shuffle. The chances were that he wouldn't be able to recall anything that had happened at the hotel. He was already suffering from total blackouts.

Berand watched. Jules propped himself against the rail, his total interest the *Saturn*. It was almost incredible that the man who had been put to bed could have rallied so soon, and now he'd be about as approachable as a bear with toothache. Berand decided to risk it. He got up and went over.

'Something wake you, Jules?'

'Eh? Oh, it's you. What the hell are you doing here?'

'Finishing your watch.'

There was no reaction to that. After a moment Jules said:

'*Saturn*'s got her engines on.'

'I don't hear them.'

'Not so easy here. You get it below decks. Definite vibration.'

His words were only slightly muzzed at their edges.

'There! Hear it now? Revving up.'

The *Saturn*'s deck lights came on. In a moment she was glowing like a cruise liner, even the towers illuminated. The display was impressive; it should have been finished off with her name in two feet high red neon over the bridge. It was a wonder Underson hadn't thought of that for advertising. He was one of the smart boys who knew that if you didn't light up your own performance no one else would. Berand now had the feeling he had come off second-best at that encounter in the hotel a few hours ago. It was something to be expected when you are apologizing for another to an angry man. And Underson had certainly been angry, with much more behind feeling than a drunk's insult to his wife.

'Sailing,' Jules said heavily, as though this troubled him. 'Turbine trouble! Like hell.'

The diesels had become clearly audible, a deep thumping, huge horse-power stirring.

'There's nothing wrong with her engines and never has been. So what, Jules?'

'They came in here to check up on us.'

'That's the drink still talking.'

'Shut up!'

'Tourin tells me you were going on about spies. Not very sensible in a public place.'

'I said shut up!'

'What's the matter with you?'

'Leave me alone. I'll finish my watch. Go to your bunk.'

'It's cooler up here.'

'I gave an order!'

'I don't accept it.'

Jules half-turned. 'Damn you, Berand!'

The dredger's anchors were being lifted, her winches sounding as though they were driven by some underpowered donkey engine. The monstrous raft had only riding lights and a feeble glimmering in her living quarters. Someone was moving around her with a powerful torch. Those buckets, in their weird white jackets, looked like washing left out overnight on a hillside bleaching green.

'The *Saturn* came here for a telephone,' Berand said.

'What are you talking about?'

'Ginole's sure they've never been on the air since putting out one message after we met up with them that night. Maybe they didn't feel the air was secure. The phone from here would be. It's a cable line.'

'Ginole doesn't listen to his boxes round the clock.'

'No, but he's been doing it for more than normal transmission hours. And picked up nothing out from the *Saturn*. But there was one in. It said in their company code that we were en route to South America.'

'What? Why the hell didn't Ginole tell me?'

'I told him not to. I thought you might be upset by that signal. It seems you are.'

'My God! It shows they're spying on us all right.'

'No Jules. Just curious. Not surprising in the circumstances. What interests me, though, is where their company office got the information that we were on the way to South America. It sounds almost like a Plentin cover hand-out.'

'What are you getting at?'

'Looking for the truth. It seems pretty well hidden. As soon as the *Saturn* anchored Underson went ashore to the hotel to use their phone. Lecren found that out. From the barmaid. Underson took a room there . . . maybe to wait for calls? The barmaid fancied him. She seems to fancy quite a few. Lecren was laughing about it. I gather he was the first from us to get satisfaction. But if we stay here for three months he won't be the last.'

'That bitch!'

'Not that I think we're going to stay here for three months. Or anything like it. Jules, what do you know about our training mission in this place that you haven't told me?'

'Nothing!'

'I don't believe you. Something happened at your meeting with Plentin that's been worrying you ever since. Perhaps something that was said about the *Saturn*?'

'Balls!'

'What's on your mind has a sharp enough edge to cut through one of your hangovers. And I've never known anything to do that before.'

'You're like a bloody nagging wife!'

'I'm waiting for you to finish the story of your interview with Henri Plentin.'

'You can wait.'

'Did he tell you that you might be getting the *Saturn*? As flagship of the new fleet?'

Jules's body seemed to roll around against the rail. Light from the *Saturn* showed him staring. He put up one hand and dragged it down over his face, as though to get slackened muscles back under control.

'What kind of dirty business is this, Jules?'

'Leave me alone!'

'Like hell I will. What did Plentin say to you?'

'Nothing! Nothing!'

'You have no flair as a liar.'

'I tell you he didn't say anything. Only . . .'

'Yes?'

'Well, the Scotch woman might sell. That's all.'

'And you've been brooding about that ever since?'

'I . . .'

'What is it?'

'Oh, God damn!'

'The fact that the Scotch woman might sell was so much on your mind that when we ran into her ship you took the kind of evasive action that happens in war, not peace. Why didn't you want the *Saturn* to identify us?'

Two big hands were massaging the wood of the railing. Jules stared again over water. The dredger was now drifting free, the tow cable to her submerged. The *Saturn* had started to move forward on her anchor chain. A forward deck winch whirred.

'I know nothing,' Jules said with a kind of dismal stubbornness.

'You've just been putting in overtime at guesswork? And all the while a small smell has been growing into a big stench.'

'That's not true! I haven't done anything. I didn't tell Plentin that . . .'

'You'd co-operate in his schemes?'

'There was *no* scheme. Not that he told me.'

'Still you now believe there was one. A plan. And you have a passive part in it. Passive at this stage. Jules . . . you're a bloody fool!'

'What?'

'Not to tell me. This training scheme. These men who are going to be flown down to us. You're going to need a new crew to take over this ship after the Plentin company has ordered us to man the *Saturn*.'

'I . . . don't know what you're talking about!'

'You know damn well what I'm talking about. We're down here to be handy for Gutongo. Henri Plentin had no idea how long he might have to wait before he can grab the *Saturn*. But he means to do it. And we're on station to help him when the time comes.'

'No! I don't believe it.'

'Listen to me, Jules. Whatever was planned in Brest Underson has somehow got on to it. And he thinks we're part of it all. He believes that we're waiting here to take over his ship.'

'It's impossible!'

'Is it? He offered you that tow, didn't he? As a kind of challenge. And you flew into a rage.'

'It was not . . .'

'It was what conscience you have left screaming!'

Berand felt exhausted by anger and heat. He didn't want to go on shouting, there was no point in it. And Jules would only continue to protest his innocence. This he had, of a kind; the negative innocence of a man who has reason to suspect an evil is being done from which he will benefit, and who faces up to the situation by going into strict neutral. Few would blame him, most might say that he had been sensible. Berand blamed him because this thing went flat against what Jules Dartan had always been as a man. That bulging dossier of noisy vices meant nothing, but a new addition to them did. It left Berand as shocked as a maiden aunt who had just learned of incest in the family.

The *Saturn*, with anchor up, was building speed, the tow hawser taut astern, her course beginning a great loop that would take her to port of the *Semirande* for the harbour entrance. Lights began to go out on her decks, as if a host was going around after a party, extinguishing the lamps. Berand felt the sailor's fleeting envy of another ship that is getting under way, escaping to the living sea from the dead, sterile calm of anchorage with engines shut down.

'Berand . . . what are you thinking?'

'It's time I had my own tug.'

# CHAPTER THIRTEEN

JESSIE LAWTON quite approved of the Brest hotel; it was provincial in feel, only superficially modernized, and in many ways reminded her of similar establishments in Edinburgh, though the food was better. That it had a name for its cuisine was obvious from the number of middle-aged businessmen using it for lunch, all of them eating large meals with serious attention to what went into their mouths. Her own order was an ungarnished fillet of steak, green salad and a single glass of red wine. Lazzari was eating hot Breton lobster washed down with a carafe of white and should have been happier than he looked.

The man's gloom had lasted for a long time. The Oriental—the Middle East was the Orient to Jessie—finds it very difficult to take a sportsmanlike attitude to defeat. She could understand, because the Scots find it very hard, too. And the unfortunate man opposite her was suffering from the additional humiliation of having been more or less bound hand and foot by a woman, a sex his ancestors had long regarded as only useful for child-bearing and doing all the rough work.

In victory she was being magnanimous and was trying to keep this occasion at least slightly social.

'I wonder whether French eating habits can have any direct bearing on their commercial activities?'

Lazzari looked up. 'What?'

'These large luncheons after a small breakfast. They must result in an early afternoon sluggishness. Particularly when taken with wine. I know I'd be half-asleep until tea-time.'

'They don't have tea-time,' Lazzari said.

'Precisely. I believe that we are more sensible eating often and less. Certainly there is too much starch in our diet, but I'm sure

that statistics would show the French indigestion rate as much
higher than ours. Probably the ulcer rate as well.'

'I don't know,' Lazzari said.

'The point I'm making,' Jessie said with great patience, 'is that
if you want to catch a French businessman at a time in the day
most advantageous to you, between half-past two and half-past
three would seem to be best. So I think we'll skip cheese.'

Jessie found her gloves and handbag, then stood. At the next
table three men looked up, not at a woman but at her diamonds.
She was wearing a few more of these than she usually did on a
business trip, with a particularly fine sunburst on the lapel of a
plain suit. It had been the first thing she had bought herself after
Arthur's death, regarding it as a mourning brooch in that gentle
Victorian tradition, even though it didn't carry his initials or
contain a lock of his hair. The brooch had been something of a
bargain, too. Her jeweller had told her recently that it was now
worth three times what she had paid for it.

They reached the door of the hotel to find that the day, which
had been grey, had turned to drizzle.

'You wait here then,' Lazzari said. 'I get the car.'

It was improbable that he would make a bolt for it at this stage,
but you never knew. Jessie said that a little walk would do her
good, opened her umbrella, and went with him.

The girl receptionist was astonished.

'But you are requesting, without the appointment, to be visiting M'sieur Henri Plentin?'

'I am.'

'But Madame, this is impossible!'

'Not at all. You have only to tell him I'm here. The name is
Lawton. Mrs Jessie Lawton, chairman of Anglo-European.'

'I am sorry. But M'sieur Plentin has the conference.'

'Hardly likely at this time of day. If you mean he isn't back
from lunch yet, say so.'

'Pardon?'

'I will wait in his office. Where is it?'

'Dieu! Please, if you will seat yourself . . .'

'I don't sit in halls.'

The girl used the intercom. She looked like a harassed booking
clerk endeavouring to get a late arrival on to a flight that is just
leaving.

'Oui. Mais, cette dame . . . ? Ah, M'sieur Claude! Oui!'

The girl rose. 'You will receive attention of M'sieur Claude
Plentin. A moment, if you please.'

She went down a passage. Jessie turned to Lazzari.

'Who's Claude?'

He shrugged. 'I don't know. I never come here. I am at the château. There is no Claude. Just the old devil.'

She looked at him.

'I have a suggestion to make, Mr Lazzari. It is that you pull yourself together. Try to look more like a man of affairs than you are doing at the moment.'

'You think I have some affair left?'

'Yes. If you play your cards right. I expect to be backed up. I thought I made this quite plain last night?'

'Oh, sure. Okay, I back you. But I don't like seeing him again, Chessie. I just don't like it.'

A young man approached. He wasn't tall, but still had a loose-limbed look, suggesting a certain lack of physical co-ordination. Jessie saw an awkward colt who held no promise at all of growing up into a winner. This minor obstacle wasn't going to hold her up for long. She allowed him to introduce himself and then took the smile from his face by asking for immediate audience with his father. It saddened him that this could not be arranged at the moment.

'Young man, I have travelled all the way from Scotland to see your father on a matter vital to one of the Plentin companies. There was no time to make appointments. If your father does not see me it will only be a very short time indeed before he bitterly regrets his mistake. Please tell him that from me.'

'Madame, this way.'

Claude opened a door and ushered Jessie and Lazzari into the map room. She stared in astonishment at the Plentin world and while she was doing this the door closed again.

'What an extraordinary way to watch your interests. They even have flags for their ships.'

'I tell you, Chessie, he's God.'

'Not quite.'

'I think maybe I go now as emigrant to California.'

'They wouldn't let you in, Mr Lazzari. Even on a visitor's visa. Your talents are particularly suited to a European environment, and in a time of change.' She looked around. 'This must be the board room. It could do with a coat of paint. I've heard he's mean with his re-fits, too. But I rather like the idea of running a huge business like this from a converted house. Upstarts would have insisted on a twelve-storey glass box.'

The door opened.

'My father will see you, Madame.'

Claude seemed astonished.

'Good. Come along, Mr Lazzari.'

'I think not the gentleman also, please.'

'Oh, yes. Where I go the gentleman goes.'

Jessie went out into the hall, nodding to the receptionist, who was staring. They climbed stairs and turned left, towards what had obviously been the better bedrooms. They went through a former dressing-room off one of these in which sat an outraged-looking female with red hair, and Claude knocked once on a door.

'*Entrez!*'

The door swung open, revealing the head of the Plentins behind his desk. Grey light from a window shone on a bust study, cut off by mahogany at chest level, the kind of head that is never seen in public life because its owner is always too busy over his private affairs. It was a face without any hint of arrogance from vanity, a smooth, neutral statement about power long held and long wielded with practised competence. Both his hands were on a blotting pad, both doing nothing. They looked like a pair of pale spiders waiting in a cave.

'*Madame Lawton.*' Claude said. '*Et . . . et un autre.*'

Henri Plentin looked first at the 'autre'. He didn't like what he saw. An expression crept on the mask, a reluctant admission of anger. A faint tinge of colour started on the pate and worked down.

'*Fermez la porte, Claude!*'

His son did what he was told, closing himself out. Jessie cleared her throat, refusing to admit to a slight twinge along nerves, like a first threat of toothache. Her French was always a literal and direct translation.

'*Bon apres-midi, Monsoor Plentin.*'

He acknowledged this with what looked like a quickly reconsidered decision to stand. Then he said:

'I think it is perhaps best to use English, Madame Lawton. Will you sit down? And your . . . ah . . . companion. His function?'

'A co-director of Anglo-European.'

'But of course. I am honoured. To have both of you.'

There were chairs to each side of the desk. Jessie took one. Lazzari was reluctant to go to the other, it was too close to coming action. She had to point.

'And now your business? There was talk to my son of vital matters? I am very occupied at the moment with affairs.'

'We won't waste time, I hope. I understand you have met Mr Lazzari before?'

'You are mistaken.'

'I think not. He sold you a quantity of arms. I have an itemized list here.'

Jessie opened her bag. Nothing happened in the Plentin face. The slight flush had gone, flesh tone again putty.

'I find this somewhat absurd.'

'There is the list.' Jessie pushed it across the desk. It was not picked up. 'That tallies exactly with a quantity of arms discovered aboard a dredger my tug *Saturn* had in tow. The guns are apparently identifiable by their numbers and can be traced to the suppliers, the grenades to their manufacturers.

Hands lifted from a pad, then fell back on it.

'Grenades? What next? No tanks?'

Jessie delved in her bag again. She produced a case and a cigarette from it which she lit with a glitter from fingers holding the gold lighter.

'There is one link that hasn't yet been fitted in the chain back to you, Monsoor Plentin. Or perhaps you might say two. I have no doubt, however, that the French and Belgian police, when alerted, will be able to do this for us. We do not yet know what happened to the goods on that list after they were delivered by Mr Lazzari's principals in this matter to an address you gave him. But we will be able to supply the police with that address, and also with a reasonable theory about how the goods were then transported to Antwerp and stowed aboard a dredger being fitted out for its trip to Gutongo.'

Henri Plentin had been so still that his movement was a surprise, and Lazzari jumped. The old man reached across the desk to an intercom with a detachable mouthpiece, lifted this, and said:

'*Gaston? Ici!*'

The Plentin sons were well trained. They never finished what they were doing when summoned to their father. It took the third in line to the throne perhaps twenty seconds to arrive. He shut the door without being told to do so. Jessie turned her head and felt something of a pang. She had no one to succeed her in the Lawton enterprises so, in real terms, they had no future. The Plentins would go on forever, or at least until the final triumph of Marxism.

Gaston asked no questions. He sensed tension in the room at once and went behind Jessie to stand alongside his father. There was a chair available but he didn't take it. His look at Jessie was penetrating, as though he assessed at once that she might be, like the Aga Khan, worth more than her weight in precious stones. He then shifted that gaze to Lazzari and the tight expression relaxed into something near to distaste.

Certainly Lazzari was not at his best, a mere shell of himself, managing still to sit fairly upright in a straight-backed chair, but not to do much more. He hadn't uttered a word since coming into the room and didn't mean to if he could help it. Actually words from him weren't called for, just his presence and this was working very well.

'Madame Lawton has come here, Gaston, with the extraordinary accusation that we have been trafficking in arms.'

'Papa?'

'I'm not surprised you fail to understand. It is my condition also. But we must allow Madame to continue with her statement.'

'I've finished that,' Jessie said. 'We now come to the proposition.'

'Ah. This will be most interesting.'

'It is. An immediate amalagamation of Anglo-European and Plentin salvage tug interests.'

The father controlled surprise but the son showed it. Henri Plentin, quite slowly, pulled in his arms and folded his hands over the knobs on the chair.

'Madame Lawton, if I did not know you by reputation as a business woman of some note in your own country, I would say that you were demented.'

'Others have thought so, too, Monsoor. One or two of them have since gone into liquidation.'

'Are you suggesting this as the fate of the house of Plentin if we decline to listen to your ridiculous proposition?'

'It's far from ridiculous. After all, this is the age of forced mergers. Though usually it is the big companies forcing the little one. I'm happy that for once that trend can be reversed.'

'I have to give you credit for remarkable confidence.'

'Thank you. My mother used to say that I was born with it. I think perhaps I was. But let me point out here that I wouldn't be coming to what we might call this marriage empty-handed.'

'So it is now a forced marriage? Splendid. And the bride's dot? What is the English word . . . settlement?'

'My dot, Monsoor, would be a modern salvage tug, plus one of the best crews in the business commanded by a young captain with a future in our specialization. Also, I would realize my available assets in other areas and add them to our joint holdings. These should amount to the cost of yet another modern tug plus a considerable reserve in hand. I am quite agreeable to having this new ship built in France, and in one of the yards in which you have an interest. Under my supervision, of course.'

'Indeed? You would supervise from Scotland?'

'No. I shall live in Brest. I've had a look at it today. It seems quite suitable. And your climate appears to be rather like ours.'

'In my long career,' Henri Plentin said, 'I have rarely been astounded. I am now.'

Jessie smiled at him for the first time.

'Well, it's an interesting proposition when you have time to look at it.'

'Papa . . . ?'

'Gaston, we must allow Madame to continue. If you will permit, however, one question? When we decline to accept your remarkable proposition, what will be your next move?'

'A signal to *Saturn*. Which is now at sea under radio silence. Telling her to alter course with her tow and come here.'

'To Brest?'

'Yes. This will be my temporary headquarters for the next few months at least. I'm thinking of changing to a suite in the Grand Hotel where we are staying. The terms are remarkably moderate out of season.'

'Brest, I'm sure, is honoured. Your plan, if we were to accept this strange new alliance with the Scots, would be to have these arms dumped at sea?'

'That's right. And I don't see our alliance as strange at all. There has been, after all, the Concorde project.'

'Which has had its stresses, Madame.'

'Oh, indeed. But I'm prepared to make big concessions. For one, you can insert an 'e' in Anglo-European if you wish.'

'Thank you,' Henri Plentin said gravely. 'When your tug arrives in Brest with its strange cargo behind, what then?'

'It will be met by the French police. Possibly even the Belgian police. I wouldn't be surprised, either, if the United Nations commission on the international traffic in arms is also interested.'

'I'm sure they will be. But I fail still to see how there is any connection with the house of Plentin?'

'The police will be able to find one.'

'I think not. And I must point out, Madame Lawton, that you have not one shred of evidence beyond the circumstantial that could be used against us. And the circumstantial is most weak, as indeed it must be since it points in the wrong direction. It is inconceivable that there could be any charge against us in this matter under French law. Laughable, in fact.'

Jessie's composure was not dented. She stubbed out her cigarette in a desk ash tray.

'So I was told in Paris this morning. Mr Lazzari and I spent some hours there before coming on to Brest by private hire plane. Consulting the legal firm of Pleytour and Merand. They're quite well known, I believe?'

For the first time old Henri and his son exchanged a look. The lawyers were not unknown to them. Jessie was glad to see this for Pleytour and Merand's fees about which she had inquired carefully, were enormous.

'I'm afraid you've mistaken what I'm aiming for, gentlemen. A criminal prosecution may be, as you say, improbable. But it is publicity I'm after. Focused on a family business which has long preferred to operate quietly out of the public eye. The kind of publicity which, if it doesn't actually kill, can cause a grave illness. Most damaging to many of your interests. Particularly to those you still have in Africa. It seems to me that if I am successful you may have to take quite a number of those green buttons out of your map. Like the one you were obliged to remove from Gutongo. All this would be the almost direct result of tremendous public interest in a libel suit. Brought against me.'

Henri Plentin did not move, but there was an audible intake of Gaston's breath, loud enough to make Lazzari lift his head. Jessie waited for the old man's ironic comment. This didn't come.

'I think you'll be forced to go to law against me,' she said, 'after my indiscretions to the press when the *Saturn* has arrived here. It will make a remarkably lurid story. All about a bid on the part of a commercial family out to recover lost rights in a former colonial territory that is now a sovereign state. By fomenting armed rebellion. And using an innocent party as carrier . . . my tug. I've always understood that one of the nice things about France is the allowances made for women in matters of this kind. Our emotionalism. We are not, after all, completely rational. It gives us a licence that wouldn't be granted to a man at all. I feel a jury would be sympathetic. I'm not young, certainly, but I'm a widow who has staked what might be claimed as very nearly my all to build and run one salvage tug.'

Suddenly Henri Plentin smiled. 'I would suggest that the effect of that appeal would be greatly improved if you left off your diamonds when appearing in court!'

Jessie had the unpleasant feeling that her momentum was slackening while the old man's increased.

'Must we listen to more of this?' Gaston asked in English.

'But I'm enjoying it. Pray continue, Madame. Though I might raise one other small point. What if our reaction to this colourful story you intend to release to the press is not to sue you for libel, but to laugh?'

Jessie badly wanted a deep breath.

'Could you afford to do that? A number of things would have come under a bright spotlight. You bought arms for some purpose that you will have to explain. Would it be the same explanation you gave Mr Lazzari, whom you deny having met before? I very much doubt whether your active French press is going to believe that explanation. Particularly in view of your family's former copper interests in Gutongo. I am sure that everyone is going to understand that you would wish to recover these, in one way or another. But there mightn't be much sympathy for the way in which you had gone about it. By backing a man with whom you have recently been in contact here in France, and who is believed to be planning to overthrow the present government. If he was successful he would naturally be most grateful for your help. Grateful enough, perhaps, to return your copper franchise? I refer to the Gutonguese Foreign Minister, Mr Wawatamba.'

The use of that name was a wild gamble. It came off. Jessie saw this from Gaston's eyes. He hadn't his father's experience in the art of concealment. And it was that flash of panic that steadied down her nerves again, though she was even more conscious than she had been of what she had taken on, a juggernaut that could crush bodies which got in its path.

But there was no doubt she had established a sharp ascendancy again. It seemed sound policy to cut and run before this started to wane. Jessie found gloves in her bag, then rose.

'Mr Lazzari and I won't take up any more of your time at the moment, gentlemen. I'm sure you'll want a few hours to consider my suggestions. Supposing we say that if I haven't heard from you at my hotel by ten p.m. this evening I'll know that you have rejected my merger proposals? Good afternoon. Come along, Mr Lazzari.'

Jessie was given the bridal suite at the Grand Hotel. There were two floral displays by courtesy of the management. The salon made a somewhat formal setting for the first night of love, heavy drapes in solemn velvets, imitation Louis Quinze chairs and a settee, plus a selection of marble-top tables that were extremely cold to the touch. Lazzari prowled up and down the room looking like a highly frightened Balkan crown prince who has just heard of his father's assassination. He was chain smoking smelly cigarettes bought in the lobby.

Jessie was finding the waiting rather trying herself. Her appetite for dinner had been small even though the hotel made rather a ceremony of this meal, with three-piece string ensemble to aid digestion. Now she watched television, with the sound turned low, vaguely conscious that programme planners over here, too, filled the yawning gaps of ever threatening nothingness with American westerns.

'Chessie, I say it before, I say it again. Why you want to do this? You do all right with *Saturn*. And you say you got money for another tug.'

'Another tug isn't enough in this business. Not nearly enough. And precarious finance ties your hands.'

'Didn't I get you money?'

'Yes. But I'd prefer to operate without the kind of backing you produce. It could prove an embarrassment, to say the least. The Plentin resources are tremendous.'

'My God! You still think they take you in?'

'I think they have no other alternative.'

'So? What about they hire a couple of gunmen from Marseilles?'

'I would be more inconvenient to them dead than alive. Now that they know we've employed Merand. Didn't you notice how the name registered? I must thank you for Merand. He probably functions within inches of being disbarred. And grows rich on it. You really have your uses, Mr Lazzari. An ideal contact man. Though we will want you slightly more respectable in future.'

'You talk about future. I don't see it.'

'You will resign from your Monte Carlo employment. To function solely as my assistant. Watching Plentins. You won't be popular, but you'll have my protection.'

'Maybe I go to Australia.'

'You'll resign yourself to living in Brest.'

'Here? This place? I go crazy.'

'Paris will be available for week-ends.'

'You don't really mean to live here?'

'Why not? It's more central than Edinburgh. And this will be the company base. Also, I'm a little uneasy about Scotland. If the nationalist movement becomes a real threat there will be a great flight of capital from the country. At least capital like mine. I have no intention of operating from behind a new barrier against the English. The English have been most useful to me.'

Lazzari sat down and looked at his shoes. Louis Quinze didn't contain him well. There was gunfire from the television set. The Brest evening traffic sounded heavy.

Jessie wondered if she had left Henri Plentin's office too soon. A good deal had been left unsaid, on the principle that there can be too clear an understanding between new partners which makes it almost impossible for them to operate together. She had no doubt in her own mind that the central portion of old Plentin's plan, at which she had only hinted obliquely, had been to get the *Saturn* away from her. On the face of it the proposition had been simple enough. If the tug with its tow cargo intact had sailed into Gutongo the chances were that she would never have sailed out again under the Anglo-European house flag. If the rebellion had failed the source of arms would have been traced to the dredger quickly enough, the ship impounded, and the crew jailed. And in the event of Plentin's party, the rebels, winning, the new rulers would be only too willing to oblige their benefactor by detaining the tug at his pleasure. In either case the unfortunate owner would be faced with a ship laid up indefinitely. The only thing that would have been left to her to do was simply to cut losses and sell. And at Plentin's price.

It would be at his price because he had chosen his time well.

Bids for an impounded ship weren't likely to be many or generous, and the Hoofstangers, who might have taken advantage of an opportunity to get the *Saturn*, had recently tied up most of their available capital in new keels, a fact that Henri Plantin knew well.

Jessie felt no bitterness. She had been able to spring a trap before it did her any damage, and set another immediately. What more could you ask? Provided, of course, that your trap snapped down when it was meant to.

As a semi-partner of the Plentins she would never be trusted. That didn't matter so long as she was effective. Further, she meant to confine her interests from now on to salvage only, and this was just a branch of the Plentin affairs. The rest of their business would be none of her concern. They could keep their map and she wouldn't ask for office space in the converted residence. Anglo-European would have its own offices, with Lazzari on duty in them. Once he got his nerve back he would be all right. What he needed was a steadying hand now and then. At the moment she wasn't providing this too well, in fact could have done with one herself, not Arthur, someone more contemporary. Such help was not available, she was alone. She was accustomed to the condition.

'Mr Lazzari, I think I'll have a little of that brandy you had sent up.'

'God, yes! I have one, too.'

There was a clinking from a marble-topped surface. The western had finished on television, replaced by an announcer reading what appeared to be the news, but in the kind of rapid French which was going to be a real problem to the new immigrant. De Gaulle's deliberations were about the pace she could take, the General's tempo almost precisely that of her former French master at an Edinburgh ladies' college. The trouble was that he was the only man in the country who had trained himself to speak slowly. It might well be a national conspiracy to discourage immigration, but she would get over that hurdle, too, even if it meant learning to jabber at her age.

Lazzari came across with two glasses. One had much more in it than the other. 'They don't phone,' he said.

'It's still sixteen minutes to ten. We have to remember the shock this has been to them. It's the first time in three hundred years that the Plentins have opened their family ranks to admit a stranger.'

'You think you join the family?'

'Perhaps, in a sense.'

'Old Henri is a widower. Maybe you marry him?'

'That is not on the agenda.'

He went and sat down. Jessie watched the screen, hoping

nerves didn't show. She had been a little surprised to note a marked pulse palpitation in her wrist.

The idea of joining the Plentin family by adoption, and with her *dot*, opened up interesting possibilities. It was, after all, a large family and there were bound to be tensions within it. Gaston was only the third son, and yet he had been called to his father's side in a crisis. What about the two older ones? Wasn't it highly probable that they resented this penetration by their junior into the old man's confidence? In time she might well be able to exploit existing stresses, even winning adherents to the Jessie Lawton party. It might have been a mistake to dismiss young Claude, so obviously used as a kind of office boy, in such a summary manner. He had the Plentin blood, after all, and possibly vestiges of the family character waiting to be discovered. Perhaps by kindness. She wasn't practised in kindness as such, but had always been prepared to learn a new trick when it looked like being useful. Her future in France, whatever it held, was certainly not going to be dull.

The phone rang. Lazzari jerked to attention in the chair, spilling brandy. Jessie resisted an impulse to snatch up the receiver. The shrilling went on for a full half minute, with Lazzari staring, before she put out her hand.

'Hello? *Madame Lawton ici.*'

'Claude Plentin speaking.'

'Good evening.'

'Madame, I have been remaining in the office, you understand? For a message from the château.'

'I see.'

'This has now come from my father. He is telling me to convey to you.'

Jessie appreciated the use of an intermediary. It preserved dignity. 'And what does your father have to say?'

'He is wishing a meeting with you tomorrow morning. For a discussion of matters outstanding. At ten of the clock. In this office.'

'I am agreeable to the time suggested, Monsoor Plentin, but not the place. I would prefer to have the conference here in my hotel suite. With my French solicitors present. Will you please tell your father that we will be expecting him here, together with any other of the family directors he cares to bring?'

'But, Madame . . .'

'That will be all, I think. *Bon soir.*'

She hung up. Lazzari was on his feet. He hadn't paled, he couldn't, but there was an alteration in skin pigment.

'Have we . . . won?'

He had joined the team again. Jessie nodded.

'I think we can say that, Mr Lazzari. Now I want you to phone Merand in Paris. He is to be here by ten o'clock tomorrow morning, bringing along the draft agreement of amalgamation. He ought to have that ready by now.'

'Chessie! We've done it!'

She looked at him thoughtfully for a moment.

'I'm going to have a bath,' she said.

## CHAPTER FOURTEEN

A FORCE FOUR WIND from almost due east had built up a considerable sea, not choppiness, but long, spaced swells that looked like an advertising gimmick, a display of plump bolsters to the horizon. Here and there one of these burst a top seam to let out white foam stuffing. Behind the *Saturn* the dredger wallowed, travelling in its own spray turbulence, with water streaming from the ungainly superstructure. The air was lively but contained no coolness, brittle dry, a fanned heat. Mark wasn't sure whether or not this was the *Harmattan* that blew from African deserts to plague the Cape Verdes, but it felt like it, and the tug, where salt water didn't reach to rinse her, carried a fine coating of gritty dust that looked almost yellow on the fingers.

The *Saturn*'s course was now due east towards Gutongo, straight into the swells, and the lift and fall of her decks seemed controlled by a time mechanism. She rose with a polite murmuring from a welded hull and sank with little groans of resignation. There wasn't much vibration, just the heavy beat of diesels under no strain at all, revved at a pitch that would be satisfactory to the Chief because he didn't have to worry about them. Every now and then the tug was subjected to a check jolt from the hawser, but this was almost gentle. Within the shell that contained the air-conditioning there was a feeling of half-bored acceptance of a dull tow, nothing interesting happening or likely to, a routine established that called for only a minimal alertness. The helmsman and the officer on watch could give most of their attention to the dolphins, who had returned, possibly the same circus trained family.

Mark stepped over a sill and shut the door at once. They had learned to be door shutters on the *Saturn*, coming to need that artificially washed and controlled atmosphere that was as protective as a womb, establishing a norm almost immune to what was outside. Mark needed it particularly, the tropics de-vitalized him, in them he invariably felt as though the tidy enough package of his usual personality had burst through sodden wrappings to spill out over a dock, like a crate dropped from a crane.

Alice felt much the same way. He remembered sitting with her in a café in Morocco, and her voice.

'I hate to admit this, darling, but I'm honestly not sorry that my plane's tomorrow. Send for me from Spitzbergen for our next sexy three days, will you?'

It was no wonder, really, that the surest way to get rich in India is to manufacture a proven aphrodisiac. And Mark's own physical reactions to heat cast a certain doubt in his mind about the performance of all those professional sun seekers, not to mention Latin lovers. Alice had a down quilt from Norway. Her real home was under it. In the London flat she switched off bedroom heating to get the full benefit of cosiness. In her own setting no woman could be more welcoming. But not in Morocco. That had been a fizz, palms and beach and all. It wasn't just one of those phases in a marriage, it was too much sweat.

Alice wouldn't have liked the *Harmattan* at all, she would have noticed that it had a smell. Presumably this came from Africa, the body odour of a fat continent.

He wondered how she was getting on with the problem cottage. They had inspected the problems together. There were 300 of these, topped off by the roof. The Cornish slates might be authentic, but so were the holes between. Mark had put up the heretical suggestion that the slates ought all to come off to be replaced by contemporary tiles made in a factory. This had produced growls from Alice and her brother-in-law, who belonged to a couple of societies for the preservation of rural England. The societies were losing the war on all fronts and Cornish slates were something you really took a stand over, even if this meant buckets permanently in the attic. Mark had been a little depressed by the garden, too. Present wilderness suggested that it was going to be several people's whole future for a long time to come and he didn't want even a junior partnership in this at any phase in his living.

'Darling,' Alice had said, 'you simply won't recognize the place next time you see it.'

He had just been able to applaud her optimism.

Still, it wouldn't ever be really hot under that apple tree they were both determined to preserve at all cost, just bee-buzzing warm, with larkspur nodding in the beds Alice had dug. She was planning a row of cherry trees, too, along a stone wall that was going to have to be rebuilt at a cost of £800; not flowering cherries but the real ones for fruit that could be bottled, along with strawberries, rasps, pears and their own tomatoes. It was going to be quite a life, with the spacious larders full of the preserves Grandma used to make, lining the shelves in Kilner jars.

'I never want to see anything from deep-freeze again,' Alice said.

He put his elbows on the rail and looked towards a horizon that would soon have Africa coming up over it. He had seen Africa do that before and it had never been too much of a thrill, the initial excitement of sighting land wearing off quicker than it did with most continents or islands. He refused to think about Jessie Lawton, or the Plentin company and arms supplies for a revolution in Gutongo. All that was going to bear down on him soon enough and this was a moment in which to accept torpor, to deny that life has to be one punch after the other. The dolphins denied it, personally air-conditioned play fish, whose diet obviously had a high protein and vitamin content. Mark felt as though his had been all starch for a considerable time past. Some of the crew were moaning about constipation again, though not, of course, MacDonald, the stomach swinger. There was a man who was never going to die.

Perhaps the sailor is lucky with his two lives, the one a refreshment for the other. You come home bringing the promise of joy that a man ought to bring through the front door and, long before your girl has started to become really conscious of personal habits in you she could do without, you're through the door again, leaving only a photograph on the piano. There isn't time, really, for either party to explode completely the phantasy about the other. A lot of potential anger is dispelled by sweet absence. You go to bed with a dream and probably wake up the better for it. But it all raised something of a retirement problem, unless by the time that day came you would be ready to settle for pottering instead of living, with stress factors considerably reduced as a result. And if you could just rule out a niggling worry about the handsome neighbour who has started to drop in for morning sherry bringing your wife strawberries he has grown under glass, you might be rated a happy man. The answer to the niggle, of course, was to have a wife with the kind of looks a neighbour doesn't drop in to see again, but on the whole sailors don't go for that sort of girl.

Mark knew that he could be as sure of Alice as any man can be of a woman, which is not too sure. There was a history of incidents when they had been out in public together, and most of these much more significant than the one involving that lecherous old goat who captained the *Semirande*. Even up in Spitzbergen there would be hot-eyed sailors sending out the lust signals. The fact that Alice knew how to cope with these signals wasn't the point. Suppose she stopped wanting to?

'Captain?'

Mark turned. Collins was standing in the doorway wasting manufactured coolness.

'It's not from the old girl?'

'Yes, sir. And short.'

Mark took the typed sheet. Collins always used capitals. Signals were what mattered.

'THE FRUIT IS ROTTEN SIGNED LAWTON.'

Mark drew in his breath. It was back into the ring again, and the body punches.

'Any answer, Captain?'

'Acknowledge.'

'The code address was interesting. Quite a way from home.'

'What?'

'An hotel in Brest.'

Mark was startled. If the old girl had gone whizzing off to France under the impression that she would be able to deal with the Plentins on their home ground she must be out of her mind. There could only be one result from that. Anglo-European on the danger list, and unlikely to recover. Jessie Lawton was in many ways a stubborn old fool and this could be the death of her. Though why the hell should he worry?

'I'll want the dredger on R.T. I'll come to the radio cabin.'

Collins was itching to have the signal interpreted, it was in a code he knew he couldn't break. He sat down frowning and called their tow, with Mark standing behind. A voice came through in half a minute.

'Ginnis riding the iron whore.'

Mark took the handset.

'Underson here. You're to strip off all those bucket coverings. Throw the plastic into the sea. Then dump the contents after them. Everything. Ammo, guns, the lot. I know it's going to be one hell of a job in this heat. Think you can manage it?'

'If it's not a rush order, Captain.'

'Take your time. I'd send a couple of men back to help but in this sea the transfer mightn't be too easy.'

'We'll do it. Aren't you keeping anything? As evidence?'

'Not a single Czech rifle or one round. We don't want any souvenirs, so don't try to sneak back on board with one of those grenades for conversion into a bedside lamp. Your girl isn't going to believe you've been near a revolution anyway, just boozers and knocking shops. I don't want any trace of that stuff about us anywhere when we reach Gutongo. They won't know anything about the bucket protection. Incidentally, you'll have to do the under buckets, too, even though there isn't anything in them. We'll have to risk rust.'

'There's plenty coming as it is. The protective paint's just been slapped on in some places.'

'In that case we don't worry. Happy working and remember we'll be watching through glasses. Over and out.'

Ginnis's final comment wasn't heard. Collins started to get ready to send an acknowledgement to an address in Brest, still looking sulky. On the bridge MacDonald was wearing a pair of short shorts and looked all thigh. He took the news about the dumping calmly enough.

'You're going to have a couple of heat-stroke cases back there.'

'Ginnis won't go at it too hard,' Mark said. 'It's not his nature.'

The Second didn't go at it too hard. Three hours later white plastic was still being heaved from the dredger. Great floating chunks of the stuff stretched back to the horizon, like a paper-chase trail. A wind change could easily carry the indestructible synthetic on to the golden beaches of Gutongo where it might cause interest and even some excitement. But that wouldn't be for some time yet.

It was practically sunset before what seemed to be the last box of grenades splashed into the sea. There was no worry about the cargo floating, they were over 300 fathoms of water, the late fair land of Atlantis a long way down. Mark noticed that the dolphins who tended to play up at sunset, had suddenly left, perhaps in protest against all that dumping in their territory. Or maybe they were just curious and had gone down to have a look.

Africa itself was bright green, but the ocean beyond had lost its blue. The Gutongo River flowed down from sources near the great deserts carrying its by-product, mud, far out to sea. The *Saturn* had crossed an almost sharply defined edge to this stain, which was ochre coloured and had a poisonous look. Nearer land the offshore wind dwindled but still kept enough force to flutter palms on a high bluff to one side of the river mouth. On the other bank was a massive fort, whitewashed stone which dazzled the eyes. Mark looked through binoculars at gun-barrels poking out through emplacements, and these weren't antiques, more war surplus, probably artillery twenty-five pounders. They would have a fair chance of sinking even a moderate-sized ship attempting an unauthorized exit from the river, or at least doing it some nasty damage. The flag of new nationhood blew out from a pole, an orange lion with a penumbra of pastels shading out from it. He focused down on the pilot boat coming bouncing through surf to meet them.

Mark resented most pilots, often forced to use them where they weren't needed. But he knew he needed one now. The charts were uneasy about fathom depths in the Gutongo River and the navigational guide referred ominously to shifting sand-banks. He gave the order to reduce engine speed, then to stand by to take on pilot. He went aft, down to the towing deck,

checking that fenders were over. Back on the dredger Mac-
Donald was standing in swimming trunks holding on to one of
the emptied buckets, an impressionist splash of pink above
yellow water.

On the face of it everything was going well enough, their
arrival timed nicely just at the turn of the tide which put
plenty of water over the bars and should see them ready to
hand over the dredger some time in the early afternoon. This
would leave *Saturn* free to refuel at the oil depot, anchor for the
night, and then come down river again about eleven hundred
hours next day, which would be a nice quick turn around. No
snags seemed likely, and yet he would have gladly skipped a
day in his life just to be heading out into the South Atlantic
again.

The pilot launch was a converted lifeboat with an inboard
engine, and the pilot stood out from the three men in her. He
was on his feet in the bows, balancing easily, huge, broad
shouldered, in shorts and singlet, with the physique of an
Olympic shot-putter. The man signalled back with a hand
and the clumsy boat went into a wide sweep which brought
her on a course parallel to the tug's. The pilot then jumped
up on about two feet of decking over a bow locker and stood
there balancing like a surf rider on his board. As the launch
moved into a turbulence from the *Saturn*'s screws the act began
to look impossible, but the man swayed easily from flat, bare
feet that might have been equipped with suction pads.

The pilot waved away the two *Saturn* men posted to help him
aboard and jumped long before he should have done, skimming
the low rail with his heels, then landing on the deck in a half
crouch. He snapped his body straight.

'*Je m'appelle Underson,*' Mark said. '*Le Capitaine.*'

The man had ears ironed in against a head that was small
for the rest of him.

'*Le Pilote.* Ashuri. But don't strain yourself, Captain. I speak
good English.'

He turned and went for'ard without waiting to be shown
the way.

Ashuri took the wheel himself. He seemed totally unimpressed
by the *Saturn*'s navigational equipment, as though he had seen
it all often enough before, and anyway Africa would soon be
producing better. He was obviously very much part of a new
emergent nationalism, and this was all right with Mark; what
he didn't like was the pilot's attitude towards the channel marker
buoys. Every now and then the *Saturn* and her tow were taken
outside the twin lines of these, unpleasantly near one of the
banks. Mark stood it out in silence for as long as he could.

'Does the channel change often?'

'Uh?'

'You're not between the buoys?'

'That's right.'

The pilot lit a cigarette and let it droop from his lips.

'You got coke? Something to eat? I don't bring my own sandwiches.'

'There's a tray coming up.'

Ashuri scratched the inside of one thigh.

'Your markers don't seem to have lights. I suppose you don't use the night tides at all?'

'Sure. Sometimes.'

'It can't be easy on an unlit channel?'

'It's not. You pray to the Holy Virgin. If you're a good Catholic. I'm not. This river's a bitch, too.'

It was obvious that the pilot didn't much like having the Captain on the bridge behind him, but it was Mark's watch and he was staying. Further, this man seemed totally oblivious to a tow and the problems it raises, never once looking back to see the way that the dredger's wash was eroding the river banks. They were on short hawser now, the coupling almost as close as a train's, but even with this the raft was contriving to interpret that current in its own way and now and then swung wide of the tug's course. It would be a nice ending to a long haul if the thing stuck fast on a mud bar within a couple of miles of its operational base. This would almost certainly involve a mass of fine legal points about the *Saturn*'s responsibility for delivery and he could see them hanging around the river for days on wreck salvage, trying to pull clear an object he wanted out of vision range as soon as possible and forever.

The six miles up to Umtulu Pulundi took two hours. Mark felt decidedly older at the end of it. The pilot's order to drop anchor found the Captain leaning against a bulkhead with his arms tightly folded into his body, longing for a puff at one of those cigarette stubs their guest star kept dropping into a sand-box.

'Okay. That's it. Engines off.'

The pilot yawned and lifted his arms until they touched the deck above. He looked up, contemptuous of the *Saturn*'s low clearance. Then, without even glancing at her captain, he went aft through the chartroom in a long fast lope. Mark went to port to watch the launch, which had tailed them, come in along-side. Ashuri did another exhibitionist leap down into it. The lifeboat frothed away.

The current looked strong even here where the river widened like a bulge blown in a glass tube, water running with a surface

oiliness pockmarked by small, shifting whirlpools. The city was
built on what had probably once been marsh, a site chosen for
anchorage offered, and certainly not for amenity in the tropics.
Hills on both sides of the river put most of Umtulu Pulundi
into an airless cup and though wind was still blowing over trees
on high ground it certainly didn't ventilate Gutongo's capital.

The British Empire expanded from India and took into its
new territories a tropic, not London, feel for architecture, little
Poonas planked down in places like Kuala Lumpur and Burma
and Sandakan, but the French colonialists all seemed to have
come straight from Paris and stayed heartsick for it. Mark had
seen quite a few of these bids to copy France's capital, amongst
them Saigon, Dakar and Algiers. Umtulu Pulundi was another.
By the river's edge was a promenade that had first been named
after Louis Napoleon, then the Republic, after that—briefly—
General de Gaulle, but now immortalizing another General
who in three months had skipped all the intermediate ranks
from sergeant, one Joseph Makeke, established at gun-point as
the father of his people.

From the river-front drive boulevards radiated back towards
rising ground. These offered shade trees and wide pavements
with cafés. Most of the buildings in sight had balconies slung
across their second floors. At this distance the city looked more
prosperous than it probably was and that symbol of national
feeling, the Presidential palace, long in construction, now
appeared to be finished. Mark remembered that it had been
rumoured to have 200 rooms, all air-conditioned. It sat on top
of a private hill with machine-gun posts on the two approach
roads. The General meant to establish a dynasty and was said
to have twenty-three children all living with him, together
with their mothers.

The *Saturn*'s crew, or some of them, were going to want a
metropolitan night of shore leave, but the Captain hadn't quite
made up his mind about this. He didn't much like the idea of
sailing down the Gutongo River in the morning with a load of
hangovers. He would stay on board himself, playing chess with
the Chief, perhaps allowing a liberty party on a strict time
pass. It might be an occasion for one of the Captain's short
lectures. The V.D. germ's survival against penicillin was a
good text for these sermons, and he used it, beaming the message
at the young, like Ginnis, who never appeared to be listening.

Mark crossed the bridge to starboard. Two harbour tugs were
approaching, clearly to take over the dredger, these vintage
conversions from coal burners, retaining the old tall funnels.
It seemed improbable that between them they could develop
900 horse-power which was going to mean some problems with

their tow in this current. There was a small boat as well, much smarter than the pilot launch, with a cabin and a couple of gentlemen sitting in the aft cockpit wearing white caps and uniform. There was a notice that could be illumined identifying the boat—*Gendarmerie de Marine*.

Mark went through the chartroom, picking up his cap, then emerged on the narrow strip of starboard decking. It was one of the times when he missed bridge wings on which he could have appeared with dignity, at once identified. The new ship, if Jessie hadn't gone into liquidation, would have them.

A policeman was looking at him through glasses. The man took his time, then stood with a megaphone.

'*Le bâteau remorqueur Saturn?*'

With the tug's name in raised letters on her bow the question seemed a poor opener, but Mark shouted back in a loud: '*Oui!*'

'*Parlez-vous français?*'

'Not well.'

'It is necessary to be removing *la halage*. You understand?'

'Yes, that's fine with me. You can have her any time. She's not anchored, still on hawser.'

'*Pardon?*'

'The dredger is still on our tow-lines. When your tugs have secured their lines we'll release ours. *Compris?*'

'*Mais certainement.* It shall be done. But you have men on *la halage?*'

'One of our boats will take them off.'

The police launch was now close in. The senior of the two men down there seemed uninterested in the exchange, smoking a cigar and looking straight ahead, leaving everything to his junior.

It would have been possible to dispense with the megaphone but number two continued to use it. His bellows must be reaching the Promenade de General Joseph Makeke.

'You will contain yourself upon sheep.'

'I'm sorry, I don't get that?'

'It is necessary for you to rest tranquil.'

'Your meaning still escapes me!'

'It is not permitted to arrive to shore.'

'I see. We have to wait port authority clearance?'

'It is so. Also, *le médecin*.'

'When can we expect the doctor?'

Number two shrugged and put down the megaphone. His voice still carried well.

'*Demain, peut-être.*'

'You mean we can't have medical inspection today?'

'*Oui. Le médecin est occupé.*'

'But my men will want ashore tonight? We sail in the morning.'

'Impossible.'

'Do you mean we can't go ashore or can't sail?'

'Both thing, Capitaine.'

'Look, I'm just here on a turn around. I want to refuel this afternoon and sail tomorrow.'

'This is not in order.'

He had that English phrase off pat, as though he often had occasion to use it. Mark looked at the other shipping anchored, a small tanker flying the Panamanian flag and two tramps, one registered in Liberia, the other in Portugal. There was no sign of activity on any of them and he had the unpleasant feeling that they could be tied to those rusting buoys by red tape. The Saturn would not be allowed to move over to the depot to take on diesel fuel until she got her clearance some time tomorrow. And it mightn't be tomorrow either, they could sit in this stinking river for days. It wouldn't be so bad if there were clear signs that the dredger's arrival was to be celebrated with pomp, something involving her tug's crew in local hospitality, but this didn't seem scheduled at all.

The two veteran tugs had made it across the current and were nudging in towards the dredger, but in a manner which suggested they weren't quite sure what they were doing. The policeman explained that they were not to be permitted to close with the dredger to secure lines until the Saturn's men were off the raft, presumably for fear that the pink giant back there was a disease carrier. Mark went inside and shouted an order to get a boat away. Then he appeared on deck again.

The police launch had moved off, circling the tug, having a good look at her, possibly considering the uses she could be put to if she was requisitioned for the Gutonguese navy. Mark's sweat was flowing. He returned to air-conditioning and found Ginnis sitting on a chartroom settee reading Playboy which must have been acquired in the Cape Verde Islands and said a lot for the magazine's circulation.

'We're not getting ashore tonight,' he said.

What Ginnis had been thinking about as he looked at illustrations was then plain from his expression.

'How the hell?'

'Police. We're under quarantine.'

'For what?'

'Bugs from the outside world.'

'They can't do this!'

'I authorize you as Second to go out there and tell them so. But I think they can. Remind me when anyone suggests Umtulu

Pulundi again that we don't do tows to this place, whatever the old lady says.'

'Isn't there someone you could appeal to?'

'No. As neo-colonialists we carry no weight at all down here. Or anywhere along this coastline. What did you think of the pilot?'

'Sure of himself.'

'It's the new thing. You know when it was a good time to be a white man, Ginnis? Eighteen eighty. This isn't our century.'

'Travelling by windjammer wouldn't have been mine.' He put down *Playboy*. 'Oh, hell!'

MacDonald came aboard like a man who has been for some time in the wrong psychic atmosphere for his Yoga exercises and wanting privacy to get at them again. The fact that there was to be no shore leave didn't disappoint a muscle-bound near-temperance probable virgin in his thirties, all he wanted was to get cool and stay that way. He was heard asking the cook for ice. The Mate climbed up from the galley with a bowlful of cubes, to be met by Ginnis. The Second showed no respect for seniority of rank in these moments of his frustration.

'What are you going to do with that?' he asked. 'Deep freeze your balls?'

There was no answer. A door shut. Mark went into his own cabin, but couldn't settle. It was no moment for his diary of records, and there was one thing certain, he wasn't going to add Gutonguese talking drums to his disc collection.

Just before flaming sunset the two harbour tugs got the dredger across the Gutongo River to what were apparently to be her temporary moorings. It had taken them four and a half hours. According to the cook, who was running a book on it, they'd had seventeen tries, testing the current at various points and being defeated by it on sixteen occasions. Only when they had finally hit on the scheme of towing the dredger well up past Umtulu Pulundi and letting the current do half the work, did they finally get over. It was quite a show, with an audience of almost the *Saturn*'s total crew lining her rails. There was a considerable crowd along the city's promenade, too. Then, just when it seemed that the entertainment was all over, a Gutonguese girl of obviously the monied classes came out for an evening sail in the light breeze which had strayed into the depression. She was solo in a twelve-foot dinghy with a leg of mutton sail. There was no need for her to come in close to the *Saturn*, but she did, risking infection. At one point Mark considered ordering his men to chasten their language but apparently the girl didn't understand English at all, for she took no notice. She was in a bikini and had plenty to offer. From the sounds that travelled across water there would have been plenty of takers.

Mark was pretty attentive, too, particularly when the girl suddenly showed herself to be a tease. She brought the dinghy round and passed slowly within feet of the *Saturn*'s hull, looking up for the first time to smile. The din was appalling. She had oiled her skin, not against sunburn since this wasn't necessary, but to make it shine, and she knew how to handle her boat, every movement experienced. The Captain found himself beginning to regret the night life on shore. Chess was one thing, a good time was another.

'Call for assistance, sir.'

Mark stared at Collins.

'And what the hell are we supposed to be able to do about that?'

'I don't know. I worked it out as two-o-seven miles north-west from the river mouth.'

'Come inside.'

Collins was glad to do that, he didn't like getting burned.

'What is she?'

'A freighter with a latex fire. Number two hold under the bridge.'

The worst possible place to have a fire, a threat to the ship's control systems.

'Nationality?'

'British. From Malaysia. Gorton Line. Seven thousand tons. The *Gorton Queen*. Bound Liverpool. I looked her up. Crew of twenty-seven. Launched nineteen fifty-two. Originally built for Jennings and Hudson who sold her in . . .'

'All right, that's enough. We're stuck here, Collins!'

The Chief came in from the deck, still keeping his expletives mild.

'Dear me! That almost reminded me of my youth.'

Mark swung round.

'How much fuel have we got?'

'Let me think. Not enough to get back to England. We've had spells at an uneconomic turn of speed . . .'

'How far could we get?'

'Well, certainly Lisbon. Why?'

'That's where we're going. On the next tide.'

'The sun has affected you. Have you forgotten we're under a form of detention at the moment?'

'To hell with detention! We're sailing.'

'Without a pilot?'

'Yes.'

'Kindly put me ashore first. I'll risk an Umtulu Pulundi jail before I sail down that channel with you in the dark. I saw some of it coming up.'

'I was watching the pilot the whole way.'

'No doubt. But with all respect to your photographic memory, things look different on the way back. Don't be crazy!'

'I will not be cooped up in this god-damned place when there's a job to be done! A ship may be sinking, Chief. It's on fire.'

'Did you see those guns on the fort? Even if we got that far we mightn't get farther. It's my belief they don't like ships that haven't got clearance running off. They're feeling their oats these days. Anything could happen.'

'If we go down at about twenty-two hours we'll catch the full tide at the bars.'

'Which would be all right if you knew where they were.'

'I'll find where they are.'

'That's what I'm afraid of. With our hull.'

Mark made for stairs going down.

'The *Saturn* sails at twenty-two hundred hours,' he said. 'And thank God for direct engine control.'

'It isn't that we'll need,' the Chief shouted after him. 'It's an active patron saint. And you haven't earned his services!'

Mark was counting on a moon; it was the sort of thing you did in the tropics, and it was coming on to full, a good lantern. But moon was African, backing Gutongo, putting itself firmly behind an overcast about as opaque as a wool blanket. The only really bright light was from the Presidential palace which seemed to use as much electricity as the whole of the rest of the capital, the pile entirely floodlit and with all its windows glowing, too. Down the approach drives were arc-lamps glaring just in case any enemies of democracy tried to sneak past the machine-gun posts. They could get clear of the harbour all right using this illumination but the river went into a quick turn beyond bluffs and after that was the dark.

He didn't want to use the *Saturn*'s searchlights too soon, or even at all. That kind of advertising mightn't be healthy. Mark decided on two spots rigged to shine low from her bows to port and starboard, and these were put in place when dark fell. After eating he went to bed to get the rest he needed, but didn't sleep, lying on his back wanting the whisky which would kill off a few more of those brain cells he couldn't afford to lose. He wanted one of the fat cigarettes he kept in the cabin as a challenge, but didn't weaken on that front either. The highly moral abstinence didn't make him feel virtuous.

What he planned was a damn fool thing. It is part of the salvage business to do damn fool things on occasion. He wanted to get to that burning ship, motive professional not humanitarian. The *Saturn* hadn't, to date, had many calls on its highly contemporary fire-fighting equipment, and that platform that could be thrust out from the tower had been used only once. The idea had been Mark's own, an addition to the tug at her first re-fit, not really approved of by marine designers and certainly mocked by his rivals.

When fire hits a ship the first thing to be done is to try and contain it to the hold in which it started, usually with steam. Newer vessels have efficient methods of spraying this steam from nozzles in the holds, the older ships don't. It seemed probable that the *Gorton Queen* had been built without this equipment since she had been launched in fifty-two, which had still been the period of rush replacement for war tonnage losses. A spray system could have been added to her since. Chances were it hadn't been.

Mark's projecting arm was designed to have two functions. First, its railed platform for the hose operator put the man controlling salt water or chemical jet streams much nearer target, on occasion almost over it. Second, the arm also served as a boom for carrying a steam pipe to the stricken vessel. In a sea with movement on it getting that steam pipe over from tug to ship, and keeping it over, is a hazardous business, the threat all the time being rupture from the vessels suddenly moving apart. On the *Saturn* the steam pipe was suspended from a height and also from the projecting arm, which cut down greatly on the risk of a break.

The *Gorton Queen* might prove to be his first real test of this equipment. Weather reports from her area showed a Force Four wind, which meant reasonable conditions at least. Her signals indicated the fire still contained to number two hold. If it could be kept from spreading the ship would be salvaged with the bulk of her cargo intact, and that would put up the price for the job.

Mark held all this in his mind as a screen against the problem of getting down the Gutongo River and out to sea in one piece. The screws of tension were tightening again under his skull. He was able to switch on a play-back in his mind of most of their passage upstream and that would be some help tonight, in spite of what the Chief had said. Charts were useless, not even relevant to a changing river bed, and in that six or seven knot current there would be damn-all time to read them. He knew that even with the draught the *Saturn* carried he would be fighting a whirl spin all the way, that tendency in a strong flow to have your stern swung around by it, so that a ship is broadside on in seconds, being swept downriver like a beetle in a flooded drain and just about as helpless.

He was on the point of putting at risk well over a million pounds worth of plant and machinery. No owner, consulted, would say that the circumstances justified this. Owners wanted the rewards without any wild gambles. Always, too, at the back of any salvage skipper's mind is the thought of the kind of fool he is going to look in the business if he needs assistance himself. In this case it wouldn't be available anyway, at least not locally. Those two little putters would never be able to fight current and pull the *Saturn* off a bank at the same time. Possibly the *Semirande* would come over for the job. Dartan would love that.

At twelve minutes to ten by his wristwatch Mark left his cabin wearing clean shorts, a white shirt and his cap. MacDonald was on the dimmed-out bridge, pacing up and down. Yoga never seemed to relax him, nor did he ever give the impression that he was in serene communication with the ultimate. Maybe he did his exercises in the wrong sequence. Mark's appearance had apparently interrupted one of those measured miles, he gave it up and stood, shadowy, by a port window. The Captain, not wanting to crowd the man in any way, went to starboard.

Nothing moved in the harbour, the river's marked flow through the middle of it, noticeable in daylight, couldn't be seen. At some distance thunder grumbled, but it wasn't going to build up enough to cover the sound of an anchor being raised.

'Captain, a launch has just left the promenade. Looks like it's making for us.'

Mark crossed over. Besides running lights on the boat there was a long illumined board that almost certainly said 'Gendarmerie de Marine'.

'Switch on that stern flood, MacDonald. I'm going aft and I want to be able to see.'

The tow-deck was bright when he reached it, a glow that extended out over the water in a ring about the *Saturn*. The launch came nosing into that light fast, the engine going into a flurry of reverse for braking action. A man with a boat-hook stood poised in her bows. In the aft cockpit a figure leaned on the roof of the small cabin. The boat-hook came down, dug into one of the *Saturn*'s fenders, the engine cut. Slowly the launch was pulled in against the tug's side. A youngish face, on the plump side, under fair hair on the wane, was turned up to Mark.

'Hello, old boy. Had you worried, did I? Greetings and all that. Going to let me aboard?'

'Should you? We haven't had our bill of health.'

'I know. Actually, that's what my visit's about. Give a hand, will you? I'm a bit wobbly. Half a dimpled bottle before dinner, what?'

Mark helped him over the low rail.

'Must say your lighting is impressive. My name's Gorridge, by the way. Local resident, but without official status, in case you think I'm British Consul. He wouldn't touch me with a boat-hook. Can we go somewhere? Deck's a bit public.'

'You're the only one boarding us?'

'But of course, old boy. Oh, you mean the coppers? I've just had a loan of their boat, that's all. It happens when I'm on a little mission like this. They'll stay where they are.'

'Then come to my cabin.'

Gorridge was wearing a white shirt with sweat stains and white nylon trousers. In the passage he swayed somewhat and he seemed glad to be able to sit down. He looked around.

'Nice place you've got here. No expense spared, eh? I must say tugs are rather something these days. Cool air, too.'

'A whisky?'

'I've rarely been known to say no. The thing is, old boy, you've rather put your foot in it. According to local custom and all that. The big man was a bit pipped, really, when he heard.'

'Heard what?'

'Well, the niceties not observed, all that sort of thing. You understand.'

'I don't,' Mark said, giving his guest a glass.

'Cheers. Let me explain.'

Gorridge was economical about this, sentences punctuated by sips. What Mark should have done when the police launch came alongside in the afternoon was invite the two gentlemen in the aft cockpit on board for a refreshment. It was the normal practice and tended to iron out delays. And if you wanted to be absolutely certain of no delays at all you put twenty pounds in an envelope and slipped this discreetly to the lesser of the two personages as you served the second round of drinks.

'All right,' Gorridge said, 'it's the jolly old palm oil. But it's the practice and that's that. No use bashing your head against a wall, is there? In view of the fact that you slipped up it might be a good idea now to make it thirty pounds. And if you do you'll get clearance practically at dawn and be whizzing off on that tide you were after.'

'Mr Gorridge, what do you do in Umtulu Pulundi?'

'I've a garage concession here. Import new and do a big used trade, too. We have a hire service as well. It's all rather smooth really. I nipped in just after the French were chucked out. Waving the old Union Jack, you know. It was the Tricolour the locals didn't much like then. Though, of course, the French have come back since. An absolute flood. Old Daddy Makeke couldn't begin to run the place without them. But they haven't been able to budge me, though God knows they've tried hard enough.'

Mark's sympathy in this matter was with the French.

'And if I don't pay this bribe?'

'My dear chap, don't use that word, it hurts me. The answer, though, is that rather unpleasant things can happen. As a sort of last resort they've got rather a nasty tactic, really. They search you for contraband opium. And it's remarkable how they seem to find what they're looking for. Then it's the Consul and all that fuss, you know. You could be held up for weeks, old boy. After all, look at it this way, they keep their extortion moderate, wouldn't you say? What's thirty pounds?'

'Money that I can't put to company expenses.'

'Really? Where have you been living all these years?'

'Most of them at sea.'

'It's still pure out there, is it? How splendid. But you'll just have to learn to adapt to ports, I'm afraid. And the times.'

'In some things I will not. And this is one of them.'

'Yeou mean no little pourboire for the police? But my dear chap, really!'

'I am not your dear chap, Mr Gorridge. And now I'll conduct you to your borrowed launch.'

The visitor rose.

'I'm afraid you're going to regret this. Rather much.'

He went through an opened door and along the passage.

'I always thought a tug would smell of oil and bad cooking. But I suppose the air-conditioning clears all that away?'

Mark made no comment. Gorridge lost none of his bounce. On the boat-deck he said:

'When you change your mind you will let me know, won't you? A go-between is on permanent duty. Gorridge's Garage always get me. Though I'm afraid you'll find that the longer you hold out the more it will cost you. Unofficial clearance fees can be subject to the most ghastly inflation.'

Mark did not help his guest on to the launch. Gorridge leaned on the cabin roof again.

'I'm sure I'll be seeing you again in the next day or two. Cheerio for now.'

Mark watched the police boat pull away. Then he turned and went along the tow deck, up to the boats and into the deck-house. There was some curiosity waiting for him on the bridge. He ignored it.

'Oh, you're here, Ginnis. Get that aft flood off. MacDonald, anchor up, engines on.'


## CHAPTER FIFTEEN

THE *Saturn* struck river current like a car hitting black ice. Mark had the panic feeling of control lost, of mental gears not meshing quickly enough to change demanded. The wheel went slack, as though rudder cables had gone. He felt the tug's drift through his feet, the power packed into her hull neutralized simply by the angle at which he had taken her into fast water. It was mistake number one. There had better not be many more.

She came round slowly, fighting him. He had never felt his ship like this, a sense of imbalance, a design fault somewhere only now revealed under stress. His mind rejected that. There was nothing wrong with the *Saturn*, trouble was from his handling. MacDonald and Ginnis were both thinking this, too.

Umtulu Pulundi's lights came swinging into view through the starboard bridge windows, neon tinted, some of them moving, and up on the hill the palace was a glittering frosted cake. Mark had a quick look back towards the esplanade, expecting to see a red or green dot surging away from it. But no lights travelled on the water. The harbour had a closed-down look, like a suburban station on a branch line at night.

'Speed, MacDonald?'

'Nine, sir.'

Almost seven of this would be the current.

'Dead slow.'

'Dead slow it is, sir.'

'Fathom depth, Ginnis?'

'Twelve, sir.'

Formality had come into sudden bloom on the *Saturn*'s bridge, like a resurgence of protocol during a royal occasion in a normally free and easy country. Mark had a full attendance of his deck officers. They had jobs to do, these essential if he was to spend the next hour and a half with his attention glued to a river. Ginnis was on the depth finder and communications, MacDonald had engine control. Up on the tower platform two men manned the big searchlight in case this was needed, another was on bow watch equipped with walkie-talkie back to the Second. Mark had considered having Ackroyd up for'ard swinging the lead in throws that just might give them information in advance of the depth finder, but had decided against it. The speed they would be travelling at made this pointless. The only man officially off duty was the cook, and presumably he was running a sweep, odds heavily against the Skipper.

The Captain of the *Saturn* was in these moments deeply unloved. He could live with the pain of this better than the increasing grind of his headache. The fact remained, however, that everyone on board knew perfectly well that in the coming test the man at the wheel was going to be relying heavily on intuition, far too heavily by their reckoning. Mark put it at something like four parts instinct to six of assistance from navigational aids, which was turning the clock back a long way from contemporary automation. That automation, though, had its uses. Without direct bridge control of engines the idea of attempting this passage pilotless would have been unthinkable. It probably still was unthinkable.

The *Saturn* had come back to a kind of obedience again, still far from sweet about it, but accepting orders. Mark felt a little better, though he saw now that he was going to have to use those rigged lights much sooner than intended. Marker buoys were becoming difficult to pick up as the city's glow faded.

'Eight fathoms, sir.'

It wouldn't be eight for long. Mark wished that Ashuri, in fractional moments of talk, hadn't referred to rocks waiting. Mud banks were bad, but rocks sinister. The pilot had indicated them as sites of grief.

'Bow lights on.'

These were fairly tight beamed and sent out two probes like antennae ahead of *Saturn*, the one to port immediately picking up a marker. The one to starboard would be alerting shore watchers if the tug's sailing hadn't already been noted. Mark placed another buoy and knew he was all right for the moment if he kept his ship on the indicated channel; it was much further downstream that Ashuri had gone in for those deviations that might have been just carelessness but were much more likely highly significant.

'Ten fathoms, sir.'

This was good news, indicating a deepening of the river for the passage between twin bluffs. These looked like huge, buttressed foundations for a suspension bridge that had never been built. The sensation of speed was unnerving because it wasn't being delivered by the *Saturn*'s engines. As they went through those rock gates it felt as if a huge hand had reached out for the tug's stern to lift it and shove her on.

'Eleven knots, sir.'

'Stop the engines!'

'Engines stopped, sir.'

'Stand by for full astern.'

'Twelve fathoms, sir.'

A very deep channel. They lost all light from the city behind. The twin white probes seemed on the feeble side. A gleam from the useless radar screen was distracting and Mark had this switched off. The men on the *Saturn*'s bridge became shadowy, their faces expressionless blurs. It was probably better that way.

'Speed?'

'Nine and a half.'

It was still too much

'Six fathoms.'

'Half-astern!'

'Half-astern it is, sir.'

The revs of engines mounting again, on reversed screws, set up a trembling, fractionally jarring, almost as though they had hit something. Mark was conscious of MacDonald turning to look at him. He took no notice. He was peering ahead for a starboard buoy that was due and hadn't come up. He didn't remember a gap in that marker spacing, but there might have been one.

'Five fathoms, sir.'

'Thirty feet. The *Saturn* drew eighteen.

'Full astern!'

Froth from their propellers swirled past on the current. From the bulk of high ground it was clear that the *Saturn* was holding, then moving slowly stern.

'Half-astern.'

Altered revs released the ship again, but still kept her checked, like a car driven on handbrake.

'Four fathoms, sir!'

God! They were off channel. Mark guessed the error was to starboard and slammed the wheel over. The *Saturn* responded, and a bow light caught the missing *buoy*. They had almost run it down.

'Seven knots, sir.'

Mark knew that current speed was too fast, but decided to risk it. 'Ginnis, call the tower. Searchlight on. Beam it four ship's lengths ahead. If that isn't right we'll correct.'

'Sir.'

'Captain, car lights on the road up there,' MacDonald said. 'To starboard. On top of the cliff.'

'So what?'

'Travelling fast. I'd say towards the fort.'

'Gun crew, you mean? Answering a call to action stations?'

'I wouldn't know.'

'We'll worry about those guns later.'

'Five fathoms, sir.'

'Full astern!'

There was a curious sucking noise, audible even on the bridge. The *Saturn* struck. It was mud, not rocks, but the jolt enough to make a free standing man catch at his balance. MacDonald had to do that. He also swore, very softly. Mark knew that if reversed screws hadn't bitten into water at just the right moment the tug could have been held by her bows for long enough to be swung around broadside on to the flow.

He had to give up the idea of keeping current speed, settling for somewhere around four knots at a maximum. The main bends were just ahead, a series of S loops, and what the channel did in them was anyone's guess.

The searchlight came on, an avalanche of whiteness over the *Saturn*'s bows, dazzle against bridge glass.

'The bloody fools!' Mark shouted, then wished he hadn't.

The *Saturn* was holding and the light crew got range in less than half a minute. Four ship's lengths ahead showed up the scenery, though it left an almost blind area back in towards the tug's bows, a hazed-out patch. This remained, even when the rigged lights were switched off, something that had to be accepted.

Mark was now controlling a drift under reversed props, the light ahead letting him see what was coming, but at some distance. He had to take in that picture and memorize it. It was like steering a ship on slightly delayed close-circuit television, the screen his brain. The screws under his skull had tightened home, becoming the source of pulsed distress signals. One day he would have his coronary right on the bridge, and MacDonald would have to take over. Pray to that non-commissioned patron saint who seemed to have looked after them so far, that it wouldn't be tonight. Maybe, as well as reducing alcohol intake he should cut out animal fats and live on margarine. All those country fresh eggs Alice planned to add to their diet increased your cholesterol rate. Damn the writers of medical articles in news magazines!

'Seven fathoms, sir.'

That was better. That was it, in fact, on the first sharp bend. There was no doubt about the usefulness of the searchlight once you got used to the glare factor. It offered a printed pattern of surface turbulence, even pointing this up more sharply than sun would have done, and this data was then fed into the Underson mark one computer which translated it to action via wheel grips. Practically all automatic, easy if there was no power failure.

'Under four fathoms, sir!'

No panic. Something wrong again. Look at the river. Take in the clean flow. It was beyond the starboard markers, in towards the bank. This must be one of the places where Ashuri had seemed careless.

'Three and a half, sir!'

Three feet of water between them and mud, or gravel, or rock. Gamble. Don't cut speed.

Mark took the *Saturn* in towards the river bank. MacDonald started a protest, but checked this on a hissed breath.

'Five, sir.'

Mark filled his lungs with washed air.

'Seven, sir.'

Probably Ashuri kept them from moving those buoys, as a guarantee against redundancy. You wouldn't have thought the bastard would have worried. Maybe he just liked to show off.

Seven seemed about the river's norm, a good enough depth,

adequate for big liners if that dredger ever got down here to widen channels and soften bends. The trick was to watch for the smooth flow. Eddies and whirlpools were danger signals. It was simple when you knew how.

Mark was drenched with sweat, conscious of this when he moved his arms. His deodorant had packed in. MacDonald hadn't used one after his last shower. As Mate he was doing little to boost his Skipper's morale. Ginnis was better, getting his nerve back. He was beginning to sound almost as though he thought the Captain had genius.

'Just over seven, sir.'

Keep it like that, Saint, whatever your name is. Keep it sweet seven.

There hadn't been a peep from the engine-room. Maybe the Chief was down there invoking the Saint, too. After all, he'd put up the idea.

'Moonlight!' Ginnis shouted. 'On the sea!'

'What?'

'Dead ahead, sir.'

Mark couldn't really look, only vaguely conscious of another brightness beyond the one they were manufacturing. He accepted that moonlight on trust, as a kind of omen, and certainly the canyon through which they had been travelling appeared to be widening out. On the sea was light, the shining promise of it. Out there charts would have meaning again, allowing routine to come creeping back. The automatic pilot could be put on the job.

Afterwards Mark wasn't quite sure at just what point he had known they would make it, but certainly it had been rather as though their Saint had suddenly put a hand on his shoulder and said: 'You'll get down there, boyo.'

MacDonald seemed much slower to feel this than any of the rest of them, perhaps because as Mate he was nearer to total authority and suddenly had been made conscious of just what this involved. Mark wanted to tell him that with authority there is often a free issue of something extra to make it endurable, but it was hard to find the right words to put the idea over, and by the time he was really talking again the moment had gone.

They made it downriver in just over the hour, sailing into a lagoon that shallowed out in the delta to six fathoms but spread this comforting depth over a considerable area. The last hazard was a passage through the sandbar that almost formed a break-water, though covered at this tide. The gap to the ocean was pretty plainly indicated by the way the seas ran through it instead of breaking up, and the *Saturn* moved at three knots of her own power, current propulsion neutralized, towards that exit. Above them cloud was still thick, the blanket's frayed edge about six miles out. Beyond this the South Atlantic was under attack from a brisk Force Four wind and the waves glittered.

'Searchlight off.'

They were getting back to norm. Mark didn't want glare for that passage through a channel marked by buoys, though there was still a chance that these could also be jokers.

'Five knots.'

Gently increasing vibration was therapy for pulse rates at high pressure. Mark let himself think about standing under a cold shower for a long time. The ceiling speaker crackled, the first evidence for over an hour that Collins was still with them and still on duty.

'Captain? The fort has just come through on R.T. The chief up there is demanding to speak to you. What do I do about it?'

Mark slackened his hold on the wheel, half-expecting the skin on his palms to stick to the grips.

'MacDonald, take over. Hold us towards the channel.'

At the panel he said: 'Give me the fort.'

A voice came through at once. 'You are tug Captain?'

'Yes. Who are you?'

'*Le chef de fortresse.* Listen! It is immediate that you stop ship!'

'Why?'

'Listen! There is gun fixed on bridge. Your ship now under arrest for searching of contraband. Stop! Off engine immediate!'

'If I don't, what?'

'We fire gun.'

'Now *you* listen. If a shell comes out of that spout I'll put out a distress call to the whole of the South Atlantic saying I'm under wanton attack from a Gutonguese fort while on my lawful business.'

'You break laws! You escape to conceal contraband.'

Mark switched off. 'Dead slow,' he ordered.

Mark pressed the general alarm buzzer, then used the internal communications network of speakers that put his voice out on *Saturn*'s three decks.

'Attention! Captain here. We may come under fire from the fort's guns. All men to keep clear of starboard. Repeat that, keep clear of starboard. All lights that can be seen outside ship off, now. Repeat that, all lights off. Total black-out.'

He punched for the tower.

'Ginnis, running, mast and deck lights out.'

'Sir.'

'MacDonald put us on a zigzag. Nothing dramatic. But so we can't be positioned easily. We're not silhouetted against that moonlight.'

'Sir.'

Ackroyd came through from the tower.

'Stand by searchlight,' Mark ordered. 'They're going to put a beam on us before they use a gun. As soon as they do dazzle them back with our beam. Remember how we did it with the *Grooter*?'

'Yes, sir.'

'Don't take your time about it. The moment their beam comes on, blast them.'

'Sir.'

The ceiling speaker gave them Collins.

'That *chef* is making a lot of noise. Says he has a last warning, or something.'

Mark got through to the radio cabin.

'Stall him. Say I've gone aft. You're trying to get me.'

Mark turned to Ginnis.

'I'll watch the finder. You get over to port side.'

'Is that an order?'

'No.'

Ginnis stayed where he was. They were a couple of heroes defying a dictatorship by standing in number one target area. It was damn stupid.

'Do you think those bastards *will* fire?' Ginnis asked.

'I can't assess the stress factors on them. But I'm betting this is a low level affair. And about police chief level. I don't think General Makeke has told anyone to sink us. So it's a try-on.'

'You hope.'

'That's right.'

The fort used two searchlights, both groping for range, and with beams suggesting they were powered by a pretty sick dynamo. The *Saturn*'s reply was a shattering display of candlepower splashing over the fort, subjecting it to a great sheet of white fire.

Mark went to engine control and dialled full speed.

'Take her through, MacDonald. You've got eight fathoms.'

The fort did not fire. Mark stood looking at it, waiting for one or more of those glistening gun barrels to lift for range on *Saturn*. The guns didn't move.

'Seven and a half going eight again,' Ginnis called out.

'You can leave us now,' Mark said to the Saint. 'And thanks.'

Ginnis turned his head. The illuminations showed him looking startled.

The *Saturn*'s Skipper lay on his berth washed and naked. He had swallowed three buffered aspirin with the first mouthful of a treble whisky and expected to feel better soon. His mind was as slack as a body after orgasm, its only activity a rejection of recurring television pictures showing eddies and whirlpools and the stretches where the water ran fast. The screen for the reception of these was still glowing, but the frames themselves were mercifully becoming blurred as aspirin, or whisky, reached nerve endings. Mark imposed a thought between those pictures and himself. The thought was that the Hoofstangers were right to retire their skippers at sixty. That gave him another quarter of a century issuing orders and carrying the can if these weren't effective. To last out all that time he was going to have to do something about himself, maybe borrow MacDonald's book on Yoga. He could use an intensive course on how to achieve serenity. With proper training you were able to stand on your head for fifteen minutes while the blood did a rush job of re-vitalizing brain cells.

It would be cosier to be able to believe in that nameless Saint on loan from heaven for specialist assignments such as looking after tug captains under stress. To be able to do this you had to bow yourself back from the rational into mystery. In his case this would mean calling in all established mental patterns and reprocessing them. It was improbable that it could be done at his age. You had to be caught young and hooked up to the right circuits.

He wished he could sleep, but he wasn't going to.

There was a knock on the door and Collins came in without waiting to be bidden. He looked at his Captain lying there without the dignity of underpants as though startled to find the boss was human.

'I'm sorry, sir . . .'

'That's all right. Something urgent?'

'A long signal from Mrs Lawton. I've just decoded it.'

'Well?'

'I think you'll find it pretty incredible.'

Collins might almost have been suffering from shock. Mark sat up. 'Give me. And help yourself to a whisky.'

'Thanks, sir. I think I will.'

Mark took the sheet.

CAPTAIN UNDERSON SATURN STOP HAVE COMPLETED AMALGAMATION ANGLO-EUROPEAN WITH PLENTIN COMPANY SALVAGE STOP NEW COMPANY TO BE CALLED ANGLO EUROPEEN STOP WITH E STOP INCORPORATED FRANCE STOP BREST HOME PORT STOP I RESIDE THIS CITY STOP JOINT FLEET SATURN AND SEMIRANDE PLUS ARRANGED PURCHASE TWO AMERICAN TUGS STOP FURTHER PURCHASES LIKELY STOP ALSO TWO TUGS BUILDING IMMEDIATE STOP HAVE STIPULATED SATURN FLAGSHIP UNTIL SUITABLE NEW REPLACEMENT STOP YOU RETAIN COMMAND AS FLEET COMMODORE STOP CAPITAL AVAILABLE CHALLENGE WORLD SALVAGE INTERESTS STOP SIGNED LAWTON.

Mark read the signal a second time. Then he stared at the deck.

'How did she do it, sir? How did she ever pull this off? I'd have thought the Plentins would have stepped on her.'

Collins was standing there with a glass in his hand. The contents weren't mostly water.

'She got them by the short hairs,' Mark said.

## CHAPTER SIXTEEN

BERAND knocked on the Captain's door. There was no answer. He listened again at slats but heard nothing above the *Semirande*'s creakings and the whirr of an electric fan. He turned the handle.

Jules was on his back, mouth open, on the verge of snores. The berth light glared down on his face. Sleep didn't restore him to any kind of innocence. He wore trousers but no shirt, and had the fan beamed on a bare chest. Stale air was being stirred but not revived, the port-hole shut. The Mate looked around for the usual sedative, but there was no sign of a bottle or an empty tooth-glass rolling on the deck. He went close to the bunk. The Captain's breath, while not sweet, bore no trace of brandy.

The open door wasn't enough ventilation. Berand braced his knees against the edge of the bunk and leaned across Jules to unscrew the port-hole clamps. These were salt-rusted from long disuse. It took some time to prise a metal frame open a couple of inches. Berand fixed it there with the clamps and straightened. A shower spattering of spray came through. Jules rolled over and sat up.

'Hell! That was a bloody sea on top of me! Did you . . . ?'

'We need air to live.'

'What are you doing here?'

'Calling you to breakfast.'

'Eh?'

'We've all had it. We'll be at the *Gorton Queen* in under an hour. About first light. Cook wants your order.'

'It's coffee.'

'You didn't eat anything last night.'

'Been watching me, have you? Had a look round the cabin for the brandy bottle, too, I'll bet. Well, it's in the drawer.'

'It's not a good idea to fight a ship's fire on an empty stomach.'

'Clack, clack!'

'Listen to me, you bad tempered old bastard! It's about time you snapped out of the sulks!'

Jules stared.

'The *what*?'

'You've been sunk in them ever since we got that Plentin cable in St Vincent. And it's getting the men down. They're used to your foul temper, but not to this moping.'

Berand expected a shouted reaction and shut the door behind him to cut down crew participation. But all that Jules did was twist his body about and set to work closing the porthole, patient over the stiff screw clamps. Then he swung his legs out and groped with bare feet for slip-ons.

'Do you mind telling me why this amalgamation is getting you down?'

Jules lifted his head. 'You're not bothered by it?'

'I hate change, as you know. Seems I've got to take it.'

'Nothing more than that?'

'Jules, for God's sake, the sky hasn't fallen in. The Plentins have taken over another salvage company operating one ship.'

'Which happens to be the *Saturn*.'

'I wouldn't have thought the Plentins getting the *Saturn* could shock you.'

'At *that* again, are we?'

'Yes. What you mind is them getting Underson along with his ship.'

'Sure,' Jules said. 'That's what I mind. That and Henri Plentin cheating me.'

'How?'

'Spinning a line about me the senior captain. Down in those bloody islands to train crews before coming back to be the big chief. Blah, blah. I swallowed it all. You saw me getting big-headed, didn't you? And all the time the old man was laughing.'

'What does that mean?'

'That he meant to have Underson all along. Somehow. He wanted him.'

'You don't know what you're talking about.'

'I tell you I can see it all. Plain. The Plentins looking for the key man in their expansion. And it was never me, Berand.'

'Look, Jules, Underson is just another skipper in the new company!'

'Can't you look beyond your own nose in this? The *Saturn* is going to be the newest ship in the fleet. And she'll stay the newest even with these refit jobs you and I are going to. She'll be number one, we'll be two and three. She'll carry the commodore's flag.'

'For hell's sake, there isn't a commodore's flag!'

'There'll be one now. Underson will see to that.'

'You don't know the first thing about what Underson's position will be in the new company.'

'I know this . . . that man will never play second fiddle to anyone. Certainly not to me. Which makes sweet nothing of old Plentin's talk. He's got his new fleet commodore along with the *Saturn*.'

'We haven't a clue as to what's really happening in Brest. We'll find out when we get there. Then we can take action, if that's necessary.'

'*When* we get there,' Jules said. 'Don't you see? If we got to this fire we'll be wallowing around in the Atlantic with a four knot tow while Underson sails into Brest in that tin box of his for the big take-over.'

'You really believe that?'

'I know it.'

'So you don't want to go to the *Gorton Queen*?'

'Damn you! I didn't say that. I'm just telling you what will happen if Underson gets to Brest first. And anyway, it's already happened. I don't need to have it spelled out to me in a Plentin signal or interview in that damn office. I get number two ship out there in Japan. For the last few years of my service. Before honourable retirement.' He stared at the bulkhead. 'Seems I can't win, Berand. I hate Underson, do you know that? I hate his guts.'

The Mate stood very still. He knew what Jules hated, not the man, but the much younger Captain, who had climbed fast and would go on climbing. There was nothing to be said.

Jules looked up. His voice was quiet.

'The *Gorton Queen*'s going to want our steam, that's for sure. Well, we can give it to them. I've had an idea for rigging up a boom to take over our hose. It's not a bad sea running. If we can support that hose pipe half-way we ought to be able to cut down the risk of a break. You'll have the wheel. It'll be your job to hold us as close to that ship as you can. Tourin and I will go aboard her. Now you can tell the cook I want an English breakfast, bacon and egg, toast and marmalade.'

Mark stared. 'Are you saying that the *Semirande* is going to the *Gorton Queen*? And is in sight of her?'

Collins looked uneasy. 'Yes, sir. At twelve miles.'

'But how the hell could you have missed the signals between those two? There must have been some earlier?'

'I should think so.'

'Collins . . . you weren't listening?'

'Not when we were in the river. I went out on deck. You said radio silence. And I wasn't thinking about other ships.'

None of them had been, not in the river. Mark had no comment on that. Collins waited, then said:

'Now that we're the same company and the *Semirande*'s almost there, are we still going to the freighter?'

'Yes. The *Semirande* isn't adequately equipped to fight a latex fire. We are.'

'Do I signal the *Gorton Queen*? Or the *Semirande*?'

'No signals. We just arrive.'

Mark walked over to the starboard windows. He looked at a sea under a lightening sky on which the wind was only whipping up a moderate choppiness, less than Force Four now, but still enough to fan a freighter fire.

The *Semirande* must have been on her way back to Brest when she picked up that call from the *Gorton Queen*, ordered home like the *Saturn*.

Maybe they were planning a regatta in Brest, an official inspection by owners, Jessie and Henri Plentin travelling in a canopied launch between the first two ships of their fleet. It might be possible to arrange to have them piped aboard.

From five miles, and in first light, the *Gorton Queen* looked a perfectly normal cargo ship proceeding under her own power, if slowly, north towards the Canaries. The only smoke visible was a thin ribbon from her funnel. At 500 yards the black seepage was spotted from the *Semirande*. This leaked from the joins of the freighter's number two hatch cover, like steam from a badly fitting pressure-cooker lid. The wind carried a stench of old tyres burning on a dump.

Berand was already at the wheel, Jules in the radio cabin talking on R.T. to the *Gorton Queen*'s Master. He had left doors open and his voice reached the bridge, pitched high, Jules near losing his temper. Moments later there was the sound of his muttering progress through the chartroom.

'You know what that bugger wants? Our steam, not us. Says he can handle things on board.'

Berand turned his head. 'So it's not so serious?'

'Bloody serious, I'd say. Guess what he's got in the forward hold, with only a bulkhead between it and the latex? Barrelled palm oil. And the bulkhead's already hot. They've been clearing the barrels to make room for sluicing steel with sea water. Still he doesn't want me aboard.'

'Why not just give him steam and leave it at that?'

'Like hell! If he gets our steam he gets Tourin and me over there to see what happens to it.'

'Jules, this ship isn't going to be any prize.'

'Eh?'

'Look at her. You know what she'd be worth in an awards court? The breakers' price and salvaged cargo.'

'What do you mean, breakers' price? That ship was built in fifty-two.'

'Which is about as obsolete as a car built in fifty-two. She's still at sea because her replacement hasn't been commissioned. But the moment that happens its off to the scrap yard for the *Gorton Queen*. I'd say any time now.'

'Eighteen years isn't a ship's life.'

'Didn't use to be. It is now. You know that perfectly well, Jules. Fifteen knots and that thing over there blows a cylinder head. She hasn't the speed for contemporary carrying and her owners know it. Pretty paint doesn't alter the facts.'

'So?'

'Give her steam, contain her fire, seal the hold and let the Captain take her under her own power to the Canaries. Shore firemen can deal with the smouldering. We push off to Brest.'

'So you're anxious to get to Brest now, are you?'

'Yes.'

'I do this job properly, Berand. If that palm oil goes up she's a torch. And the bridge is threatened. Number two hold goes back under deck-housing. Fire has only to push up through one layer of plating to get to her main control lines.'

'All I'm saying, Jules, is that no one is going to wave any flags when you arrive with that in tow. I'd listen to her Captain. Maybe he knows best.'

'They all do, until the last minute. Then when all hell breaks loose it's over to us. I'm trying to prevent hell breaking loose. And I'm not on standby.'

'You'll have it your own way. I'm going to miss Tourin on the bridge.'

'Lecren's coming up when he's got the boom fixed. He'll manage engine-room control for you and have the walkie-talkie to me. How near can you take us for a steady hold alongside?'

'About fifteen metres.'

'The boom will reach nearly half that. Then we'll have slack to the well-deck. I'll leave enough for a three or four metre roll play. But you won't have more than that.'

'I'm going to be busy.'

'That's why I'm giving you Lecren. I can't spare anyone else. We'll need every available man to handle the hose.'

'Has the *Gorton Queen* got spray nozzles in that hold?'

'No. It's a pipe feed. They're trying to power water hoses along with the steam. It's too much for them. I don't think the Captain knows what he's doing. But he's a snooty bastard. It's the old business, bleat for a tug to help and when she shows up try to stay boss yourself.'

'But he agreed to the form?'

'I made him. Berand, close now for the position you can hold. When you've got it I'll send over the line for the sling cradle.

Tourin will be by me when we're on the freighter. We'll keep in touch.'

'Jules . . . ?'

There was no answer. The Captain was out on the port wing supervising a swing out of his boom contraption. He began to bellow instructions.

The *Gorton Queen* was still just making way, holding her bow into the wind. The *Semirande* was close in, on the same course and at the same speed. Now and again Berand was aware of magnetic attraction between the two hulls, the pull of this not really neutralized by the rush of water separating them.

Jules's boom device seemed to be working all right. For half the distance to the freighter a reinforced canvas and rubber pipe was slung through loose rope rings, sagging between each. The hose had play for tightening and slackening off along its suspension from the boom, as well as from the big droop between the end of this and the *Gorton Queen*'s well-deck. Wind was dropping and the seas going down. Everything looked all right, too good; Berand was uneasy.

Jules's voice came loud through a speaker. 'Dartan here. Get me Berand.'

Lecren came nearer with the walkie-talkie.

'Yes, Jules?'

'Hah! They didn't need us. Know what I've just found out? Number two hold's aft bulkhead is buckling, too. I went down to have a look, through the engine-room. The thing's reinforced, but that's not going to hold it.'

'God! Have they still got bridge control?'

'You'd notice if they'd lost it! By some miracle that's all right. How long I can't say. But the centre of heat seems to be low in the hold. Don't ask me how it started. The real nightmare isn't losing bridge control, it's the main fuel tank. Shoved in across ship. Next to that hot bulkhead.'

'Are you emptying it?'

'The Captain doesn't want me to. That fuel's to get him to Liverpool. Or at least the Canaries. He's used his other tanks. Pour it out on the sea and he's a hulk in a couple of hours.'

'Can't you pump it into the empty tanks?'

'You'd have thought that, wouldn't you? But oh, no. There's no way of doing this. Apparently the designers were worried about upsetting ship's trim or something. Bloody fools! Also, that goes for putting a main tank right up against a hold bulkhead. Not that we haven't seen that before a few hundred times. No worry about fire risk at all.'

'Explosion risk ought to be worrying Captain Ellis!'

'He's determined not to lose fuel. Still clinging to the idea we'll bring number two under control. Then he seals it, says "thanks very much, send in your bill for steam", and sails away. Maybe he thinks he can get back to England like this. Wouldn't put it past him to try. He only sees what he wants to, like a civil servant. Talks like one, too.'

'So what do you do?'

'Have a look at the burning latex.'

'*What?*'

'Don't get excited, Berand. Watch your steering. That's your job. We brought over respirators.'

'They won't help you in that smouldering hell! The heat, man!'

'I'm just going to nip in through the inspection hatch for a quick look. There's a platform just under it I can stand on. And it's on a level with the top of the cargo.'

'Jules, what good is this going to do?'

'Let me see whether there's glowing up top. And how much heat at high levels. Then I can come out and tell the Captain just exactly what the situation is. And what he has to do. I think controls are still functioning because the fire's low down. The deck above the aft part of the hold isn't very hot, I've just checked. It's fine for the bridge if the fire's deep in her belly, but hell for the fuel tank. Get it?'

'You're mad if you open that inspection hatch!'

'Why? Rubber doesn't flare. That's not the way it burns. We can risk the little air I'll let in.'

'You mean you're going to have the hatch cover closed after you? Listen to me! You're wearing a rope round your middle if you go down in there. And if you don't say you'll do that I'll swing the *Semirande* out and break your bloody steam pipe!'

'All right! Don't get hysterical. I'll wear a rope.'

'Hang on a minute. Ginole's just come with a signal.'

'*Saturn* on R.T.,' Ginole said.

Berand made a fractional correction on course.

'How is that posible?'

'Range twelve miles. Coming over horizon. Towers to starboard.'

Berand continued to watch the freighter's hull.

'Jules? You hear that? The *Saturn*'s nearing us.'

There was no answer from the box. Lecren tried a call over but all he got was static.

'Out on the wing, Ginole! Tell me what you see.'

The radio operator took his time. He didn't sound too interested.

'Their crew at hose pipe. Nothing else.'

Berand remembered that the well-deck bulwarks took a long curve as it reached midships deck-housing. The inspection hatch was probably in behind that steel shelter screen.

'Lecren calling Tourin. Over.'

The Second came through.

'Sorry we lost contact. The Skipper put the set down.'

'Does he know the *Saturn*'s coming?' Berand asked.

'Good God! Is she? He didn't say anything. I'll tell him.'

'Can't you keep him out of that hold?'

'When has he ever listened to me?'

There was only one answer to that. The grips of the wheel felt damp against the Mate's hands. His shirt stuck to his back.

'I'm off,' Ginole said. 'Message to *Saturn*?'

'Yes. Acknowledge. Tell them what's happening here. Say we're supplying steam but could do with more. Tell her to come up to the *Gorton Queen*'s port. But keep well clear of us in approach. And dead slow from half a mile. Any kind of wash from her could mean our pipe going. Got all that?'

'Yes.'

'Lecren, have you still contact with Tourin?'

'No.'

Berand's eyes measured the channel between two ships. Jules must have heard Ginole reporting *Saturn*. He knew perfectly well that the ship bearing down on them was far better equipped to fight a latex fire than the *Semirande*. But the stubborn old fool would never admit this. He wouldn't admit, either, that the two tugs had become allies.

Climbing sun had turned small waves ahead into burnished, dented copper. Under glare there was no blue in sky or sea, the only shadow made by two hulls, the water in it purple. That metallic veneer on the ocean looked rigid, as though clamped down to suffocate all living things under it, but a flying fish broke through, coming in glittering over the *Semirande*'s bows to smack down on her forepeak. It lay stunned for seconds, then started to flop about, just missing a scupper that would have let it back into the sea, writhing against a bulwark, trying jerks into the air which weren't high enough to carry it over the rail. The surrender to death was sudden, the bright fish still, that strange sail fin—which had failed it—remaining elevated.

Jules Dartan knotted the rope around his waist. The respirator hung on his chest.

'I'll try to keep tension on the rope,' he said. 'Two tugs mean I want to be pulled up quickly. One means pay it out. You'd better have your mask on, too. There'll be plenty of smoke coming out of that hatch crack.'

'Captain, if the *Saturn*'s coming up why can't you wait? Between us we could just pour in the steam. She's only four miles off now.'

Jules said nothing. He tested the knot, then walked, trailing rope, to where the well-deck bulkhead dropped to waist height. He stared at the approaching tug.

'I'll find out if they've had any more signals from *Saturn*, sir.'

'No! Tell them to shut off steam. Now.'

Tourin picked the walkie-talkie out of a deck drain. He got Lecren, then Berand. The Mate had questions. Under stress his voice was thin and tight, sounding angry. Jules took no notice of the exchange, though he must have heard most of it. Tourin didn't try to relay any messages from the *Semirande*.

'The Captain wants steam off. Now. Over and out.'

He switched off the set and put it back in the drain. Jules had his back to *Saturn*. He shouted over to the ship's Bos'n who had three sailors on a pipe-watching detail.

'We finish steam. For inspection. See?'

The Bos'n nodded. His men stared. Tourin thought the freighter's crew a surly lot. They stood about like street corner idlers, not really doing anything, or even pretending to. They might have had a deep grudge against the ship which had betrayed them to an invader and didn't give a damn now what became of her. It could, of course, be English phlegm that made them appear indifferent to the threat of fire but certainly the ones up by the opened number one hold, taking a break from sluicing a hot bulkhead, lay about looking more like sun bathers than men recovering from heat exhaustion. They seemed to be denying, all of them, a state of crisis on the *Gorton Queen*. This was just something the Frenchies had worked up in their own interest.

Tourin knew that they had all been living with their latex fire for more than a week now, as the ship ran north for the Canaries. In a period of time like that you can get used to most things. It still wasn't clear what had made Captain Ellis suddenly decide he had a situation he couldn't handle himself, perhaps the slow heating up of that bulkhead to the forward hold which told him that all the steam he could muster wasn't going to be enough.

Except for the Mate, who came down from time to time, the other officers stayed clear of the well-deck, tending to line the bridge rail like mildly interested cruise passengers. Now and then they were joined by the Captain, a puffy-faced man whose head seemed set straight on the collar of his starched tunic. The Master made no inquiries about progress below, in dignified withdrawal, apparently still angry that his simple prescription for the situation had not been accepted by the tug. Jules roamed the ship, unassisted and unaided, testing decks and bulkheads for heat, and during his absences Tourin stood alone, feeling not unlike a traveller who has strayed into a mountain village still hostile to contemporary tourism, watched but not greeted.

The hissing from the *Semirande*'s steam pipe died away. Jules, with a tail of rope behind him crossed to port and turned a valve to cut off the freighter's own contribution. The slow beat of the *Gorton Queen*'s engines produced almost no vibration at all and it was suddenly quiet enough to hear the rush of that water channelled between two hulls. Jules walked back, looking up. Captain Ellis chose that moment to look down.

'I shut off all steam, see?' Jules shouted. 'Because I am for inspection. Now there is volcano. If you wish to keep clean your shirts seclude yourself into wheel-house.'

The meaning of this message seemed to baffle the men up top, though one or two withdrew. Captain Ellis did not, he leaned farther over the rail, for the first time looking anxious.

Jules opened the hatch himself, unclamping a round metal lid like a man-hole cover, flinging this back on to the deck. Smoke was an eruption, an obscene column fattening as it shot up, at bridge level pushed back by wind. There was shouting from above. Tourin shouted, too.

'Captain! You can't go into that!'

'Ach, wait. You'll see vapour.'

This came, a lightening of the blackness, a dilution of it, a dirty grey steam cloud that billowed along the well-deck without that first smoke's urgent need to rise. The stench was hideous. Tourin started to cough. So did the men at the hose.

'Put on your respirator!' Jules roared. 'When I'm in drop the lid back on to the clamp. I've fixed it as a check. To leave room for the rope. But not too much air down. Get it?'

Jules went into a spasm of coughing. Then he came stumbling out of the cloud with respirator fitted, masked for his job. Tourin, fumbling to fit his own protection, caught a glimpse of eyes behind glass windows, a stranger's eyes, and huge, as though magnified by lenses. Already Jules had the remoteness of a diver, with gear fitted, on the verge of a plunge into dark from the known world and the sun. His voice came as a weird gobbling.

'Ready?'

Tourin nodded, then coughed inside his respirator, steaming up the eye-pieces. He felt the rope put in his hands. When he could see again there was no sign of the Captain. The rope went over the lip of that man-hole and out of sight. He got down on his knees to pull forward the lid and lower this on to the check clamp. He fumbled with the rope for tension and after a moment believed he had this, holding the line like a fisherman who thinks he may have hooked something big, but still isn't certain. He stood up, keeping tension, hearing shouting from the bridge, but paying it no attention, behind that respirator and centred in the smoke he couldn't be approached, almost as isolated as Jules. The passing seconds pulsed in his ears.

The line jerked. Tourin paid out a few feet of rope, keeping it taut through his fingers. The second signal was stronger, a demand for more room to manœuvre. The Skipper must be planning to move off from the small platform under the hatch. He couldn't step out on to the latex, it would be like putting weight on the top layer of a newly stoked bonfire, a quick crumbling away into the glowing core underneath. But there might well be a steel strut across the hold he could walk on. Tourin had the sensation of being in sudden telepathic communication with Jules, knowing much more than signals along a line could tell him. The old man now had some intent involving wild risk. Tourin wanted to shout down through the hatch, but couldn't risk pulling off the respirator. He felt fear for Jules that was much more than tension from these moments, or reflected terror. It might have come from love. He couldn't understand it.

The rope jerked again. Tourin had to pay out, hating what he was doing. Jules was cheating down there, collecting line for some sortie, neutralizing this check on him which Berand had demanded. He mustn't be allowed to get away with it. Tourin started a haul back again. At once there was a tug.

Damn him! Damn the old bastard!

Sweat streamed down Tourin's cheeks. He couldn't see much. How could Jules see anything?

The line went slack in his fingers. The pull in began to show just how much rope Jules had contrived to get down into that hold. Tourin's breathing rattled. Then he had tension again. Against a dead weight.

For seconds his brain refused to accept what this meant. His hands sent signals down into the hold, his own signals, from no code agreed on. He braced feet against the edge of the hatch and began to pull. The dead weight stayed fixed.

Tourin twisted the rope around one arm in a bid to keep tension, then backed through smoke, the line biting into his wrist as he moved along it. One hand yanked at the respirator. It seemed clamped to his head. It was a long time before he could shout.

'Help me! This rope. Hold! Hold!'

His eyes were streaming.

'What's this then?'

It was the Bos'n.

'Take this rope! Keep tight for me. With your men. Then pulling. I must go in hold.'

'Something's happened to your skipper?'

'I think so. You must pull. Alone I cannot.'

'I get it.'

Tourin handed over the rope. He re-fitted the respirator. He groped forward again towards the man-hole. He was terrified. The hatch rim was hot. He had to force his feet over the edge, to the first rung of a steel ladder. He went down, feeling the rope, this taut but not moving. There was shouting behind him.

He hated black holes. Caves were a horror, darkening corridors to death. The platform, solid enough, was like the inner lip of an oven. He groped out for the rope. It was moving. They were pulling Jules up.

He could see nothing, no glow from smouldering cargo. He put out one foot, then the other, to the edge of the narrow platform. The rope went past him, still moving. He got down on his knees, hot metal biting through cloth, fingers groping along the line. They touched a double knot.

Tourin got a hold on trousers and a shirt, rolling an inert weight over on to the platform bars. Then he guided the lift, reaching out to protect Jules's head from the rungs of the ladder. The Skipper's respirator had gone.

There was someone by the hatch opening, risking smoke, coughing. Light was blocked out, then returned. Tourin was alone in the hold. He began to climb, suddenly certain that he wouldn't make it up eight rungs. All he could hear was his heart. And he couldn't breathe. The respirator had packed in!

Coughing came again, and a voice. 'Grab my hand.'

Tourin didn't really need the hand, just the contact. He pulled himself up and out, crawling on to the deck. The hatch cover clanged behind him.

For seconds after he got the respirator off he couldn't see at all, sweat stinging in his eyes. Someone had him by the arm. They walked along. He could feel the uneven decking, boards warped by heat from the steel under them.

They had laid Jules out on his back. His face had gone slack, mouth open, a sailor's weather-hardened skin softened to putty. His eyes stared at the sky.

'Quick!' Tourin called out. 'The kiss for life. We must give him. He must be made to breathe!'

'No one can do that now, chum,' the Bos'n said. 'Your old man's had it.'

MacDonald lowered binoculars.

'They seem to be getting steam over all right.'

Mark wasn't impressed. 'That dodge wouldn't work in any kind of sea. Today's been a gift.'

He took the glasses and read the lettering on two sterns, '*Gorton Queen, Liverpool*', '*Semirande, Brest*'. The after-decks of both ships were completely deserted and the connection between the two hulls suggested some grotesque, elephantine sex act, with the *Saturn* about to intrude on an essential privacy.

'At about a mile cut to half-ahead, MacDonald. Ready for dead slow. Make it a pretty wide turn, too. We don't want to rock them. I'll be up on the platform. If you'd like it I can talk you to a close in on fenders.'

Mark saw that MacDonald wouldn't like to be talked in. He was always giving his Mate too detailed instructions. The Captain turned away and went through the chartroom, pausing at the table to look at their position. Ginnis had marked a little cross for the freighter. This put them about two hundred and seventy miles south-west of Gran Canaria, and the reasonable facilities at Las Palmas where the *Gorton Queen* would probably be left if she was taken under tow at all. Her screws were still turning over in a continuing declaration of independence.

The bridge ceiling speaker gave its little sigh before a voice.

'Captain Underson wanted on R.T.'

Mark went to the radio cabin.

'The *Semirande* or the *Gorton Queen*?'

'*Semirande*, sir. Her Skipper's dead.'

'Dartan? *Dead?*'

'Suffocated in the hold.'

'Oh, my God! Who's that on the line?'

'Second Engineer Lecren. The Mate's at the wheel.'

Mark's shock was professional, like one policeman hearing that another he didn't know very well had been killed on duty. He picked up the handset.

'M'sieur Lecren? I've just heard the news from my radioman. We're shocked here.'

'Yes, sir. It is most terrible. So quick. I have apologies of the First Officer, he is . . .'

'I understand. Please tell him how sorry we all are.'

'Thank you.'

'Do you know what happened?'

'Well, not so clearly. Tourin, the Second, he is with the Capitaine. He assists him from the hold. The Capitaine must have fallen in a narrow place between the cargo.'

'Was he roped?'

'Yes. For inspection. He insists he must see the state of the cargo. In falling the respirator is knocked from his head.'

Mark stared out of the square port.

'In that stuff he wouldn't be conscious for long.'

'No. We think that, too.'

'You must all be under a kind of shock, M'sieur Lecren.'

'It is true, yes. But we manage.'

'We'd like to do anything we can to help. And, after all, we're now the same company.'

'That's so, Capitaine.'

'Perhaps you can help me first. I've been on to the freighter on short wave and R.T. We can't raise them. What is the position on board? Fire still contained to number two?'

'To this moment. But main fuel tank is up against hot bulkhead. The diesel oil cannot be moved. Only discharged to sea. And the Master will not. For it would make him a hulk and he does not wish to be towed.'

'One of those buggers,' Mark said, forgetting Dartan.

Then he remembered. A situation that had seemed to threaten some kind of flare-up, the first meeting between *Saturn* and *Semirande* under a common house flag, now looked like being oiled into perfect smoothness, a happy collaboration. It wouldn't have been anything like that with Jules Dartan alive.

Mark hung up.

'What a helluva way for the poor old sod to go,' Collins said. Mark nodded and went out.

The *Gorton Queen* didn't provide any real test of the *Saturn*'s fire-fighting equipment. The freighter was serviced with steam and that was about all there was to it. The *Saturn* pushed on a fender cushion between two hulls, her bows south to enable the port tower platform to be used, her engines on slow astern. The platform had been ejected to eight feet over the *Gorton Queen*'s well-deck and steam pipes went straight down from it to valve connections for number two hold. Mark estimated that he was supplying twice as much steam as the cargo ship and *Semirande* had produced between them, but he didn't brag about this; he was treading very lightly indeed in the matter of first relations with a new colleague.

The *Semirande* continued to hold position at a distance from the freighter, though with wind practically gone and the sea down there was no longer the slightest need for this, she could have closed on her fenders without risk. Mark had the feeling that what he was seeing here was almost a ritual act of mourning, the Mate over there in that wheel-house adhering to the last orders received from Dartan as though by so doing he could somehow delay acceptance of what had happened.

There were some odd stories about the pair of them. In Rotterdam bars it was said that Berand used to sit in bordello parlours reading a newspaper waiting for Jules to put in time with one of the girls. Probably the two men had been psychic complements; Mark didn't think there was any question of sexual aberration though a Freudian might have found it. They always find what they're looking for. Personally he had no feeling for these male friendships with a high emotional content, and he couldn't see himself training up MacDonald as a supplement to Alice. If he tried it there would soon be no Alice. And quite right, too. He had never been a boy for the other boys, possibly because he had so much enforced male company in his work patterns, all of which was going to make it a shade difficult to get in tune with the very special grief over there on the *Semirande*. With luck he mightn't have to witness it.

Mark took a beef sandwich from a plate on the chartroom table, the cook's gesture towards lunch, and chewed carefully. He thought about Captain Ellis. The man hadn't proved an endearing character. His game was obvious and he was playing his part cleverly, his ship was not a hulk, it never had been, and never would be under his command. The diesel was still in his main tank and he could sail away under his own power at any time. He would, too, God bless him.

MacDonald came in from the bridge and took a beef sandwich. 'Is there any coffee?'

'No, just beer.'

'Our cook really knows how to rise to an emergency. They've still got Dartan wrapped in a blanket up on the *Gorton*'s forepeak.'

Mark looked up.

'Well?'

'In these latitudes you don't leave a corpse in the sun any longer than you have to. When are they going to transfer him to the *Semirande*?'

'I don't know.'

'Another thing, why don't you just give them back their pipe and say they're not needed any more?'

'Maybe out of respect to the dead.'

'What?'

'This was Dartan's party. He would have coped without us. And his Mate seems to want to go on holding ship there.'

'It's weird. How the hell are we ever going to mix with this kind of mob, Captain?'

'I shouldn't think we'll be going for mixed crews. Not at first, anyway.'

'I speak French like nothing.'

'Maybe we can get you a berth on a Thames river-tug. You can go home every night.'

MacDonald took another sandwich.

'I could marry a French girl.'

'I'm sure she'd appreciate the body beautiful.'

'We couldn't talk, so we might get on all right. I can't talk to girls.' MacDonald stared out of a port. 'They'll have to bury him at sea.'

'Yes.'

'The sailor's end. Was he married?'

'I think his wife's dead.'

'Kids?'

'I don't know. But they'd be grown up.'

'How old was he?'

'Past his middle fifties, I should think.'

'Well, he's had his life then. It's funny about that respirator.'

'What?'

'The way it came off. Those things fit like scuba masks.'

'So?'

'You can't knock them off. A fall wouldn't do it.'

'How about a rope tightening suddenly past his head?'

'Not that, either.'

'What's in your mind?'

'I don't know. Just that he . . . well, he must have taken it off himself for some reason.'

Mark was suddenly colder than the air-conditioning warranted.

'That's a stupid idea! That smoke was like ink. He wouldn't . . .'

'All right, Captain. I just don't see it any other way, that's all. Anyhow, he's dead. And that's that. Have another sandwich?'

At seventeen hundred hours the inspection hatch was opened. Very little smoke, but a great deal of stinking grey vapour came out. Mark ordered the hold sealed and then went in search of Captain Ellis. They had fifteen minutes acrimonious contact in the Master's day-cabin which ended with Ellis putting his signature to something not unlike an itemized account of services rendered. Mark wasn't offered a drink. He went out on deck and stood for a moment looking at the *Semirande* which was now on standby at a quarter of a mile. Her boom was inboard, a steam hose invisible, a small salvage job finished. Jules Dartan's body would be back in his own cabin and the Bos'n sewing canvas.

He went down two flights and out on to the warped planking of the well-deck, along this to where a rope ladder led down on to one of the *Saturn*'s fat fenders with a scramble net draped over it. Mark boarded his own ship without dignity. Ginnis was waiting for him.

'All our crew back?'

'You're the last, sir. So that's over?'

'Yes. We get costs and a week's drink money, if we're lucky. And don't want to drink much.'

'They never really made us feel wanted.'

Mark grinned. 'Take her away. Set course for Brest. I see the *Semirande* seems to be waiting for us.'

'For your orders, Fleet Commodore.'

'Before I start throwing rank about I'll wait to have that appointment confirmed by the rest of our new directors. If we're going in convoy we'd better watch speed. I suppose eighteen would be too much for the *Semirande*?'

'She'd blow up.'

'And fifteen would be an insult. Make it sixteen.'

'Aye, aye, sir.'

Mark raised an eyebrow at the Second. From his own cabin he got through to Collins.

'Get me the *Semirande* on R.T. Switch the call here.'

He went and sat on the sofa, ready to reach out for the instrument on his desk. The burring came in under a minute.

'*Semirande* for you, sir.'

'Thanks. Captain Underson here. Calling *Semirande*. Over.'

'This is First Officer Berand.'

'Captain now.'

'Yes. I'm sorry, Captain Underson, that we have not been in touch before.'

'That's all right. I knew you were busy.'

'The message from you was given to me.'

'You know how sorry we are.'

'Thank you.'

'I thought we might stay together to Brest. Unless there's a call for one of us on the way.'

'If that is your order.'

'It was my idea, Captain. That's all. When do you plan to have the funeral?'

'In the morning. Early. It seems the weather will stay calm. But not, perhaps, what you would call a funeral.'

'I don't understand?'

'The position is difficult. I will, of course, have all the crew. But there is not, shall we say, a ritual for it.'

'Wasn't he a Catholic?'

'Perhaps. A poor one.'

'But . . . surely you have some form?'

'If so I am not aware of it. There are some areas of my knowledge which are deficient. Also, I cannot act a priest. And in my time at sea there has been no death on a ship. This is perhaps lucky for me. You have experience of such things?'

'Yes. Though not as Captain.'
'And what is done?'
'We read the Anglican service for the dead.'
'Would you wish to read such a service for Jules?'
'God, no!'
'In that case I say some words only. For a friend.'
'I thought I would like to come over.'
'We'd be honoured.'
'Look . . . Berand, if you'd really like me to read that service
I will.'
There was a silence.
'Yes, I would like it.'

The words meant nothing to Mark at first, he heard his own voice
taken from him into the vast emptiness of a morning sky and
sea, commented on for their unimportance by space. And then
he came to the quiet lines that wrench the heart, which say everything without flourish and leave a pause at their end for stillness.
   ' "The days of man are but as grass; for he flourisheth as a
flower of the field. For as soon as the wind goeth over it, it is
gone: and the place thereof shall know it no more." '
   It was the words again which committed the body of Captain
Jules Dartan to the sea. Mark closed the prayer book.
   They had found a board on the *Semirande* wide enough to
hold a body sewn into canvas. Somehow, even with that extra
room for weights at the feet, the bundle looked too small to
contain a man. It was precariously balanced. Two sailors raised
the plank, but Jules didn't seem to want to go. He had to be
pushed.
   The splash was scarcely heard above engines at dead slow.
There were no bubbles, just the *Semirande*'s wake on wind-
brushed ocean. Mark looked for sharks' fins but couldn't see any.
   There was a scuffing on the deck.
   'Thank you for what you have done,' Berand said.
   He seemed perfectly composed, his face showing no strain, as
though his night's sleep had been normal. Mark groped for something to say.
   'I'm sorry I didn't really know him.'
   'No, you did not know him. Jules was not easy to know. How
do I say it in English? He would have wished to be clever at
the tricks of the world. But he was not so.'

A funeral makes you hungry. Mark wanted his breakfast. He told
the cook to bring a tray to his cabin and went there to wait for it.
A typewritten signal had been left on the glass table. The old girl
again. But it was from Alice.

PLUMBERS NOT PLUMBING STOP CARPENTERS NOT CARPENTERING
STOP AM ONLY ONE ON SCHEDULE STOP OR AHEAD OF IT STOP IF
IT IS GIRL HAVE NAME READY STOP NOT ALICE STOP BUT FEEL
CERTAIN WILL PRODUCE ANOTHER SAILOR STOP YOU CONSIDER
NAME YOUR SON STOP PLENTY TIME STOP SEE YOU LOVE STOP ALICE

If he had been with his wife he would have poured them both
drinks. Alone he didn't want one. He sat down and stared at a
bulkhead. He saw a foetus, tiny, curled, secure. His.

The buzzer went. He walked over.

'Underson.'

'Collins here, sir. There's a Hoofstanger on the rocks.'

'What? I didn't get that?'

'A Hoofstanger tug in the Azores, badly holed. Returning from
a tow of storage tanks. They're holding security on the new
company code. They think. Though this doesn't look like something they can keep in the family. Wait a minute, sir. I'm getting
another signal. I'll call back.'

Mark went for his marine atlas. He made the Azores roughly
1,200 miles from the *Saturn*'s position. It was at least 1,400 to
Milford Haven, the nearest Hoofstanger base and the *Marie
Grooter*, if she was there. They might, of course, have ships much
nearer, and there was certainly a Greek salvage tug permanently
stationed at St Michael's, the largest of the Azores.

Collins came through on the telephone.

'They *are* keeping it in the family, Captain. Hushing up the
scandal, maybe. The *Marie Grooter* has sailed from Milford
Haven. That was Scherner's "I'm coming" signal.'

'What's the tug on the rocks?'

'The *Groenlo*. I'll look her up for you. I think she is newish.
She was coming out of Villa do Porto on St Mary's. She hit at
Castello Point.'

Mark looked at the atlas. St Mary's was the most southerly
island of the group. Advantage *Saturn*. He reckoned he could be
at the *Groenlo* ten hours before Scherner made it. Would the
*Groenlo* hang on for an extra ten hours waiting for family help
in an area subject to violent storms at practically no notice? It
seemed improbable if she was really badly holed. Anyway, it was
an interesting gamble.

'Captain, there's usually a Greek tug stationed in the islands . . .'

'I know. They probably mean to call her in if things look bad.'

'They can't,' Collins said. 'She's in Brazil on a job. And that's
worrying them.'

Mark smiled. It would be nice to have another round with
Scherner before he retired.

'Collins, get the *Semirande* on R.T. Explain the position to them fully. They can report for us when they're somewhere off Portugal. But they're not to do it before then. We go on radio silence as from now. Without putting Mrs Lawton in the picture.'

'You mean we're going?'

'Yes.'

Mark put the handset back on its hooks. He stood and took a deep breath. A Hoofstanger on the rocks! He walked over and punched the bridge communication button.

'MacDonald? Underson. Set course for the Azores. Now. Speed maximum.'